MW01579719

Fresh Start

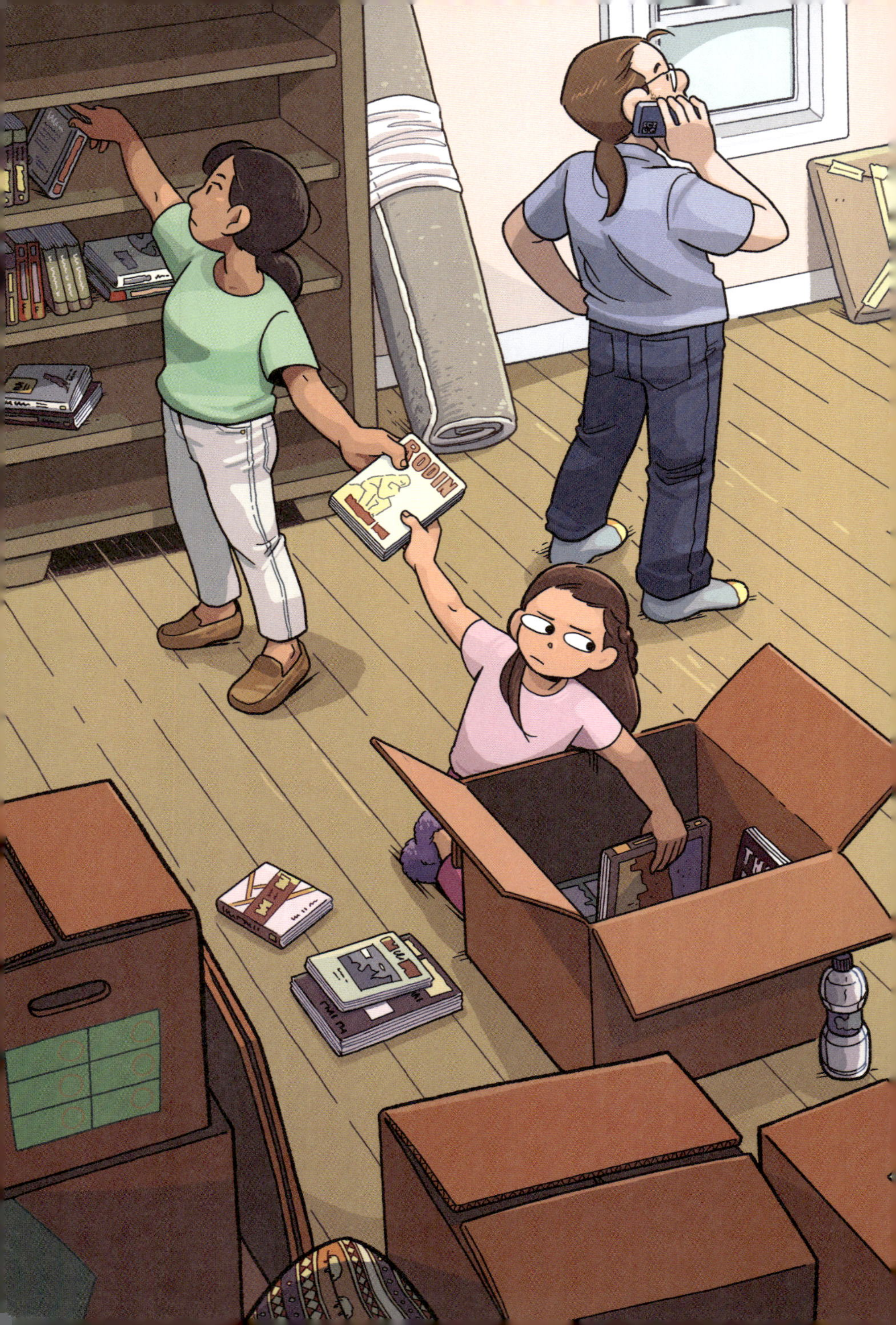
RODIN

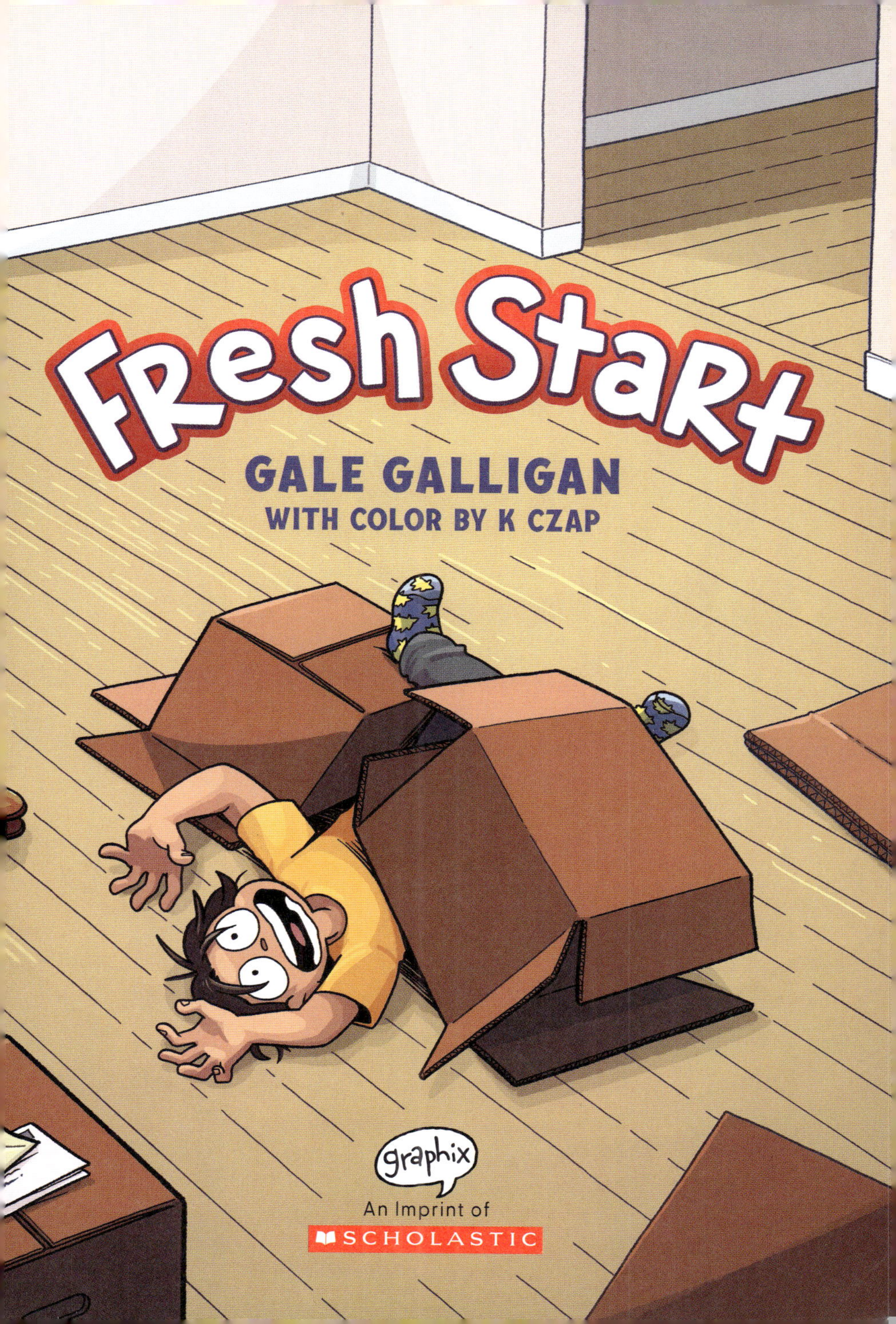
Fresh Start
GALE GALLIGAN
WITH COLOR BY K CZAP
graphix
An Imprint of
SCHOLASTIC

Copyright © 2025 by Gale Galligan

All rights reserved. Published by Graphix, an imprint of Scholastic Inc., *Publishers since 1920*. SCHOLASTIC, GRAPHIX, and associated logos are trademarks and/or registered trademarks of Scholastic Inc.

The publisher does not have any control over and does not assume any responsibility for author or third-party websites or their content.

No part of this publication may be reproduced, stored in a retrieval system, or transmitted in any form or by any means, electronic, mechanical, photocopying, recording, or otherwise, or used to train any artificial intelligence technologies, without written permission of the publisher. For information regarding permission, write to Scholastic Inc., Attention: Permissions Department, 557 Broadway, New York, NY 10012.

This book is a work of fiction. Names, characters, places, and incidents are either the product of the author's imagination or are used fictitiously, and any resemblance to actual persons, living or dead, business establishments, events, or locales is entirely coincidental.

Library of Congress Control Number: 2023947632

ISBN 978-1-338-04586-4 (hardcover)
ISBN 978-1-338-04584-0 (paperback)

10 9 8 7 6 5 4 3 2 1   25 26 27 28 29

Printed in China 62
First edition, January 2025

Edited by Cassandra Pelham Fulton
Book design by Carina Taylor
Creative Director: Phil Falco
Publisher: David Saylor

To Lori

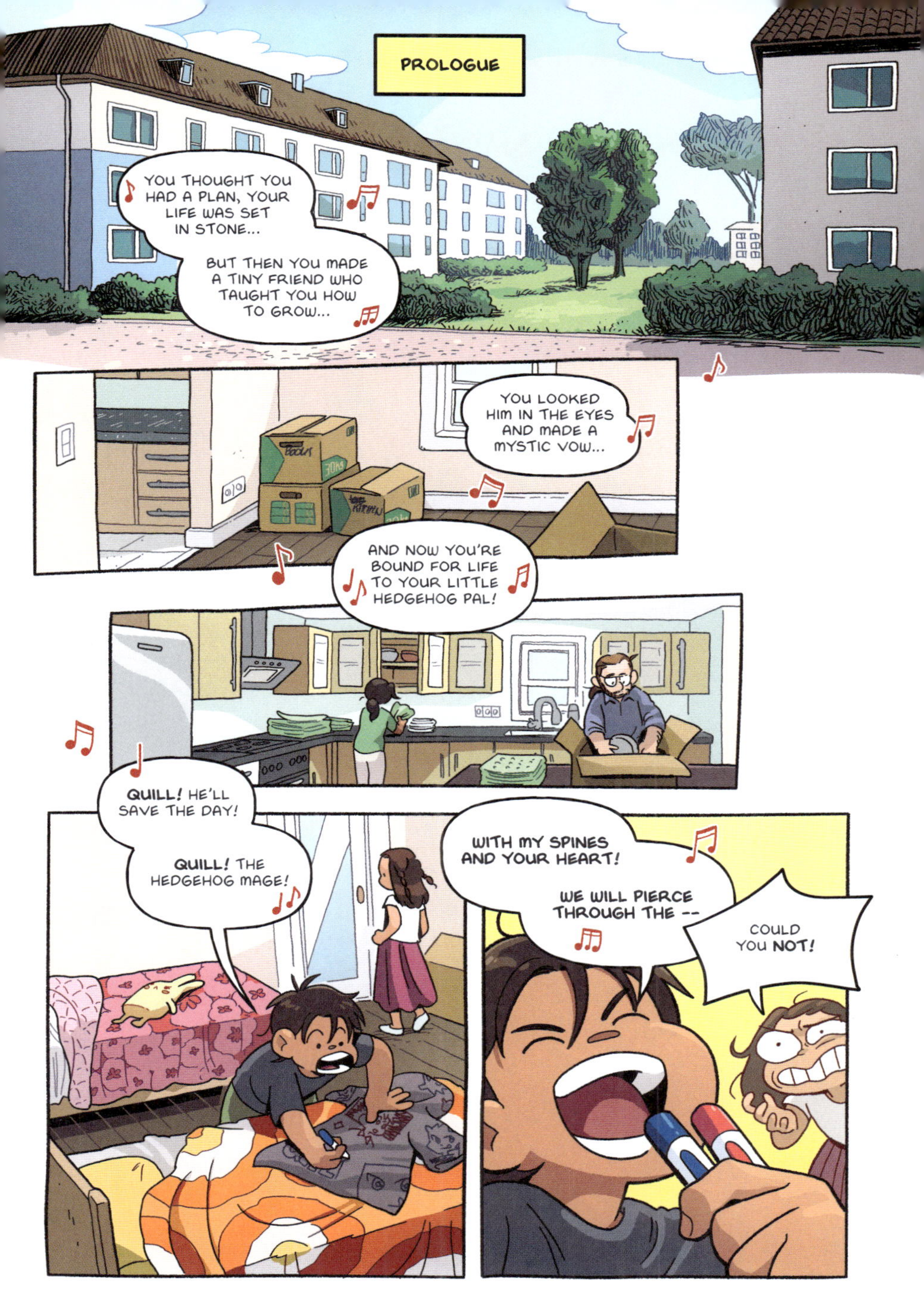
PROLOGUE
YOU THOUGHT YOU HAD A PLAN, YOUR LIFE WAS SET IN STONE...
BUT THEN YOU MADE A TINY FRIEND WHO TAUGHT YOU HOW TO GROW...
YOU LOOKED HIM IN THE EYES AND MADE A MYSTIC VOW...
AND NOW YOU'RE BOUND FOR LIFE TO YOUR LITTLE HEDGEHOG PAL!
QUILL! HE'LL SAVE THE DAY!
QUILL! THE HEDGEHOG MAGE!
WITH MY SPINES AND YOUR HEART!
WE WILL PIERCE THROUGH THE --
COULD YOU NOT!

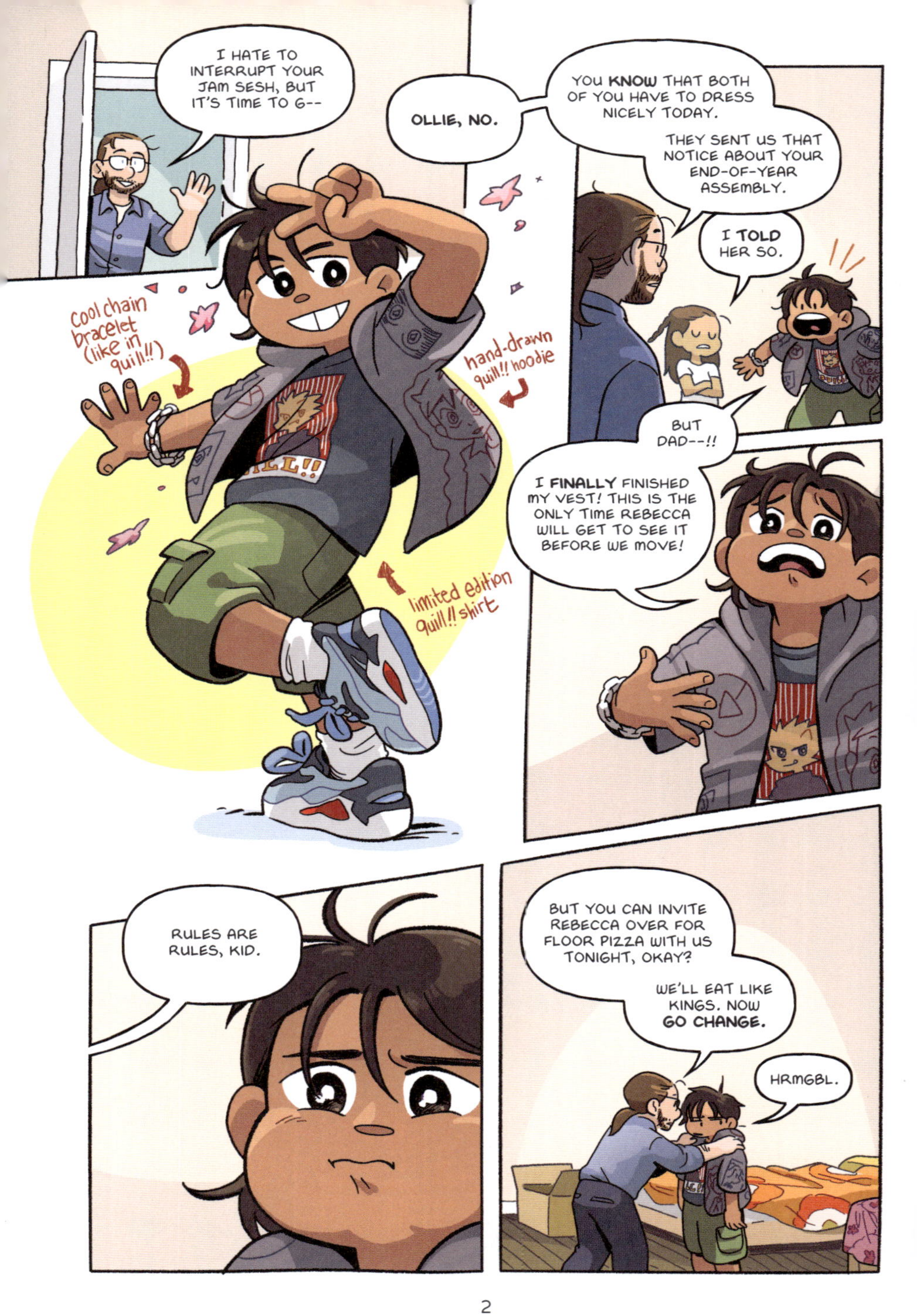
I HATE TO INTERRUPT YOUR JAM SESH, BUT IT'S TIME TO G--
cool chain bracelet (like in quill!!)
hand-drawn quill!! hoodie
limited edition quill!! shirt
OLLIE, NO.
YOU **KNOW** THAT BOTH OF YOU HAVE TO DRESS NICELY TODAY.
THEY SENT US THAT NOTICE ABOUT YOUR END-OF-YEAR ASSEMBLY.
I **TOLD** HER SO.
BUT DAD--!!
I **FINALLY** FINISHED MY VEST! THIS IS THE ONLY TIME REBECCA WILL GET TO SEE IT BEFORE WE MOVE!
RULES ARE RULES, KID.
BUT YOU CAN INVITE REBECCA OVER FOR FLOOR PIZZA WITH US TONIGHT, OKAY?
WE'LL EAT LIKE KINGS. NOW **GO CHANGE.**
HRMGBL.

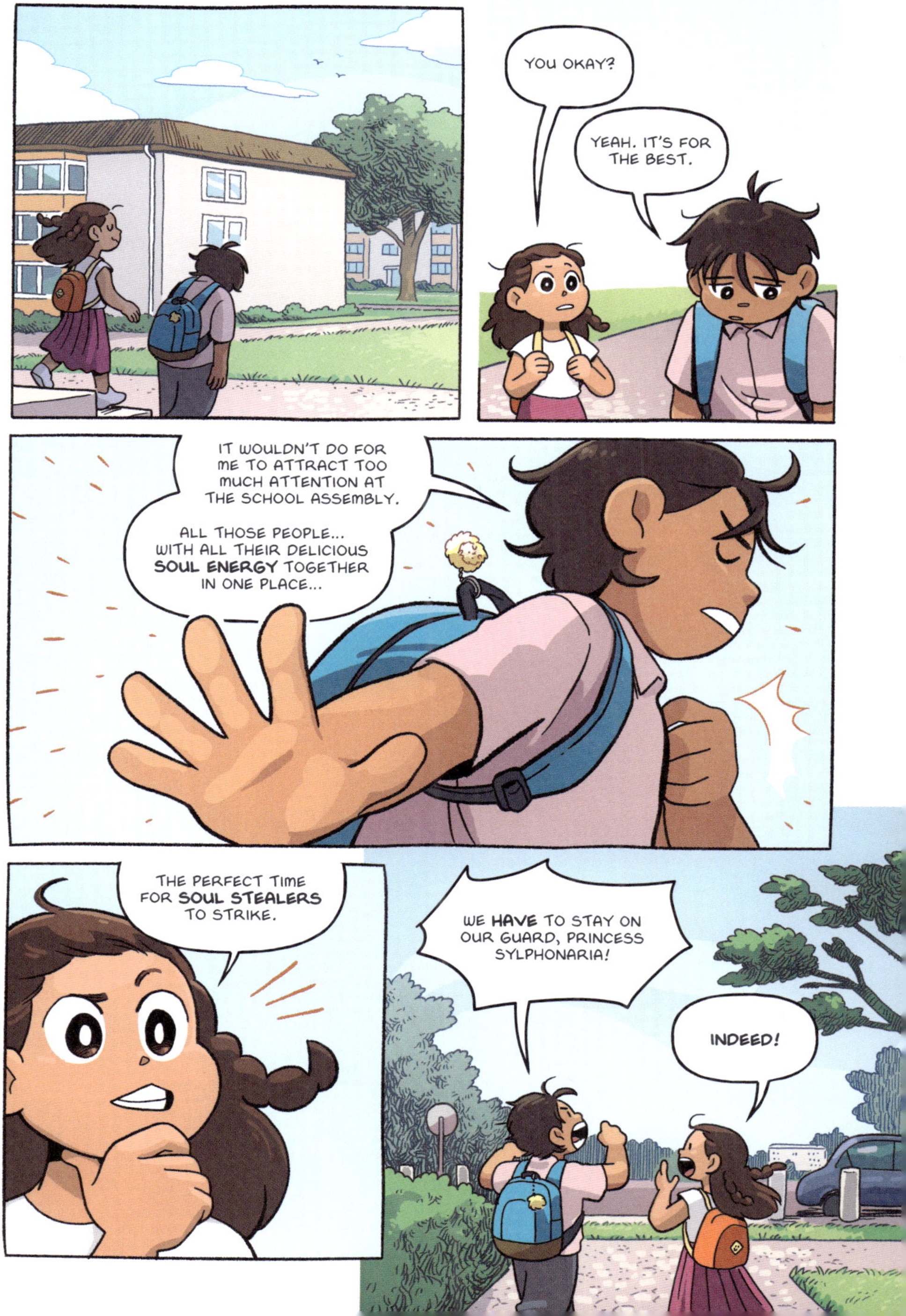
YOU OKAY?
YEAH. IT'S FOR THE BEST.
IT WOULDN'T DO FOR ME TO ATTRACT TOO MUCH ATTENTION AT THE SCHOOL ASSEMBLY.
ALL THOSE PEOPLE... WITH ALL THEIR DELICIOUS **SOUL ENERGY** TOGETHER IN ONE PLACE...
THE PERFECT TIME FOR **SOUL STEALERS** TO STRIKE.
WE **HAVE** TO STAY ON OUR GUARD, PRINCESS SYLPHONARIA!
INDEED!

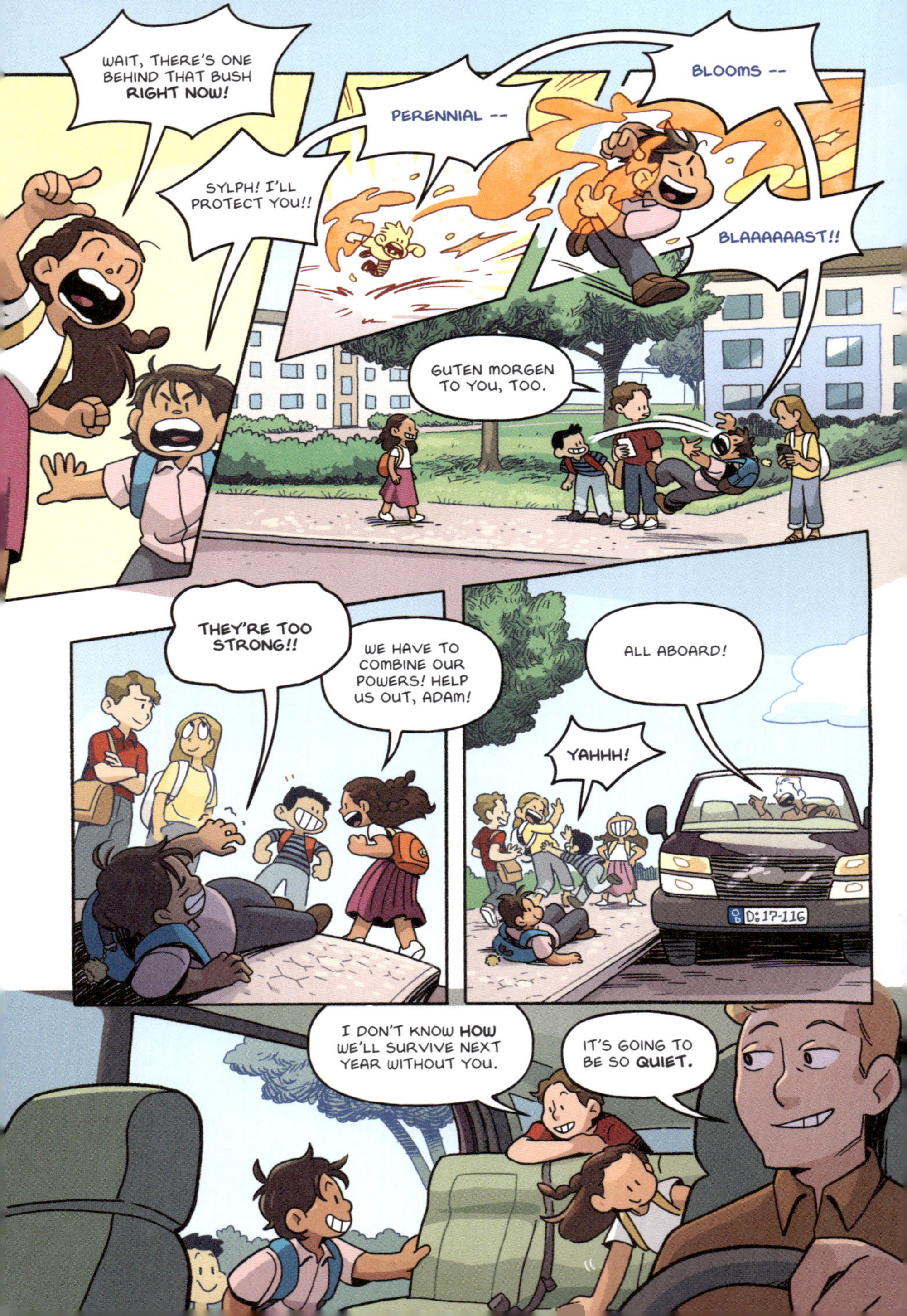
WAIT, THERE'S ONE BEHIND THAT BUSH **RIGHT NOW!**
SYLPH! I'LL PROTECT YOU!!
PERENNIAL --
BLOOMS --
BLAAAAAAST!!
GUTEN MORGEN TO YOU, TOO.
THEY'RE TOO STRONG!!
WE HAVE TO COMBINE OUR POWERS! HELP US OUT, ADAM!
ALL ABOARD!
YAHHH!
D 17-116
I DON'T KNOW **HOW** WE'LL SURVIVE NEXT YEAR WITHOUT YOU.
IT'S GOING TO BE SO **QUIET.**

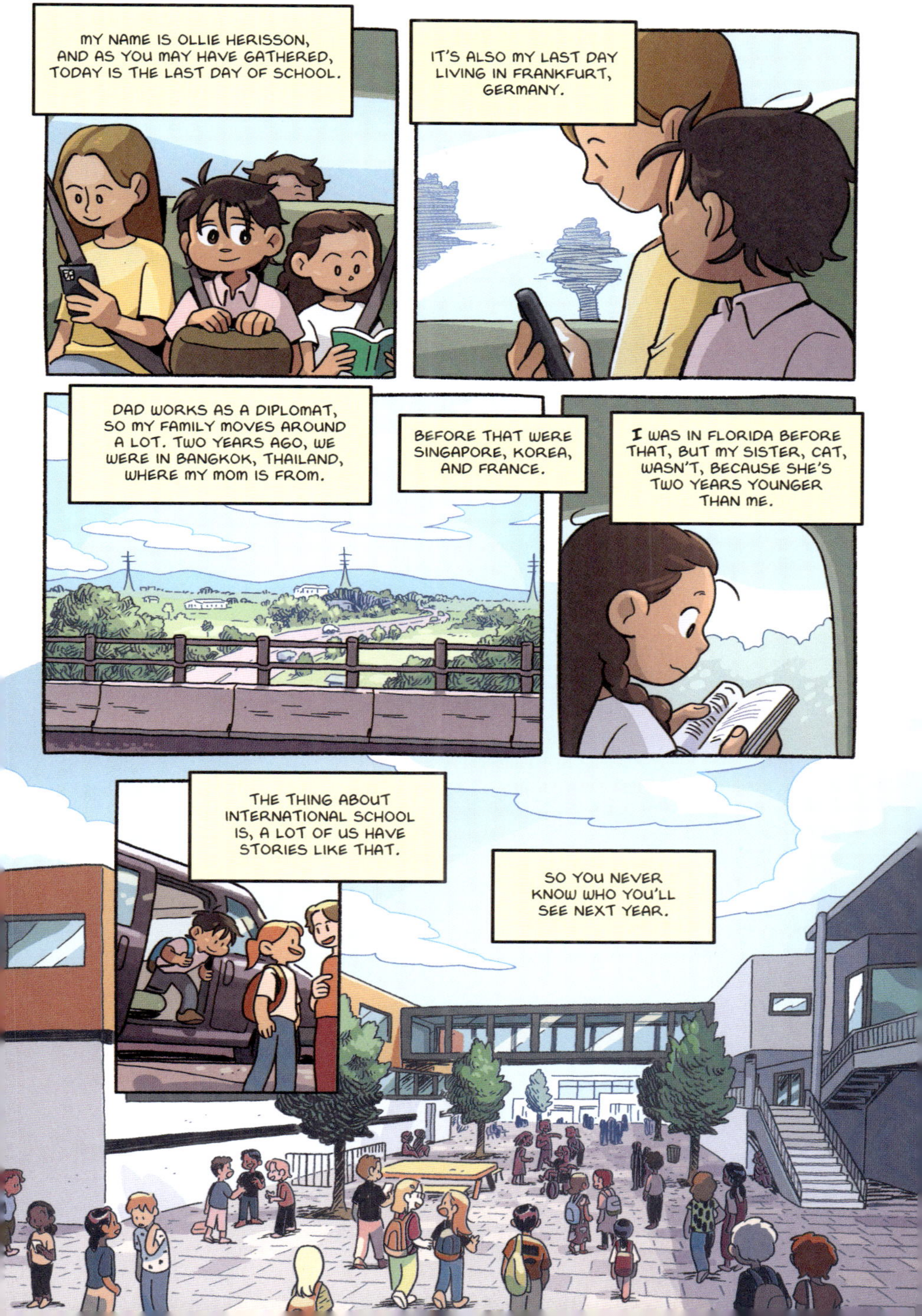
MY NAME IS OLLIE HERISSON, AND AS YOU MAY HAVE GATHERED, TODAY IS THE LAST DAY OF SCHOOL.
IT'S ALSO MY LAST DAY LIVING IN FRANKFURT, GERMANY.
DAD WORKS AS A DIPLOMAT, SO MY FAMILY MOVES AROUND A LOT. TWO YEARS AGO, WE WERE IN BANGKOK, THAILAND, WHERE MY MOM IS FROM.
BEFORE THAT WERE SINGAPORE, KOREA, AND FRANCE.
I WAS IN FLORIDA BEFORE THAT, BUT MY SISTER, CAT, WASN'T, BECAUSE SHE'S TWO YEARS YOUNGER THAN ME.
THE THING ABOUT INTERNATIONAL SCHOOL IS, A LOT OF US HAVE STORIES LIKE THAT.
SO YOU NEVER KNOW WHO YOU'LL SEE NEXT YEAR.

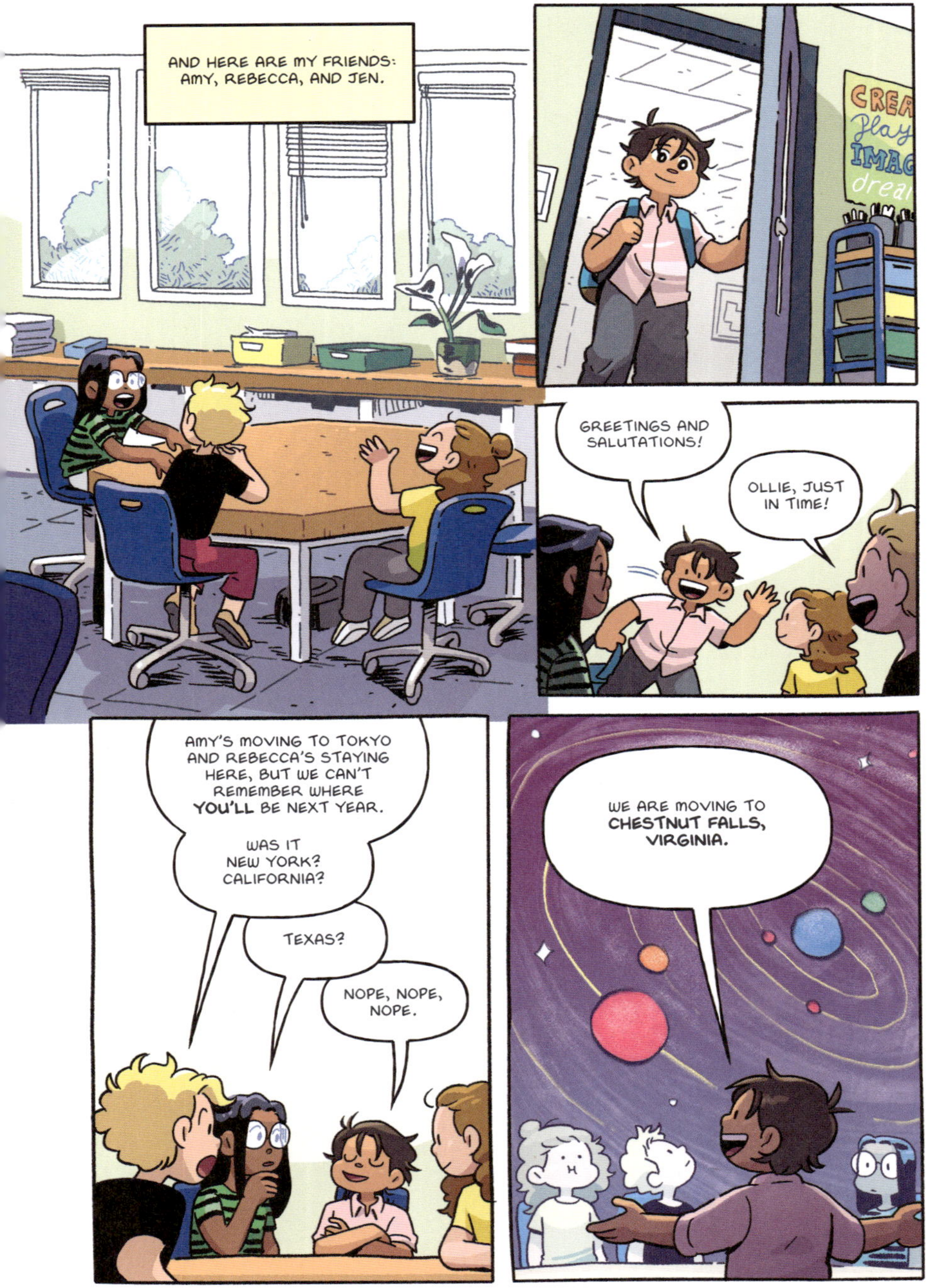
AND HERE ARE MY FRIENDS: AMY, REBECCA, AND JEN.
GREETINGS AND SALUTATIONS!
OLLIE, JUST IN TIME!
AMY'S MOVING TO TOKYO AND REBECCA'S STAYING HERE, BUT WE CAN'T REMEMBER WHERE **YOU'LL** BE NEXT YEAR.
WAS IT NEW YORK? CALIFORNIA?
TEXAS?
NOPE, NOPE, NOPE.
WE ARE MOVING TO **CHESTNUT FALLS, VIRGINIA.**

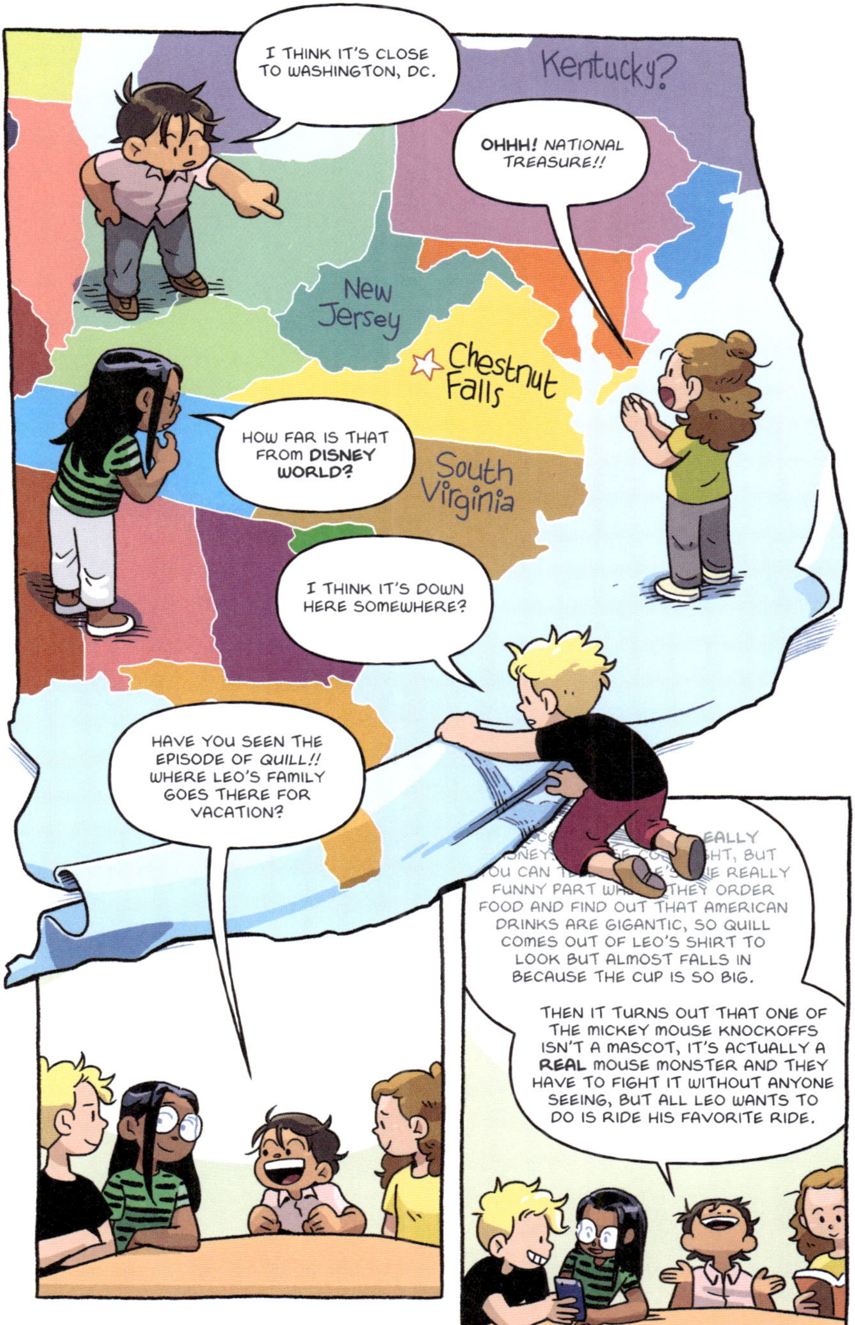
I THINK IT'S CLOSE TO WASHINGTON, DC.
Kentucky?
OHHH! NATIONAL TREASURE!!
New Jersey
Chestnut Falls
HOW FAR IS THAT FROM DISNEY WORLD?
South Virginia
I THINK IT'S DOWN HERE SOMEWHERE?
HAVE YOU SEEN THE EPISODE OF QUILL!! WHERE LEO'S FAMILY GOES THERE FOR VACATION?
FOOD AND FIND OUT THAT AMERICAN DRINKS ARE GIGANTIC, SO QUILL COMES OUT OF LEO'S SHIRT TO LOOK BUT ALMOST FALLS IN BECAUSE THE CUP IS SO BIG.
THEN IT TURNS OUT THAT ONE OF THE MICKEY MOUSE KNOCKOFFS ISN'T A MASCOT, IT'S ACTUALLY A REAL MOUSE MONSTER AND THEY HAVE TO FIGHT IT WITHOUT ANYONE SEEING, BUT ALL LEO WANTS TO DO IS RIDE HIS FAVORITE RIDE.

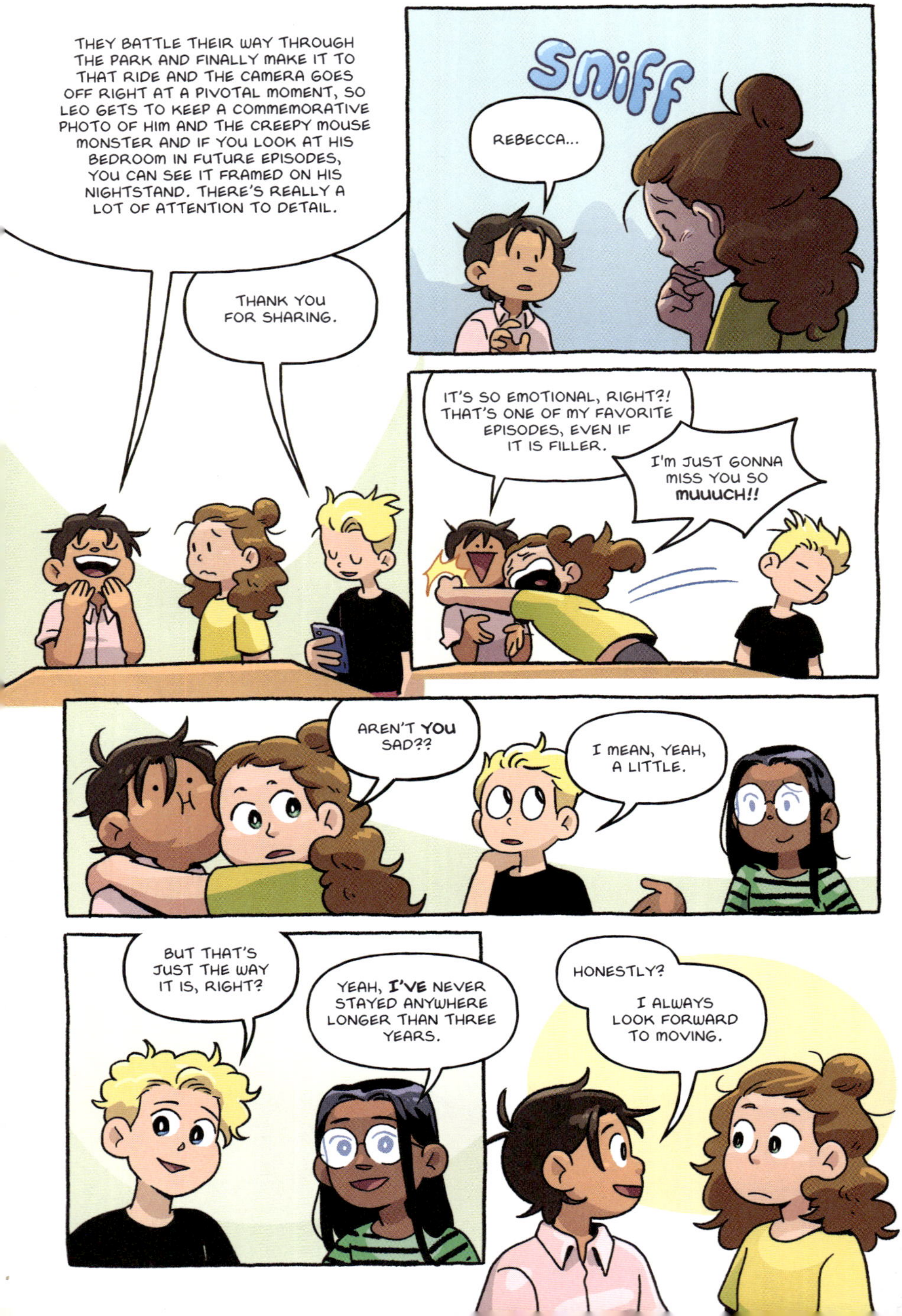
THEY BATTLE THEIR WAY THROUGH THE PARK AND FINALLY MAKE IT TO THAT RIDE AND THE CAMERA GOES OFF RIGHT AT A PIVOTAL MOMENT, SO LEO GETS TO KEEP A COMMEMORATIVE PHOTO OF HIM AND THE CREEPY MOUSE MONSTER AND IF YOU LOOK AT HIS BEDROOM IN FUTURE EPISODES, YOU CAN SEE IT FRAMED ON HIS NIGHTSTAND. THERE'S REALLY A LOT OF ATTENTION TO DETAIL.
THANK YOU FOR SHARING.
SNIFF
REBECCA...
IT'S SO EMOTIONAL, RIGHT?! THAT'S ONE OF MY FAVORITE EPISODES, EVEN IF IT IS FILLER.
I'M JUST GONNA MISS YOU SO MUUUCH!!
AREN'T YOU SAD??
I MEAN, YEAH, A LITTLE.
BUT THAT'S JUST THE WAY IT IS, RIGHT?
YEAH, I'VE NEVER STAYED ANYWHERE LONGER THAN THREE YEARS.
HONESTLY?
I ALWAYS LOOK FORWARD TO MOVING.

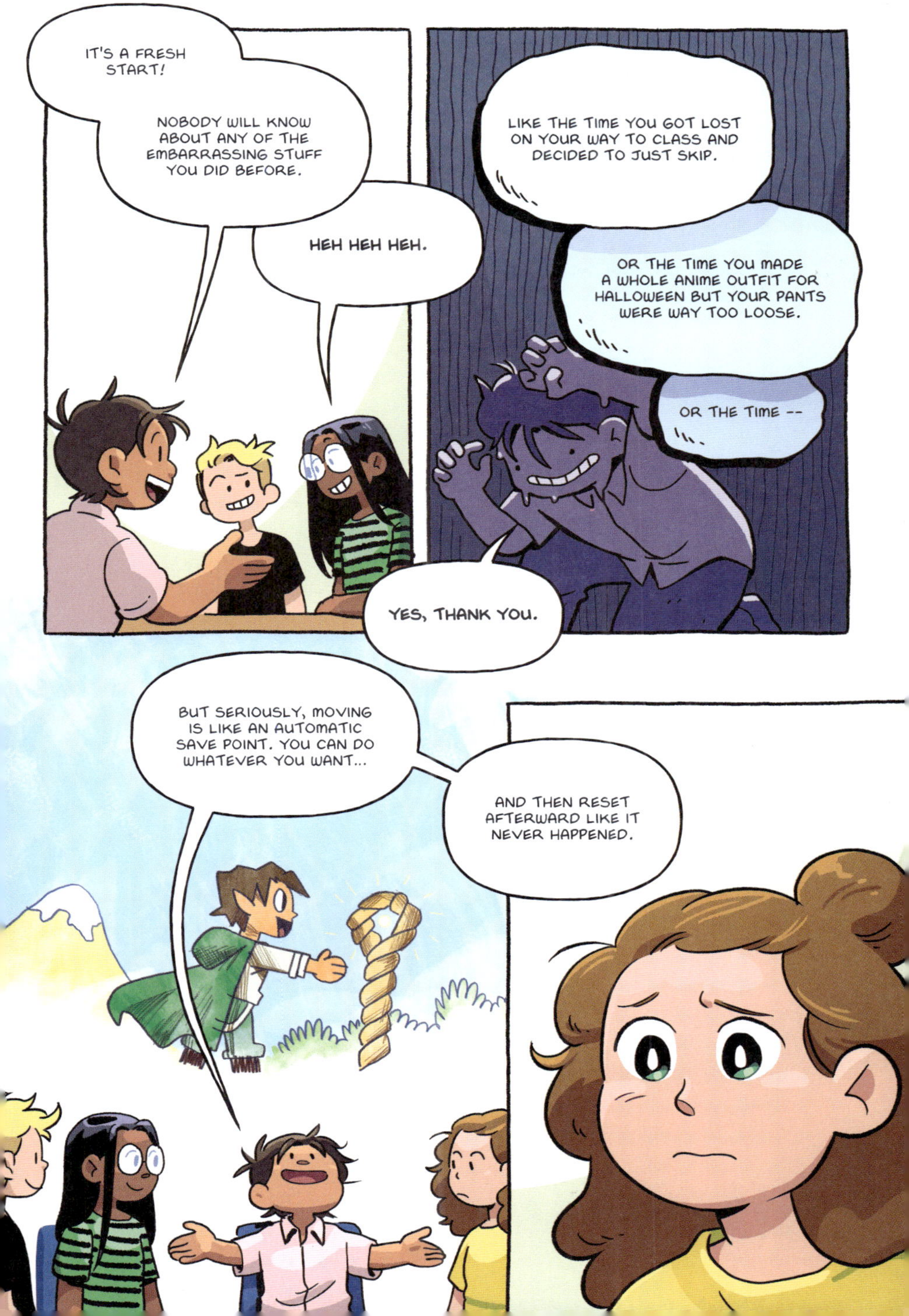
IT'S A FRESH START!
NOBODY WILL KNOW ABOUT ANY OF THE EMBARRASSING STUFF YOU DID BEFORE.
HEH HEH HEH.
LIKE THE TIME YOU GOT LOST ON YOUR WAY TO CLASS AND DECIDED TO JUST SKIP.
OR THE TIME YOU MADE A WHOLE ANIME OUTFIT FOR HALLOWEEN BUT YOUR PANTS WERE WAY TOO LOOSE.
OR THE TIME --
YES, THANK YOU.
BUT SERIOUSLY, MOVING IS LIKE AN AUTOMATIC SAVE POINT. YOU CAN DO WHATEVER YOU WANT...
AND THEN RESET AFTERWARD LIKE IT NEVER HAPPENED.

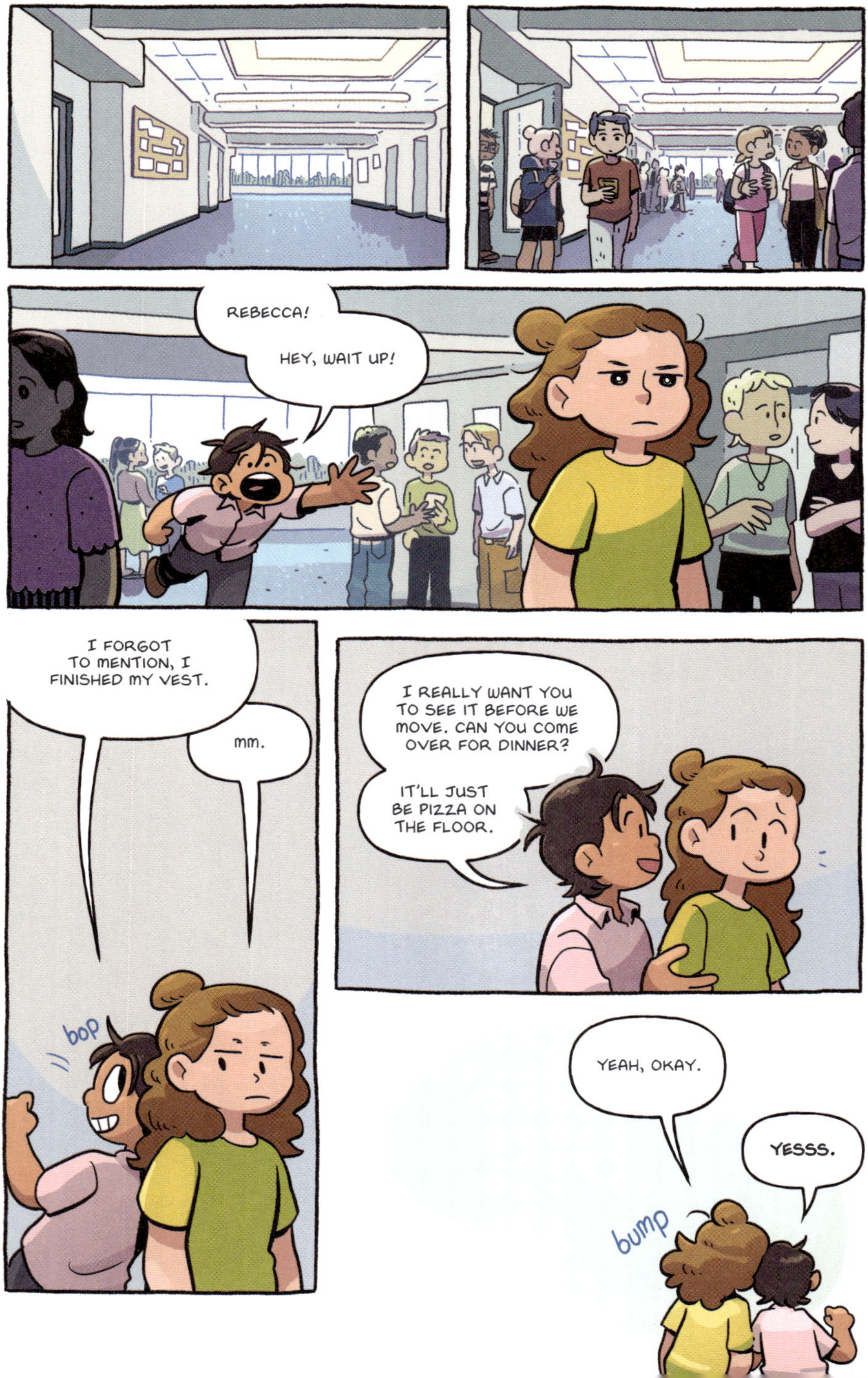
REBECCA!
HEY, WAIT UP!
I FORGOT TO MENTION, I FINISHED MY VEST.
mm.
I REALLY WANT YOU TO SEE IT BEFORE WE MOVE. CAN YOU COME OVER FOR DINNER?
IT'LL JUST BE PIZZA ON THE FLOOR.
bop
YEAH, OKAY.
YESSS.
bump

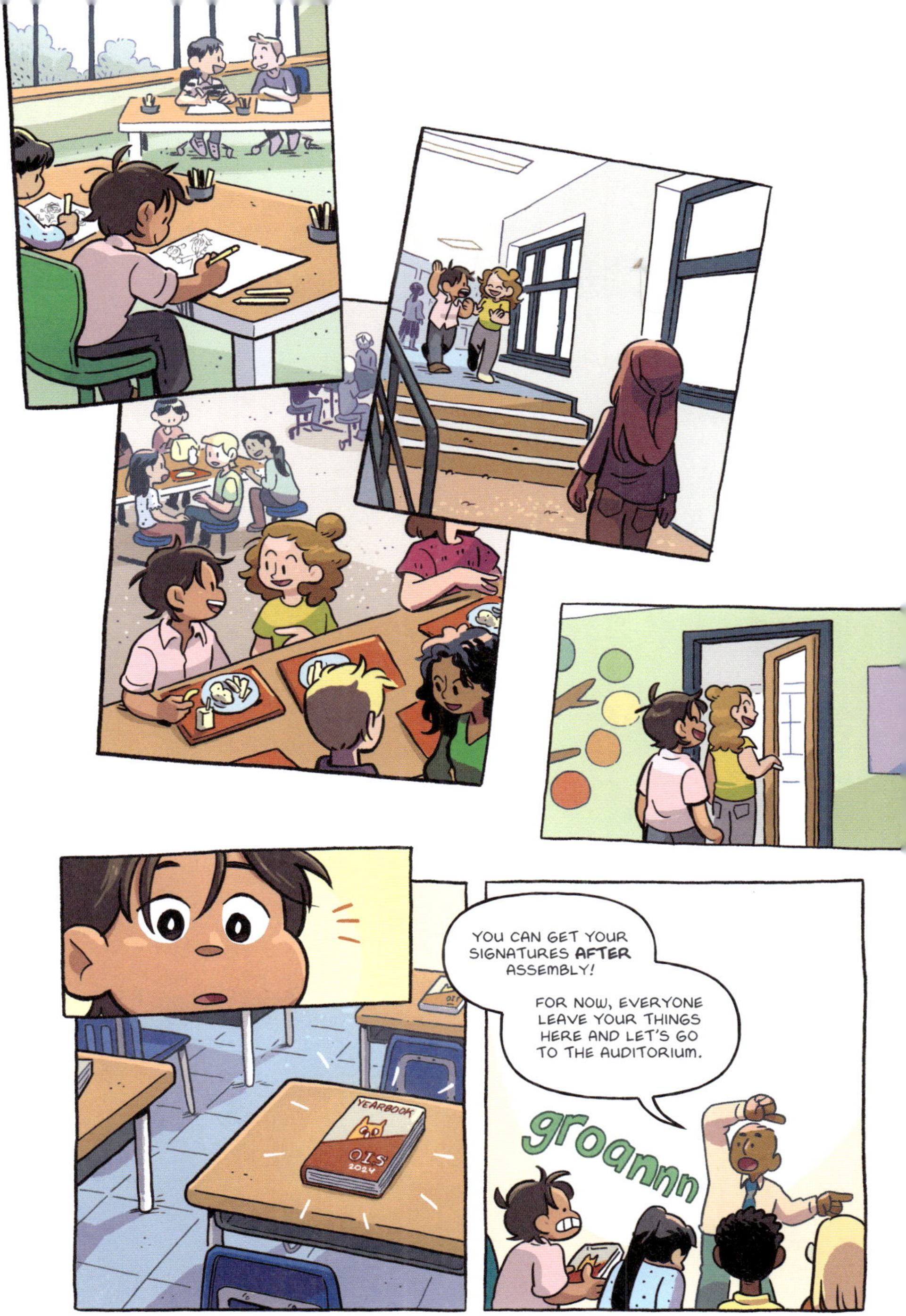
YEARBOOK
OIS
2024
YOU CAN GET YOUR SIGNATURES **AFTER** ASSEMBLY!
FOR NOW, EVERYONE LEAVE YOUR THINGS HERE AND LET'S GO TO THE AUDITORIUM.
groannn

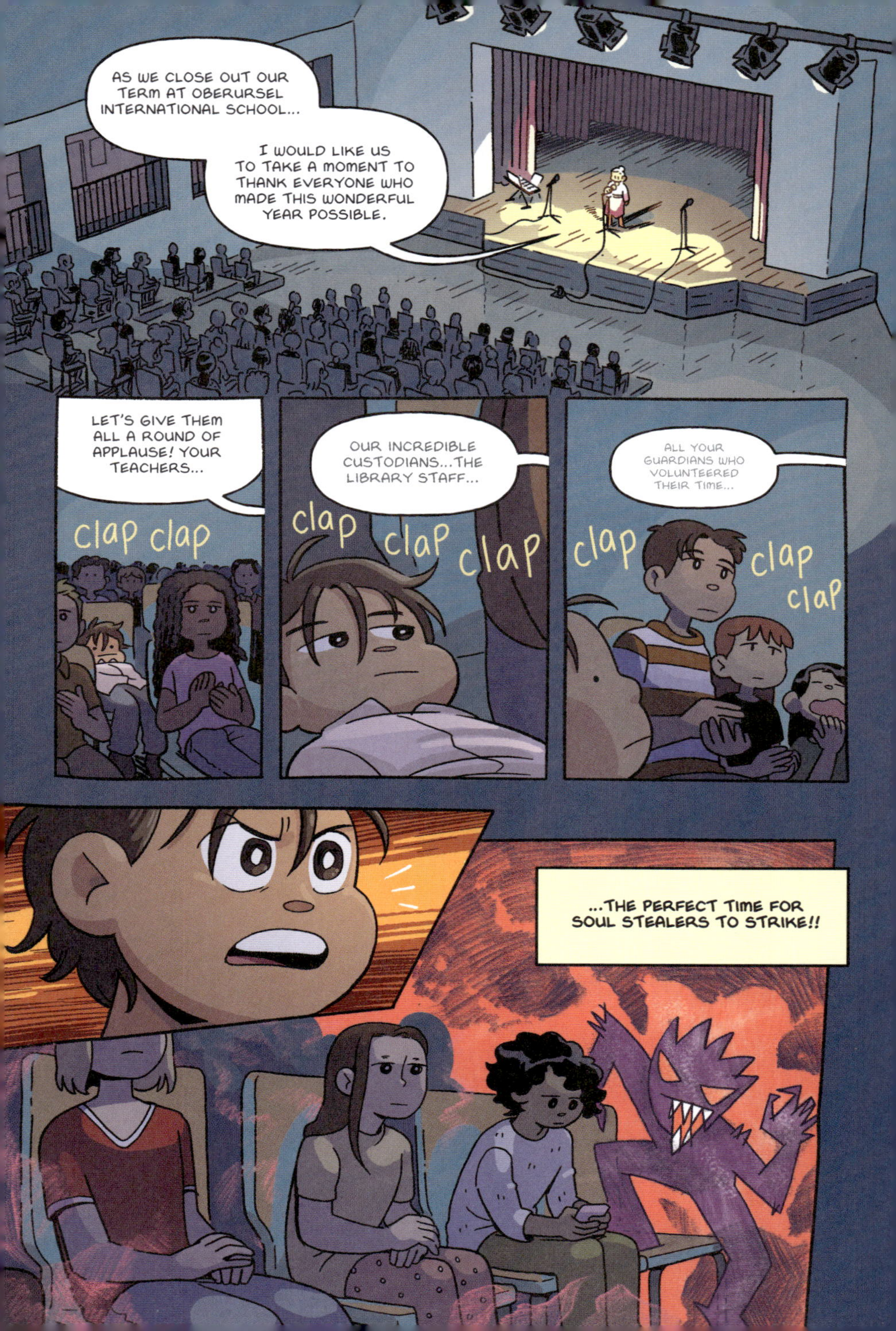
AS WE CLOSE OUT OUR TERM AT OBERURSEL INTERNATIONAL SCHOOL...
I WOULD LIKE US TO TAKE A MOMENT TO THANK EVERYONE WHO MADE THIS WONDERFUL YEAR POSSIBLE.
LET'S GIVE THEM ALL A ROUND OF APPLAUSE! YOUR TEACHERS...
clap clap
OUR INCREDIBLE CUSTODIANS...THE LIBRARY STAFF...
clap clap clap
ALL YOUR GUARDIANS WHO VOLUNTEERED THEIR TIME...
clap clap clap
...THE PERFECT TIME FOR SOUL STEALERS TO STRIKE!!

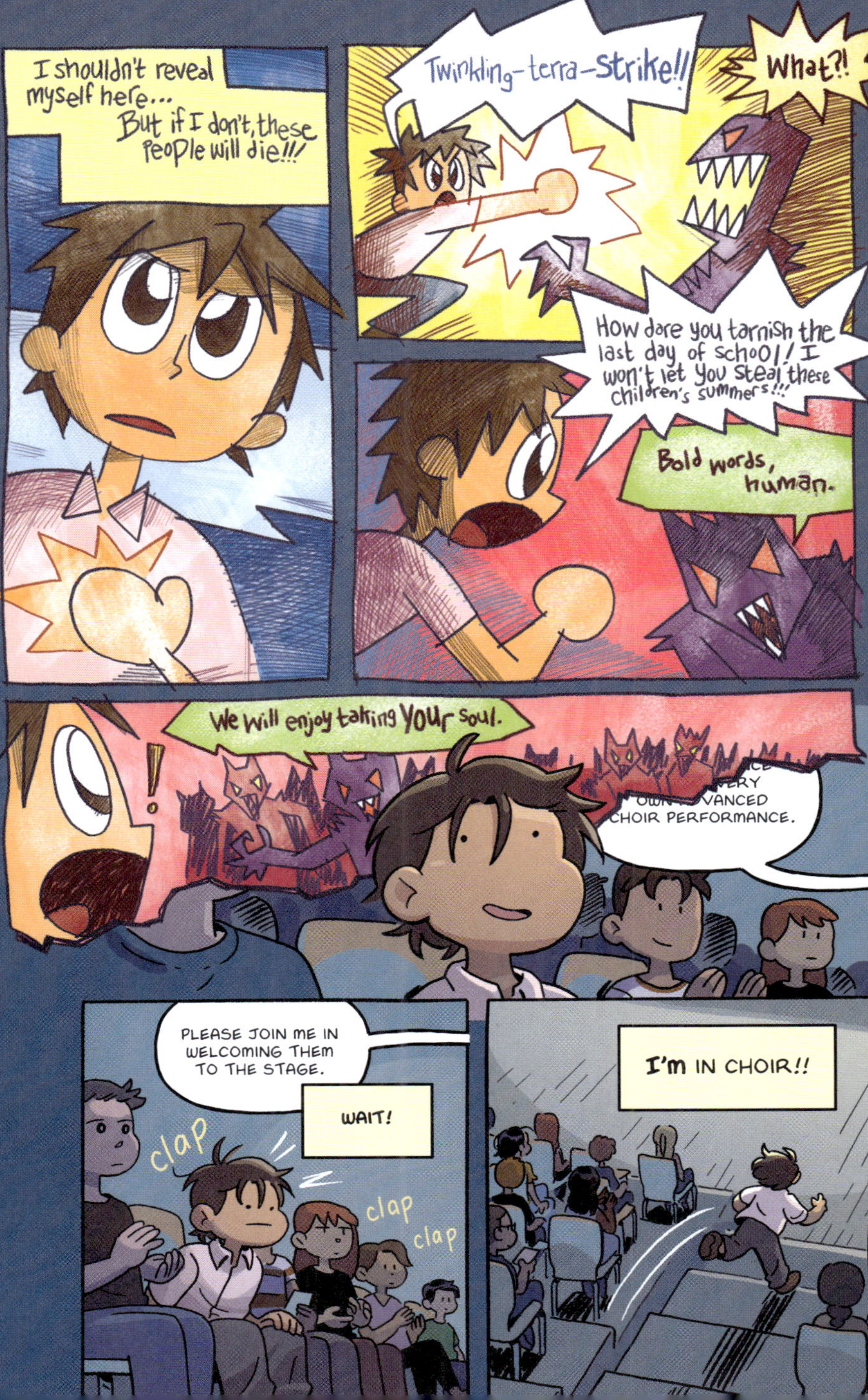
I shouldn't reveal myself here... But if I don't, these people will die!!!
Twinkling-terra-Strike!!
What?!
How dare you tarnish the last day of school! I won't let you steal these children's summers!!!
Bold words, human.
We will enjoy taking your soul.
CHOIR PERFORMANCE.
PLEASE JOIN ME IN WELCOMING THEM TO THE STAGE.
WAIT!
clap
clap
clap
I'M IN CHOIR!!

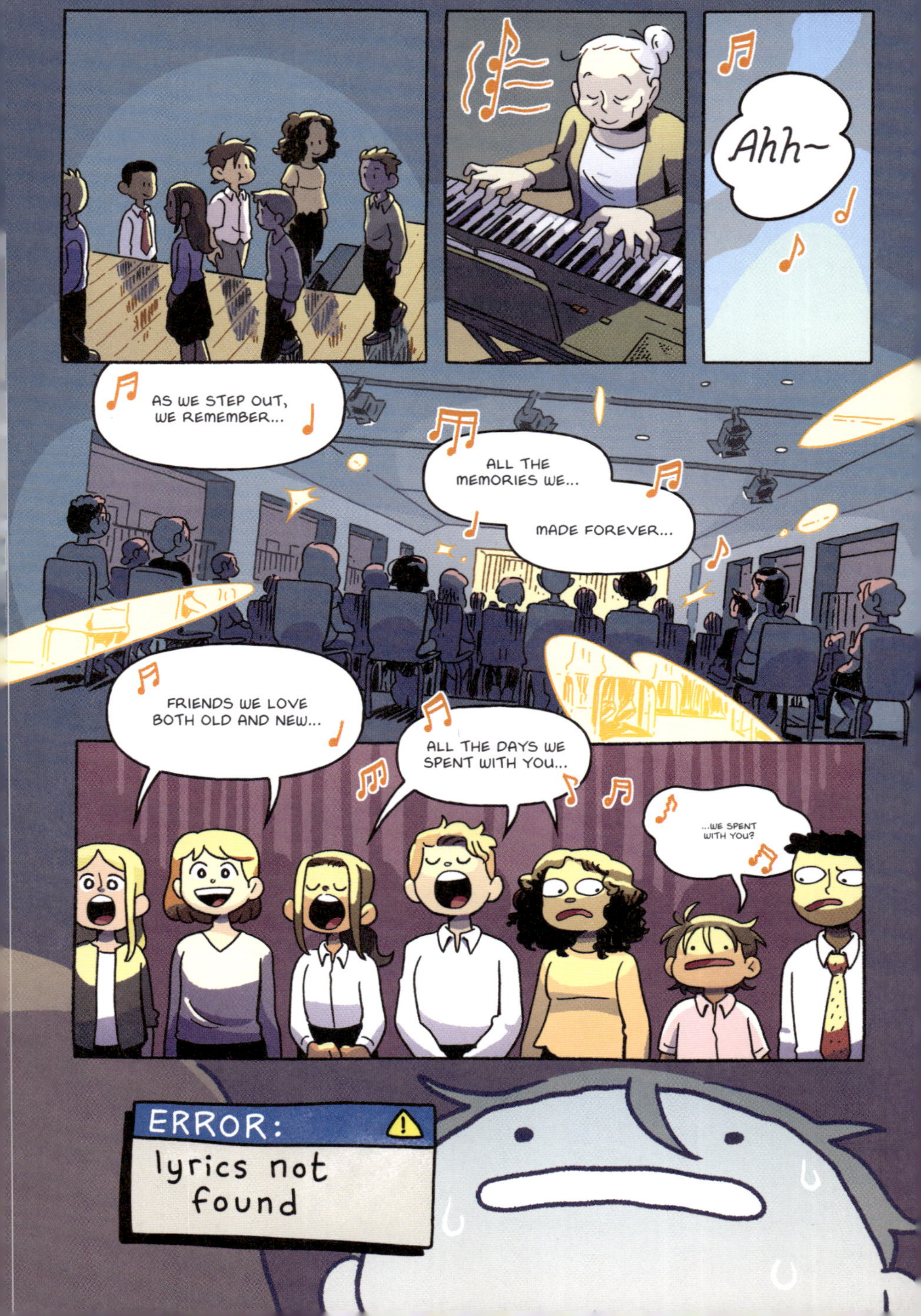
Ahh~
AS WE STEP OUT, WE REMEMBER...
ALL THE MEMORIES WE...
MADE FOREVER...
FRIENDS WE LOVE BOTH OLD AND NEW...
ALL THE DAYS WE SPENT WITH YOU...
...WE SPENT WITH YOU?
ERROR:
lyrics not found

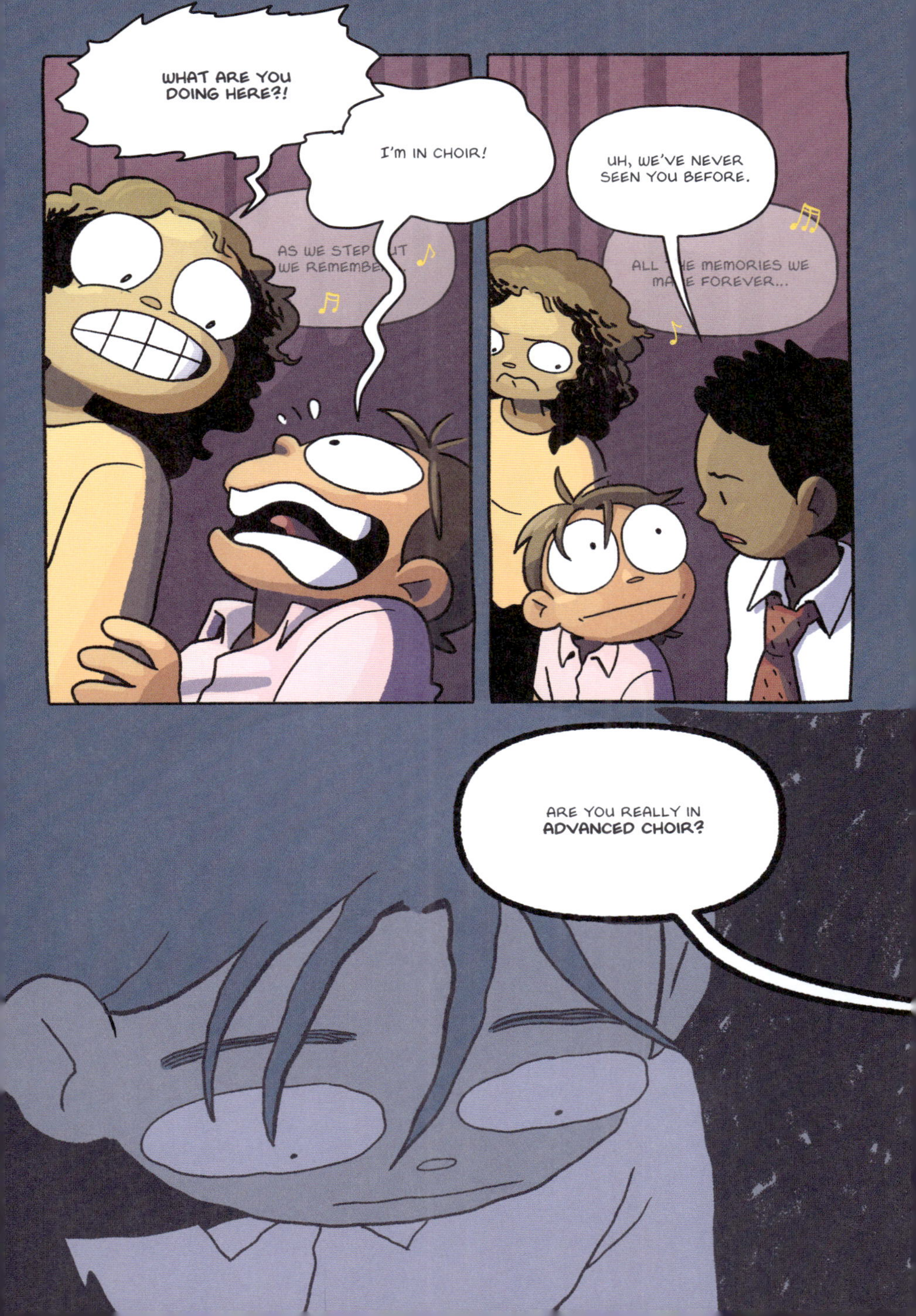
WHAT ARE YOU DOING HERE?!
I'M IN CHOIR!
UH, WE'VE NEVER SEEN YOU BEFORE.
ARE YOU REALLY IN **ADVANCED CHOIR?**

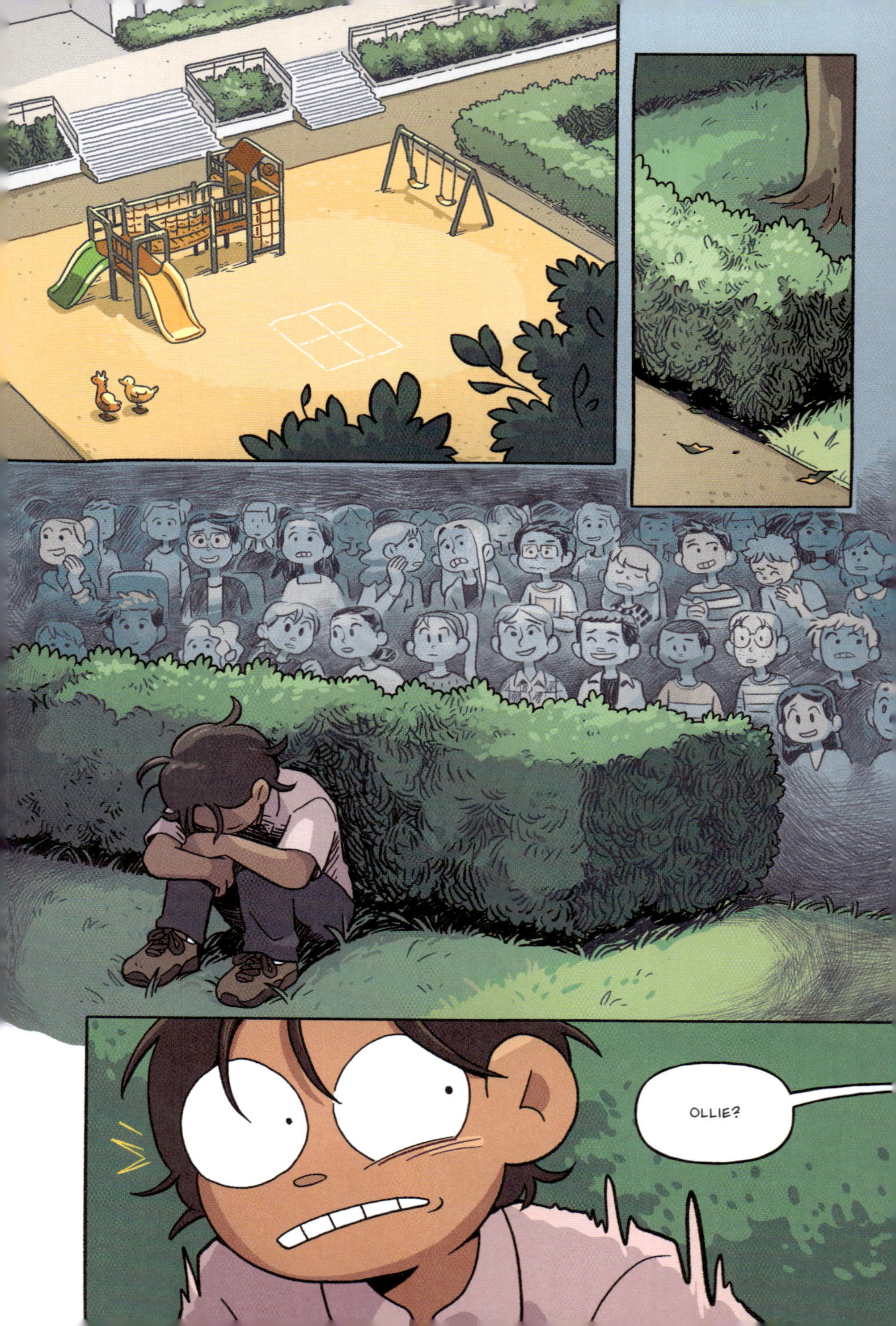
OLLIE?

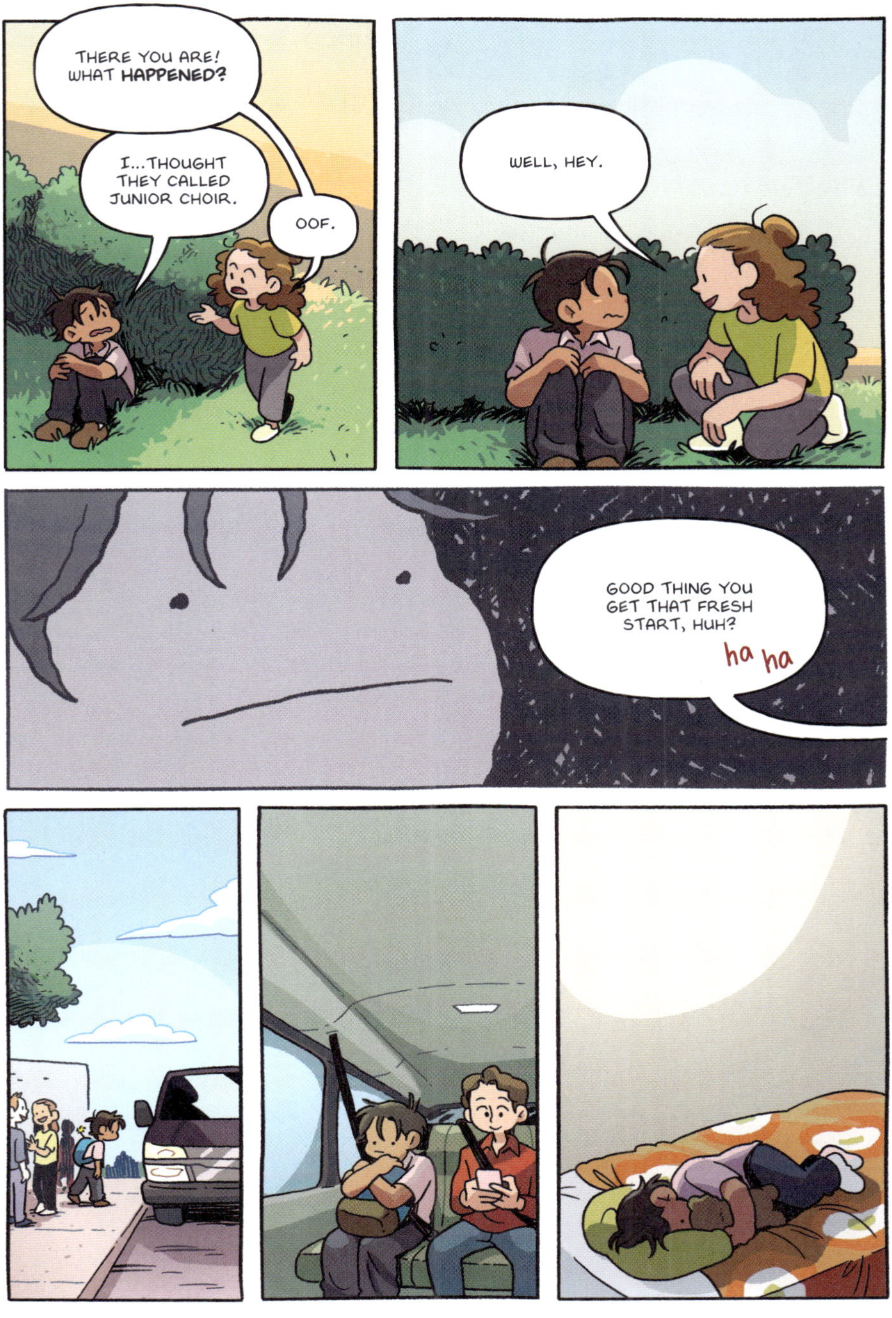
THERE YOU ARE! WHAT **HAPPENED?**
I...THOUGHT THEY CALLED JUNIOR CHOIR.
OOF.
WELL, HEY.
GOOD THING YOU GET THAT FRESH START, HUH?
ha ha

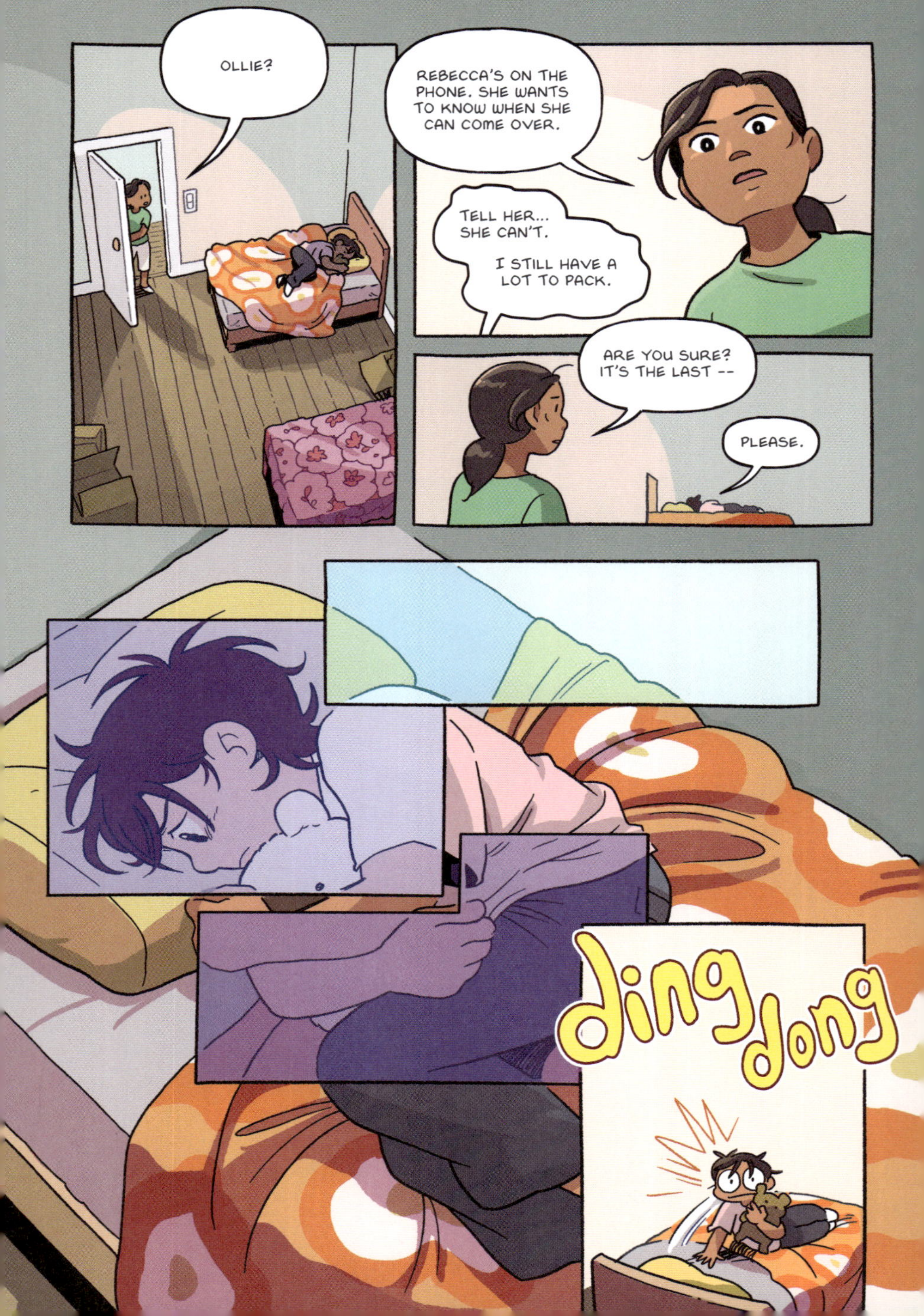
OLLIE?
REBECCA'S ON THE PHONE. SHE WANTS TO KNOW WHEN SHE CAN COME OVER.
TELL HER... SHE CAN'T.
I STILL HAVE A LOT TO PACK.
ARE YOU SURE? IT'S THE LAST --
PLEASE.
ding dong

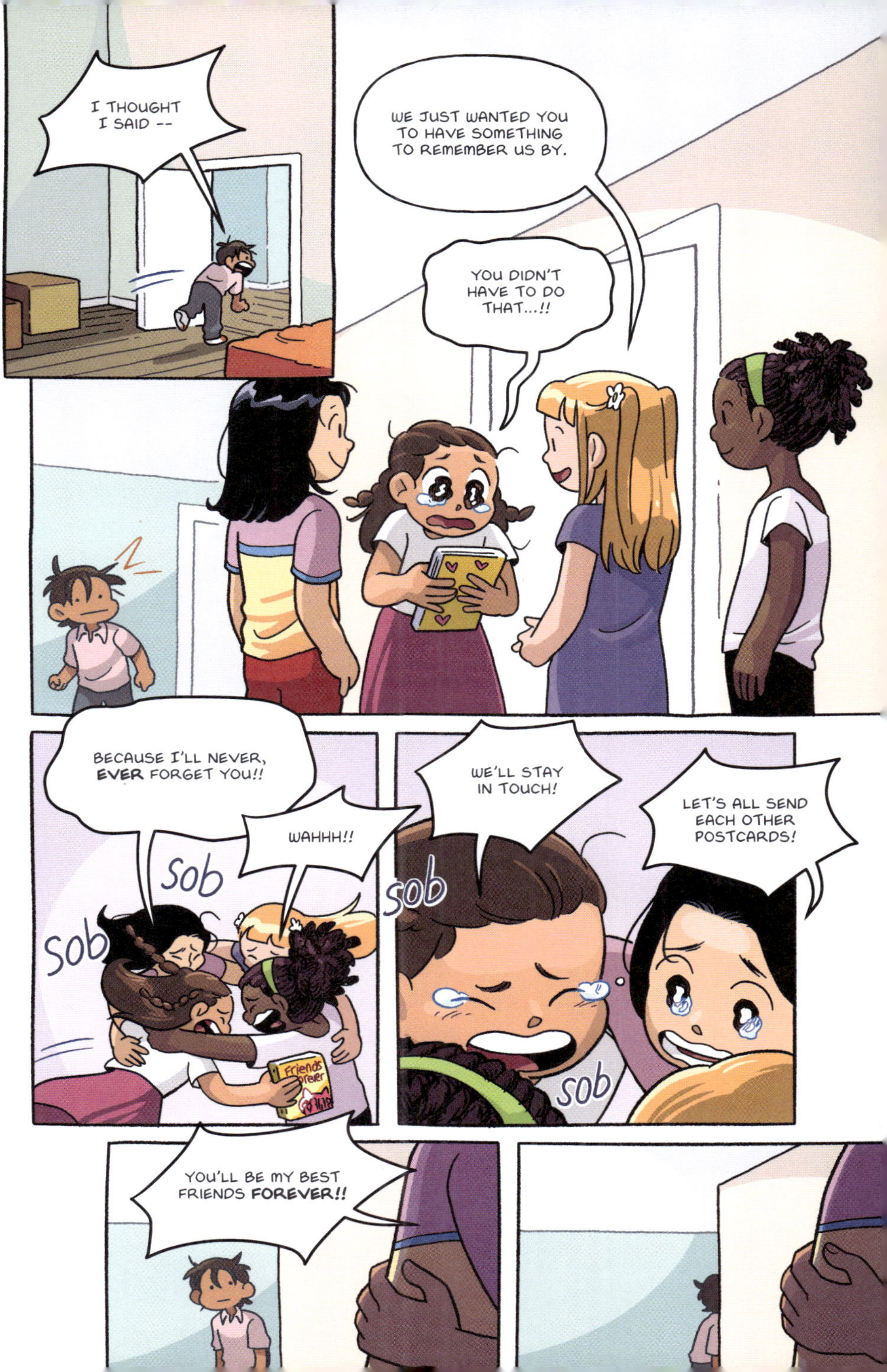
I THOUGHT I SAID --
WE JUST WANTED YOU TO HAVE SOMETHING TO REMEMBER US BY.
YOU DIDN'T HAVE TO DO THAT...!!
BECAUSE I'LL NEVER, **EVER** FORGET YOU!!
WAHHH!!
sob
sob
Friends Forever
WE'LL STAY IN TOUCH!
LET'S ALL SEND EACH OTHER POSTCARDS!
sob
sob
YOU'LL BE MY BEST FRIENDS **FOREVER!!**

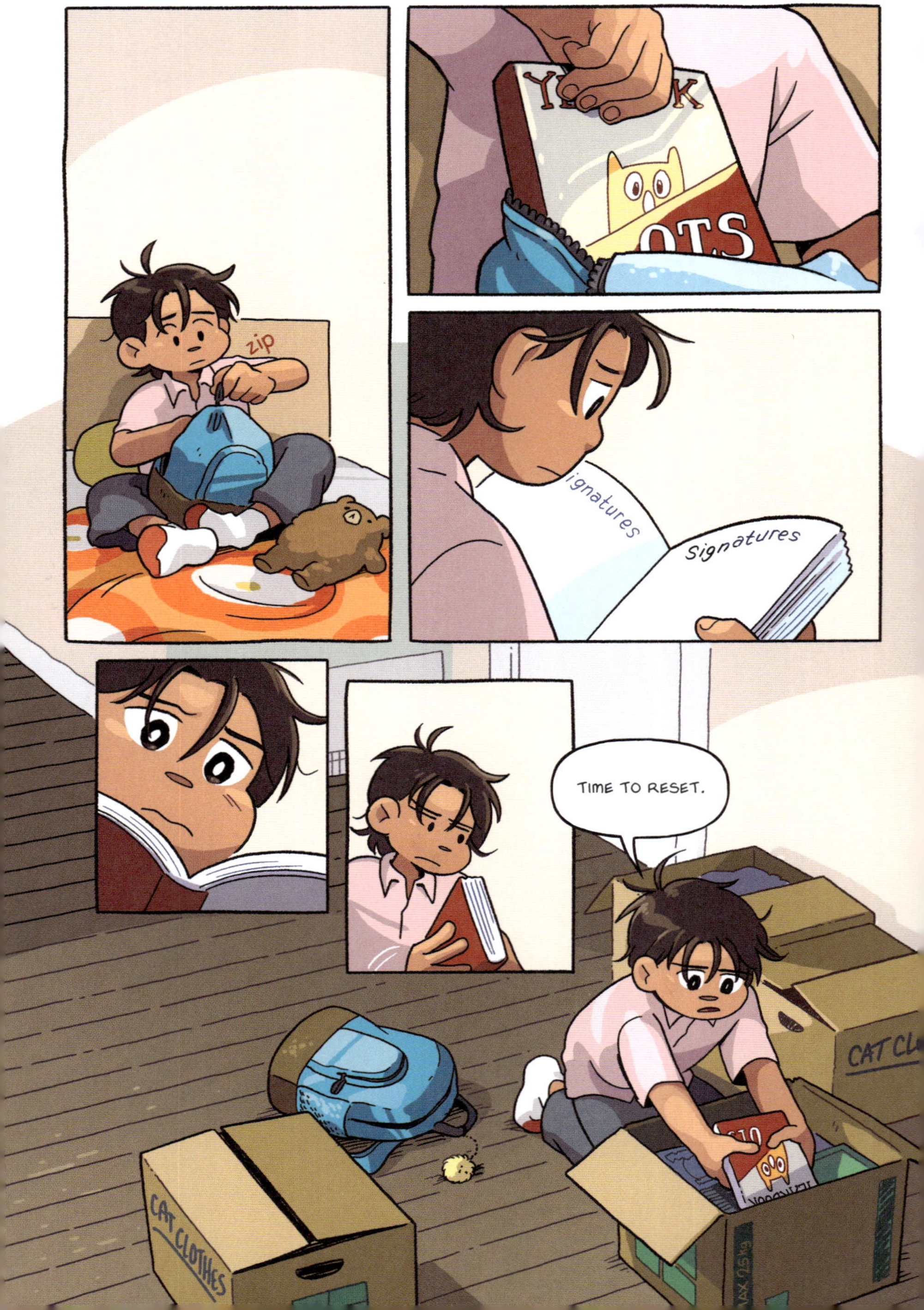
zip
Signatures
Signatures
TIME TO RESET.
CAT CLOTHES

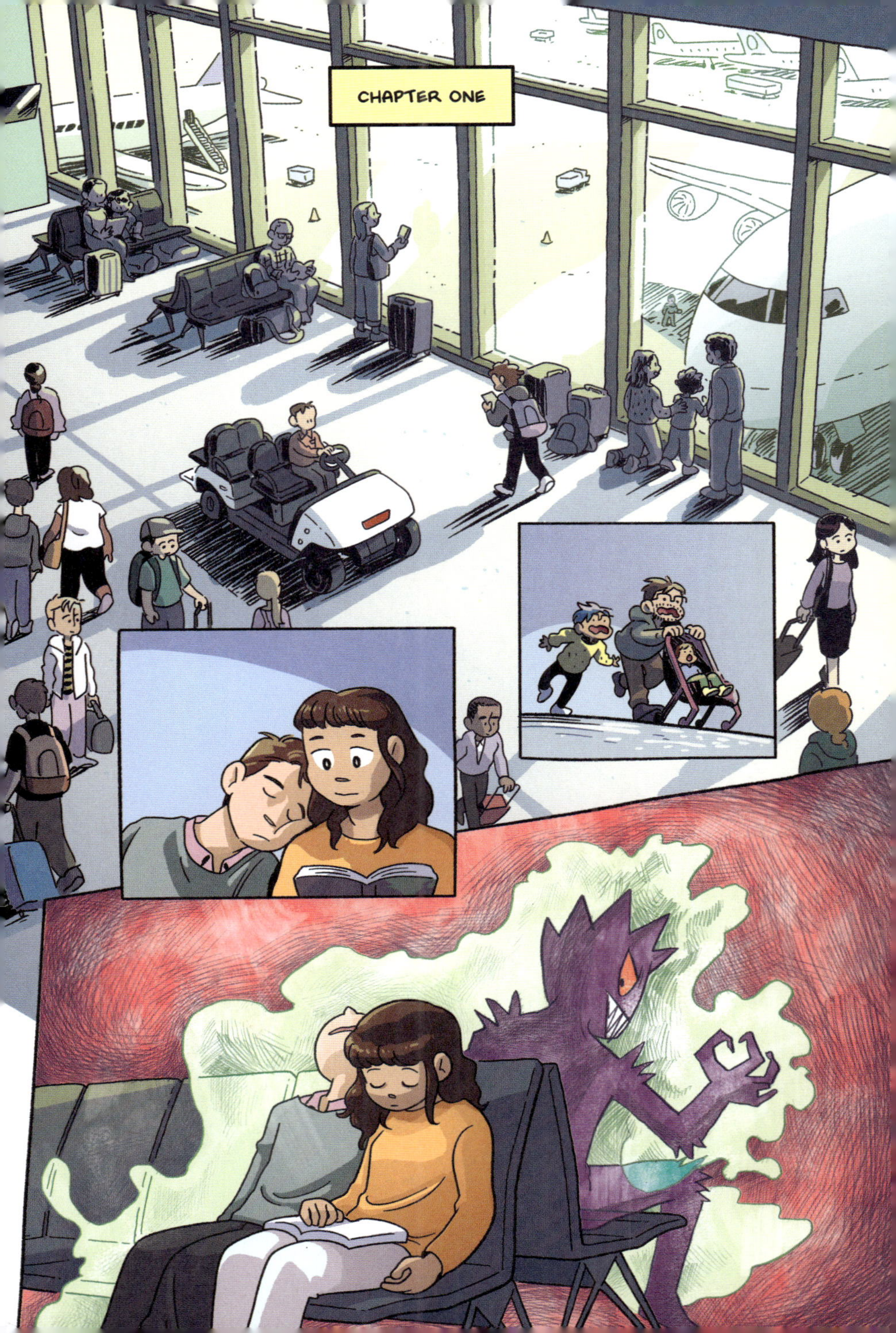
CHAPTER ONE

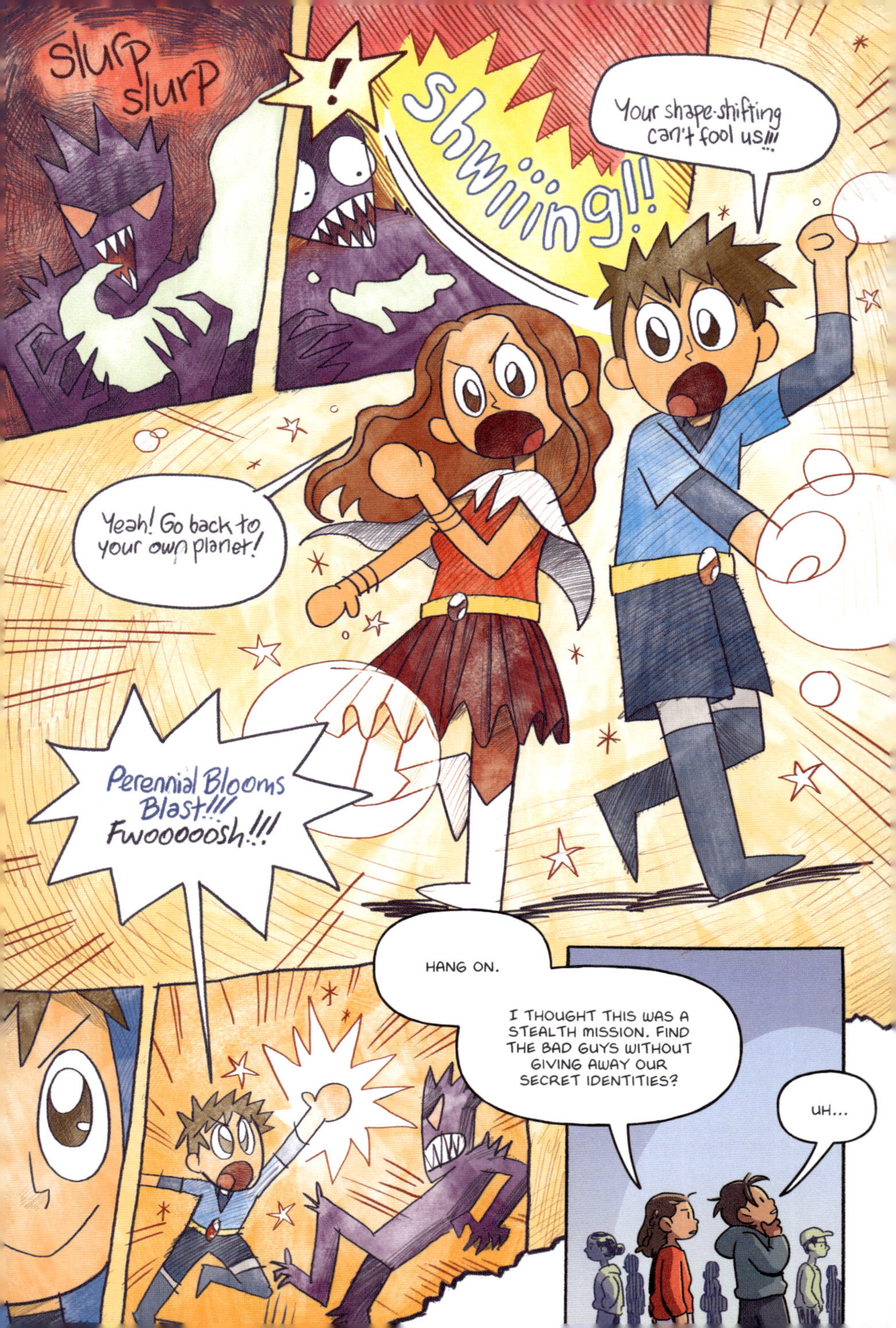
slurp slurp
!
shwiiing!!
Your shape-shifting can't fool us!!!
Yeah! Go back to your own planet!
Perennial Blooms Blast!!!
Fwoooooosh!!!
HANG ON.
I THOUGHT THIS WAS A STEALTH MISSION. FIND THE BAD GUYS WITHOUT GIVING AWAY OUR SECRET IDENTITIES?
UH...

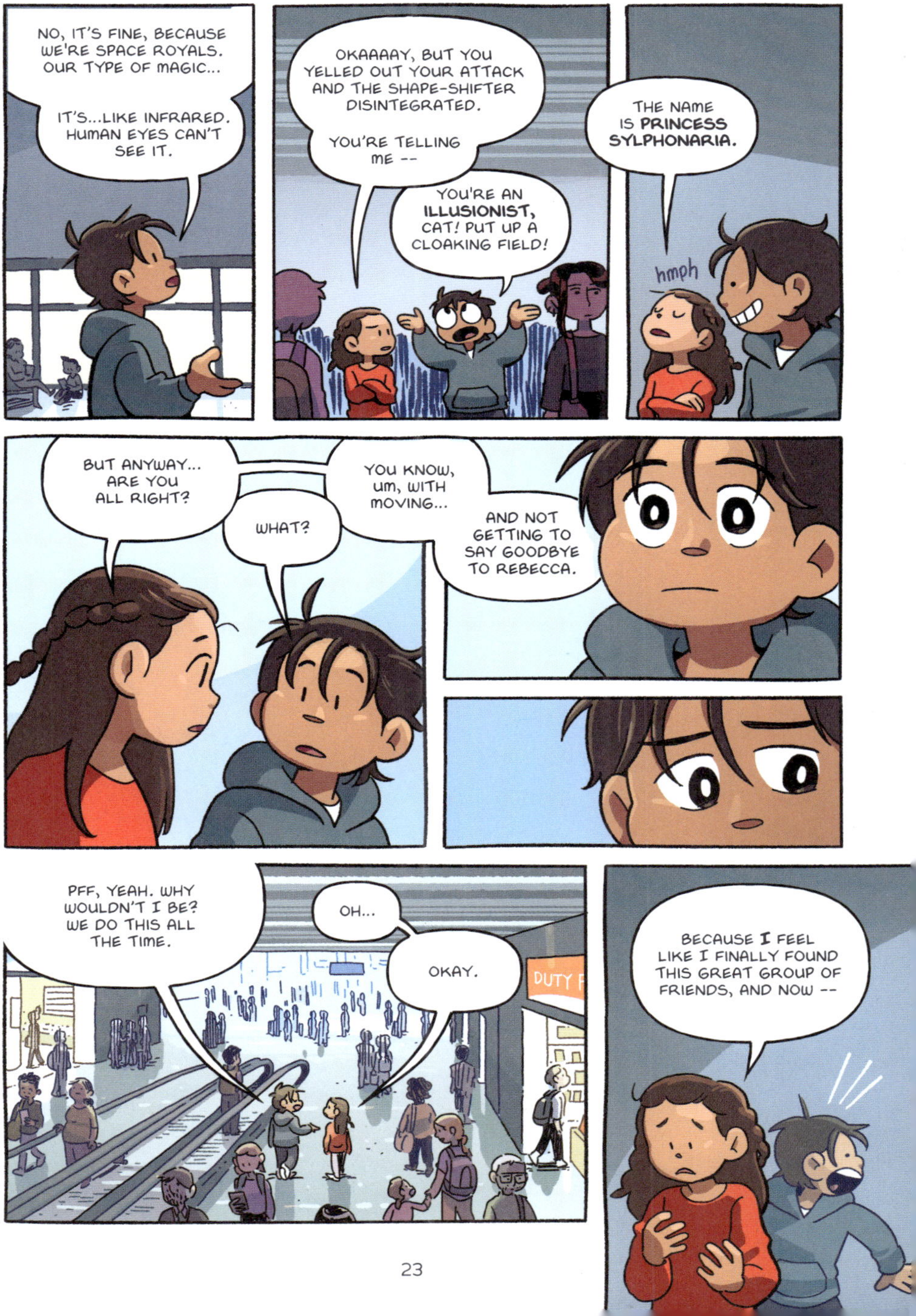
NO, IT'S FINE, BECAUSE WE'RE SPACE ROYALS. OUR TYPE OF MAGIC...
IT'S...LIKE INFRARED. HUMAN EYES CAN'T SEE IT.
OKAAAAY, BUT YOU YELLED OUT YOUR ATTACK AND THE SHAPE-SHIFTER DISINTEGRATED.
YOU'RE TELLING ME --
YOU'RE AN **ILLUSIONIST,** CAT! PUT UP A CLOAKING FIELD!
THE NAME IS **PRINCESS SYLPHONARIA.**
hmph
BUT ANYWAY... ARE YOU ALL RIGHT?
WHAT?
YOU KNOW, UM, WITH MOVING...
AND NOT GETTING TO SAY GOODBYE TO REBECCA.
PFF, YEAH. WHY WOULDN'T I BE? WE DO THIS ALL THE TIME.
OH...
OKAY.
DUTY F
BECAUSE **I** FEEL LIKE I FINALLY FOUND THIS GREAT GROUP OF FRIENDS, AND NOW --

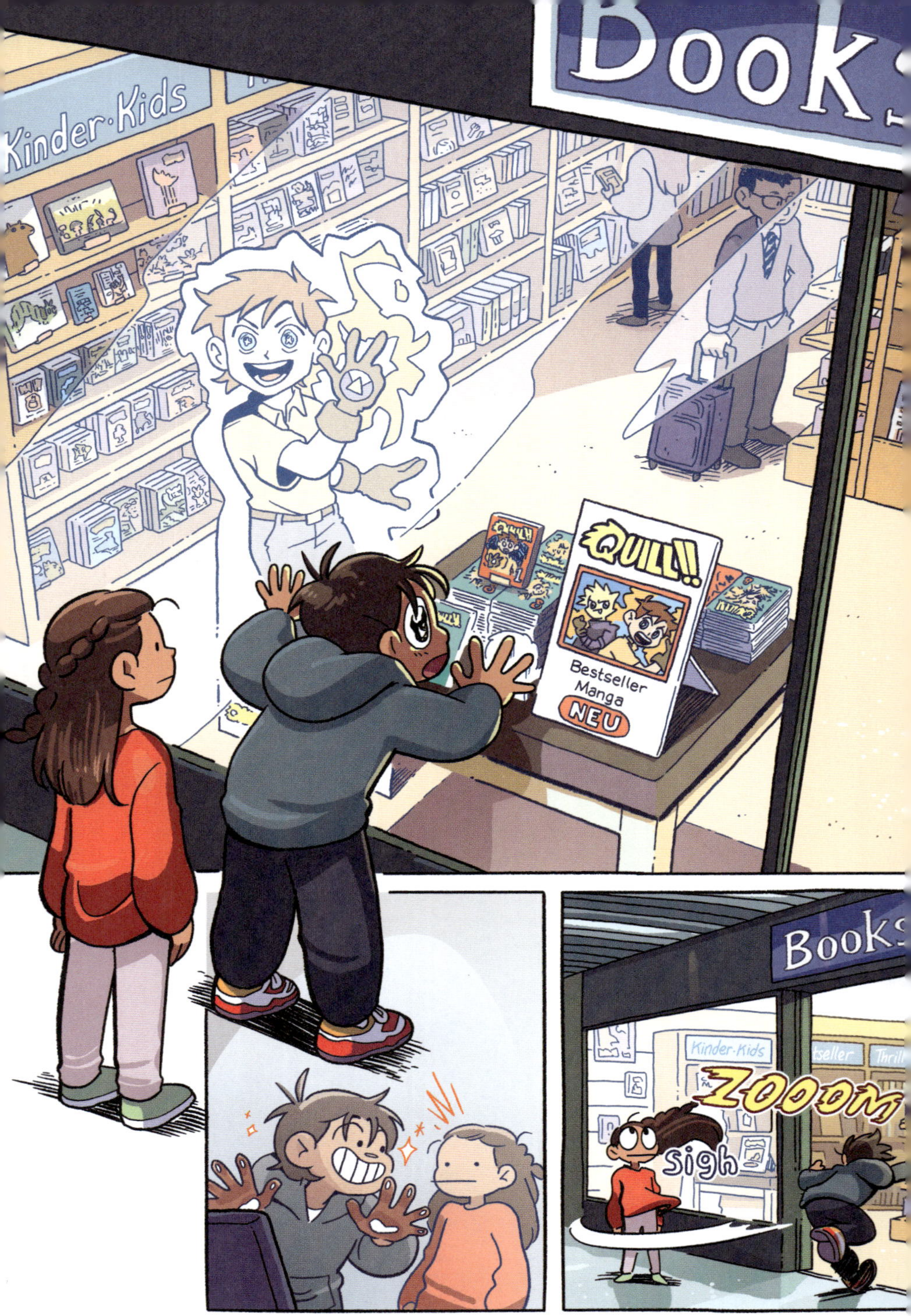
Books
Kinder·Kids
QUILL!!
Bestseller
Manga
NEU
Books
Kinder·Kids
ZOOOM
Sigh

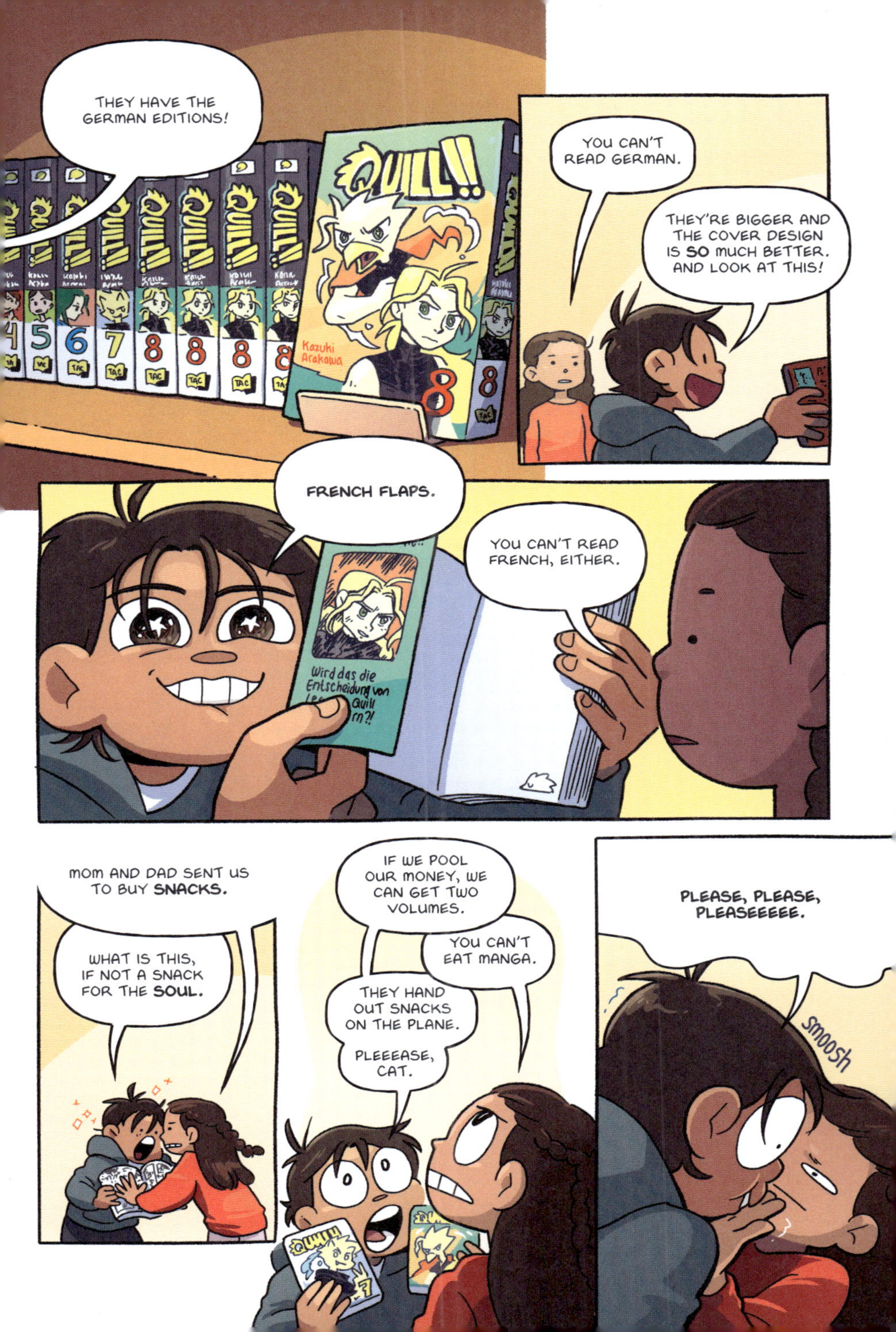
THEY HAVE THE GERMAN EDITIONS!
QUILL!!
Kazuki Arakawa
8
YOU CAN'T READ GERMAN.
THEY'RE BIGGER AND THE COVER DESIGN IS **SO** MUCH BETTER. AND LOOK AT THIS!
FRENCH FLAPS.
Wird das die Entscheidung von
YOU CAN'T READ FRENCH, EITHER.
MOM AND DAD SENT US TO BUY **SNACKS.**
WHAT IS THIS, IF NOT A SNACK FOR THE **SOUL.**
IF WE POOL OUR MONEY, WE CAN GET TWO VOLUMES.
YOU CAN'T EAT MANGA.
THEY HAND OUT SNACKS ON THE PLANE.
PLEEEASE, CAT.
PLEASE, PLEASE, PLEASEEEEE.
smoosh

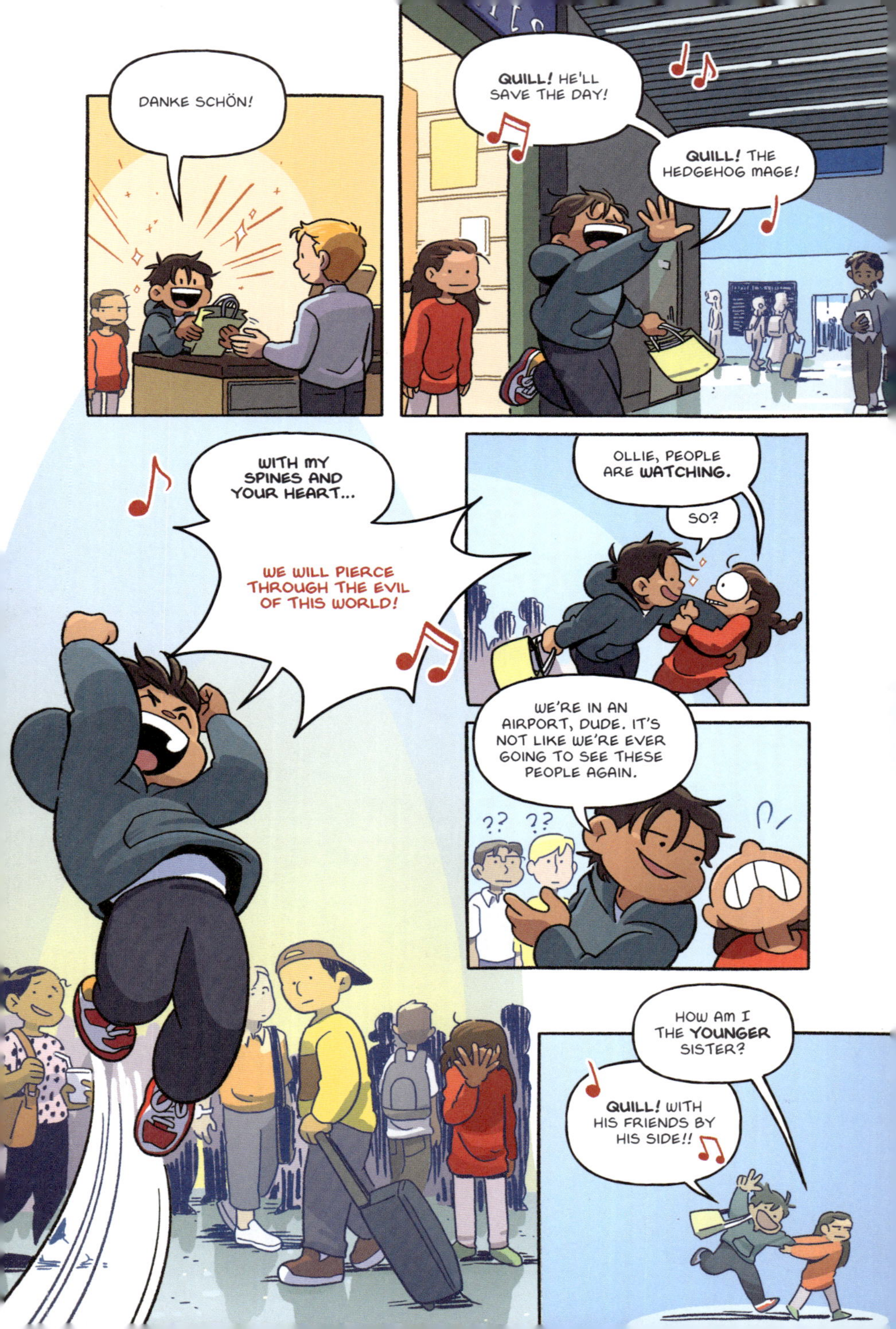
DANKE SCHÖN!
QUILL! HE'LL SAVE THE DAY!
QUILL! THE HEDGEHOG MAGE!
WITH MY SPINES AND YOUR HEART...
WE WILL PIERCE THROUGH THE EVIL OF THIS WORLD!
OLLIE, PEOPLE ARE WATCHING.
SO?
WE'RE IN AN AIRPORT, DUDE. IT'S NOT LIKE WE'RE EVER GOING TO SEE THESE PEOPLE AGAIN.
??
??
HOW AM I THE YOUNGER SISTER?
QUILL! WITH HIS FRIENDS BY HIS SIDE!!

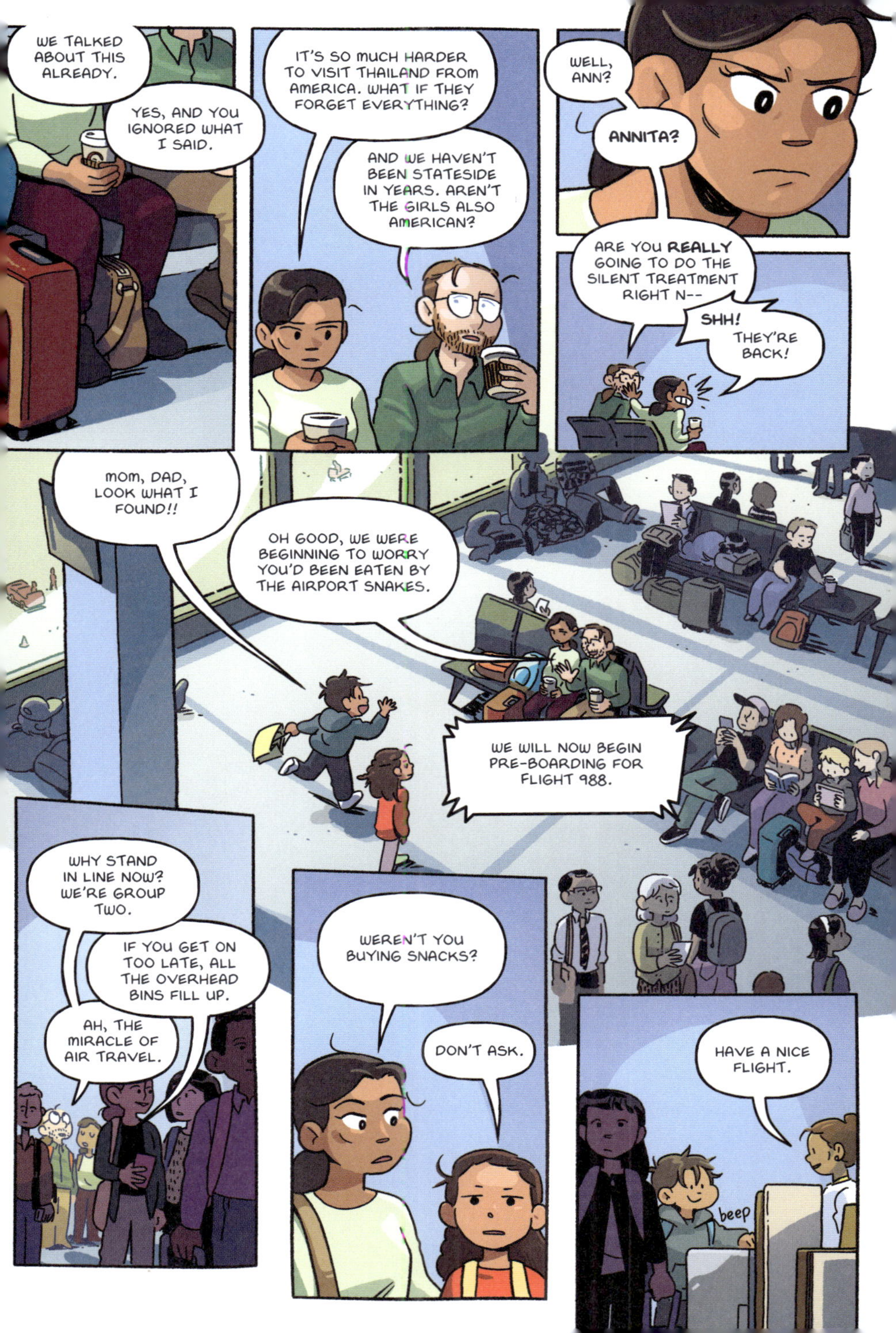
WE TALKED ABOUT THIS ALREADY.
YES, AND YOU IGNORED WHAT I SAID.
IT'S SO MUCH HARDER TO VISIT THAILAND FROM AMERICA. WHAT IF THEY FORGET EVERYTHING?
AND WE HAVEN'T BEEN STATESIDE IN YEARS. AREN'T THE GIRLS ALSO AMERICAN?
WELL, ANN?
ANNITA?
ARE YOU REALLY GOING TO DO THE SILENT TREATMENT RIGHT N--
SHH! THEY'RE BACK!
MOM, DAD, LOOK WHAT I FOUND!!
OH GOOD, WE WERE BEGINNING TO WORRY YOU'D BEEN EATEN BY THE AIRPORT SNAKES.
WE WILL NOW BEGIN PRE-BOARDING FOR FLIGHT 988.
WHY STAND IN LINE NOW? WE'RE GROUP TWO.
IF YOU GET ON TOO LATE, ALL THE OVERHEAD BINS FILL UP.
AH, THE MIRACLE OF AIR TRAVEL.
WEREN'T YOU BUYING SNACKS?
DON'T ASK.
HAVE A NICE FLIGHT.
beep

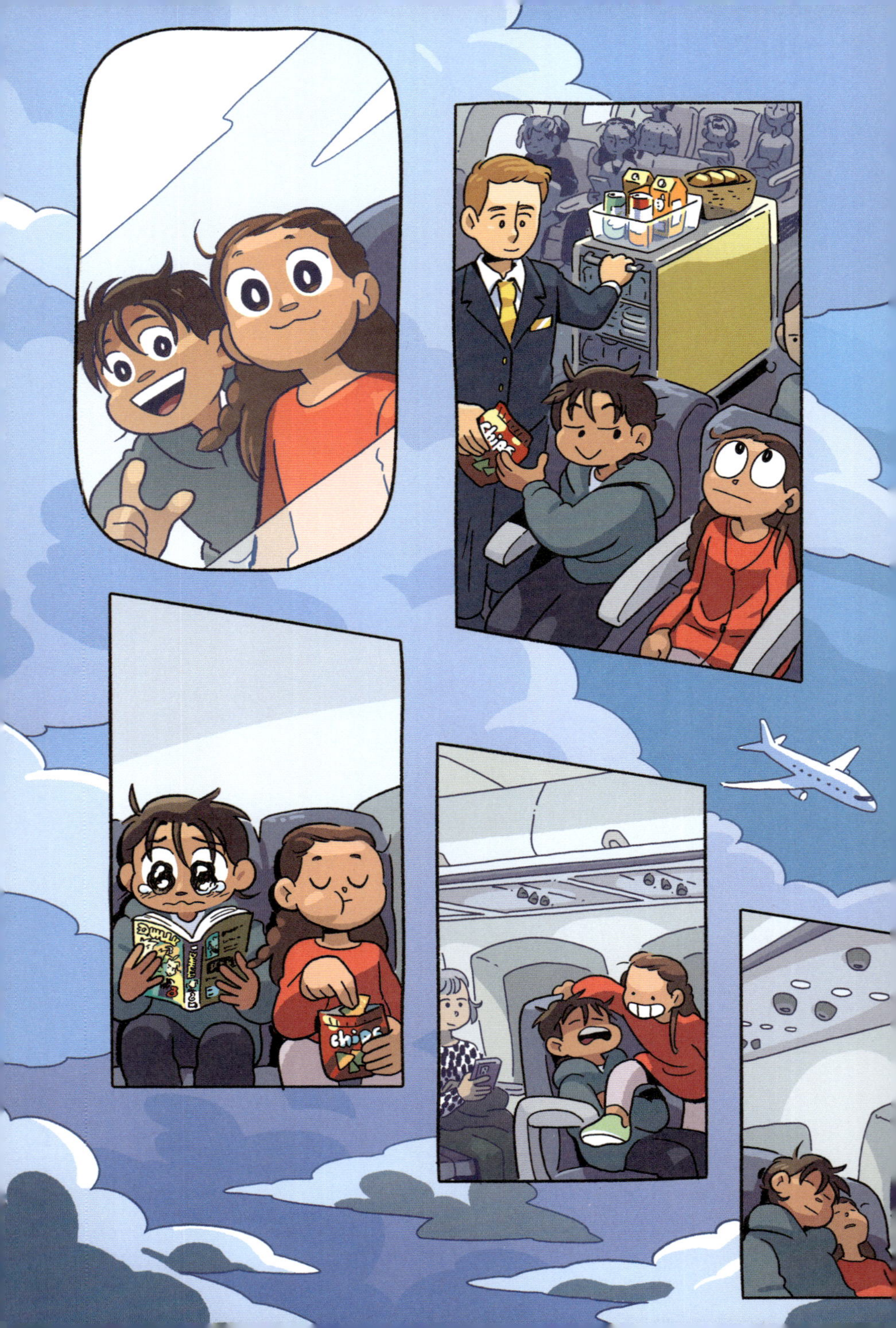
chips
chips

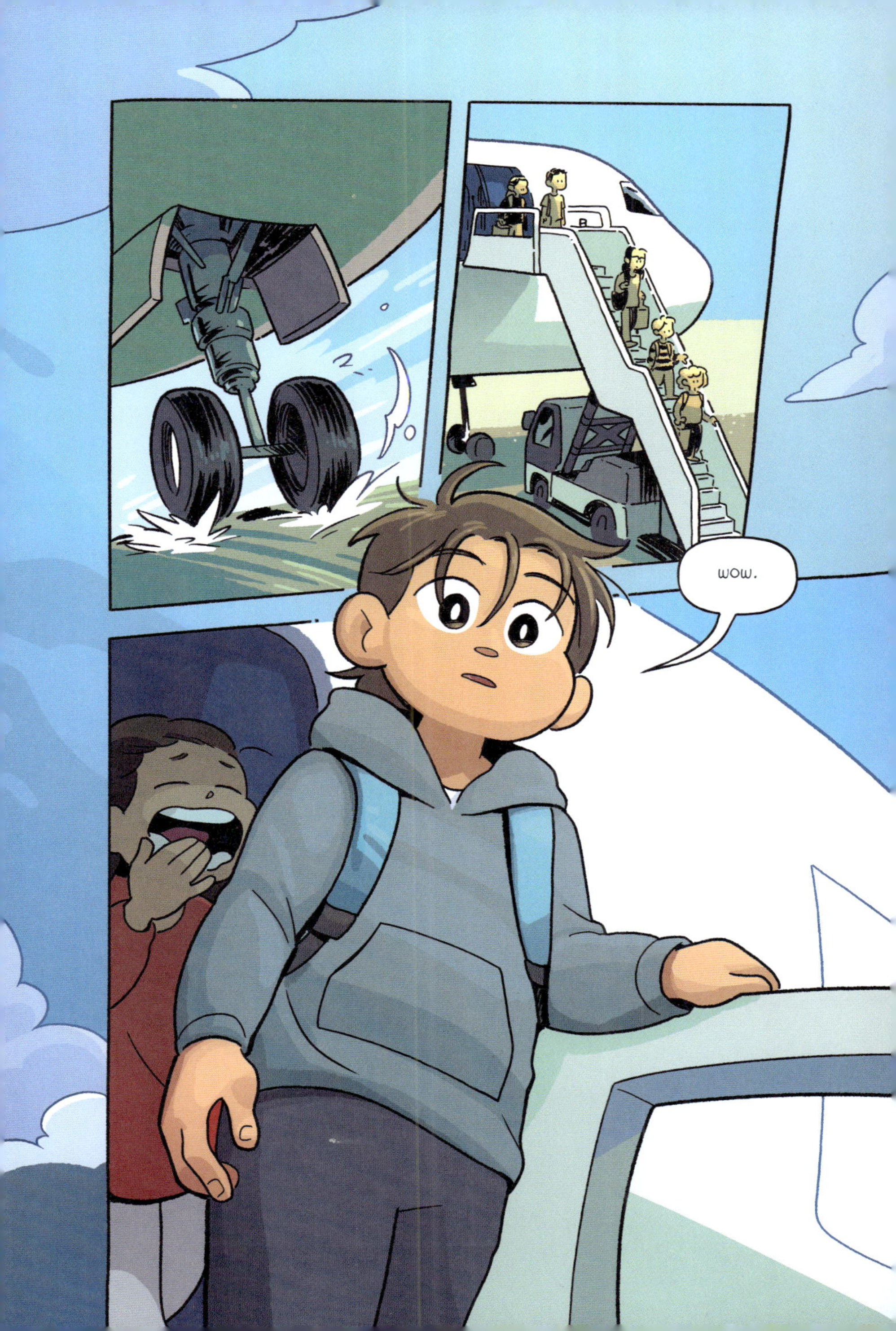
WOW.

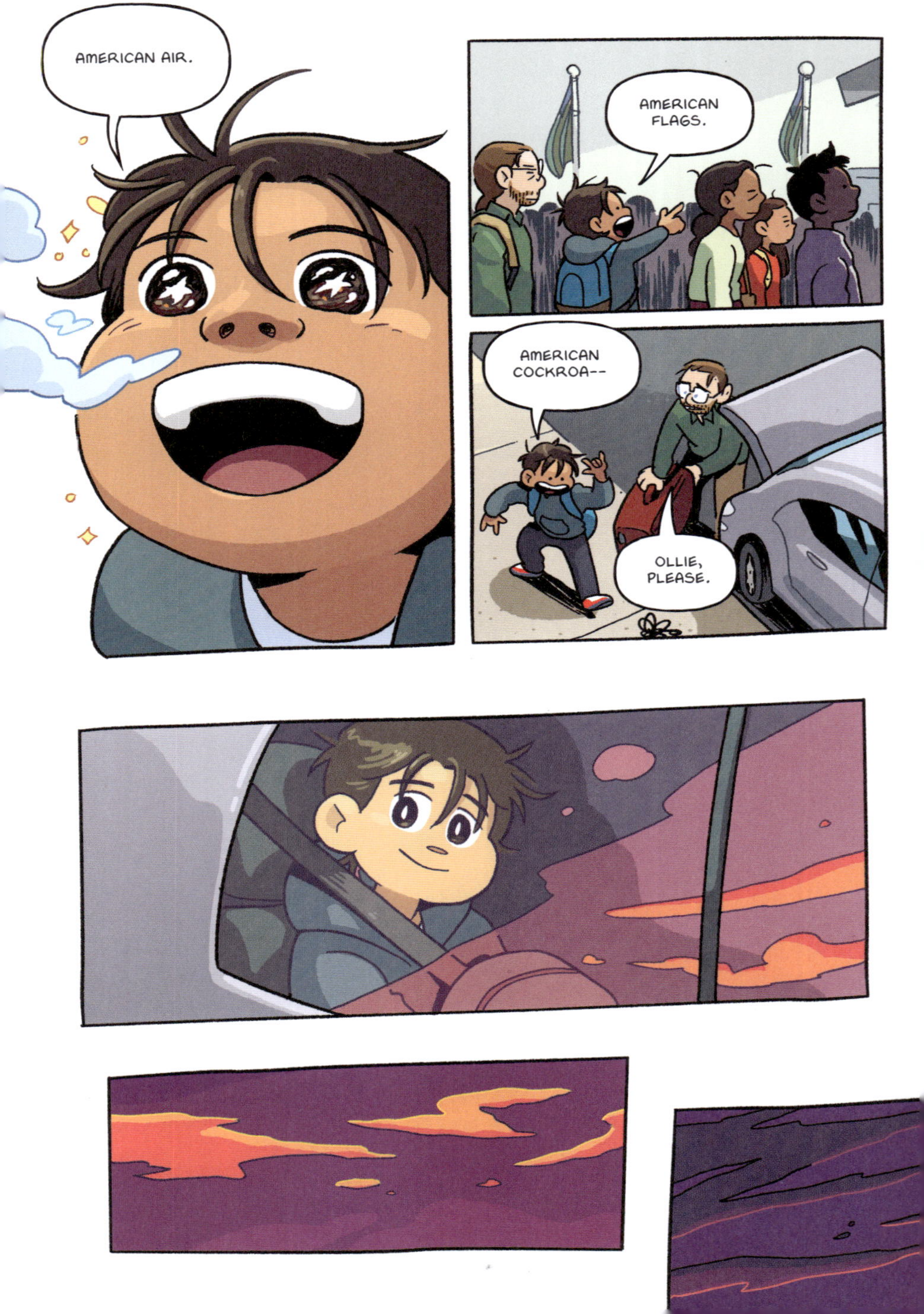
AMERICAN AIR.
AMERICAN FLAGS.
AMERICAN COCKROA--
OLLIE, PLEASE.

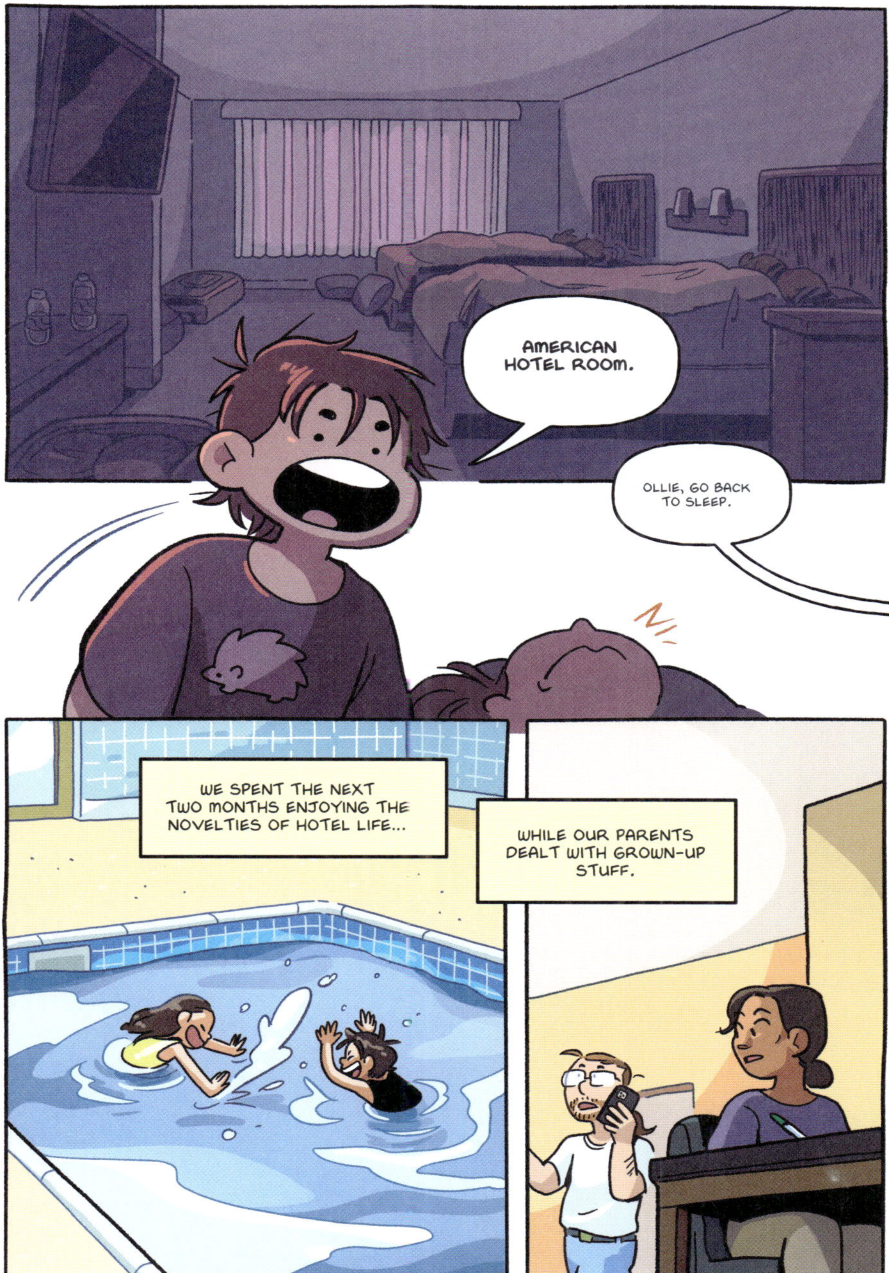
AMERICAN HOTEL ROOM.
OLLIE, GO BACK TO SLEEP.
WE SPENT THE NEXT TWO MONTHS ENJOYING THE NOVELTIES OF HOTEL LIFE...
WHILE OUR PARENTS DEALT WITH GROWN-UP STUFF.

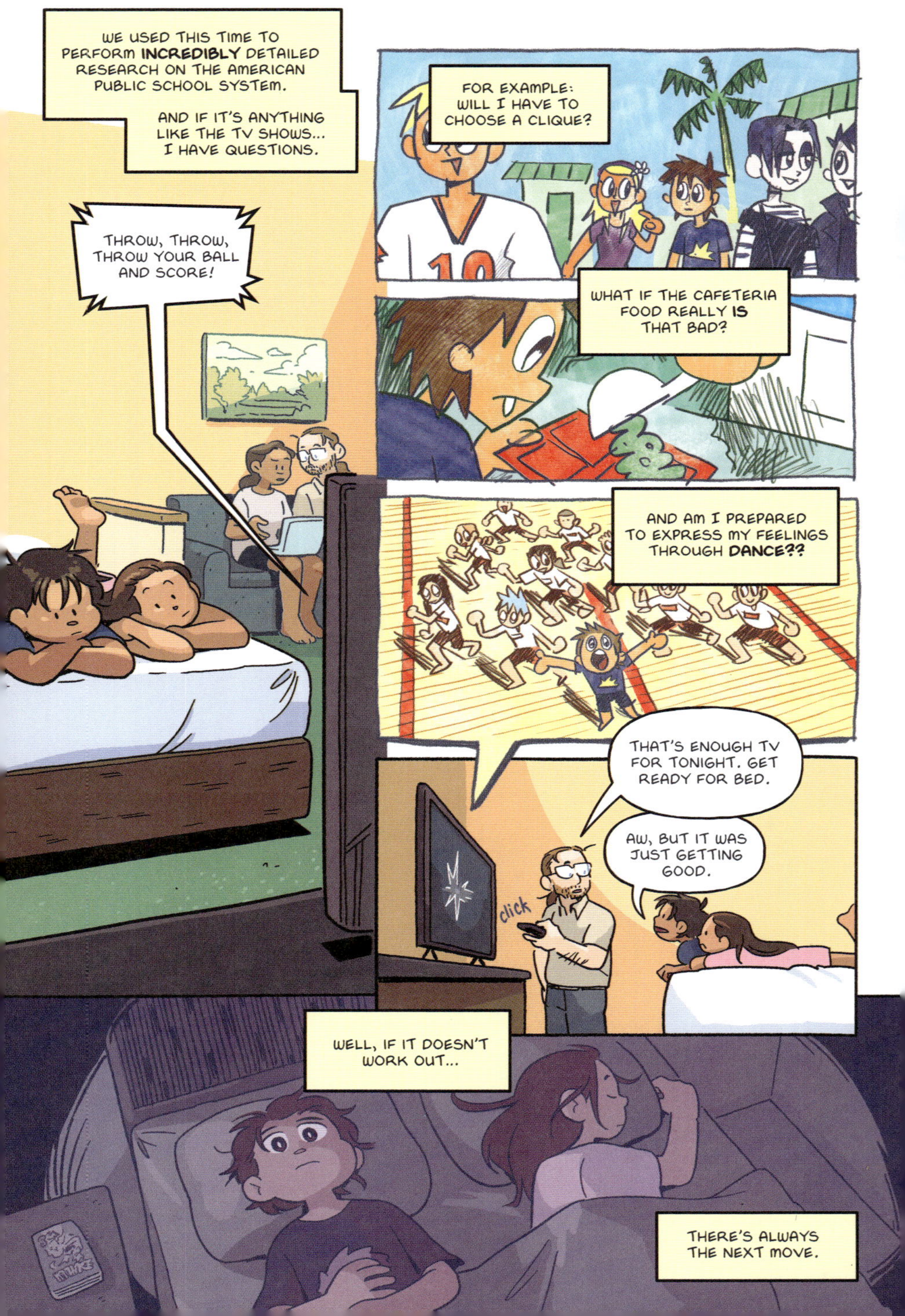
WE USED THIS TIME TO PERFORM **INCREDIBLY** DETAILED RESEARCH ON THE AMERICAN PUBLIC SCHOOL SYSTEM.
AND IF IT'S ANYTHING LIKE THE TV SHOWS... I HAVE QUESTIONS.
FOR EXAMPLE: WILL I HAVE TO CHOOSE A CLIQUE?
THROW, THROW, THROW YOUR BALL AND SCORE!
WHAT IF THE CAFETERIA FOOD REALLY **IS** THAT BAD?
AND AM I PREPARED TO EXPRESS MY FEELINGS THROUGH **DANCE??**
THAT'S ENOUGH TV FOR TONIGHT. GET READY FOR BED.
click
AW, BUT IT WAS JUST GETTING GOOD.
WELL, IF IT DOESN'T WORK OUT...
THERE'S ALWAYS THE NEXT MOVE.

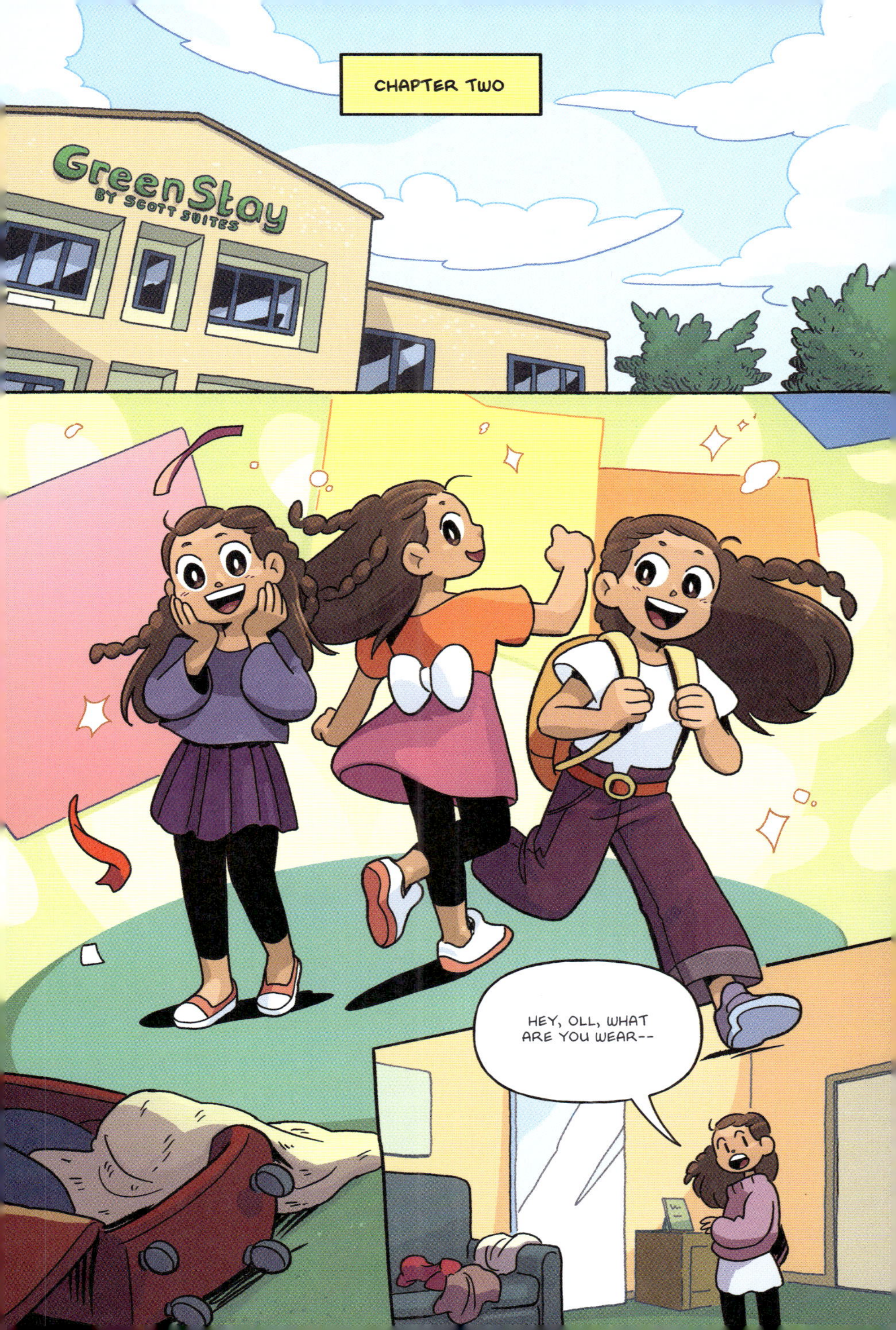
CHAPTER TWO
GreenStay
BY SCOTT SUITES
HEY, OLL, WHAT ARE YOU WEAR--

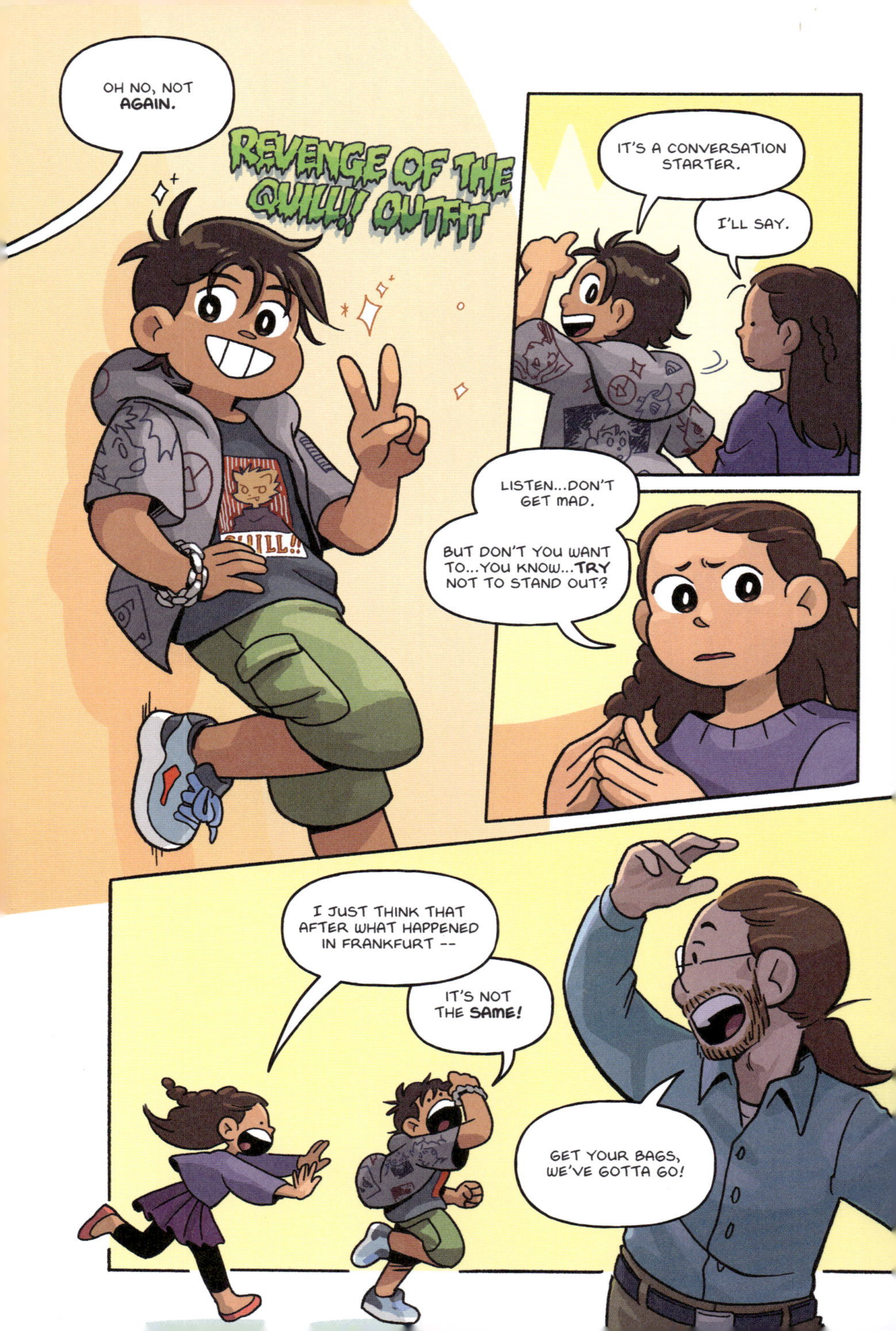
OH NO, NOT **AGAIN.**
REVENGE OF THE QUILL!! OUTFIT
QUILL!!
IT'S A CONVERSATION STARTER.
I'LL SAY.
LISTEN...DON'T GET MAD.
BUT DON'T YOU WANT TO...YOU KNOW...**TRY** NOT TO STAND OUT?
I JUST THINK THAT AFTER WHAT HAPPENED IN FRANKFURT --
IT'S NOT THE **SAME!**
GET YOUR BAGS, WE'VE GOTTA GO!

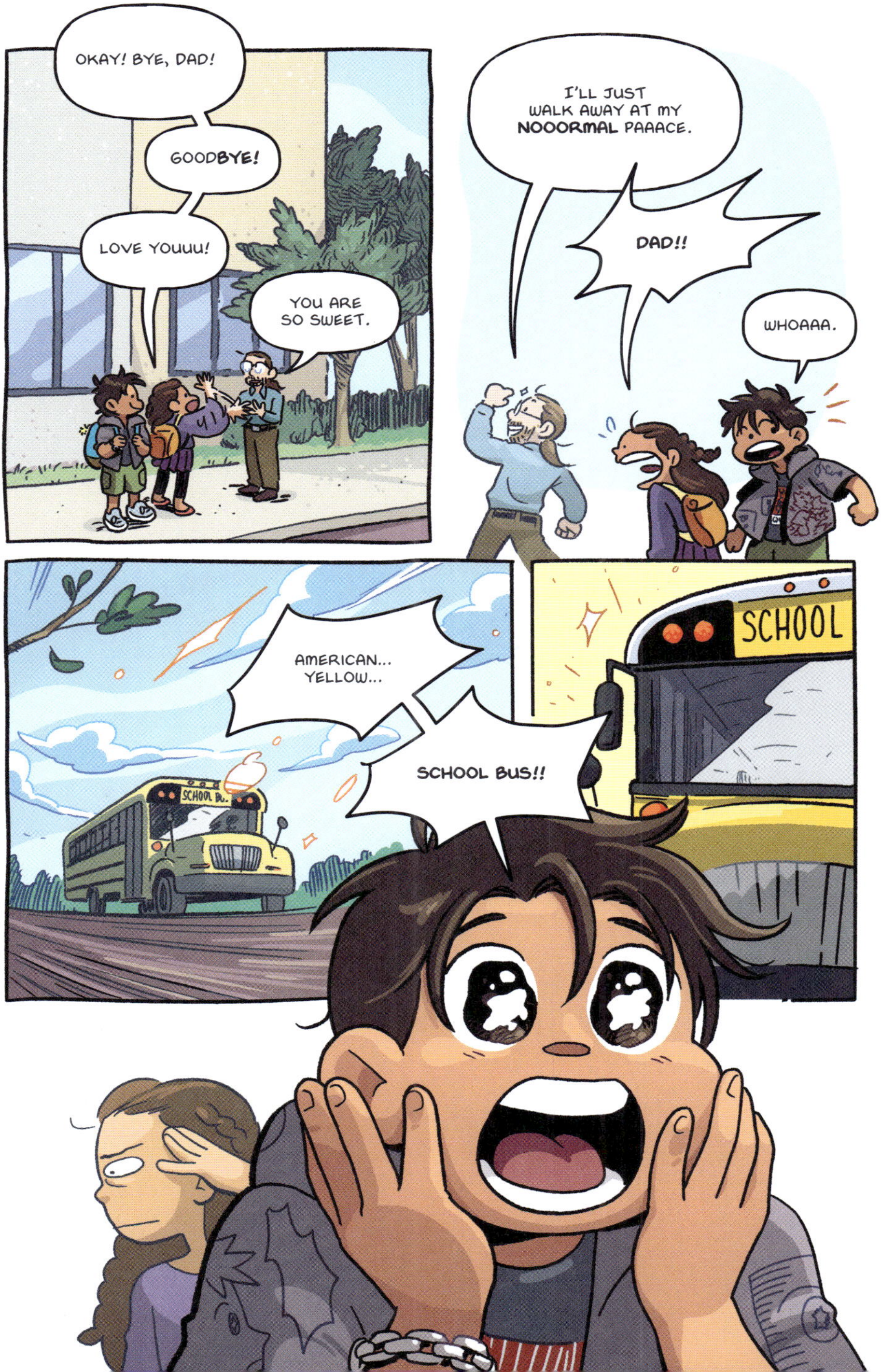
OKAY! BYE, DAD!
GOODBYE!
LOVE YOUUU!
YOU ARE SO SWEET.
I'LL JUST WALK AWAY AT MY NOOORMAL PAAACE.
DAD!!
WHOAAA.
AMERICAN... YELLOW...
SCHOOL BUS!!
SCHOOL

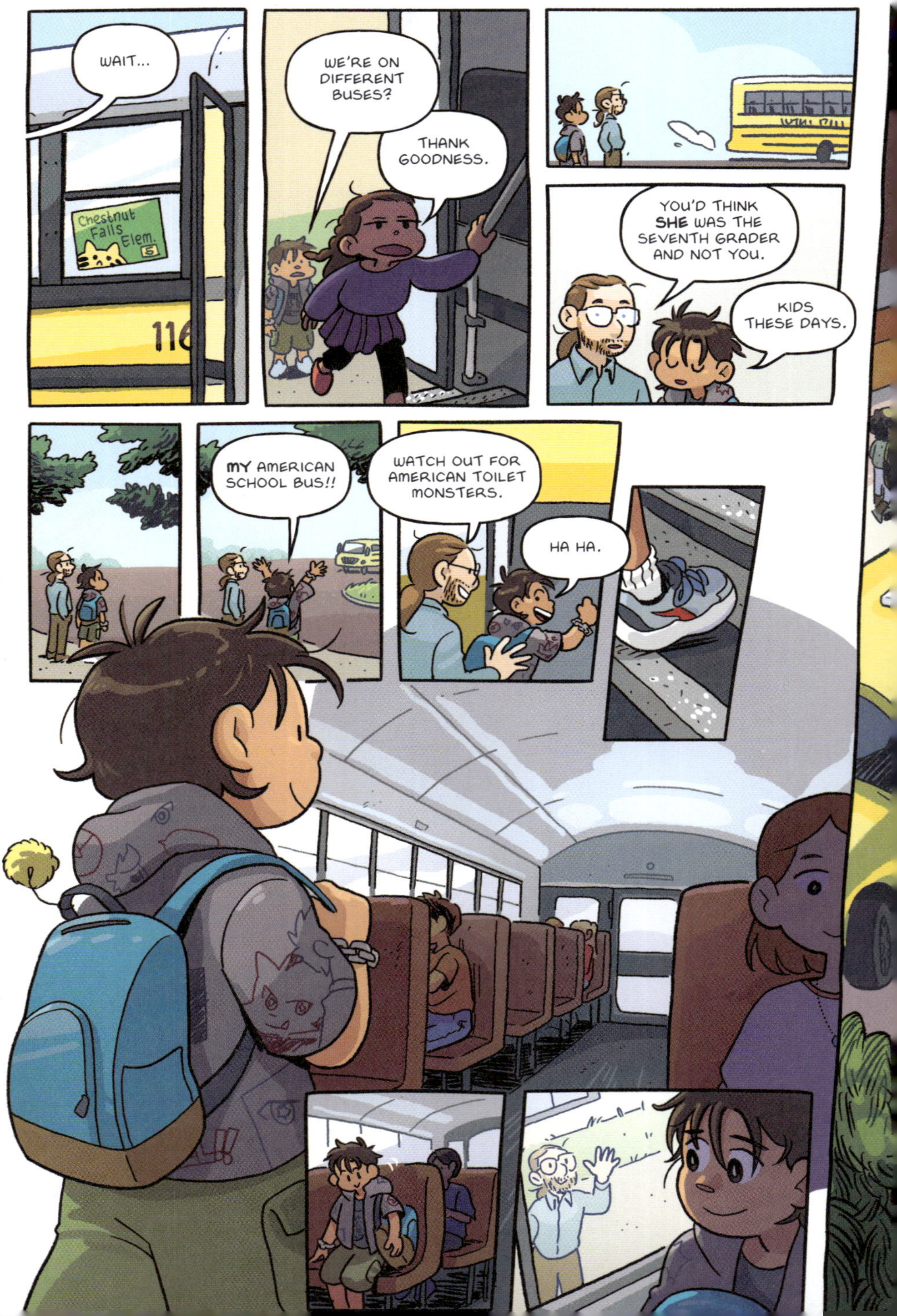
WAIT...
Chestnut Falls Elem.
WE'RE ON DIFFERENT BUSES?
THANK GOODNESS.
YOU'D THINK **SHE** WAS THE SEVENTH GRADER AND NOT YOU.
KIDS THESE DAYS.
MY AMERICAN SCHOOL BUS!!
WATCH OUT FOR AMERICAN TOILET MONSTERS.
HA HA.

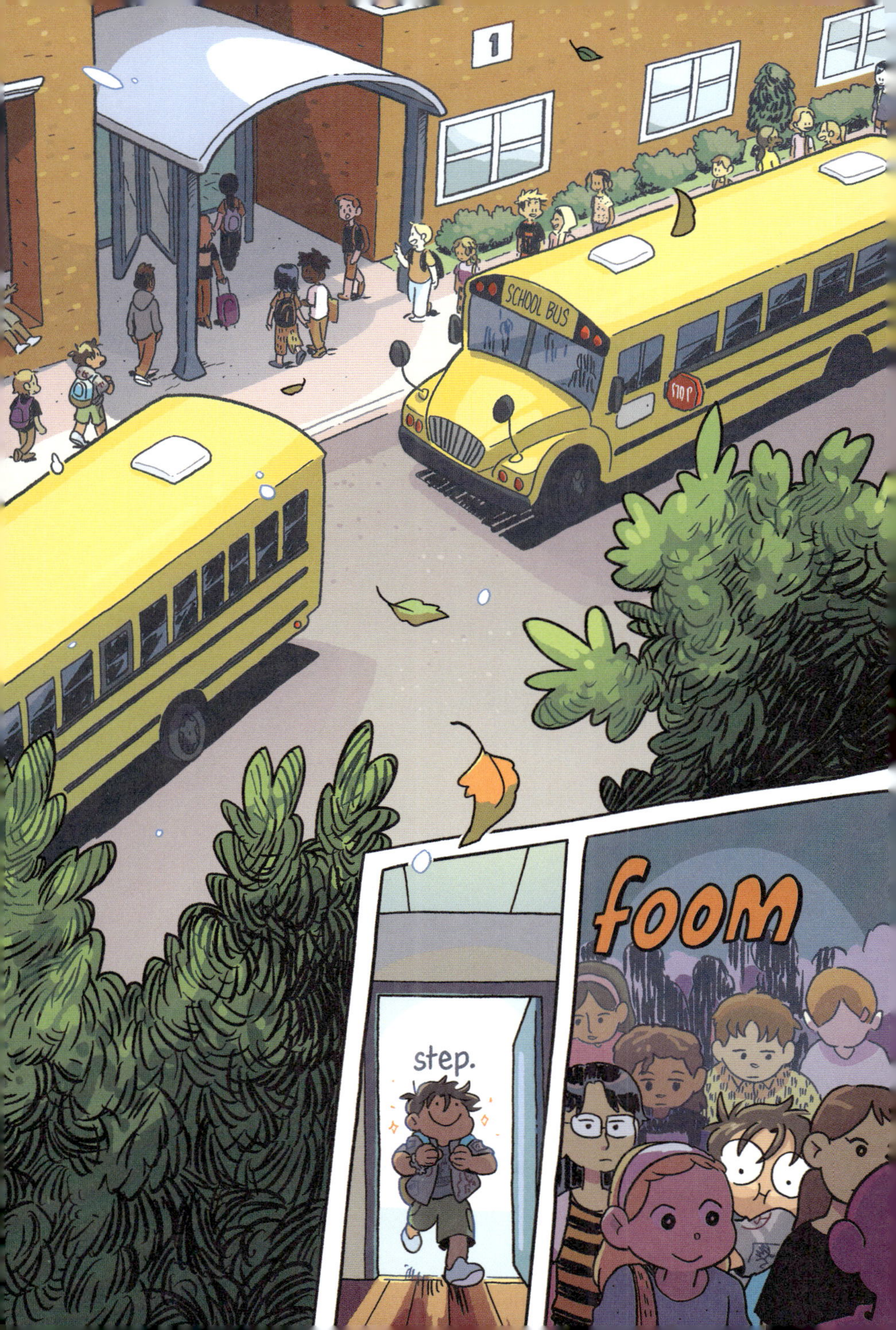
1
SCHOOL BUS
STOP
step.
foom

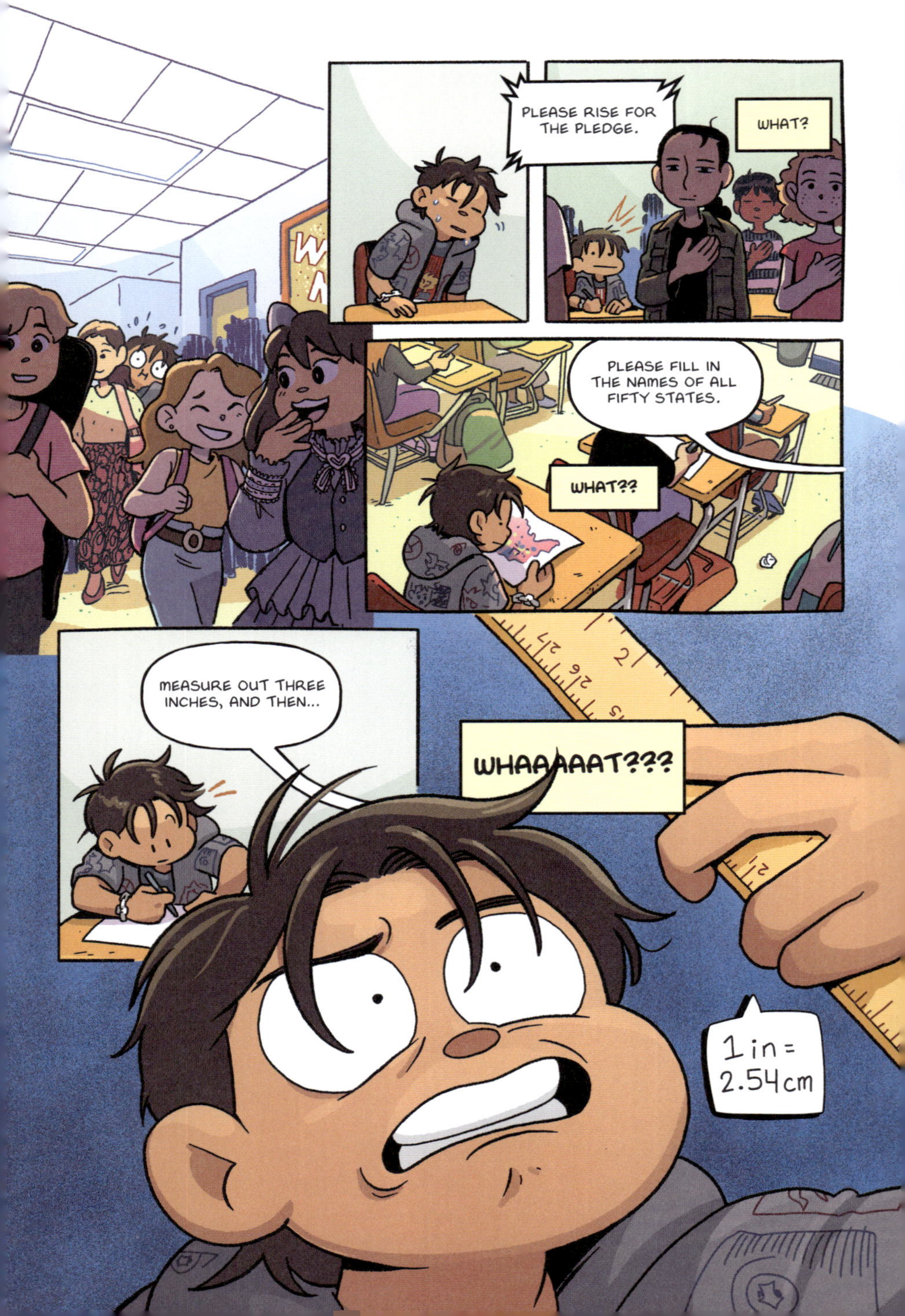
PLEASE RISE FOR THE PLEDGE.
WHAT?
PLEASE FILL IN THE NAMES OF ALL FIFTY STATES.
WHAT??
MEASURE OUT THREE INCHES, AND THEN...
WHAAAAAT???
1 in = 2.54 cm

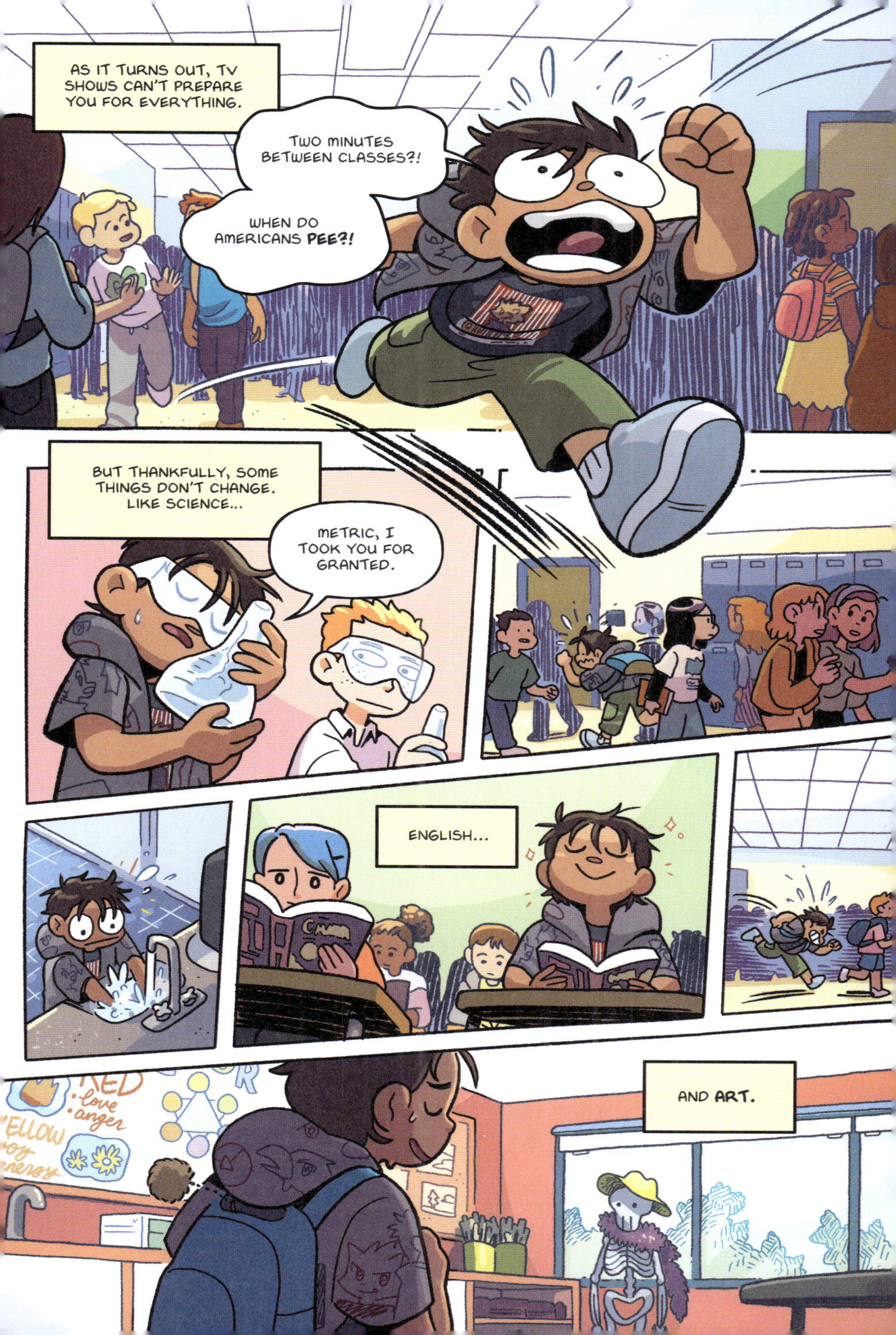

AS IT TURNS OUT, TV SHOWS CAN'T PREPARE YOU FOR EVERYTHING.
TWO MINUTES BETWEEN CLASSES?!
WHEN DO AMERICANS **PEE?!**
BUT THANKFULLY, SOME THINGS DON'T CHANGE. LIKE SCIENCE...
METRIC, I TOOK YOU FOR GRANTED.
ENGLISH...
RED
love
anger
YELLOW
AND **ART.**

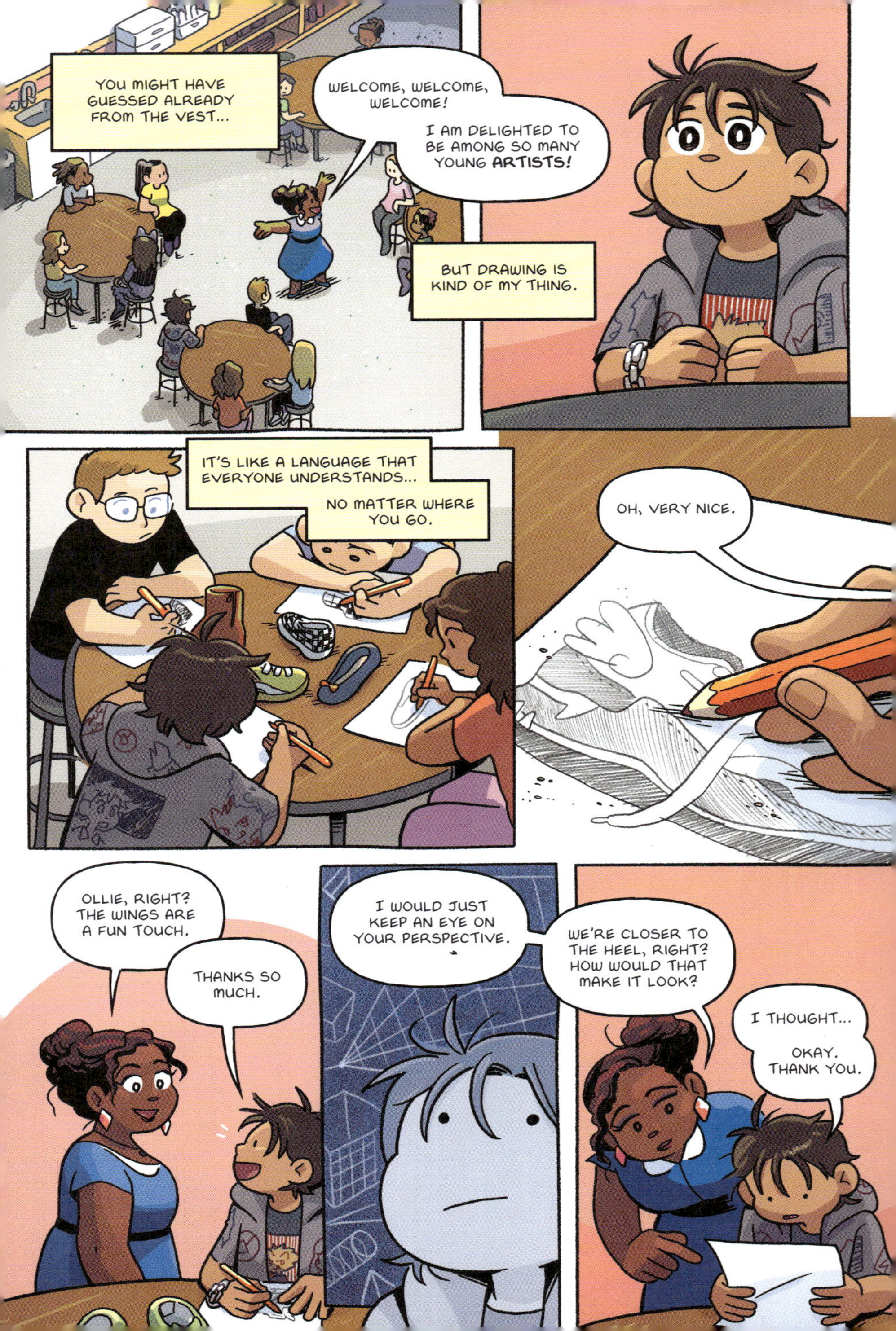
YOU MIGHT HAVE GUESSED ALREADY FROM THE VEST...
WELCOME, WELCOME, WELCOME!
I AM DELIGHTED TO BE AMONG SO MANY YOUNG ARTISTS!
BUT DRAWING IS KIND OF MY THING.
IT'S LIKE A LANGUAGE THAT EVERYONE UNDERSTANDS...
NO MATTER WHERE YOU GO.
OH, VERY NICE.
OLLIE, RIGHT? THE WINGS ARE A FUN TOUCH.
THANKS SO MUCH.
I WOULD JUST KEEP AN EYE ON YOUR PERSPECTIVE.
WE'RE CLOSER TO THE HEEL, RIGHT? HOW WOULD THAT MAKE IT LOOK?
I THOUGHT...
OKAY. THANK YOU.

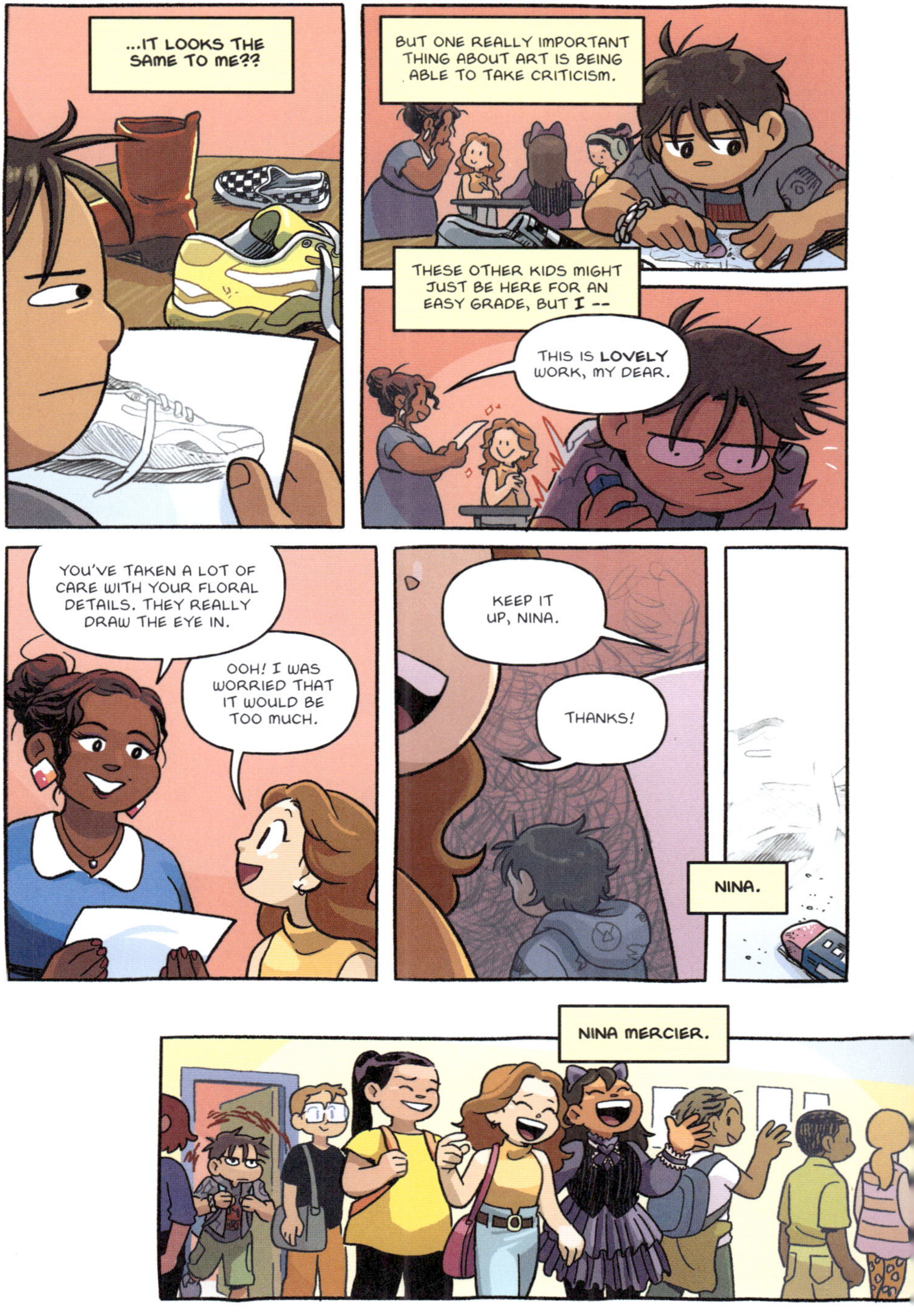
...IT LOOKS THE SAME TO ME??
BUT ONE REALLY IMPORTANT THING ABOUT ART IS BEING ABLE TO TAKE CRITICISM.
THESE OTHER KIDS MIGHT JUST BE HERE FOR AN EASY GRADE, BUT I --
THIS IS LOVELY WORK, MY DEAR.
YOU'VE TAKEN A LOT OF CARE WITH YOUR FLORAL DETAILS. THEY REALLY DRAW THE EYE IN.
OOH! I WAS WORRIED THAT IT WOULD BE TOO MUCH.
KEEP IT UP, NINA.
THANKS!
NINA.
NINA MERCIER.

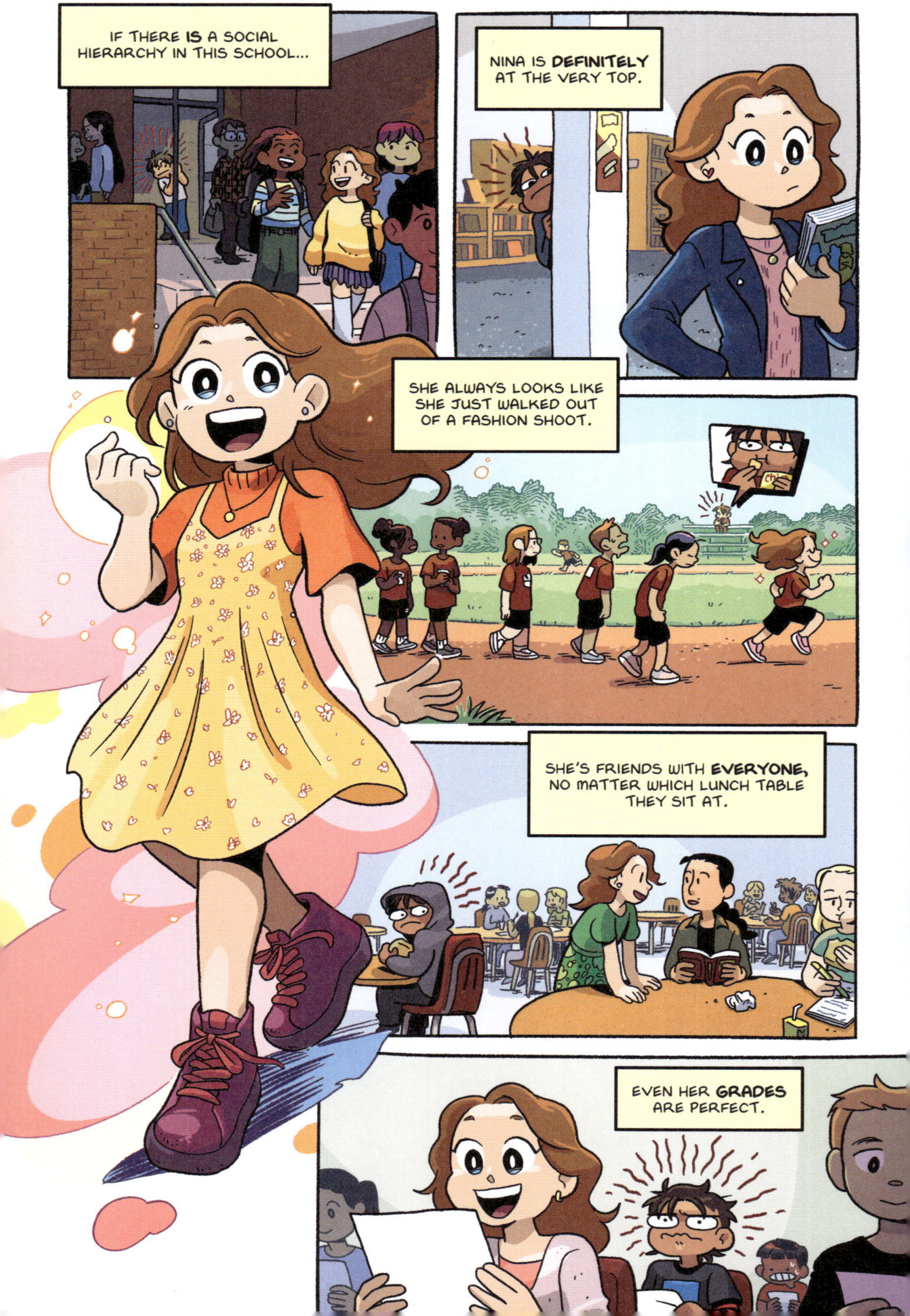
IF THERE IS A SOCIAL HIERARCHY IN THIS SCHOOL...
NINA IS DEFINITELY AT THE VERY TOP.
SHE ALWAYS LOOKS LIKE SHE JUST WALKED OUT OF A FASHION SHOOT.
SHE'S FRIENDS WITH EVERYONE, NO MATTER WHICH LUNCH TABLE THEY SIT AT.
EVEN HER GRADES ARE PERFECT.

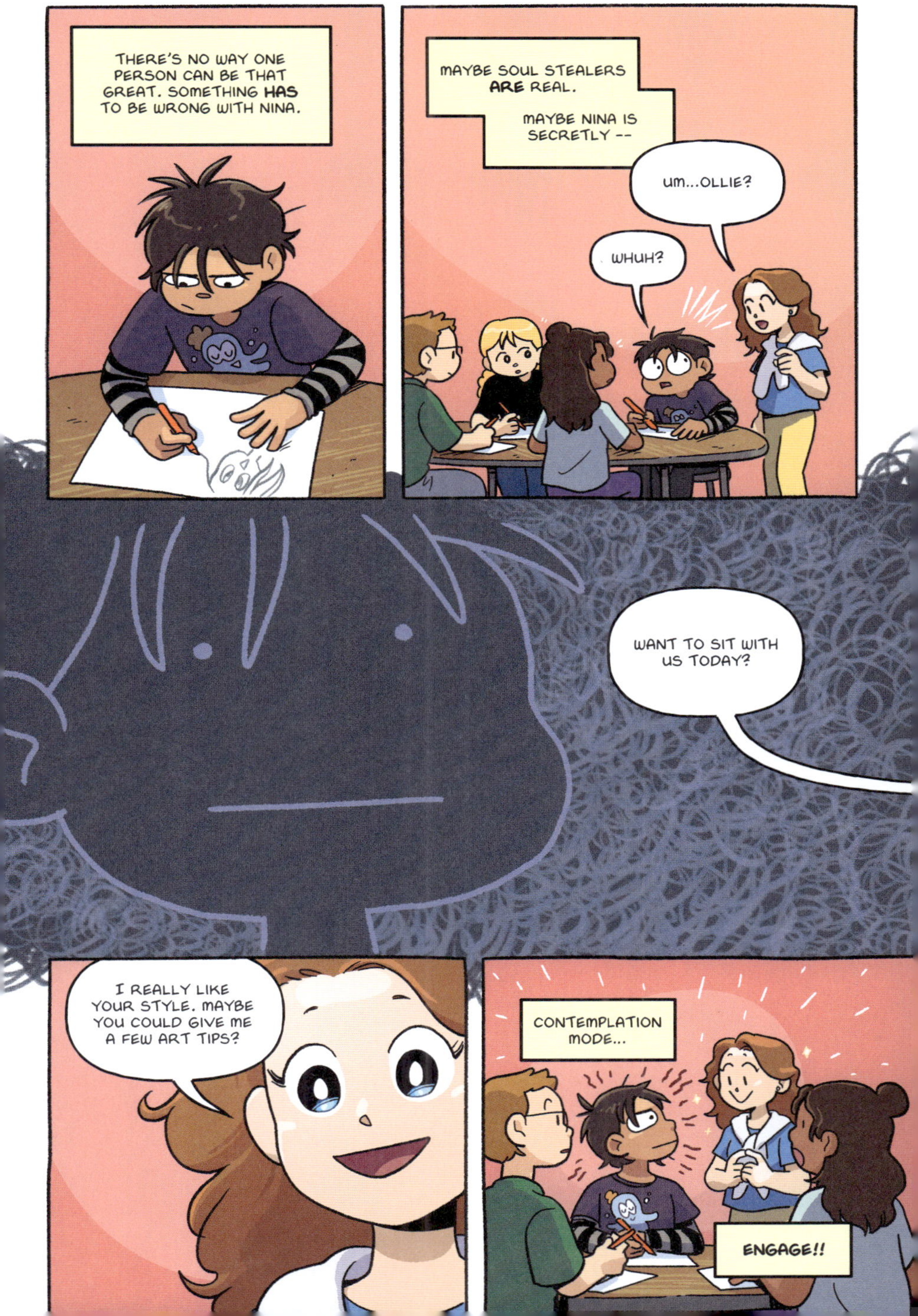
THERE'S NO WAY ONE PERSON CAN BE THAT GREAT. SOMETHING **HAS** TO BE WRONG WITH NINA.
MAYBE SOUL STEALERS **ARE** REAL.
MAYBE NINA IS SECRETLY --
UM...OLLIE?
WHUH?
WANT TO SIT WITH US TODAY?
I REALLY LIKE YOUR STYLE. MAYBE YOU COULD GIVE ME A FEW ART TIPS?
CONTEMPLATION MODE...
ENGAGE!!

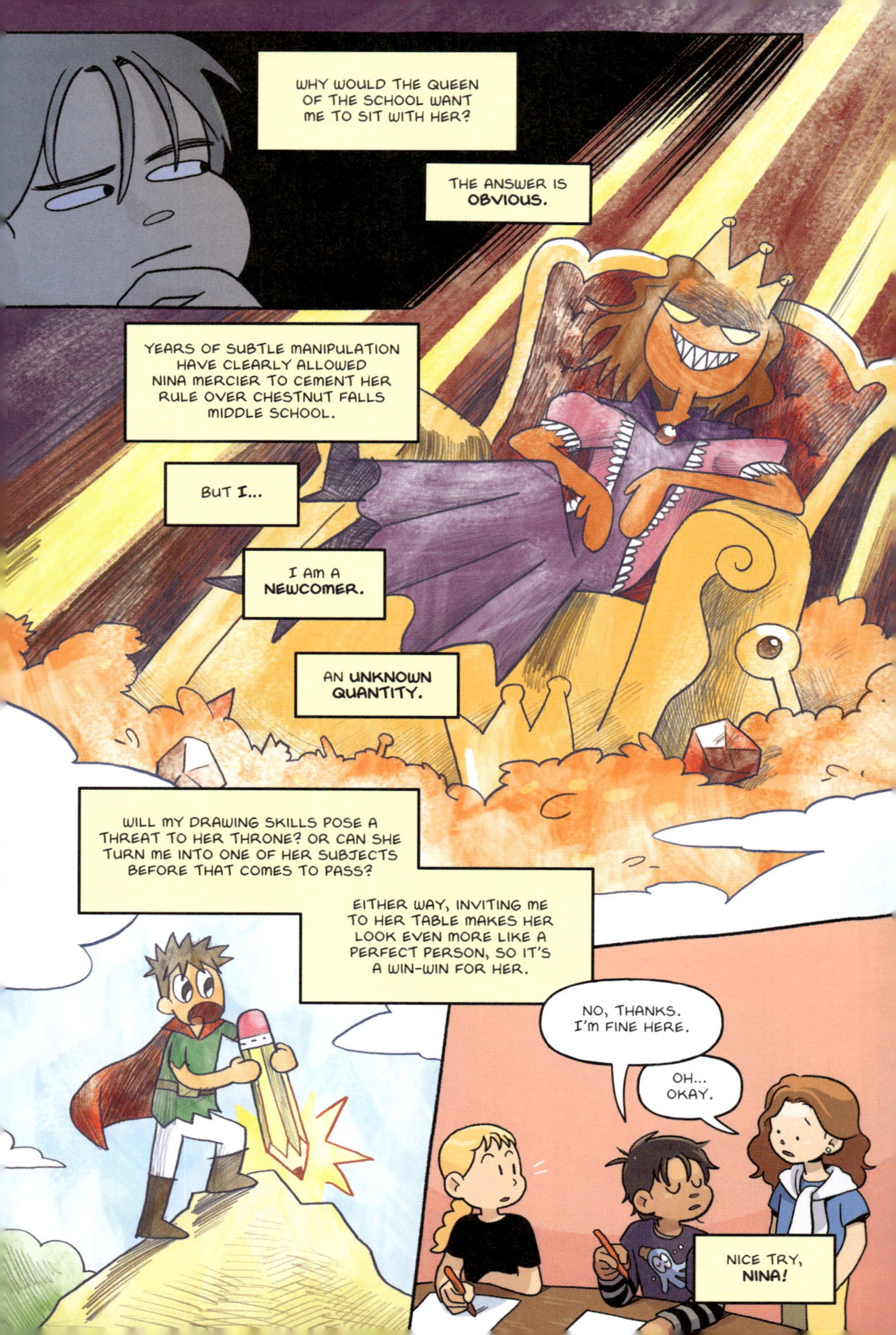
WHY WOULD THE QUEEN OF THE SCHOOL WANT ME TO SIT WITH HER?
THE ANSWER IS **OBVIOUS.**
YEARS OF SUBTLE MANIPULATION HAVE CLEARLY ALLOWED NINA MERCIER TO CEMENT HER RULE OVER CHESTNUT FALLS MIDDLE SCHOOL.
BUT **I**...
I AM A **NEWCOMER.**
AN **UNKNOWN QUANTITY.**
WILL MY DRAWING SKILLS POSE A THREAT TO HER THRONE? OR CAN SHE TURN ME INTO ONE OF HER SUBJECTS BEFORE THAT COMES TO PASS?
EITHER WAY, INVITING ME TO HER TABLE MAKES HER LOOK EVEN MORE LIKE A PERFECT PERSON, SO IT'S A WIN-WIN FOR HER.
NO, THANKS. I'M FINE HERE.
OH... OKAY.
NICE TRY, **NINA!**

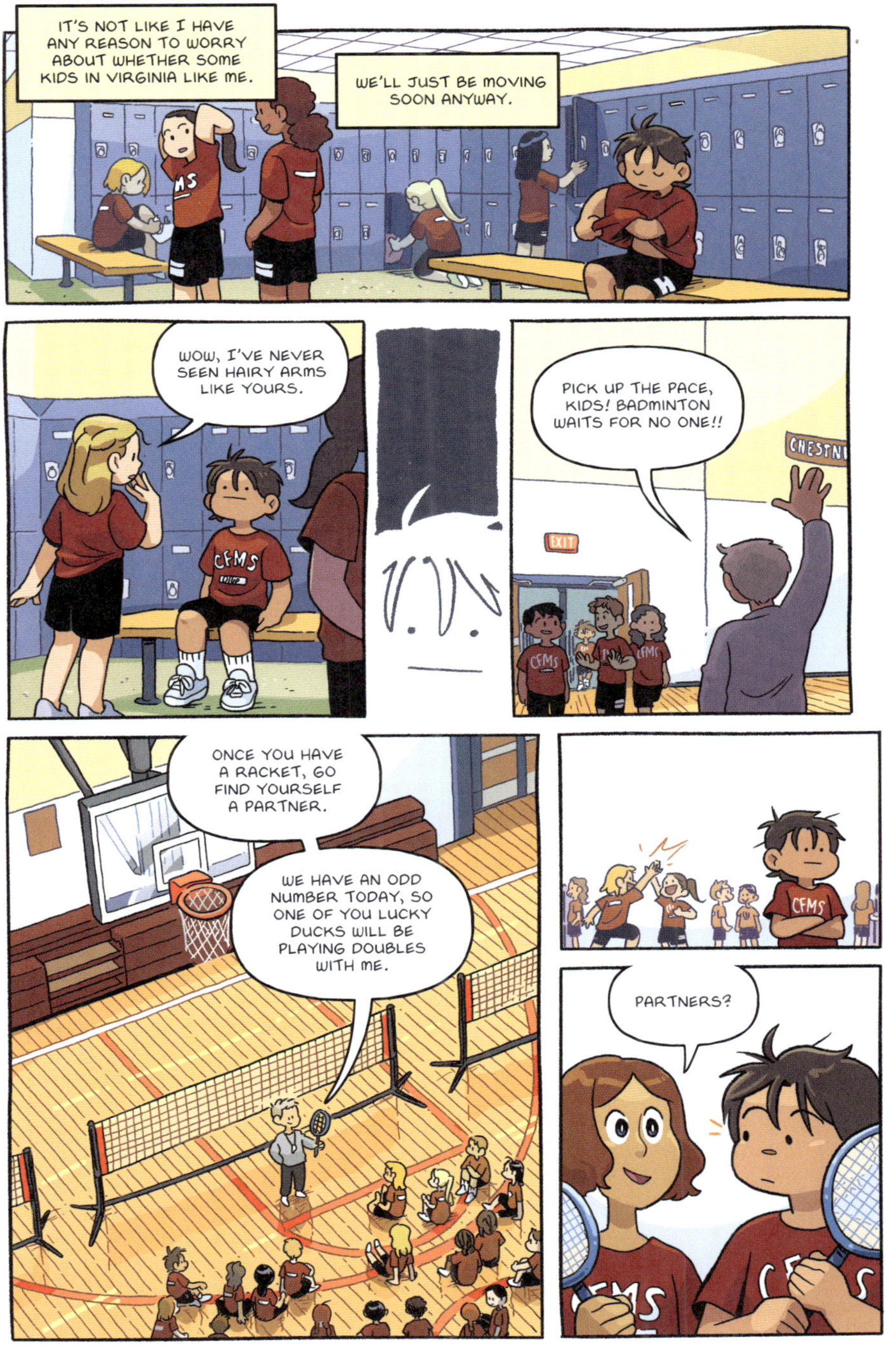
IT'S NOT LIKE I HAVE ANY REASON TO WORRY ABOUT WHETHER SOME KIDS IN VIRGINIA LIKE ME.
WE'LL JUST BE MOVING SOON ANYWAY.
WOW, I'VE NEVER SEEN HAIRY ARMS LIKE YOURS.
PICK UP THE PACE, KIDS! BADMINTON WAITS FOR NO ONE!!
EXIT
ONCE YOU HAVE A RACKET, GO FIND YOURSELF A PARTNER.
WE HAVE AN ODD NUMBER TODAY, SO ONE OF YOU LUCKY DUCKS WILL BE PLAYING DOUBLES WITH ME.
CFMS
PARTNERS?

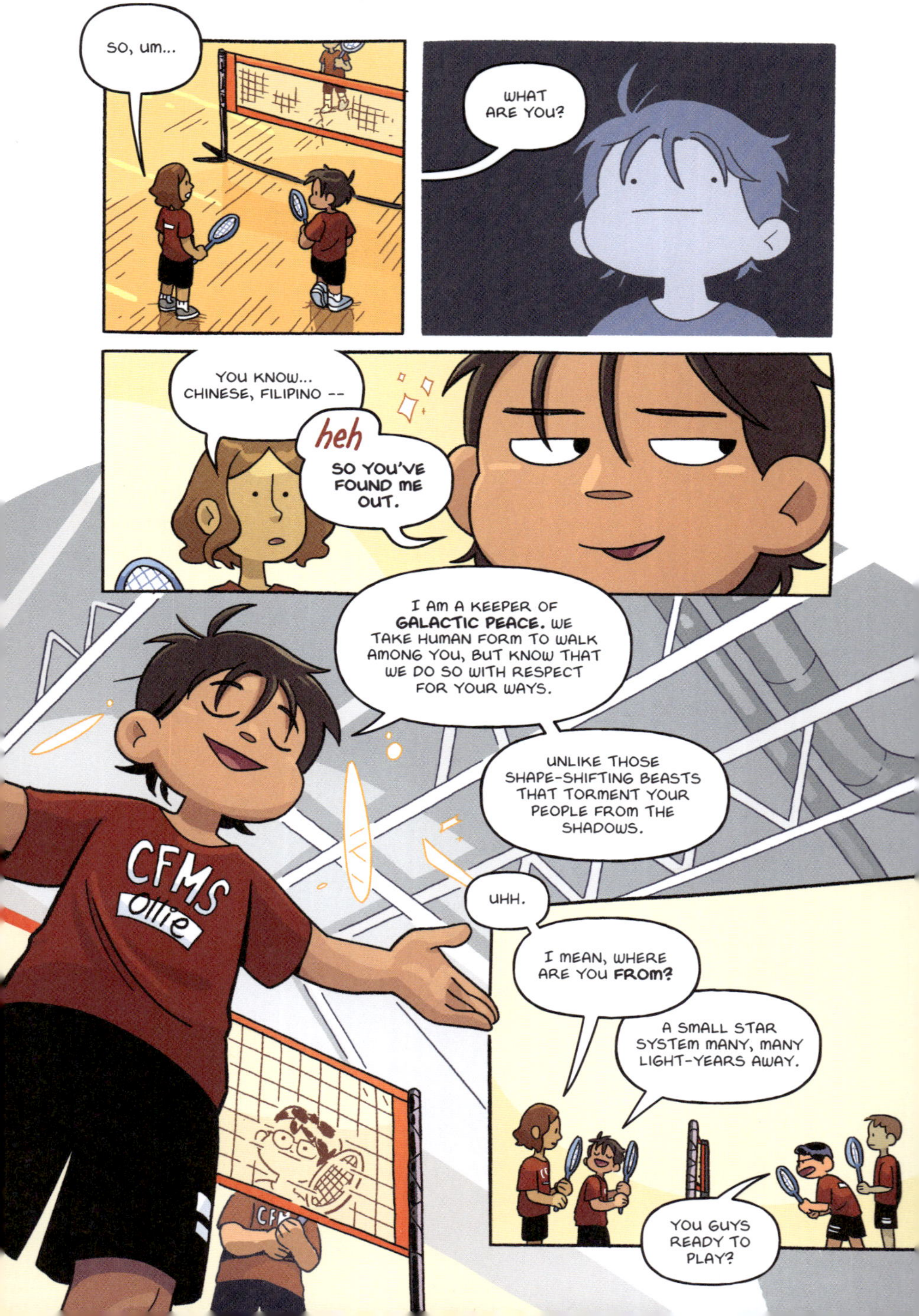
SO, UM...
WHAT ARE YOU?
YOU KNOW... CHINESE, FILIPINO --
heh
SO YOU'VE FOUND ME OUT.
I AM A KEEPER OF GALACTIC PEACE. WE TAKE HUMAN FORM TO WALK AMONG YOU, BUT KNOW THAT WE DO SO WITH RESPECT FOR YOUR WAYS.
UNLIKE THOSE SHAPE-SHIFTING BEASTS THAT TORMENT YOUR PEOPLE FROM THE SHADOWS.
CFMS
ollie
UHH.
I MEAN, WHERE ARE YOU FROM?
A SMALL STAR SYSTEM MANY, MANY LIGHT-YEARS AWAY.
YOU GUYS READY TO PLAY?

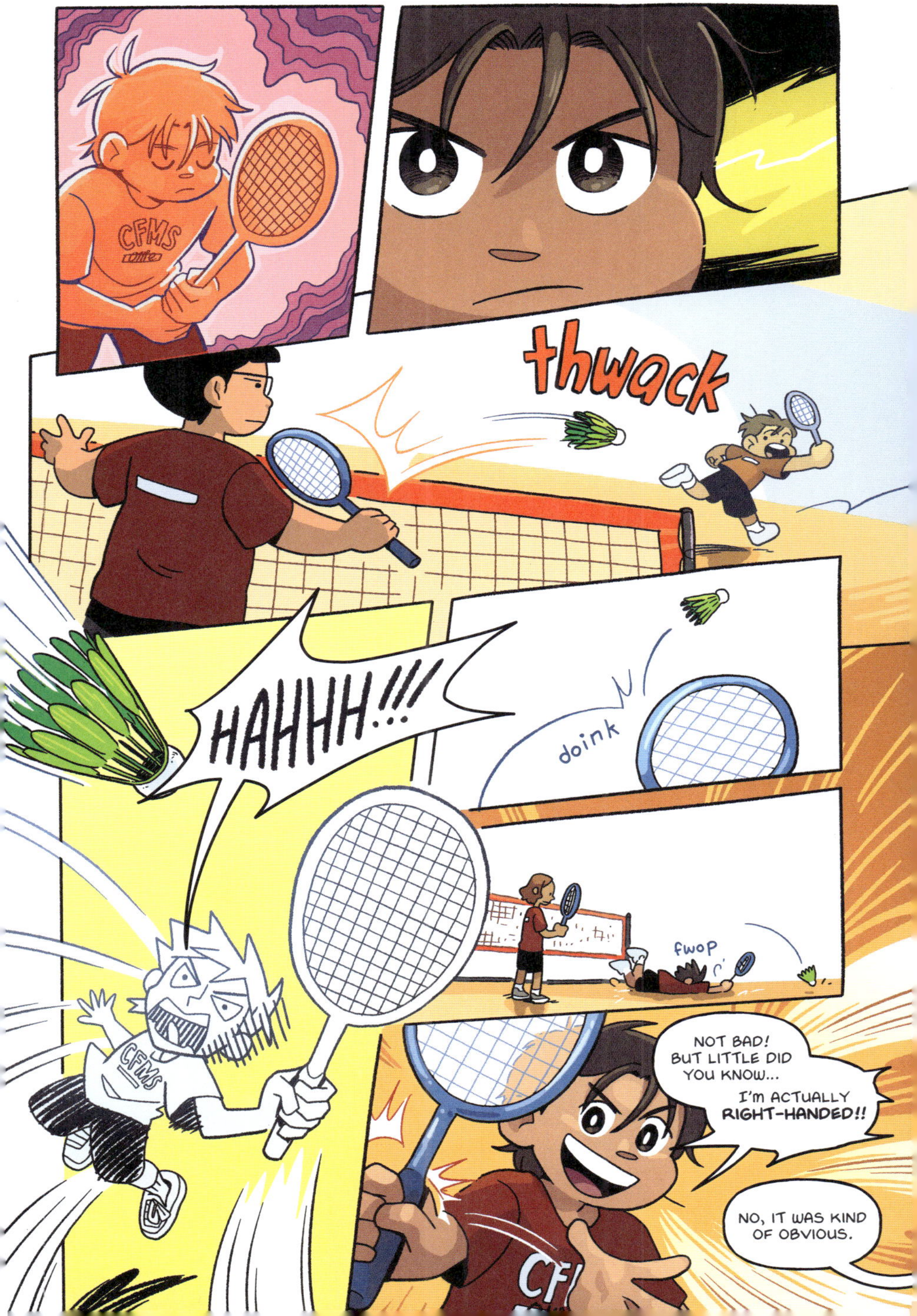
CFMS
thwack
HAHHH!!!
doink
fwop
NOT BAD! BUT LITTLE DID YOU KNOW...
I'M ACTUALLY **RIGHT-HANDED!!**
NO, IT WAS KIND OF OBVIOUS.

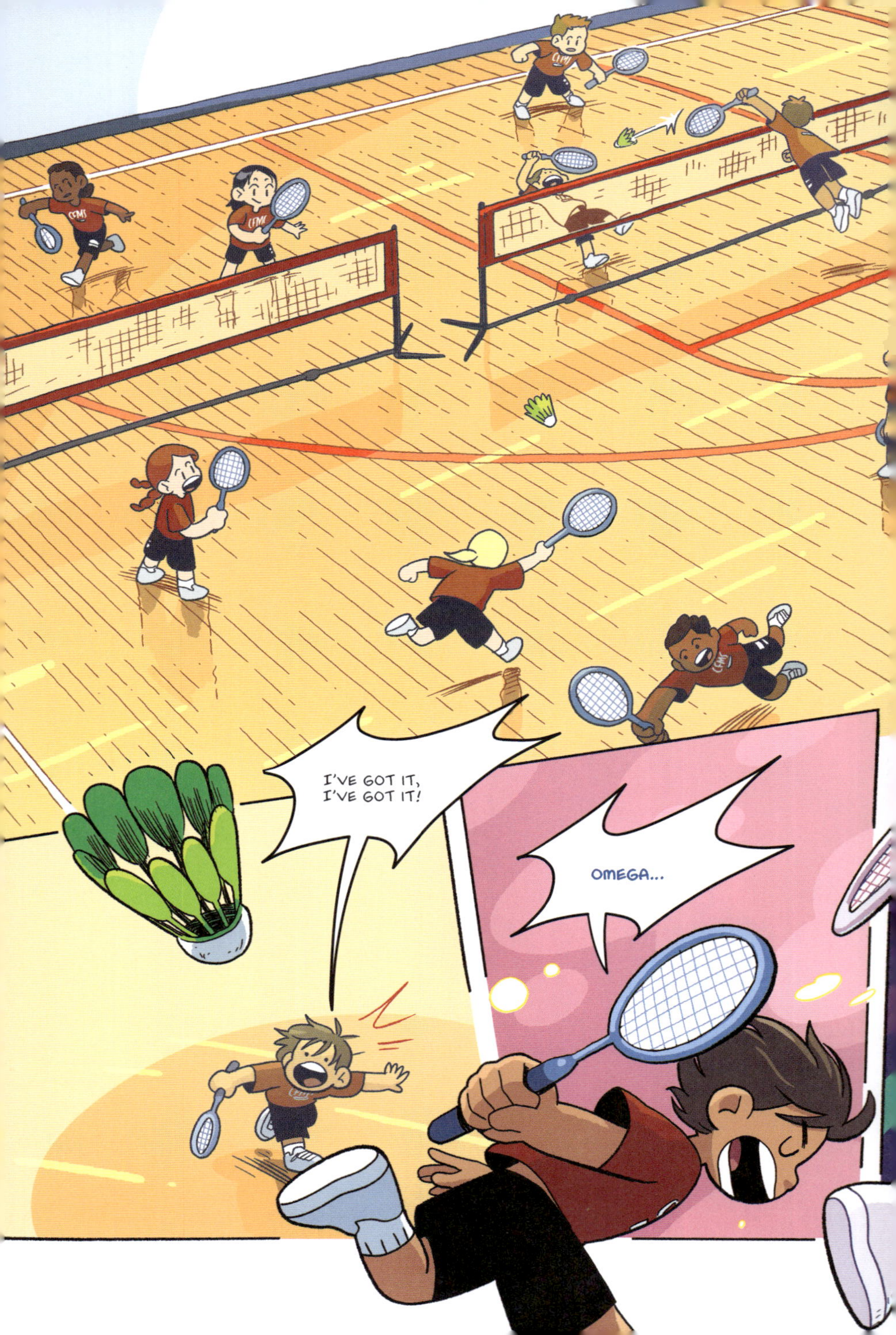
I'VE GOT IT, I'VE GOT IT!
OMEGA...

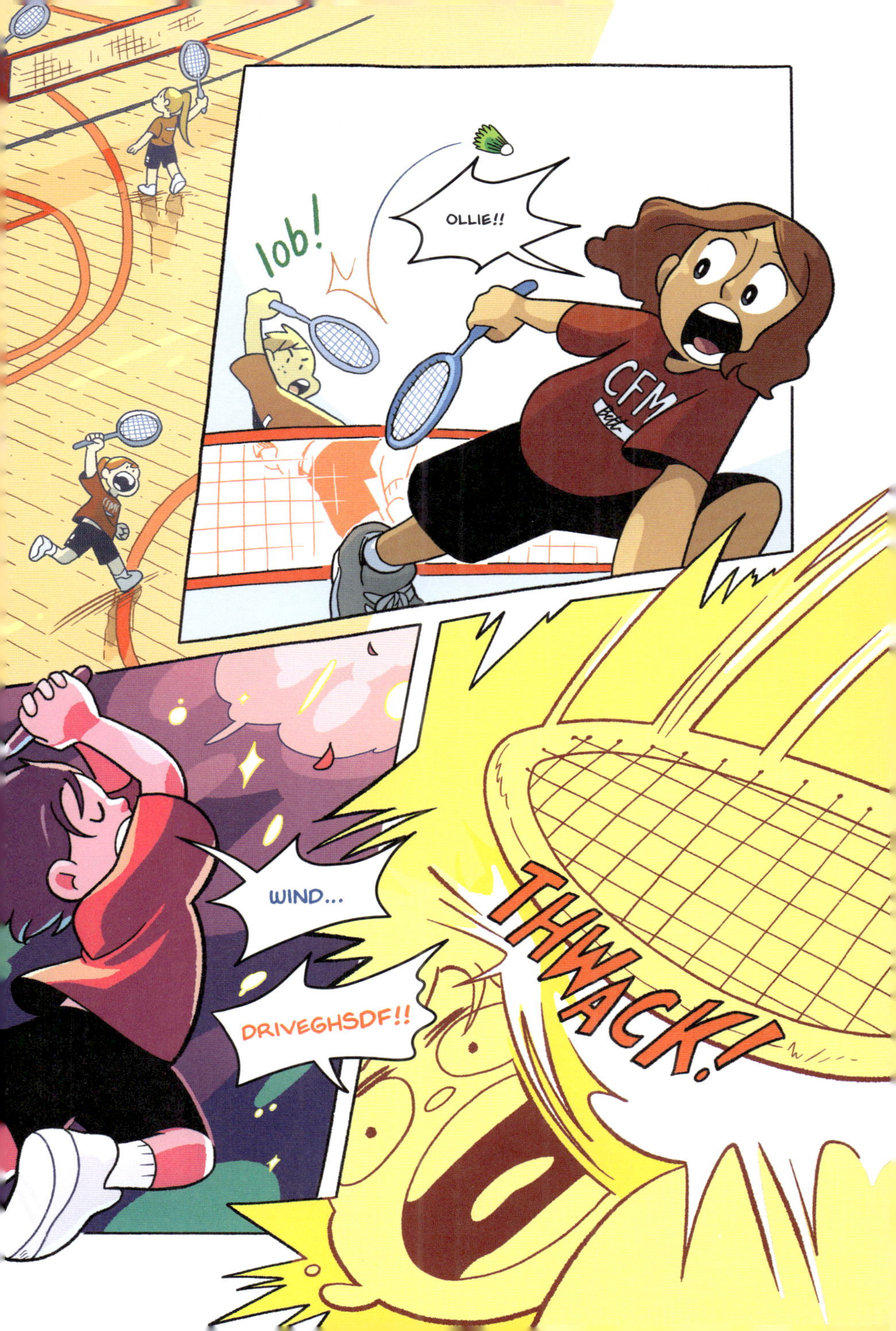
lob!
OLLIE!!
WIND...
DRIVEGHSDF!!
THWACK!

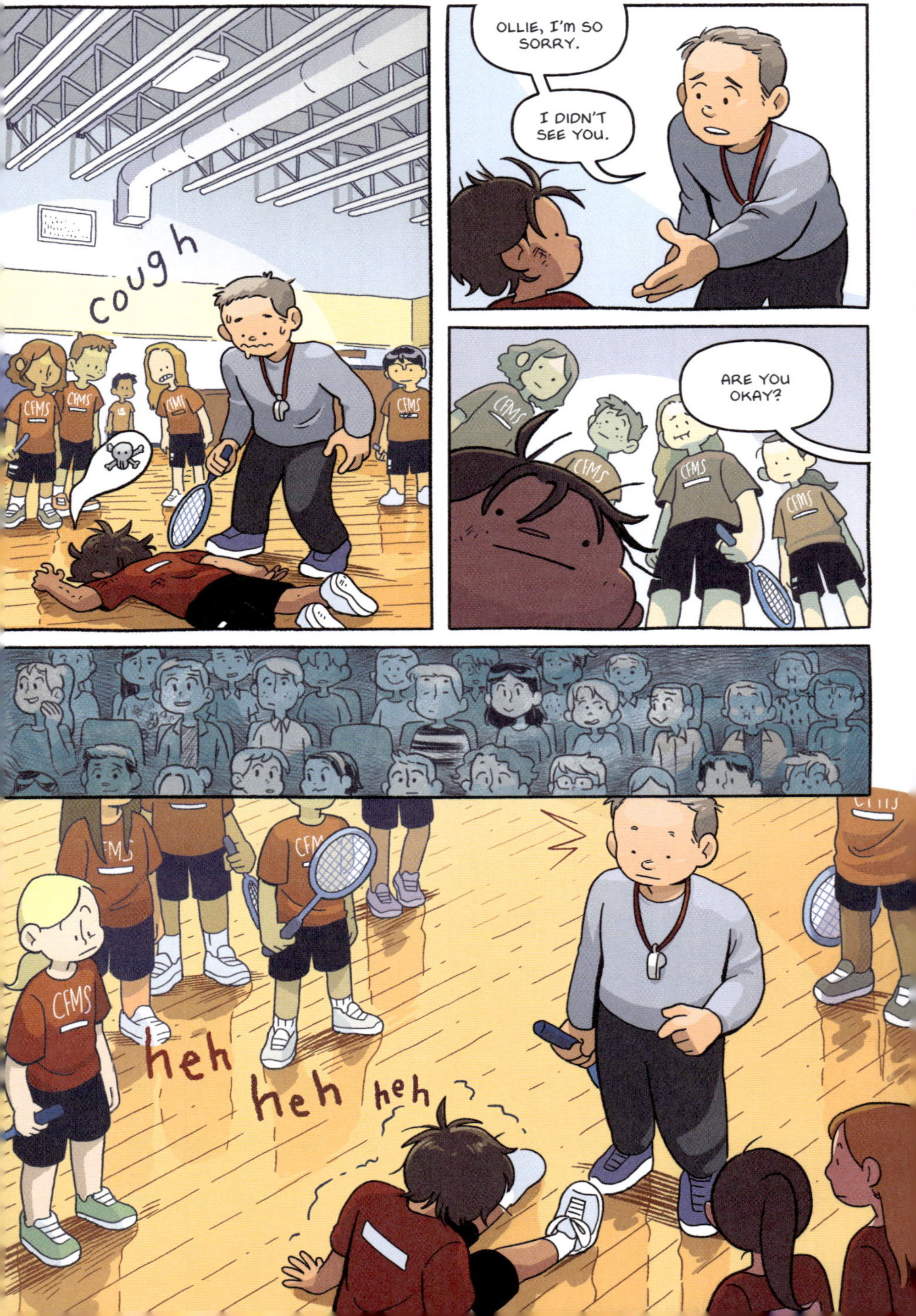
cough
OLLIE, I'M SO SORRY.
I DIDN'T SEE YOU.
ARE YOU OKAY?
heh
heh
heh

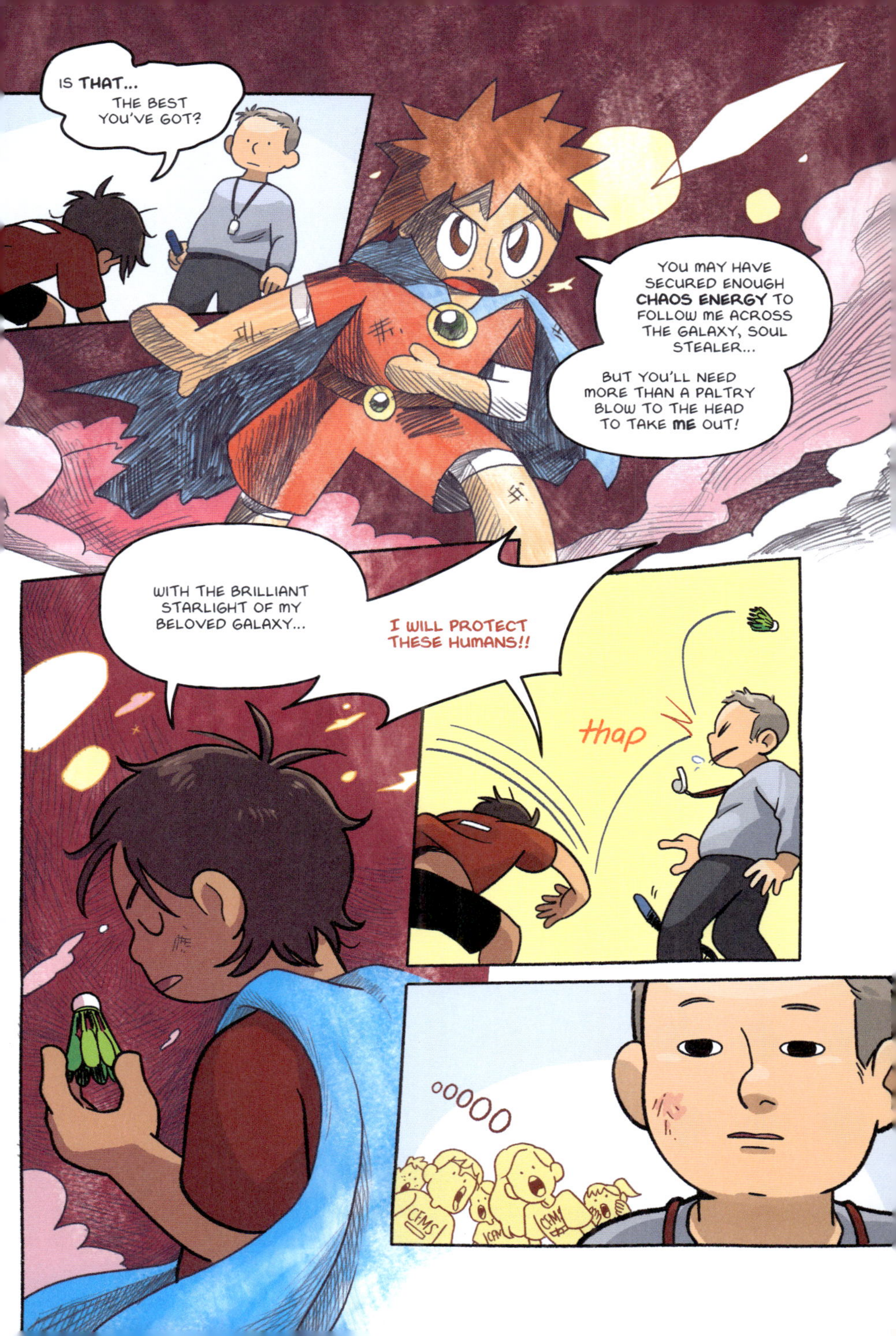
IS THAT... THE BEST YOU'VE GOT?
YOU MAY HAVE SECURED ENOUGH CHAOS ENERGY TO FOLLOW ME ACROSS THE GALAXY, SOUL STEALER...
BUT YOU'LL NEED MORE THAN A PALTRY BLOW TO THE HEAD TO TAKE ME OUT!
WITH THE BRILLIANT STARLIGHT OF MY BELOVED GALAXY...
I WILL PROTECT THESE HUMANS!!
thap
OOOOO
CFMS
CFMS
CFMS

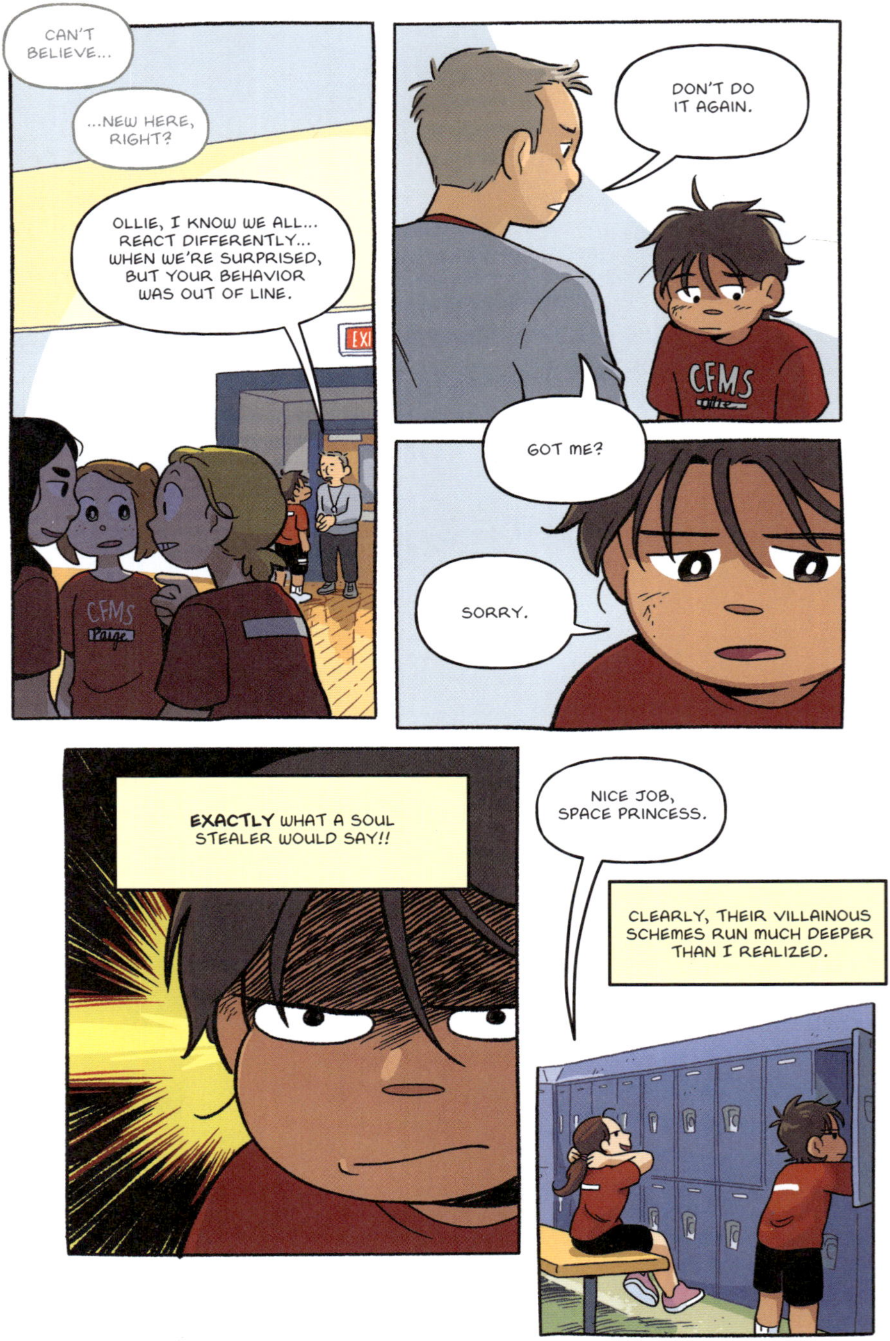
CAN'T BELIEVE...
...NEW HERE, RIGHT?
OLLIE, I KNOW WE ALL... REACT DIFFERENTLY... WHEN WE'RE SURPRISED, BUT YOUR BEHAVIOR WAS OUT OF LINE.
CFMS
Paige
DON'T DO IT AGAIN.
CFMS
GOT ME?
SORRY.
EXACTLY WHAT A SOUL STEALER WOULD SAY!!
NICE JOB, SPACE PRINCESS.
CLEARLY, THEIR VILLAINOUS SCHEMES RUN MUCH DEEPER THAN I REALIZED.

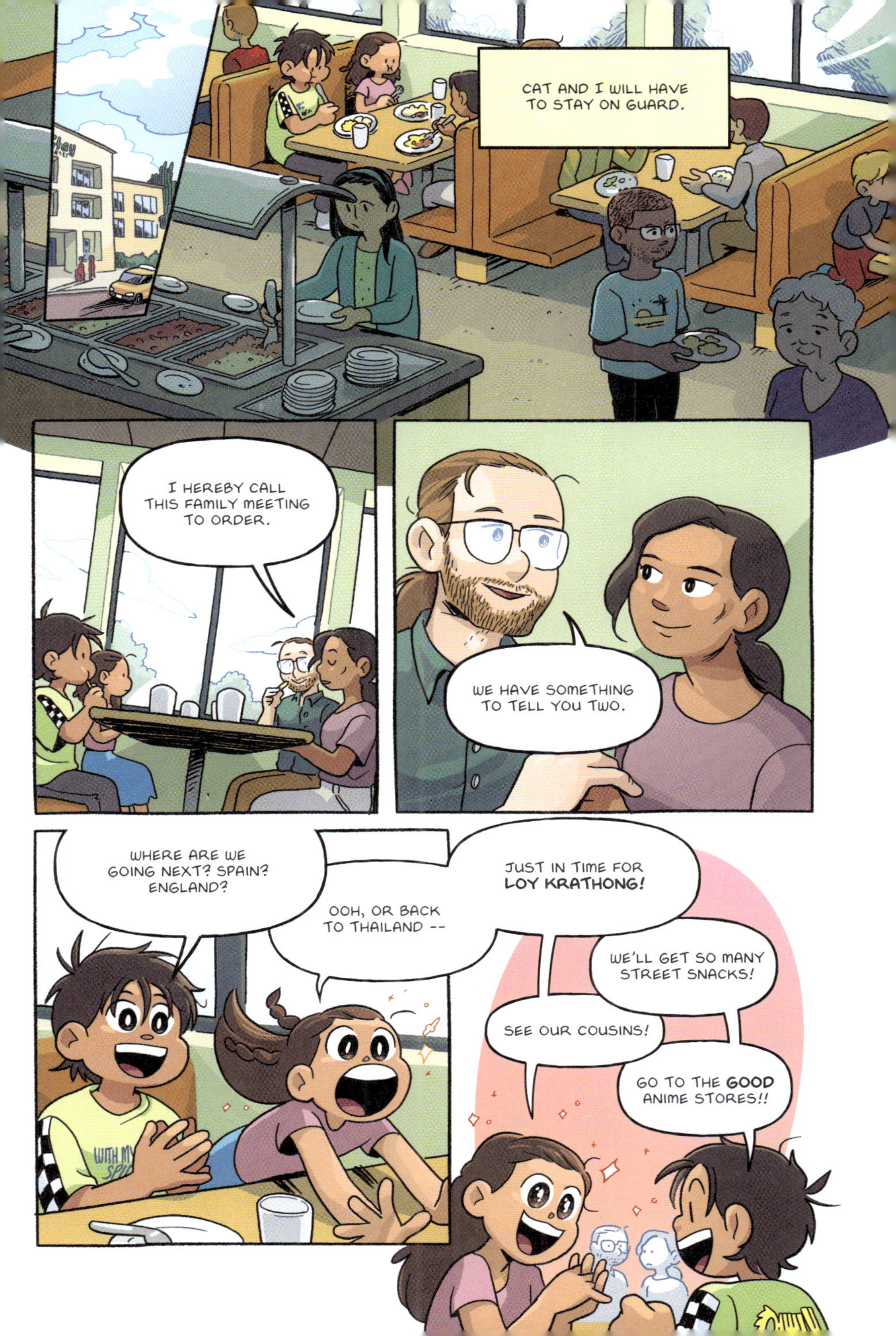
CAT AND I WILL HAVE TO STAY ON GUARD.
I HEREBY CALL THIS FAMILY MEETING TO ORDER.
WE HAVE SOMETHING TO TELL YOU TWO.
WHERE ARE WE GOING NEXT? SPAIN? ENGLAND?
OOH, OR BACK TO THAILAND --
JUST IN TIME FOR **LOY KRATHONG!**
WE'LL GET SO MANY STREET SNACKS!
SEE OUR COUSINS!
GO TO THE **GOOD** ANIME STORES!!

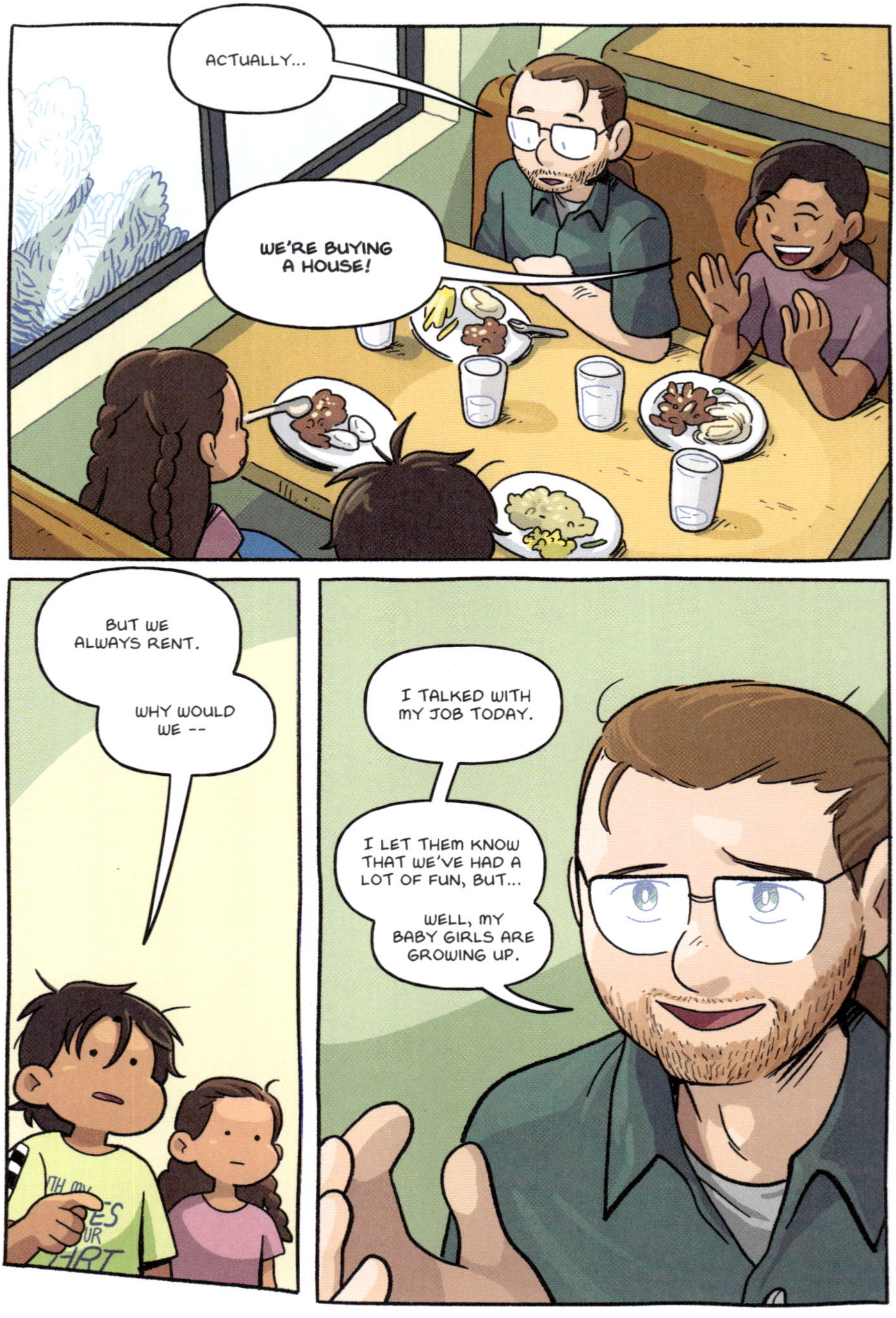
ACTUALLY...
WE'RE BUYING A HOUSE!
BUT WE ALWAYS RENT.
WHY WOULD WE --
I TALKED WITH MY JOB TODAY.
I LET THEM KNOW THAT WE'VE HAD A LOT OF FUN, BUT...
WELL, MY BABY GIRLS ARE GROWING UP.

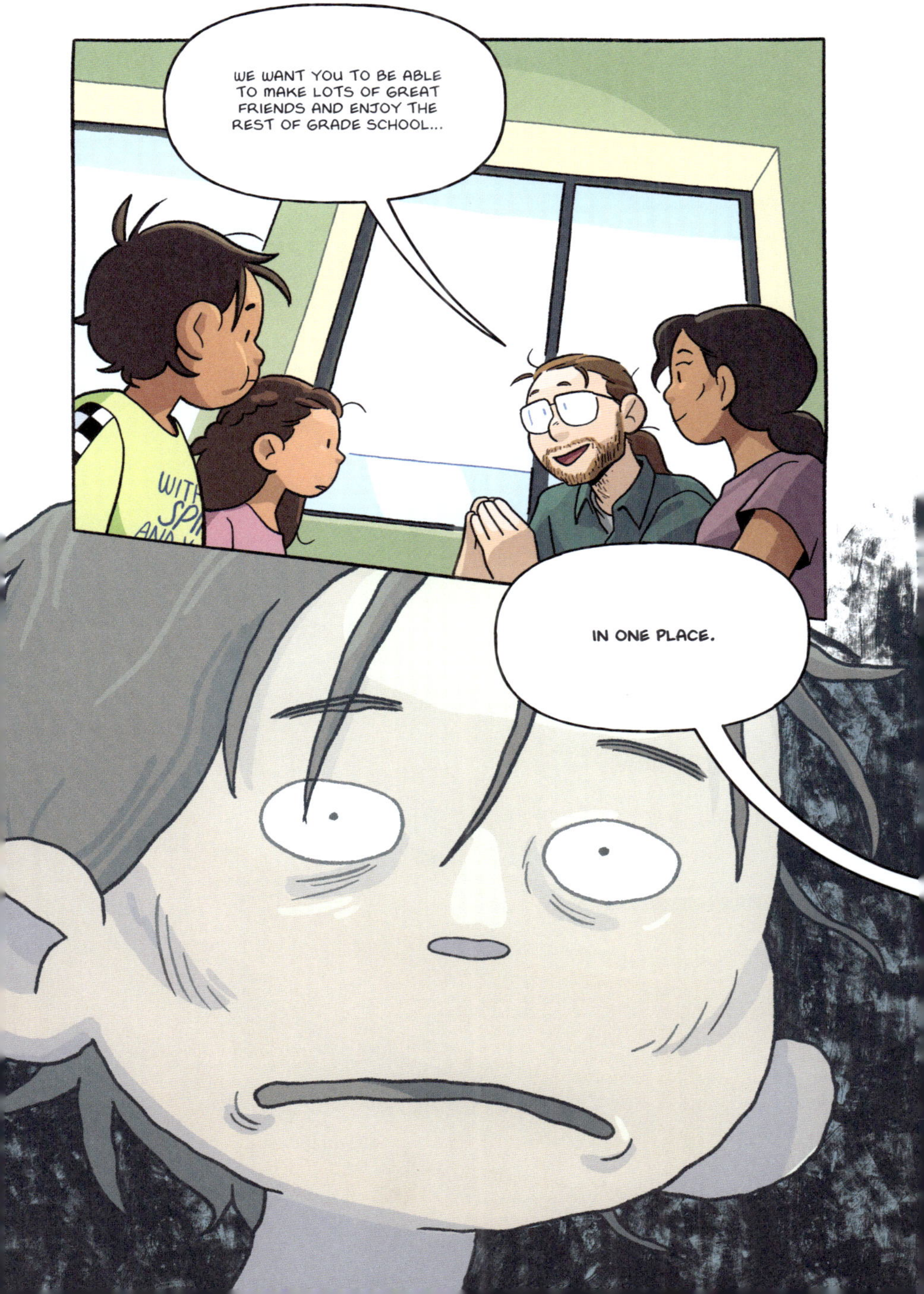
WE WANT YOU TO BE ABLE TO MAKE LOTS OF GREAT FRIENDS AND ENJOY THE REST OF GRADE SCHOOL...
IN ONE PLACE.

CHAPTER THREE

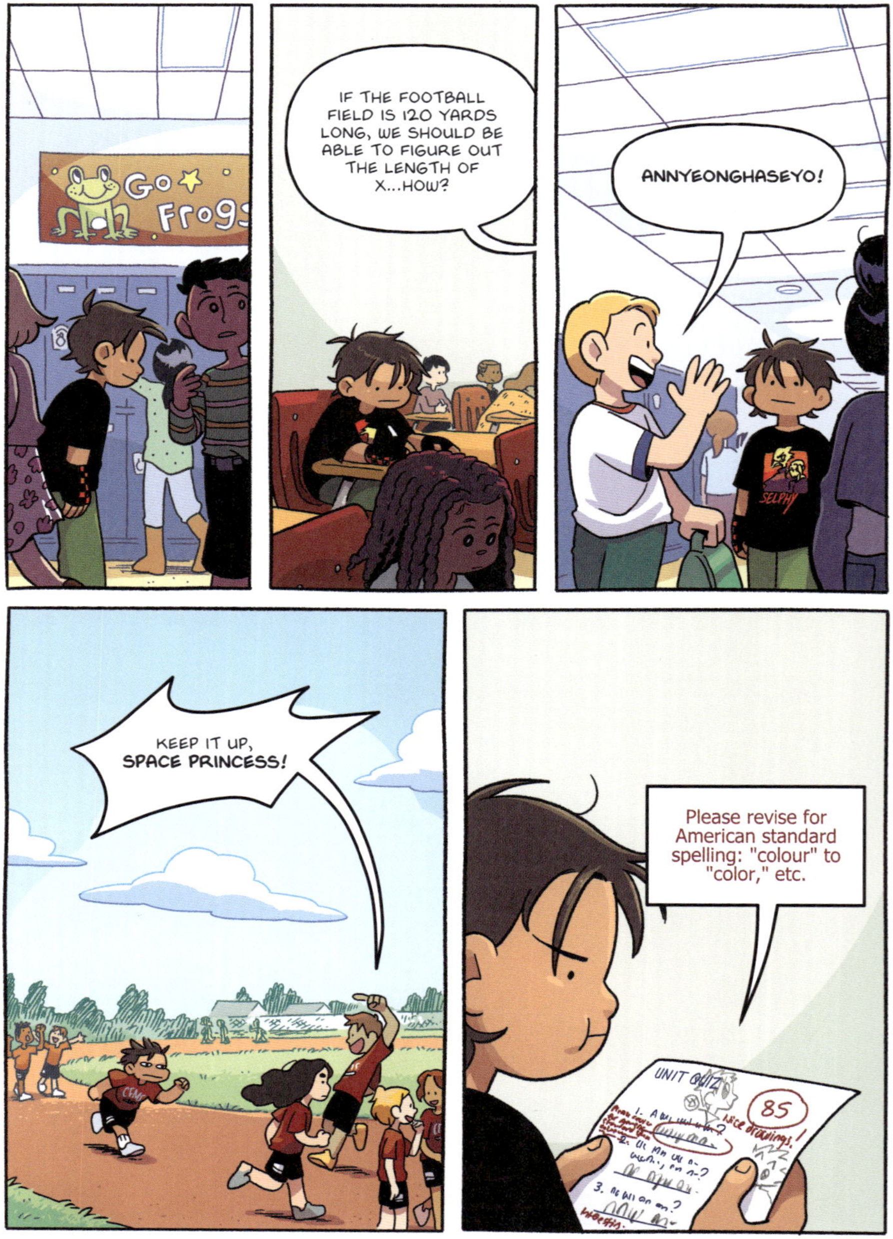
Go Frogs
IF THE FOOTBALL FIELD IS 120 YARDS LONG, WE SHOULD BE ABLE TO FIGURE OUT THE LENGTH OF X...HOW?
ANNYEONGHASEYO!
SELPHY
KEEP IT UP, **SPACE PRINCESS!**
Please revise for American standard spelling: "colour" to "color," etc.
UNIT QUIZ
85
Nice drawings!

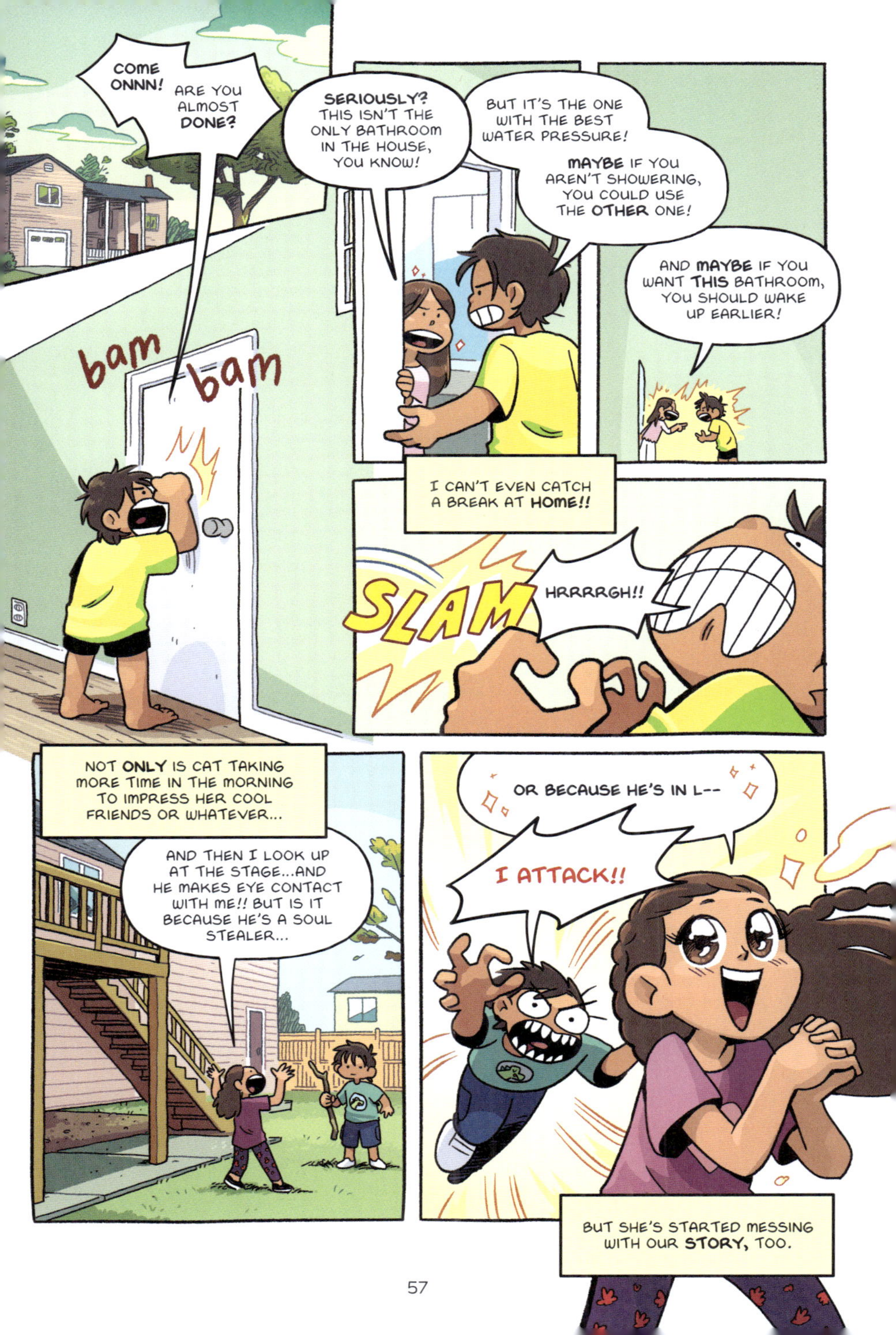

COME ONNN!
ARE YOU ALMOST DONE?
bam
bam
SERIOUSLY? THIS ISN'T THE ONLY BATHROOM IN THE HOUSE, YOU KNOW!
BUT IT'S THE ONE WITH THE BEST WATER PRESSURE!
MAYBE IF YOU AREN'T SHOWERING, YOU COULD USE THE OTHER ONE!
AND MAYBE IF YOU WANT THIS BATHROOM, YOU SHOULD WAKE UP EARLIER!
I CAN'T EVEN CATCH A BREAK AT HOME!!
SLAM
HRRRRGH!!
NOT ONLY IS CAT TAKING MORE TIME IN THE MORNING TO IMPRESS HER COOL FRIENDS OR WHATEVER...
AND THEN I LOOK UP AT THE STAGE...AND HE MAKES EYE CONTACT WITH ME!! BUT IS IT BECAUSE HE'S A SOUL STEALER...
OR BECAUSE HE'S IN L--
I ATTACK!!
BUT SHE'S STARTED MESSING WITH OUR STORY, TOO.

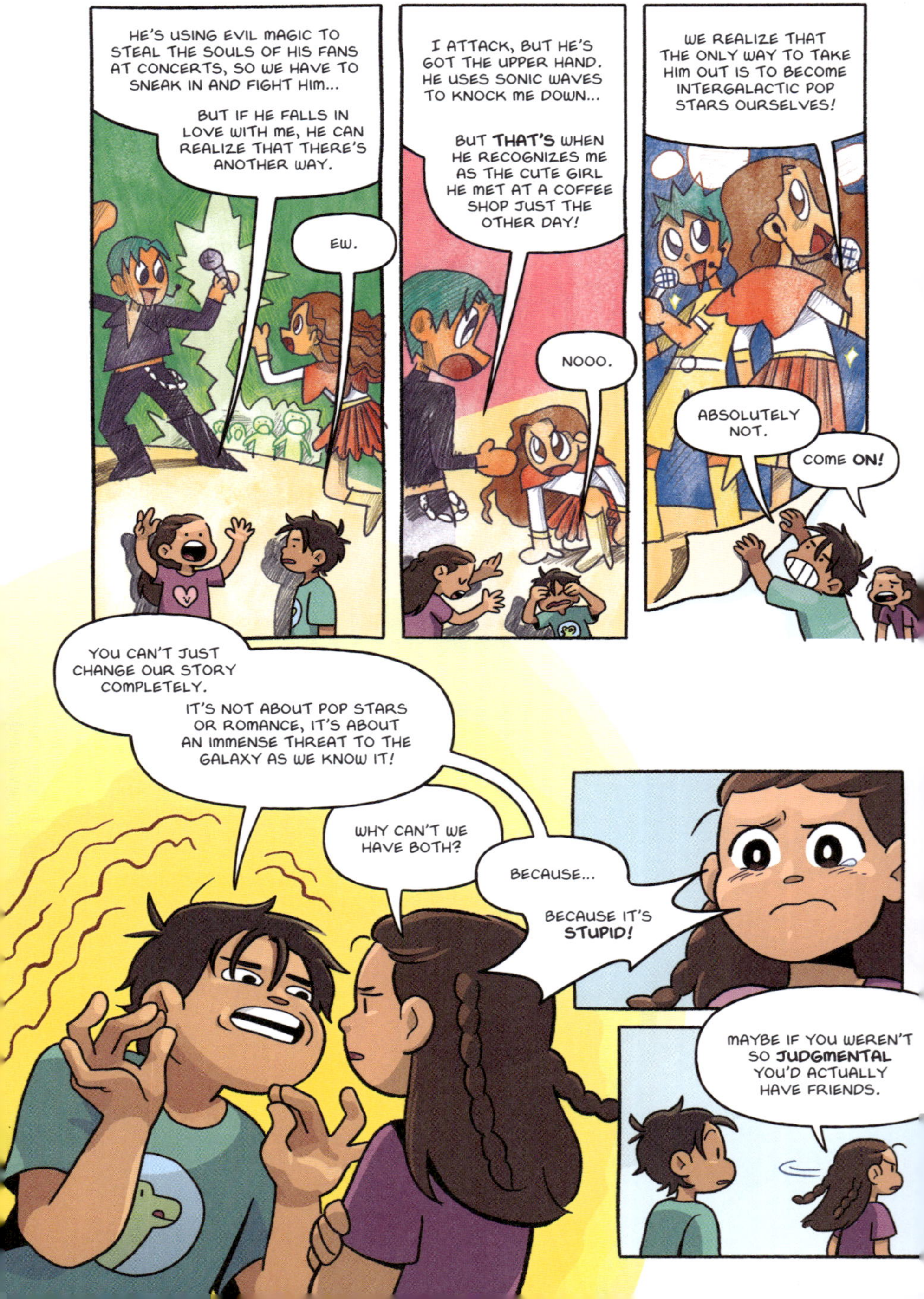
HE'S USING EVIL MAGIC TO STEAL THE SOULS OF HIS FANS AT CONCERTS, SO WE HAVE TO SNEAK IN AND FIGHT HIM...
BUT IF HE FALLS IN LOVE WITH ME, HE CAN REALIZE THAT THERE'S ANOTHER WAY.
EW.
I ATTACK, BUT HE'S GOT THE UPPER HAND. HE USES SONIC WAVES TO KNOCK ME DOWN...
BUT **THAT'S** WHEN HE RECOGNIZES ME AS THE CUTE GIRL HE MET AT A COFFEE SHOP JUST THE OTHER DAY!
NOOO.
WE REALIZE THAT THE ONLY WAY TO TAKE HIM OUT IS TO BECOME INTERGALACTIC POP STARS OURSELVES!
ABSOLUTELY NOT.
COME **ON!**
YOU CAN'T JUST CHANGE OUR STORY COMPLETELY.
IT'S NOT ABOUT POP STARS OR ROMANCE, IT'S ABOUT AN IMMENSE THREAT TO THE GALAXY AS WE KNOW IT!
WHY CAN'T WE HAVE BOTH?
BECAUSE...
BECAUSE IT'S **STUPID!**
MAYBE IF YOU WEREN'T SO **JUDGMENTAL** YOU'D ACTUALLY HAVE FRIENDS.

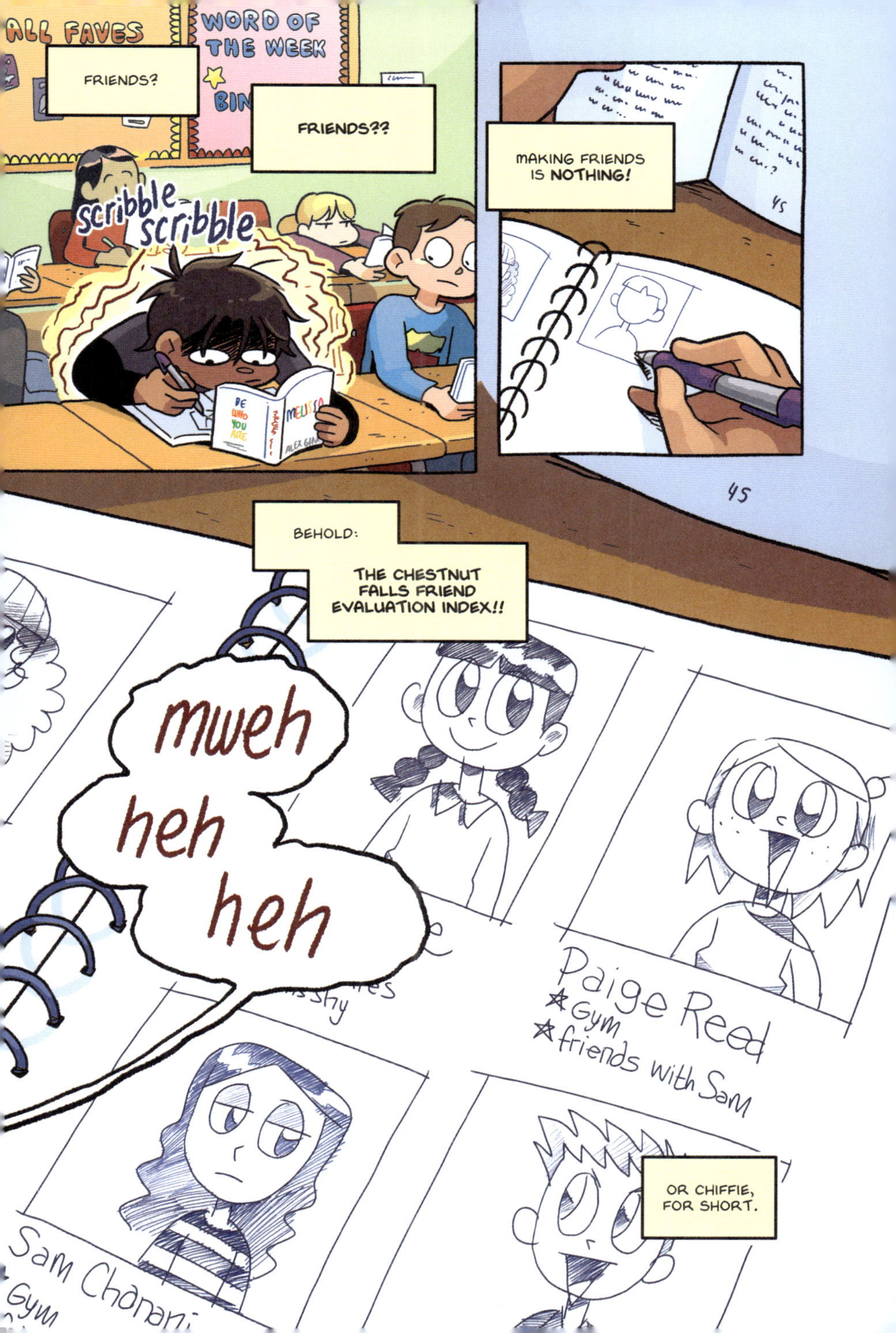
ALL FAVES
WORD OF THE WEEK
FRIENDS?
FRIENDS??
scribble scribble
BE WHO YOU ARE
MELISSA
ALEX GINO
MAKING FRIENDS IS **NOTHING!**
45
45
BEHOLD:
THE CHESTNUT FALLS FRIEND EVALUATION INDEX!!
mweh heh heh
Paige Reed
☆Gym
☆friends with Sam
OR CHIFFIE, FOR SHORT.
Sam Chanani
Gym

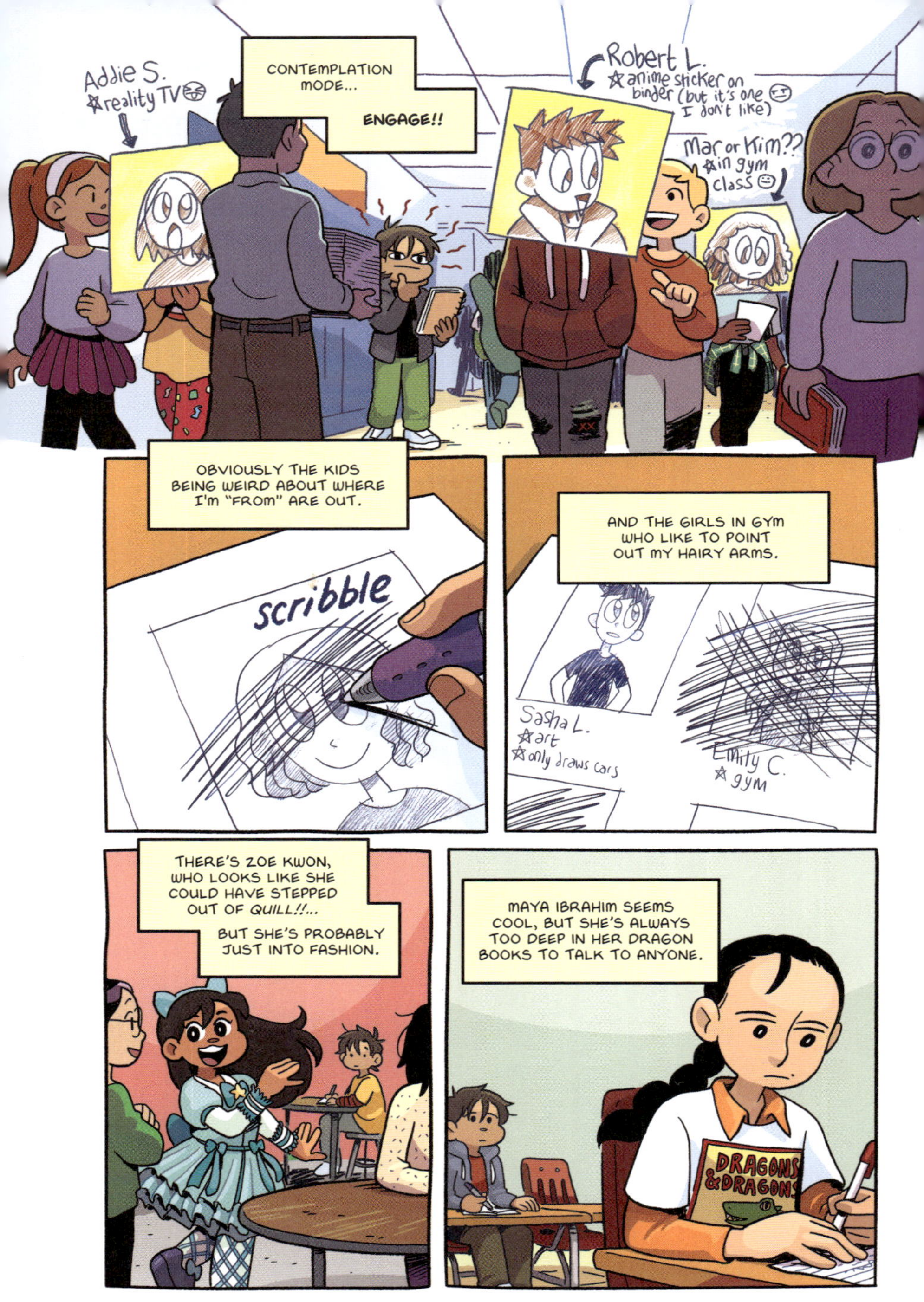
CONTEMPLATION MODE...
ENGAGE!!
Addie S.
☆reality TV
Robert L.
☆anime sticker on binder (but it's one I don't like)
Mar or Kim??
☆in gym class
OBVIOUSLY THE KIDS BEING WEIRD ABOUT WHERE I'M "FROM" ARE OUT.
scribble
AND THE GIRLS IN GYM WHO LIKE TO POINT OUT MY HAIRY ARMS.
Sasha L.
☆art
☆only draws cars
Emily C.
☆gym
THERE'S ZOE KWON, WHO LOOKS LIKE SHE COULD HAVE STEPPED OUT OF *QUILL!!*...
BUT SHE'S PROBABLY JUST INTO FASHION.
MAYA IBRAHIM SEEMS COOL, BUT SHE'S ALWAYS TOO DEEP IN HER DRAGON BOOKS TO TALK TO ANYONE.
DRAGONS &DRAGONS

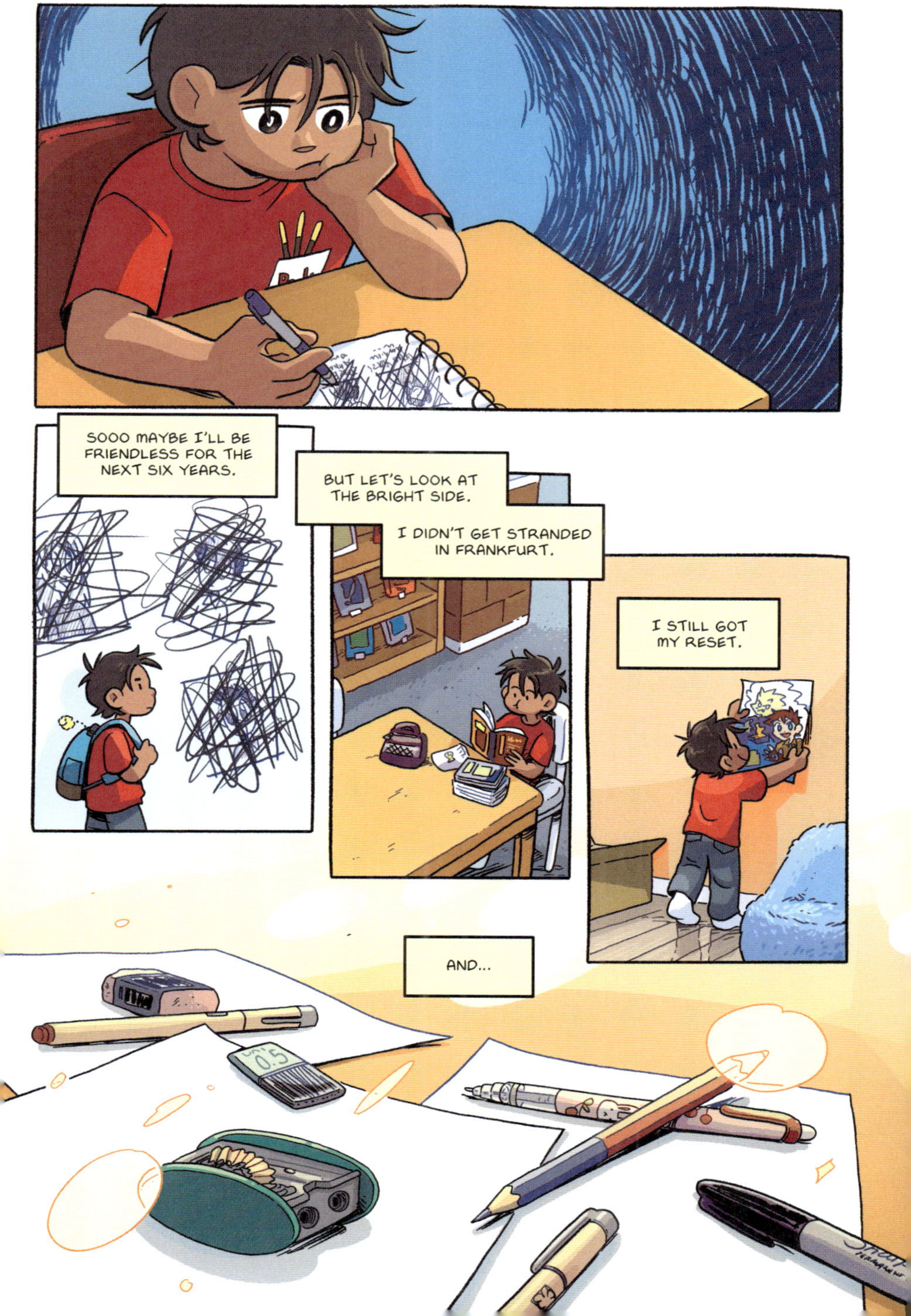
SOOO MAYBE I'LL BE FRIENDLESS FOR THE NEXT SIX YEARS.
BUT LET'S LOOK AT THE BRIGHT SIDE.
I DIDN'T GET STRANDED IN FRANKFURT.
I STILL GOT MY RESET.
AND...

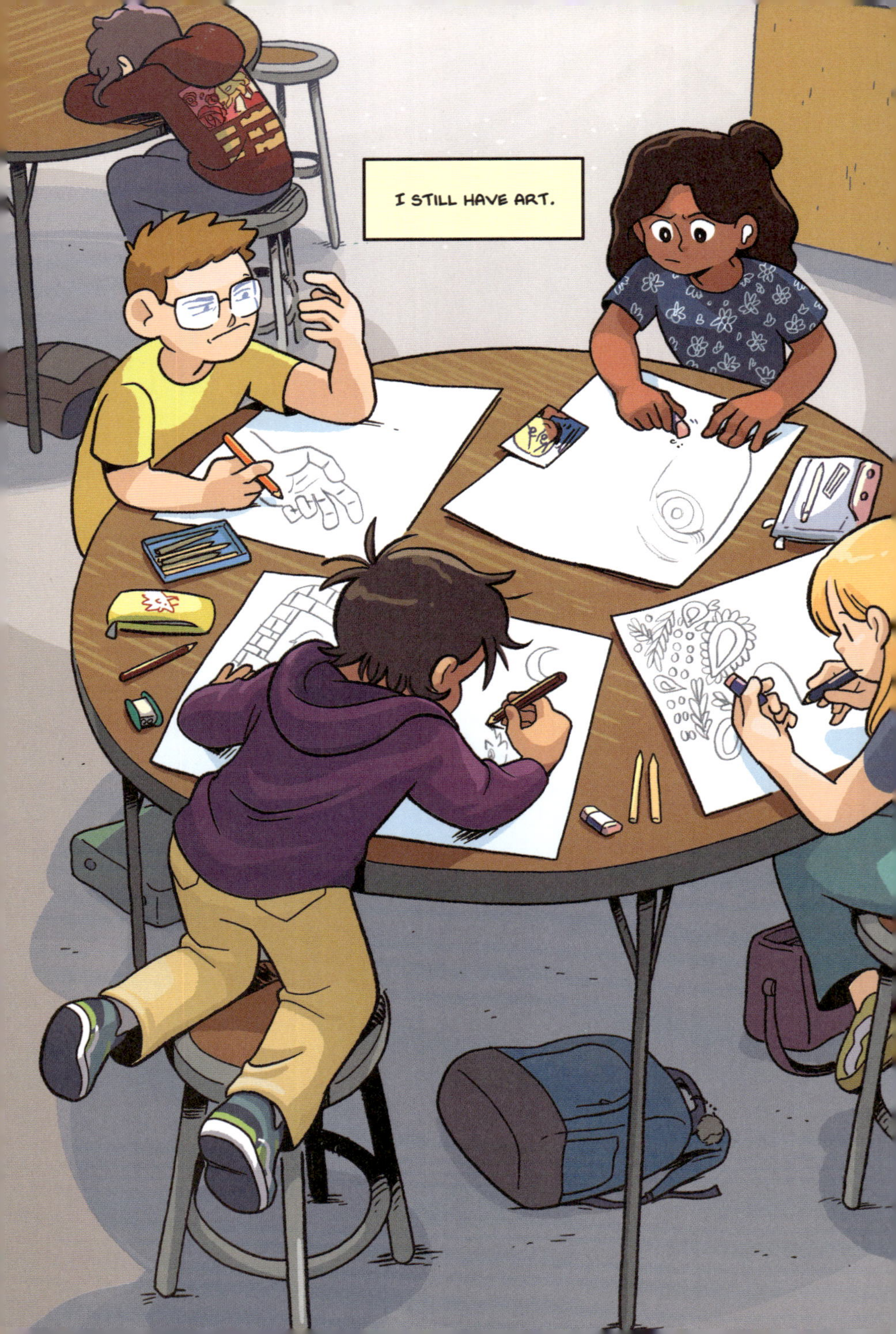
I STILL HAVE ART.

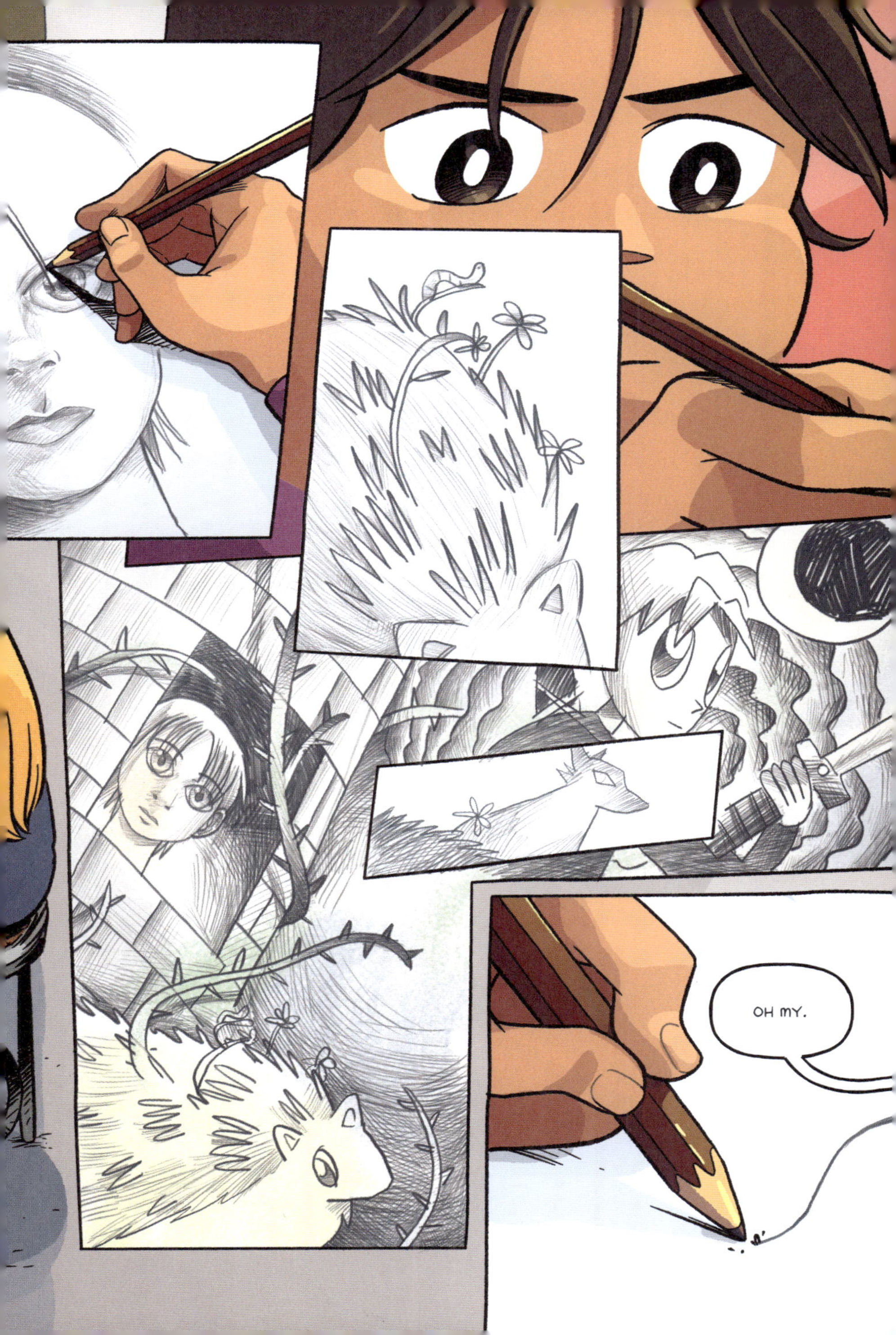
OH MY.

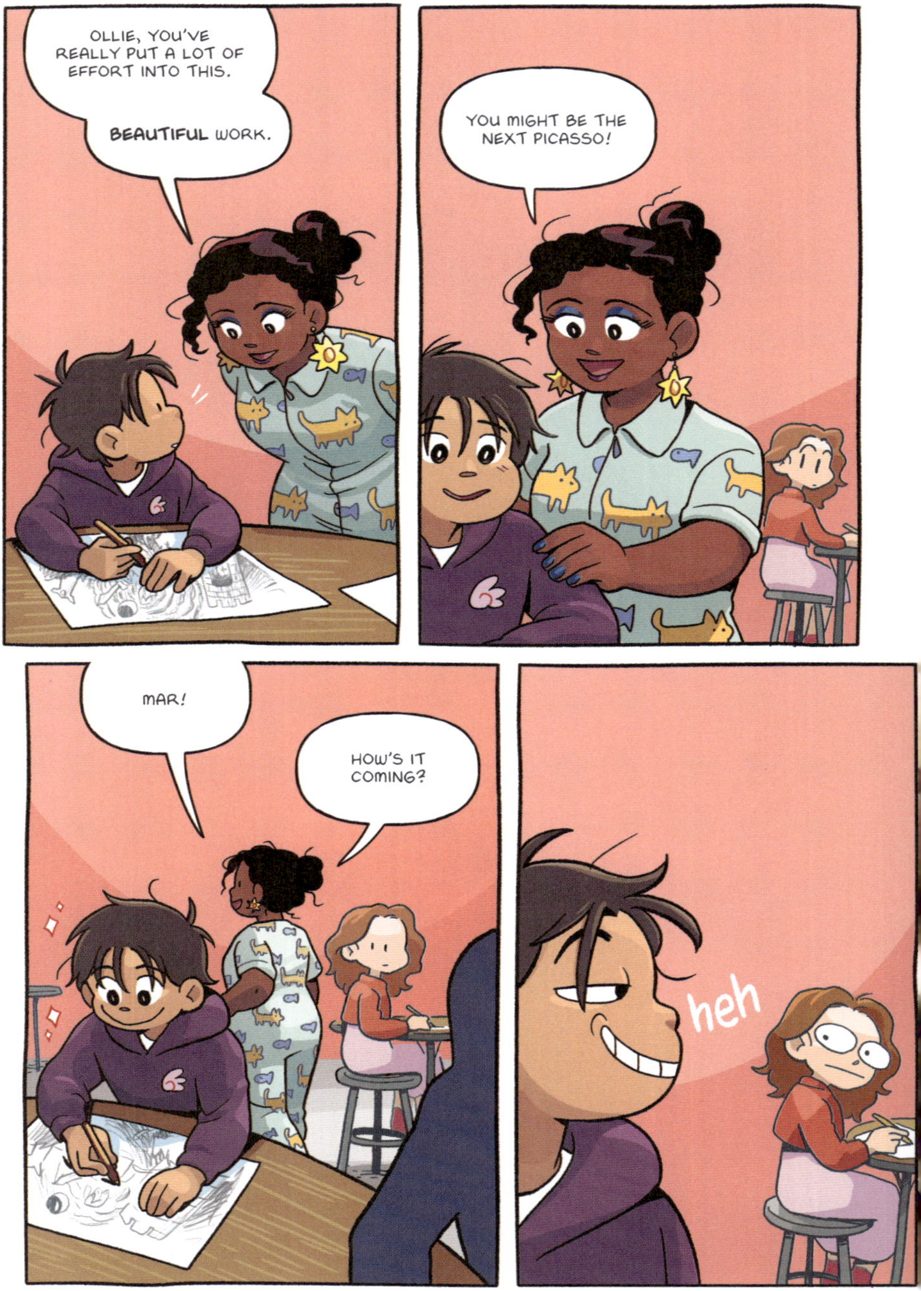
OLLIE, YOU'VE REALLY PUT A LOT OF EFFORT INTO THIS.
BEAUTIFUL WORK.
YOU MIGHT BE THE NEXT PICASSO!
MAR!
HOW'S IT COMING?
heh

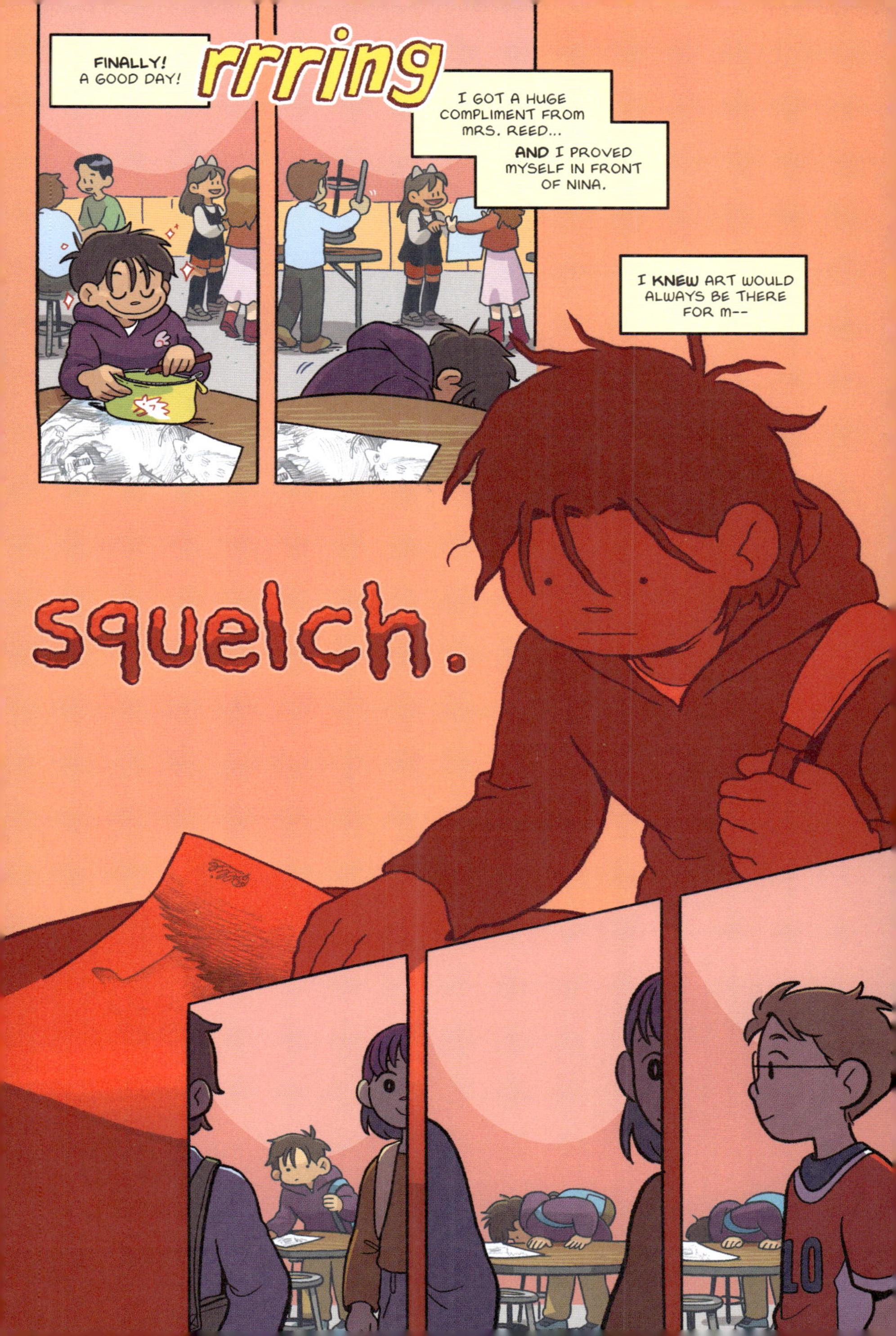
FINALLY! A GOOD DAY!
rrring
I GOT A HUGE COMPLIMENT FROM MRS. REED...
AND I PROVED MYSELF IN FRONT OF NINA.
I KNEW ART WOULD ALWAYS BE THERE FOR M--
squelch.

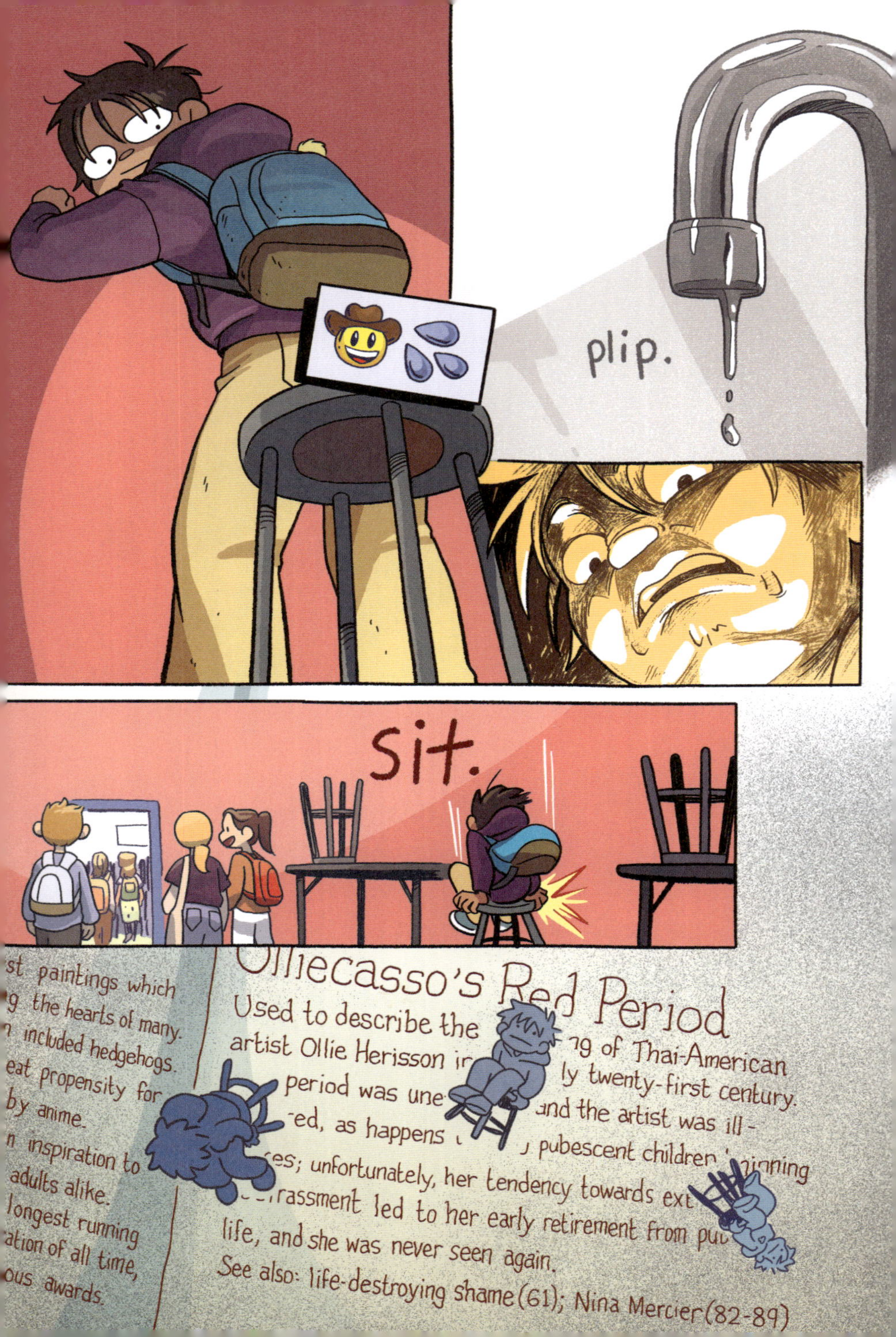
plip.
sit.
st paintings which
g the hearts of many.
n included hedgehogs.
eat propensity for
by anime.
n inspiration to
adults alike.
longest running
ation of all time,
ous awards.
Olliecasso's Red Period
Used to describe the
artist Ollie Herisson in
ng of Thai-American
ly twenty-first century.
period was une
and the artist was ill-
ed, as happens
pubescent children
es; unfortunately, her tendency towards ext
rassment led to her early retirement from pu
life, and she was never seen again.
See also: life-destroying shame (61); Nina Mercier (82-89)

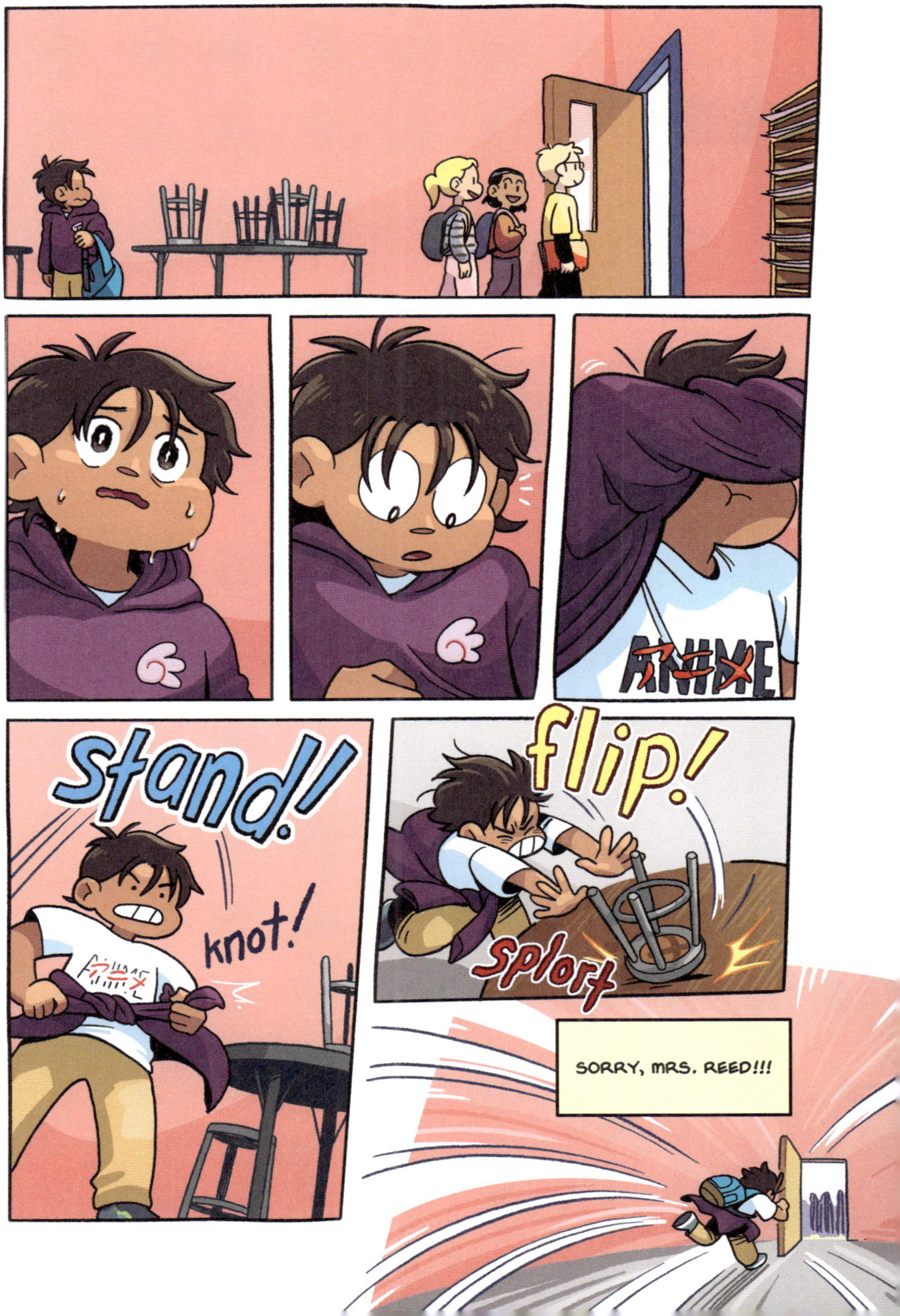
ANIME
アニメ
stand!
knot!
flip!
splort
SORRY, MRS. REED!!!

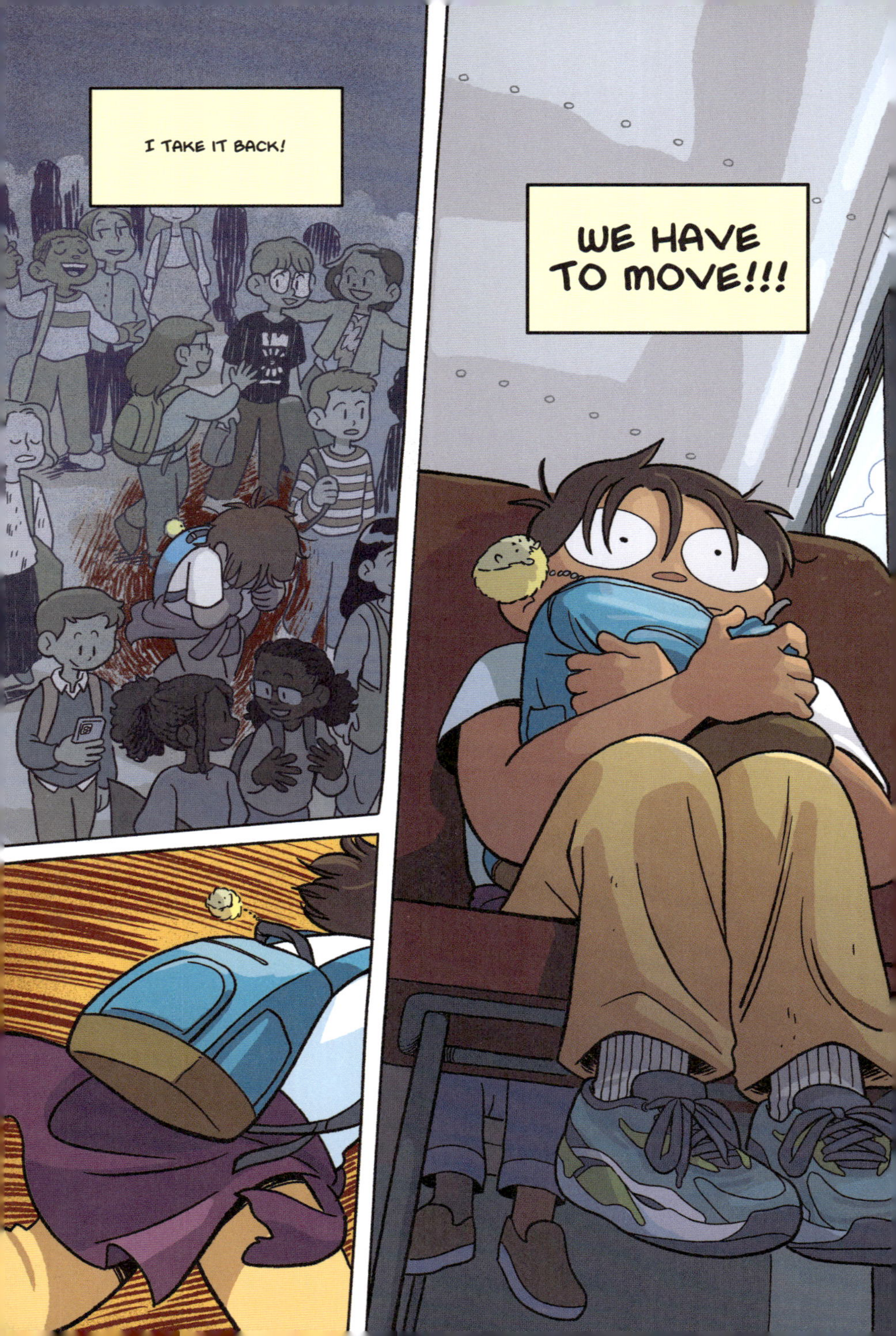
I TAKE IT BACK!
WE HAVE TO MOVE!!!

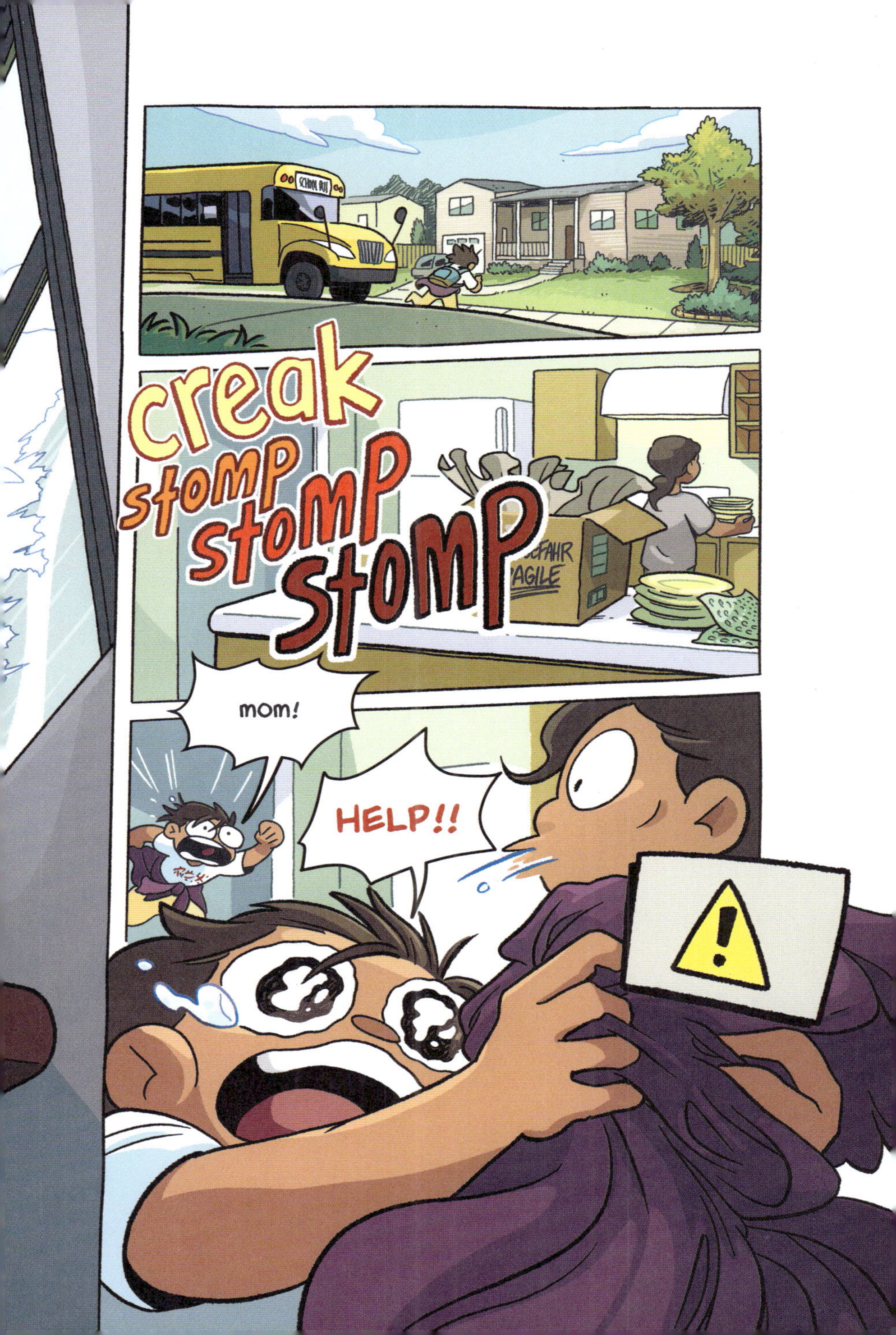
creak
stomp
stomp
stomp
mom!
HELP!!

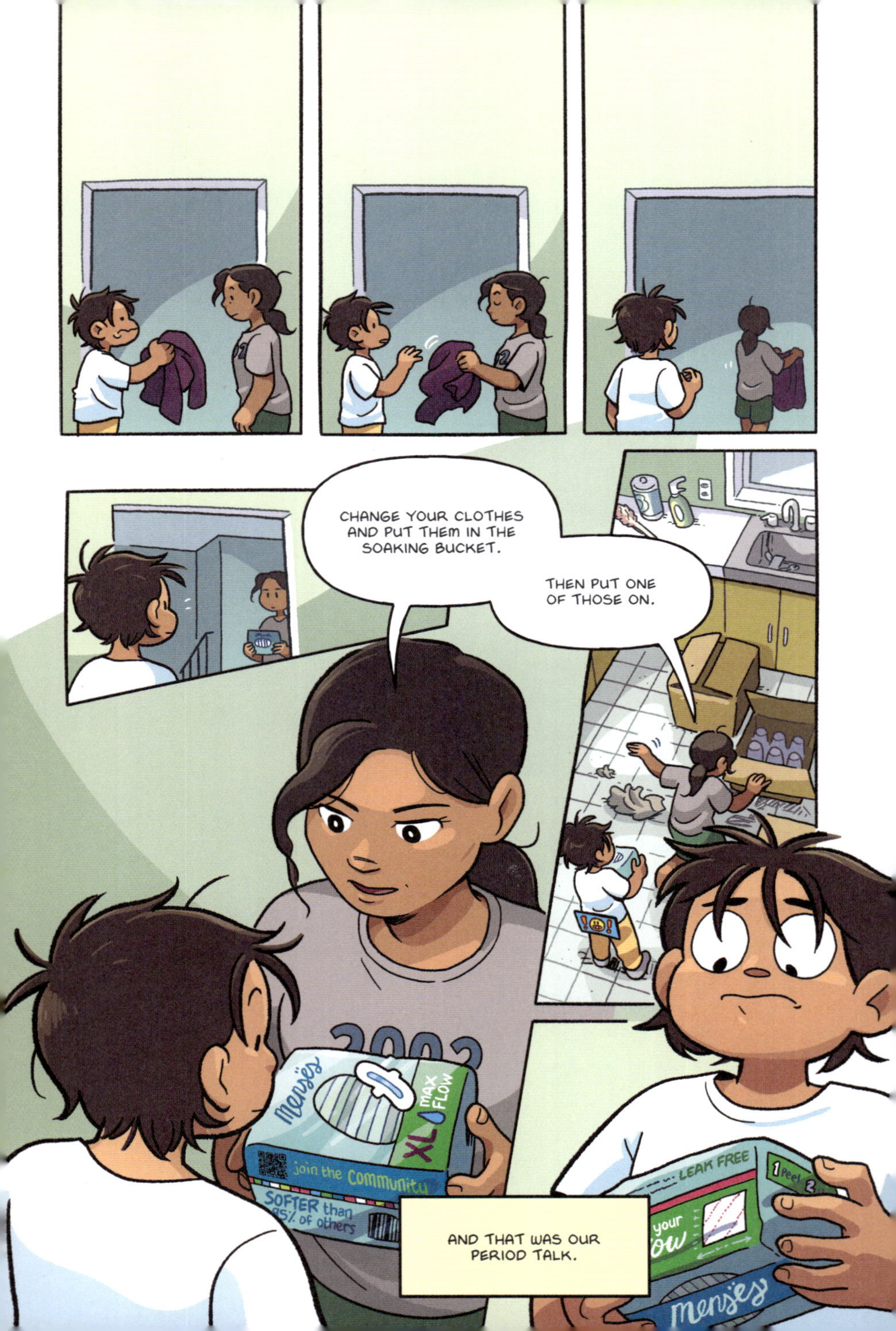
CHANGE YOUR CLOTHES AND PUT THEM IN THE SOAKING BUCKET.
THEN PUT ONE OF THOSE ON.
Mensës
MAX FLOW
XL
join the Community
SOFTER than 95% of others
LEAK FREE
AND THAT WAS OUR PERIOD TALK.

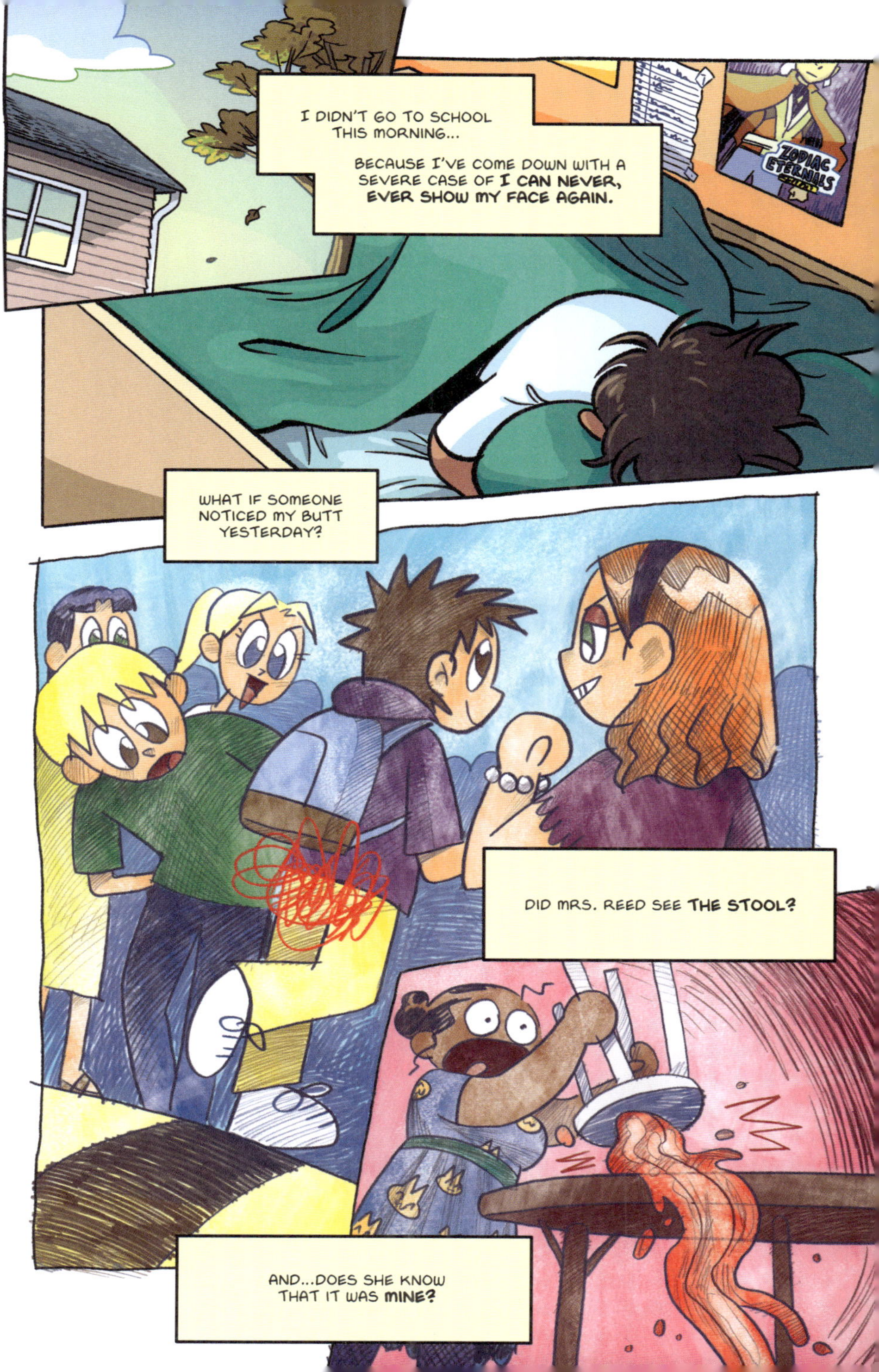

I DIDN'T GO TO SCHOOL THIS MORNING...
BECAUSE I'VE COME DOWN WITH A SEVERE CASE OF I CAN NEVER, EVER SHOW MY FACE AGAIN.
ZODIAC ETERNALS
WHAT IF SOMEONE NOTICED MY BUTT YESTERDAY?
DID MRS. REED SEE THE STOOL?
AND...DOES SHE KNOW THAT IT WAS MINE?

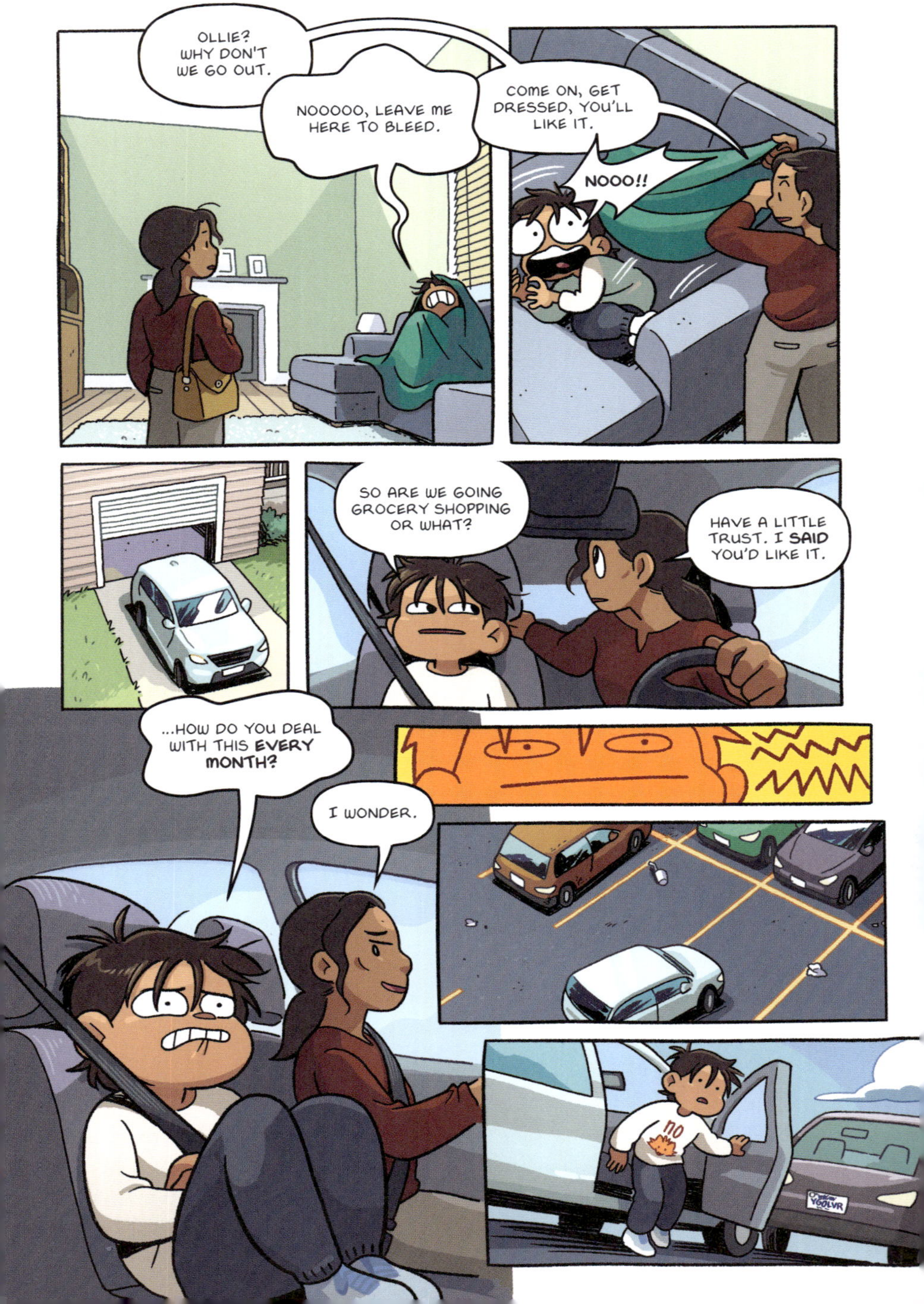
OLLIE? WHY DON'T WE GO OUT.
NOOOOO, LEAVE ME HERE TO BLEED.
COME ON, GET DRESSED, YOU'LL LIKE IT.
NOOO!!
SO ARE WE GOING GROCERY SHOPPING OR WHAT?
HAVE A LITTLE TRUST. I **SAID** YOU'D LIKE IT.
...HOW DO YOU DEAL WITH THIS **EVERY MONTH?**
I WONDER.
NO

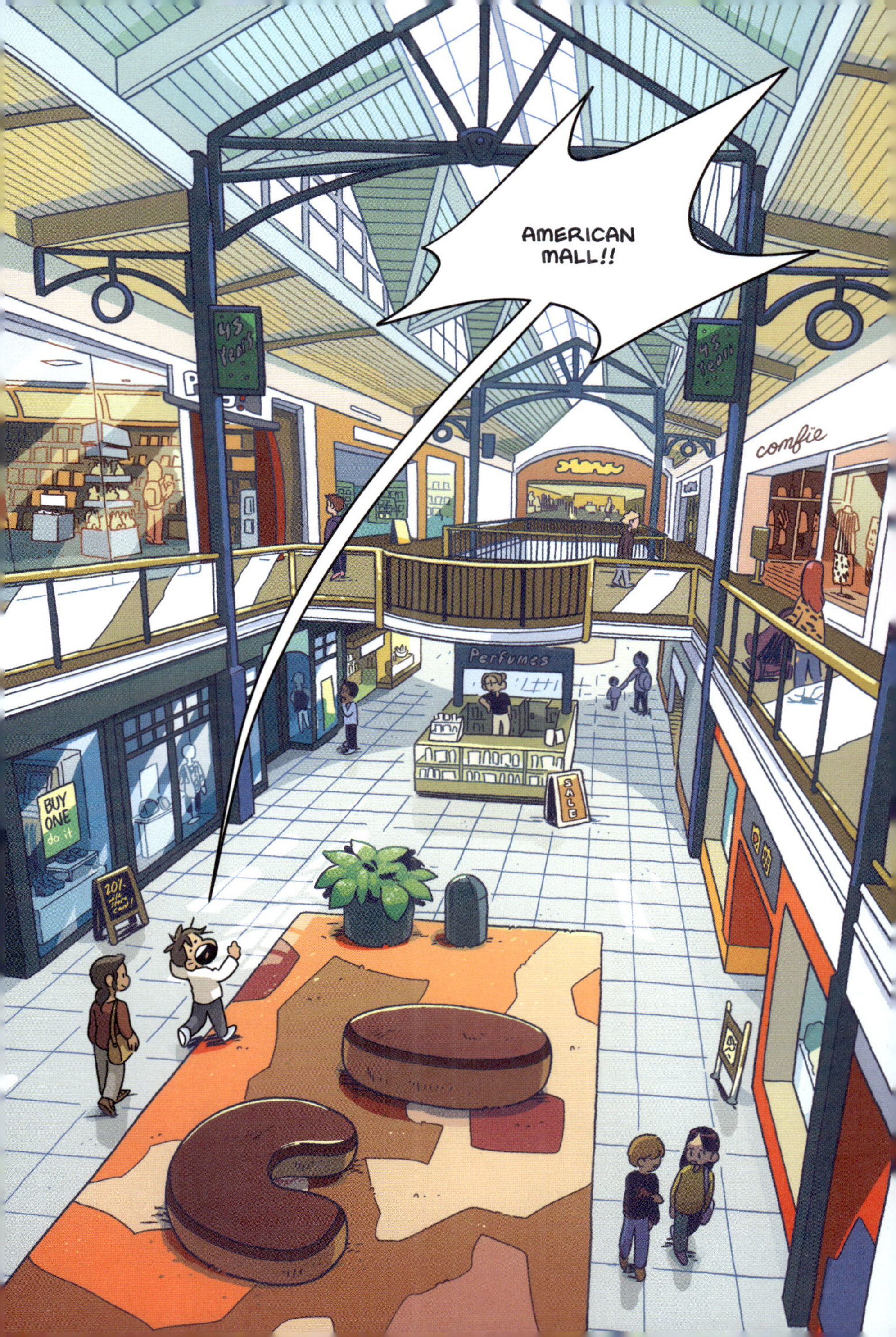

AMERICAN MALL!!
comfie
Perfumes
BUY ONE
do it
SALE

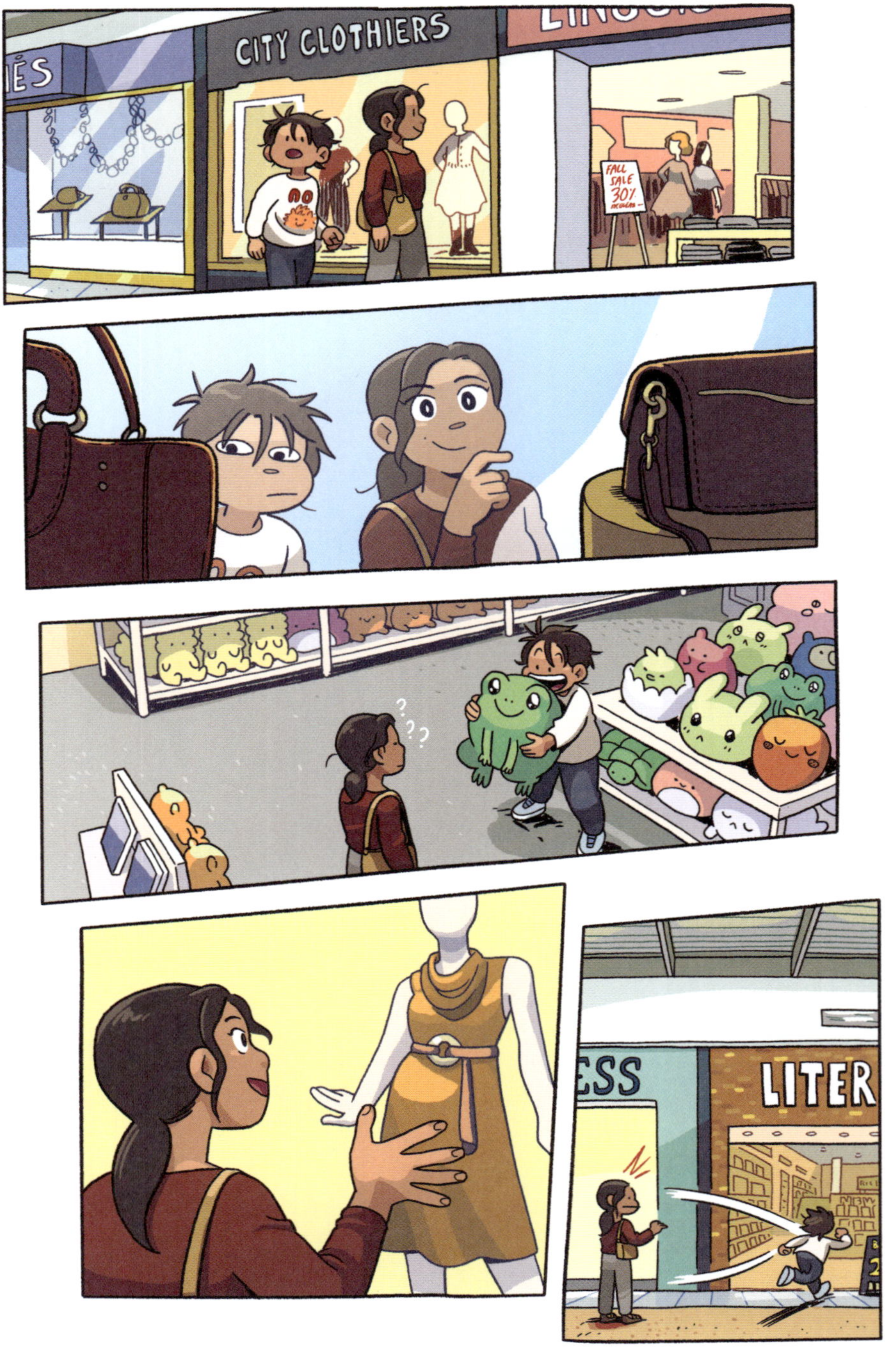
CITY CLOTHIERS
FALL SALE 30%
???
ESS
LITER

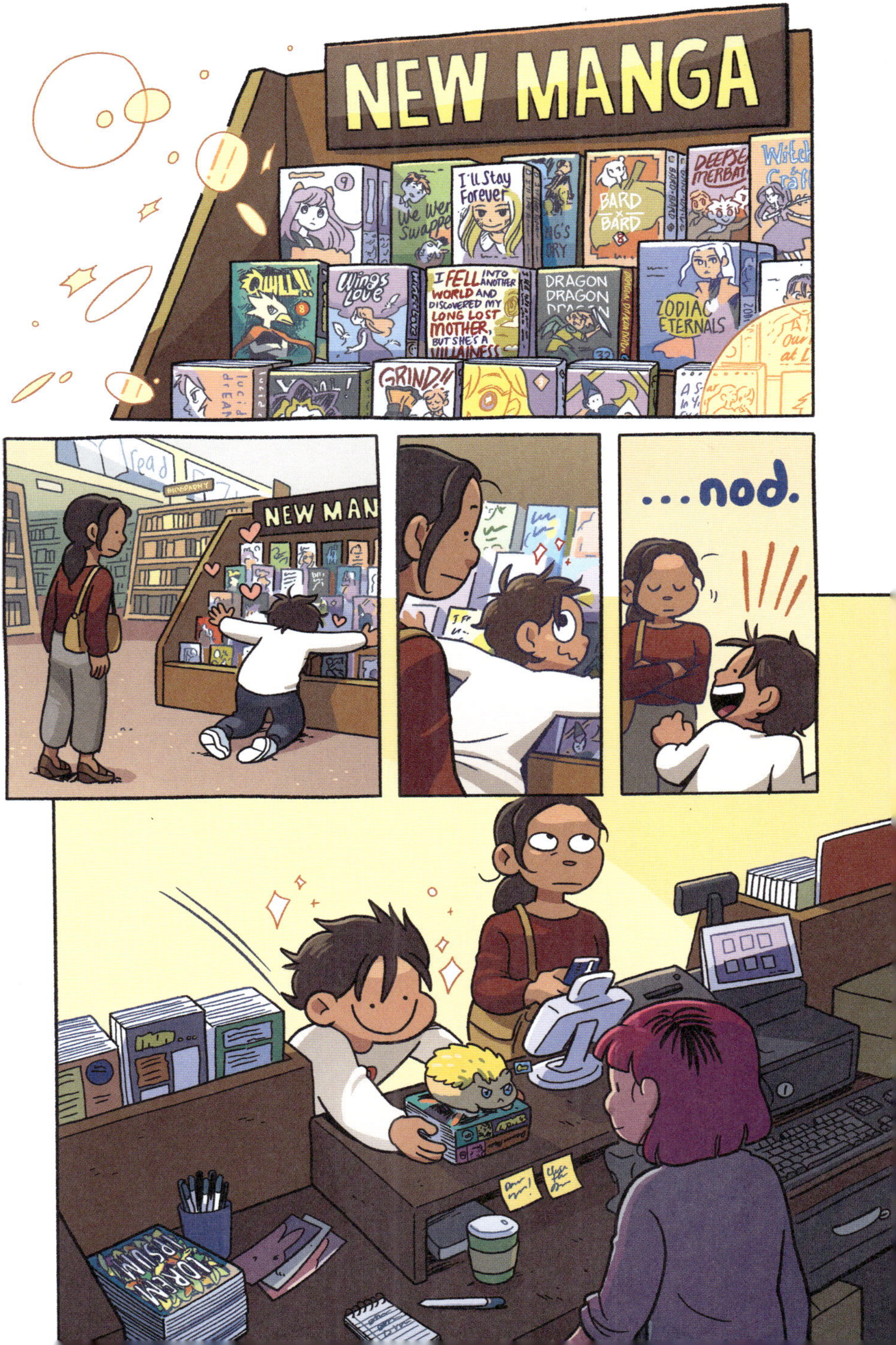
NEW MANGA
I'll Stay Forever
BARD x BARD
QUILL!!
I FELL INTO ANOTHER WORLD AND DISCOVERED MY LONG LOST MOTHER, BUT SHE'S A VILLAINESS
DRAGON DRAGON
ZODIAC ETERNALS
GRIND!!
NEW MAN
...nod.
LOREM IPSUM

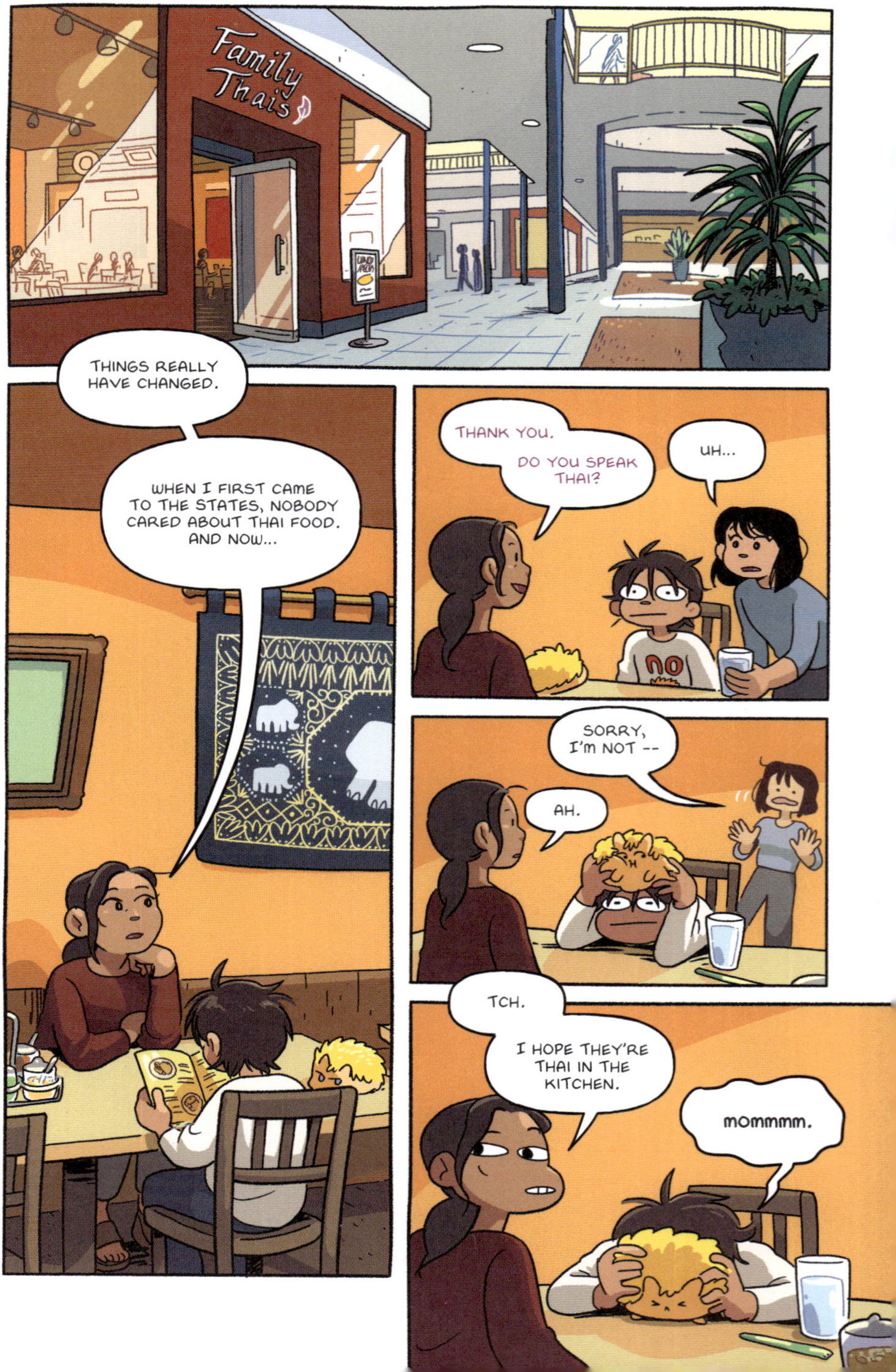
Family Thais
THINGS REALLY HAVE CHANGED.
WHEN I FIRST CAME TO THE STATES, NOBODY CARED ABOUT THAI FOOD. AND NOW...
THANK YOU.
DO YOU SPEAK THAI?
UH...
SORRY, I'M NOT --
AH.
TCH.
I HOPE THEY'RE THAI IN THE KITCHEN.
MOMMMM.

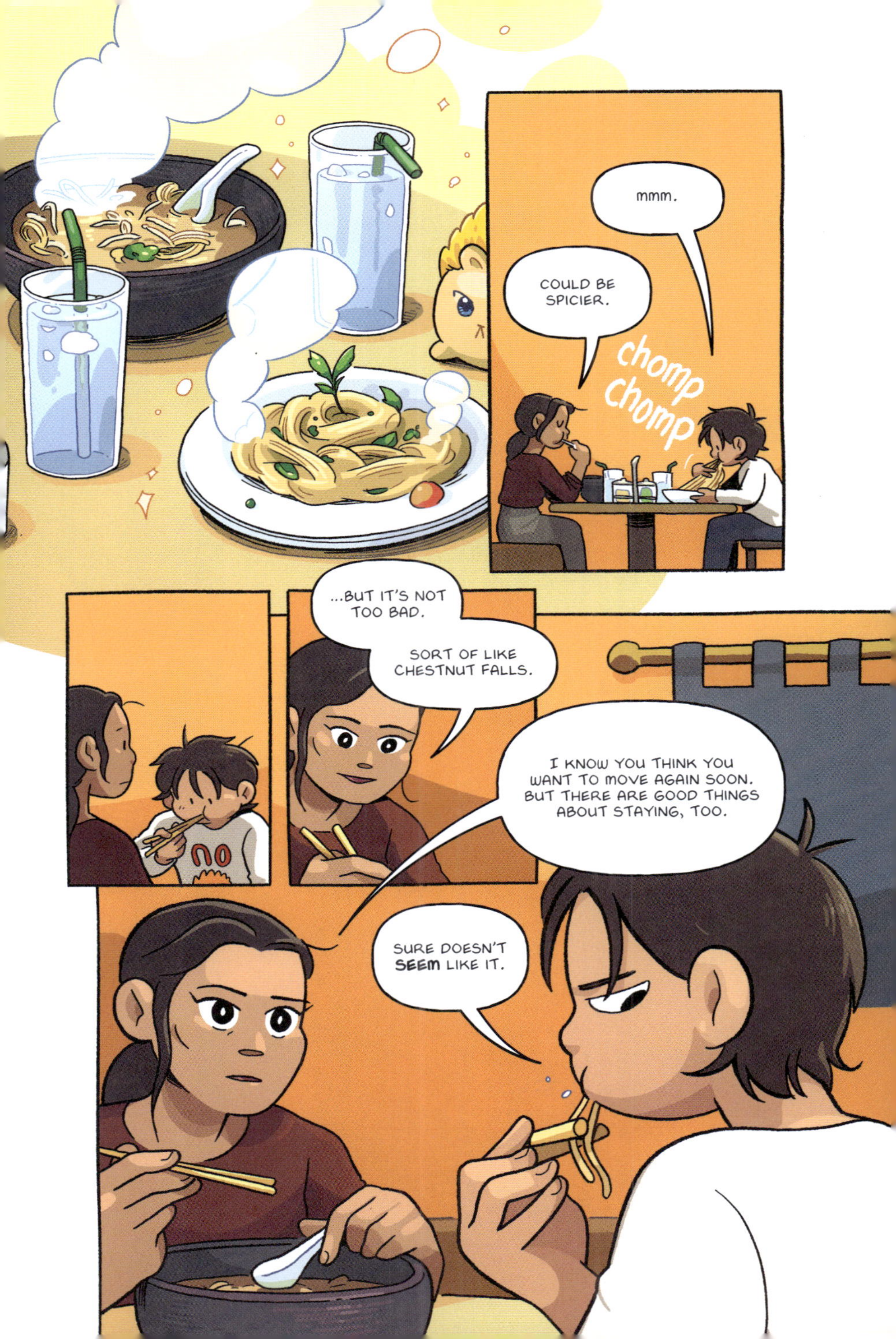

COULD BE SPICIER.
mmm.
chomp chomp
...BUT IT'S NOT TOO BAD.
SORT OF LIKE CHESTNUT FALLS.
no
I KNOW YOU THINK YOU WANT TO MOVE AGAIN SOON. BUT THERE ARE GOOD THINGS ABOUT STAYING, TOO.
SURE DOESN'T **SEEM** LIKE IT.

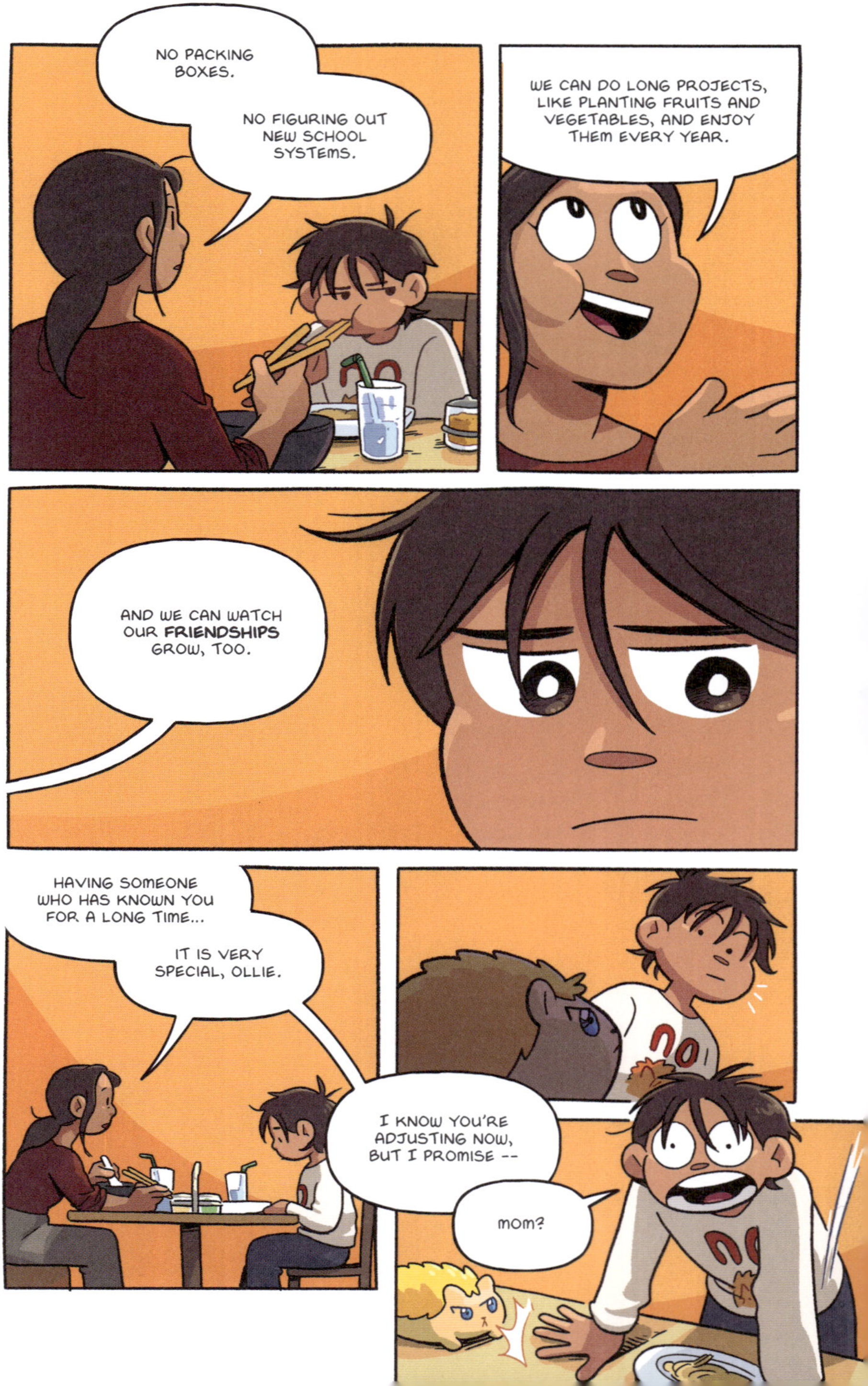
NO PACKING BOXES.
NO FIGURING OUT NEW SCHOOL SYSTEMS.
WE CAN DO LONG PROJECTS, LIKE PLANTING FRUITS AND VEGETABLES, AND ENJOY THEM EVERY YEAR.
AND WE CAN WATCH OUR **FRIENDSHIPS** GROW, TOO.
HAVING SOMEONE WHO HAS KNOWN YOU FOR A LONG TIME...
IT IS VERY SPECIAL, OLLIE.
I KNOW YOU'RE ADJUSTING NOW, BUT I PROMISE --
mom?

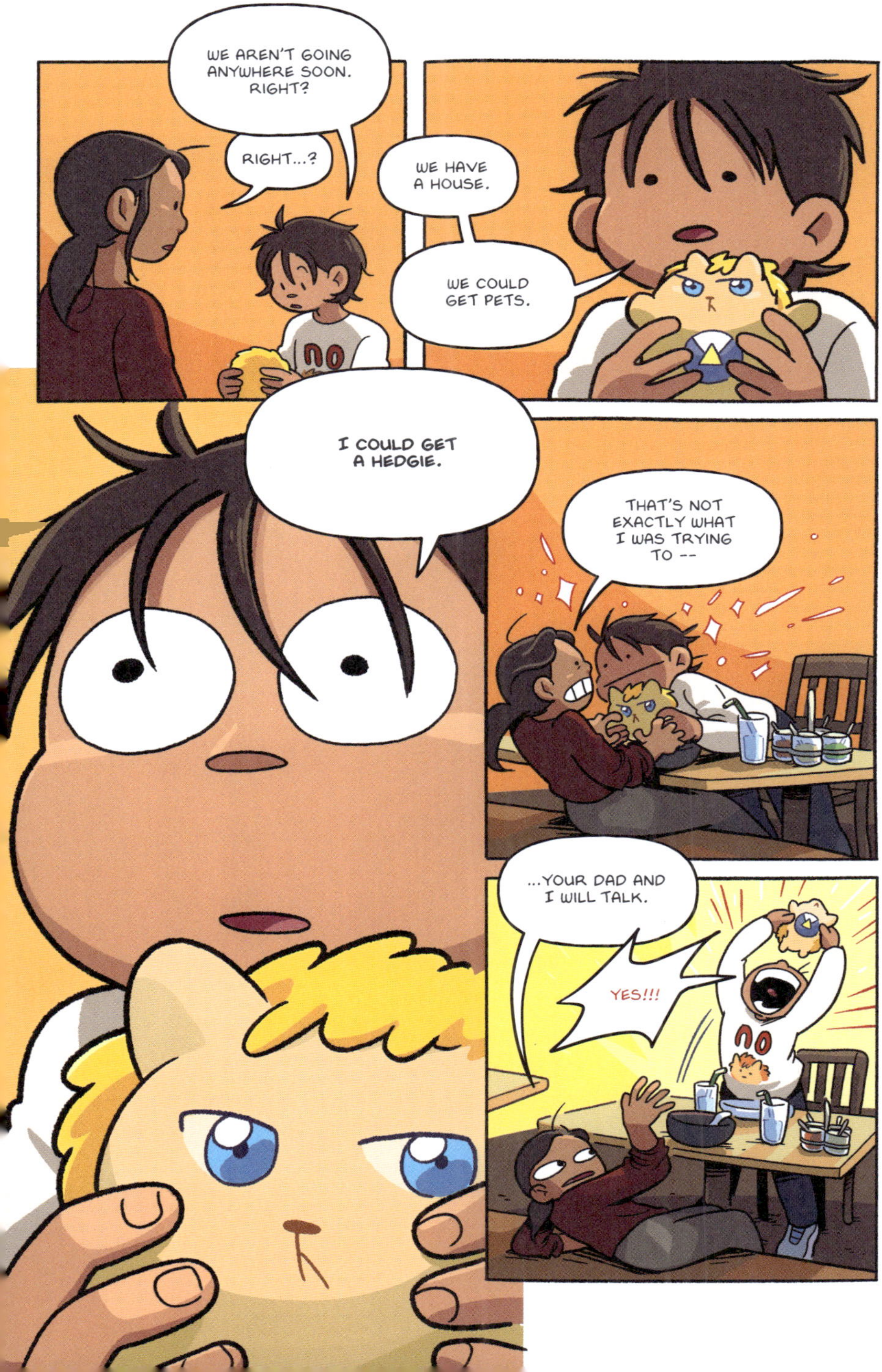
WE AREN'T GOING ANYWHERE SOON. RIGHT?
RIGHT...?
WE HAVE A HOUSE.
WE COULD GET PETS.
I COULD GET A HEDGIE.
THAT'S NOT EXACTLY WHAT I WAS TRYING TO --
...YOUR DAD AND I WILL TALK.
YES!!!

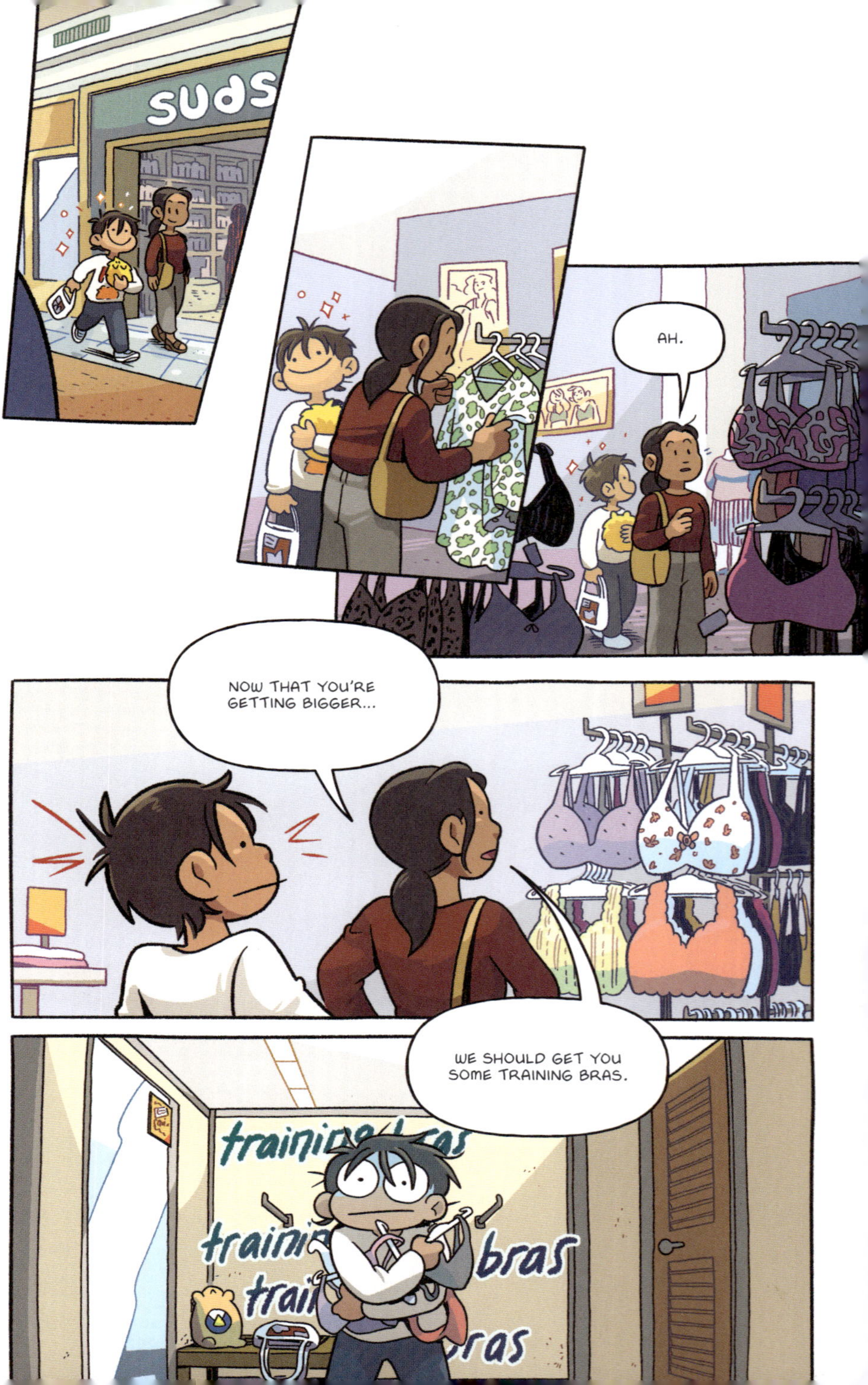
suds
AH.
NOW THAT YOU'RE GETTING BIGGER...
WE SHOULD GET YOU SOME TRAINING BRAS.
training bras
bras

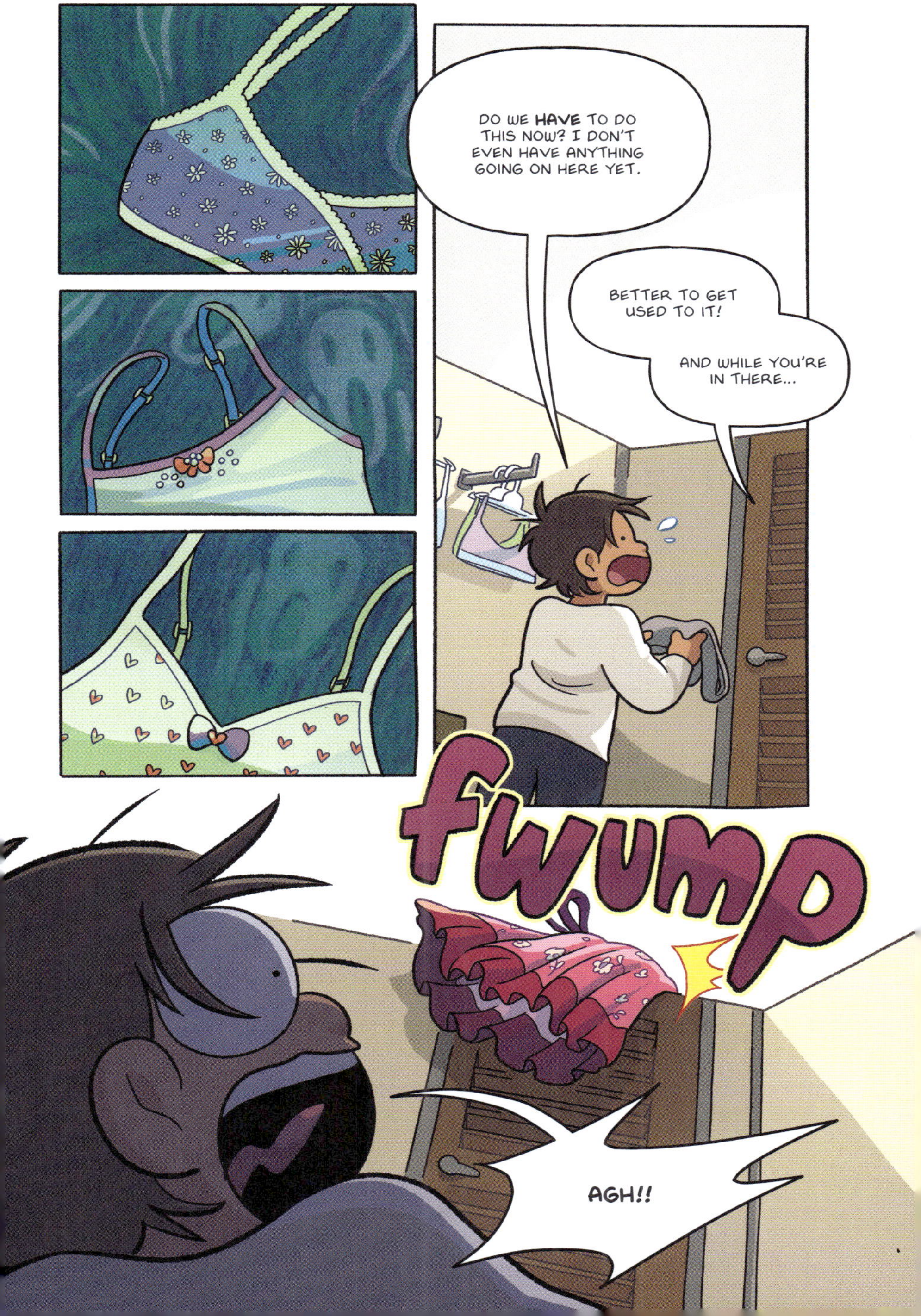
DO WE **HAVE** TO DO THIS NOW? I DON'T EVEN HAVE ANYTHING GOING ON HERE YET.
BETTER TO GET USED TO IT!
AND WHILE YOU'RE IN THERE...
FWUMP
AGH!!

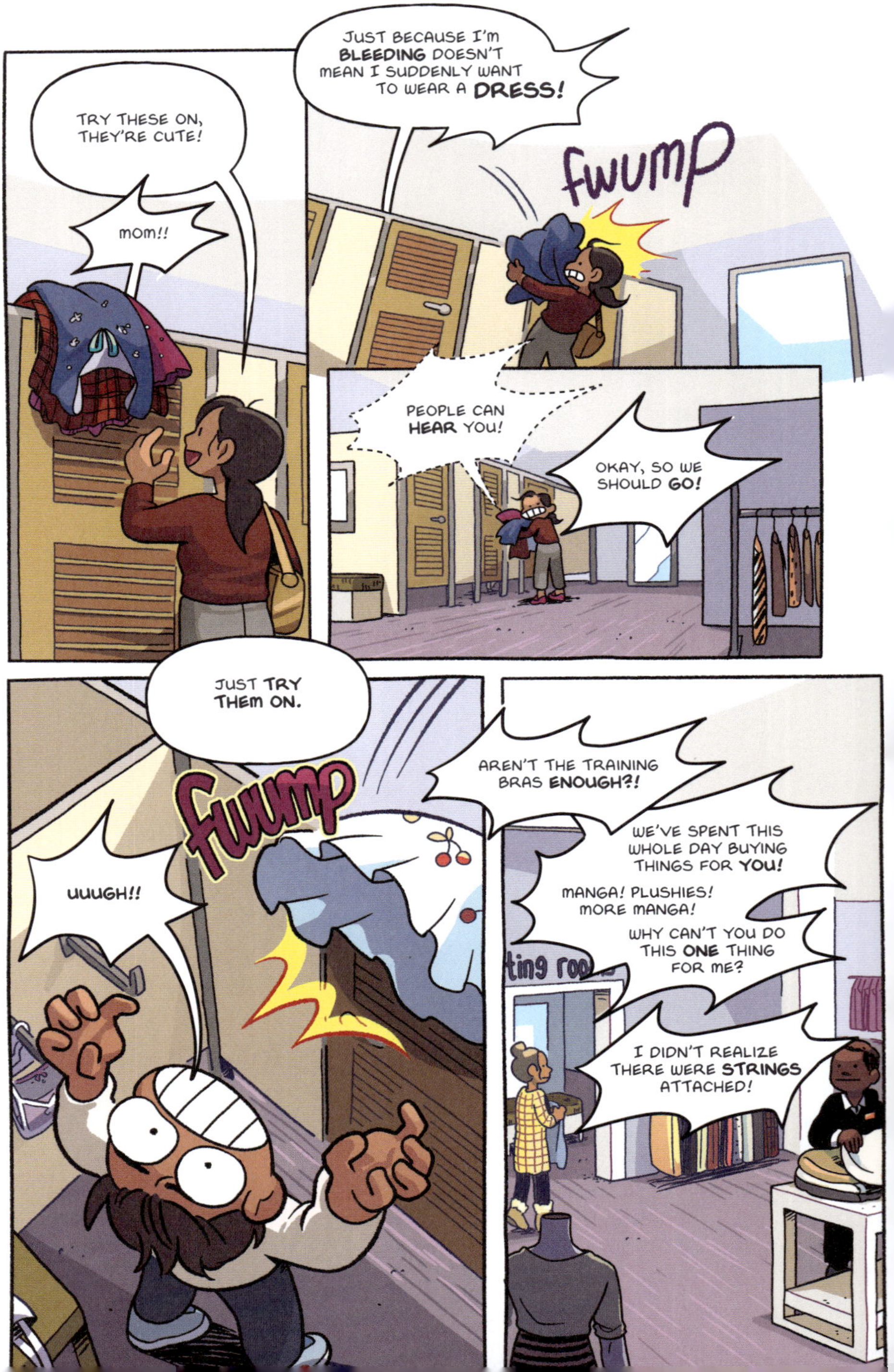
TRY THESE ON, THEY'RE CUTE!
MOM!!
JUST BECAUSE I'M BLEEDING DOESN'T MEAN I SUDDENLY WANT TO WEAR A DRESS!
FWUMP
PEOPLE CAN HEAR YOU!
OKAY, SO WE SHOULD GO!
JUST TRY THEM ON.
FWUMP
UUUGH!!
AREN'T THE TRAINING BRAS ENOUGH?!
WE'VE SPENT THIS WHOLE DAY BUYING THINGS FOR YOU!
MANGA! PLUSHIES! MORE MANGA!
WHY CAN'T YOU DO THIS ONE THING FOR ME?
I DIDN'T REALIZE THERE WERE STRINGS ATTACHED!

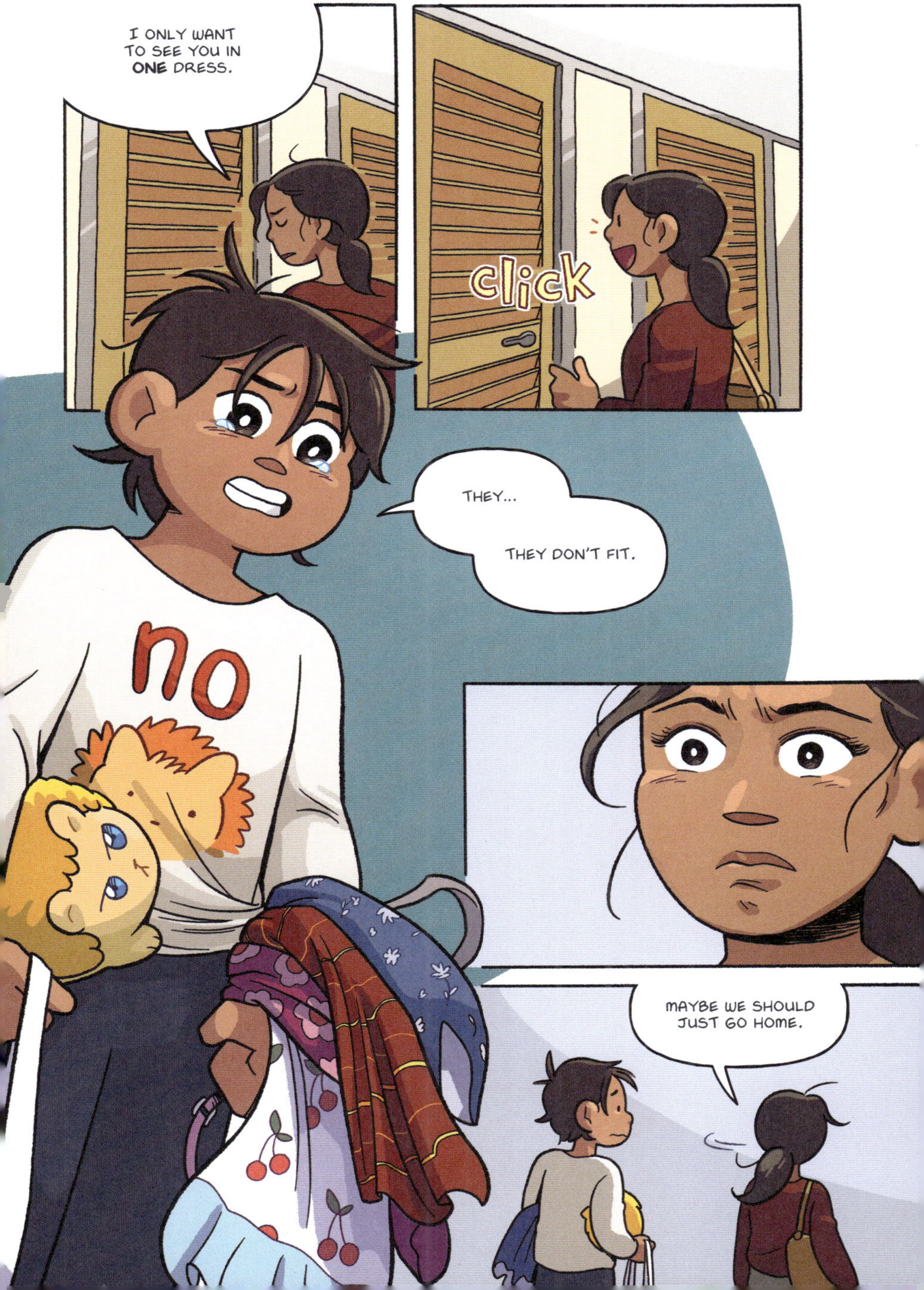
I ONLY WANT TO SEE YOU IN ONE DRESS.
click
THEY...
THEY DON'T FIT.
no
MAYBE WE SHOULD JUST GO HOME.

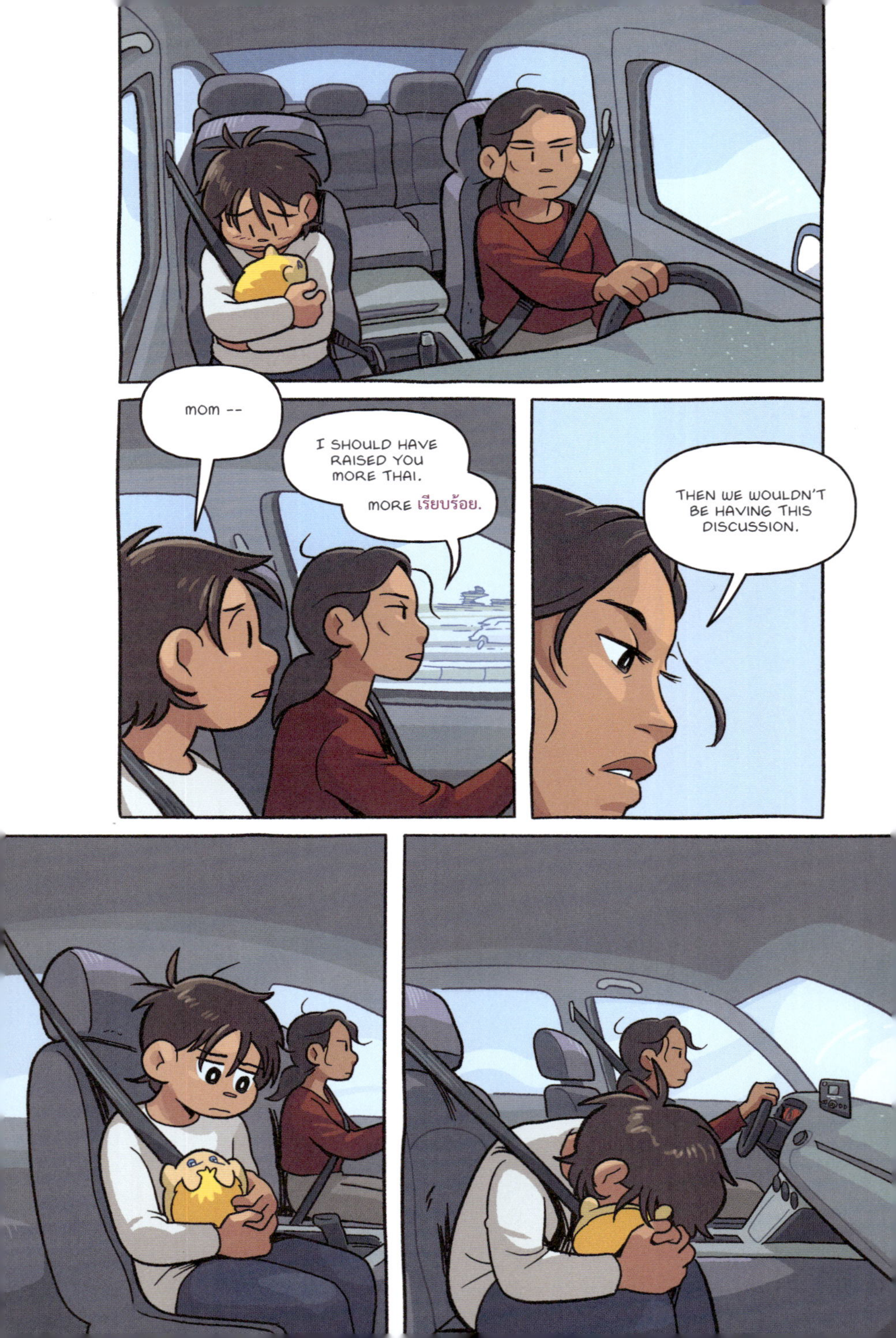
mom --
I SHOULD HAVE RAISED YOU MORE THAI.
MORE เรียบร้อย.
THEN WE WOULDN'T BE HAVING THIS DISCUSSION.

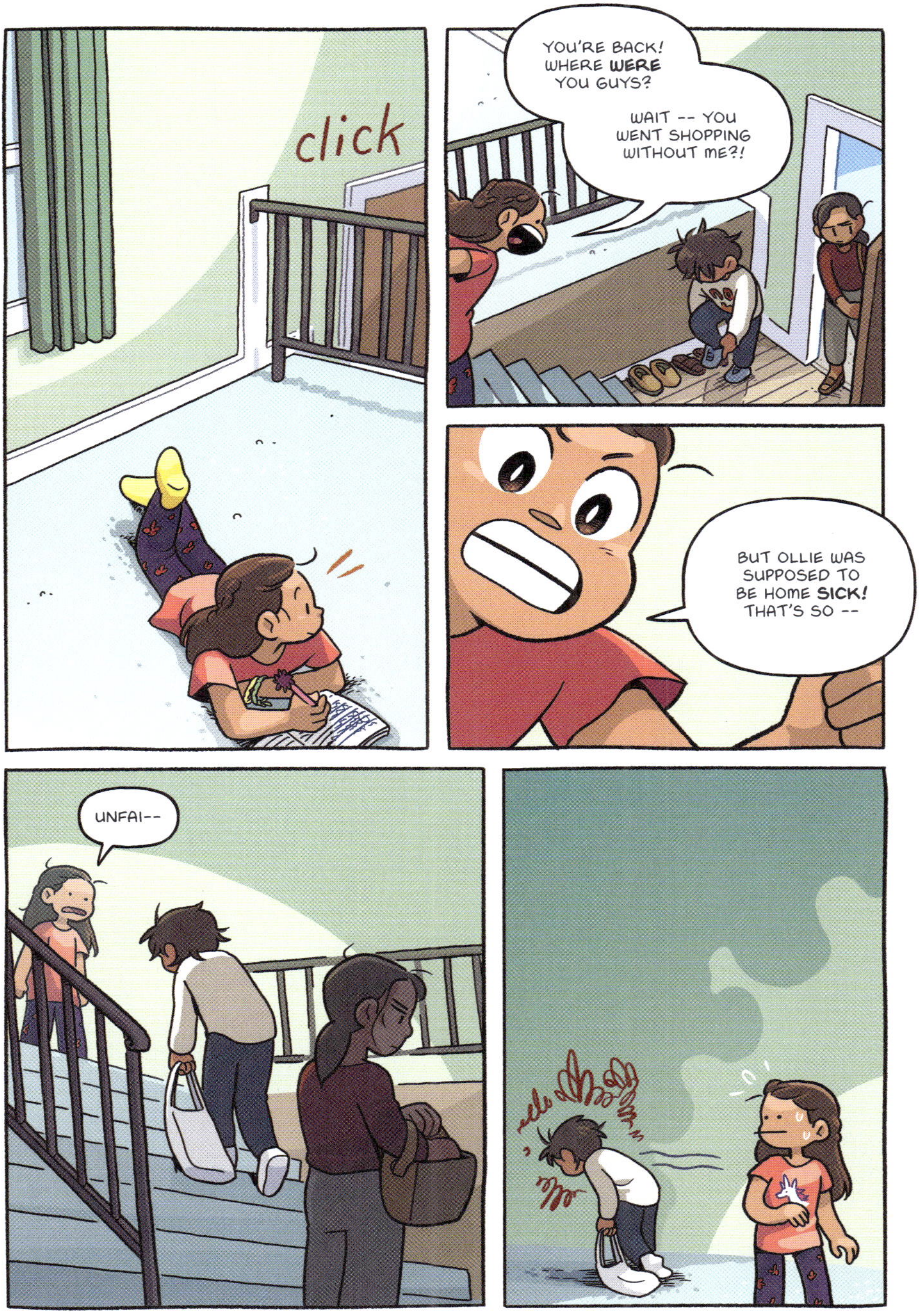
click
YOU'RE BACK! WHERE WERE YOU GUYS?
WAIT -- YOU WENT SHOPPING WITHOUT ME?!
BUT OLLIE WAS SUPPOSED TO BE HOME SICK! THAT'S SO --
UNFAI--

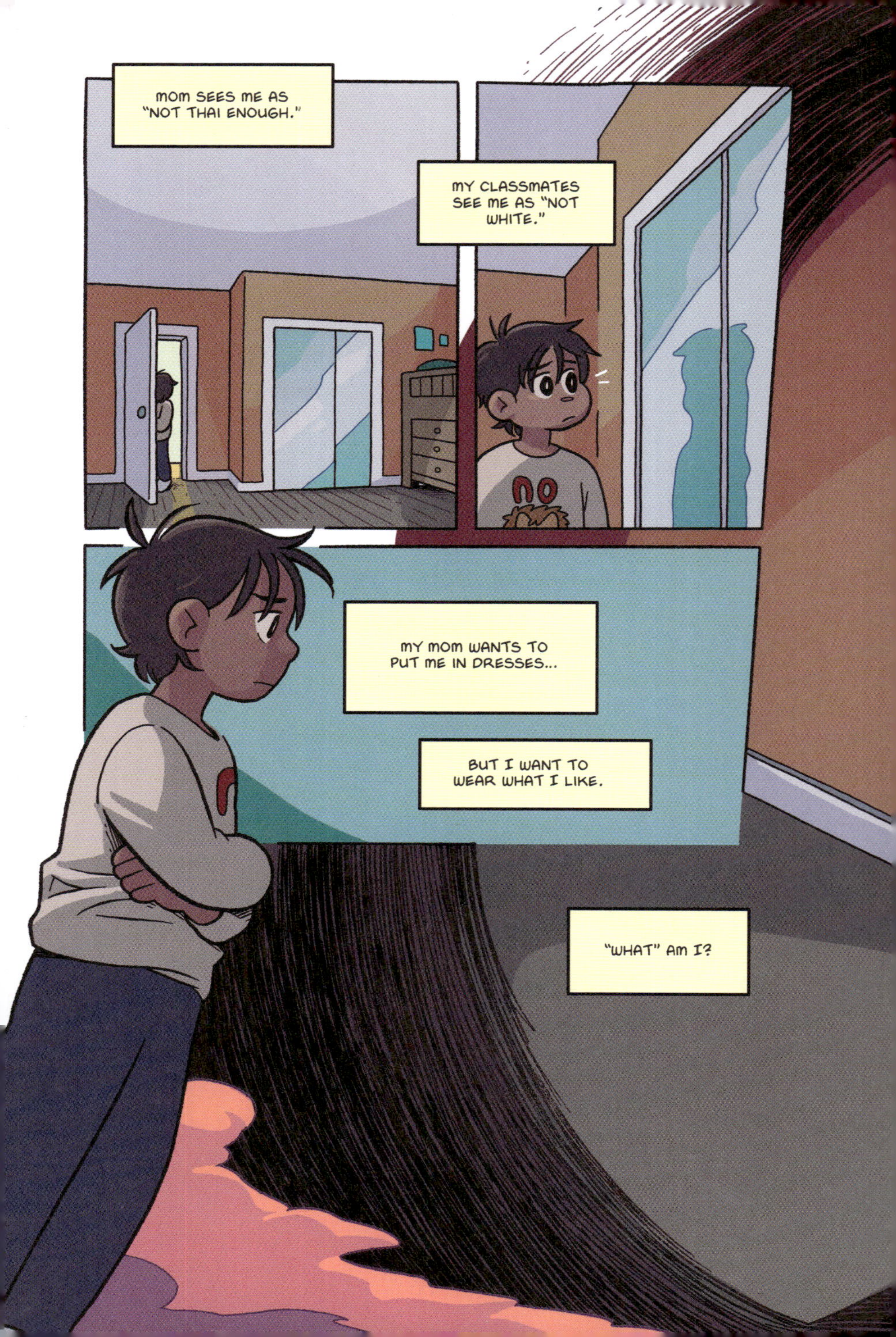
MOM SEES ME AS "NOT THAI ENOUGH."
MY CLASSMATES SEE ME AS "NOT WHITE."
NO
MY MOM WANTS TO PUT ME IN DRESSES...
BUT I WANT TO WEAR WHAT I LIKE.
"WHAT" AM I?

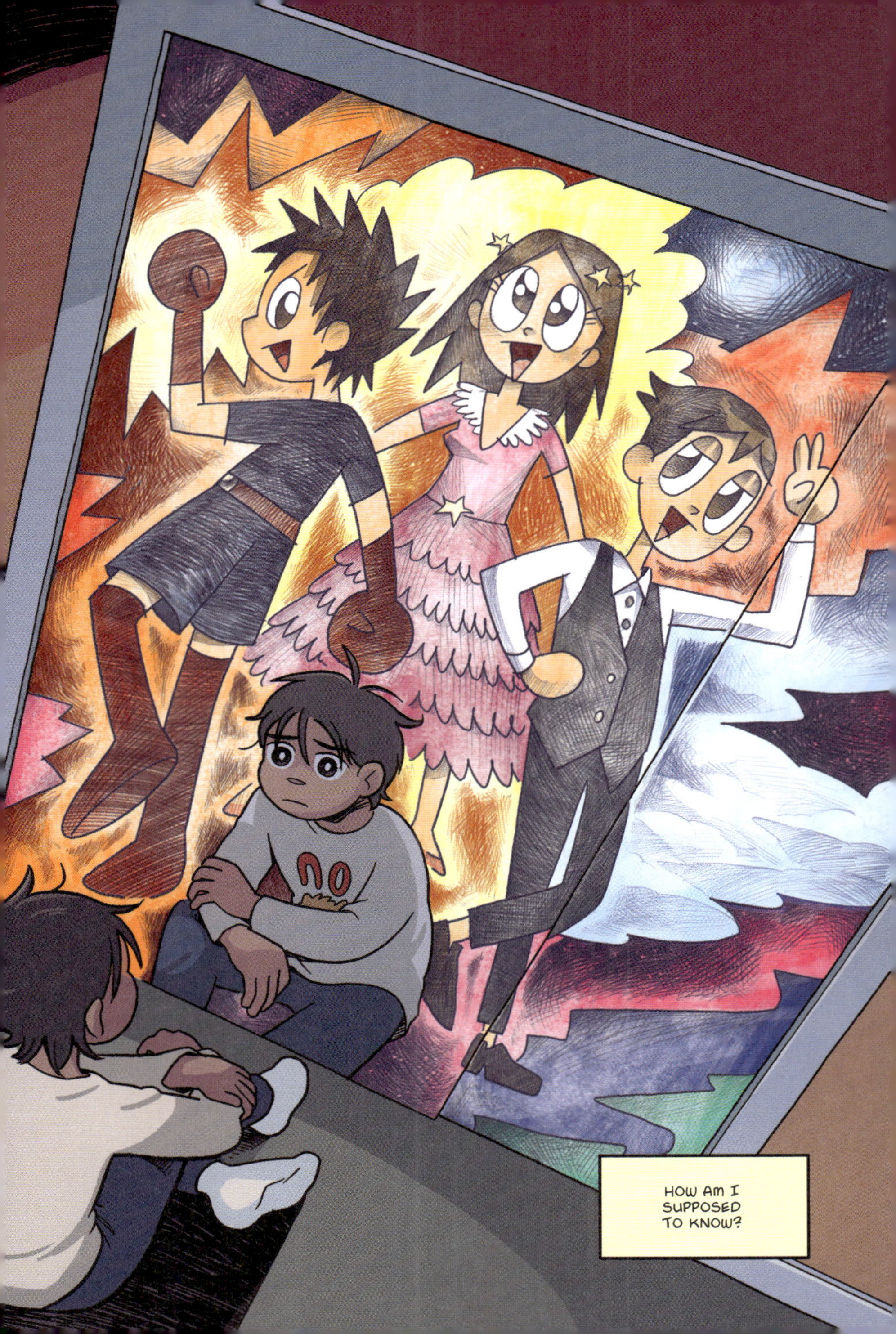

HOW AM I SUPPOSED TO KNOW?

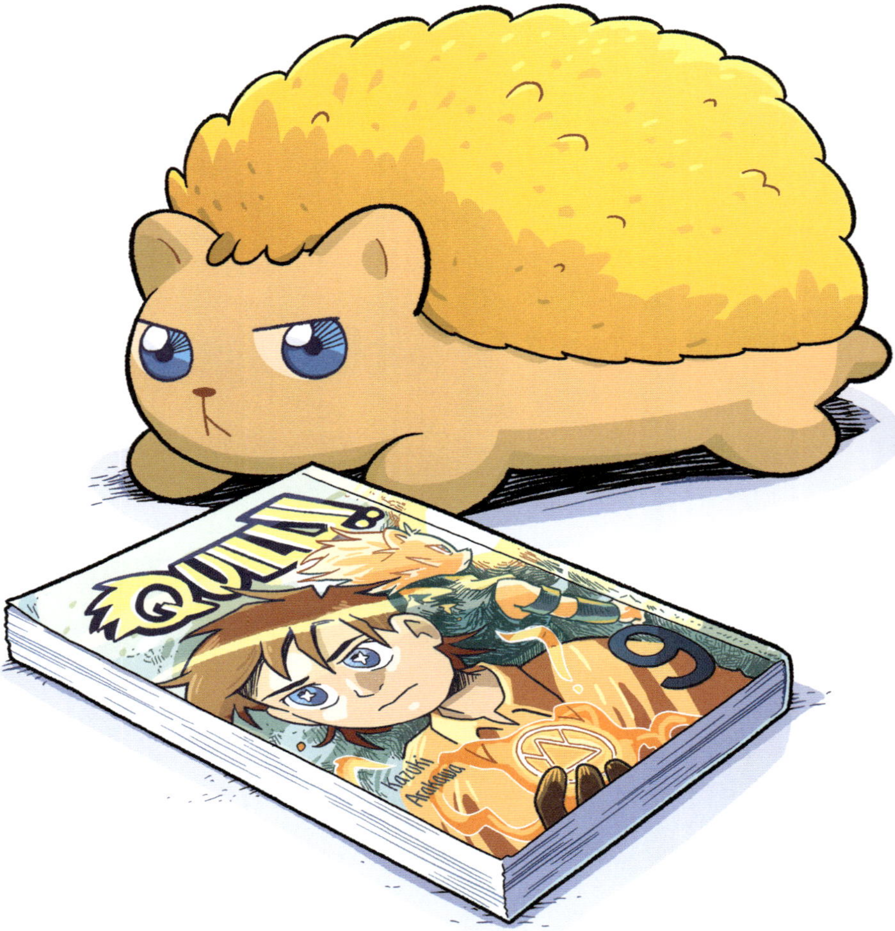
9
Kazuki
Arakawa

CHAPTER FOUR

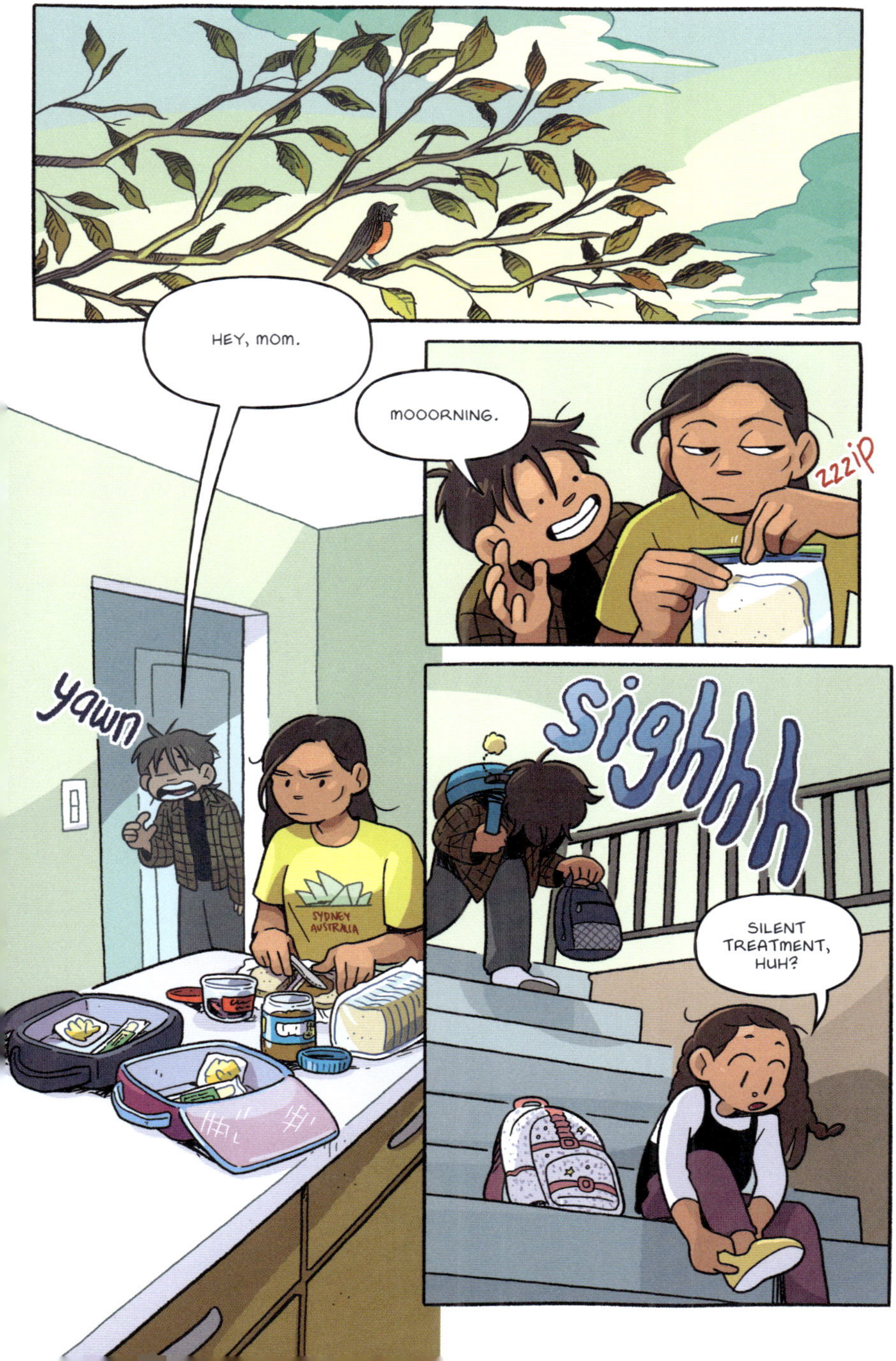
HEY, MOM.
yawn
MOOORNING.
zzzip
Sighhhh
SYDNEY AUSTRALIA
SILENT TREATMENT, HUH?

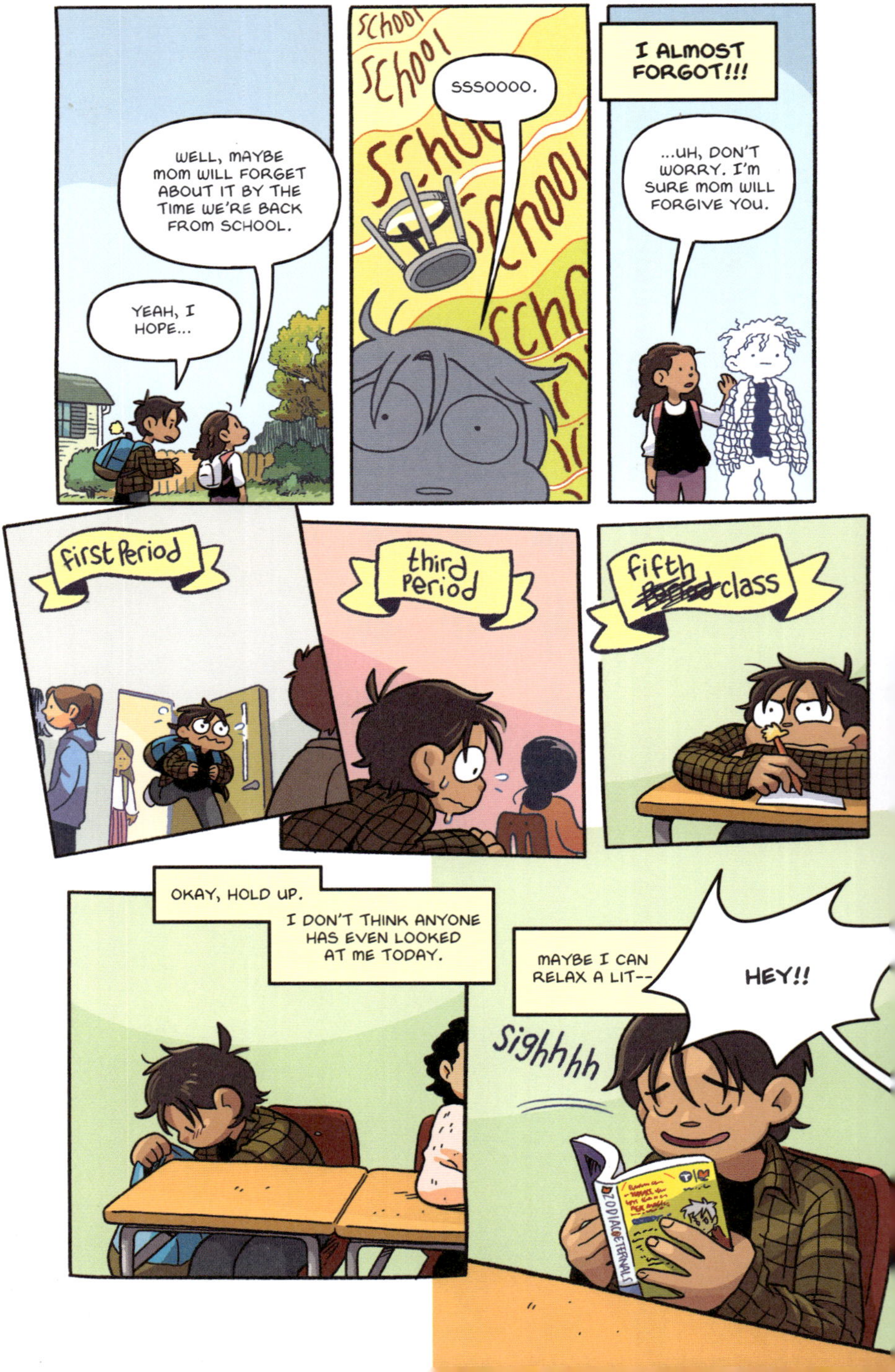
WELL, MAYBE MOM WILL FORGET ABOUT IT BY THE TIME WE'RE BACK FROM SCHOOL.
YEAH, I HOPE...
SSSOOOO.
I ALMOST FORGOT!!!
...UH, DON'T WORRY. I'M SURE MOM WILL FORGIVE YOU.
first Period
third Period
fifth period class
OKAY, HOLD UP.
I DON'T THINK ANYONE HAS EVEN LOOKED AT ME TODAY.
MAYBE I CAN RELAX A LIT--
HEY!!
Sighhhh
ZODIAC ETERNALS

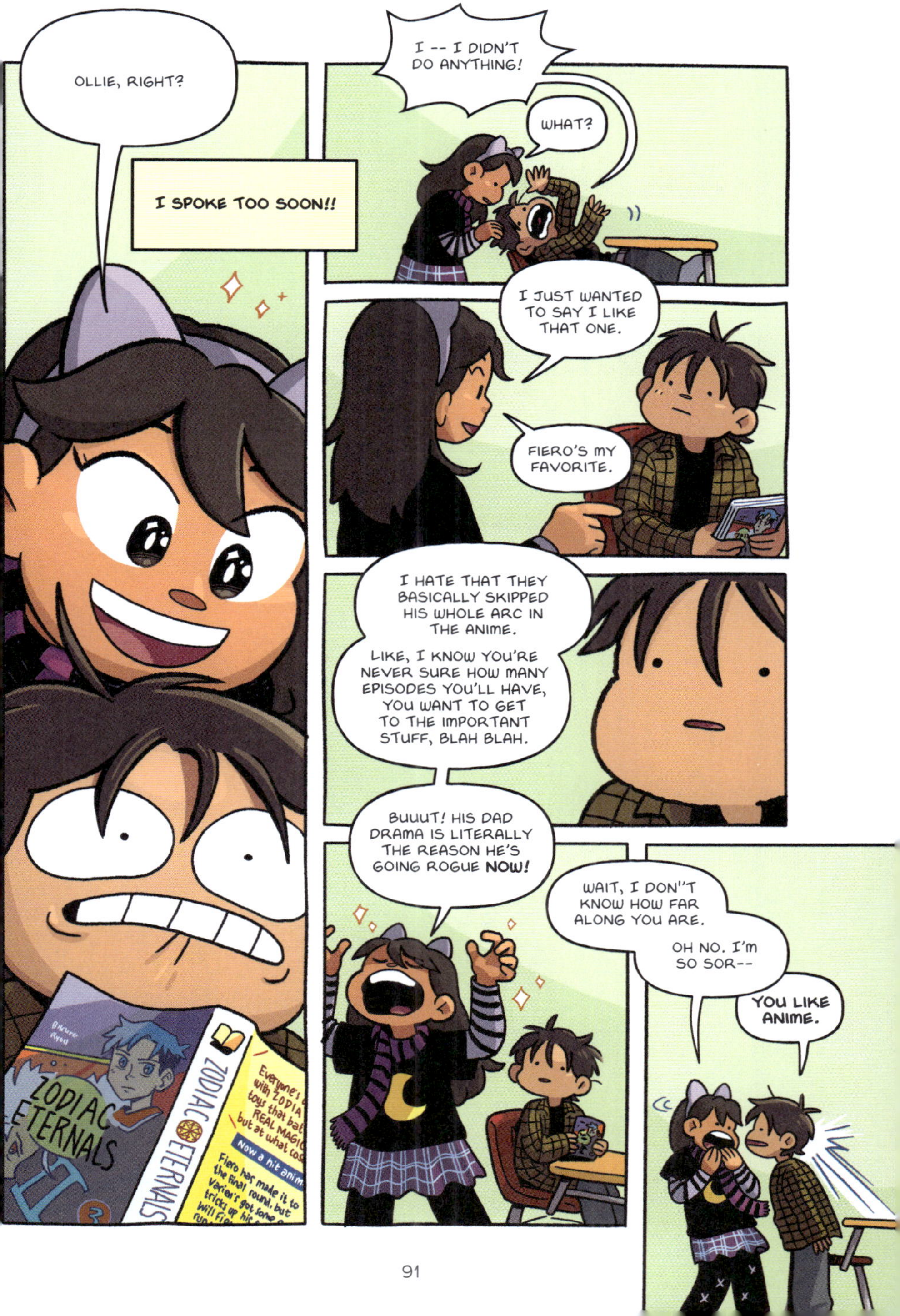
OLLIE, RIGHT?
I SPOKE TOO SOON!!
ZODIAC ETERNALS
I -- I DIDN'T DO ANYTHING!
WHAT?
I JUST WANTED TO SAY I LIKE THAT ONE.
FIERO'S MY FAVORITE.
I HATE THAT THEY BASICALLY SKIPPED HIS WHOLE ARC IN THE ANIME.
LIKE, I KNOW YOU'RE NEVER SURE HOW MANY EPISODES YOU'LL HAVE, YOU WANT TO GET TO THE IMPORTANT STUFF, BLAH BLAH.
BUUUT! HIS DAD DRAMA IS LITERALLY THE REASON HE'S GOING ROGUE **NOW!**
WAIT, I DON'T KNOW HOW FAR ALONG YOU ARE.
OH NO. I'M SO SOR--
YOU LIKE ANIME.

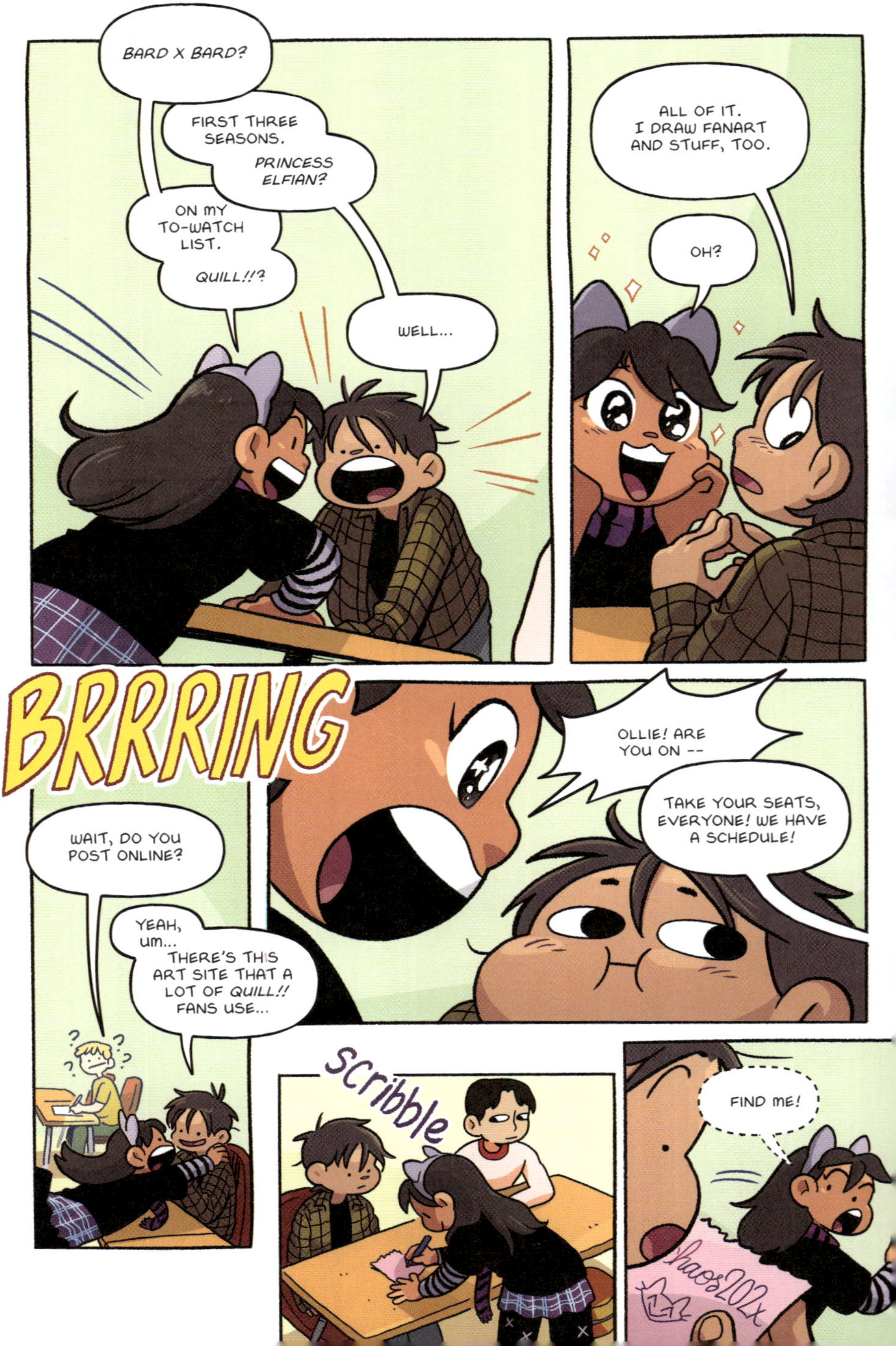
BARD X BARD?
FIRST THREE SEASONS.
PRINCESS ELFIAN?
ON MY TO-WATCH LIST.
QUILL!!?
WELL...
ALL OF IT. I DRAW FANART AND STUFF, TOO.
OH?
BRRRING
OLLIE! ARE YOU ON --
TAKE YOUR SEATS, EVERYONE! WE HAVE A SCHEDULE!
WAIT, DO YOU POST ONLINE?
YEAH, um... THERE'S THIS ART SITE THAT A LOT OF QUILL!! FANS USE...
scribble
FIND ME!
chaos202x

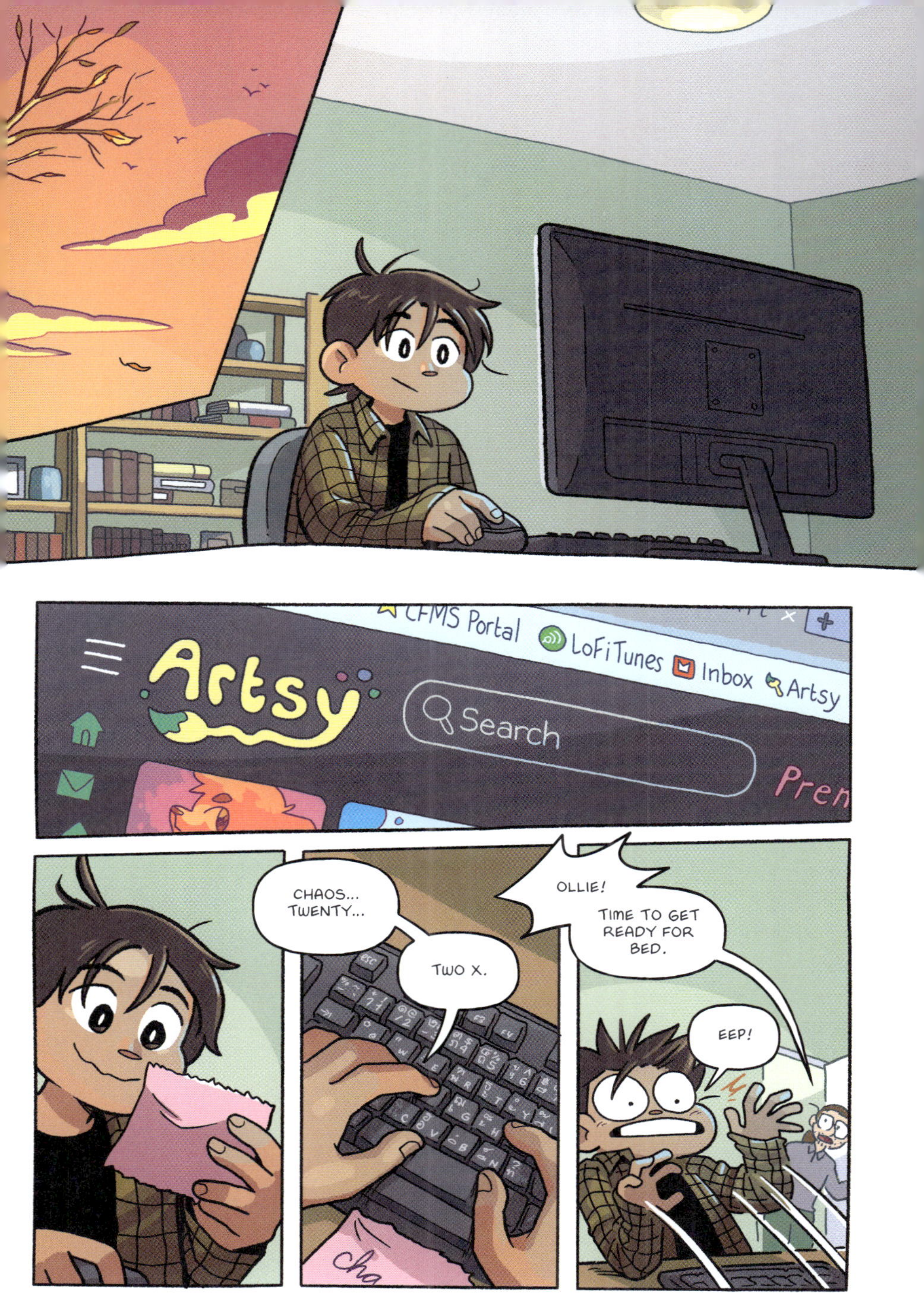
CFMS Portal
LoFiTunes
Inbox
Artsy
Artsy
Search
CHAOS... TWENTY...
TWO X.
OLLIE!
TIME TO GET READY FOR BED.
EEP!

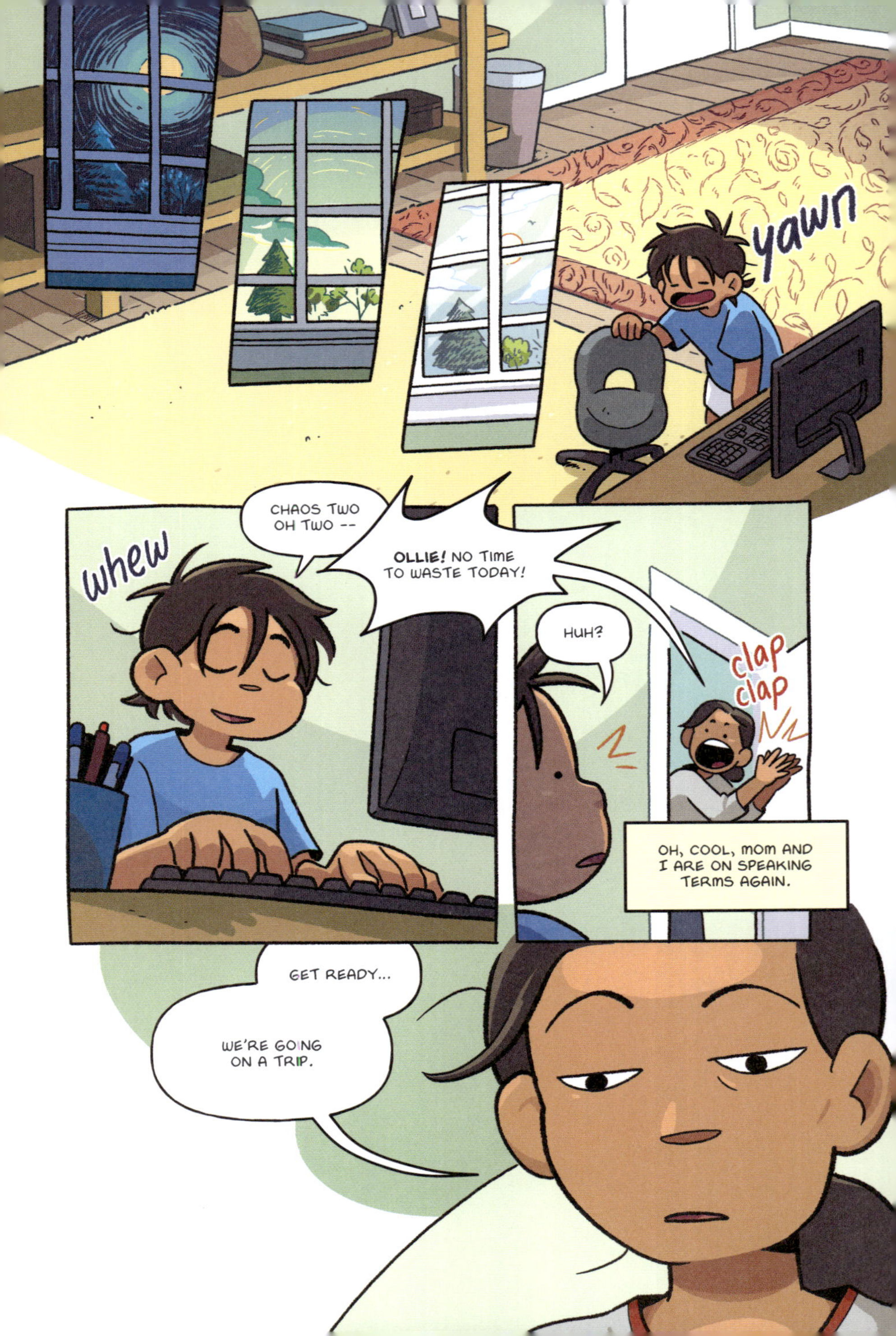

yawn
whew
CHAOS TWO OH TWO --
OLLIE! NO TIME TO WASTE TODAY!
HUH?
clap clap
OH, COOL, MOM AND I ARE ON SPEAKING TERMS AGAIN.
GET READY...
WE'RE GOING ON A TRIP.

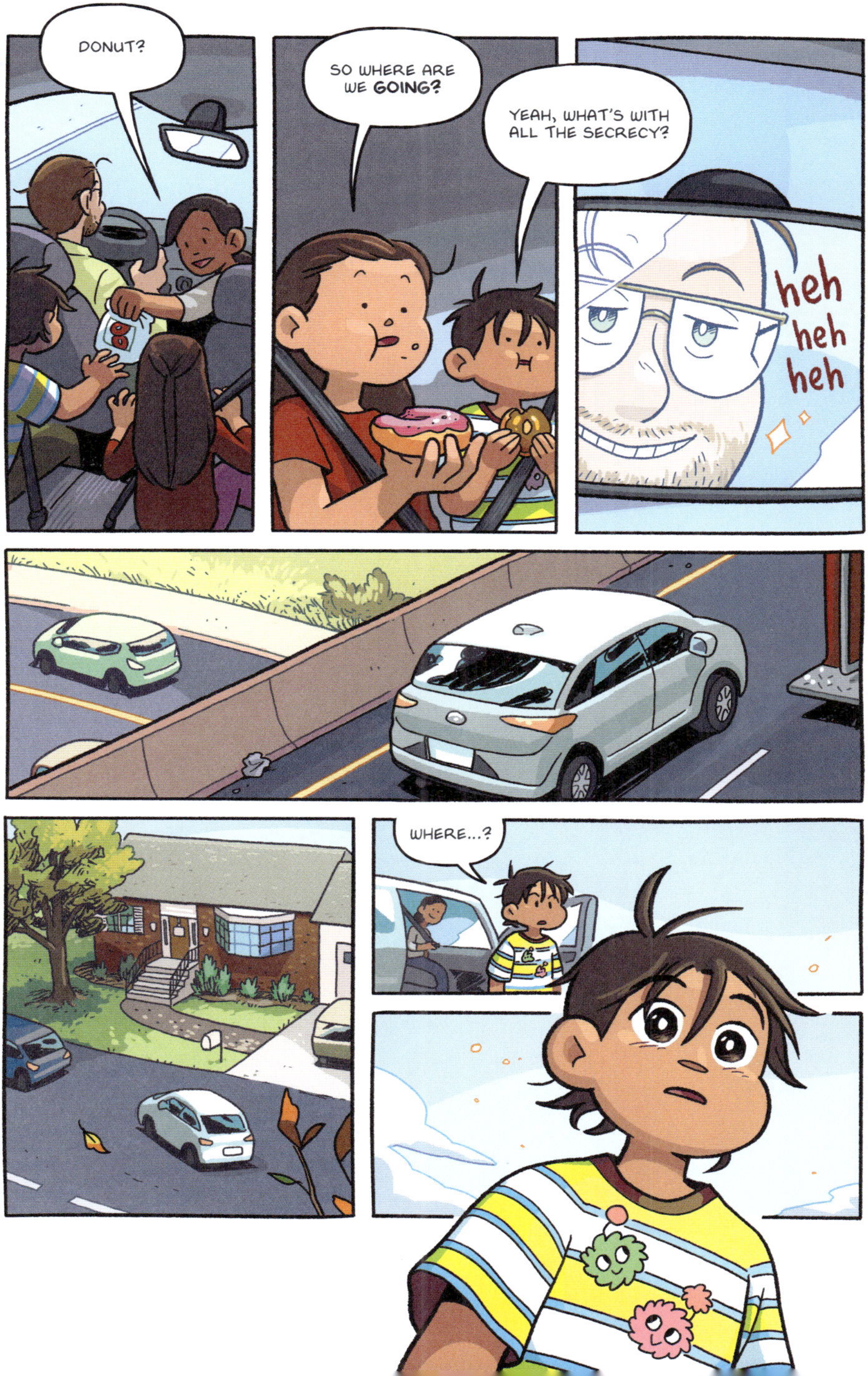
DONUT?
SO WHERE ARE WE **GOING?**
YEAH, WHAT'S WITH ALL THE SECRECY?
heh heh heh
WHERE...?

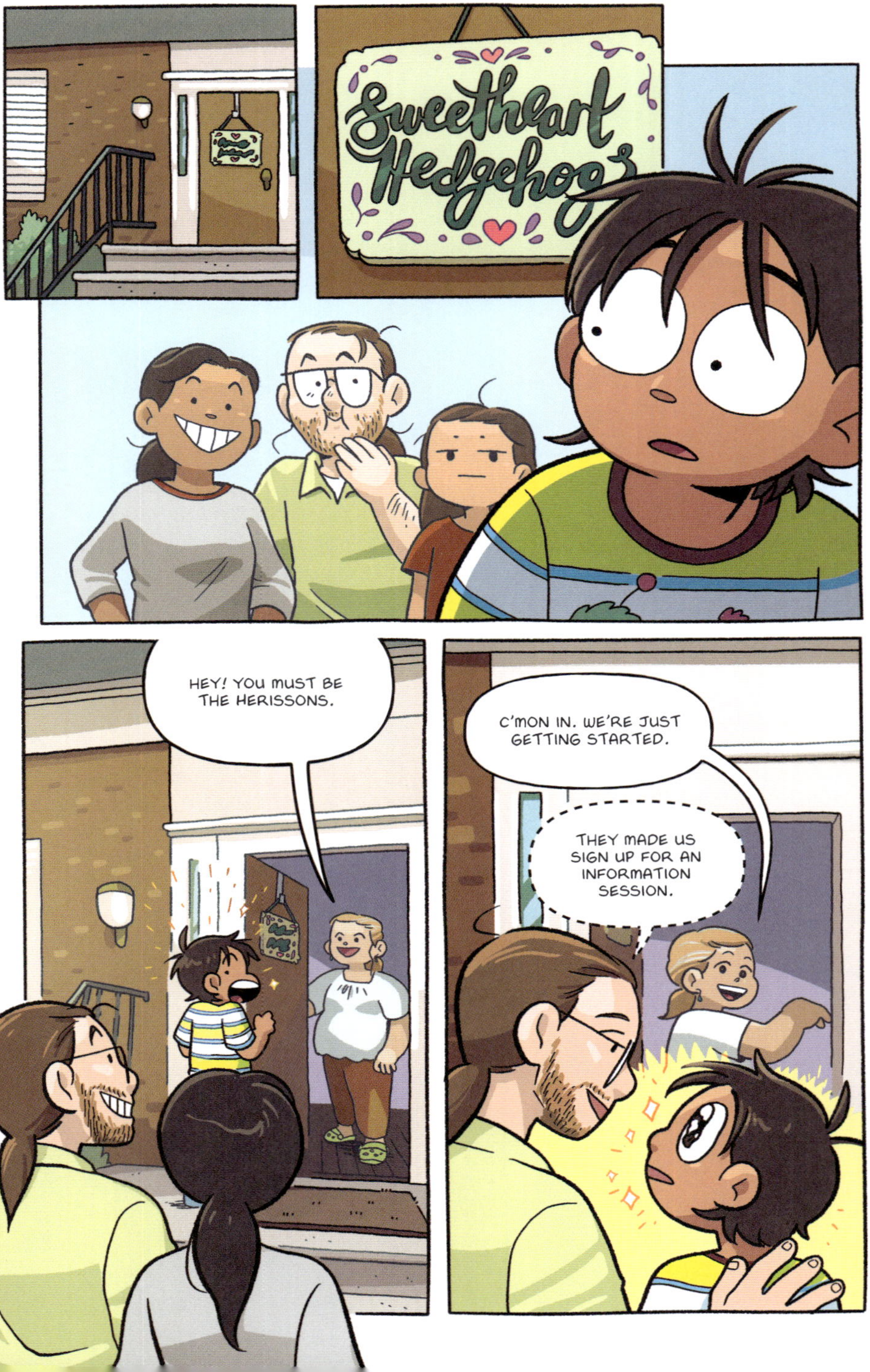
Sweetheart Hedgehogs
HEY! YOU MUST BE THE HERISSONS.
C'MON IN. WE'RE JUST GETTING STARTED.
THEY MADE US SIGN UP FOR AN INFORMATION SESSION.

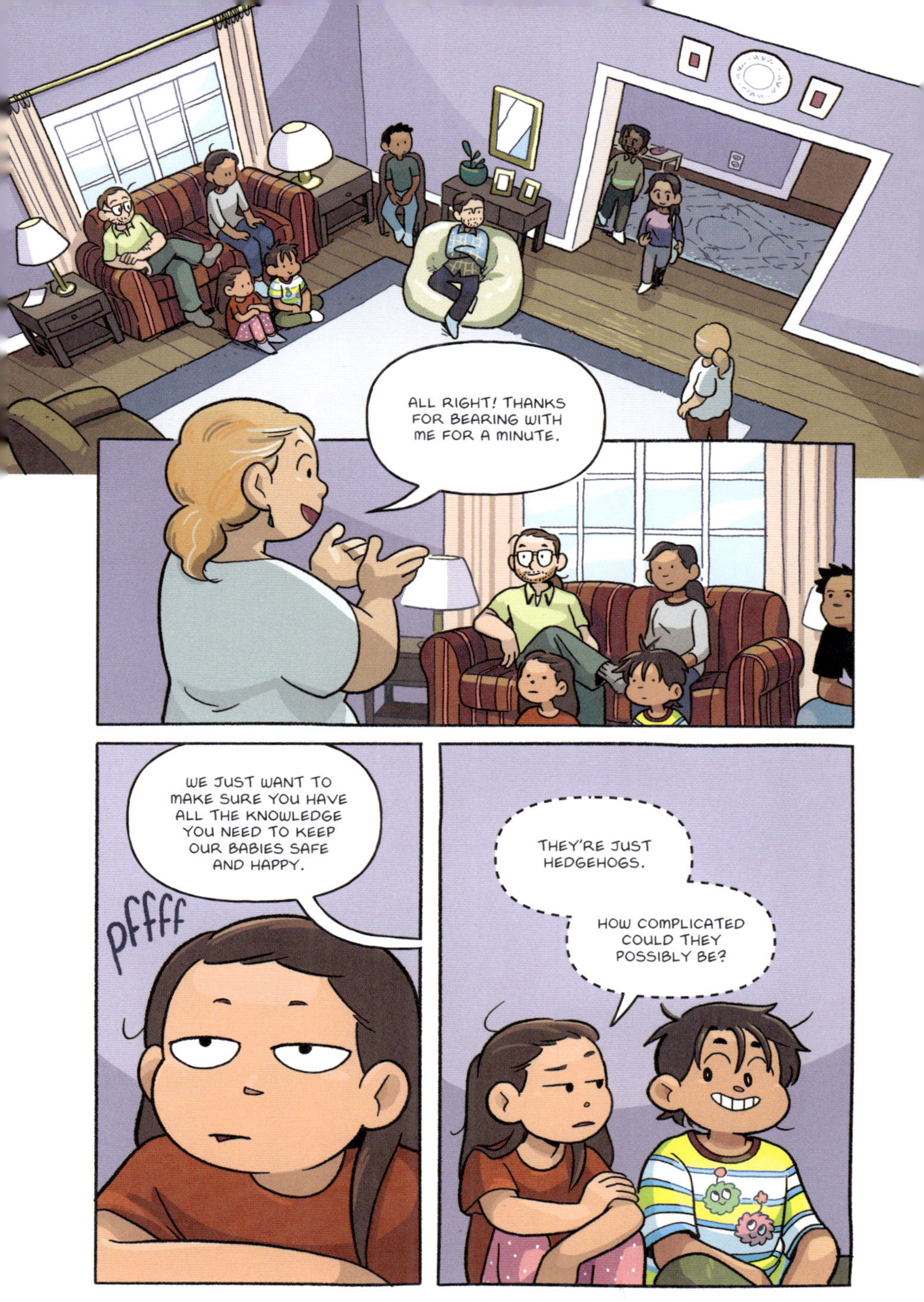
ALL RIGHT! THANKS FOR BEARING WITH ME FOR A MINUTE.
WE JUST WANT TO MAKE SURE YOU HAVE ALL THE KNOWLEDGE YOU NEED TO KEEP OUR BABIES SAFE AND HAPPY.
pffff
THEY'RE JUST HEDGEHOGS.
HOW COMPLICATED COULD THEY POSSIBLY BE?

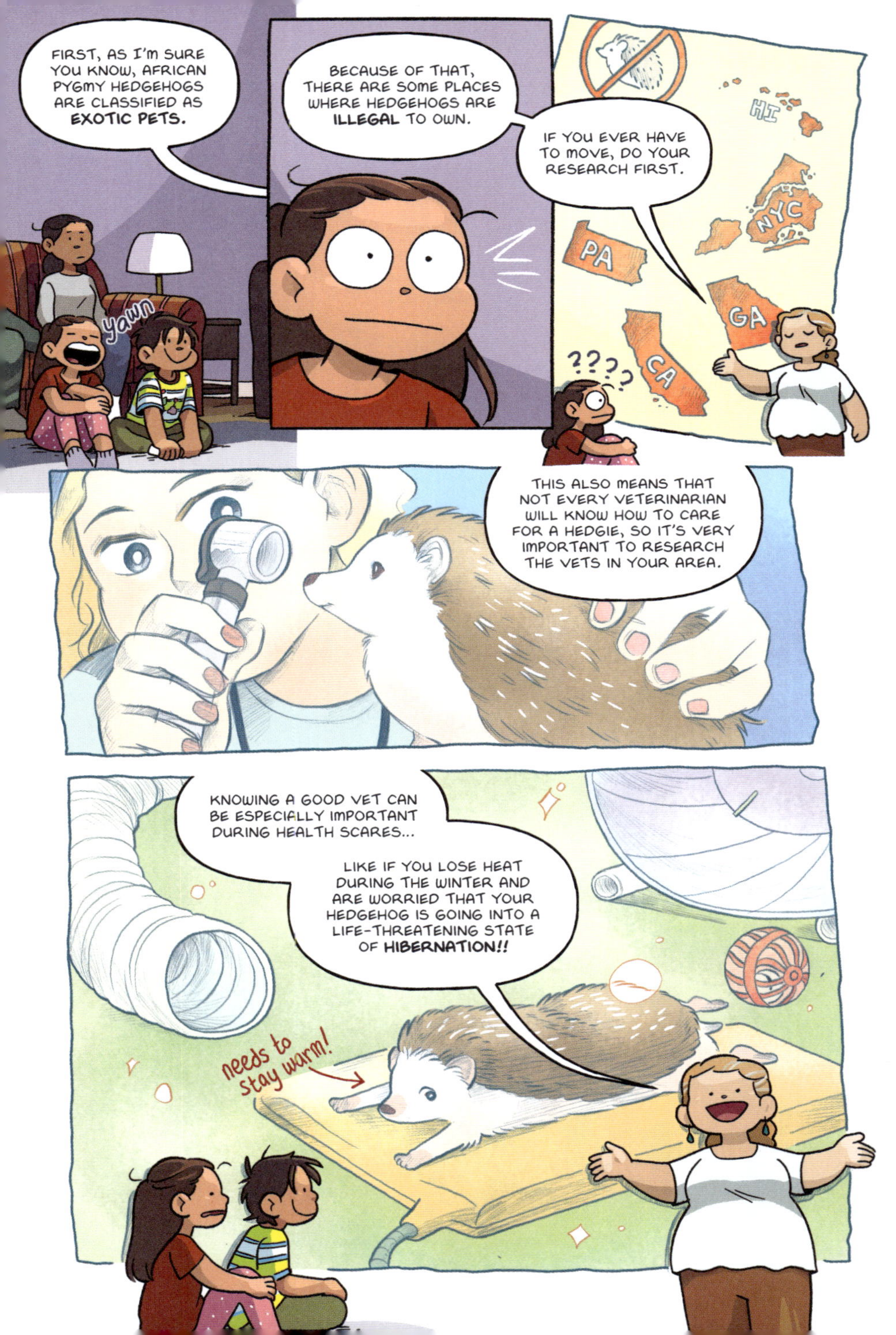
FIRST, AS I'M SURE YOU KNOW, AFRICAN PYGMY HEDGEHOGS ARE CLASSIFIED AS **EXOTIC PETS.**
yawn
BECAUSE OF THAT, THERE ARE SOME PLACES WHERE HEDGEHOGS ARE **ILLEGAL** TO OWN.
IF YOU EVER HAVE TO MOVE, DO YOUR RESEARCH FIRST.
HI
NYC
PA
GA
CA
????
THIS ALSO MEANS THAT NOT EVERY VETERINARIAN WILL KNOW HOW TO CARE FOR A HEDGIE, SO IT'S VERY IMPORTANT TO RESEARCH THE VETS IN YOUR AREA.
KNOWING A GOOD VET CAN BE ESPECIALLY IMPORTANT DURING HEALTH SCARES...
LIKE IF YOU LOSE HEAT DURING THE WINTER AND ARE WORRIED THAT YOUR HEDGEHOG IS GOING INTO A LIFE-THREATENING STATE OF **HIBERNATION!!**
needs to stay warm!

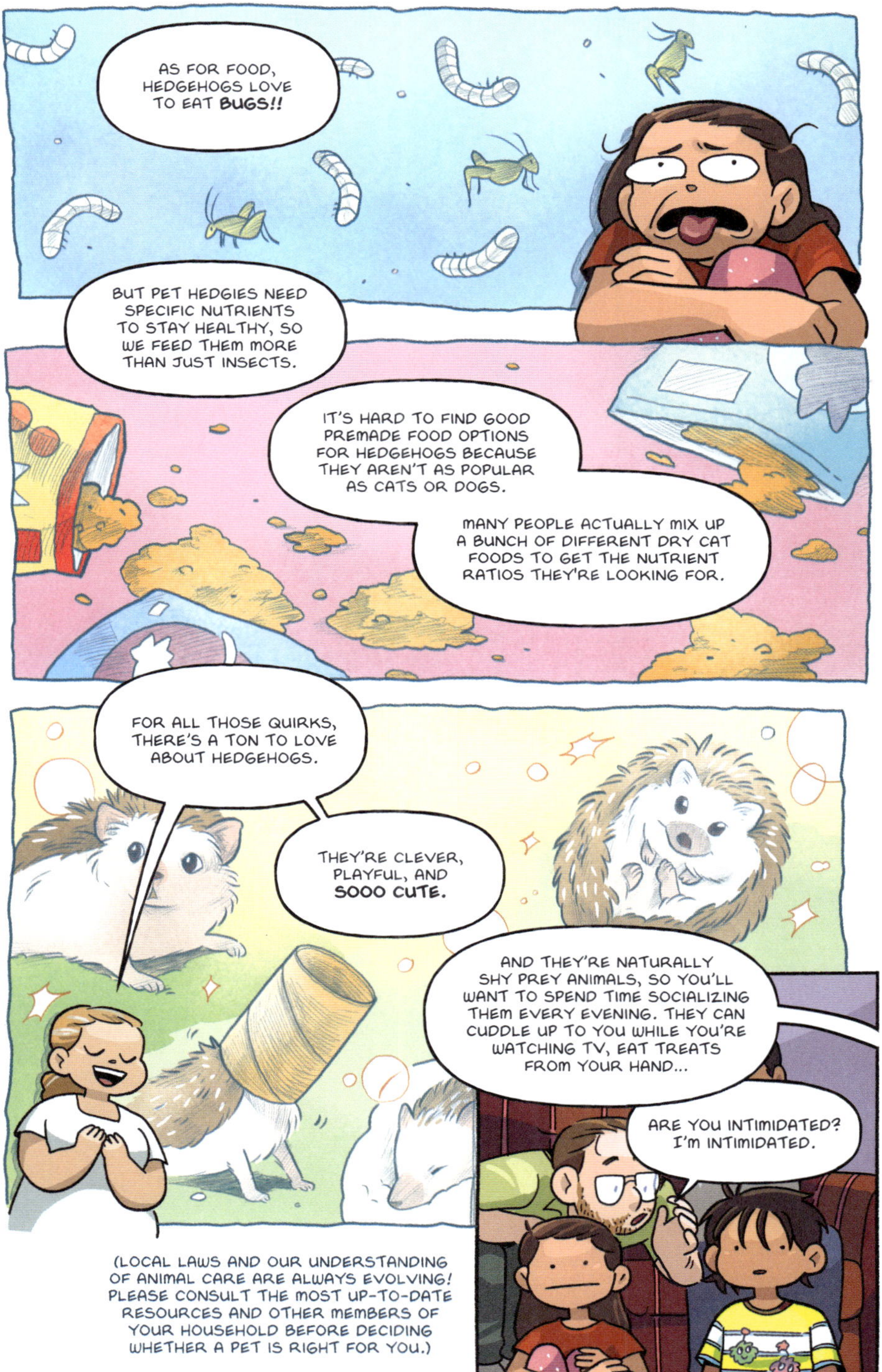
AS FOR FOOD, HEDGEHOGS LOVE TO EAT **BUGS!!**
BUT PET HEDGIES NEED SPECIFIC NUTRIENTS TO STAY HEALTHY, SO WE FEED THEM MORE THAN JUST INSECTS.
IT'S HARD TO FIND GOOD PREMADE FOOD OPTIONS FOR HEDGEHOGS BECAUSE THEY AREN'T AS POPULAR AS CATS OR DOGS.
MANY PEOPLE ACTUALLY MIX UP A BUNCH OF DIFFERENT DRY CAT FOODS TO GET THE NUTRIENT RATIOS THEY'RE LOOKING FOR.
FOR ALL THOSE QUIRKS, THERE'S A TON TO LOVE ABOUT HEDGEHOGS.
THEY'RE CLEVER, PLAYFUL, AND **SOOO CUTE.**
AND THEY'RE NATURALLY SHY PREY ANIMALS, SO YOU'LL WANT TO SPEND TIME SOCIALIZING THEM EVERY EVENING. THEY CAN CUDDLE UP TO YOU WHILE YOU'RE WATCHING TV, EAT TREATS FROM YOUR HAND...
ARE YOU INTIMIDATED? I'M INTIMIDATED.
(LOCAL LAWS AND OUR UNDERSTANDING OF ANIMAL CARE ARE ALWAYS EVOLVING! PLEASE CONSULT THE MOST UP-TO-DATE RESOURCES AND OTHER MEMBERS OF YOUR HOUSEHOLD BEFORE DECIDING WHETHER A PET IS RIGHT FOR YOU.)

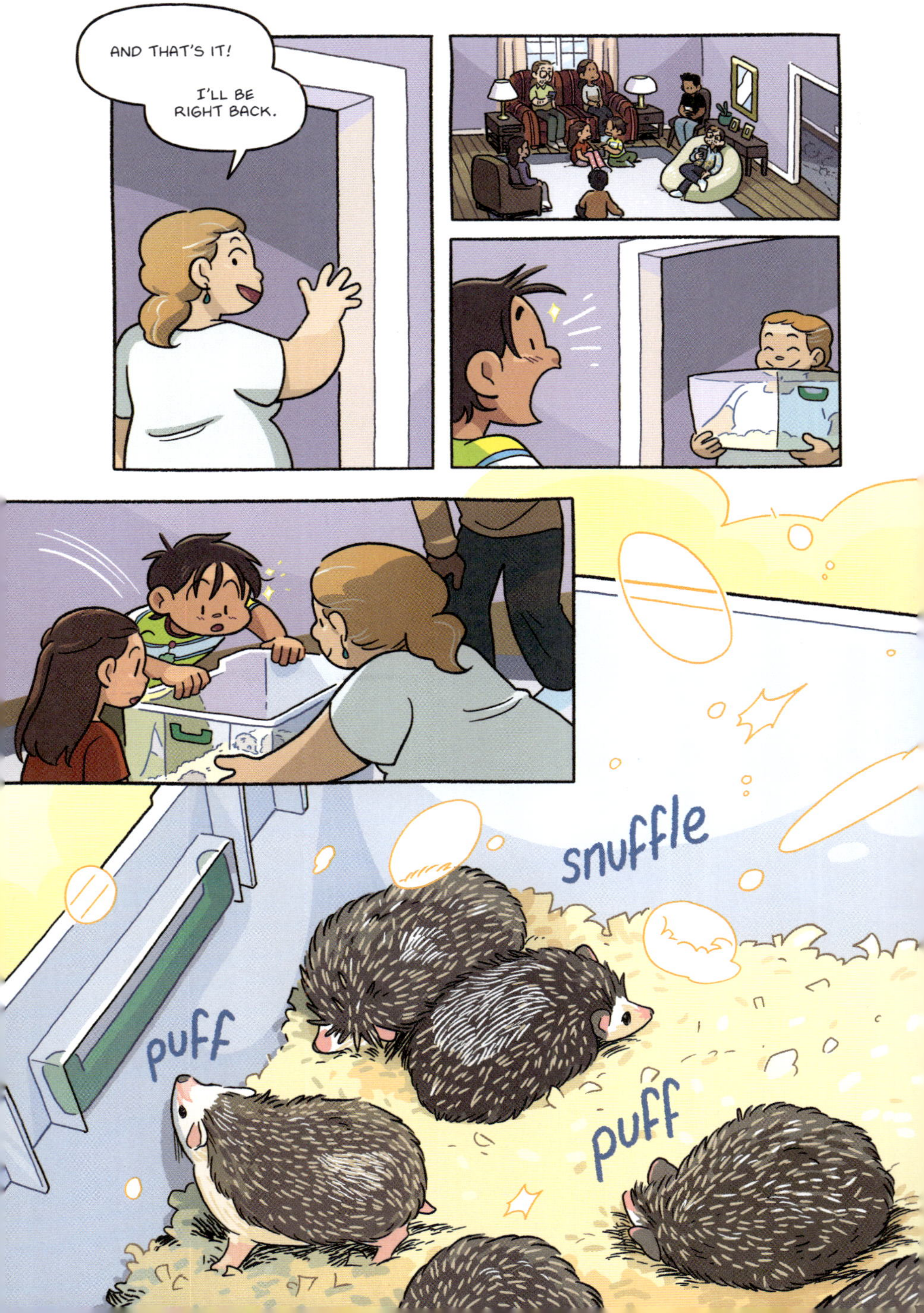
AND THAT'S IT!
I'LL BE RIGHT BACK.
snuffle
puff
puff

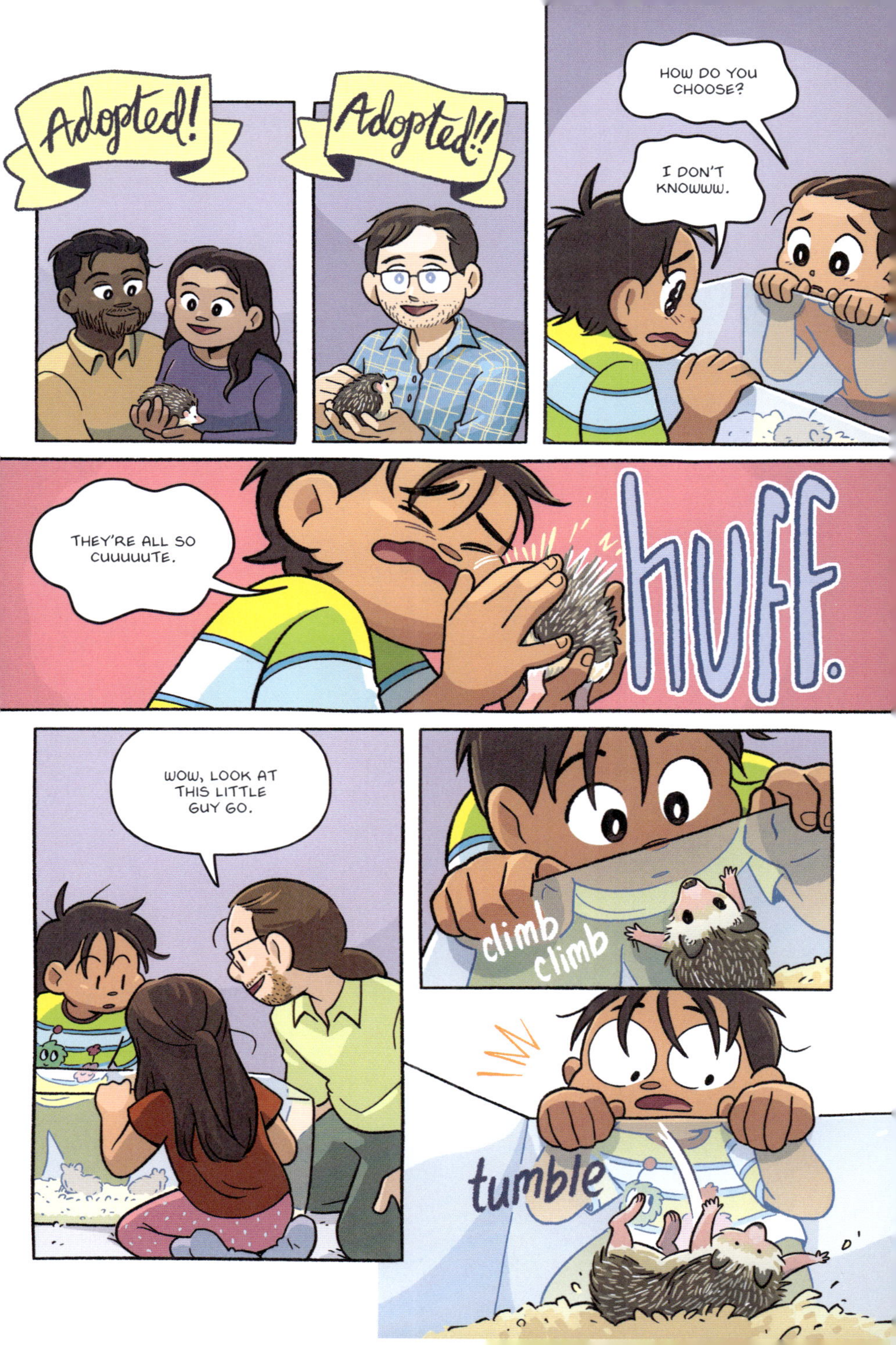
Adopted!
Adopted!!
HOW DO YOU CHOOSE?
I DON'T KNOWWW.
THEY'RE ALL SO CUUUUUTE.
huff.
WOW, LOOK AT THIS LITTLE GUY GO.
climb
climb
tumble

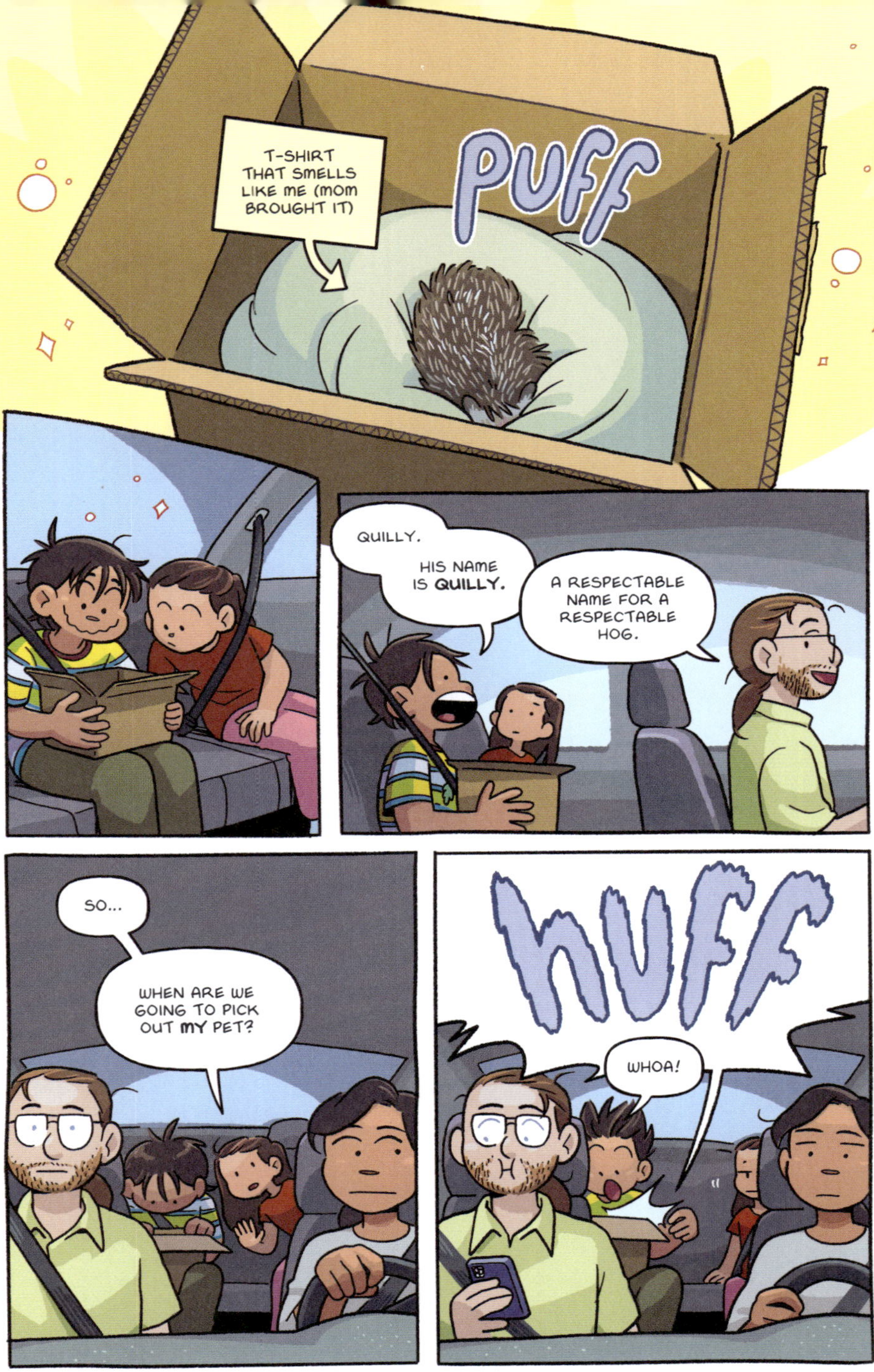
T-SHIRT THAT SMELLS LIKE ME (MOM BROUGHT IT)
PUFF
QUILLY.
HIS NAME IS **QUILLY.**
A RESPECTABLE NAME FOR A RESPECTABLE HOG.
SO...
WHEN ARE WE GOING TO PICK OUT **MY** PET?
HUFF
WHOA!

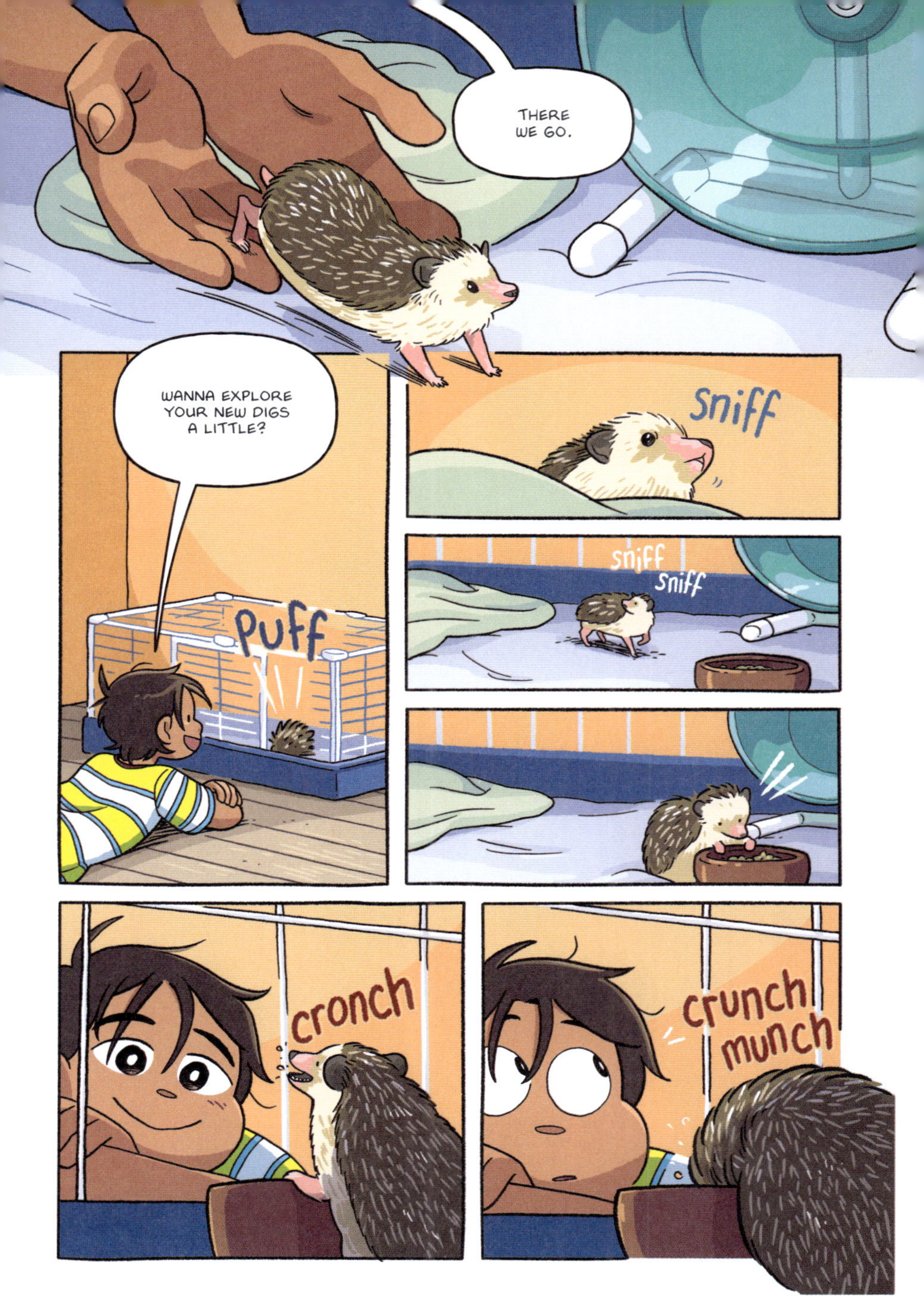
THERE WE GO.
WANNA EXPLORE YOUR NEW DIGS A LITTLE?
PUFF
SNIFF
SNIFF
SNIFF
CRONCH
CRUNCH
MUNCH

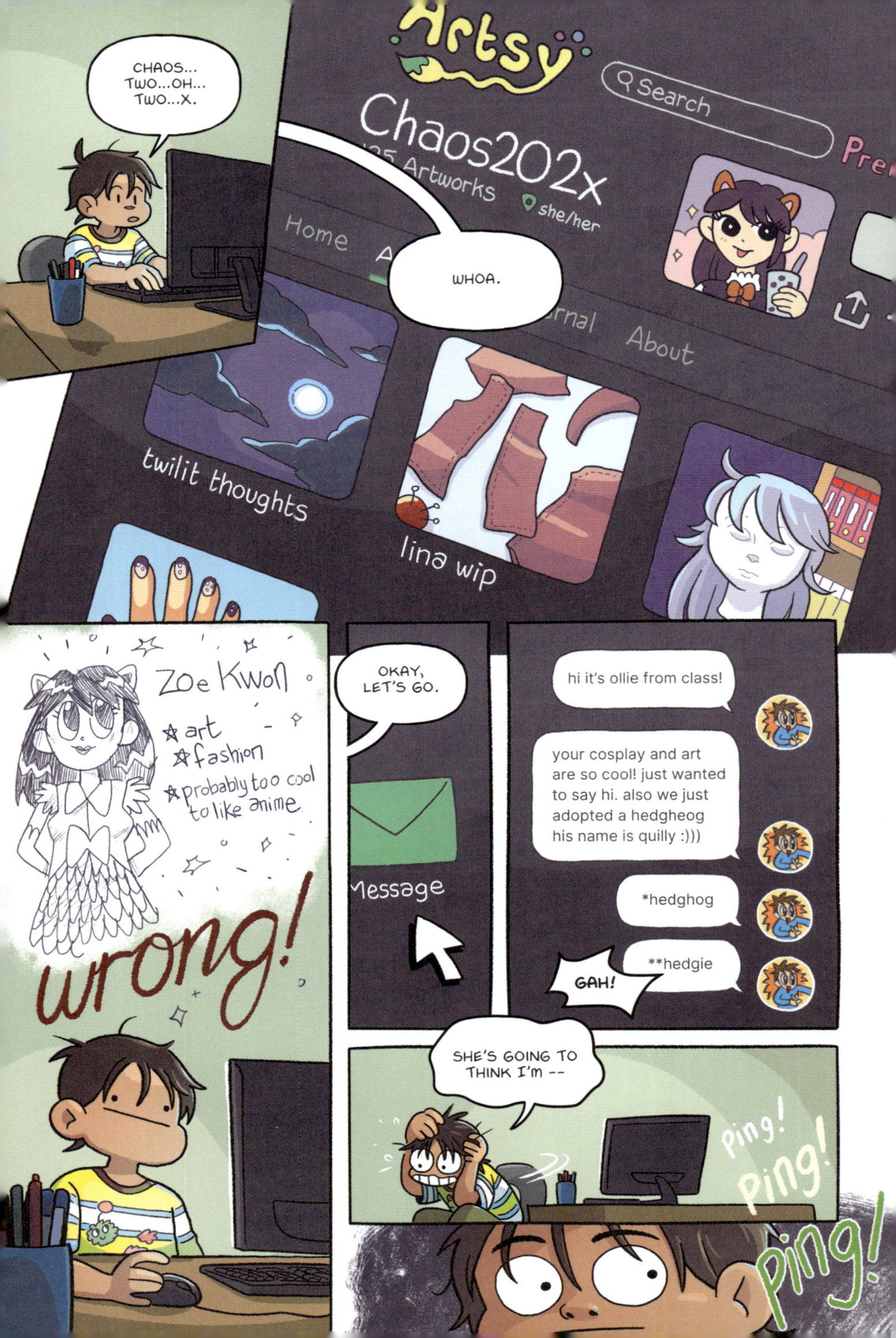
CHAOS... TWO...OH... TWO...X.
Artsy
Search
Chaos202x
she/her
Home
About
WHOA.
twilit thoughts
lina wip
Zoe Kwon
art
fashion
probably too cool to like anime
wrong!
OKAY, LET'S GO.
Message
hi it's ollie from class!
your cosplay and art are so cool! just wanted to say hi. also we just adopted a hedgheog his name is quilly :)))
*hedghog
**hedgie
GAH!
SHE'S GOING TO THINK I'M --
ping!
ping!
ping!

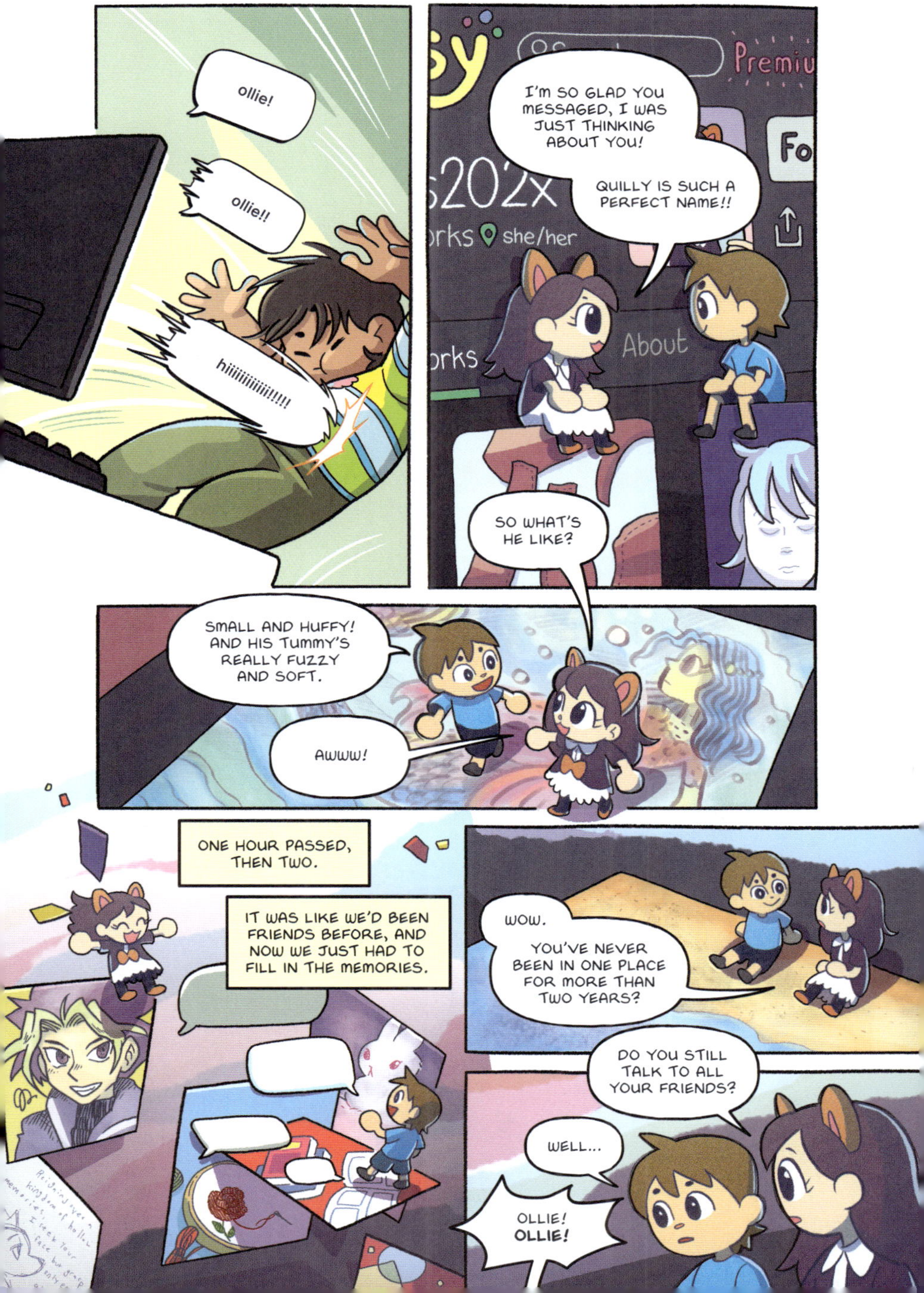
ollie!
ollie!!
hiiiiiiiiiiiiii!!!!!
I'M SO GLAD YOU MESSAGED, I WAS JUST THINKING ABOUT YOU!
QUILLY IS SUCH A PERFECT NAME!!
SO WHAT'S HE LIKE?
SMALL AND HUFFY! AND HIS TUMMY'S REALLY FUZZY AND SOFT.
AWWW!
ONE HOUR PASSED, THEN TWO.
IT WAS LIKE WE'D BEEN FRIENDS BEFORE, AND NOW WE JUST HAD TO FILL IN THE MEMORIES.
WOW.
YOU'VE NEVER BEEN IN ONE PLACE FOR MORE THAN TWO YEARS?
DO YOU STILL TALK TO ALL YOUR FRIENDS?
WELL...
OLLIE!
OLLIE!

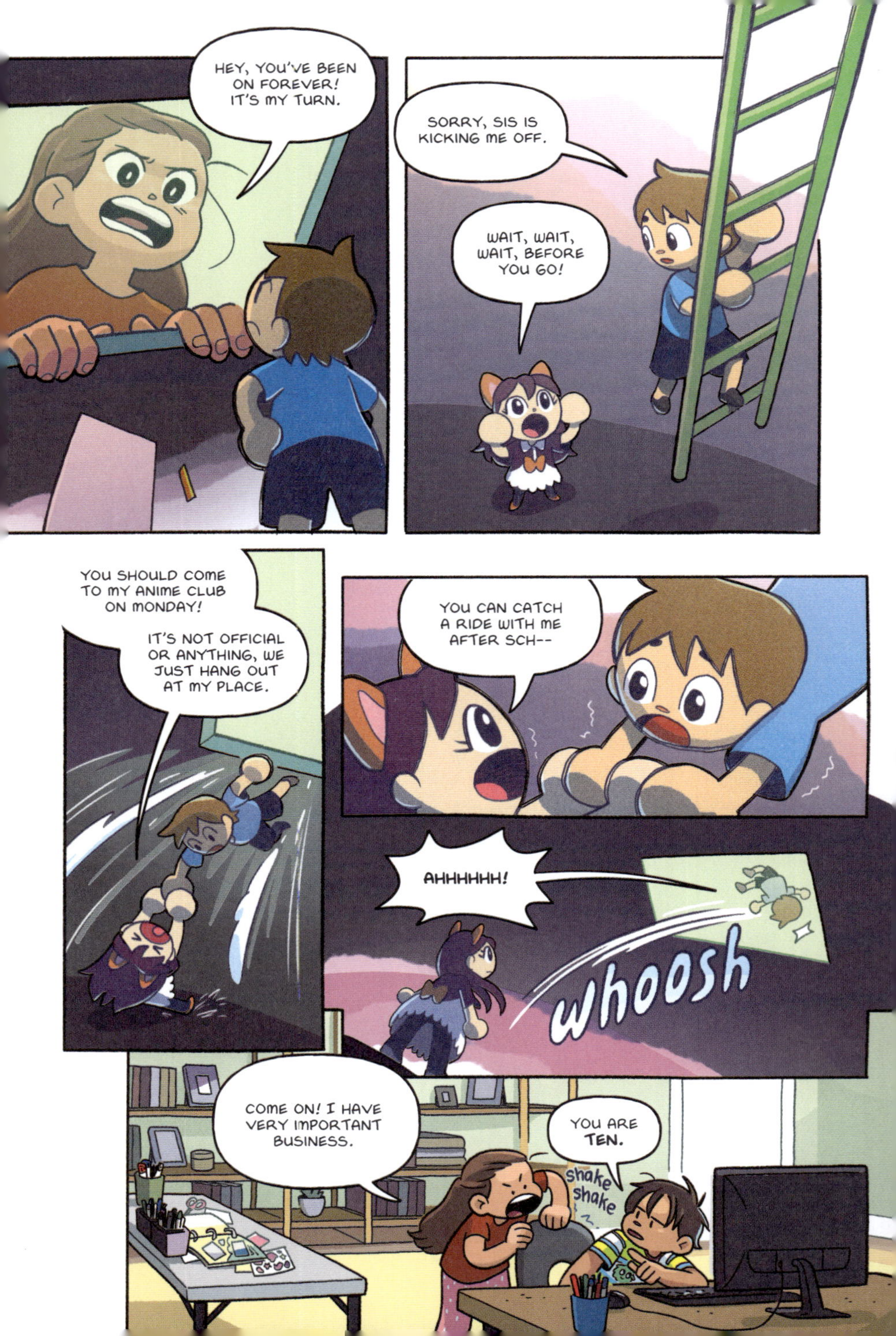
HEY, YOU'VE BEEN ON FOREVER! IT'S MY TURN.
SORRY, SIS IS KICKING ME OFF.
WAIT, WAIT, WAIT, BEFORE YOU GO!
YOU SHOULD COME TO MY ANIME CLUB ON MONDAY!
IT'S NOT OFFICIAL OR ANYTHING, WE JUST HANG OUT AT MY PLACE.
YOU CAN CATCH A RIDE WITH ME AFTER SCH--
AHHHHHH!
whoosh
COME ON! I HAVE VERY IMPORTANT BUSINESS.
YOU ARE **TEN.**
shake shake

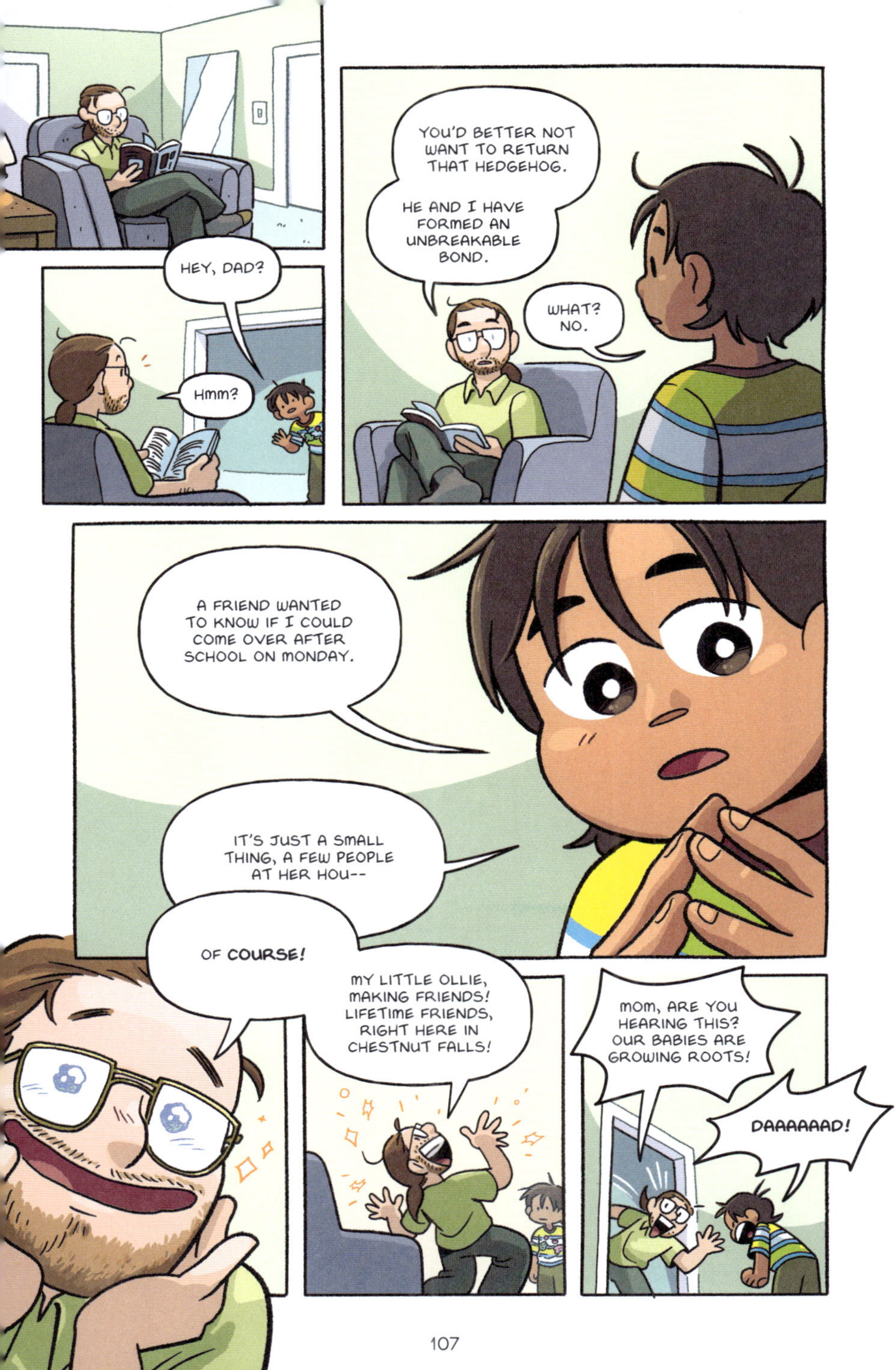
HEY, DAD?
Hmm?
YOU'D BETTER NOT WANT TO RETURN THAT HEDGEHOG.
HE AND I HAVE FORMED AN UNBREAKABLE BOND.
WHAT? NO.
A FRIEND WANTED TO KNOW IF I COULD COME OVER AFTER SCHOOL ON MONDAY.
IT'S JUST A SMALL THING, A FEW PEOPLE AT HER HOU--
OF **COURSE!**
MY LITTLE OLLIE, MAKING FRIENDS! LIFETIME FRIENDS, RIGHT HERE IN CHESTNUT FALLS!
MOM, ARE YOU HEARING THIS? OUR BABIES ARE GROWING ROOTS!
DAAAAAAD!

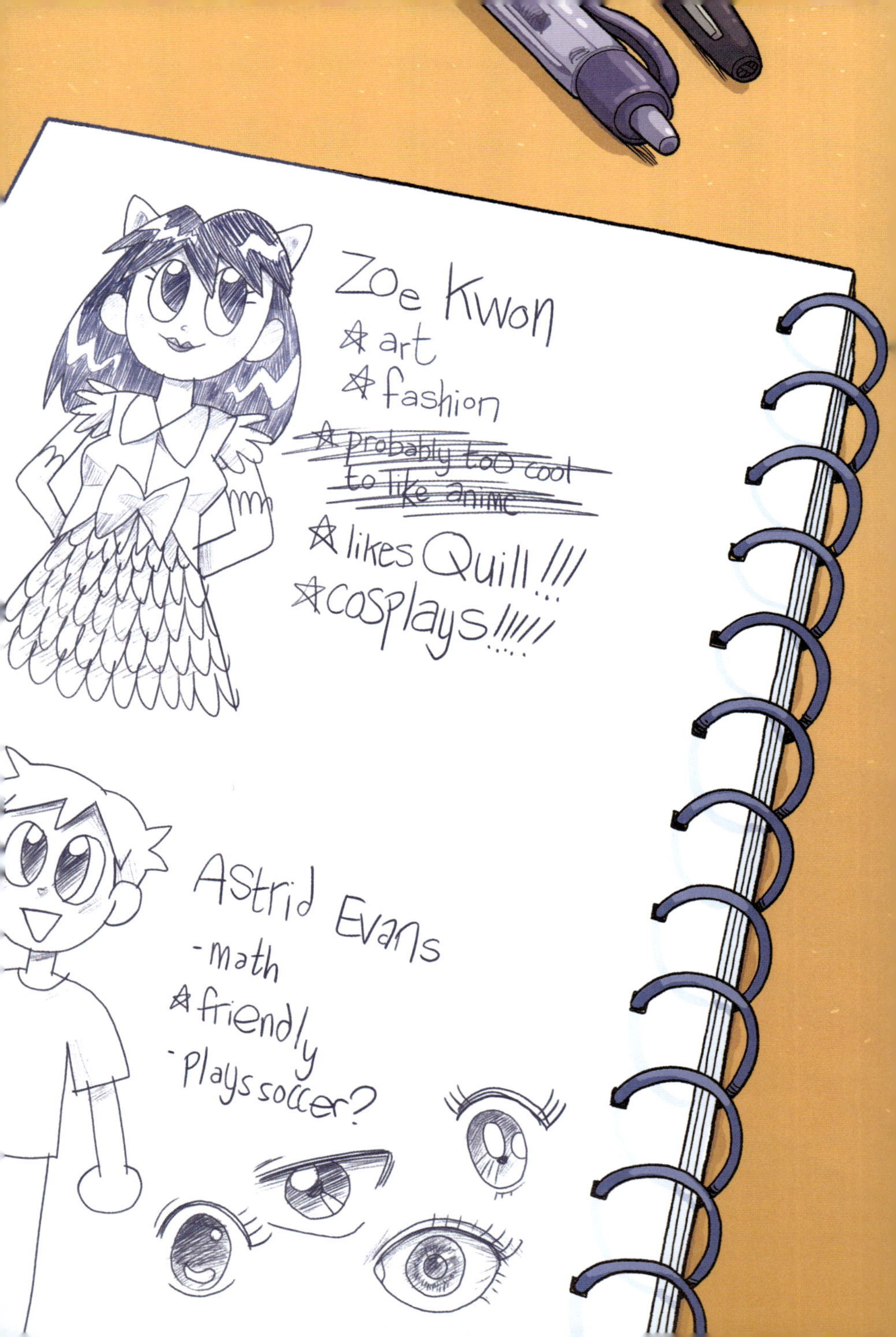

Zoe Kwon
☆ art
☆ fashion
☆ probably too cool to like anime
☆ likes Quill!!!
☆ cosplays!!!!!
Astrid Evans
- math
☆ friendly
- plays soccer?

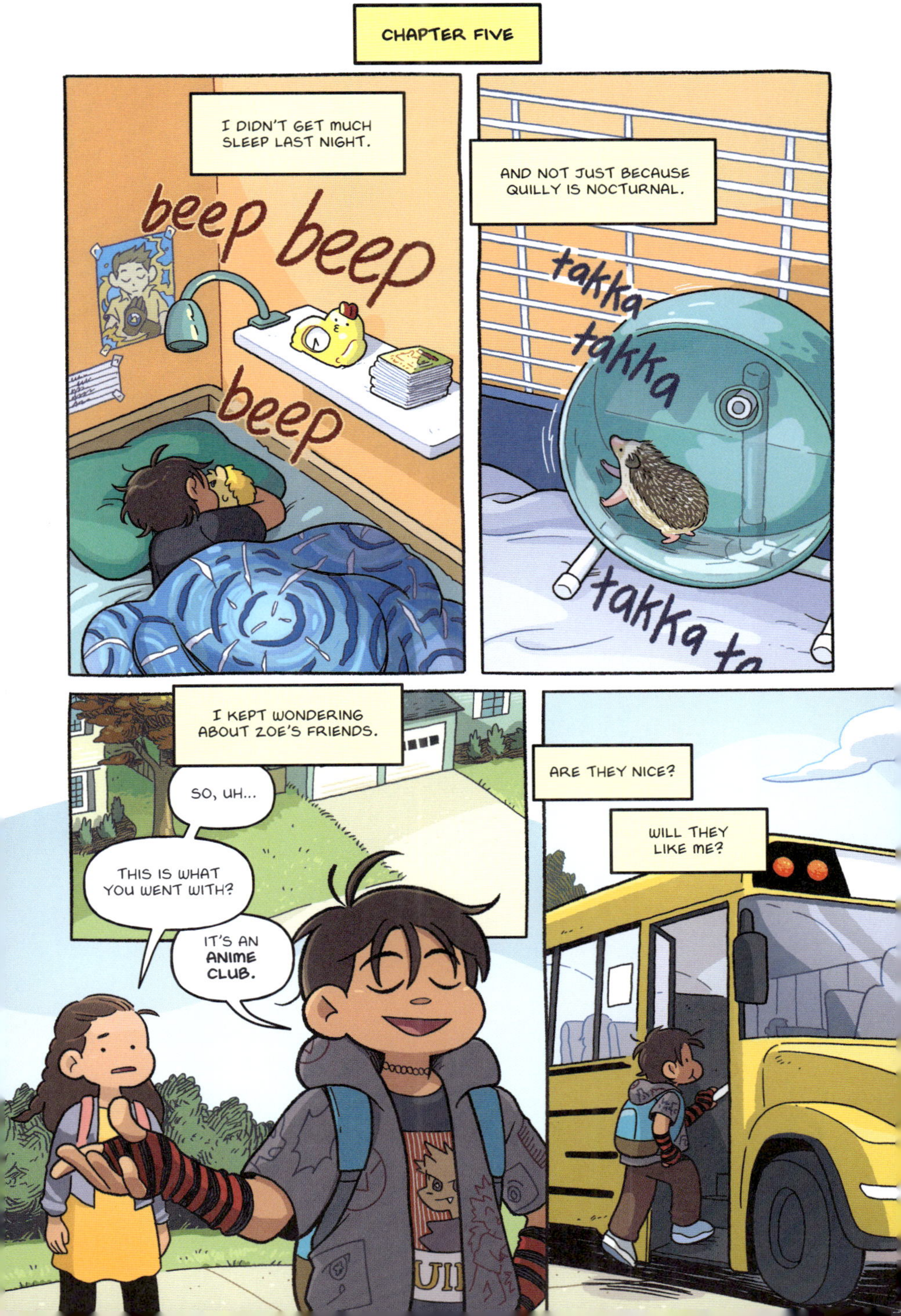

CHAPTER FIVE
I DIDN'T GET MUCH SLEEP LAST NIGHT.
beep beep
beep
AND NOT JUST BECAUSE QUILLY IS NOCTURNAL.
takka
takka
takka ta
I KEPT WONDERING ABOUT ZOE'S FRIENDS.
SO, UH...
THIS IS WHAT YOU WENT WITH?
IT'S AN ANIME CLUB.
ARE THEY NICE?
WILL THEY LIKE ME?

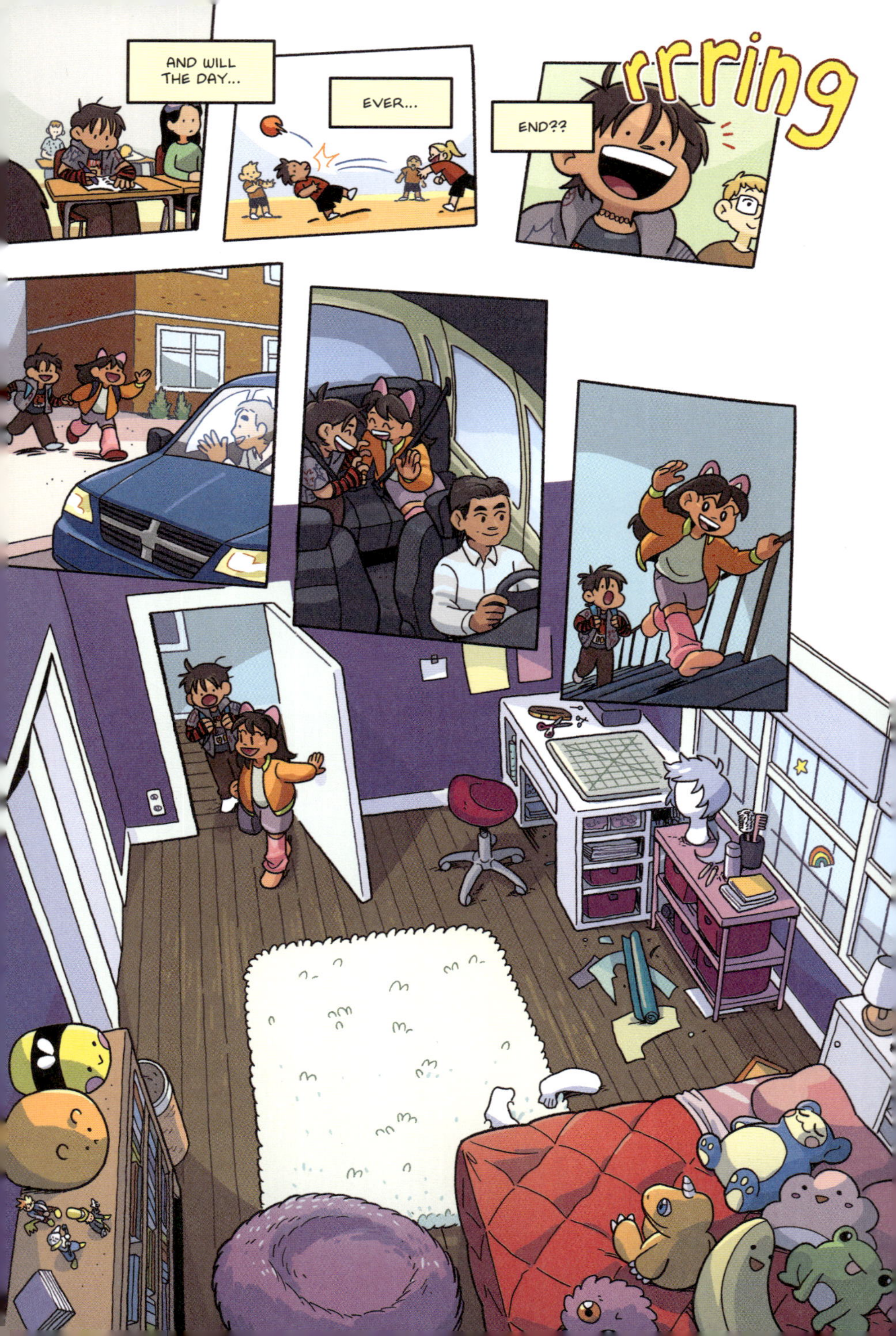
AND WILL THE DAY...
EVER...
END??
rrring

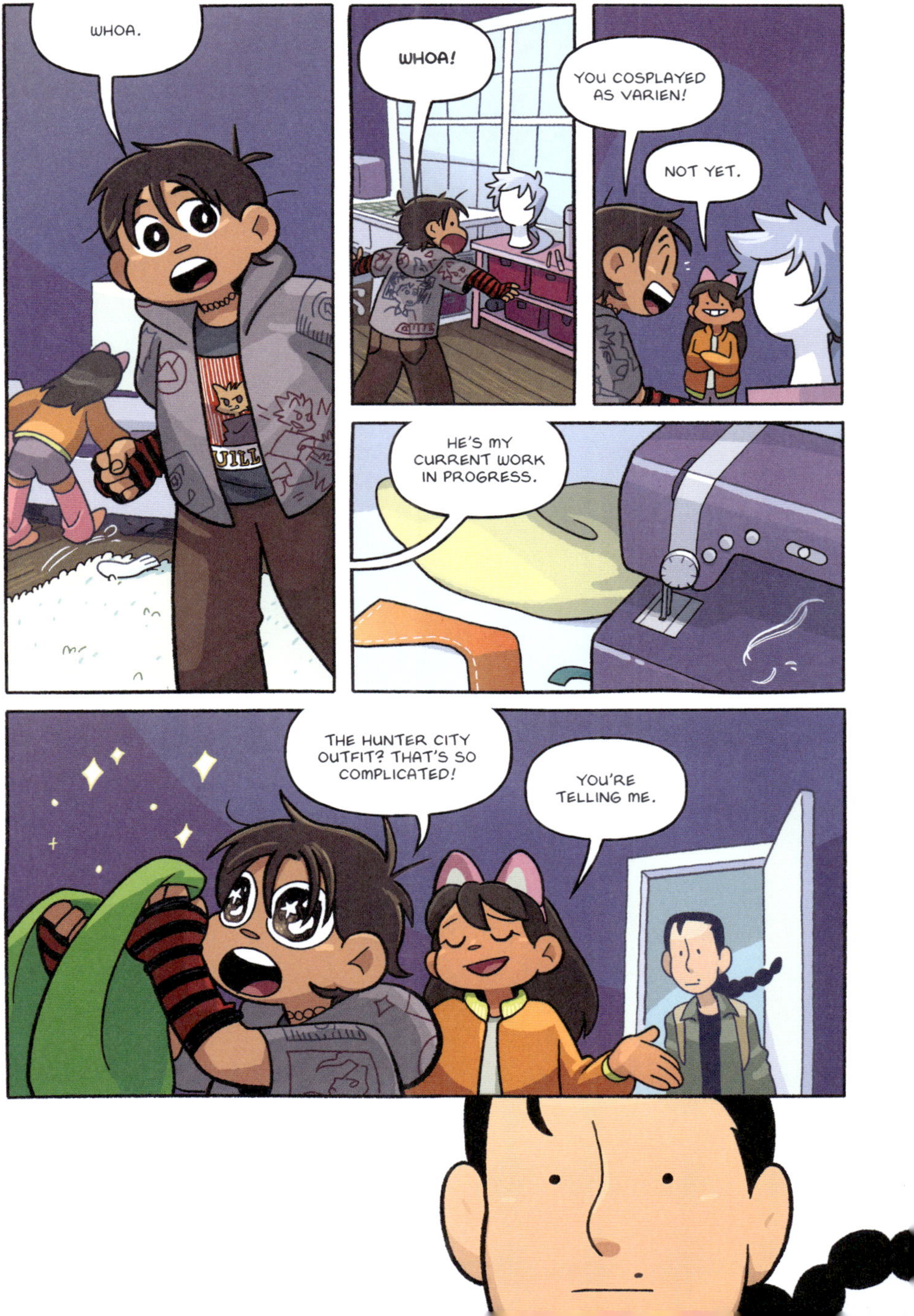
WHOA.
WHOA!
YOU COSPLAYED AS VARIEN!
NOT YET.
HE'S MY CURRENT WORK IN PROGRESS.
THE HUNTER CITY OUTFIT? THAT'S SO COMPLICATED!
YOU'RE TELLING ME.

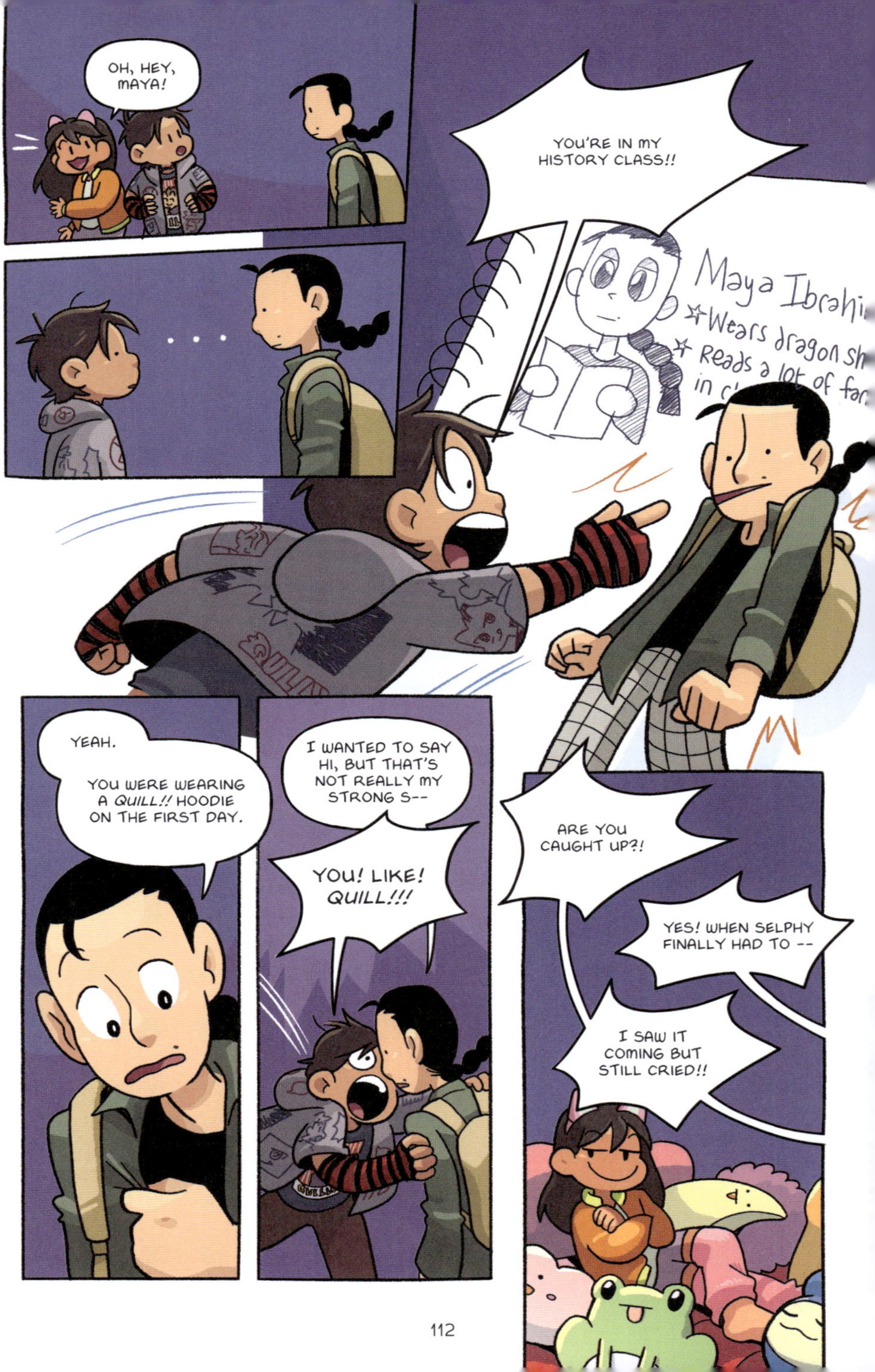
OH, HEY, MAYA!
YOU'RE IN MY HISTORY CLASS!!
Maya Ibrahi
☆Wears dragon
☆Reads a lot of
YEAH.
YOU WERE WEARING A *QUILL!!* HOODIE ON THE FIRST DAY.
I WANTED TO SAY HI, BUT THAT'S NOT REALLY MY STRONG S--
YOU! LIKE! *QUILL!!!*
ARE YOU CAUGHT UP?!
YES! WHEN SELPHY FINALLY HAD TO --
I SAW IT COMING BUT STILL CRIED!!

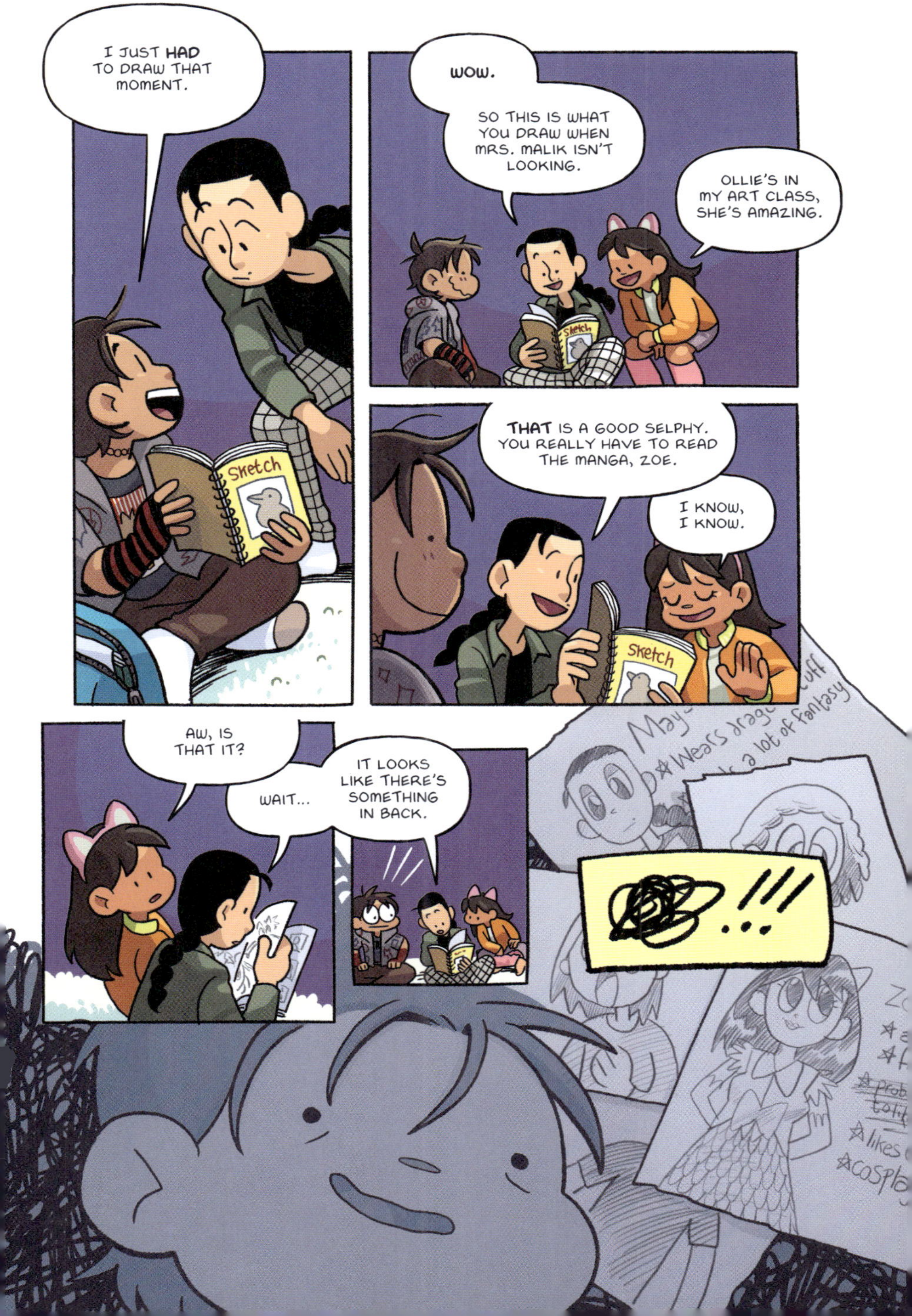
I JUST HAD TO DRAW THAT MOMENT.
SKETCH
WOW.
SO THIS IS WHAT YOU DRAW WHEN MRS. MALIK ISN'T LOOKING.
OLLIE'S IN MY ART CLASS, SHE'S AMAZING.
THAT IS A GOOD SELPHY. YOU REALLY HAVE TO READ THE MANGA, ZOE.
I KNOW, I KNOW.
SKETCH
AW, IS THAT IT?
WAIT...
IT LOOKS LIKE THERE'S SOMETHING IN BACK.
!!!...
☆ likes
☆cosplay

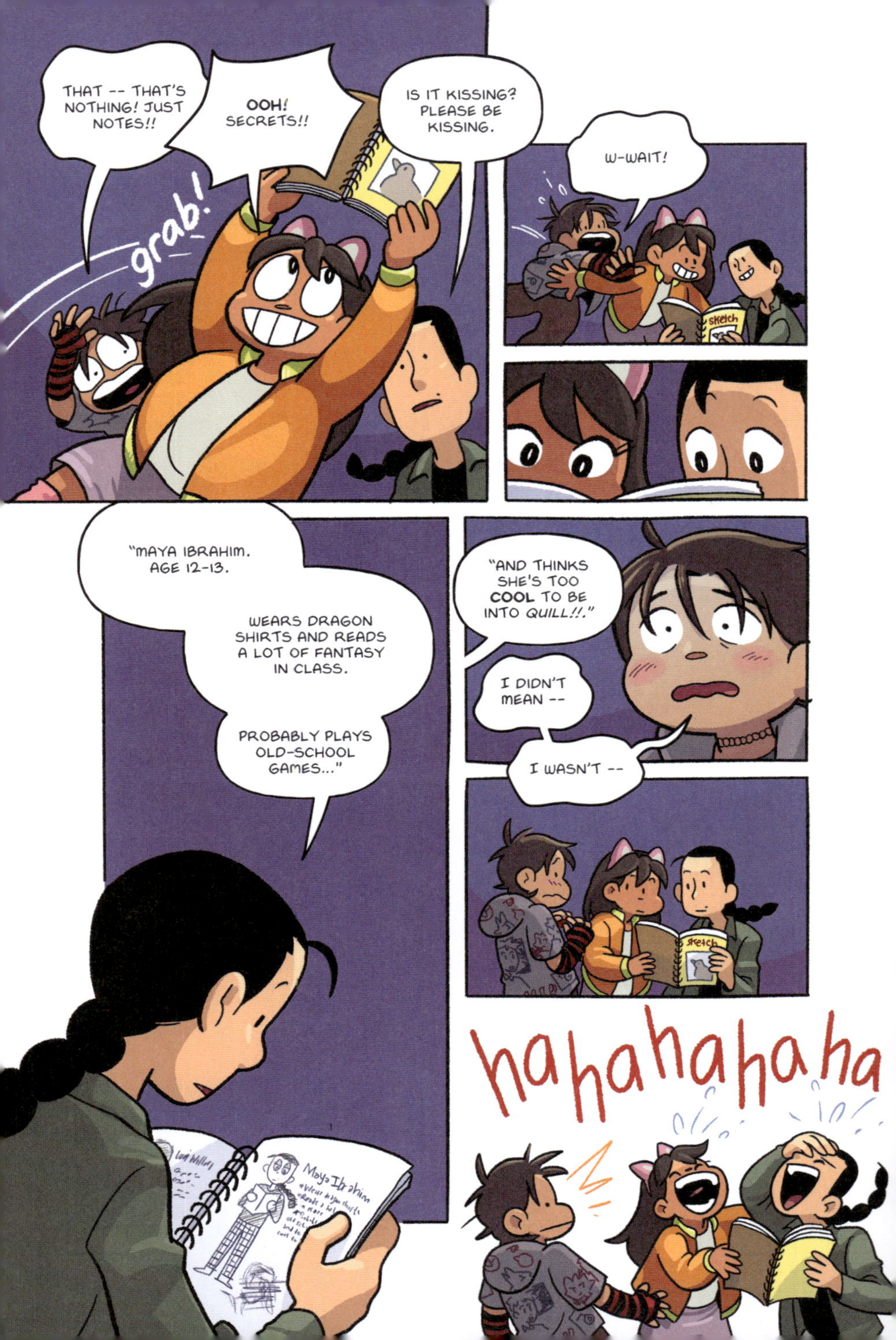

THAT -- THAT'S NOTHING! JUST NOTES!!
OOH! SECRETS!!
IS IT KISSING? PLEASE BE KISSING.
grab!
W-WAIT!
sketch
"MAYA IBRAHIM. AGE 12-13.
WEARS DRAGON SHIRTS AND READS A LOT OF FANTASY IN CLASS.
PROBABLY PLAYS OLD-SCHOOL GAMES..."
Maya Ibrahim
"AND THINKS SHE'S TOO COOL TO BE INTO QUILL!!."
I DIDN'T MEAN --
I WASN'T --
sketch
hahahahaha

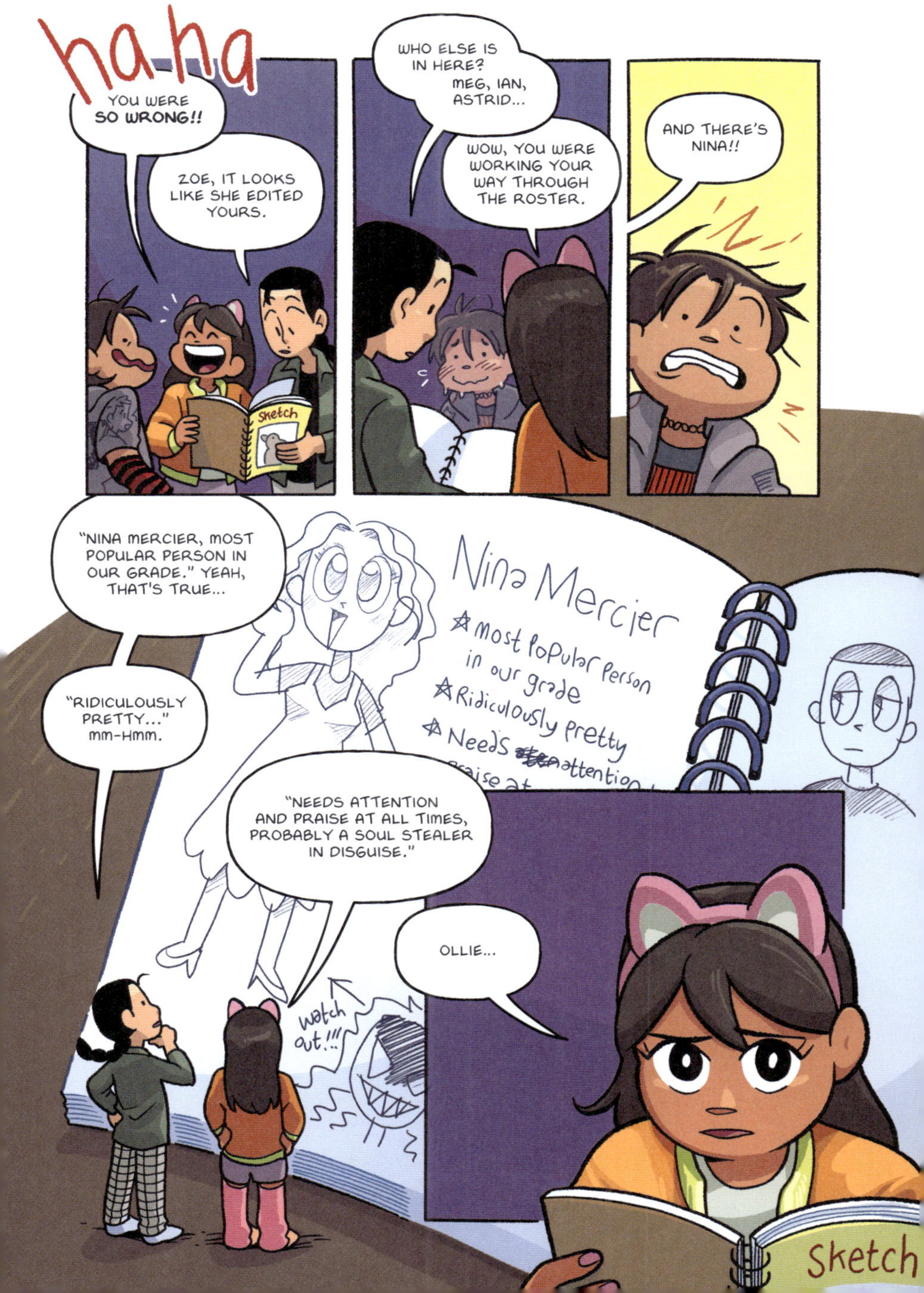

ha-ha
YOU WERE SO WRONG!!
ZOE, IT LOOKS LIKE SHE EDITED YOURS.
Sketch
WHO ELSE IS IN HERE? MEG, IAN, ASTRID...
WOW, YOU WERE WORKING YOUR WAY THROUGH THE ROSTER.
AND THERE'S NINA!!
"NINA MERCIER, MOST POPULAR PERSON IN OUR GRADE." YEAH, THAT'S TRUE...
Nina Mercier
most popular person in our grade
Ridiculously pretty
Needs attention
"RIDICULOUSLY PRETTY..." mm-Hmm.
"NEEDS ATTENTION AND PRAISE AT ALL TIMES, PROBABLY A SOUL STEALER IN DISGUISE."
watch out!!!
OLLIE...
Sketch

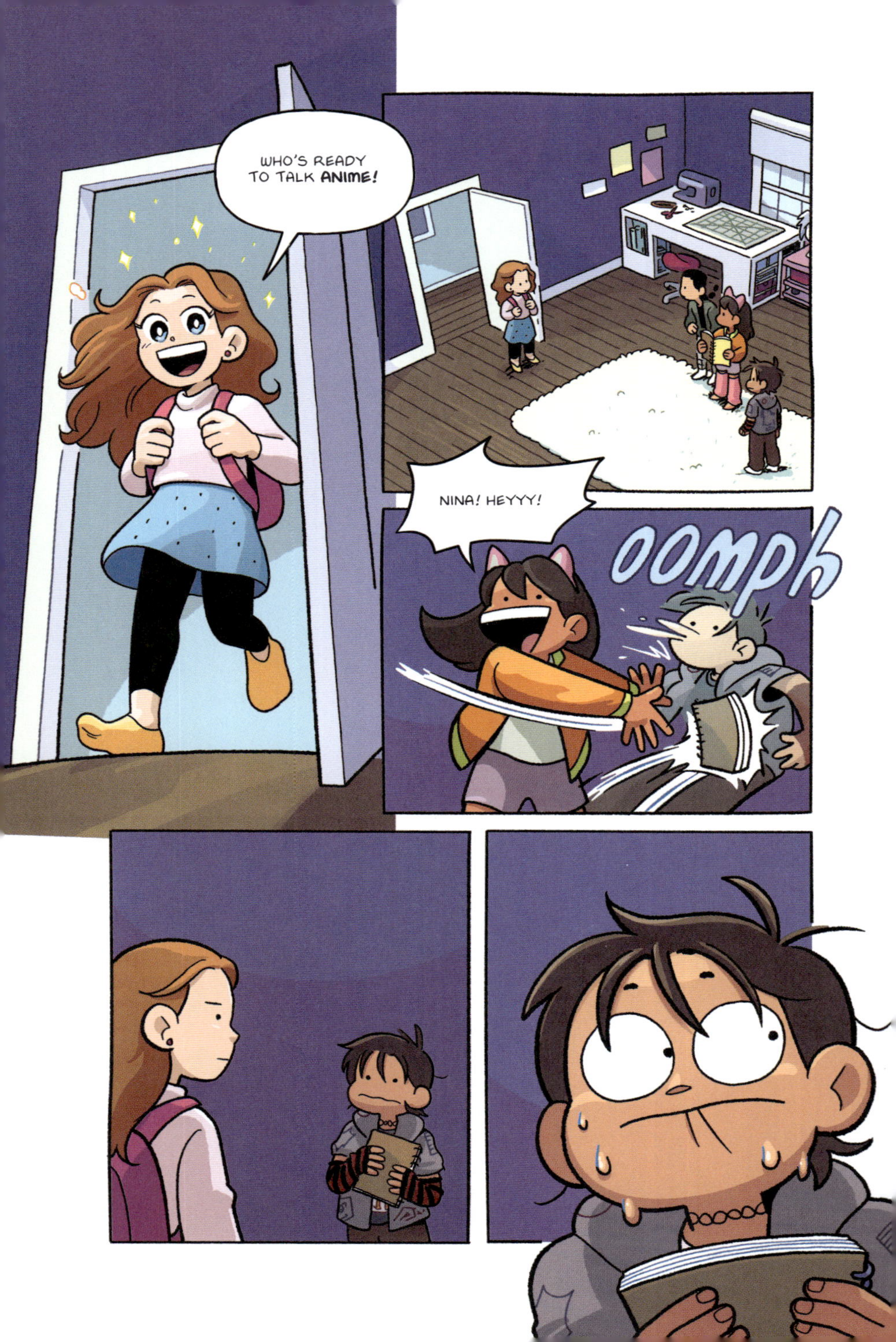
WHO'S READY TO TALK **ANIME!**
NINA! HEYYY!
OOMPH

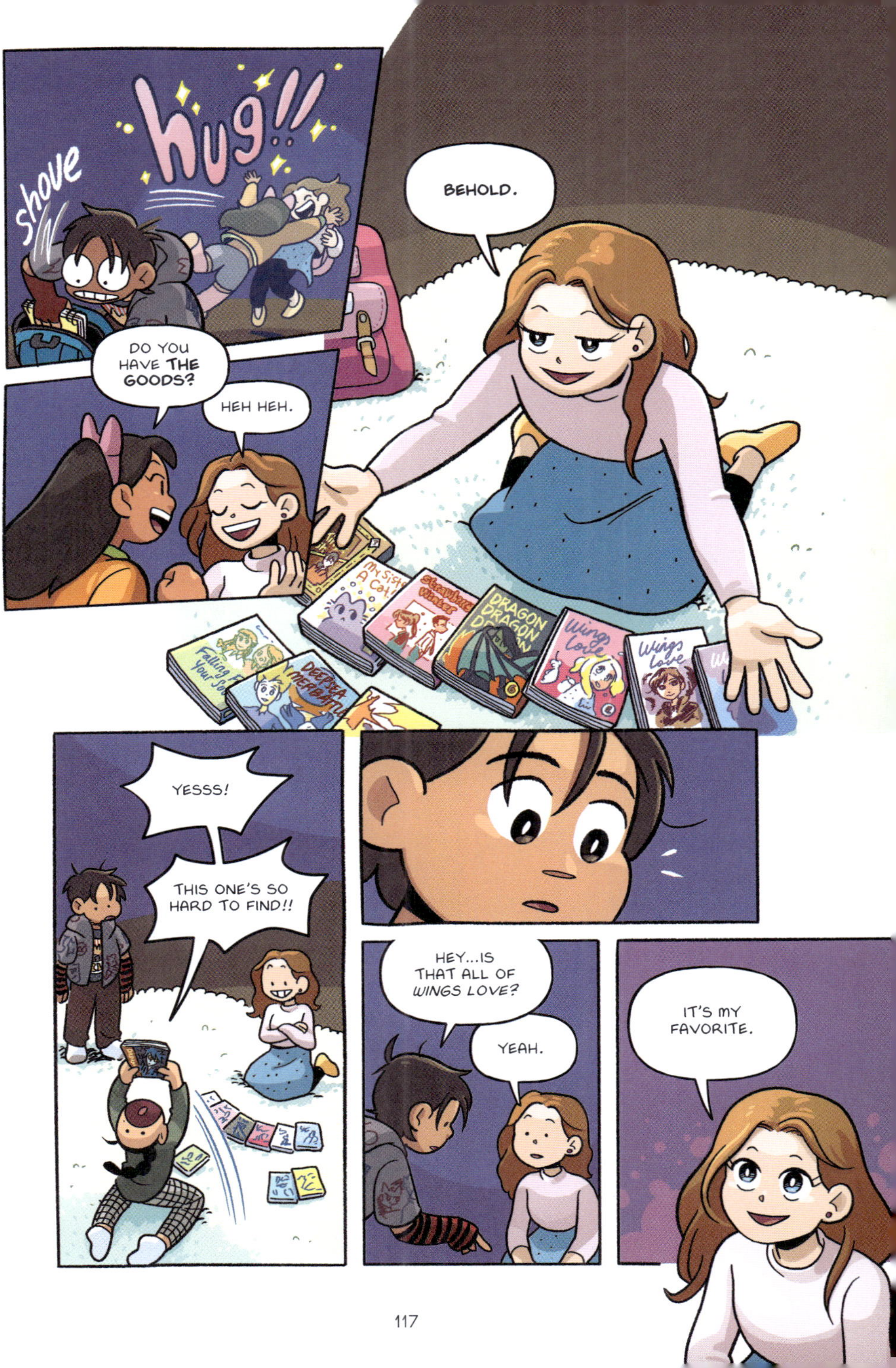
shove
hug!!
BEHOLD.
DO YOU HAVE THE GOODS?
HEH HEH.
YESSS!
THIS ONE'S SO HARD TO FIND!!
HEY...IS THAT ALL OF WINGS LOVE?
YEAH.
IT'S MY FAVORITE.

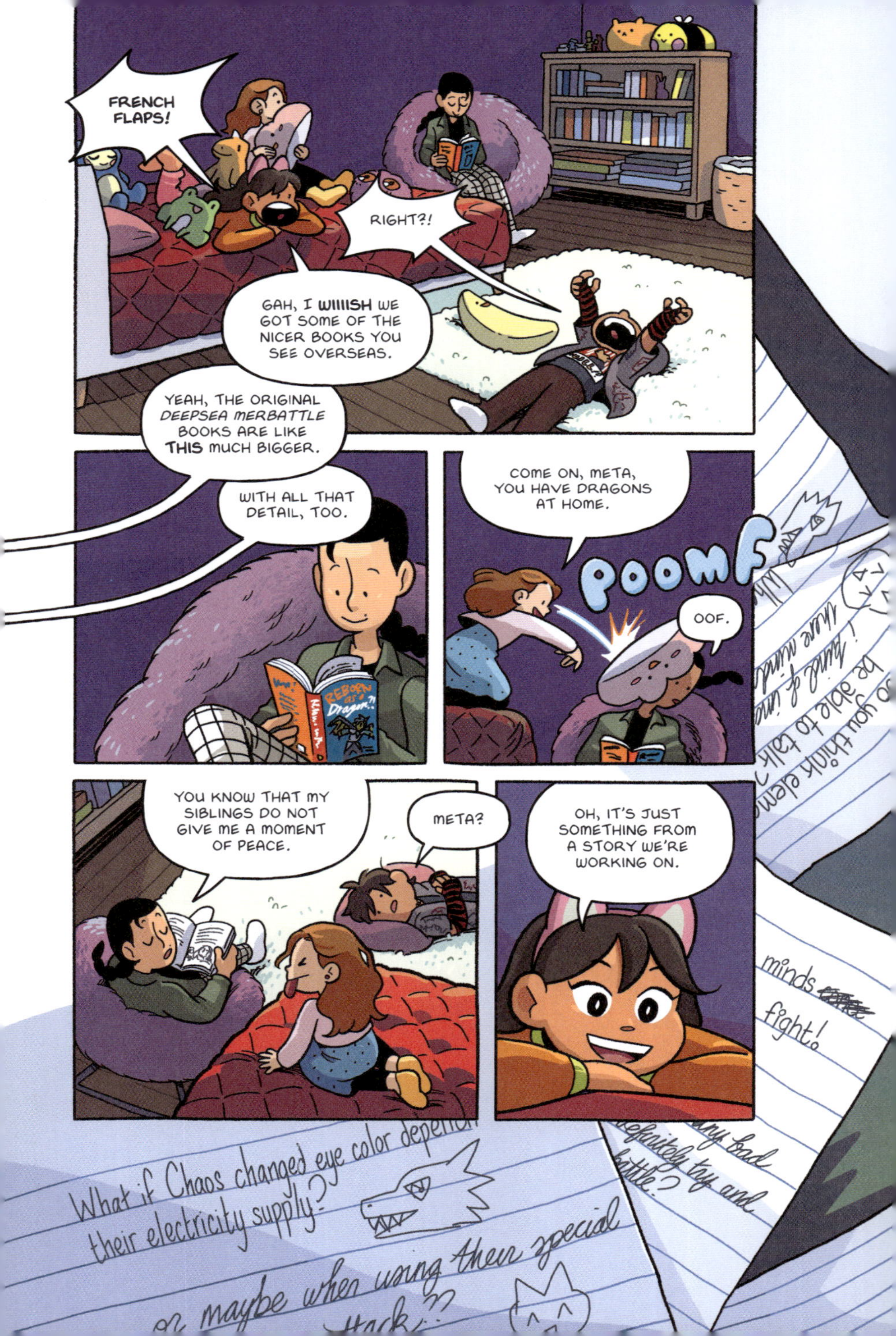
FRENCH FLAPS!
RIGHT?!
GAH, I WIIIISH WE GOT SOME OF THE NICER BOOKS YOU SEE OVERSEAS.
YEAH, THE ORIGINAL DEEPSEA MERBATTLE BOOKS ARE LIKE THIS MUCH BIGGER.
WITH ALL THAT DETAIL, TOO.
REBORN as a Dragon?!
COME ON, META, YOU HAVE DRAGONS AT HOME.
POOMF
OOF.
YOU KNOW THAT MY SIBLINGS DO NOT GIVE ME A MOMENT OF PEACE.
META?
OH, IT'S JUST SOMETHING FROM A STORY WE'RE WORKING ON.
minds
fight!
What if Chaos changed eye color depending on their electricity supply?
or maybe when using their special

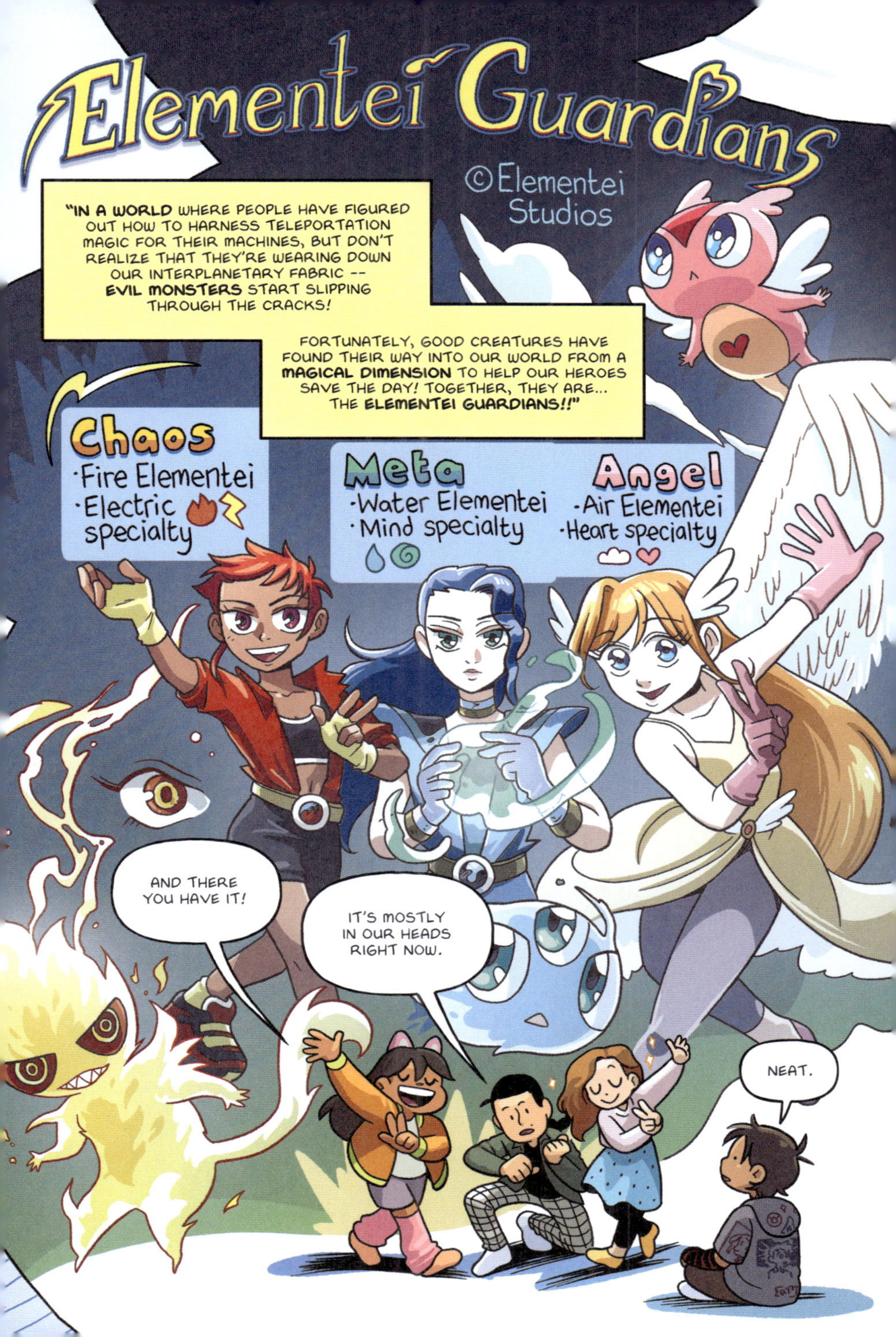
Elementei Guardians
©Elementei Studios
"IN A WORLD WHERE PEOPLE HAVE FIGURED OUT HOW TO HARNESS TELEPORTATION MAGIC FOR THEIR MACHINES, BUT DON'T REALIZE THAT THEY'RE WEARING DOWN OUR INTERPLANETARY FABRIC -- EVIL MONSTERS START SLIPPING THROUGH THE CRACKS!
FORTUNATELY, GOOD CREATURES HAVE FOUND THEIR WAY INTO OUR WORLD FROM A MAGICAL DIMENSION TO HELP OUR HEROES SAVE THE DAY! TOGETHER, THEY ARE... THE ELEMENTEI GUARDIANS!!"
Chaos ·Fire Elementei ·Electric specialty
Meta ·Water Elementei ·Mind specialty
Angel ·Air Elementei ·Heart specialty
AND THERE YOU HAVE IT!
IT'S MOSTLY IN OUR HEADS RIGHT NOW.
NEAT.

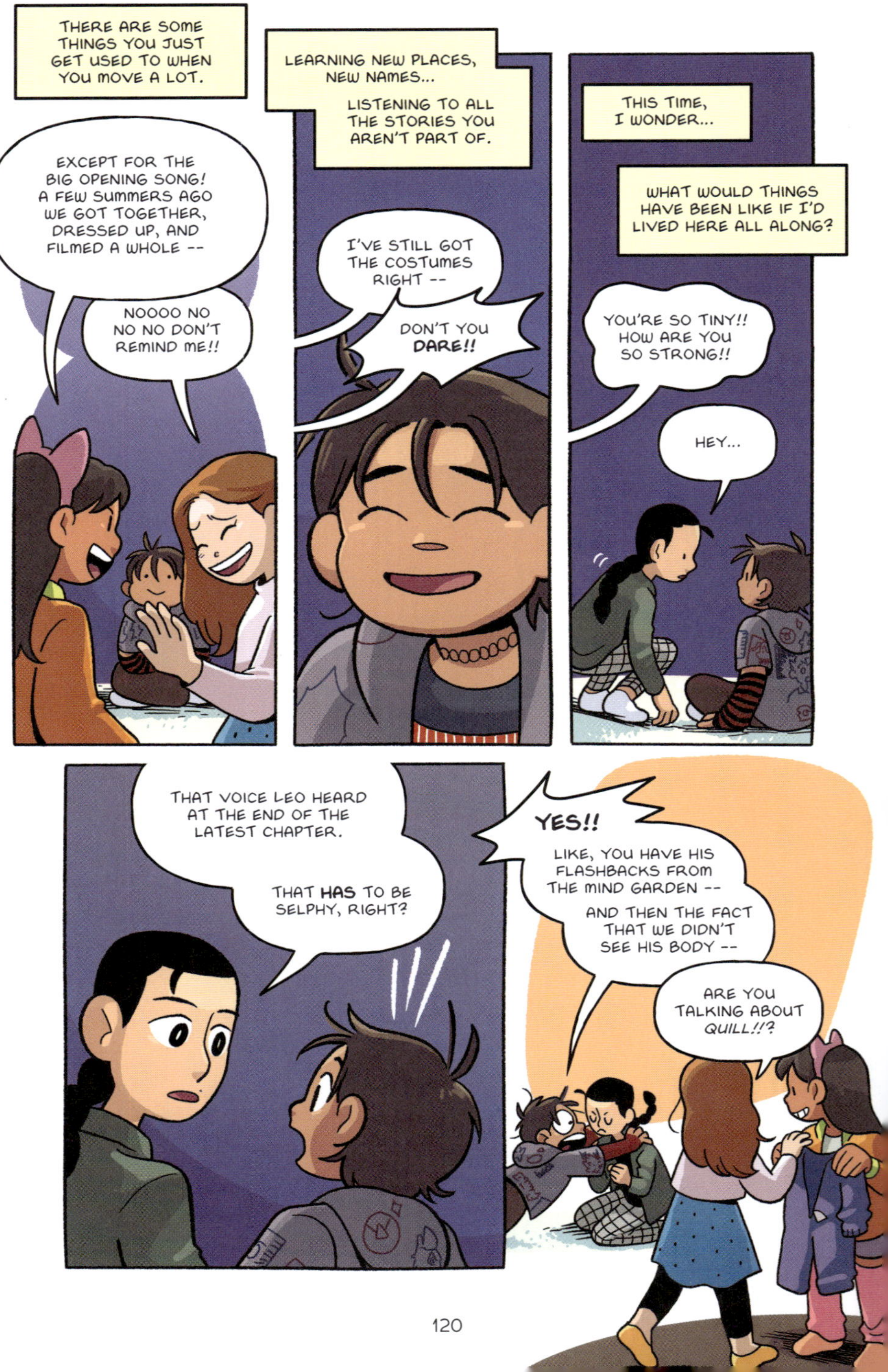
THERE ARE SOME THINGS YOU JUST GET USED TO WHEN YOU MOVE A LOT.
EXCEPT FOR THE BIG OPENING SONG! A FEW SUMMERS AGO WE GOT TOGETHER, DRESSED UP, AND FILMED A WHOLE --
NOOOO NO NO NO DON'T REMIND ME!!
LEARNING NEW PLACES, NEW NAMES...
LISTENING TO ALL THE STORIES YOU AREN'T PART OF.
I'VE STILL GOT THE COSTUMES RIGHT --
DON'T YOU **DARE!!**
THIS TIME, I WONDER...
WHAT WOULD THINGS HAVE BEEN LIKE IF I'D LIVED HERE ALL ALONG?
YOU'RE SO TINY!! HOW ARE YOU SO STRONG!!
HEY...
THAT VOICE LEO HEARD AT THE END OF THE LATEST CHAPTER.
THAT **HAS** TO BE SELPHY, RIGHT?
YES!!
LIKE, YOU HAVE HIS FLASHBACKS FROM THE MIND GARDEN --
AND THEN THE FACT THAT WE DIDN'T SEE HIS BODY --
ARE YOU TALKING ABOUT *QUILL!!?*

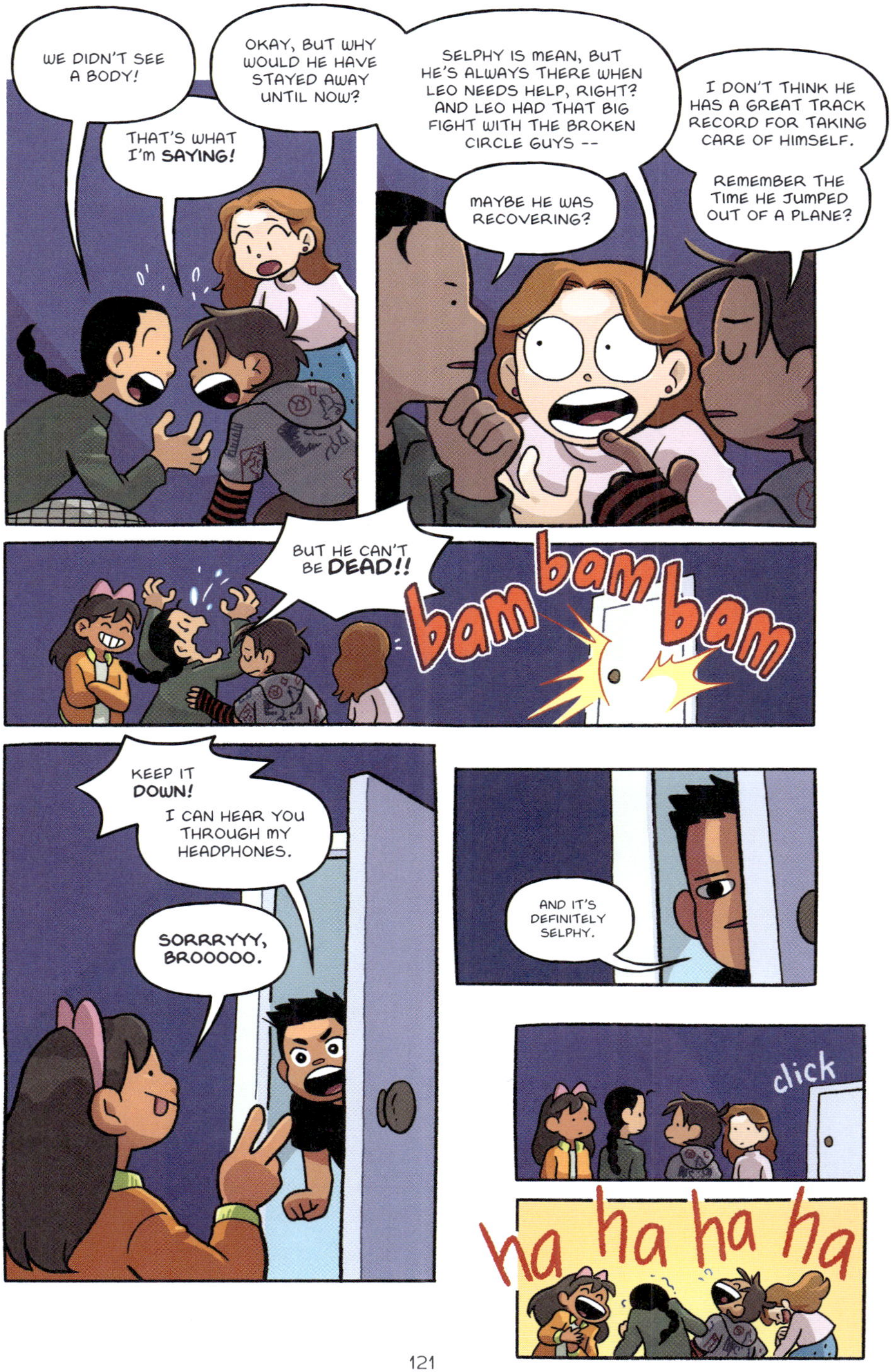
WE DIDN'T SEE A BODY!
THAT'S WHAT I'm SAYING!
OKAY, BUT WHY WOULD HE HAVE STAYED AWAY UNTIL NOW?
SELPHY IS MEAN, BUT HE'S ALWAYS THERE WHEN LEO NEEDS HELP, RIGHT? AND LEO HAD THAT BIG FIGHT WITH THE BROKEN CIRCLE GUYS --
MAYBE HE WAS RECOVERING?
I DON'T THINK HE HAS A GREAT TRACK RECORD FOR TAKING CARE OF HIMSELF.
REMEMBER THE TIME HE JUMPED OUT OF A PLANE?
BUT HE CAN'T BE DEAD!!
bam bam bam
KEEP IT DOWN!
I CAN HEAR YOU THROUGH MY HEADPHONES.
SORRRYYY, BROOOOO.
AND IT'S DEFINITELY SELPHY.
click
ha ha ha ha

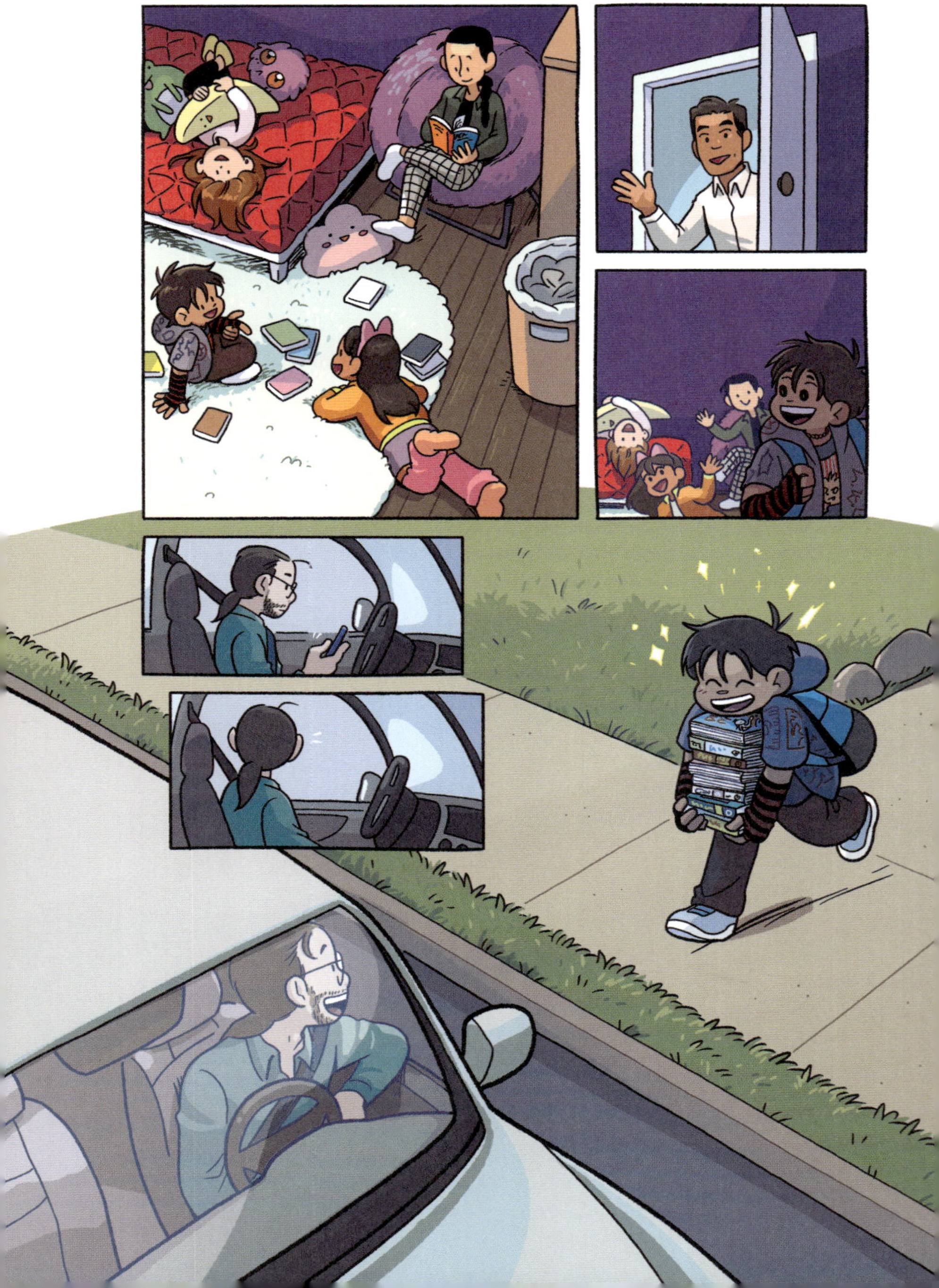

CHAPTER SIX

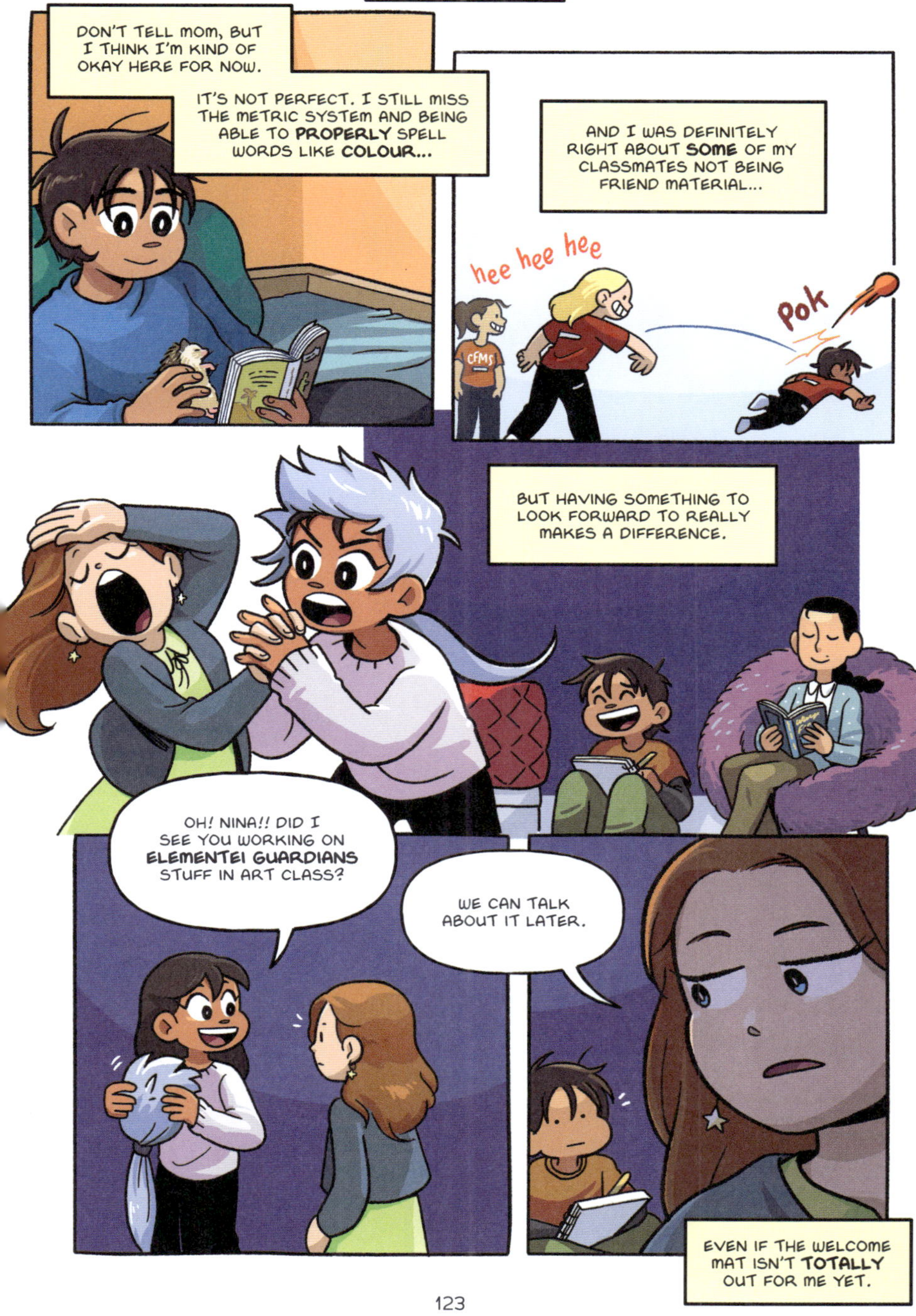

DON'T TELL MOM, BUT I THINK I'M KIND OF OKAY HERE FOR NOW.
IT'S NOT PERFECT. I STILL MISS THE METRIC SYSTEM AND BEING ABLE TO **PROPERLY** SPELL WORDS LIKE **COLOUR...**
AND I WAS DEFINITELY RIGHT ABOUT **SOME** OF MY CLASSMATES NOT BEING FRIEND MATERIAL...
hee hee hee
CFMS
Pok
BUT HAVING SOMETHING TO LOOK FORWARD TO REALLY MAKES A DIFFERENCE.
OH! NINA!! DID I SEE YOU WORKING ON **ELEMENTEI GUARDIANS** STUFF IN ART CLASS?
WE CAN TALK ABOUT IT LATER.
EVEN IF THE WELCOME MAT ISN'T **TOTALLY** OUT FOR ME YET.

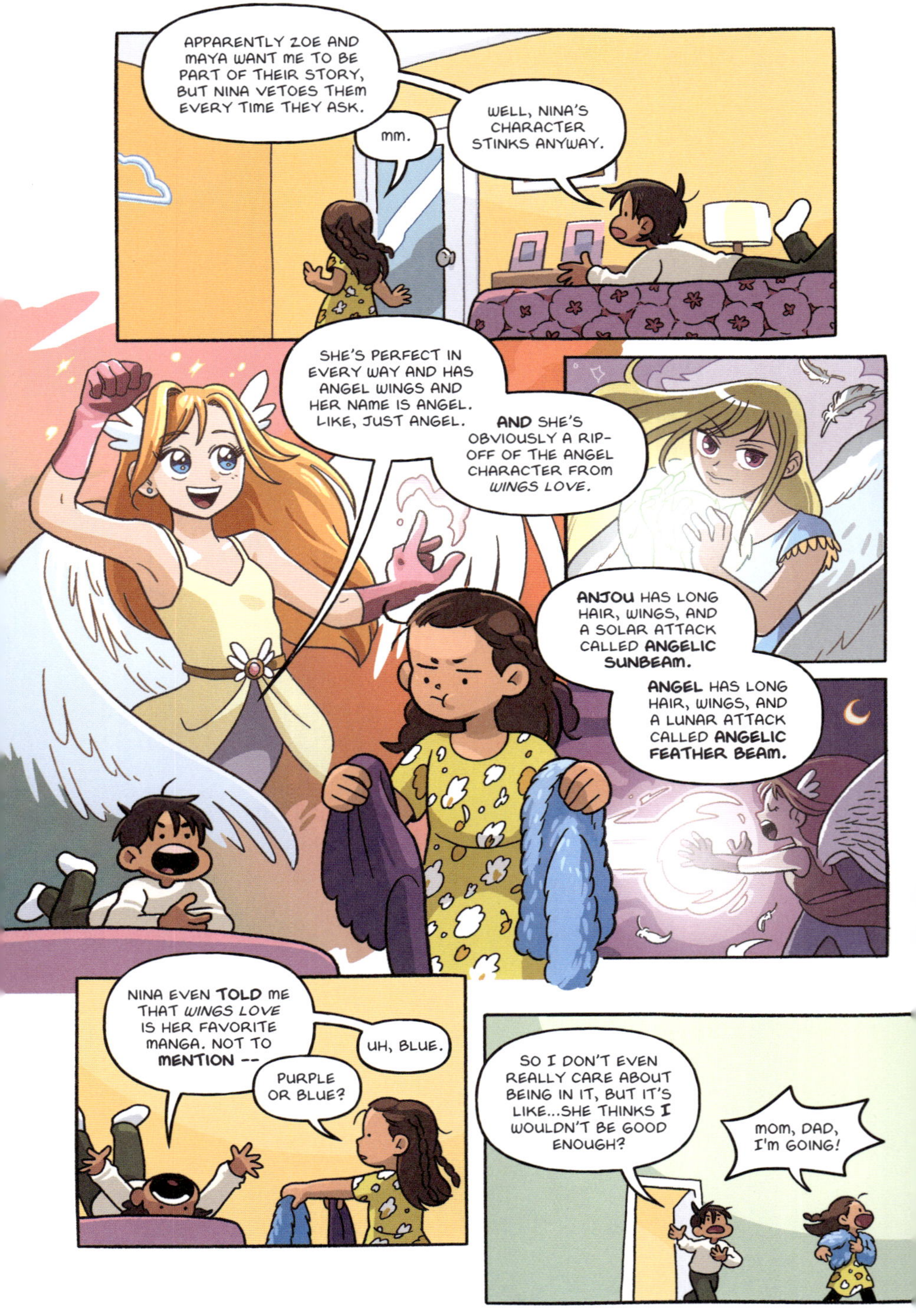
APPARENTLY ZOE AND MAYA WANT ME TO BE PART OF THEIR STORY, BUT NINA VETOES THEM EVERY TIME THEY ASK.
MM.
WELL, NINA'S CHARACTER STINKS ANYWAY.
SHE'S PERFECT IN EVERY WAY AND HAS ANGEL WINGS AND HER NAME IS ANGEL. LIKE, JUST ANGEL.
AND SHE'S OBVIOUSLY A RIP-OFF OF THE ANGEL CHARACTER FROM WINGS LOVE.
ANJOU HAS LONG HAIR, WINGS, AND A SOLAR ATTACK CALLED ANGELIC SUNBEAM.
ANGEL HAS LONG HAIR, WINGS, AND A LUNAR ATTACK CALLED ANGELIC FEATHER BEAM.
NINA EVEN TOLD ME THAT WINGS LOVE IS HER FAVORITE MANGA. NOT TO MENTION --
UH, BLUE.
PURPLE OR BLUE?
SO I DON'T EVEN REALLY CARE ABOUT BEING IN IT, BUT IT'S LIKE...SHE THINKS I WOULDN'T BE GOOD ENOUGH?
MOM, DAD, I'M GOING!

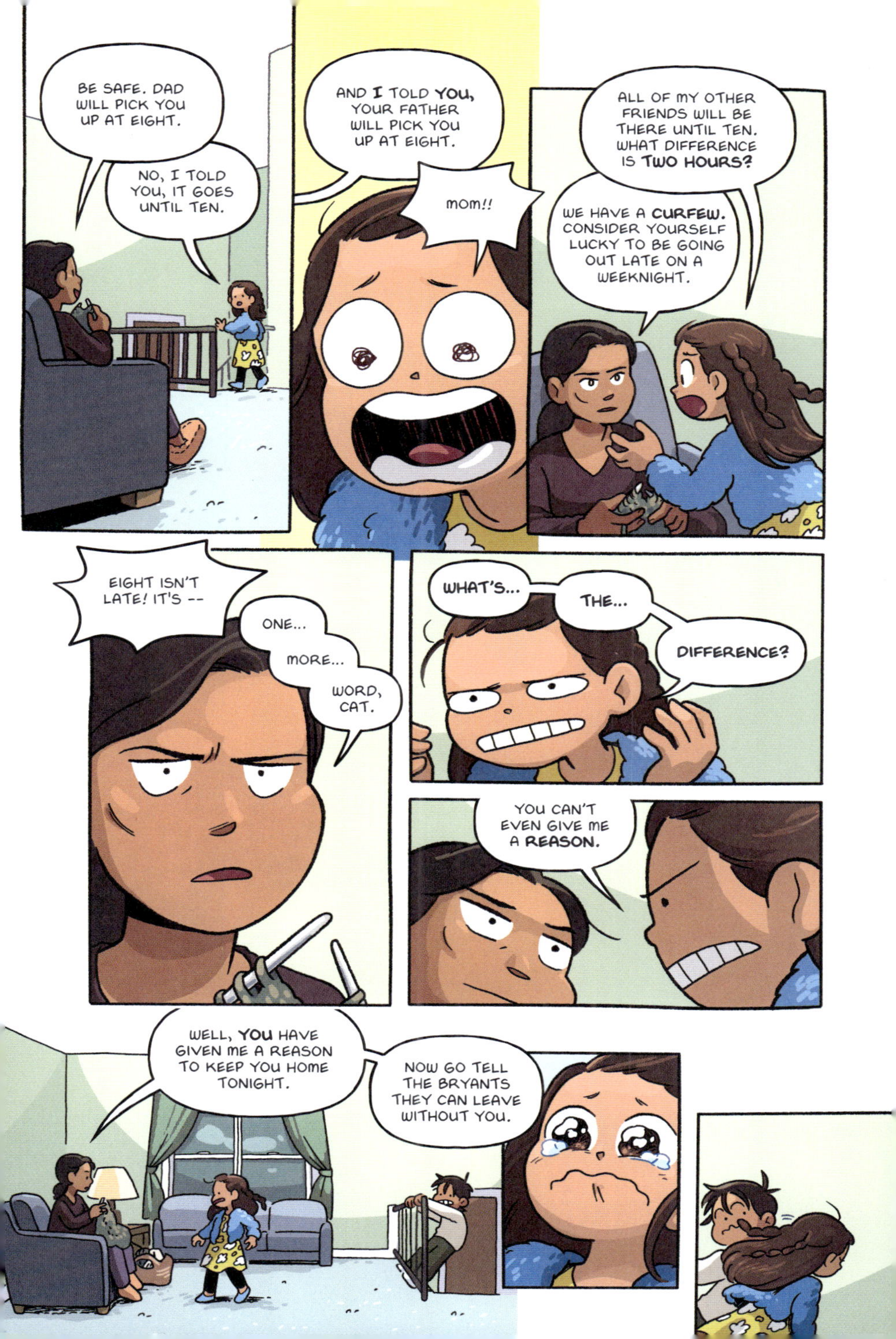
BE SAFE. DAD WILL PICK YOU UP AT EIGHT.
NO, I TOLD YOU, IT GOES UNTIL TEN.
AND I TOLD YOU, YOUR FATHER WILL PICK YOU UP AT EIGHT.
MOM!!
ALL OF MY OTHER FRIENDS WILL BE THERE UNTIL TEN. WHAT DIFFERENCE IS TWO HOURS?
WE HAVE A CURFEW. CONSIDER YOURSELF LUCKY TO BE GOING OUT LATE ON A WEEKNIGHT.
EIGHT ISN'T LATE! IT'S --
ONE...
MORE...
WORD, CAT.
WHAT'S...
THE...
DIFFERENCE?
YOU CAN'T EVEN GIVE ME A REASON.
WELL, YOU HAVE GIVEN ME A REASON TO KEEP YOU HOME TONIGHT.
NOW GO TELL THE BRYANTS THEY CAN LEAVE WITHOUT YOU.

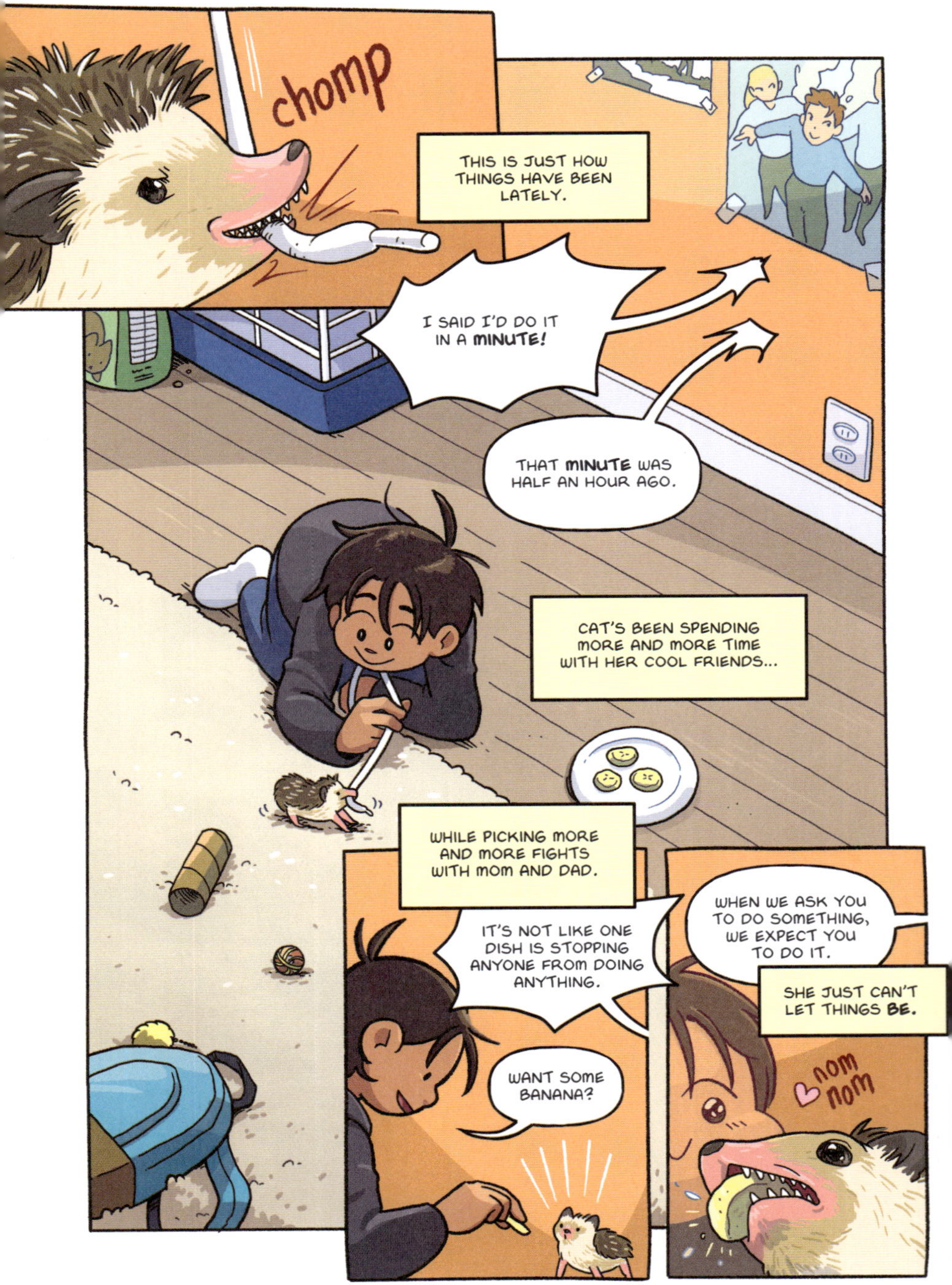
chomp
THIS IS JUST HOW THINGS HAVE BEEN LATELY.
I SAID I'D DO IT IN A **MINUTE!**
THAT **MINUTE** WAS HALF AN HOUR AGO.
CAT'S BEEN SPENDING MORE AND MORE TIME WITH HER COOL FRIENDS...
WHILE PICKING MORE AND MORE FIGHTS WITH MOM AND DAD.
IT'S NOT LIKE ONE DISH IS STOPPING ANYONE FROM DOING ANYTHING.
WANT SOME BANANA?
WHEN WE ASK YOU TO DO SOMETHING, WE EXPECT YOU TO DO IT.
SHE JUST CAN'T LET THINGS **BE.**
nom nom

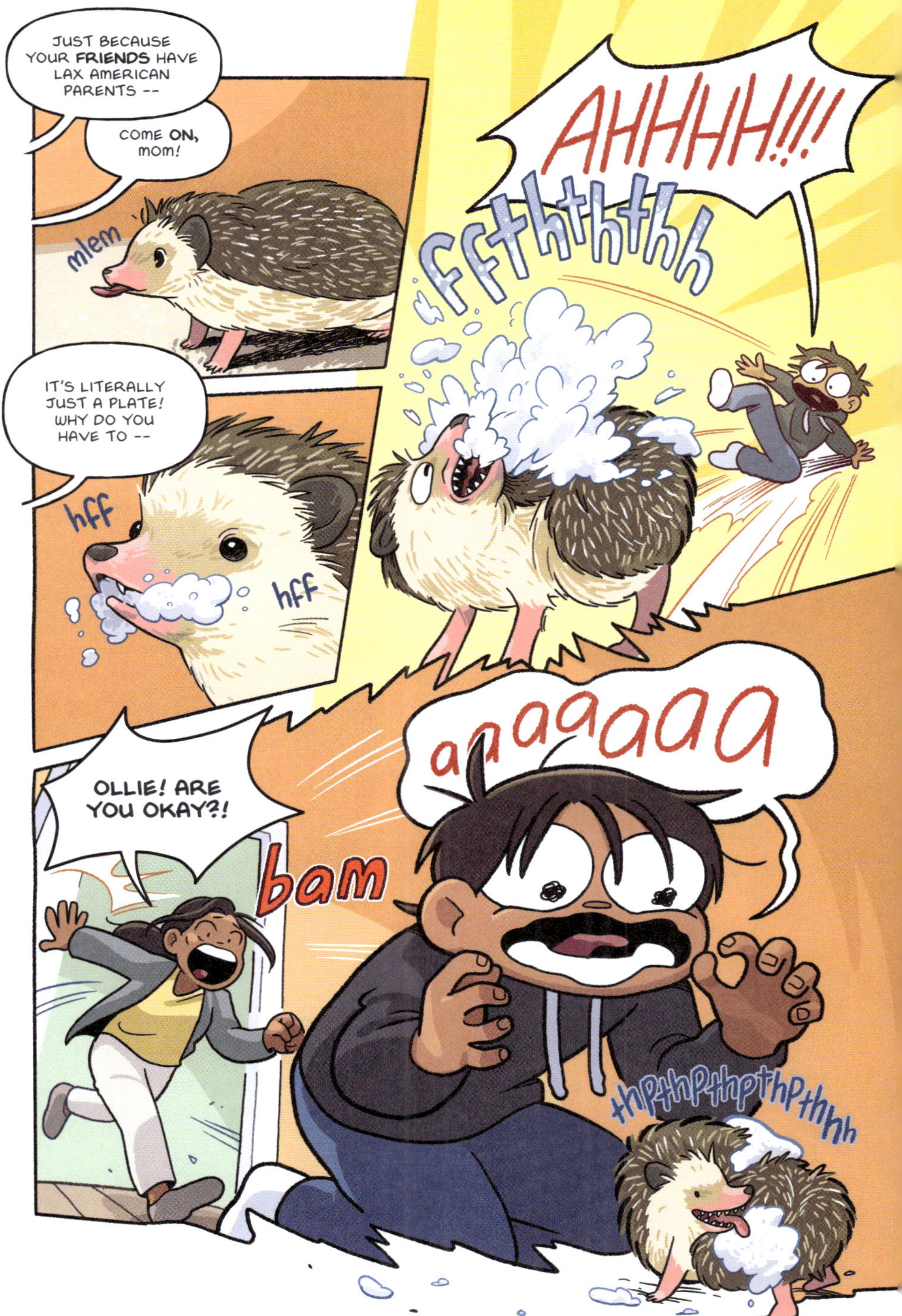
JUST BECAUSE YOUR **FRIENDS** HAVE LAX AMERICAN PARENTS --
COME **ON**, MOM!
mlem
IT'S LITERALLY JUST A PLATE! WHY DO YOU HAVE TO --
hff
hff
AHHHH!!!
ffthththhh
OLLIE! ARE YOU OKAY?!
bam
aaaaaaa
thpthpthpthpthhh

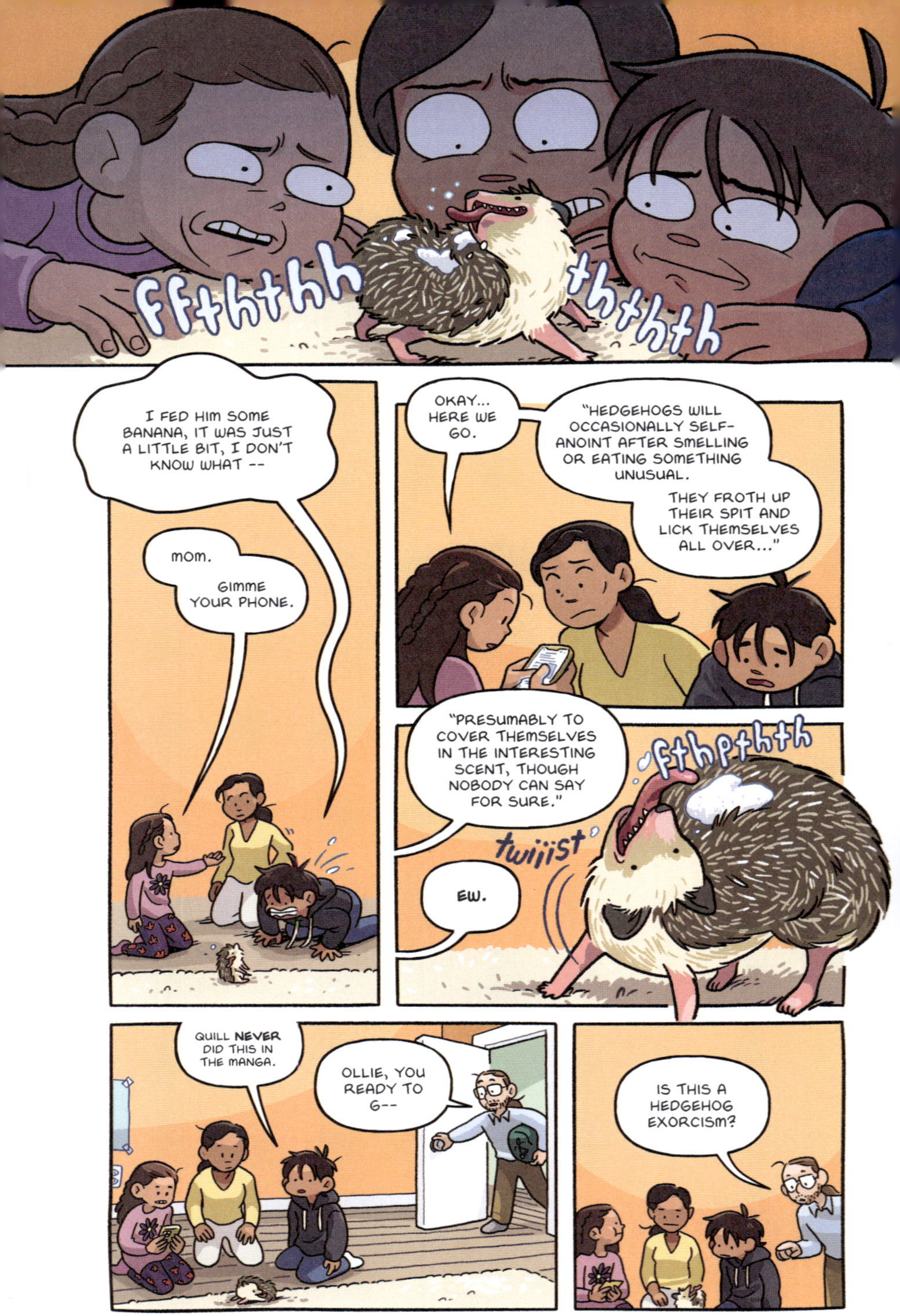

FFTHTHH THTHTH
I FED HIM SOME BANANA, IT WAS JUST A LITTLE BIT, I DON'T KNOW WHAT --
MOM.
GIMME YOUR PHONE.
OKAY... HERE WE GO.
"HEDGEHOGS WILL OCCASIONALLY SELF-ANOINT AFTER SMELLING OR EATING SOMETHING UNUSUAL.
THEY FROTH UP THEIR SPIT AND LICK THEMSELVES ALL OVER..."
"PRESUMABLY TO COVER THEMSELVES IN THE INTERESTING SCENT, THOUGH NOBODY CAN SAY FOR SURE."
FTHPTHTH
TWIIIST
EW.
QUILL **NEVER** DID THIS IN THE MANGA.
OLLIE, YOU READY TO G--
IS THIS A HEDGEHOG EXORCISM?

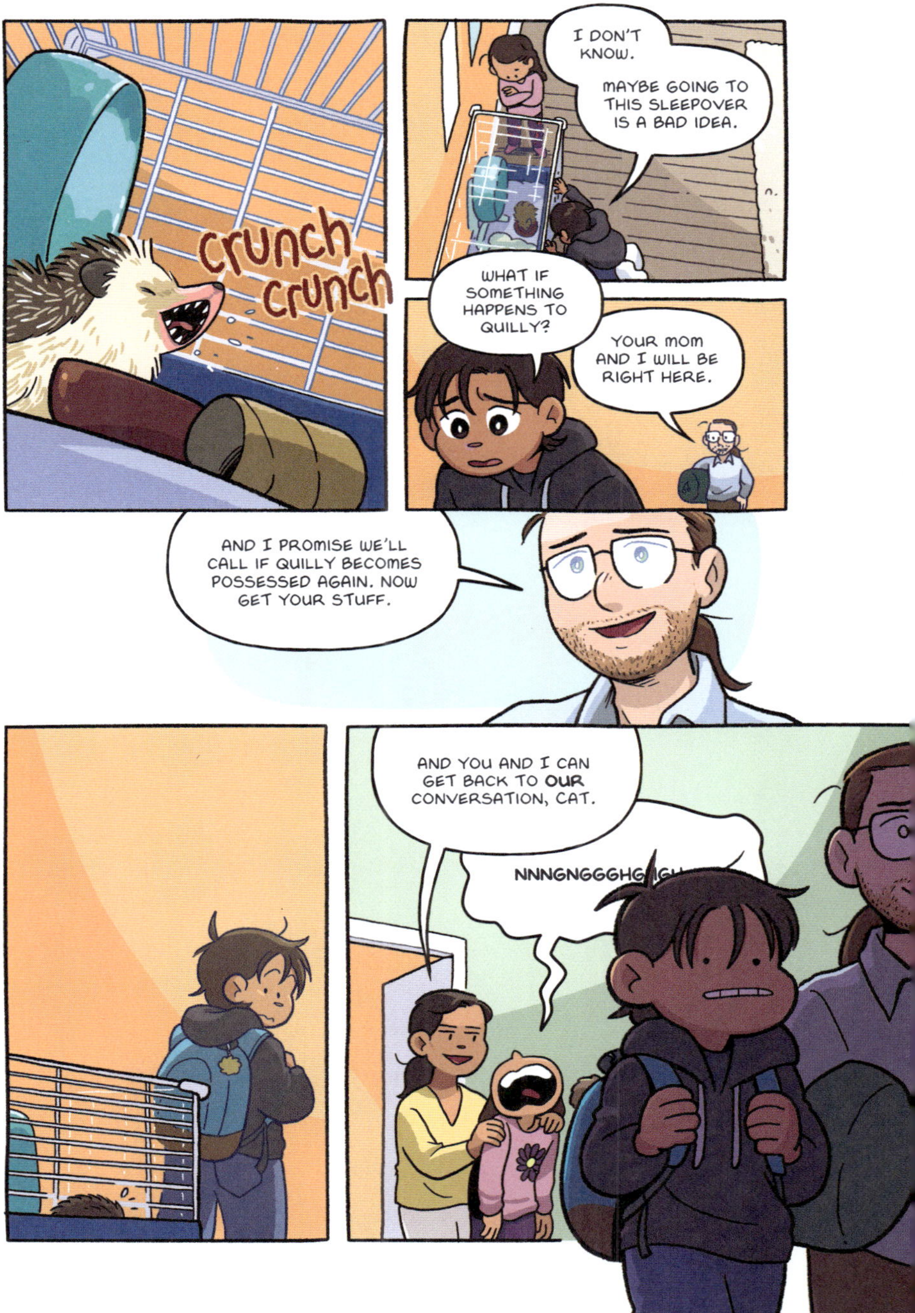
crunch crunch
I DON'T KNOW.
MAYBE GOING TO THIS SLEEPOVER IS A BAD IDEA.
WHAT IF SOMETHING HAPPENS TO QUILLY?
YOUR MOM AND I WILL BE RIGHT HERE.
AND I PROMISE WE'LL CALL IF QUILLY BECOMES POSSESSED AGAIN. NOW GET YOUR STUFF.
AND YOU AND I CAN GET BACK TO **OUR** CONVERSATION, CAT.
NNNGNGGGHG

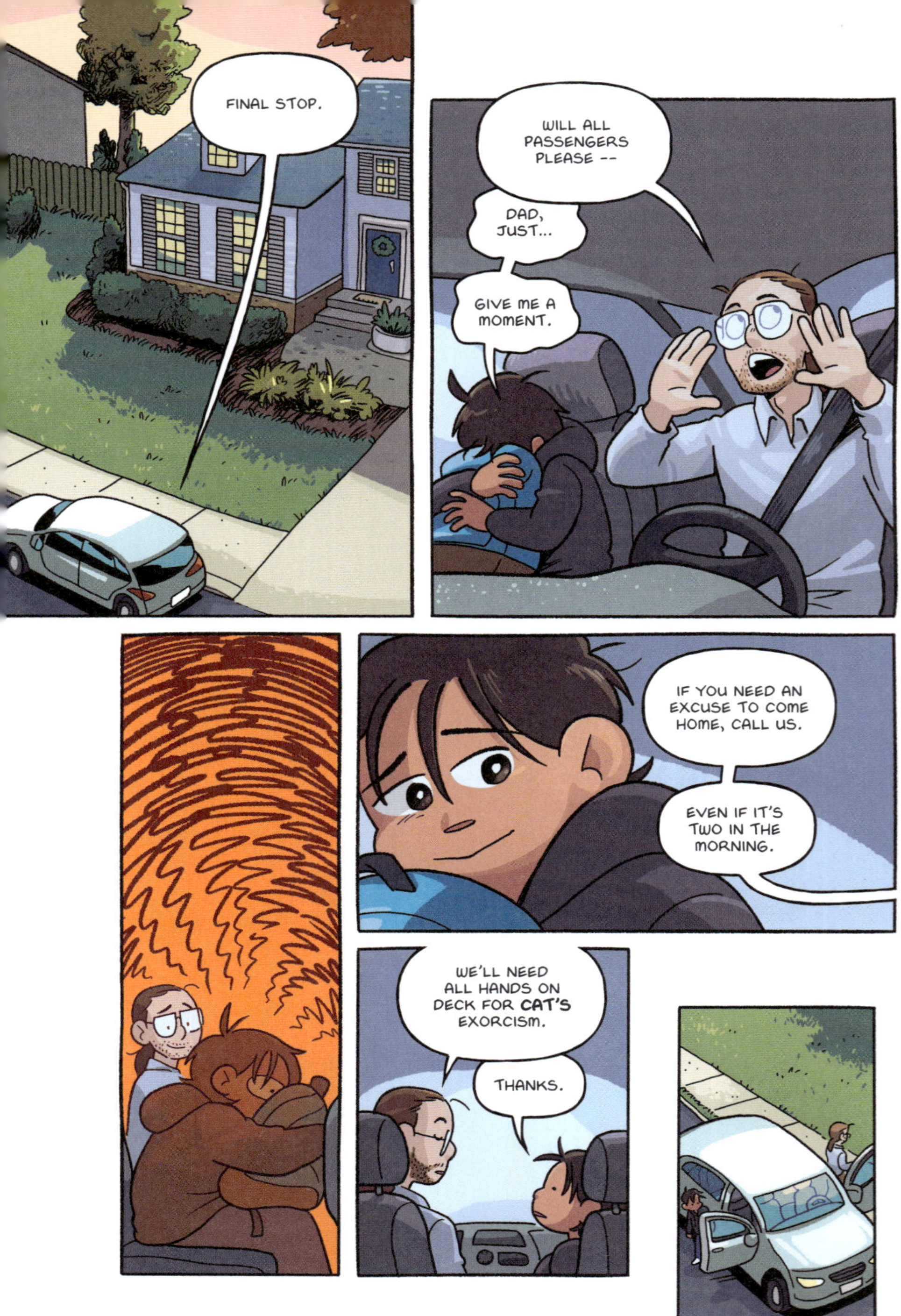
FINAL STOP.
WILL ALL PASSENGERS PLEASE --
DAD, JUST...
GIVE ME A MOMENT.
IF YOU NEED AN EXCUSE TO COME HOME, CALL US.
EVEN IF IT'S TWO IN THE MORNING.
WE'LL NEED ALL HANDS ON DECK FOR **CAT'S** EXORCISM.
THANKS.

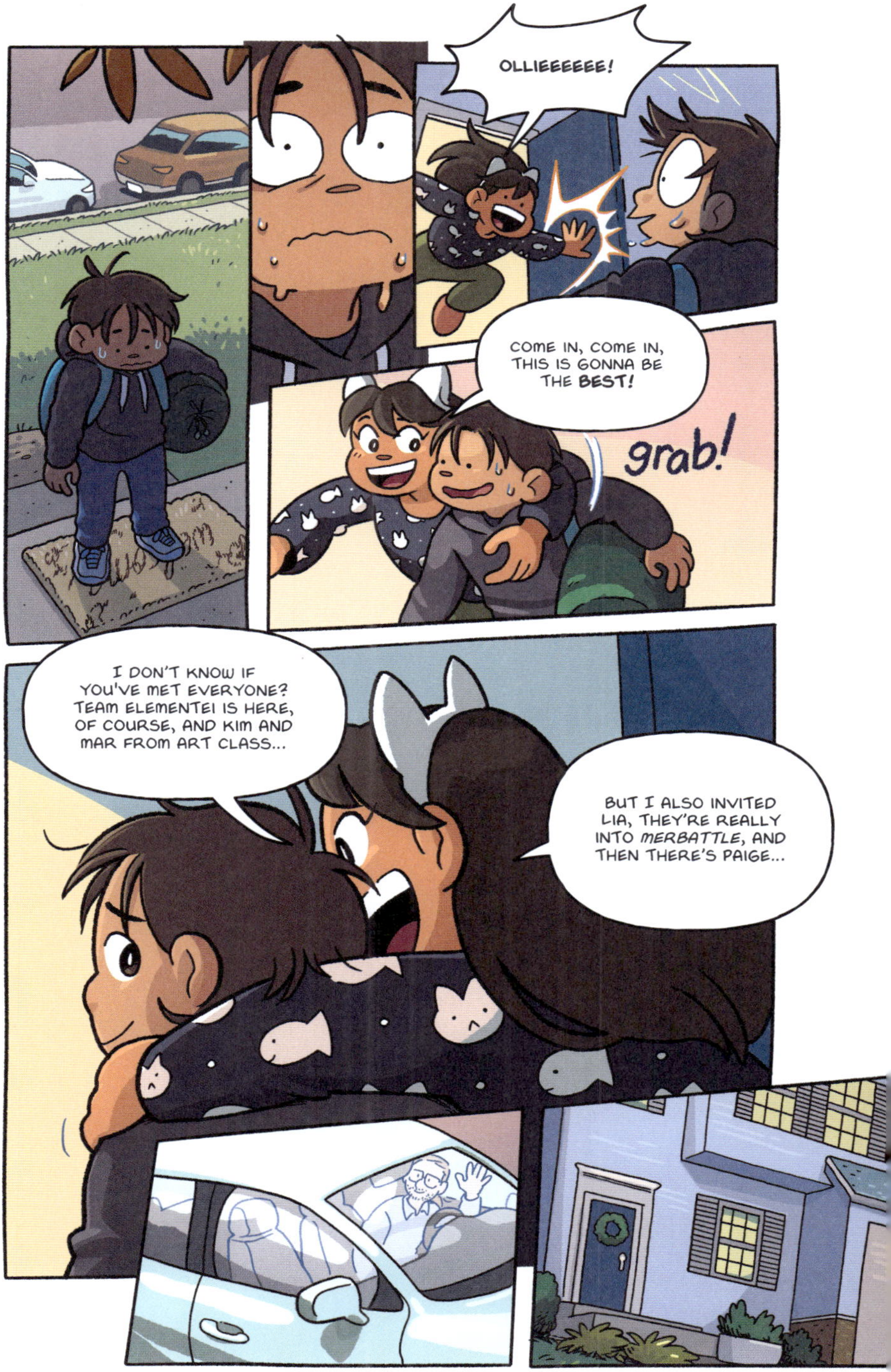
OLLIEEEEEE!
COME IN, COME IN, THIS IS GONNA BE THE **BEST!**
grab!
I DON'T KNOW IF YOU'VE MET EVERYONE? TEAM ELEMENTEI IS HERE, OF COURSE, AND KIM AND MAR FROM ART CLASS...
BUT I ALSO INVITED LIA, THEY'RE REALLY INTO *MERBATTLE*, AND THEN THERE'S PAIGE...

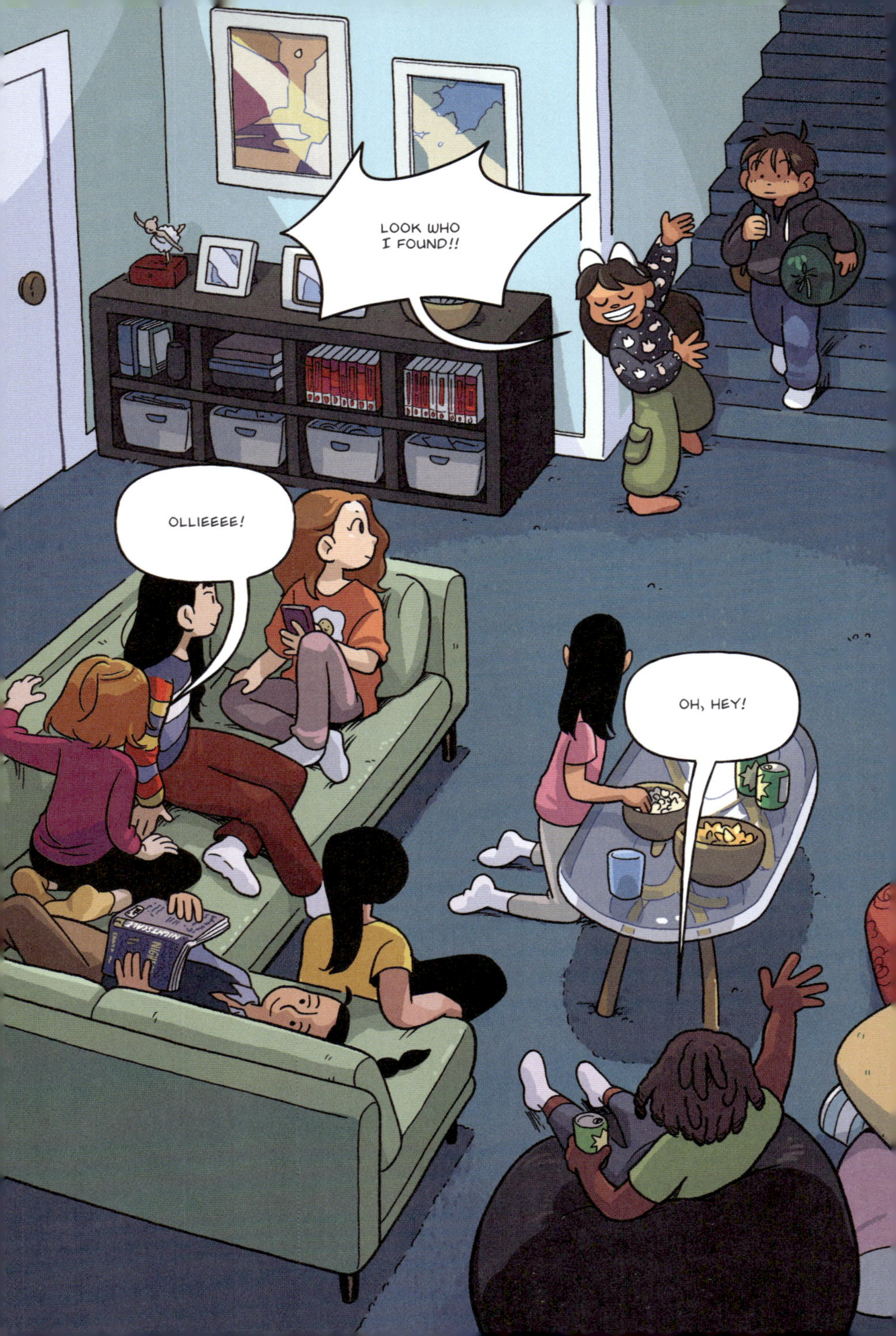
LOOK WHO I FOUND!!
OLLIEEEE!
OH, HEY!

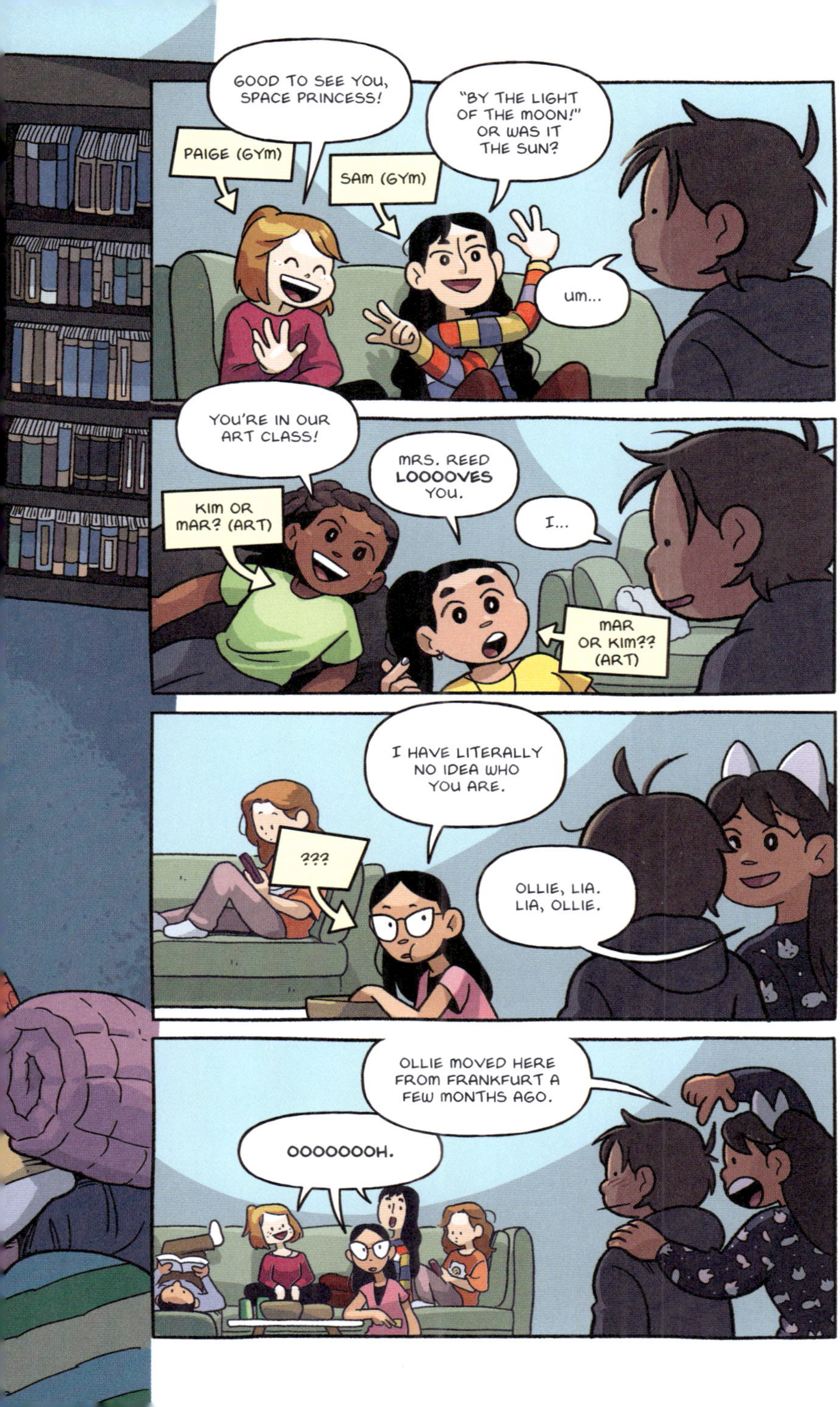
GOOD TO SEE YOU, SPACE PRINCESS!
PAIGE (GYM)
"BY THE LIGHT OF THE MOON!" OR WAS IT THE SUN?
SAM (GYM)
UM...
YOU'RE IN OUR ART CLASS!
KIM OR MAR? (ART)
MRS. REED **LOOOOVES** YOU.
I...
MAR OR KIM?? (ART)
I HAVE LITERALLY NO IDEA WHO YOU ARE.
???
OLLIE, LIA. LIA, OLLIE.
OLLIE MOVED HERE FROM FRANKFURT A FEW MONTHS AGO.
OOOOOOOH.

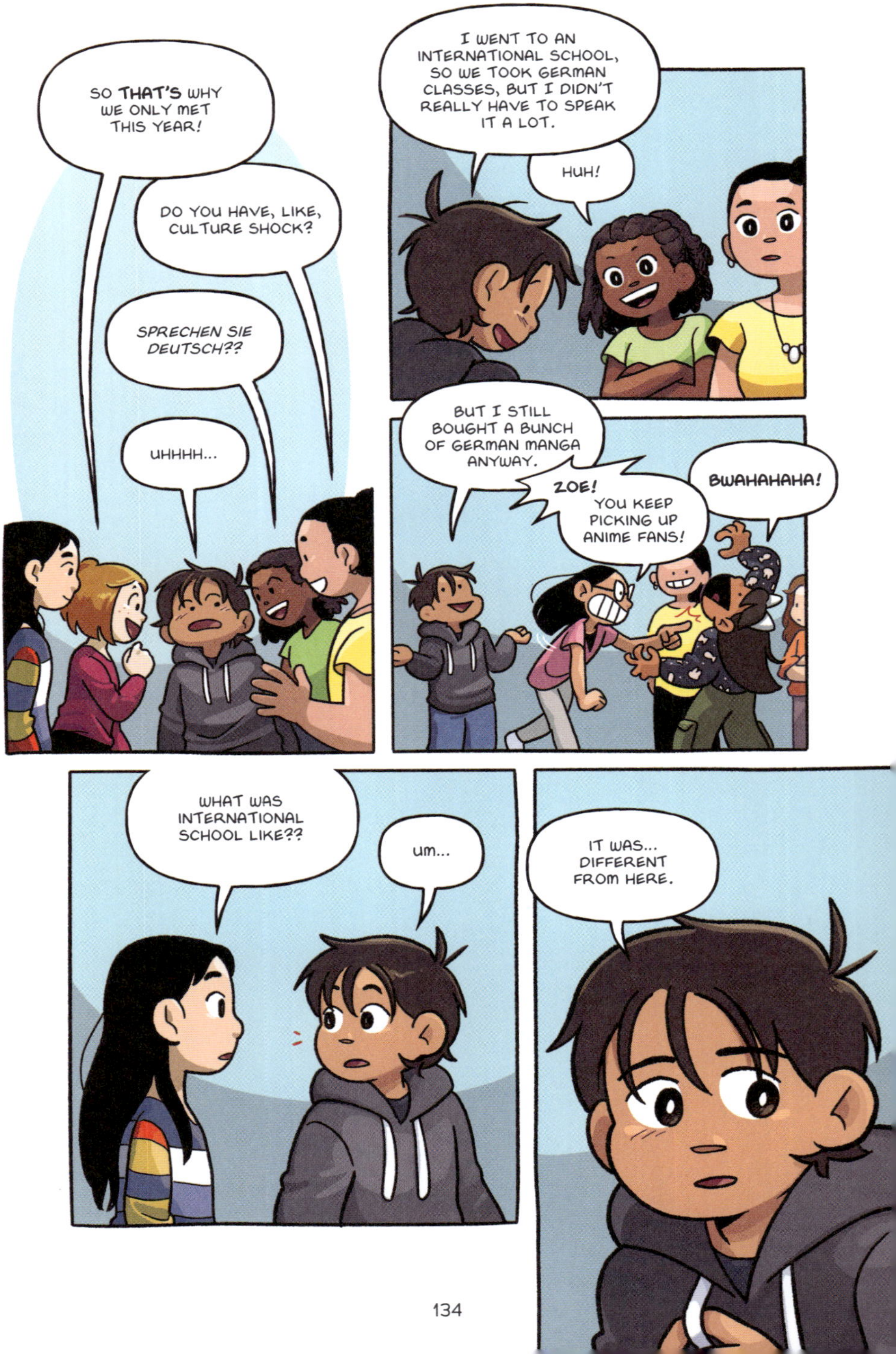
SO **THAT'S** WHY WE ONLY MET THIS YEAR!
DO YOU HAVE, LIKE, CULTURE SHOCK?
SPRECHEN SIE DEUTSCH??
UHHHH...
I WENT TO AN INTERNATIONAL SCHOOL, SO WE TOOK GERMAN CLASSES, BUT I DIDN'T REALLY HAVE TO SPEAK IT A LOT.
HUH!
BUT I STILL BOUGHT A BUNCH OF GERMAN MANGA ANYWAY.
ZOE!
YOU KEEP PICKING UP ANIME FANS!
BWAHAHAHA!
WHAT WAS INTERNATIONAL SCHOOL LIKE??
um...
IT WAS... DIFFERENT FROM HERE.

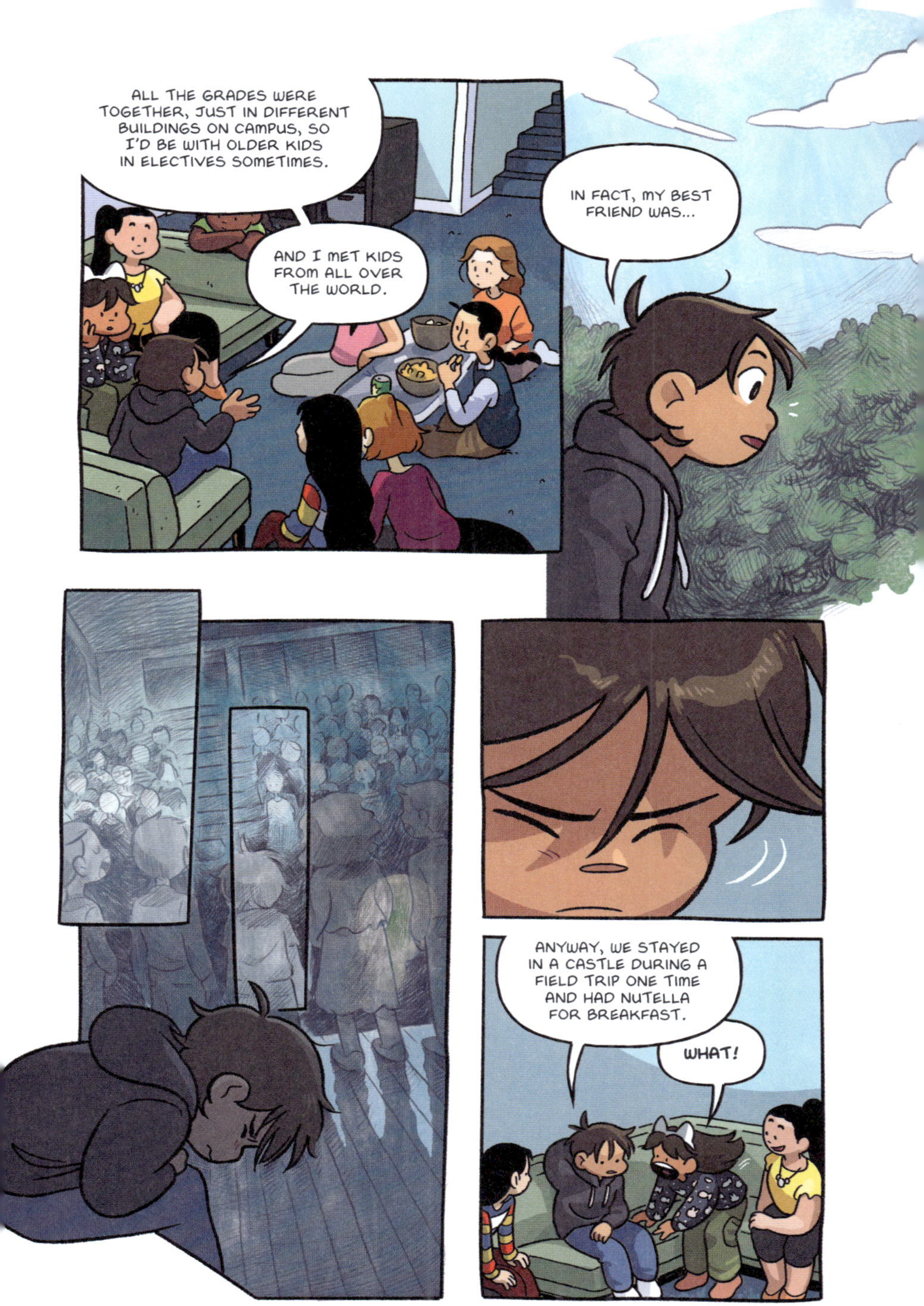
ALL THE GRADES WERE TOGETHER, JUST IN DIFFERENT BUILDINGS ON CAMPUS, SO I'D BE WITH OLDER KIDS IN ELECTIVES SOMETIMES.
AND I MET KIDS FROM ALL OVER THE WORLD.
IN FACT, MY BEST FRIEND WAS...
ANYWAY, WE STAYED IN A CASTLE DURING A FIELD TRIP ONE TIME AND HAD NUTELLA FOR BREAKFAST.
WHAT!

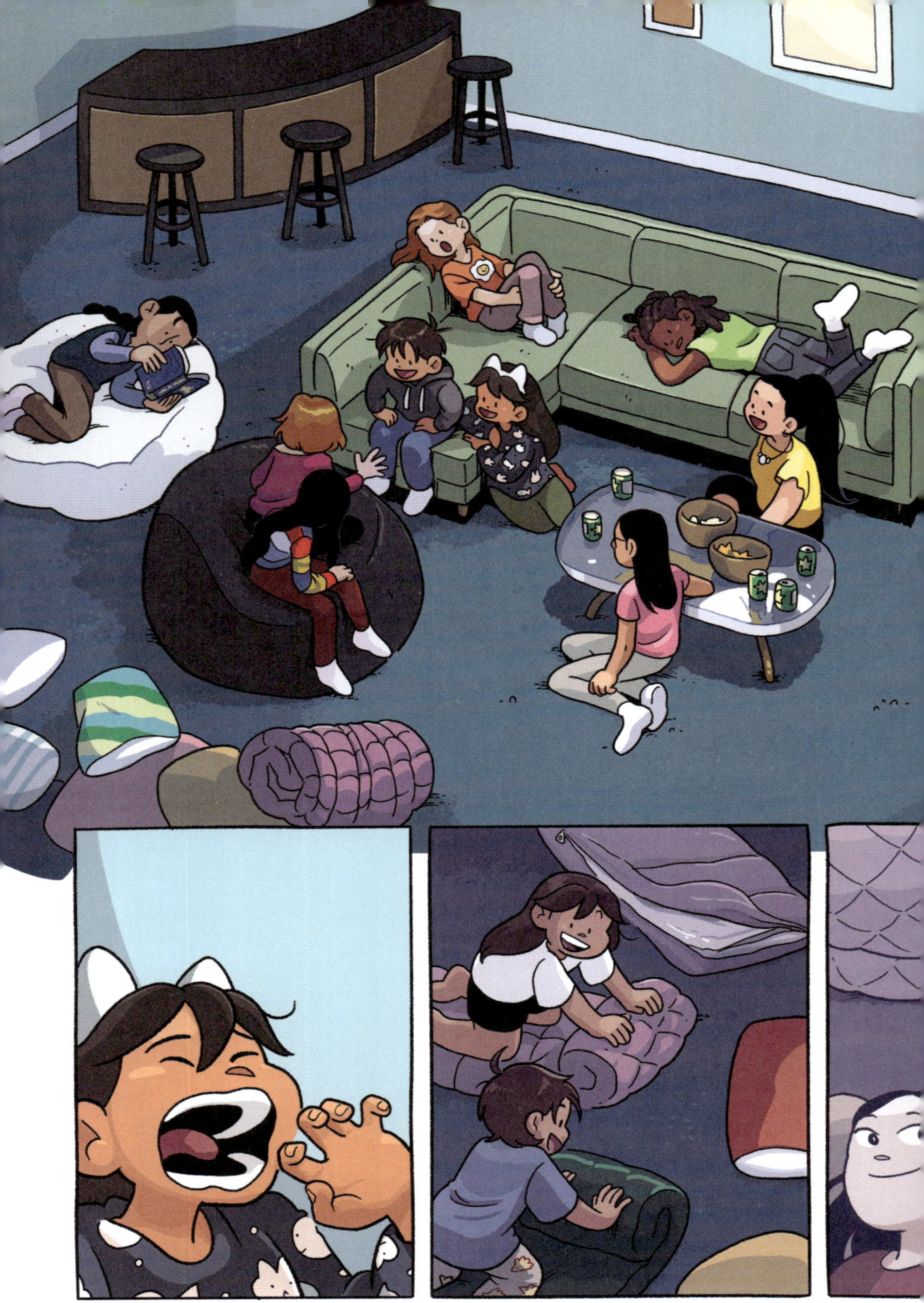

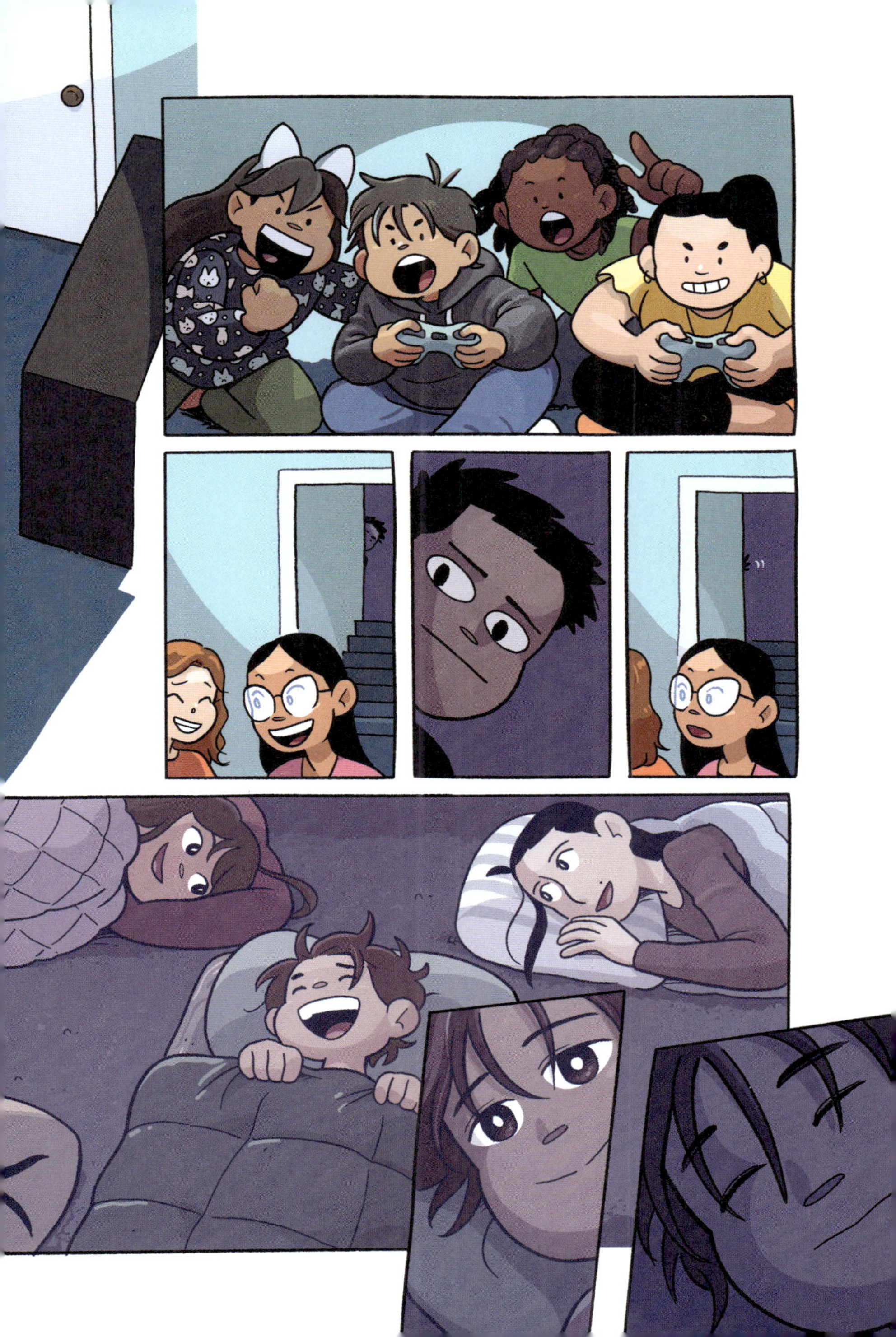

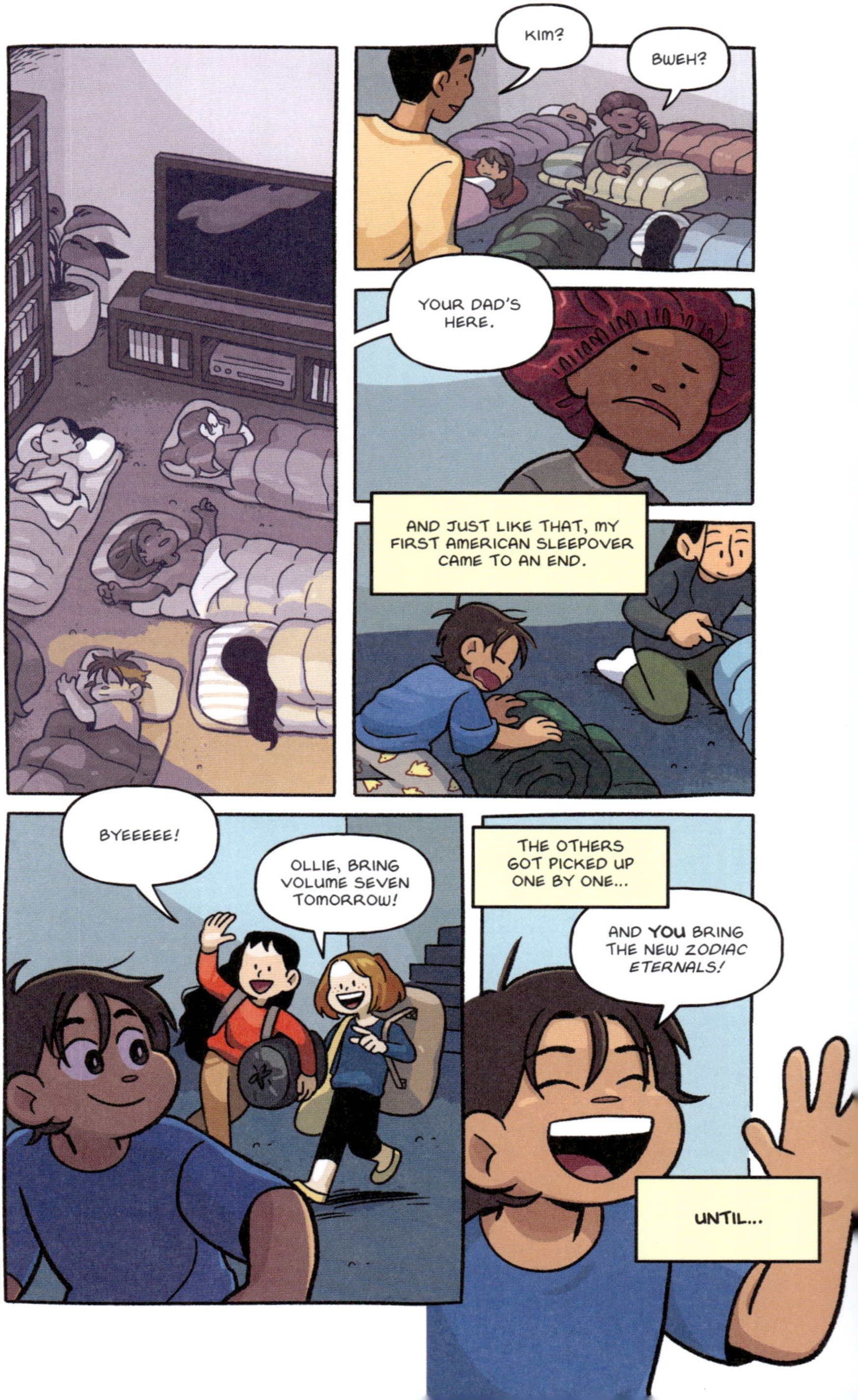
KIM?
BWEH?
YOUR DAD'S HERE.
AND JUST LIKE THAT, MY FIRST AMERICAN SLEEPOVER CAME TO AN END.
BYEEEEE!
OLLIE, BRING VOLUME SEVEN TOMORROW!
THE OTHERS GOT PICKED UP ONE BY ONE...
AND **YOU** BRING THE NEW *ZODIAC ETERNALS!*
UNTIL...

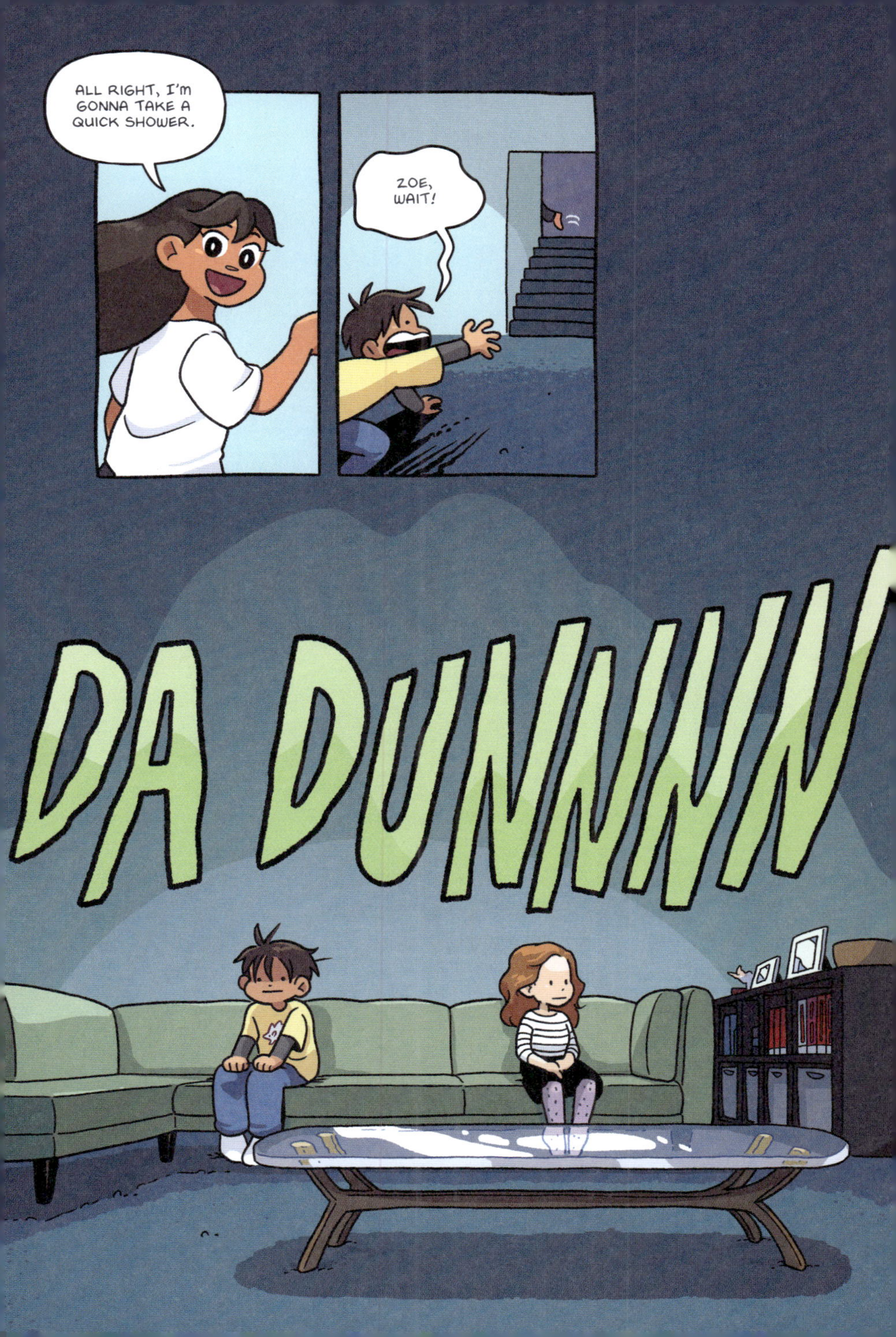
ALL RIGHT, I'M GONNA TAKE A QUICK SHOWER.
ZOE, WAIT!
DA DUNNNN

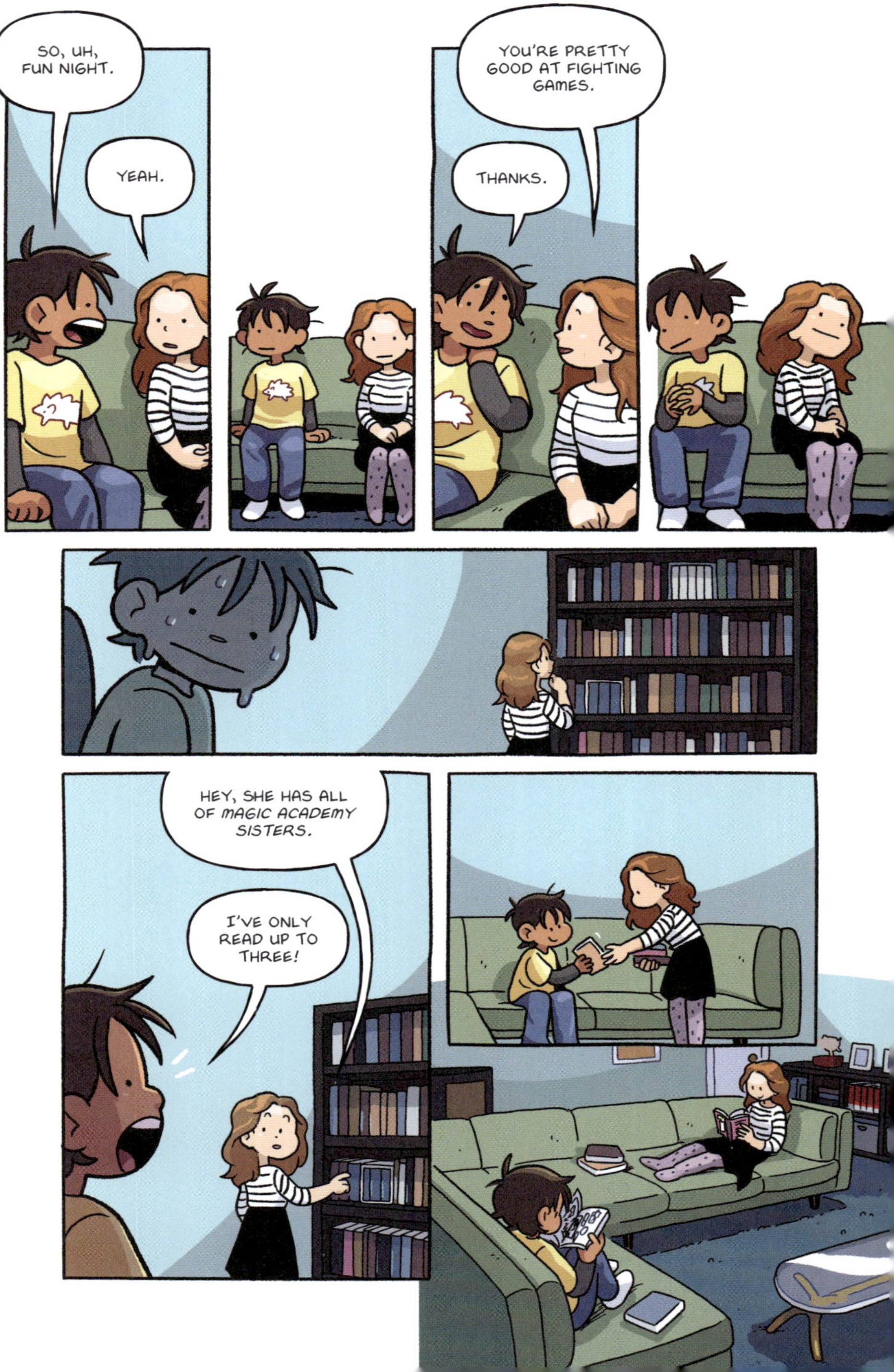
SO, UH, FUN NIGHT.
YEAH.
YOU'RE PRETTY GOOD AT FIGHTING GAMES.
THANKS.
HEY, SHE HAS ALL OF *MAGIC ACADEMY SISTERS*.
I'VE ONLY READ UP TO THREE!

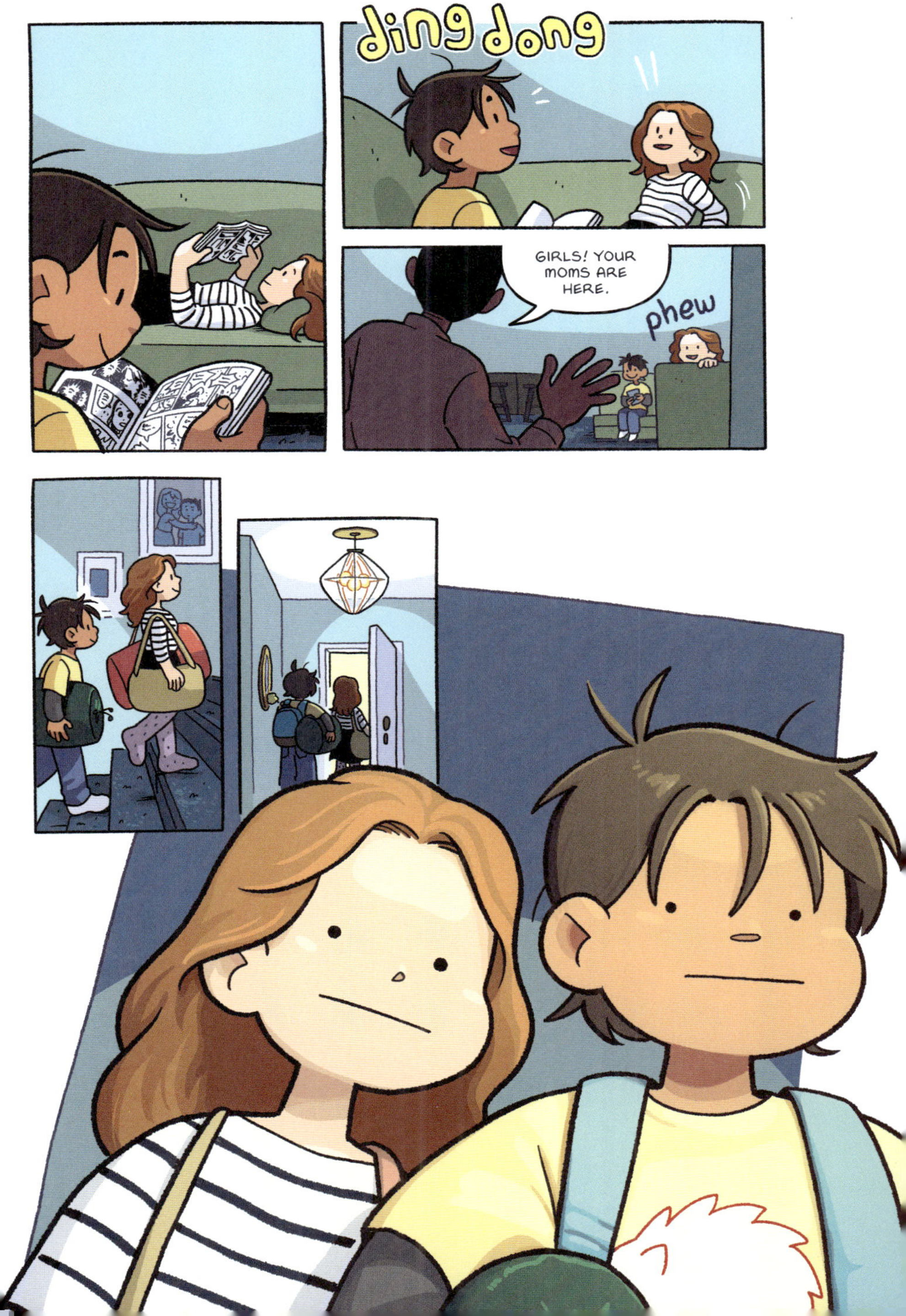
ding dong
GIRLS! YOUR MOMS ARE HERE.
phew

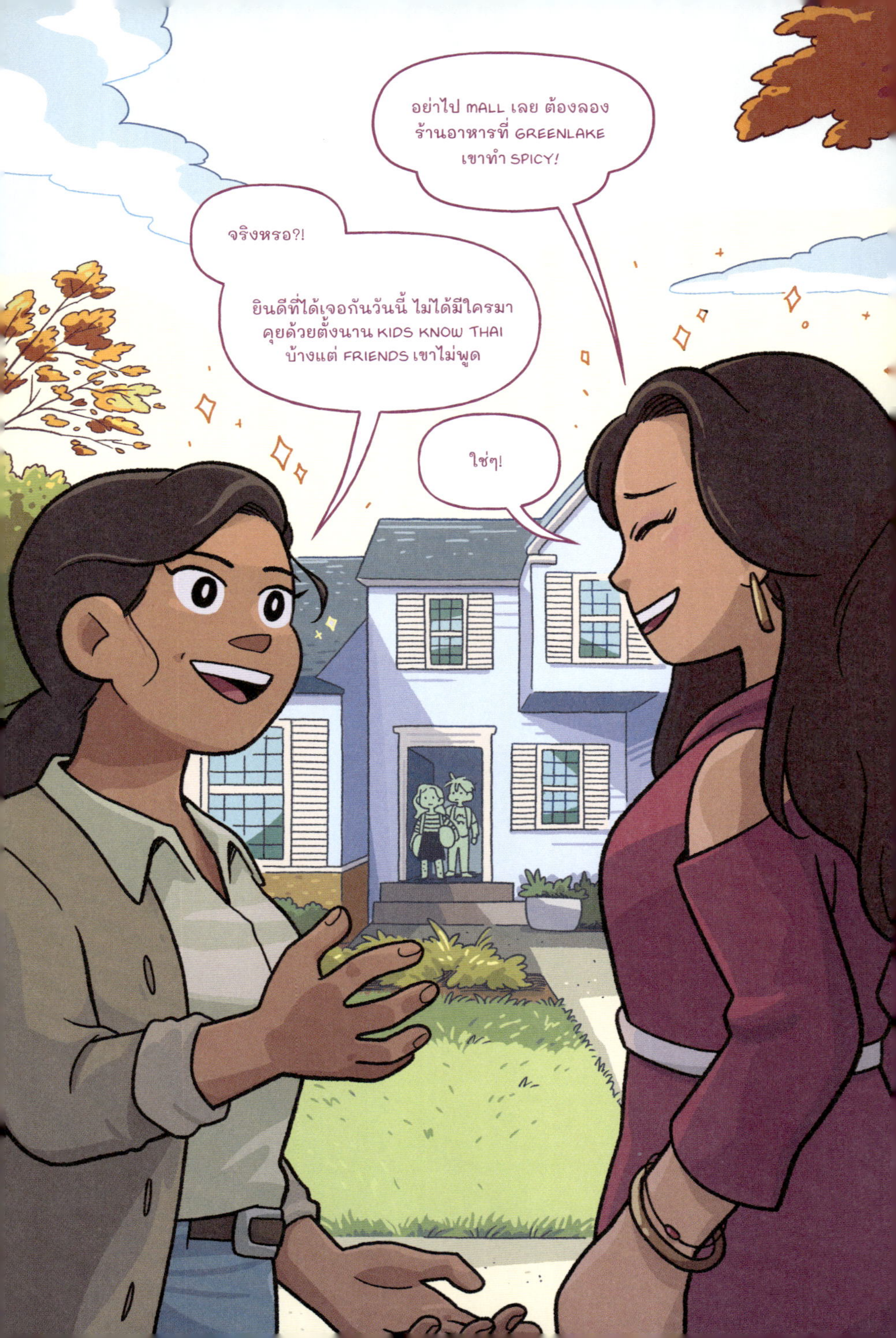
อย่าไป MALL เลย ต้องลอง ร้านอาหารที่ GREENLAKE เขาทำ SPICY!
จริงหรอ?!
ยินดีที่ได้เจอกันวันนี้ ไม่ได้มีใครมาคุยด้วยตั้งนาน KIDS KNOW THAI บ้างแต่ FRIENDS เขาไม่พูด
ใช่ๆ!

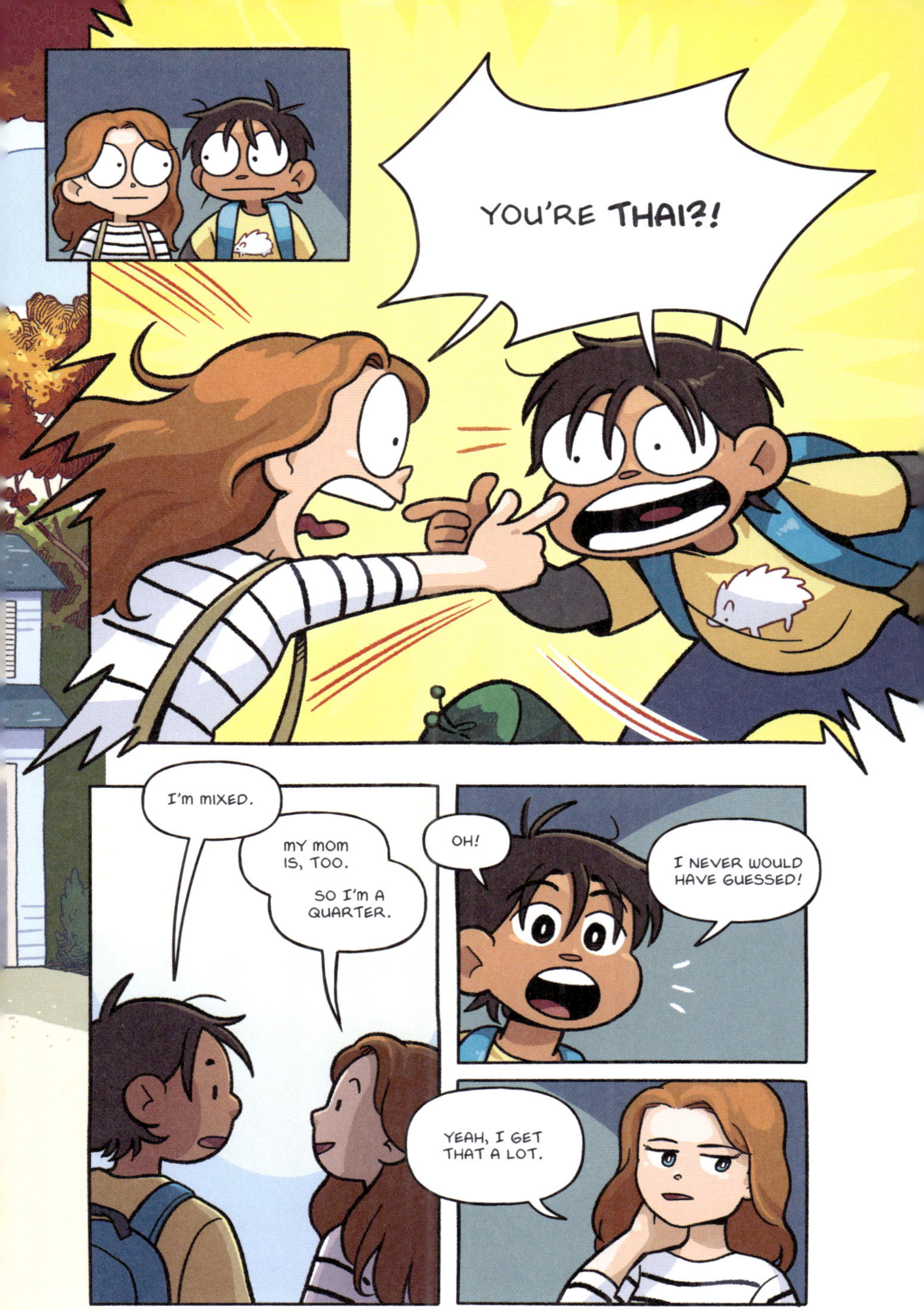
YOU'RE THAI?!
I'm MIXED.
MY MOM IS, TOO.
SO I'm A QUARTER.
OH!
I NEVER WOULD HAVE GUESSED!
YEAH, I GET THAT A LOT.

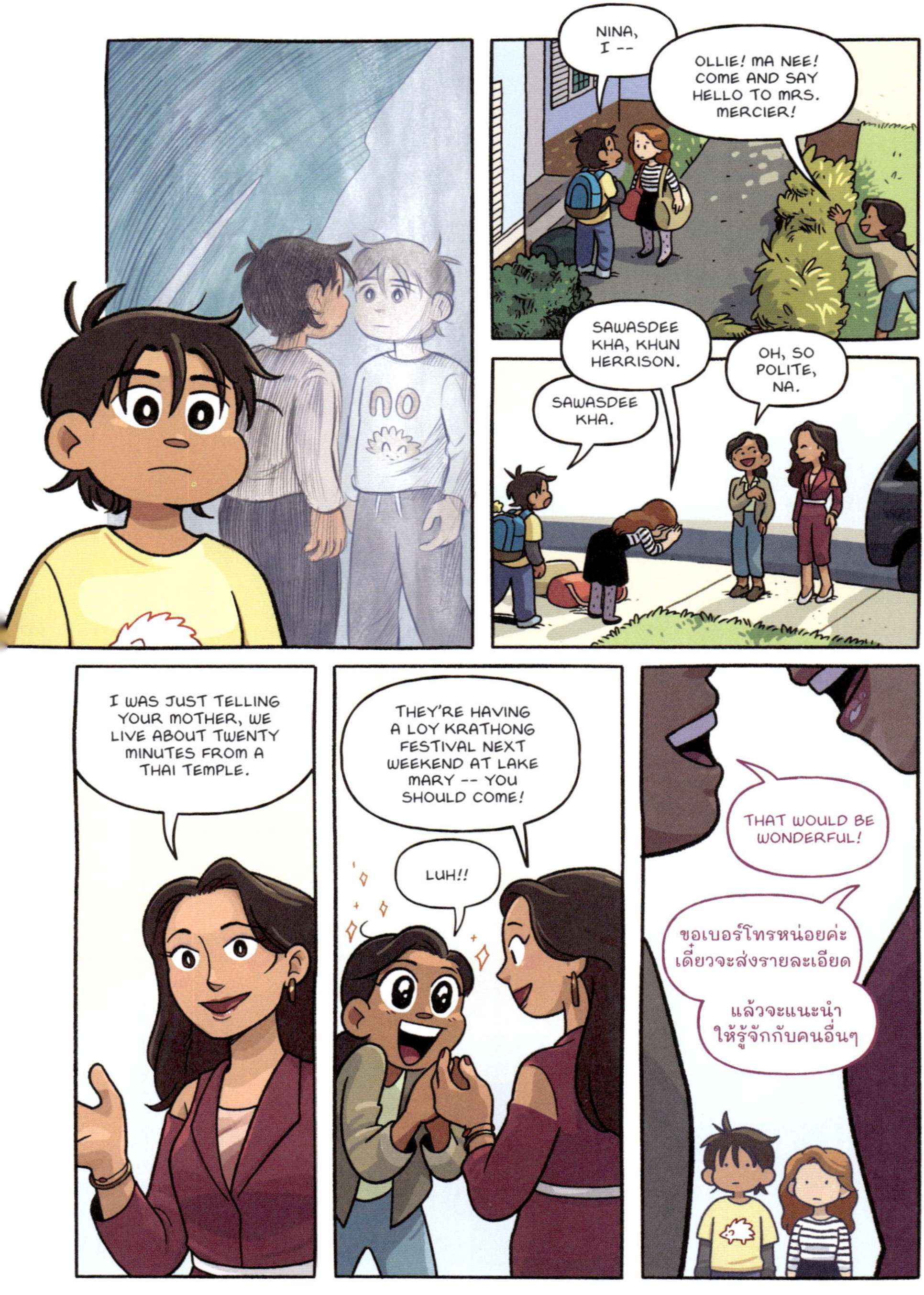
NINA, I --
OLLIE! MA NEE! COME AND SAY HELLO TO MRS. MERCIER!
SAWASDEE KHA, KHUN HERRISON.
SAWASDEE KHA.
OH, SO POLITE, NA.
I WAS JUST TELLING YOUR MOTHER, WE LIVE ABOUT TWENTY MINUTES FROM A THAI TEMPLE.
THEY'RE HAVING A LOY KRATHONG FESTIVAL NEXT WEEKEND AT LAKE MARY -- YOU SHOULD COME!
LUH!!
THAT WOULD BE WONDERFUL!
ขอเบอร์โทรหน่อยค่ะ เดี๋ยวจะส่งรายละเอียด
แล้วจะแนะนำ ให้รู้จักกับคนอื่นๆ

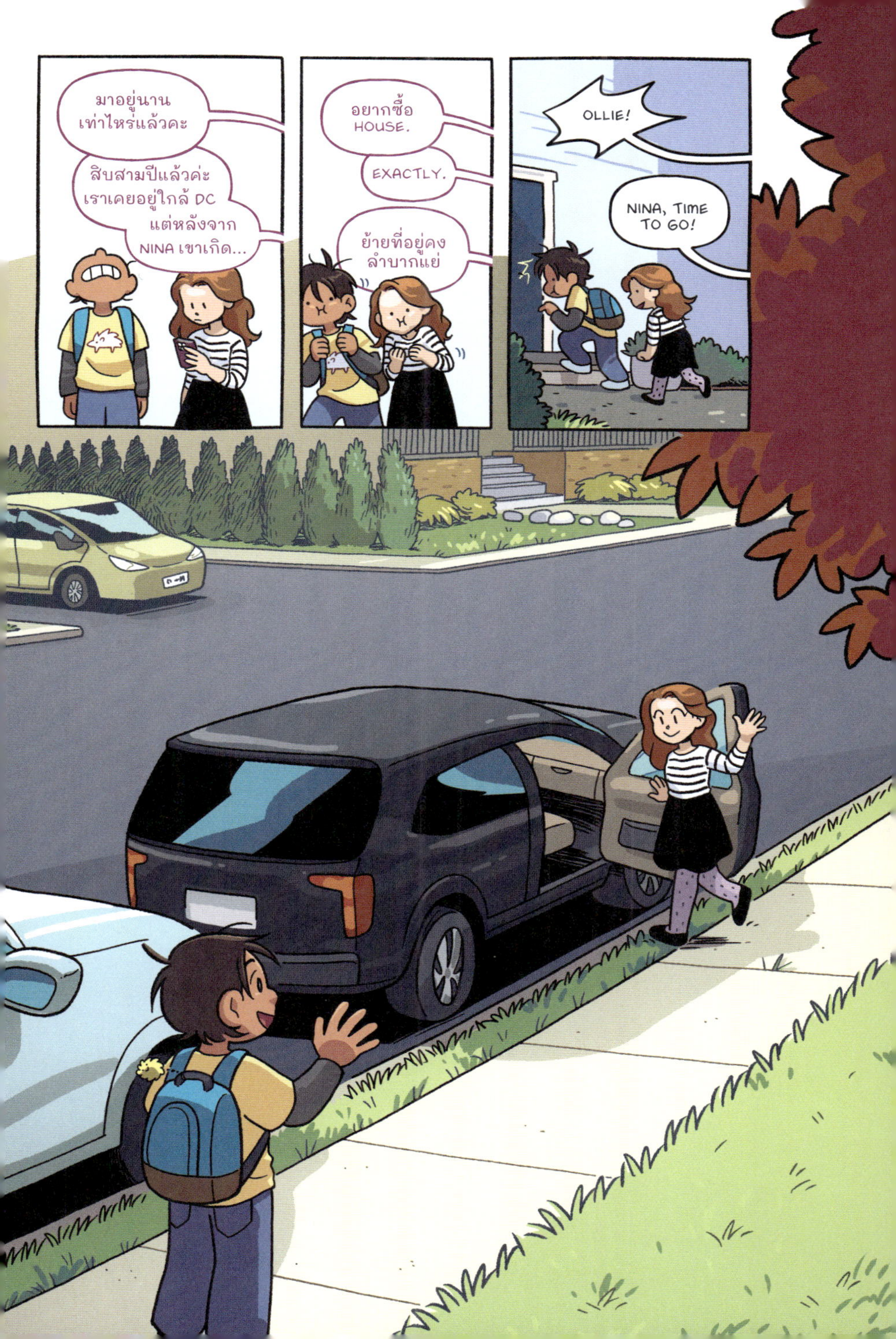
มาอยู่นาน เท่าไหร่แล้วคะ
สิบสามปีแล้วค่ะ เราเคยอยู่ใกล้ DC แต่หลังจาก NINA เขาเกิด...
อยากซื้อ HOUSE.
EXACTLY.
ย้ายที่อยู่คงลำบากแย่
OLLIE!
NINA, TIME TO GO!

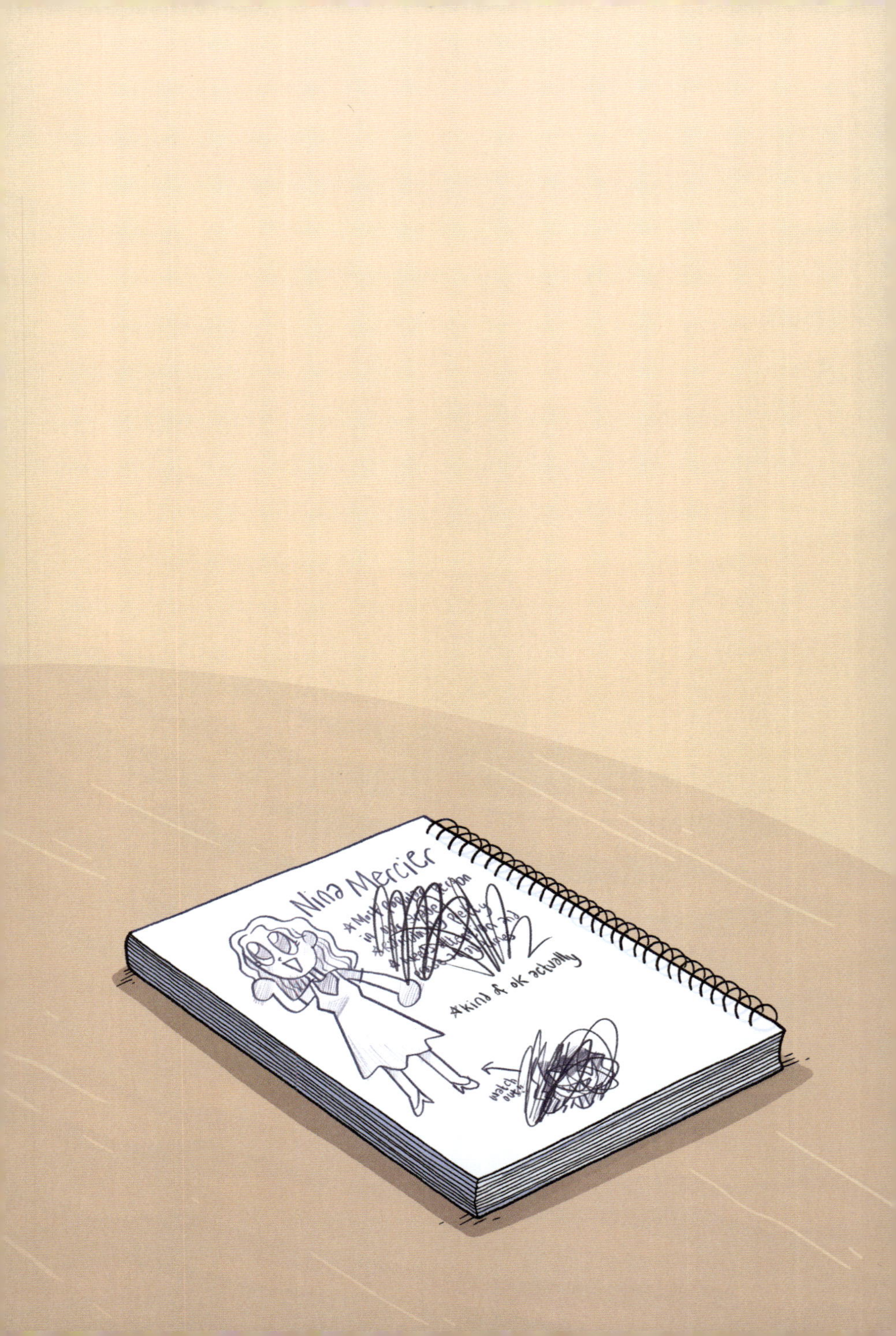
Nina Mercier
*kind & ok actually
watch out!

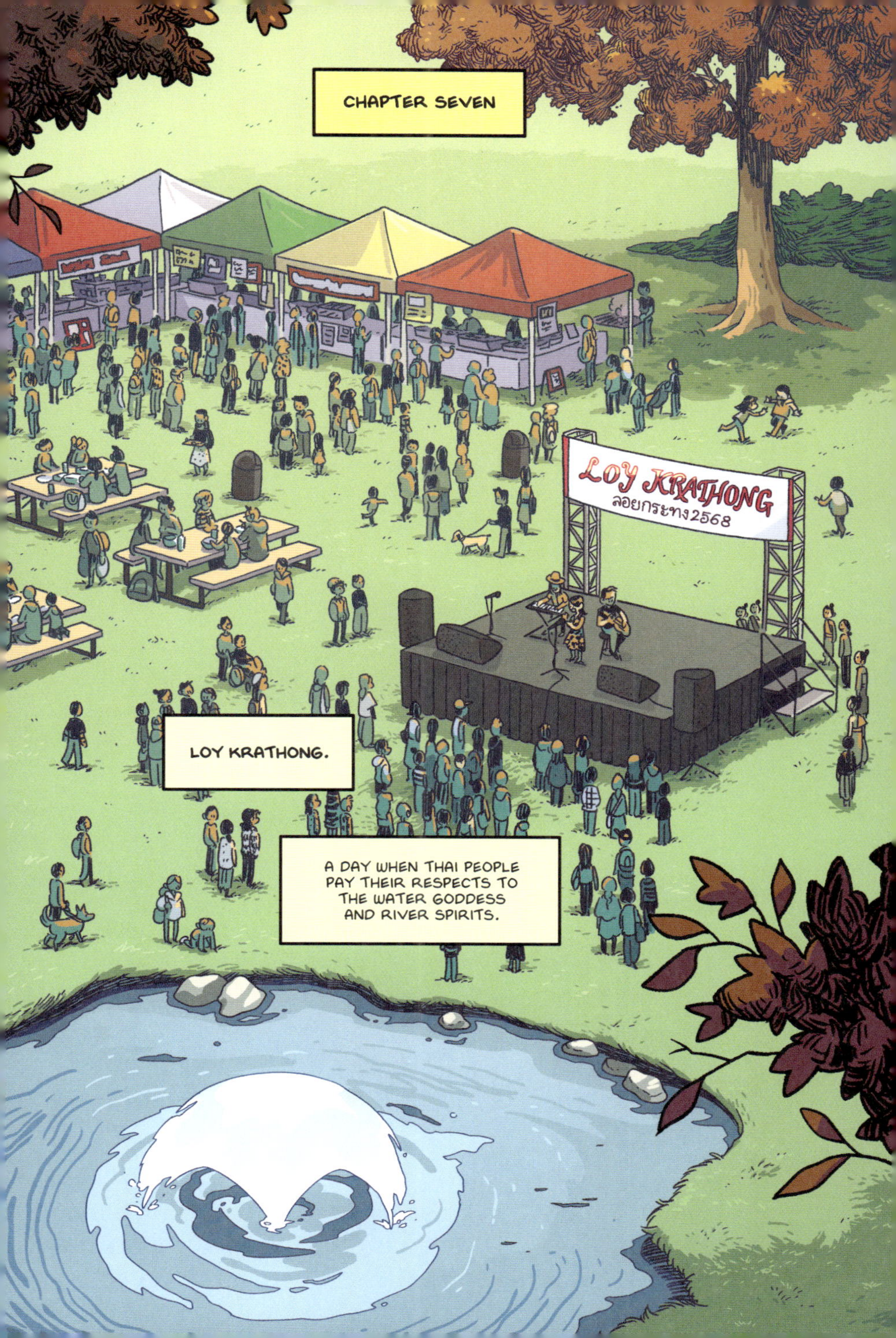
CHAPTER SEVEN
LOY KRATHONG
ลอยกระทง2568
LOY KRATHONG.
A DAY WHEN THAI PEOPLE PAY THEIR RESPECTS TO THE WATER GODDESS AND RIVER SPIRITS.

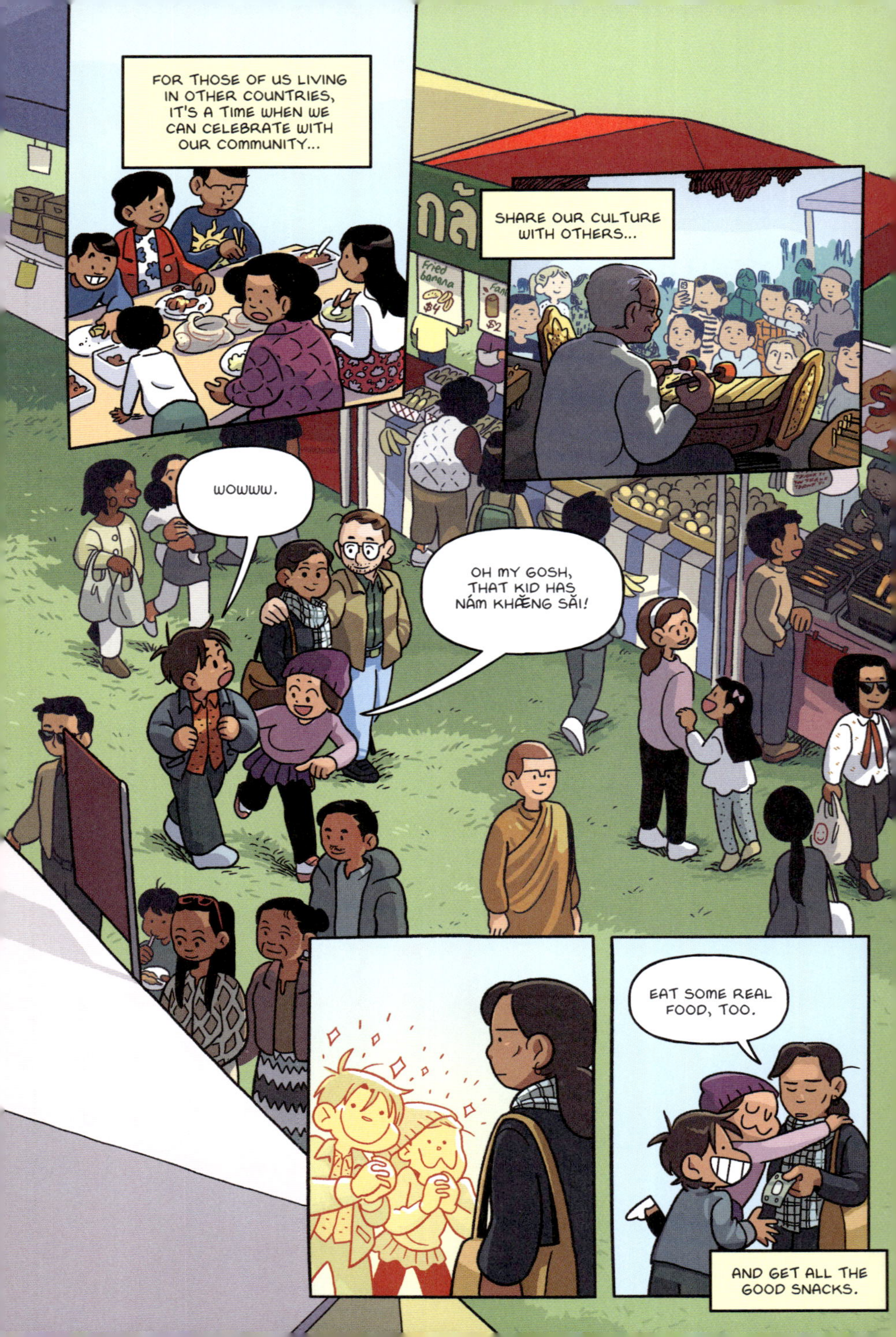
FOR THOSE OF US LIVING IN OTHER COUNTRIES, IT'S A TIME WHEN WE CAN CELEBRATE WITH OUR COMMUNITY...
SHARE OUR CULTURE WITH OTHERS...
Fried banana
$4
$2
WOWWW.
OH MY GOSH, THAT KID HAS NÁM KHĂENG SĂI!
EAT SOME REAL FOOD, TOO.
AND GET ALL THE GOOD SNACKS.

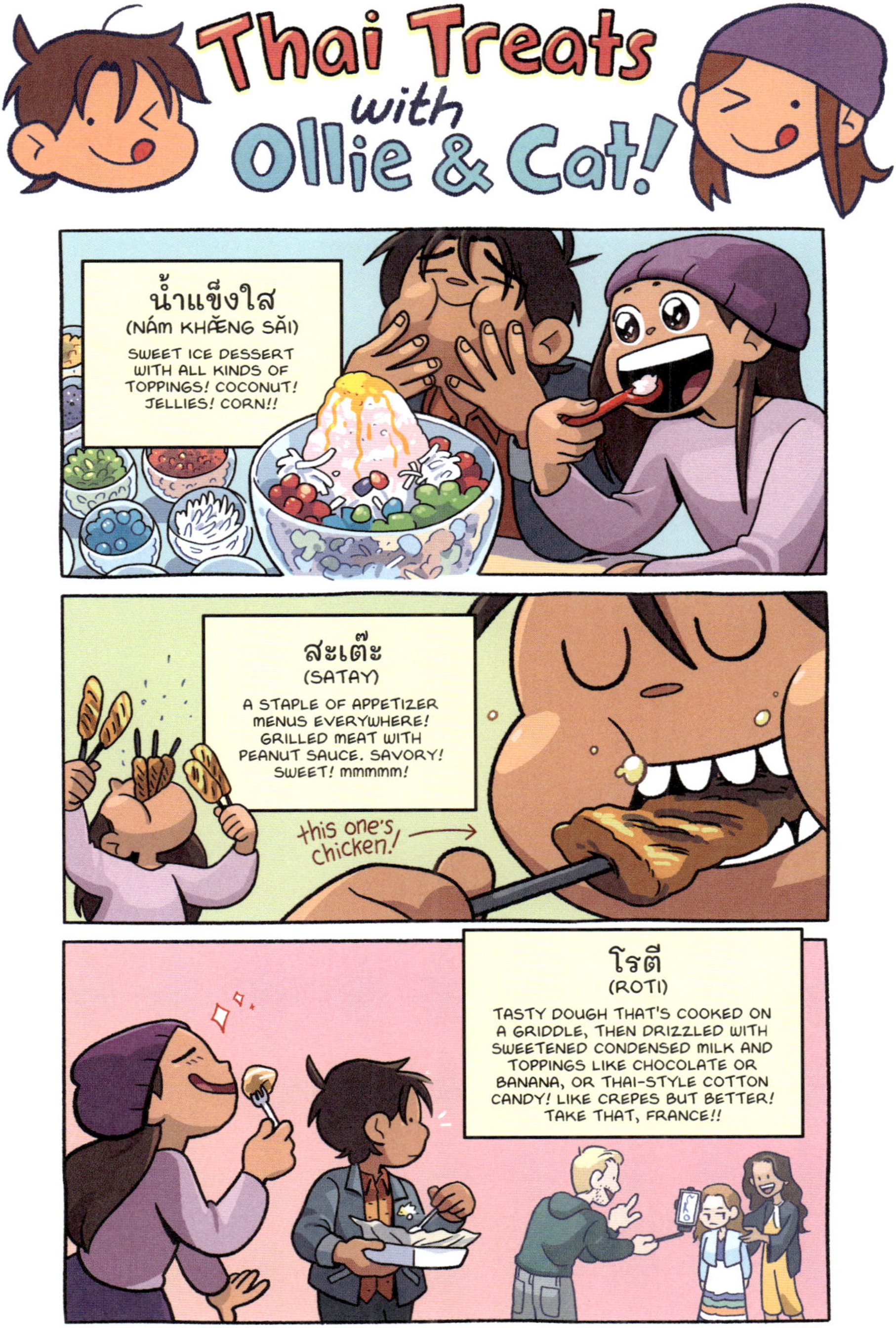
Thai Treats with Ollie & Cat!
น้ำแข็งใส
(NÁM KHĚNG SǍI)
SWEET ICE DESSERT WITH ALL KINDS OF TOPPINGS! COCONUT! JELLIES! CORN!!
สะเต๊ะ
(SATAY)
A STAPLE OF APPETIZER MENUS EVERYWHERE! GRILLED MEAT WITH PEANUT SAUCE. SAVORY! SWEET! mmmmm!
this one's chicken!
โรตี
(ROTI)
TASTY DOUGH THAT'S COOKED ON A GRIDDLE, THEN DRIZZLED WITH SWEETENED CONDENSED MILK AND TOPPINGS LIKE CHOCOLATE OR BANANA, OR THAI-STYLE COTTON CANDY! LIKE CREPES BUT BETTER! TAKE THAT, FRANCE!!

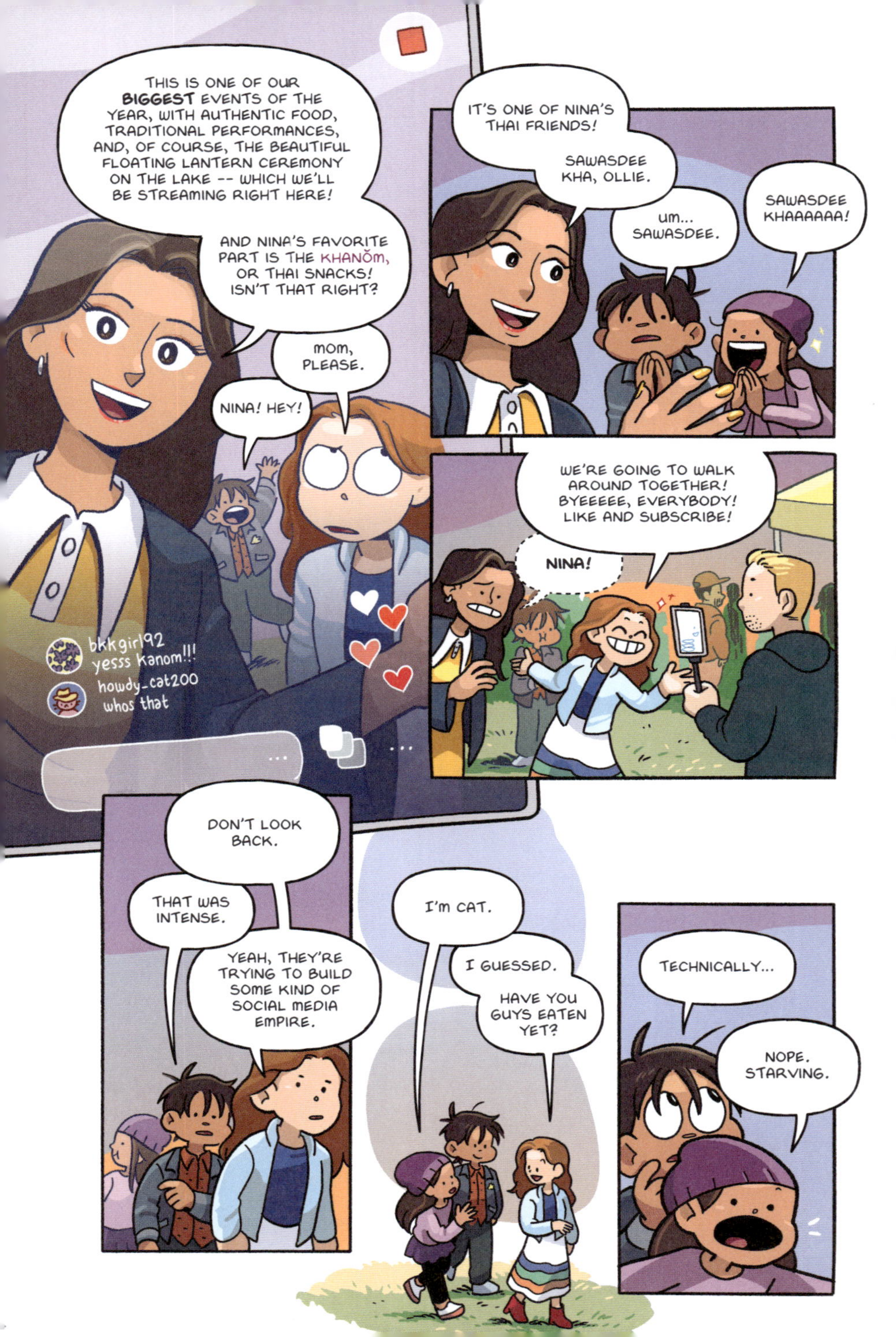
THIS IS ONE OF OUR **BIGGEST** EVENTS OF THE YEAR, WITH AUTHENTIC FOOD, TRADITIONAL PERFORMANCES, AND, OF COURSE, THE BEAUTIFUL FLOATING LANTERN CEREMONY ON THE LAKE -- WHICH WE'LL BE STREAMING RIGHT HERE!
AND NINA'S FAVORITE PART IS THE KHANŎM, OR THAI SNACKS! ISN'T THAT RIGHT?
MOM, PLEASE.
NINA! HEY!
bkkgirl92
yesss kanom!!!
howdy_cat200
whos that
IT'S ONE OF NINA'S THAI FRIENDS!
SAWASDEE KHA, OLLIE.
UM... SAWASDEE.
SAWASDEE KHAAAAAA!
WE'RE GOING TO WALK AROUND TOGETHER! BYEEEEE, EVERYBODY! LIKE AND SUBSCRIBE!
NINA!
DON'T LOOK BACK.
THAT WAS INTENSE.
YEAH, THEY'RE TRYING TO BUILD SOME KIND OF SOCIAL MEDIA EMPIRE.
I'M CAT.
I GUESSED.
HAVE YOU GUYS EATEN YET?
TECHNICALLY...
NOPE. STARVING.

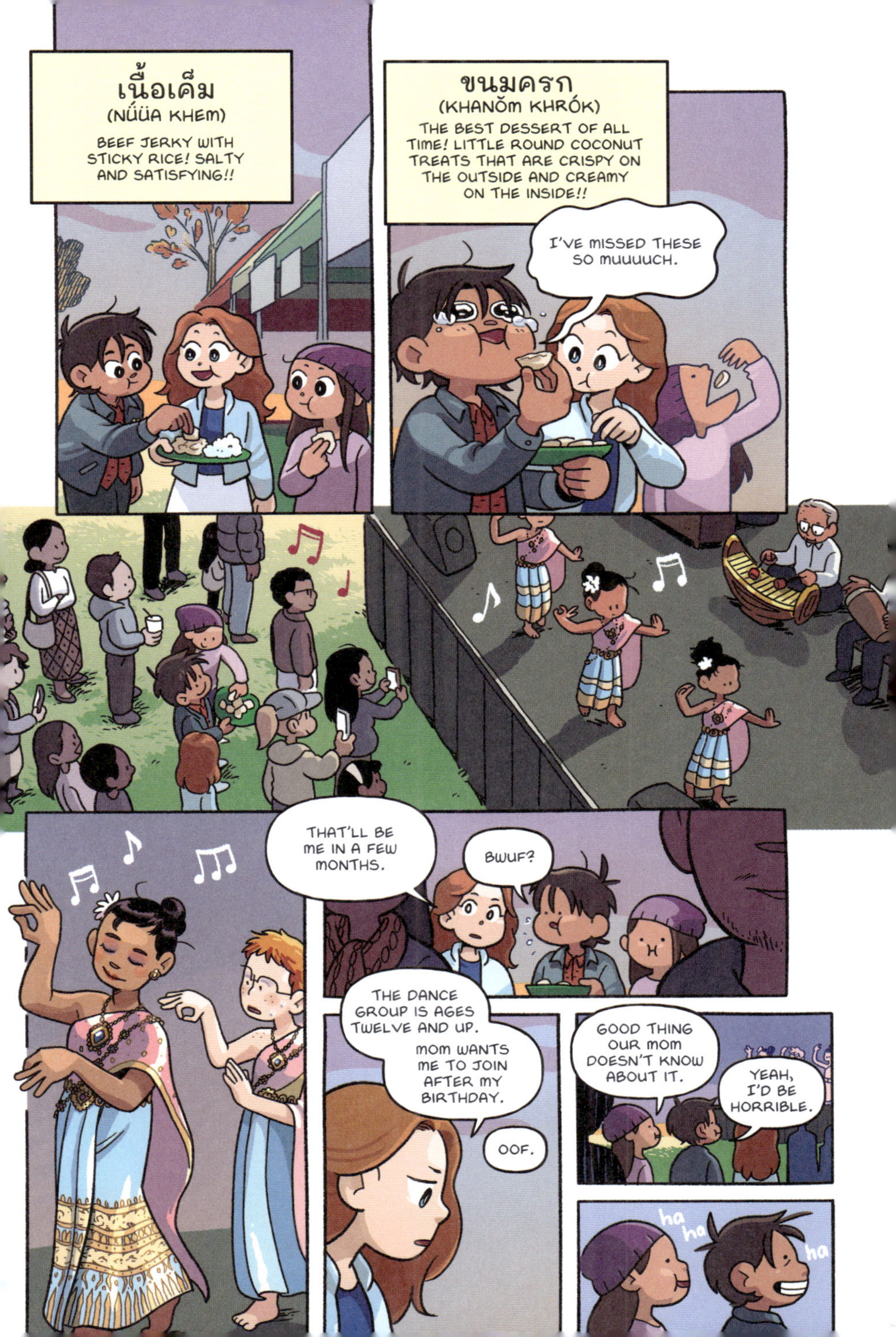

เนื้อเค็ม
(NŨÜA KHEM)
BEEF JERKY WITH STICKY RICE! SALTY AND SATISFYING!!
ขนมครก
(KHANŎM KHRÓK)
THE BEST DESSERT OF ALL TIME! LITTLE ROUND COCONUT TREATS THAT ARE CRISPY ON THE OUTSIDE AND CREAMY ON THE INSIDE!!
I'VE MISSED THESE SO MUUUUCH.
THAT'LL BE ME IN A FEW MONTHS.
BWUF?
THE DANCE GROUP IS AGES TWELVE AND UP.
MOM WANTS ME TO JOIN AFTER MY BIRTHDAY.
OOF.
GOOD THING OUR MOM DOESN'T KNOW ABOUT IT.
YEAH, I'D BE HORRIBLE.
ha ha
ha

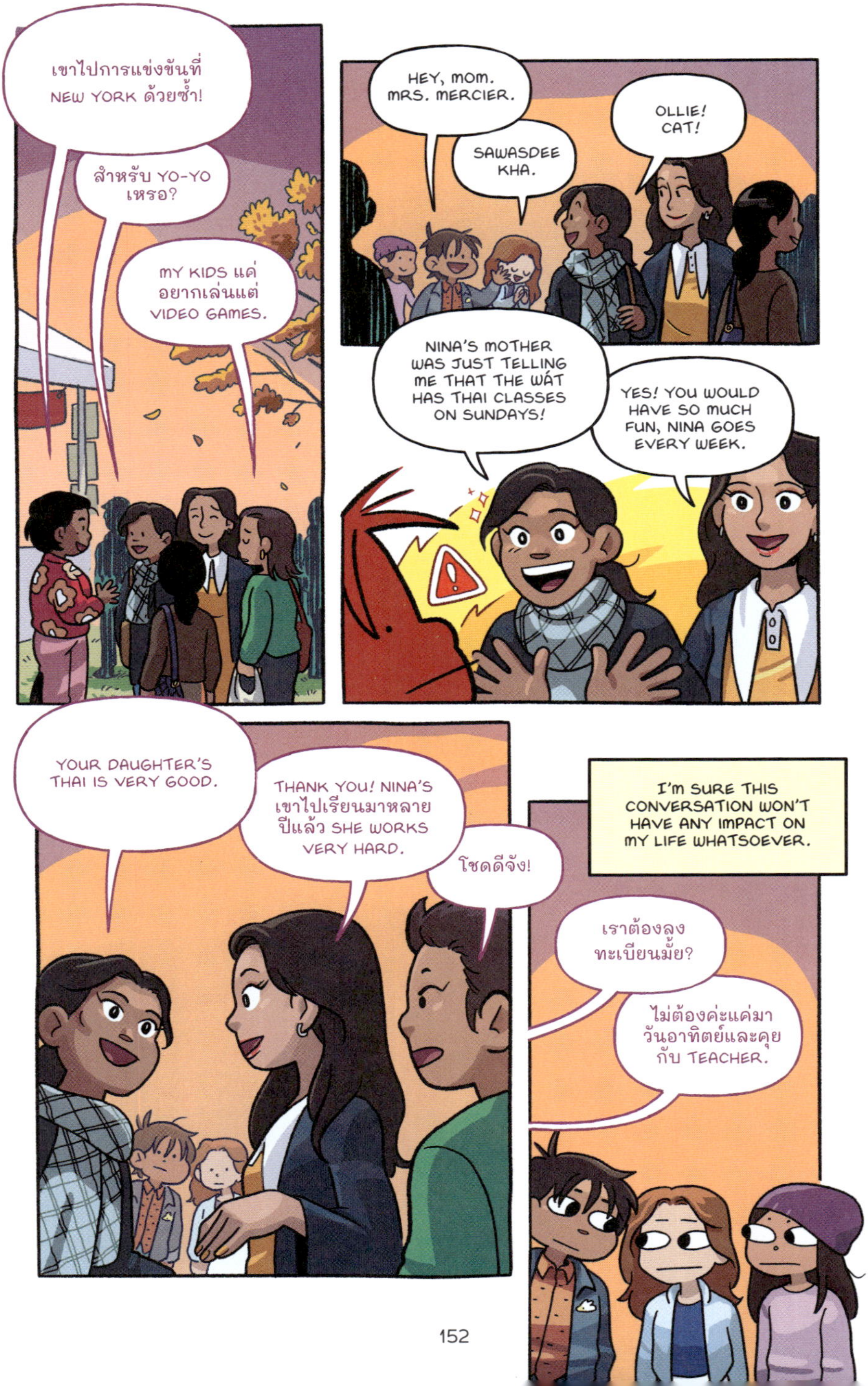

เขาไปการแข่งขันที่ NEW YORK ด้วยซ้ำ!
สำหรับ YO-YO เหรอ?
MY KIDS แค่ อยากเล่นแต่ VIDEO GAMES.
HEY, MOM. MRS. MERCIER.
SAWASDEE KHA.
OLLIE! CAT!
NINA'S MOTHER WAS JUST TELLING ME THAT THE WÁT HAS THAI CLASSES ON SUNDAYS!
YES! YOU WOULD HAVE SO MUCH FUN, NINA GOES EVERY WEEK.
YOUR DAUGHTER'S THAI IS VERY GOOD.
THANK YOU! NINA'S เขาไปเรียนมาหลายปีแล้ว SHE WORKS VERY HARD.
โชคดีจัง!
I'M SURE THIS CONVERSATION WON'T HAVE ANY IMPACT ON MY LIFE WHATSOEVER.
เราต้องลงทะเบียนมั้ย?
ไม่ต้องค่ะแค่มา วันอาทิตย์และคุย กับ TEACHER.

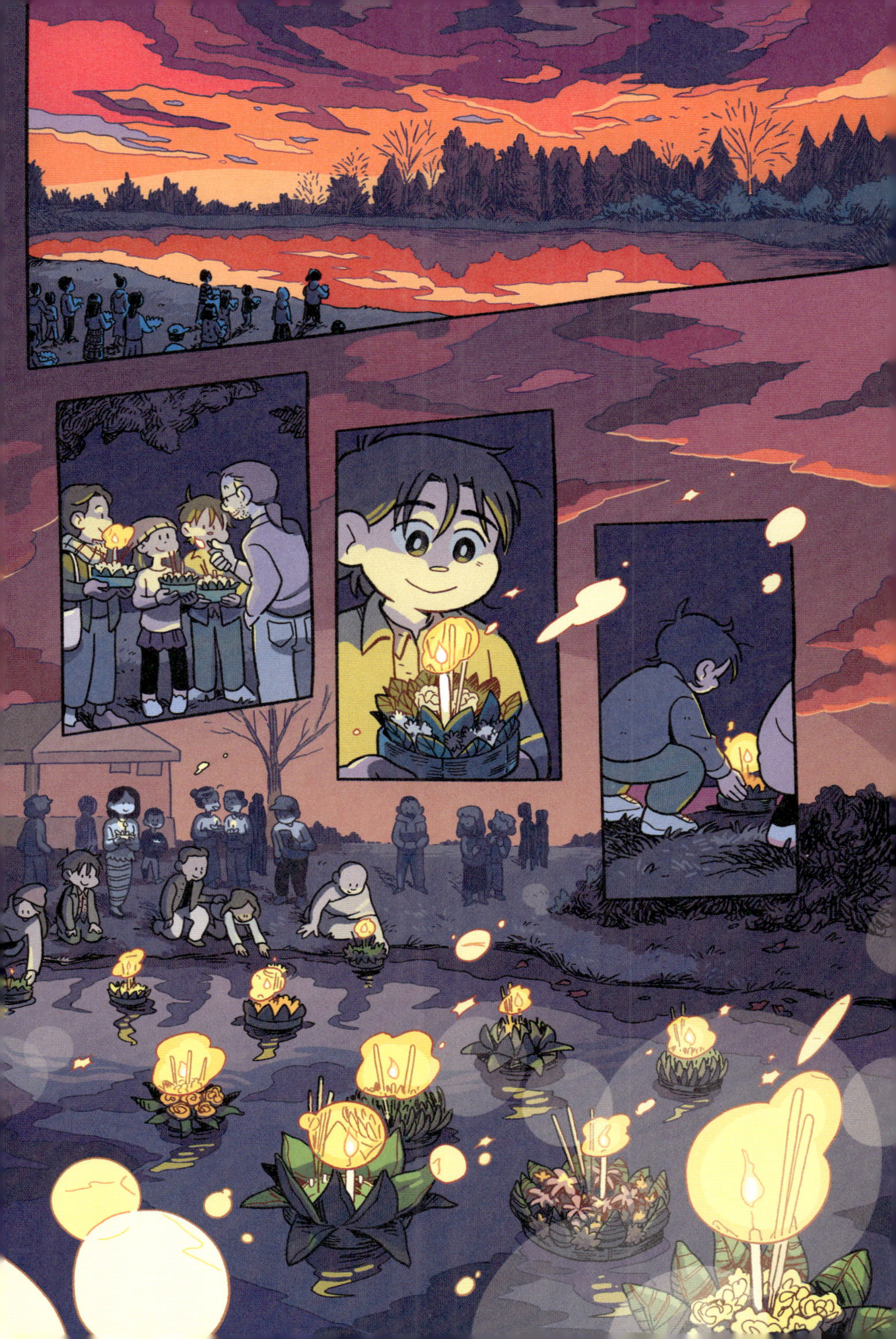

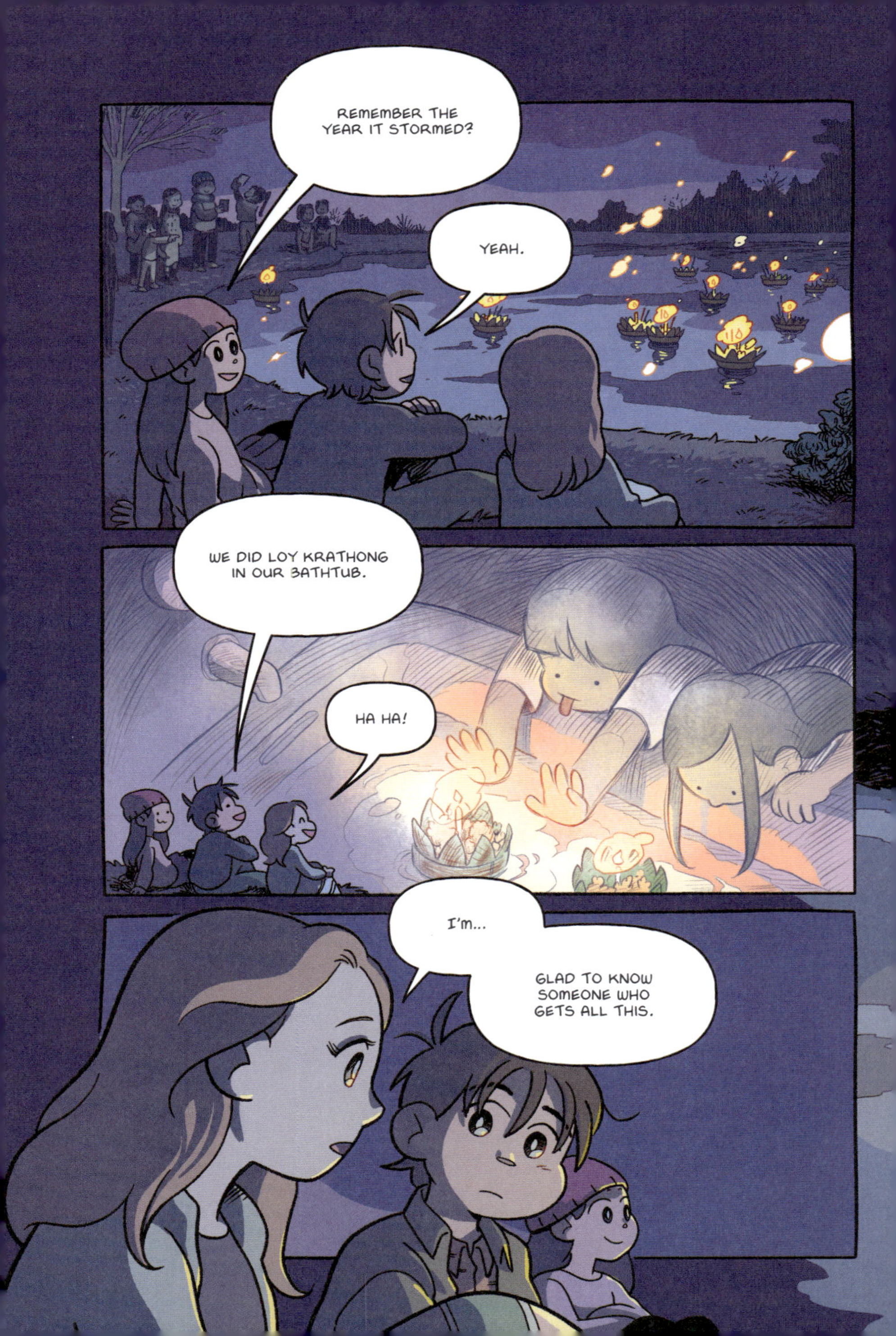
REMEMBER THE YEAR IT STORMED?
YEAH.
WE DID LOY KRATHONG IN OUR BATHTUB.
HA HA!
I'm...
GLAD TO KNOW SOMEONE WHO GETS ALL THIS.

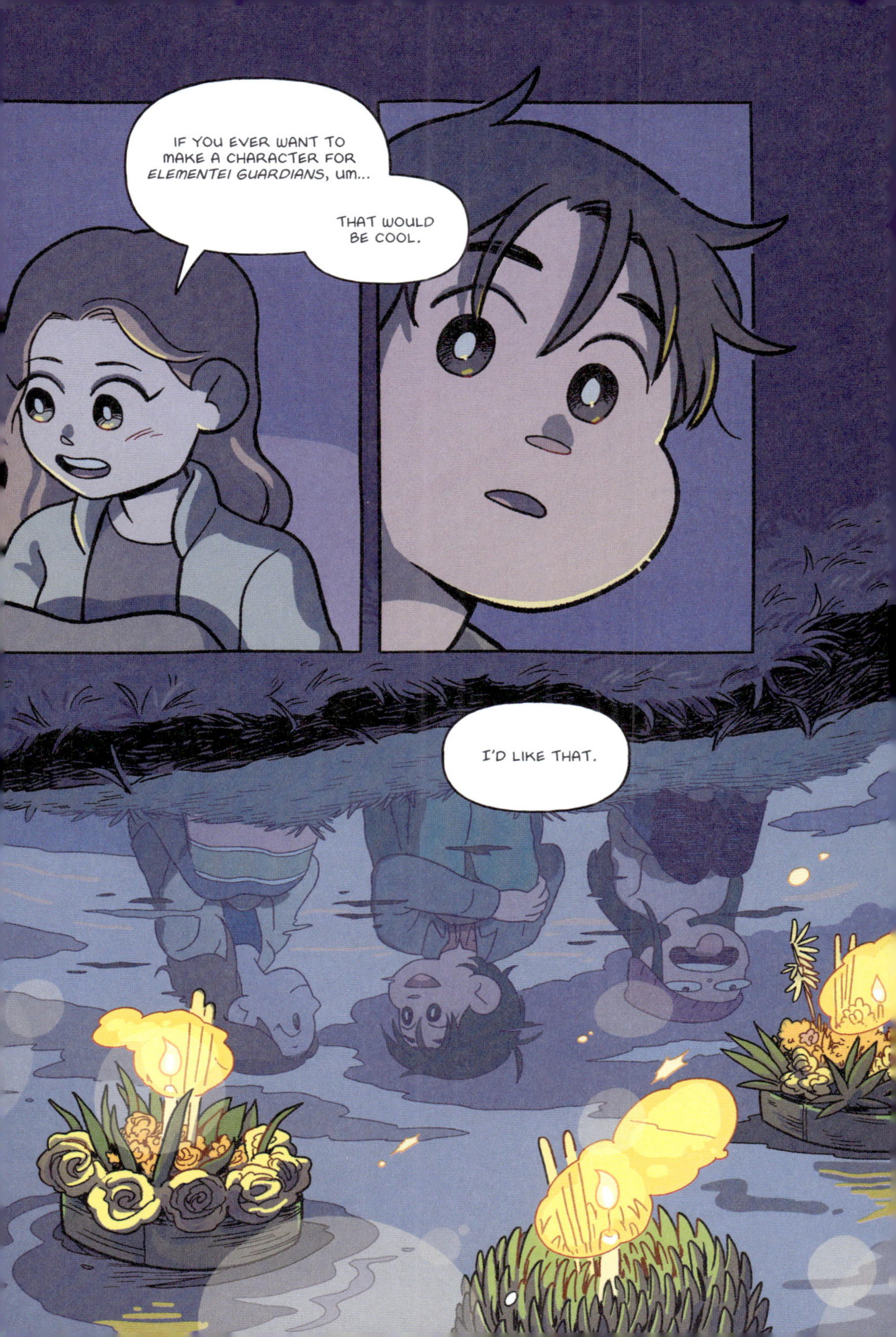
IF YOU EVER WANT TO MAKE A CHARACTER FOR ELEMENTEI GUARDIANS, um...
THAT WOULD BE COOL.
I'D LIKE THAT.

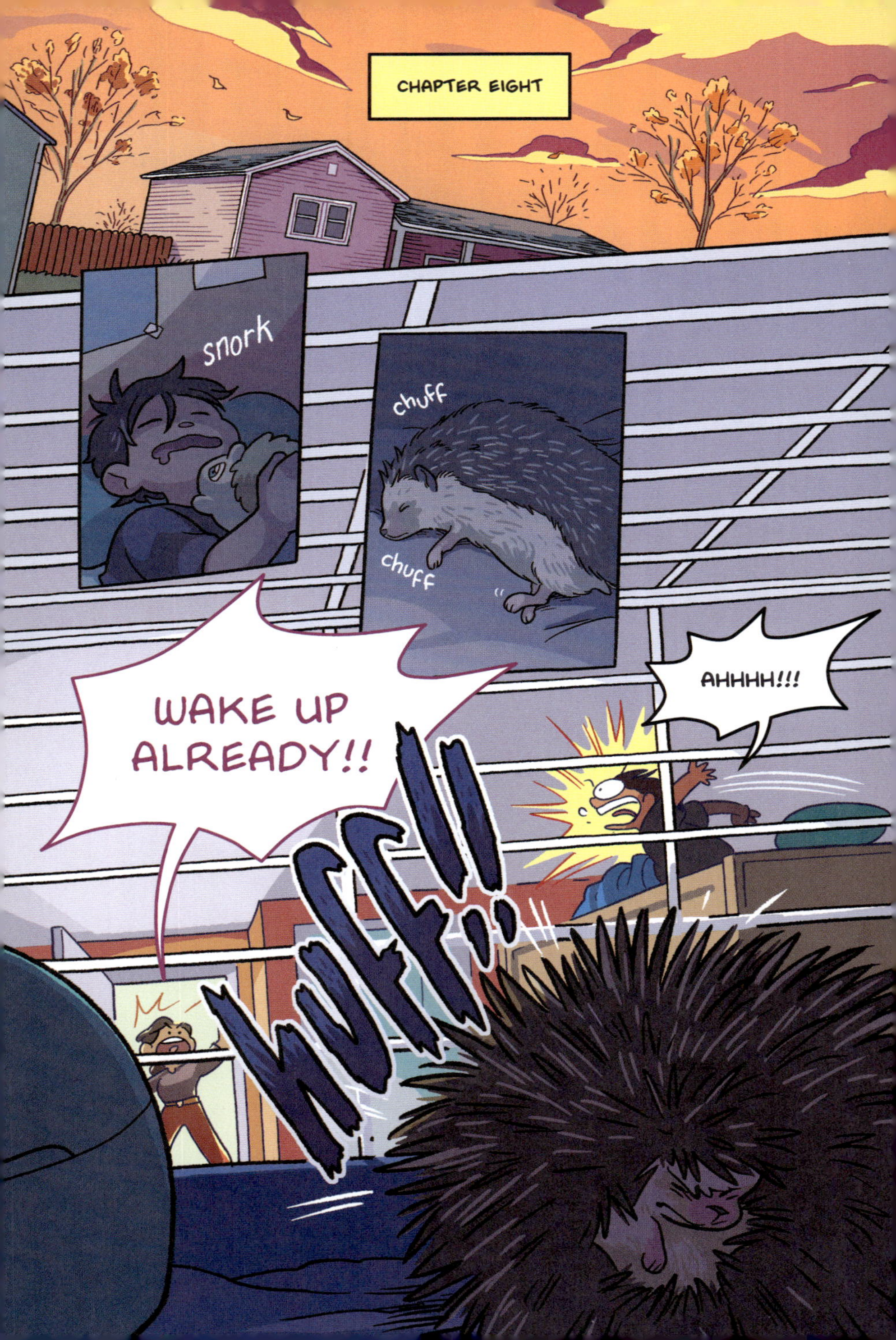
CHAPTER EIGHT
snork
chuff
chuff
WAKE UP ALREADY!!
HUFF!!
AHHHH!!!

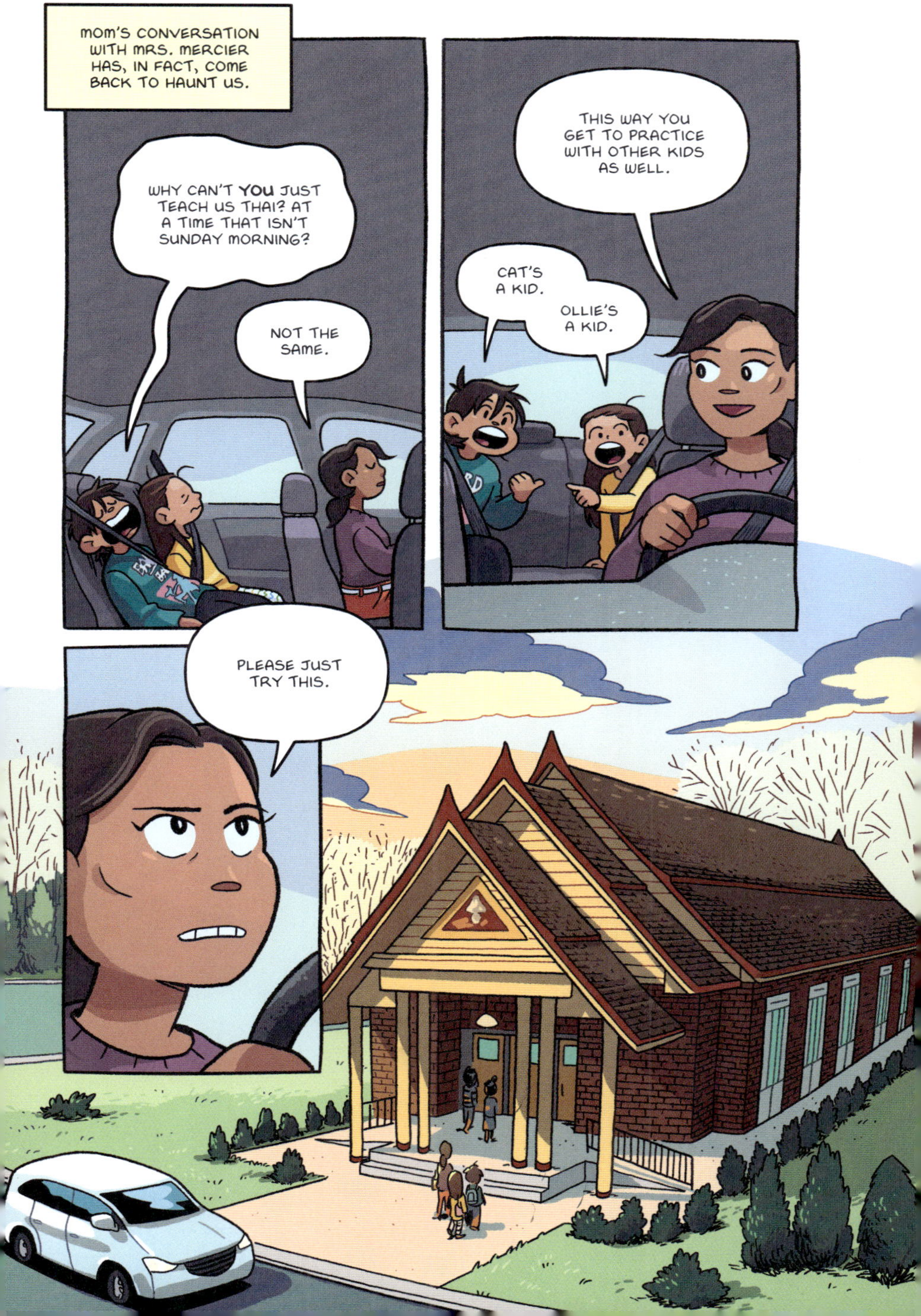
MOM'S CONVERSATION WITH MRS. MERCIER HAS, IN FACT, COME BACK TO HAUNT US.
WHY CAN'T **YOU** JUST TEACH US THAI? AT A TIME THAT ISN'T SUNDAY MORNING?
NOT THE SAME.
THIS WAY YOU GET TO PRACTICE WITH OTHER KIDS AS WELL.
CAT'S A KID.
OLLIE'S A KID.
PLEASE JUST TRY THIS.

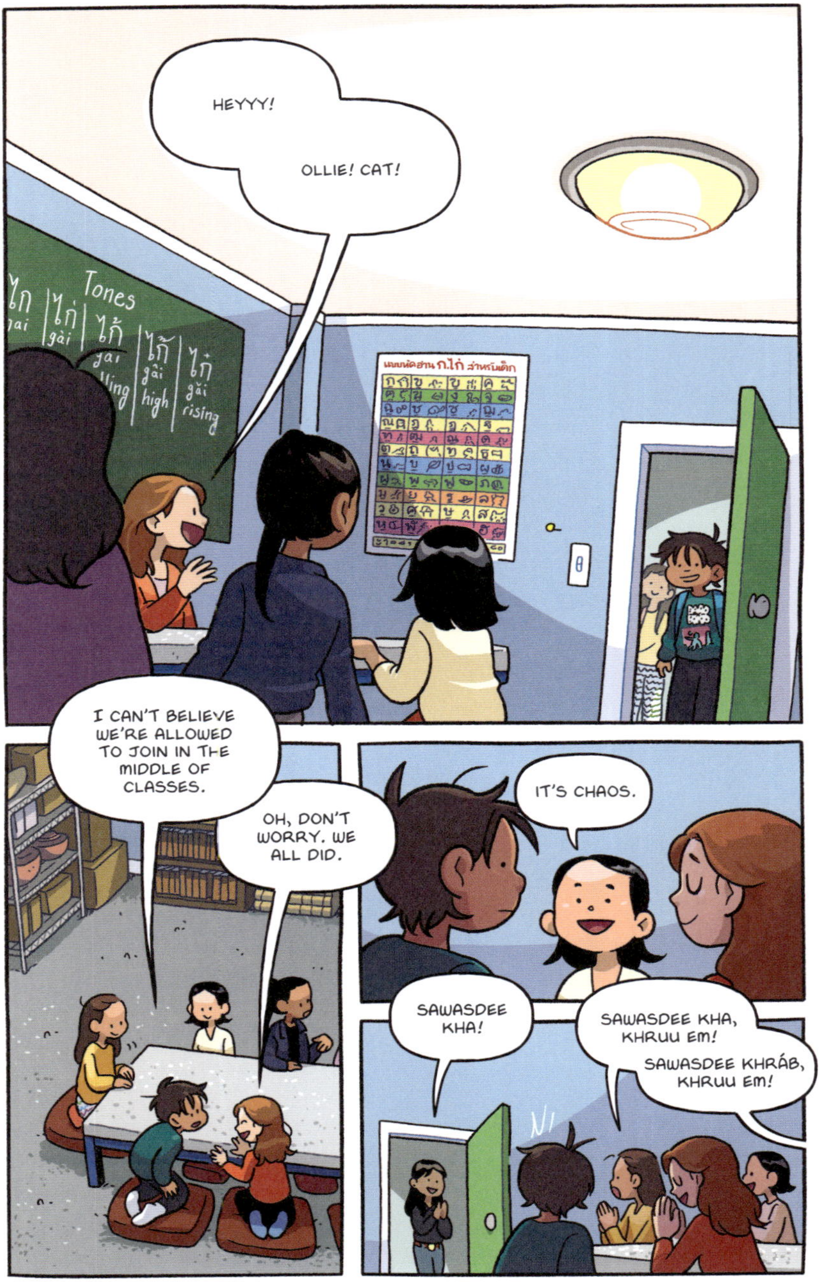
Tones
ไก่ gài
ไก๊ gâi high
ไก๋ găi rising
HEYYY!
OLLIE! CAT!
I CAN'T BELIEVE WE'RE ALLOWED TO JOIN IN THE MIDDLE OF CLASSES.
OH, DON'T WORRY. WE ALL DID.
IT'S CHAOS.
SAWASDEE KHA!
SAWASDEE KHA, KHRUU EM!
SAWASDEE KHRÁB, KHRUU EM!

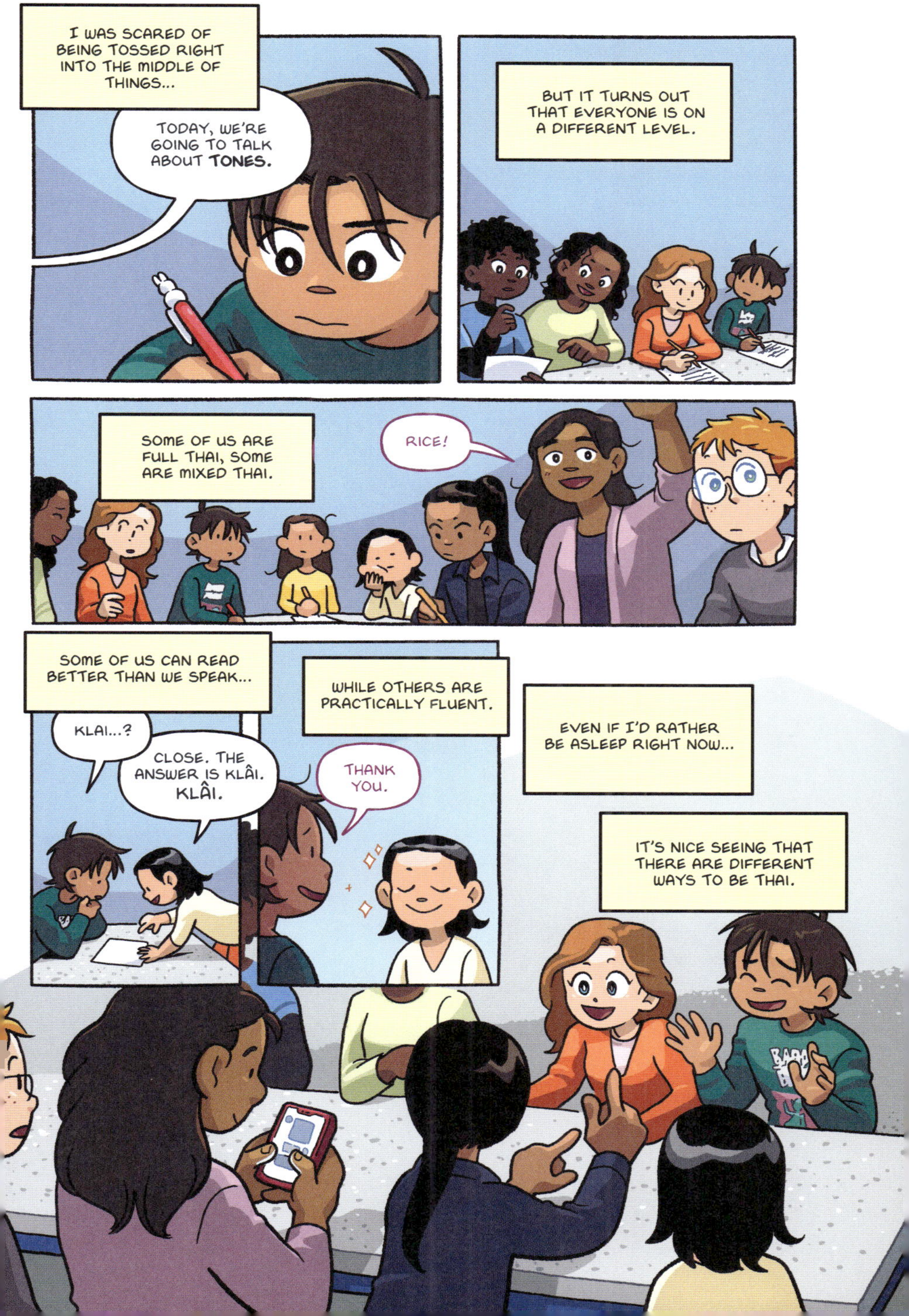

I WAS SCARED OF BEING TOSSED RIGHT INTO THE MIDDLE OF THINGS...
TODAY, WE'RE GOING TO TALK ABOUT TONES.
BUT IT TURNS OUT THAT EVERYONE IS ON A DIFFERENT LEVEL.
SOME OF US ARE FULL THAI, SOME ARE MIXED THAI.
RICE!
SOME OF US CAN READ BETTER THAN WE SPEAK...
KLAI...?
CLOSE. THE ANSWER IS KLÂI. KLÂI.
WHILE OTHERS ARE PRACTICALLY FLUENT.
THANK YOU.
EVEN IF I'D RATHER BE ASLEEP RIGHT NOW...
IT'S NICE SEEING THAT THERE ARE DIFFERENT WAYS TO BE THAI.

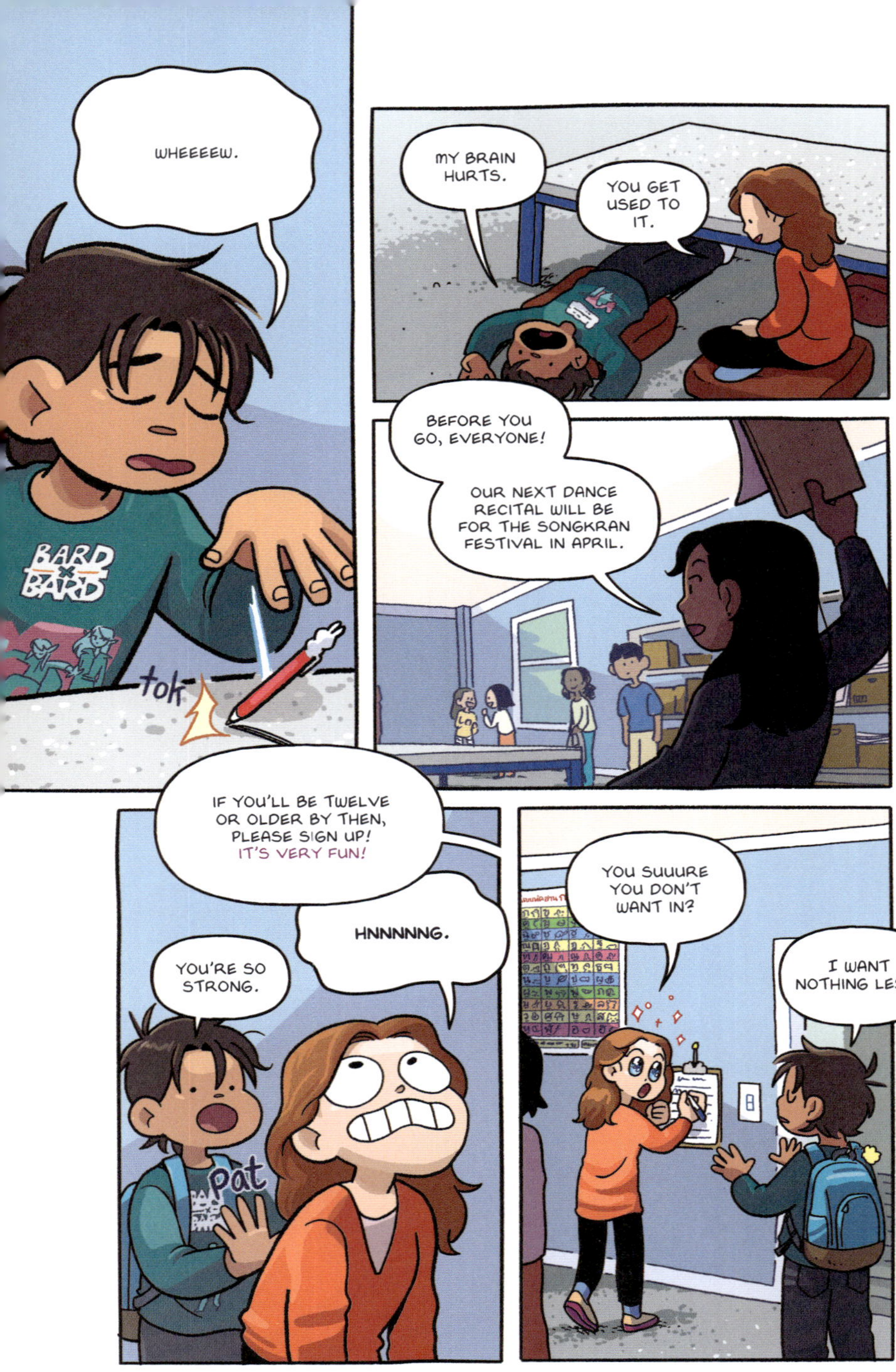
WHEEEEW.
tok
MY BRAIN HURTS.
YOU GET USED TO IT.
BEFORE YOU GO, EVERYONE!
OUR NEXT DANCE RECITAL WILL BE FOR THE SONGKRAN FESTIVAL IN APRIL.
IF YOU'LL BE TWELVE OR OLDER BY THEN, PLEASE SIGN UP! IT'S VERY FUN!
HNNNNNG.
YOU'RE SO STRONG.
pat
YOU SUUURE YOU DON'T WANT IN?
I WANT NOTHING LESS.

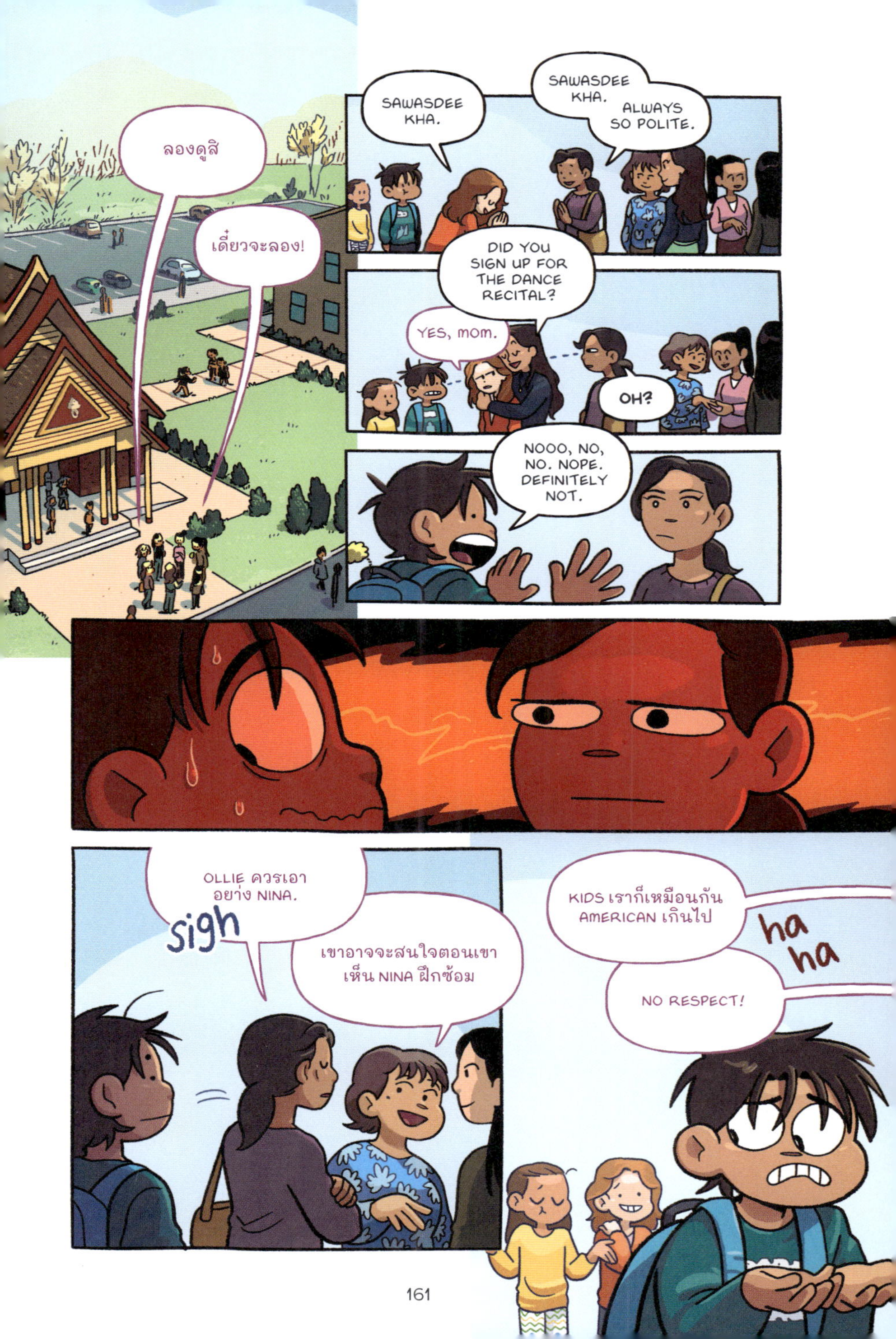

ลองดูสิ
เดี๋ยวจะลอง!
SAWASDEE KHA.
SAWASDEE KHA.
ALWAYS SO POLITE.
DID YOU SIGN UP FOR THE DANCE RECITAL?
YES, MOM.
OH?
NOOO, NO, NO. NOPE. DEFINITELY NOT.
OLLIE ควรเอาอย่าง NINA.
sigh
เขาอาจจะสนใจตอนเขาเห็น NINA ฝึกซ้อม
KIDS เราก็เหมือนกัน AMERICAN เกินไป
ha ha
NO RESPECT!

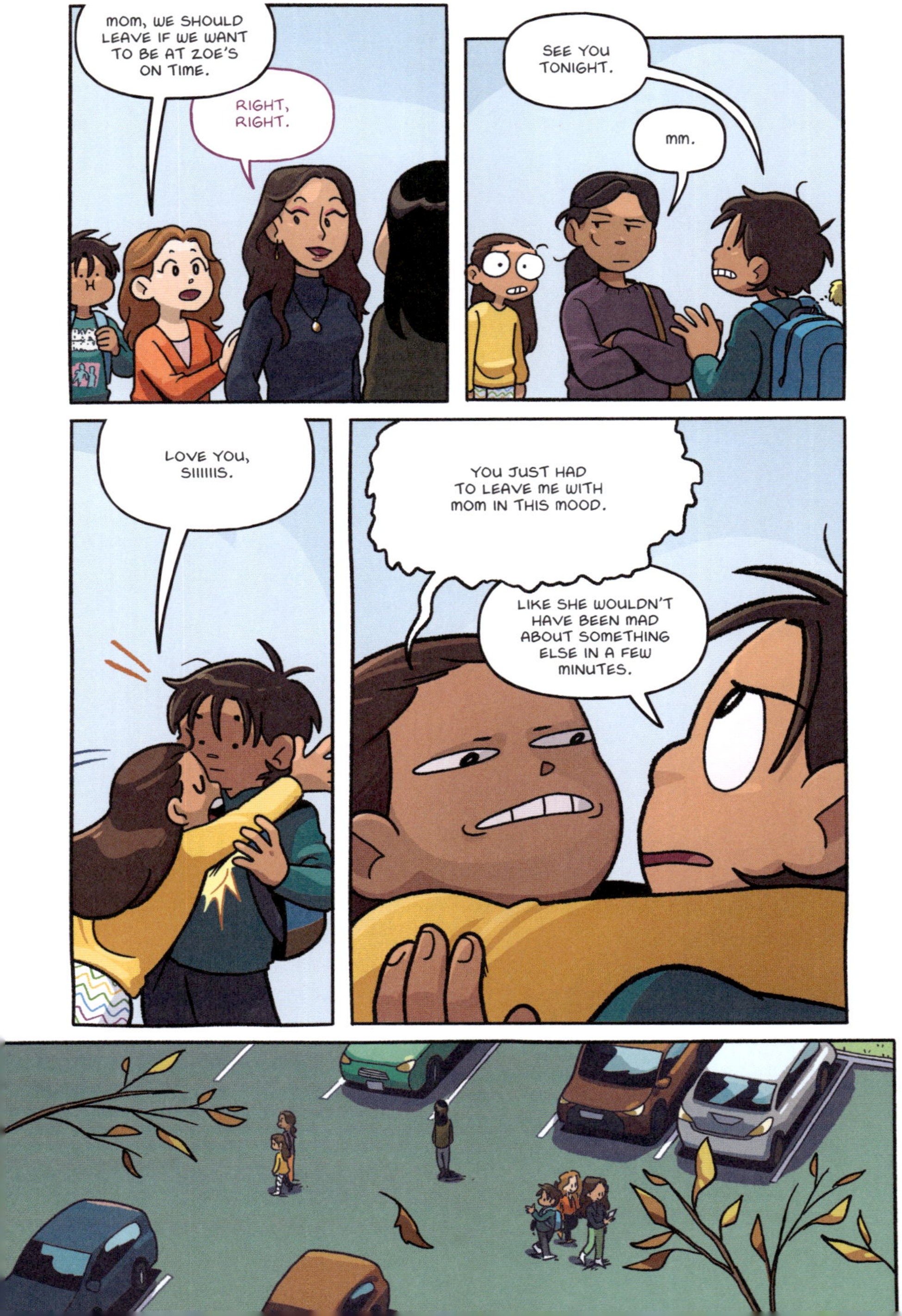
MOM, WE SHOULD LEAVE IF WE WANT TO BE AT ZOE'S ON TIME.
RIGHT, RIGHT.
SEE YOU TONIGHT.
MM.
LOVE YOU, SIIIIIIS.
YOU JUST HAD TO LEAVE ME WITH MOM IN THIS MOOD.
LIKE SHE WOULDN'T HAVE BEEN MAD ABOUT SOMETHING ELSE IN A FEW MINUTES.

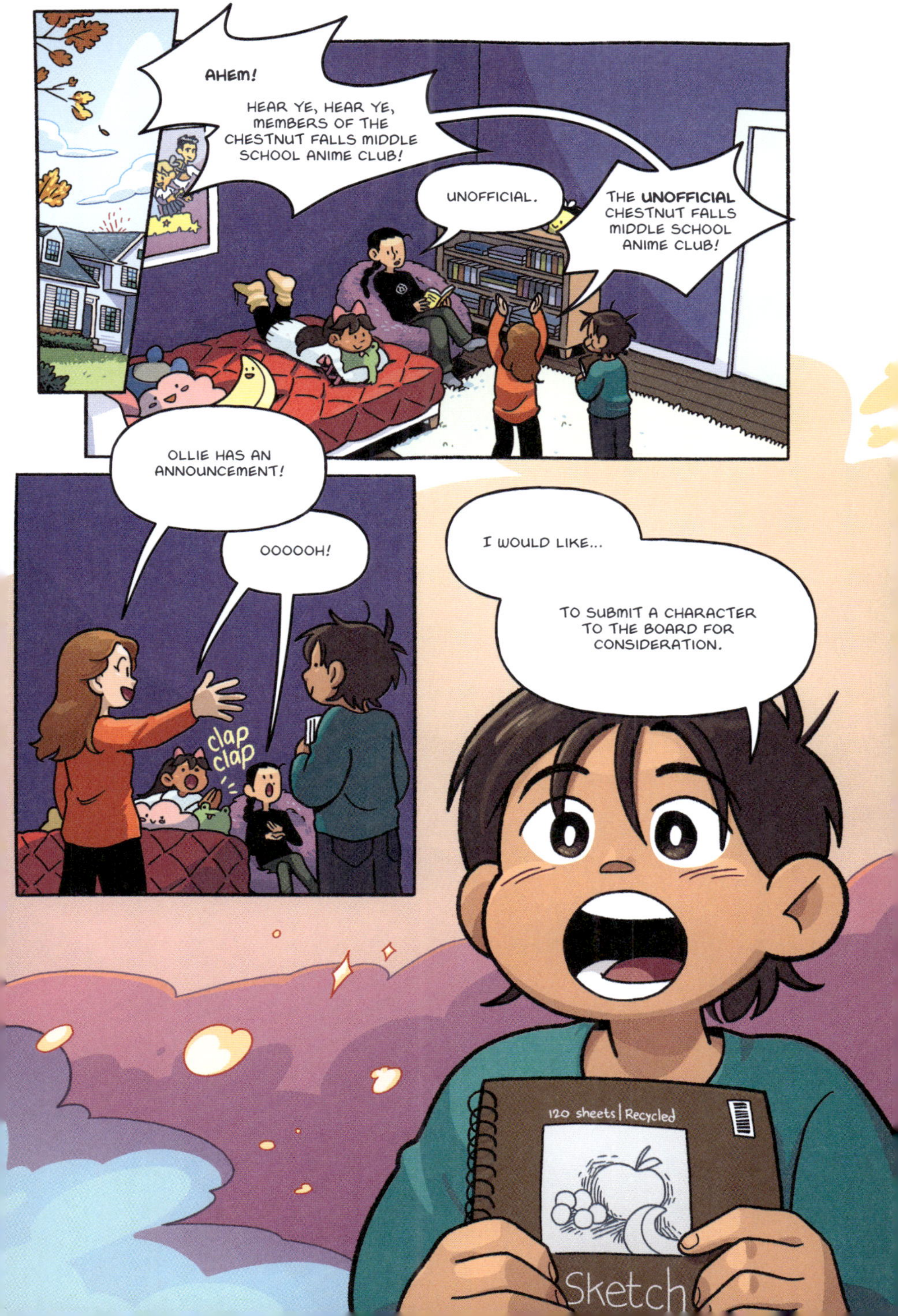
AHEM!
HEAR YE, HEAR YE, MEMBERS OF THE CHESTNUT FALLS MIDDLE SCHOOL ANIME CLUB!
UNOFFICIAL.
THE **UNOFFICIAL** CHESTNUT FALLS MIDDLE SCHOOL ANIME CLUB!
OLLIE HAS AN ANNOUNCEMENT!
OOOOOH!
clap clap
I WOULD LIKE...
TO SUBMIT A CHARACTER TO THE BOARD FOR CONSIDERATION.
120 sheets | Recycled
Sketch

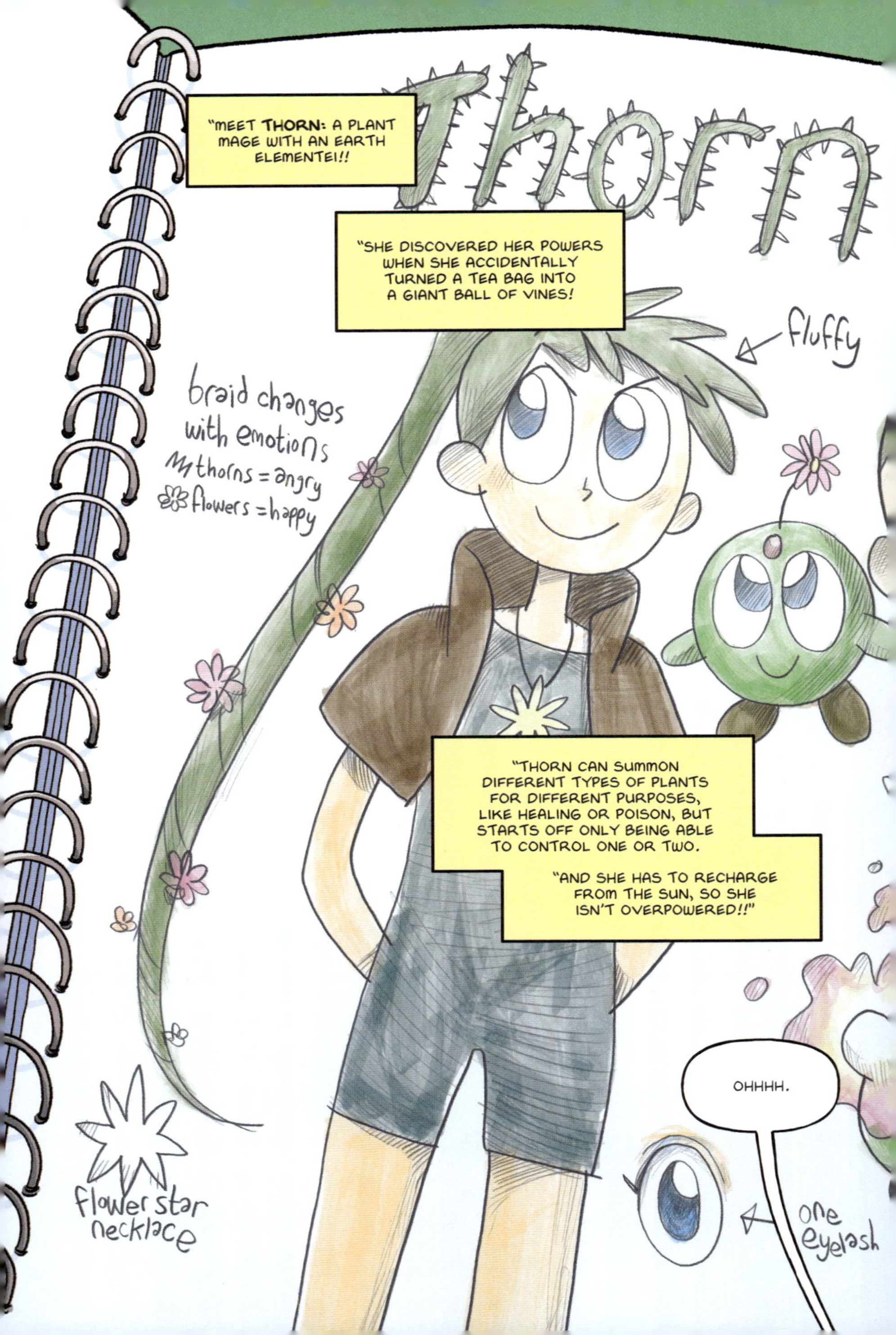
"MEET **THORN:** A PLANT MAGE WITH AN EARTH ELEMENTEI!!
Thorn
"SHE DISCOVERED HER POWERS WHEN SHE ACCIDENTALLY TURNED A TEA BAG INTO A GIANT BALL OF VINES!
fluffy
braid changes with emotions
thorns = angry
flowers = happy
"THORN CAN SUMMON DIFFERENT TYPES OF PLANTS FOR DIFFERENT PURPOSES, LIKE HEALING OR POISON, BUT STARTS OFF ONLY BEING ABLE TO CONTROL ONE OR TWO.
"AND SHE HAS TO RECHARGE FROM THE SUN, SO SHE ISN'T OVERPOWERED!!"
flower star necklace
OHHHH.
one eyelash

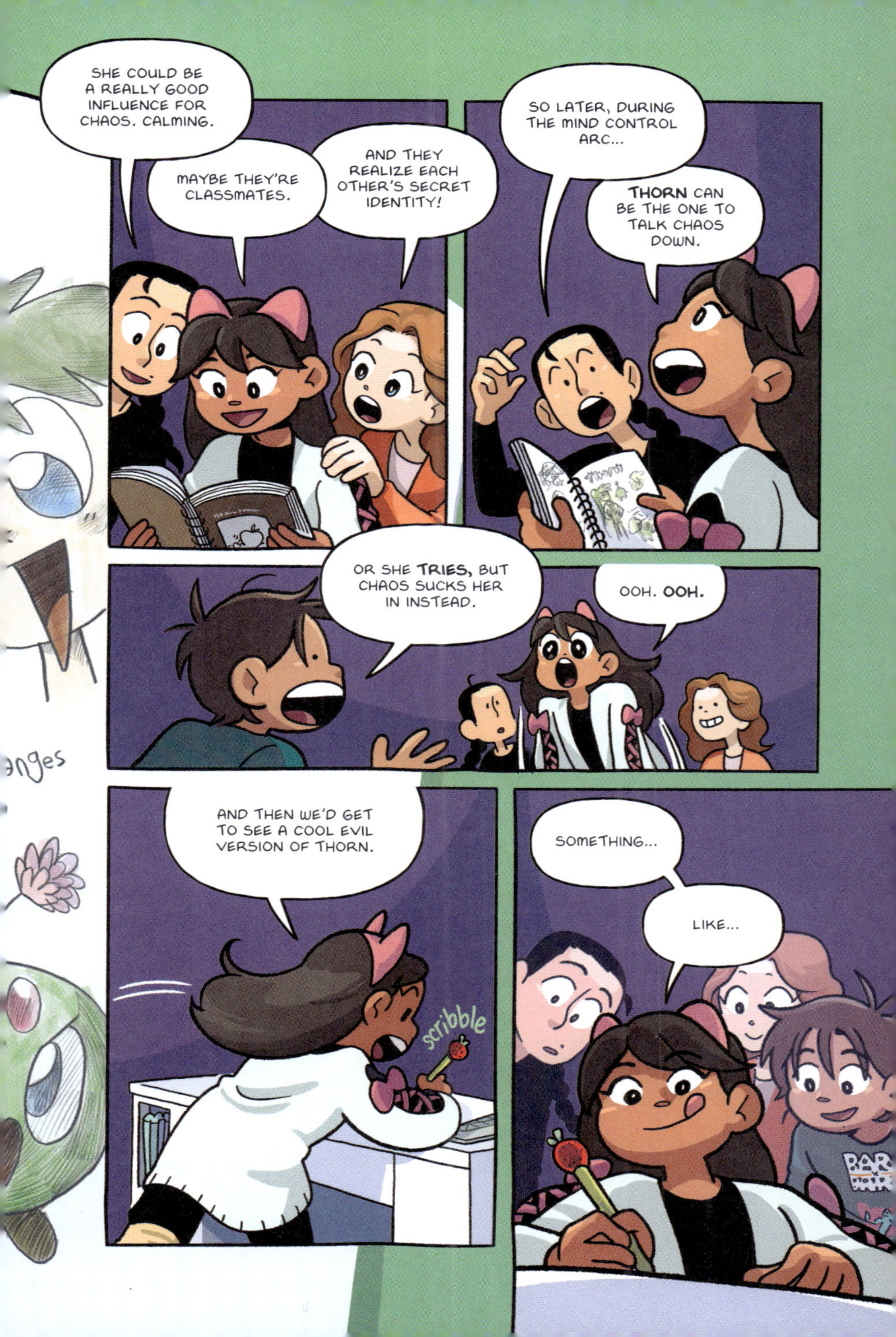

SHE COULD BE A REALLY GOOD INFLUENCE FOR CHAOS. CALMING.
MAYBE THEY'RE CLASSMATES.
AND THEY REALIZE EACH OTHER'S SECRET IDENTITY!
SO LATER, DURING THE MIND CONTROL ARC...
THORN CAN BE THE ONE TO TALK CHAOS DOWN.
OR SHE **TRIES,** BUT CHAOS SUCKS HER IN INSTEAD.
OOH. **OOH.**
AND THEN WE'D GET TO SEE A COOL EVIL VERSION OF THORN.
scribble
SOMETHING...
LIKE...

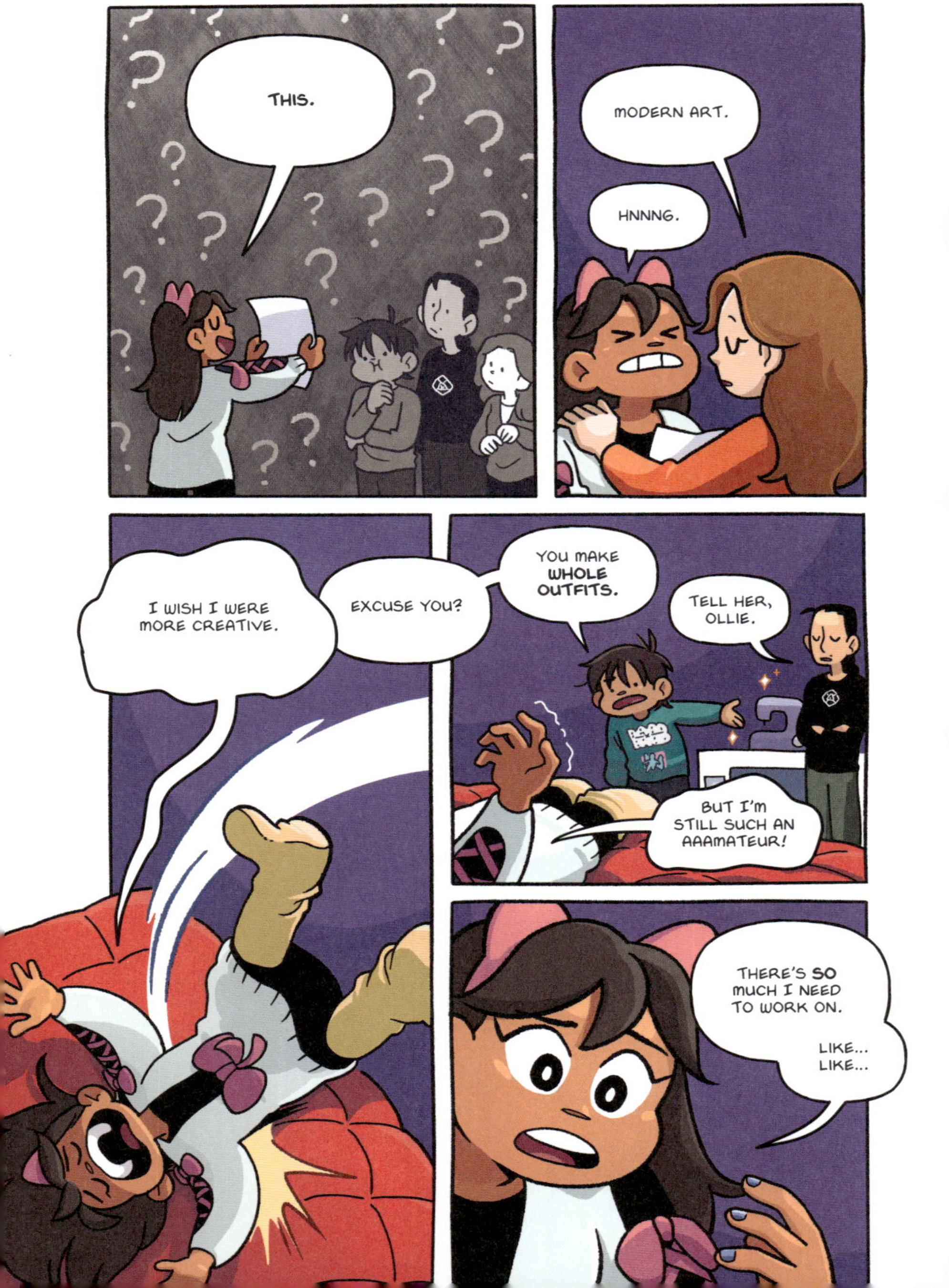
THIS.
MODERN ART.
HNNNG.
I WISH I WERE MORE CREATIVE.
EXCUSE YOU?
YOU MAKE **WHOLE OUTFITS.**
TELL HER, OLLIE.
BUT I'M STILL SUCH AN AAAMATEUR!
THERE'S **SO** MUCH I NEED TO WORK ON.
LIKE... LIKE...

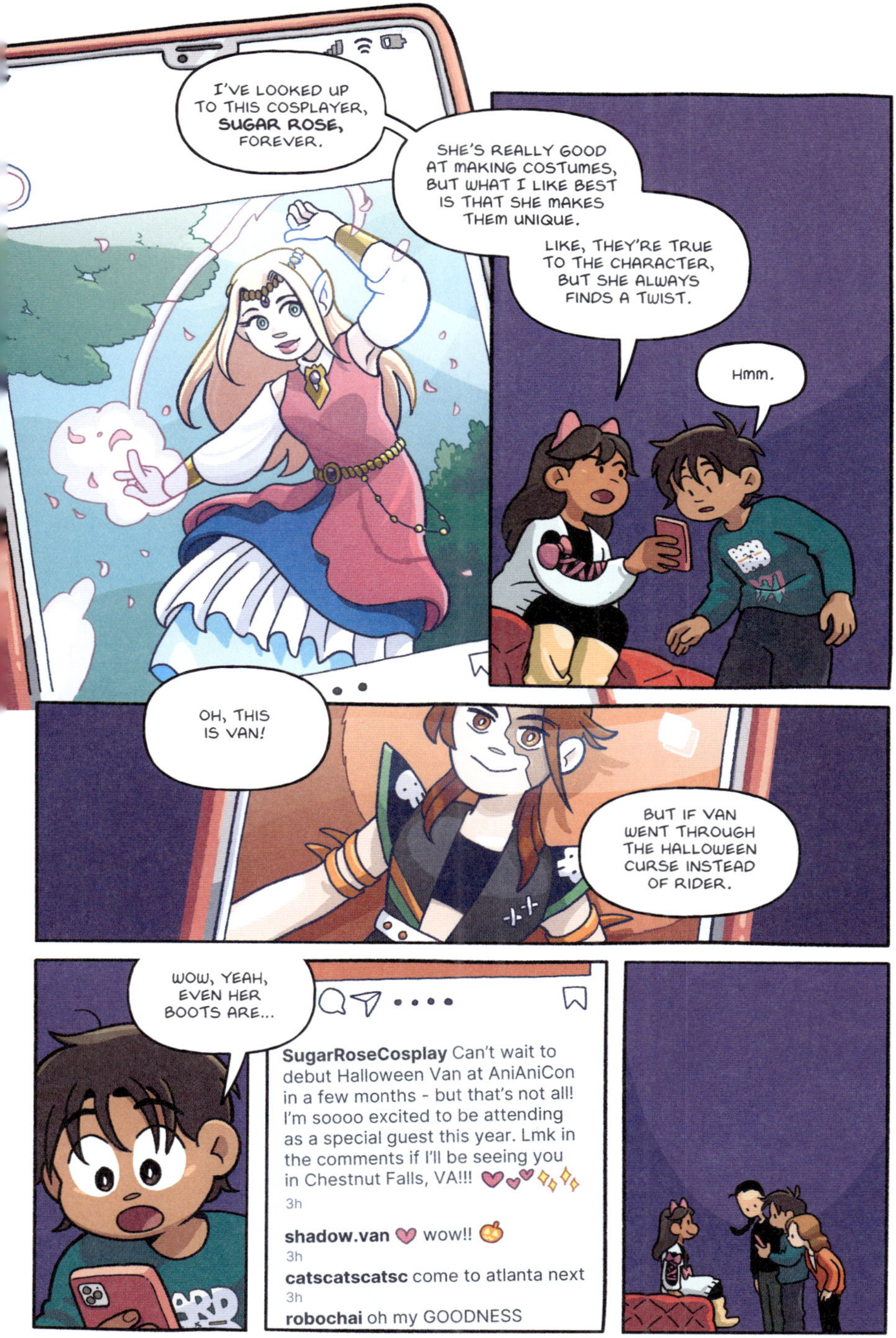
I'VE LOOKED UP TO THIS COSPLAYER, **SUGAR ROSE,** FOREVER.
SHE'S REALLY GOOD AT MAKING COSTUMES, BUT WHAT I LIKE BEST IS THAT SHE MAKES THEM UNIQUE.
LIKE, THEY'RE TRUE TO THE CHARACTER, BUT SHE ALWAYS FINDS A TWIST.
Hmm.
OH, THIS IS VAN!
BUT IF VAN WENT THROUGH THE HALLOWEEN CURSE INSTEAD OF RIDER.
WOW, YEAH, EVEN HER BOOTS ARE...
SugarRoseCosplay Can't wait to debut Halloween Van at AniAniCon in a few months - but that's not all! I'm soooo excited to be attending as a special guest this year. Lmk in the comments if I'll be seeing you in Chestnut Falls, VA!!!
3h
shadow.van wow!!
3h
catscatscatsc come to atlanta next
3h
robochai oh my GOODNESS

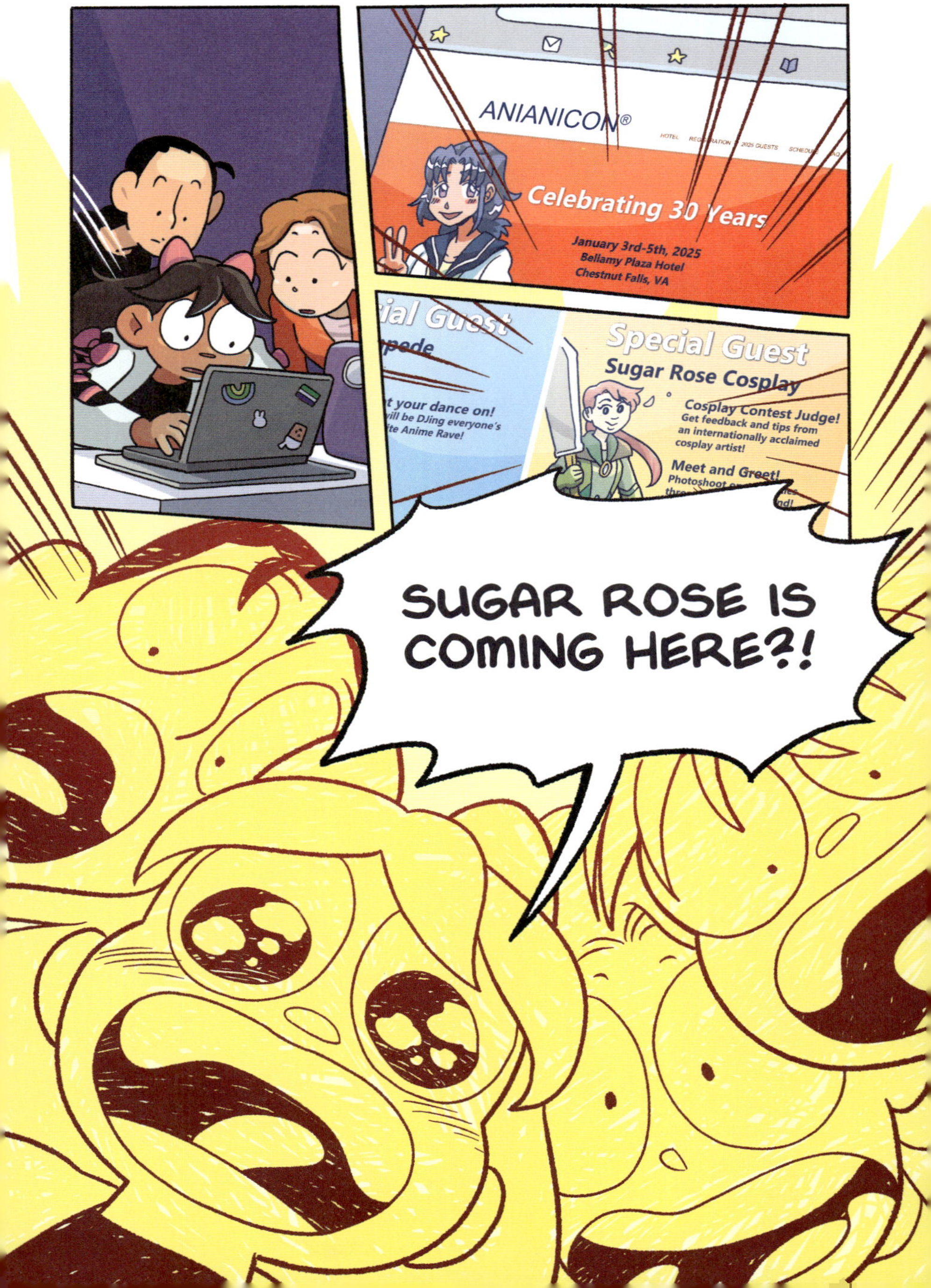
ANIANICON®
HOTEL
2025 GUESTS
Celebrating 30 Years
January 3rd-5th, 2025
Bellamy Plaza Hotel
Chestnut Falls, VA
Special Guest
Sugar Rose Cosplay
Cosplay Contest Judge!
Get feedback and tips from an internationally acclaimed cosplay artist!
Meet and Greet!
SUGAR ROSE IS COMING HERE?!

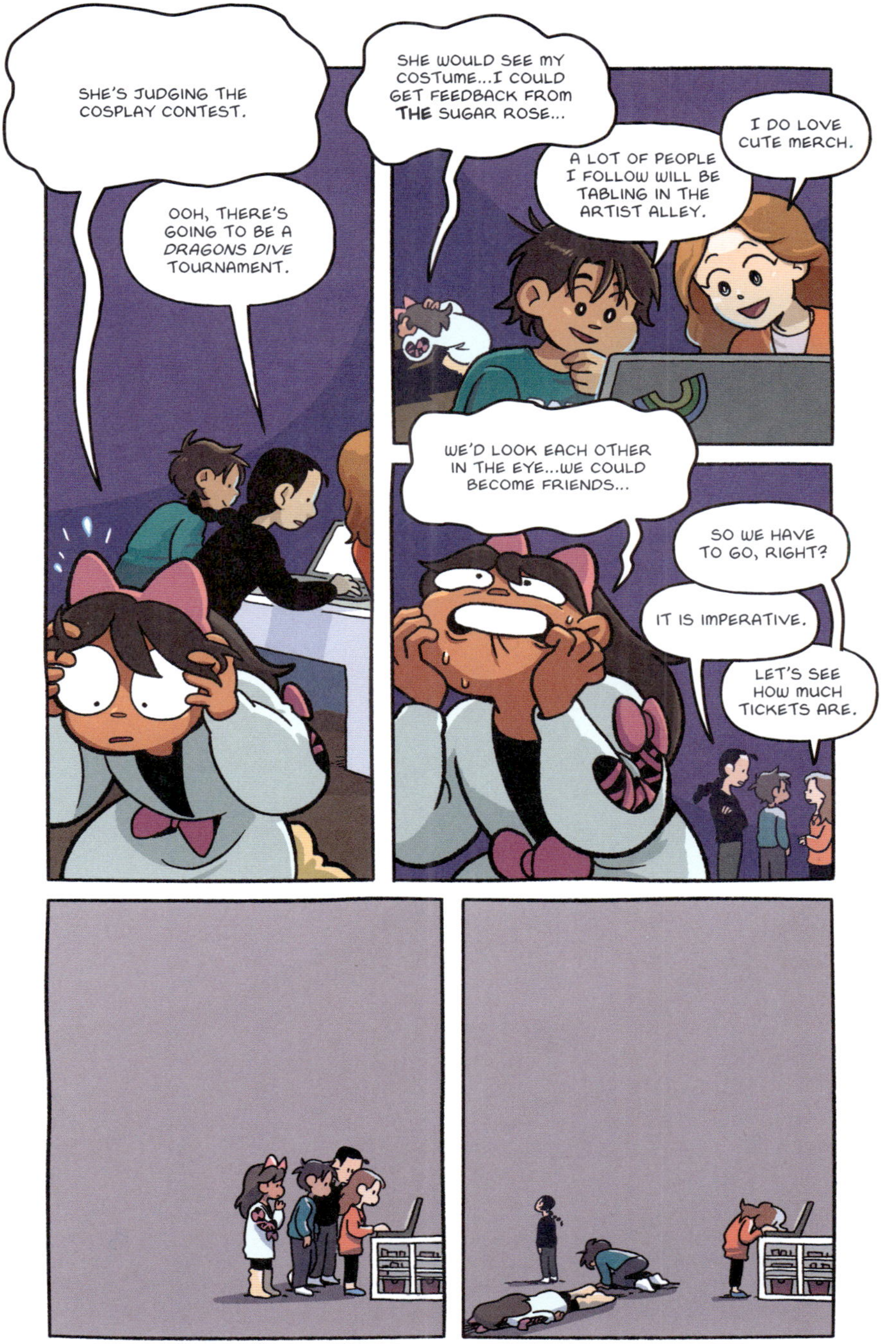
SHE'S JUDGING THE COSPLAY CONTEST.
OOH, THERE'S GOING TO BE A *DRAGONS DIVE* TOURNAMENT.
SHE WOULD SEE MY COSTUME...I COULD GET FEEDBACK FROM **THE** SUGAR ROSE...
A LOT OF PEOPLE I FOLLOW WILL BE TABLING IN THE ARTIST ALLEY.
I DO LOVE CUTE MERCH.
WE'D LOOK EACH OTHER IN THE EYE...WE COULD BECOME FRIENDS...
SO WE HAVE TO GO, RIGHT?
IT IS IMPERATIVE.
LET'S SEE HOW MUCH TICKETS ARE.

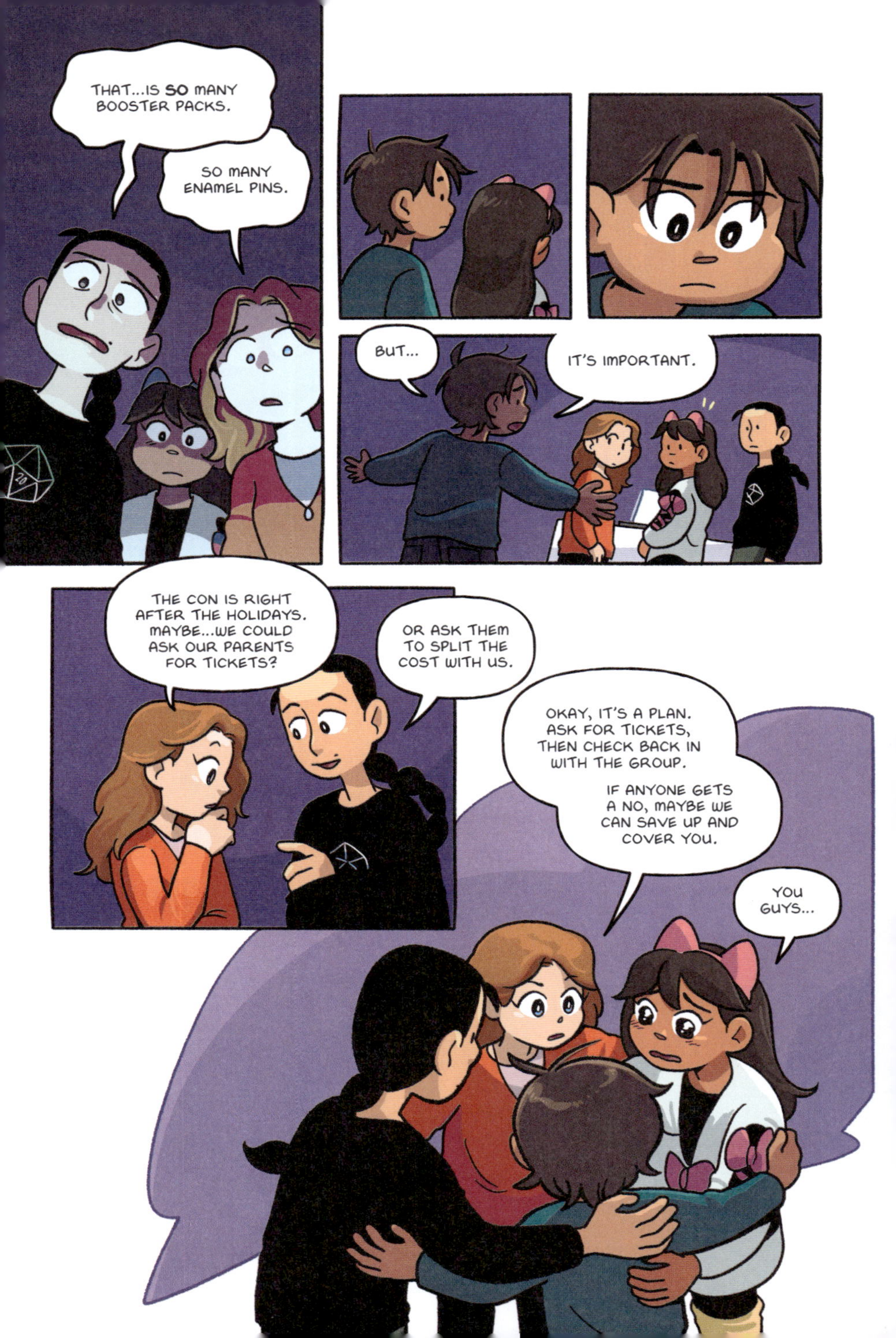
THAT...IS SO MANY BOOSTER PACKS.
SO MANY ENAMEL PINS.
BUT...
IT'S IMPORTANT.
THE CON IS RIGHT AFTER THE HOLIDAYS. MAYBE...WE COULD ASK OUR PARENTS FOR TICKETS?
OR ASK THEM TO SPLIT THE COST WITH US.
OKAY, IT'S A PLAN. ASK FOR TICKETS, THEN CHECK BACK IN WITH THE GROUP.
IF ANYONE GETS A NO, MAYBE WE CAN SAVE UP AND COVER YOU.
YOU GUYS...

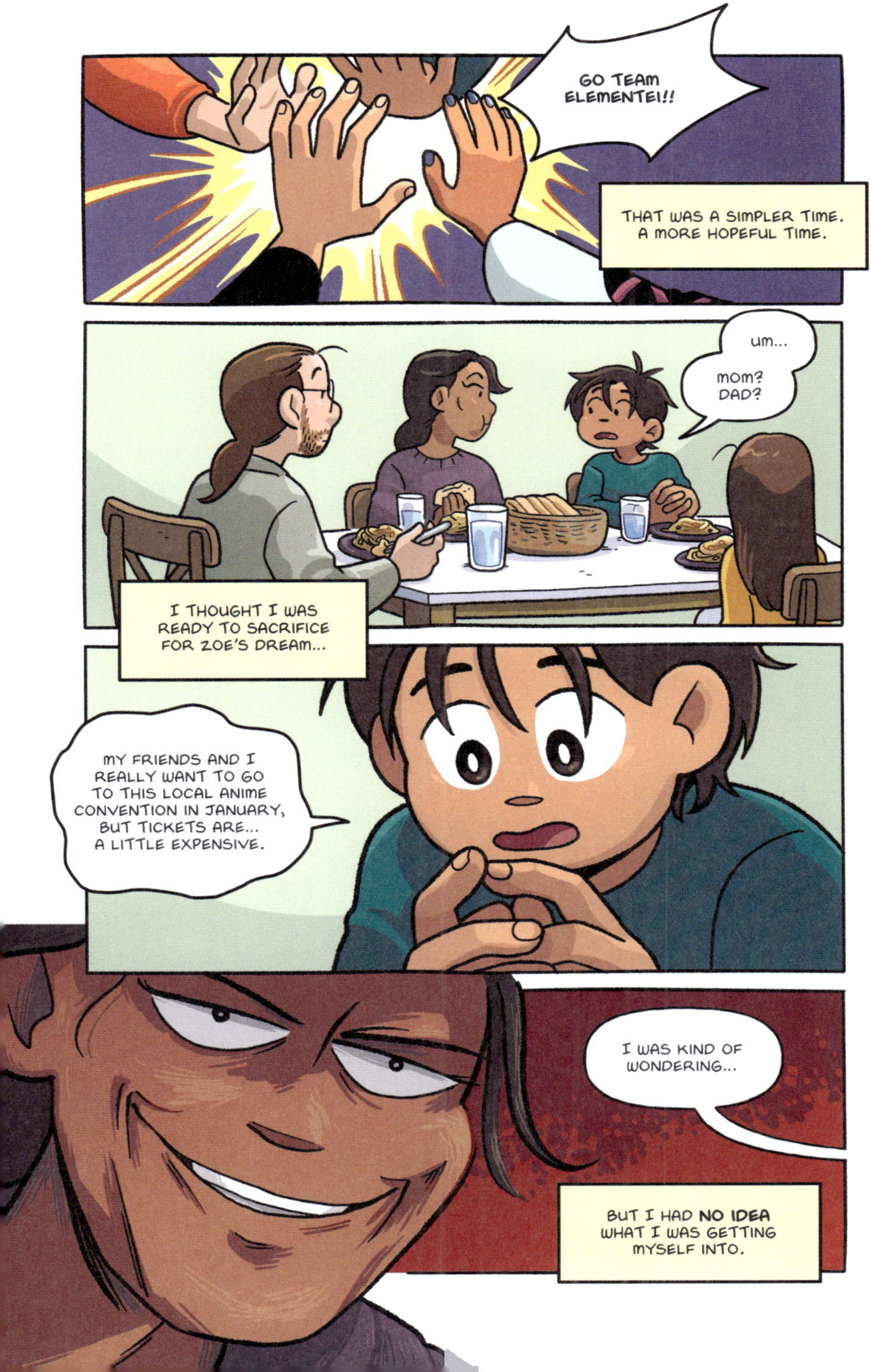
GO TEAM ELEMENTEI!!
THAT WAS A SIMPLER TIME. A MORE HOPEFUL TIME.
um...
mom? DAD?
I THOUGHT I WAS READY TO SACRIFICE FOR ZOE'S DREAM...
MY FRIENDS AND I REALLY WANT TO GO TO THIS LOCAL ANIME CONVENTION IN JANUARY, BUT TICKETS ARE... A LITTLE EXPENSIVE.
I WAS KIND OF WONDERING...
BUT I HAD **NO IDEA** WHAT I WAS GETTING MYSELF INTO.

CHAPTER NINE

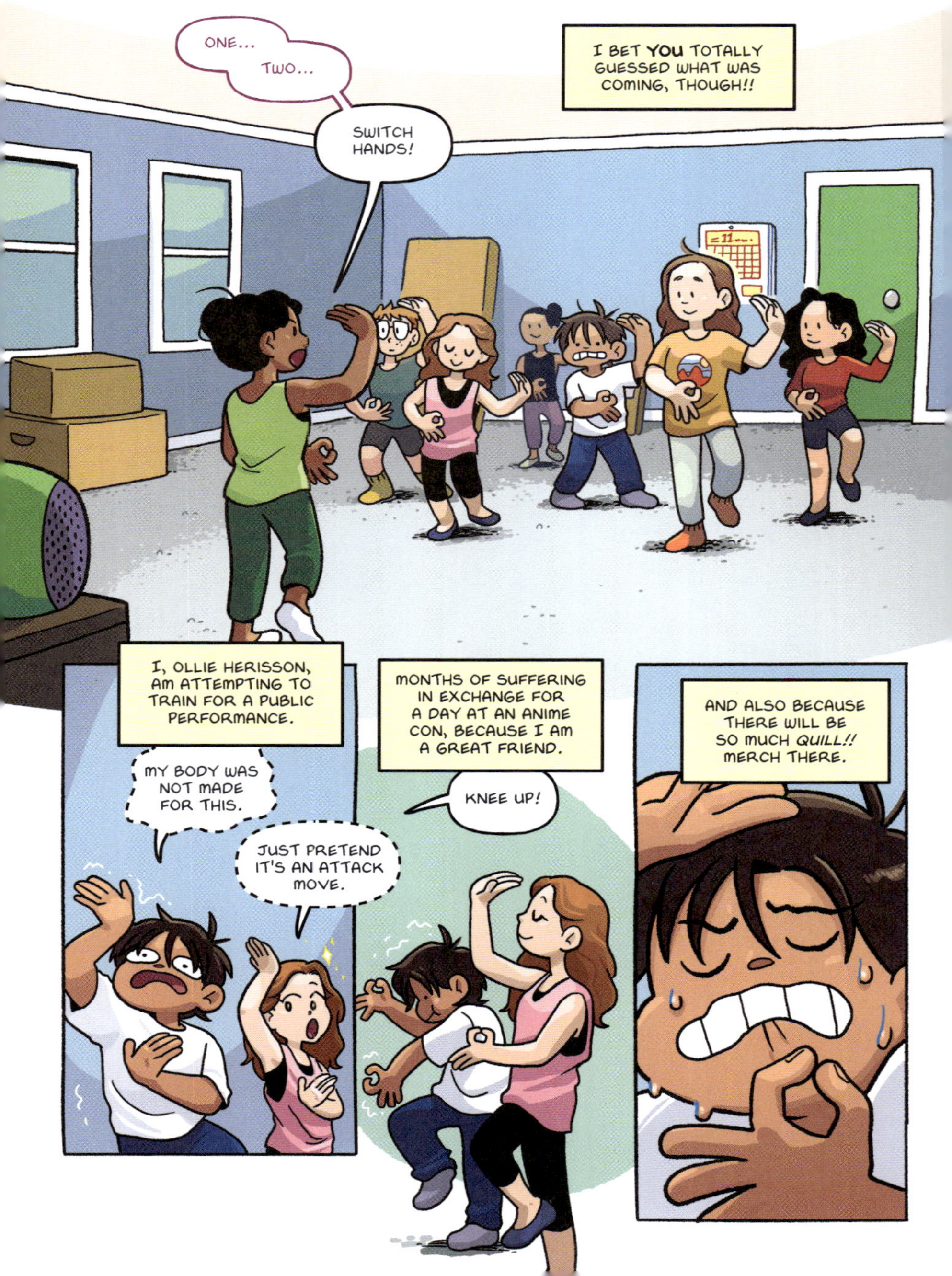
I BET **YOU** TOTALLY GUESSED WHAT WAS COMING, THOUGH!!
ONE... TWO...
SWITCH HANDS!
I, OLLIE HERISSON, AM ATTEMPTING TO TRAIN FOR A PUBLIC PERFORMANCE.
MY BODY WAS NOT MADE FOR THIS.
JUST PRETEND IT'S AN ATTACK MOVE.
MONTHS OF SUFFERING IN EXCHANGE FOR A DAY AT AN ANIME CON, BECAUSE I AM A GREAT FRIEND.
KNEE UP!
AND ALSO BECAUSE THERE WILL BE SO MUCH *QUILL!!* MERCH THERE.

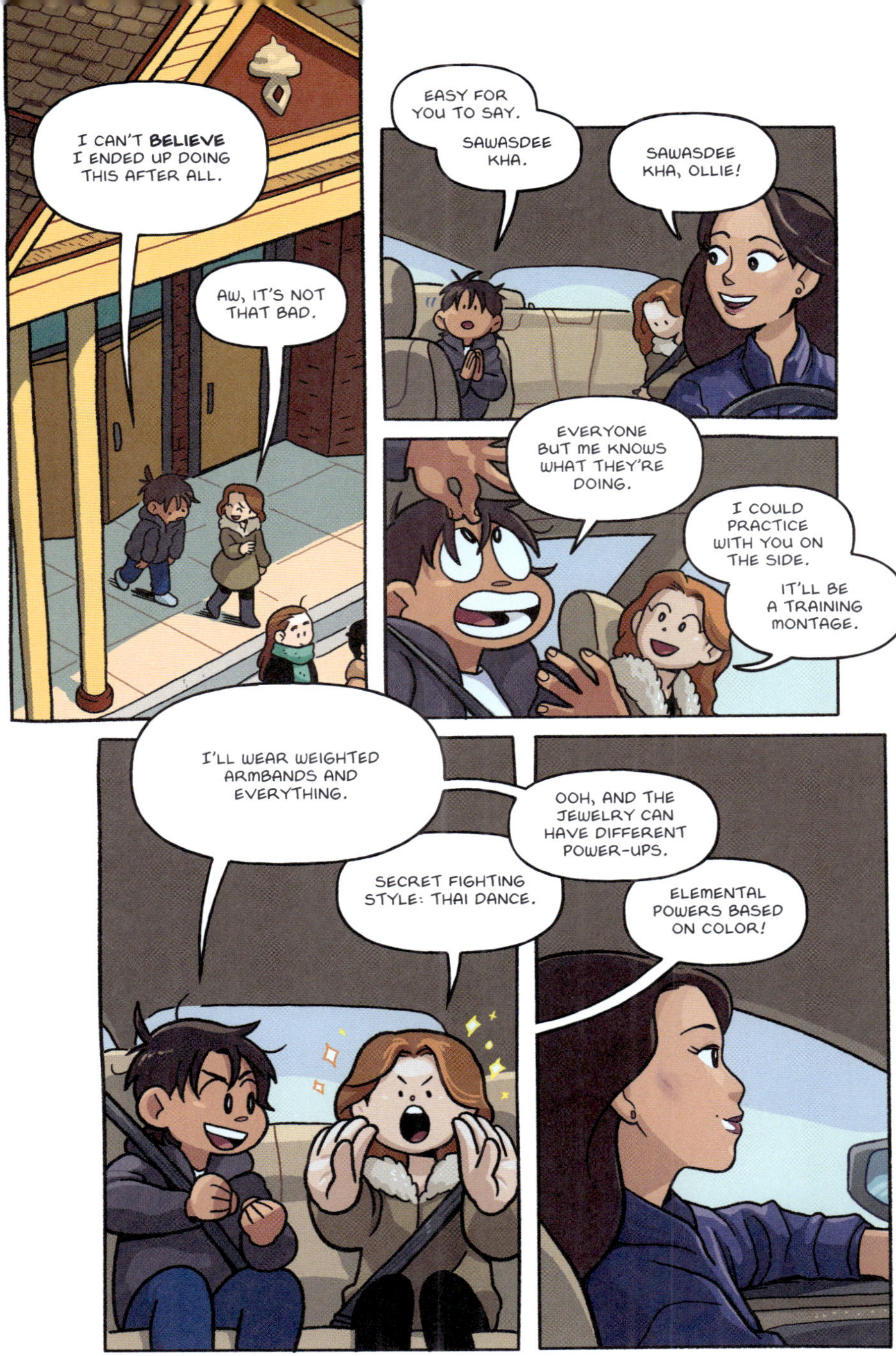
I CAN'T **BELIEVE** I ENDED UP DOING THIS AFTER ALL.
AW, IT'S NOT THAT BAD.
EASY FOR YOU TO SAY.
SAWASDEE KHA.
SAWASDEE KHA, OLLIE!
EVERYONE BUT ME KNOWS WHAT THEY'RE DOING.
I COULD PRACTICE WITH YOU ON THE SIDE.
IT'LL BE A TRAINING MONTAGE.
I'LL WEAR WEIGHTED ARMBANDS AND EVERYTHING.
SECRET FIGHTING STYLE: THAI DANCE.
OOH, AND THE JEWELRY CAN HAVE DIFFERENT POWER-UPS.
ELEMENTAL POWERS BASED ON COLOR!

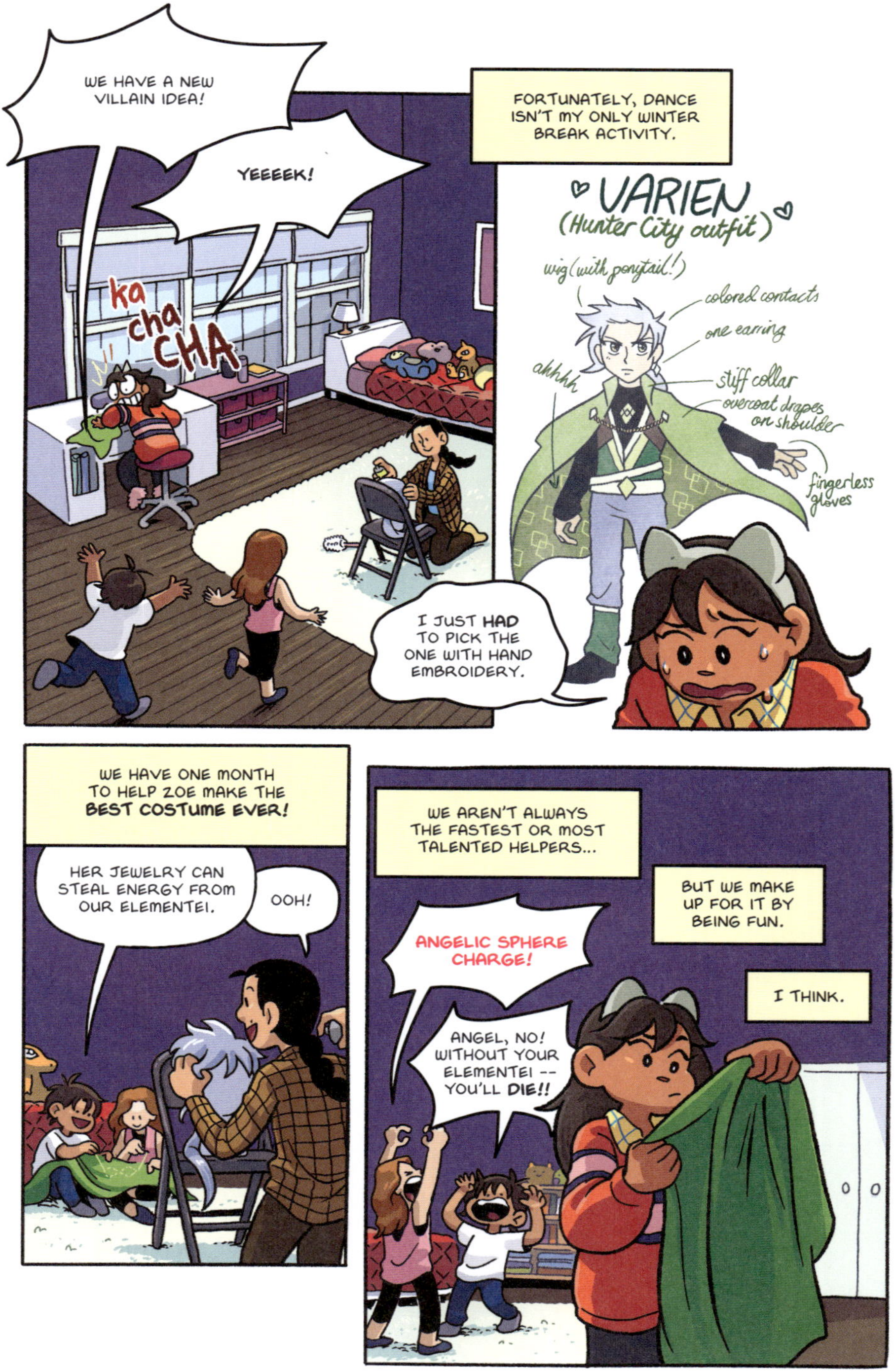
WE HAVE A NEW VILLAIN IDEA!
YEEEEK!
ka cha CHA
FORTUNATELY, DANCE ISN'T MY ONLY WINTER BREAK ACTIVITY.
VARIEN (Hunter City outfit)
wig (with ponytail!)
colored contacts
one earring
ahhhh
stiff collar
overcoat drapes on shoulder
fingerless gloves
I JUST HAD TO PICK THE ONE WITH HAND EMBROIDERY.
WE HAVE ONE MONTH TO HELP ZOE MAKE THE BEST COSTUME EVER!
HER JEWELRY CAN STEAL ENERGY FROM OUR ELEMENTEI.
OOH!
WE AREN'T ALWAYS THE FASTEST OR MOST TALENTED HELPERS...
BUT WE MAKE UP FOR IT BY BEING FUN.
ANGELIC SPHERE CHARGE!
I THINK.
ANGEL, NO! WITHOUT YOUR ELEMENTEI -- YOU'LL DIE!!

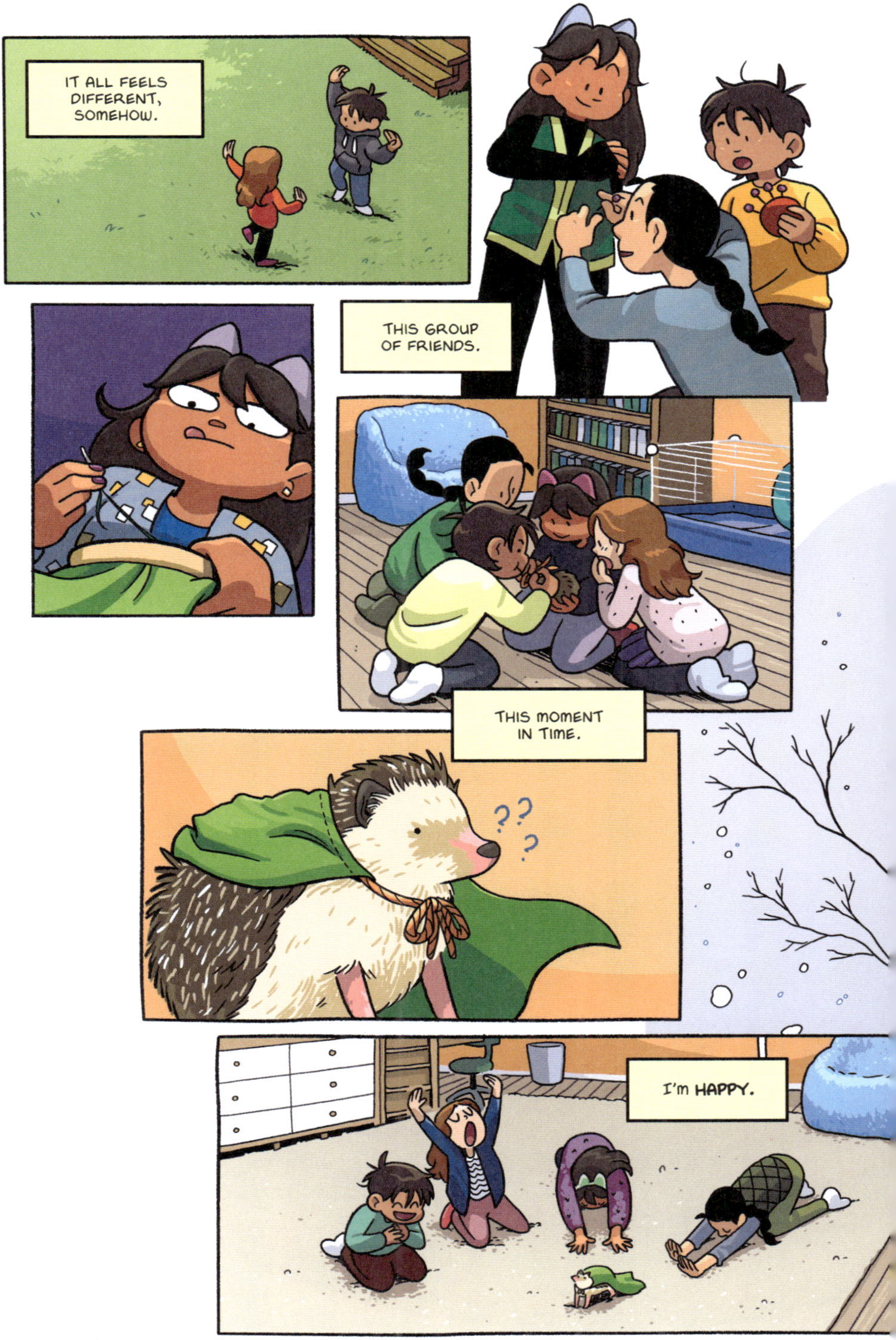
IT ALL FEELS DIFFERENT, SOMEHOW.
THIS GROUP OF FRIENDS.
THIS MOMENT IN TIME.
??
?
I'm **HAPPY.**

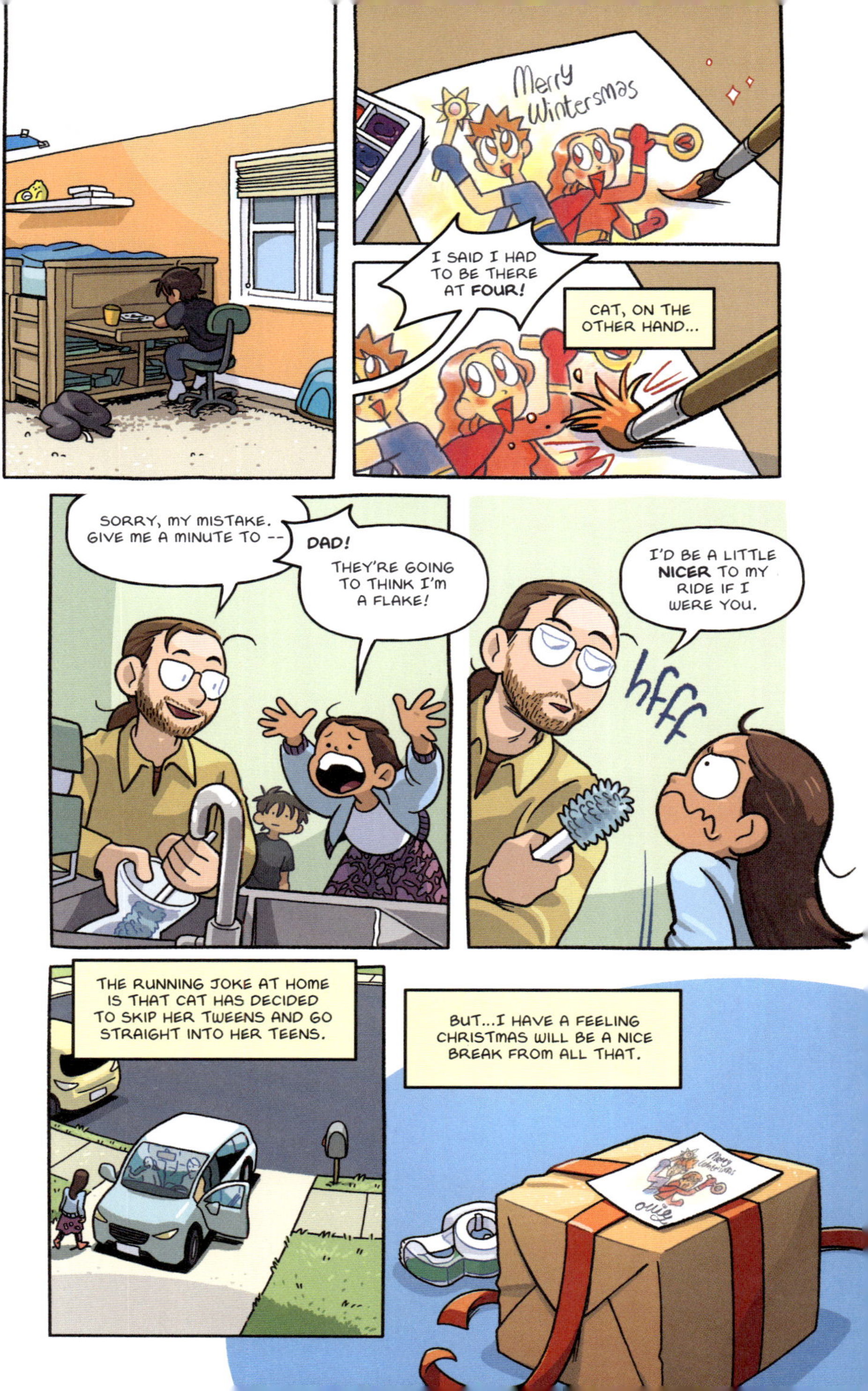

Merry Wintersmas
I SAID I HAD TO BE THERE AT **FOUR!**
CAT, ON THE OTHER HAND...
SORRY, MY MISTAKE. GIVE ME A MINUTE TO --
DAD! THEY'RE GOING TO THINK I'M A FLAKE!
I'D BE A LITTLE **NICER** TO MY RIDE IF I WERE YOU.
hfff
THE RUNNING JOKE AT HOME IS THAT CAT HAS DECIDED TO SKIP HER TWEENS AND GO STRAIGHT INTO HER TEENS.
BUT...I HAVE A FEELING CHRISTMAS WILL BE A NICE BREAK FROM ALL THAT.

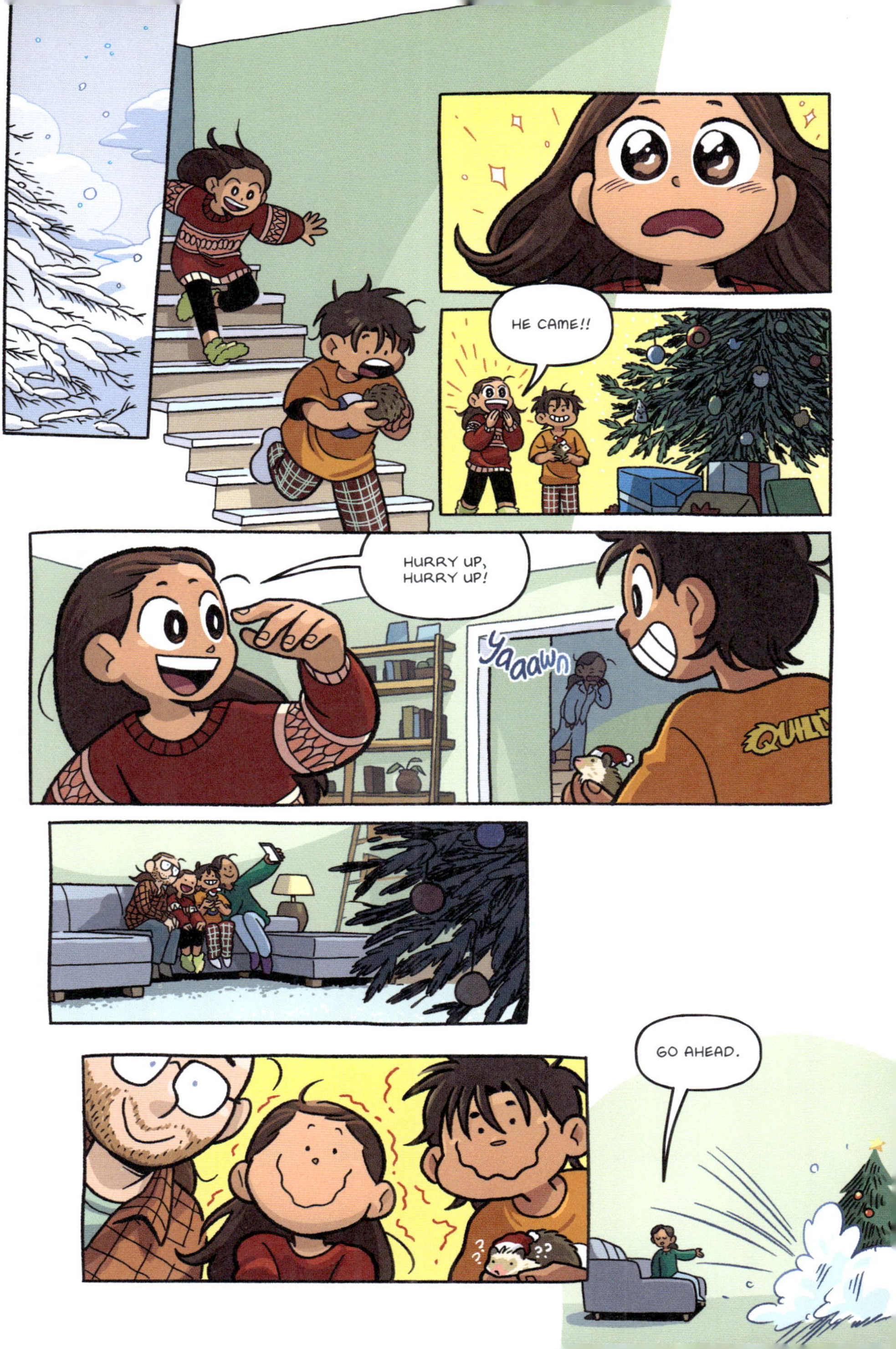
HE CAME!!
HURRY UP, HURRY UP!
Yaaawn
QUILL
GO AHEAD.

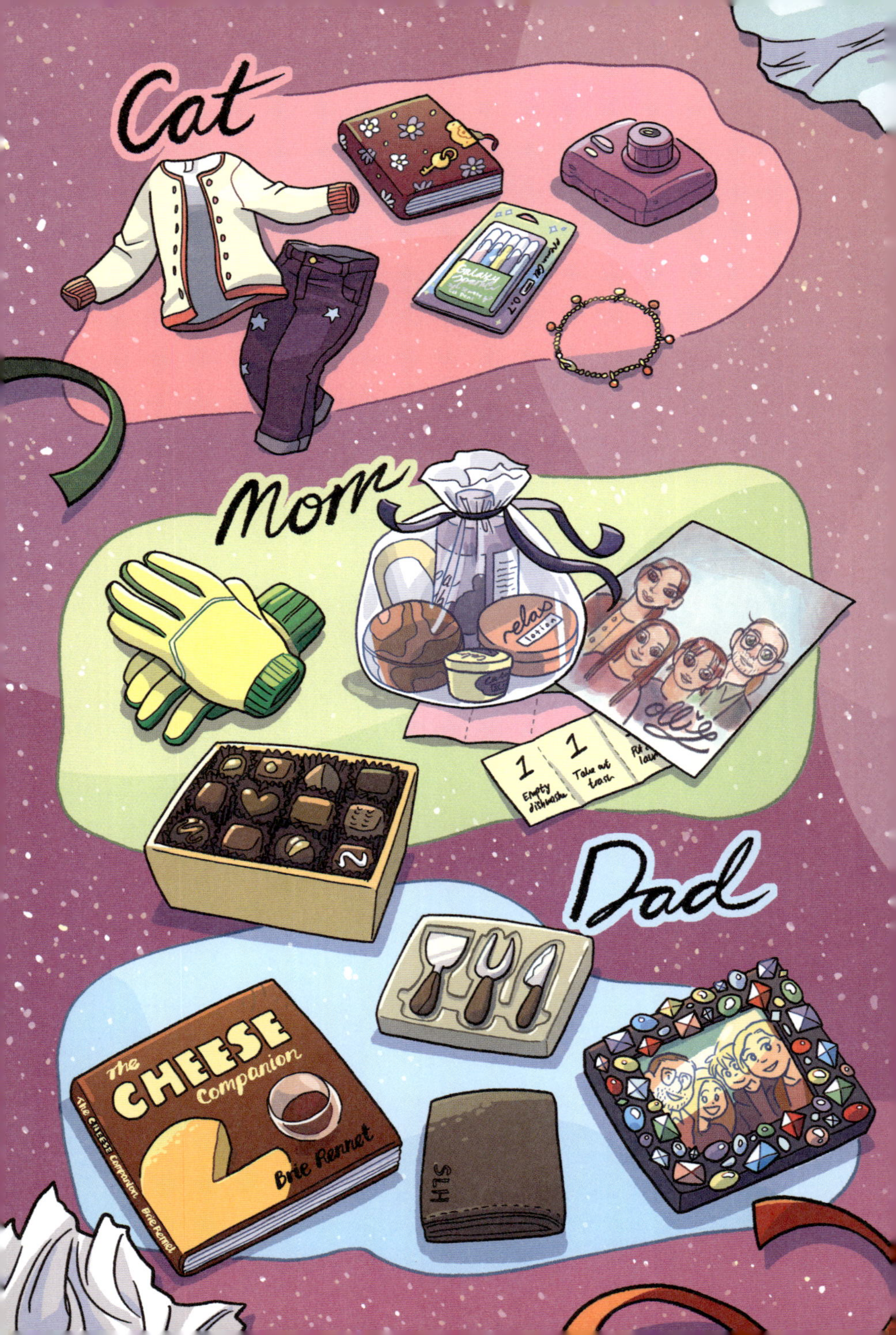

Cat
Galaxy Sparkle
0.7
Mom
relax lotion
1 Empty dishwashe
1 Take out trash
ollie
Dad
The CHEESE Companion
Brie Rennet
The CHEESE Companion Brie Rennet
HS

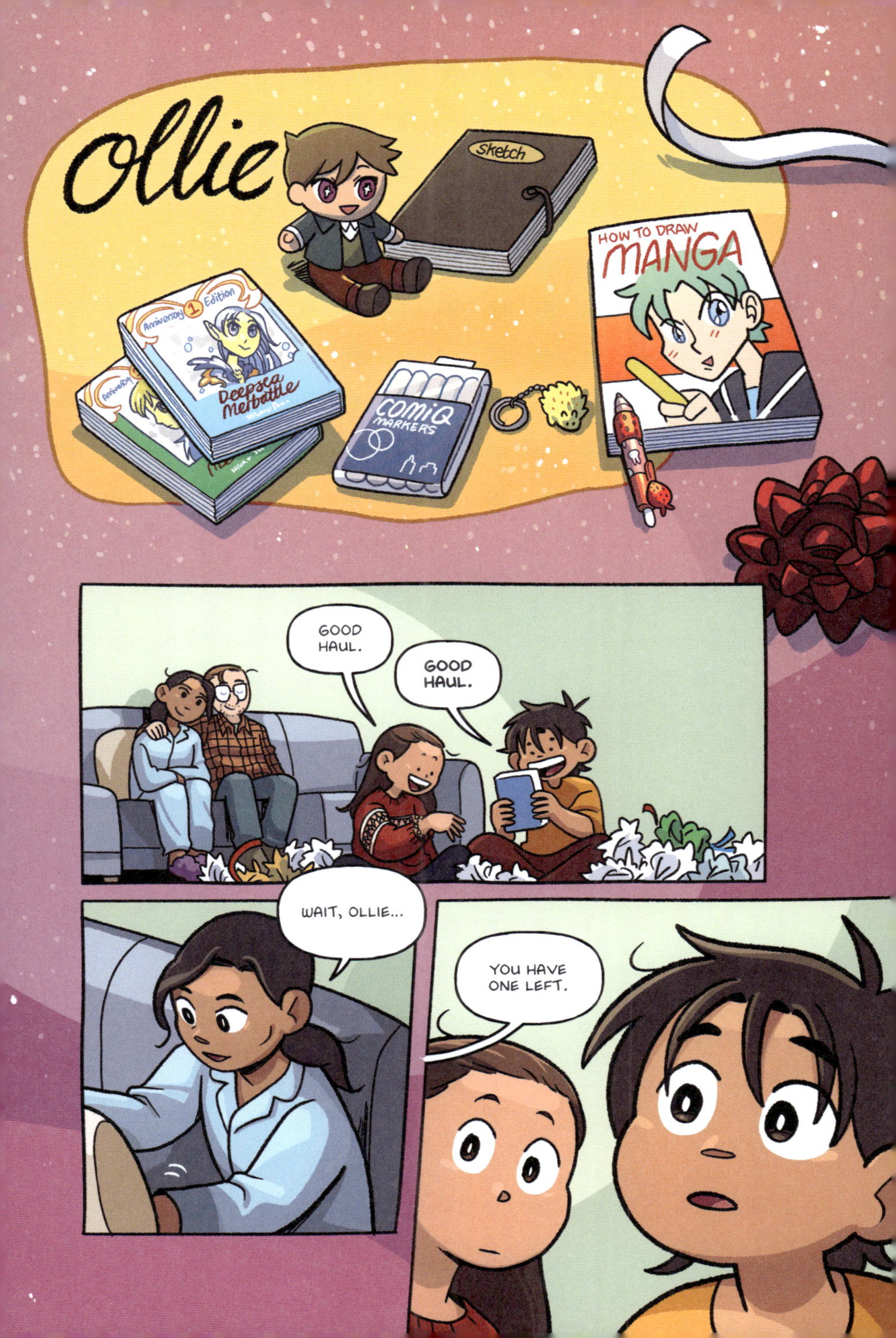
Ollie
sketch
HOW TO DRAW MANGA
Anniversary 1 Edition
Deepsea Merbattle
COMIQ MARKERS
GOOD HAUL.
GOOD HAUL.
WAIT, OLLIE...
YOU HAVE ONE LEFT.

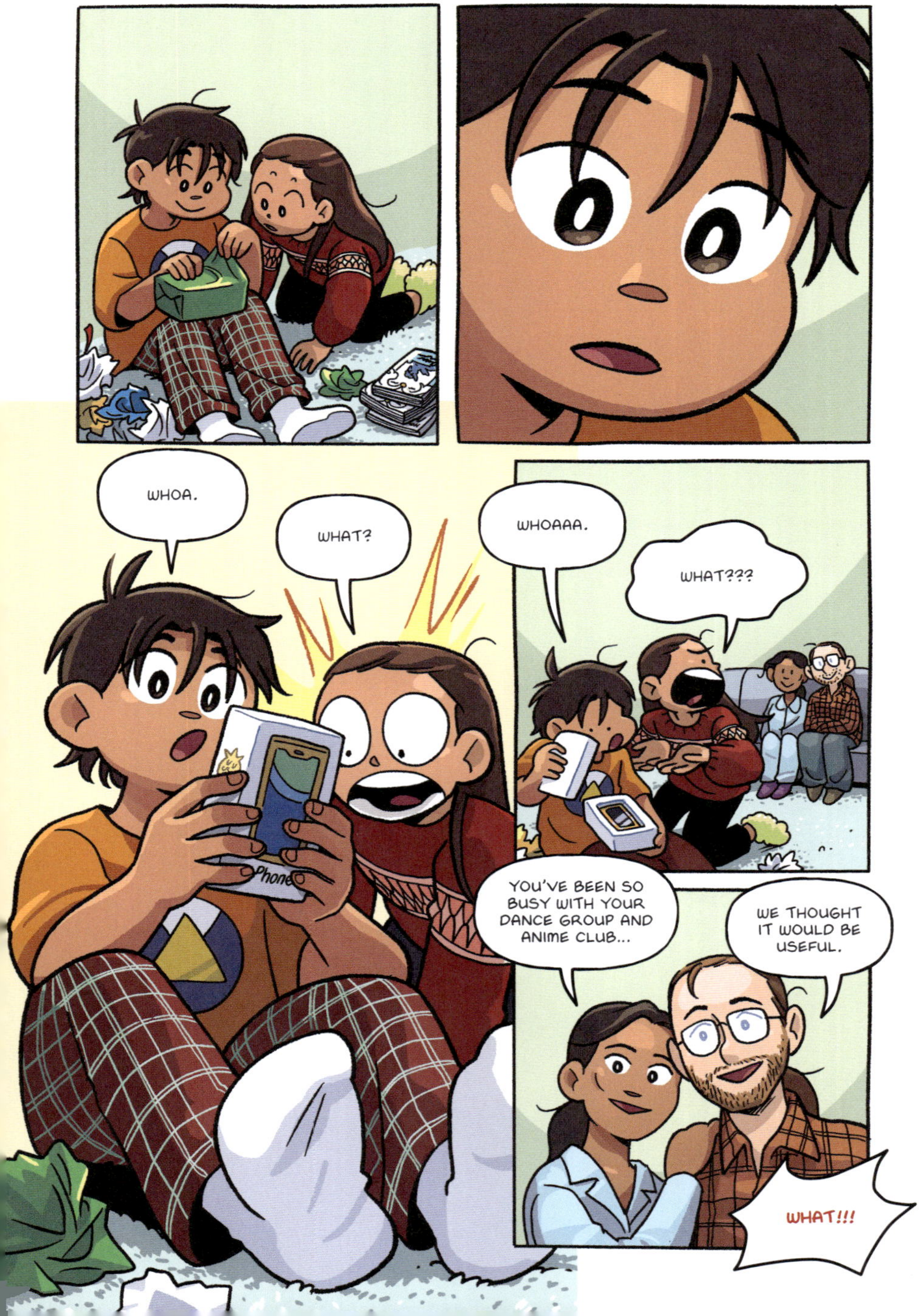
WHOA.
WHAT?
WHOAAA.
WHAT???
YOU'VE BEEN SO BUSY WITH YOUR DANCE GROUP AND ANIME CLUB...
WE THOUGHT IT WOULD BE USEFUL.
WHAT!!!

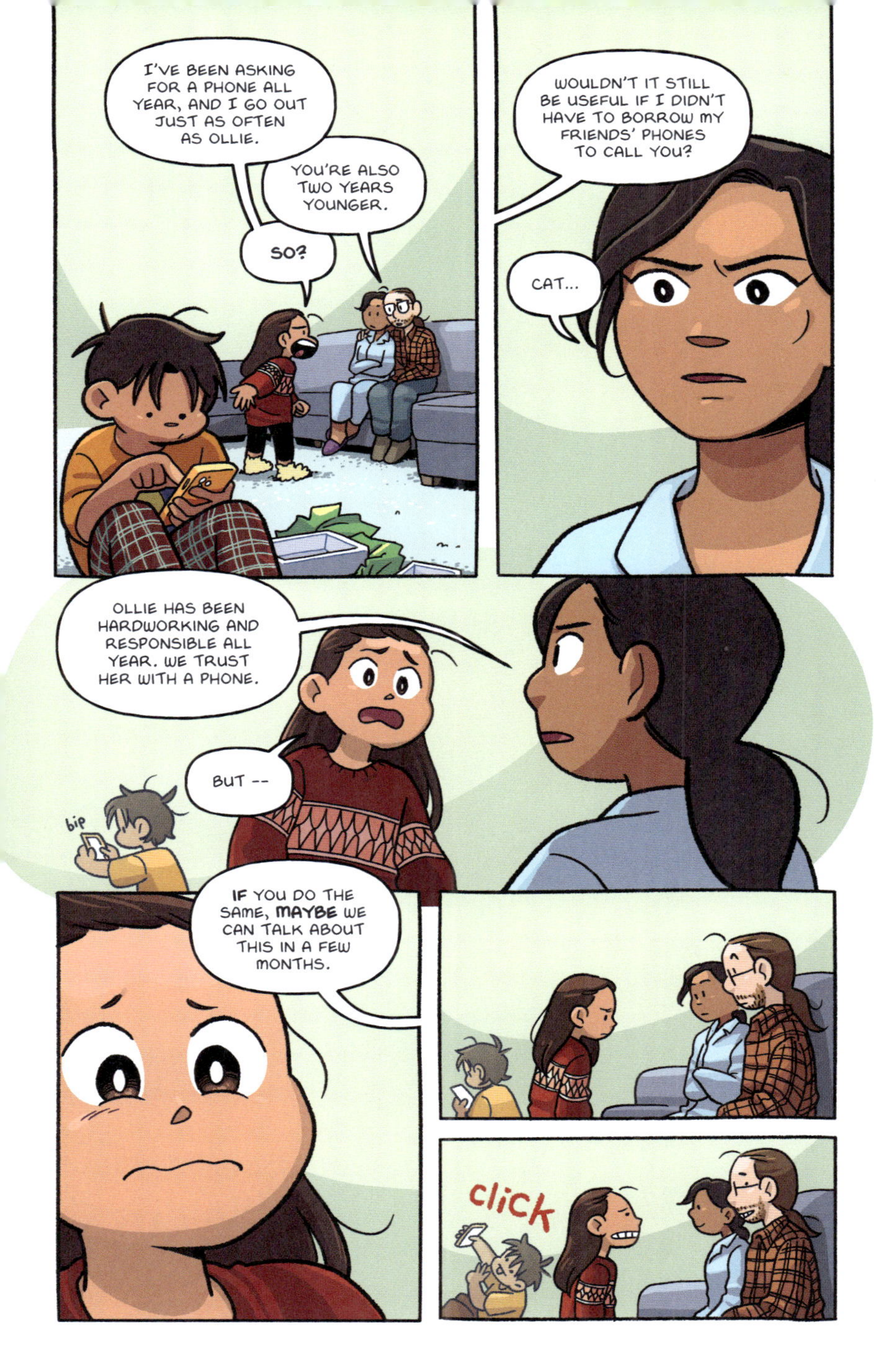
I'VE BEEN ASKING FOR A PHONE ALL YEAR, AND I GO OUT JUST AS OFTEN AS OLLIE.
YOU'RE ALSO TWO YEARS YOUNGER.
SO?
WOULDN'T IT STILL BE USEFUL IF I DIDN'T HAVE TO BORROW MY FRIENDS' PHONES TO CALL YOU?
CAT...
OLLIE HAS BEEN HARDWORKING AND RESPONSIBLE ALL YEAR. WE TRUST HER WITH A PHONE.
BUT --
bip
IF YOU DO THE SAME, **MAYBE** WE CAN TALK ABOUT THIS IN A FEW MONTHS.
click

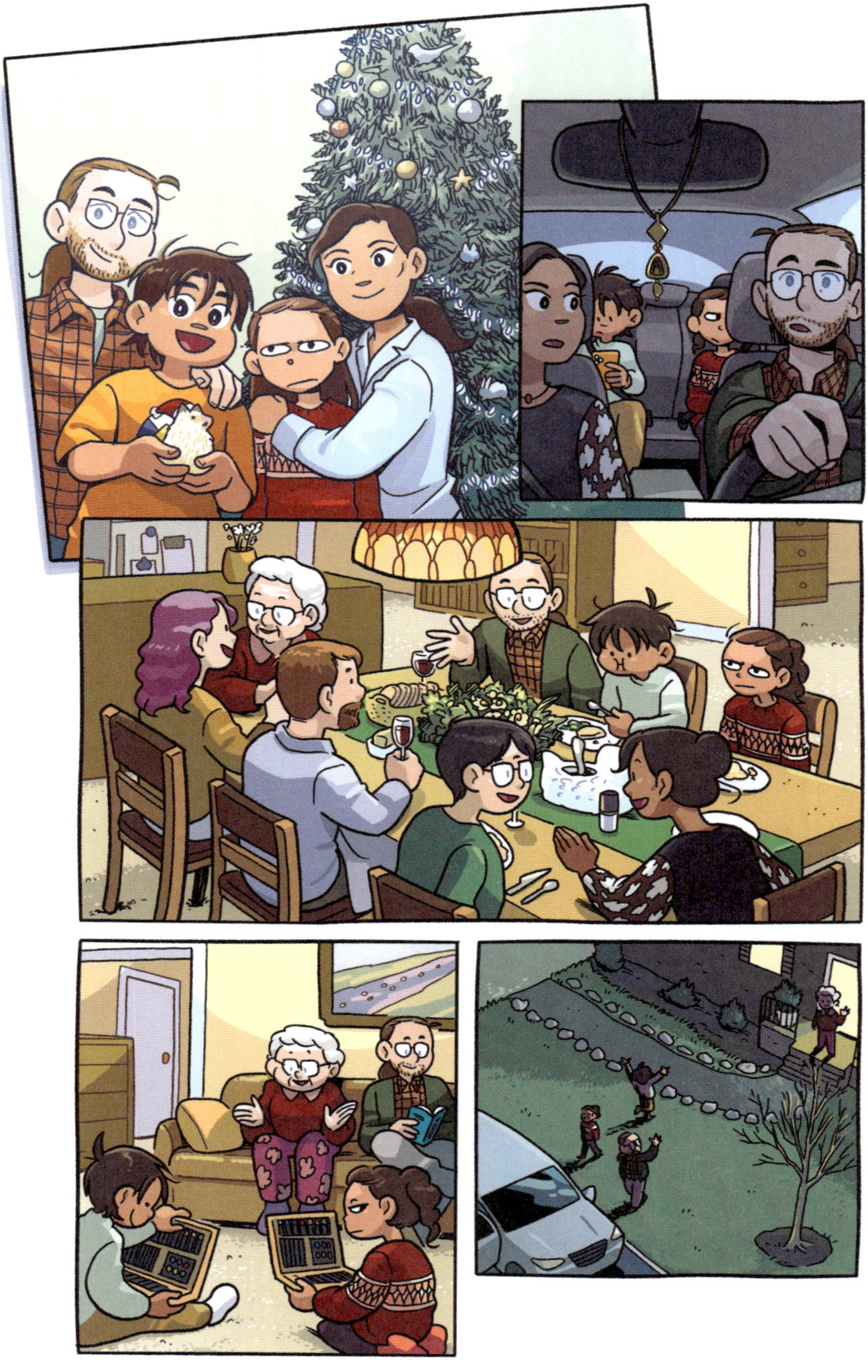

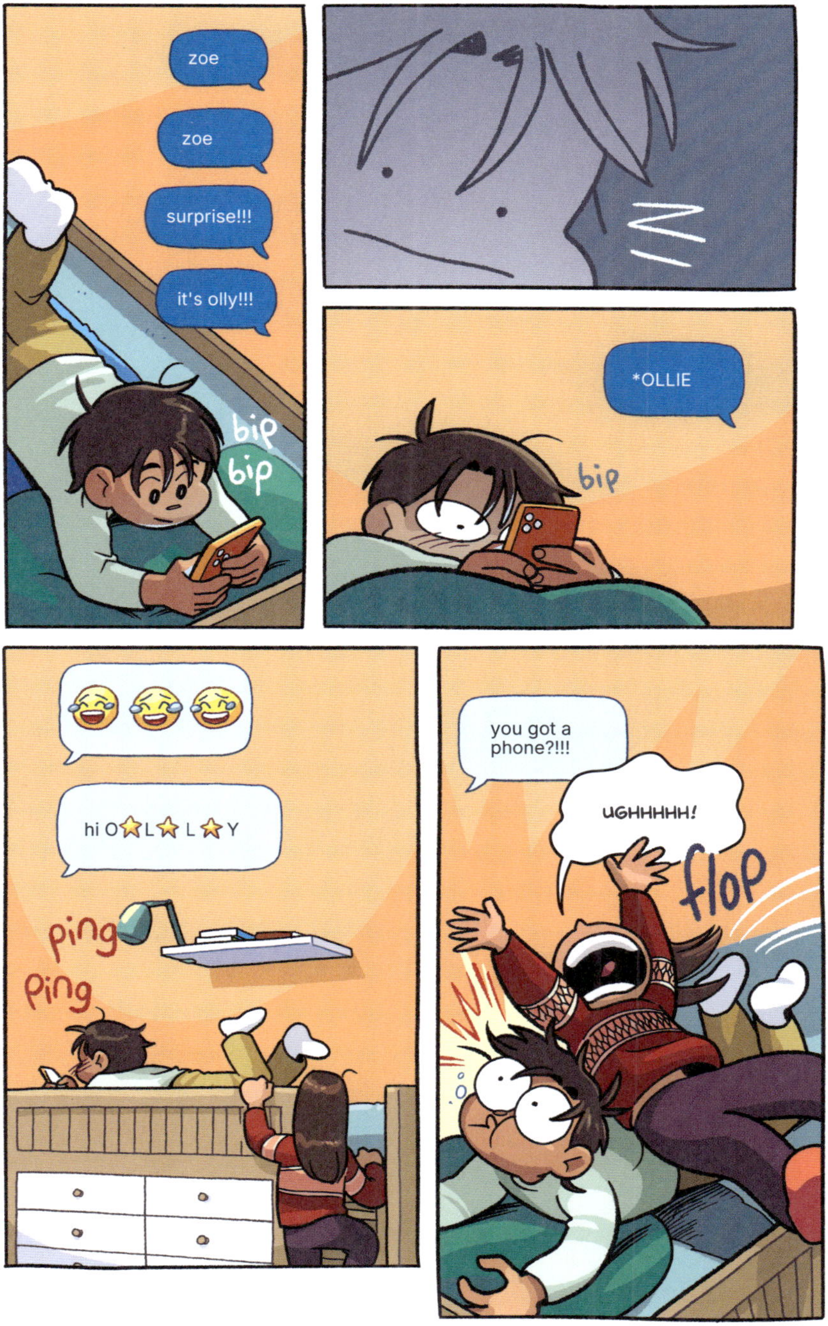
zoe
zoe
surprise!!!
it's olly!!!
bip
bip
*OLLIE
bip
hi O⭐L⭐L⭐Y
ping
ping
you got a phone?!!!
UGHHHHH!
flop

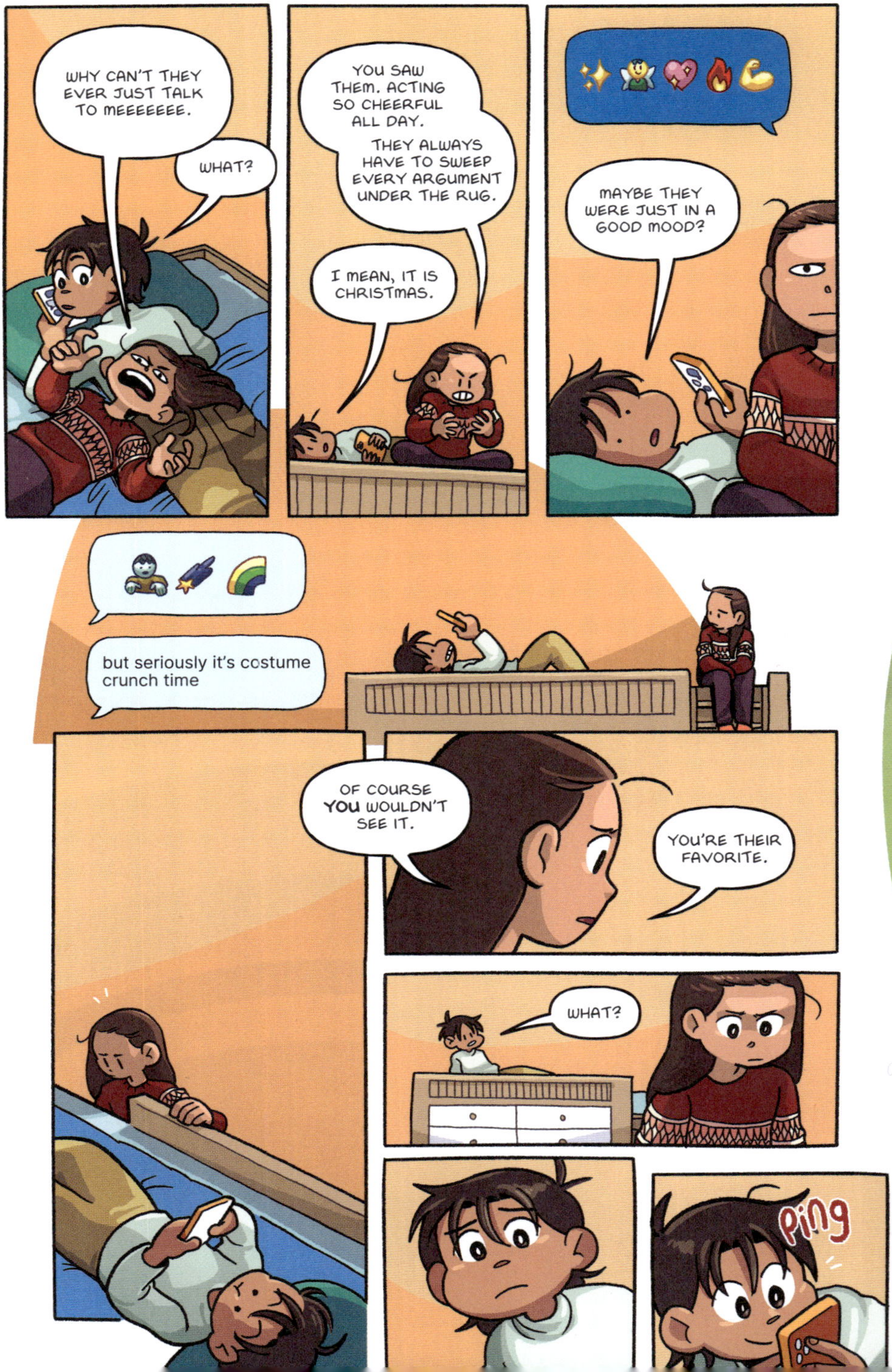
WHY CAN'T THEY EVER JUST TALK TO MEEEEEEE.
WHAT?
YOU SAW THEM. ACTING SO CHEERFUL ALL DAY.
THEY ALWAYS HAVE TO SWEEP EVERY ARGUMENT UNDER THE RUG.
I MEAN, IT IS CHRISTMAS.
MAYBE THEY WERE JUST IN A GOOD MOOD?
but seriously it's costume crunch time
OF COURSE YOU WOULDN'T SEE IT.
YOU'RE THEIR FAVORITE.
WHAT?
PING

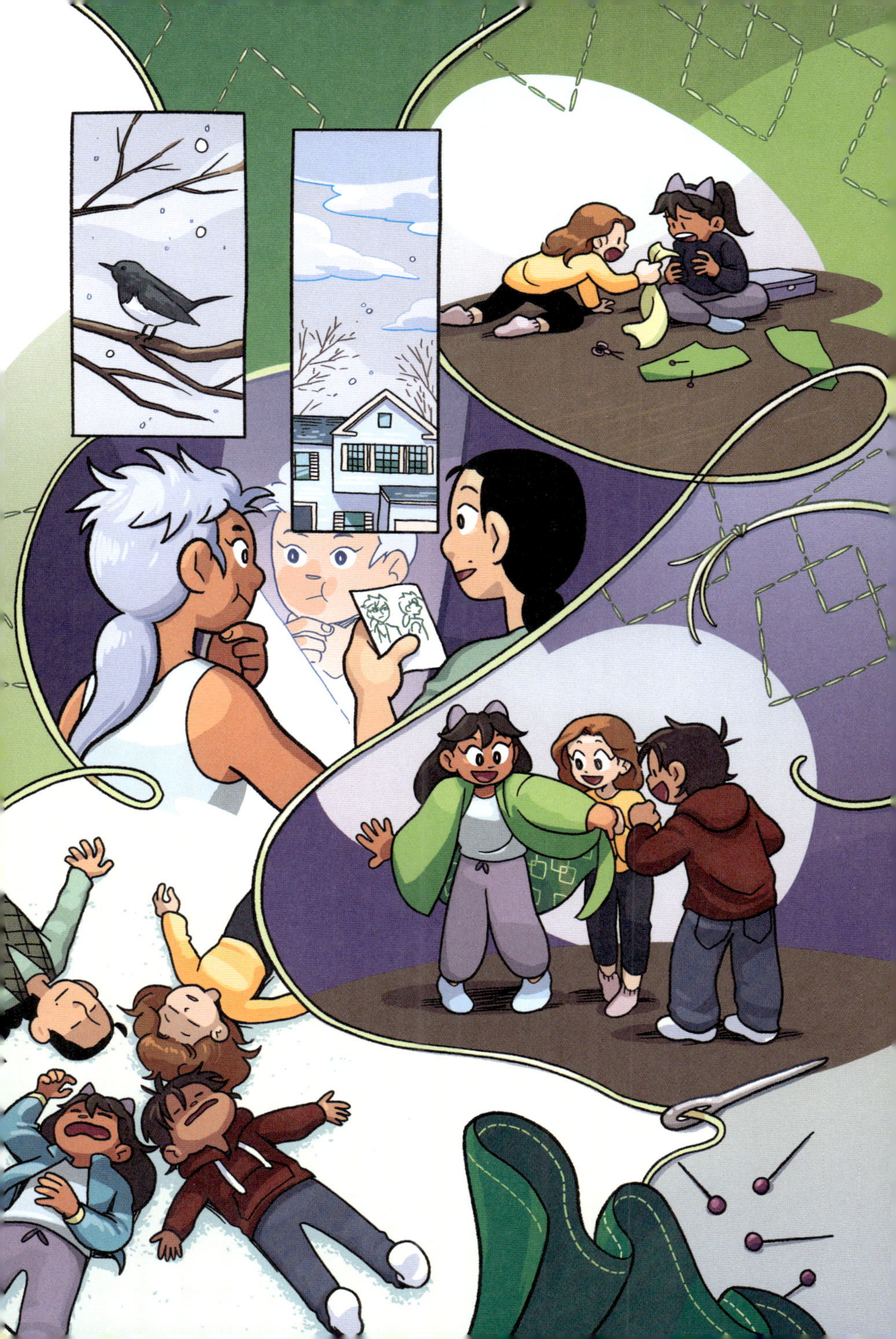

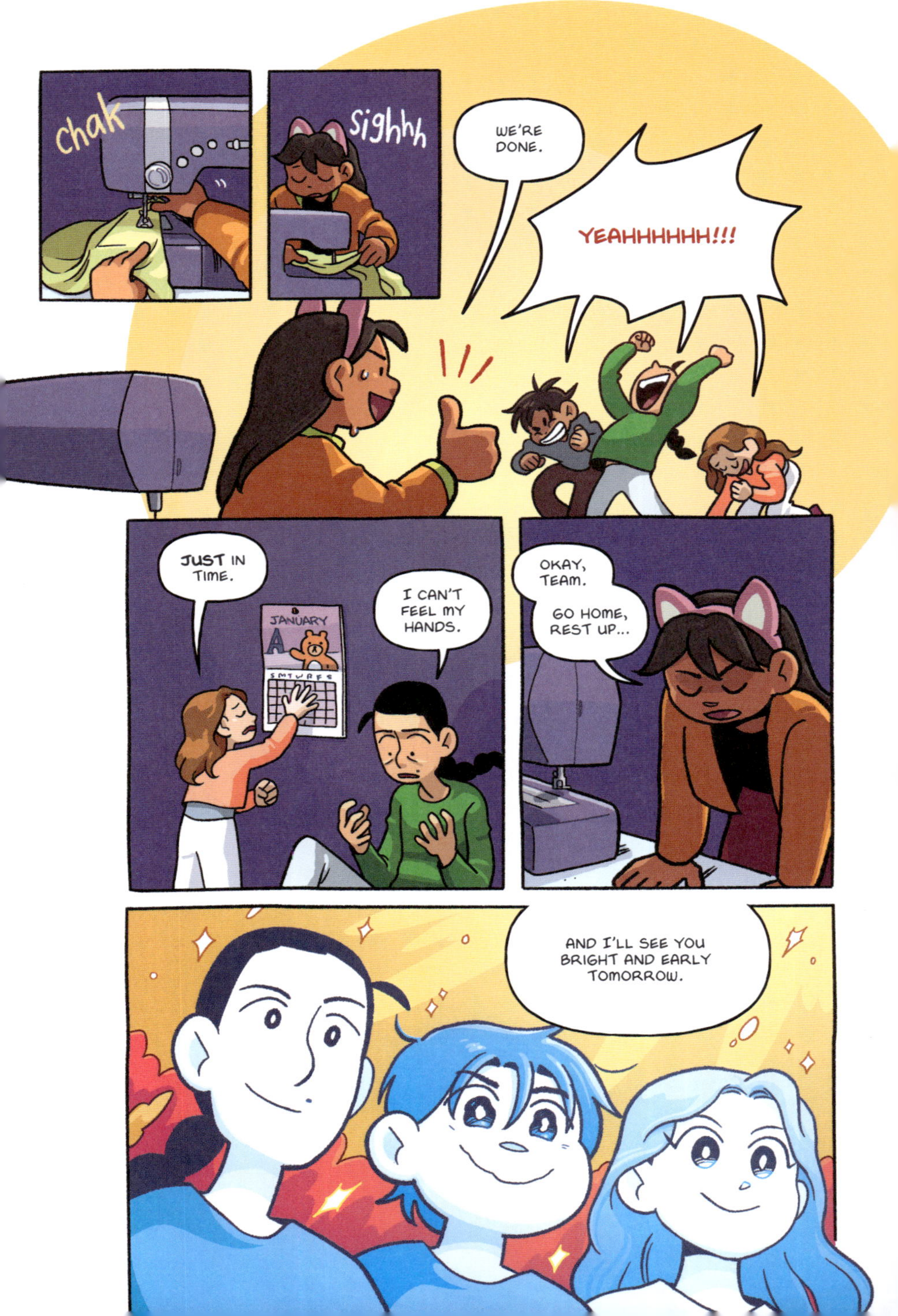
chak
sighhh
WE'RE DONE.
YEAHHHHHH!!!
JUST IN TIME.
JANUARY
I CAN'T FEEL MY HANDS.
OKAY, TEAM.
GO HOME, REST UP...
AND I'LL SEE YOU BRIGHT AND EARLY TOMORROW.

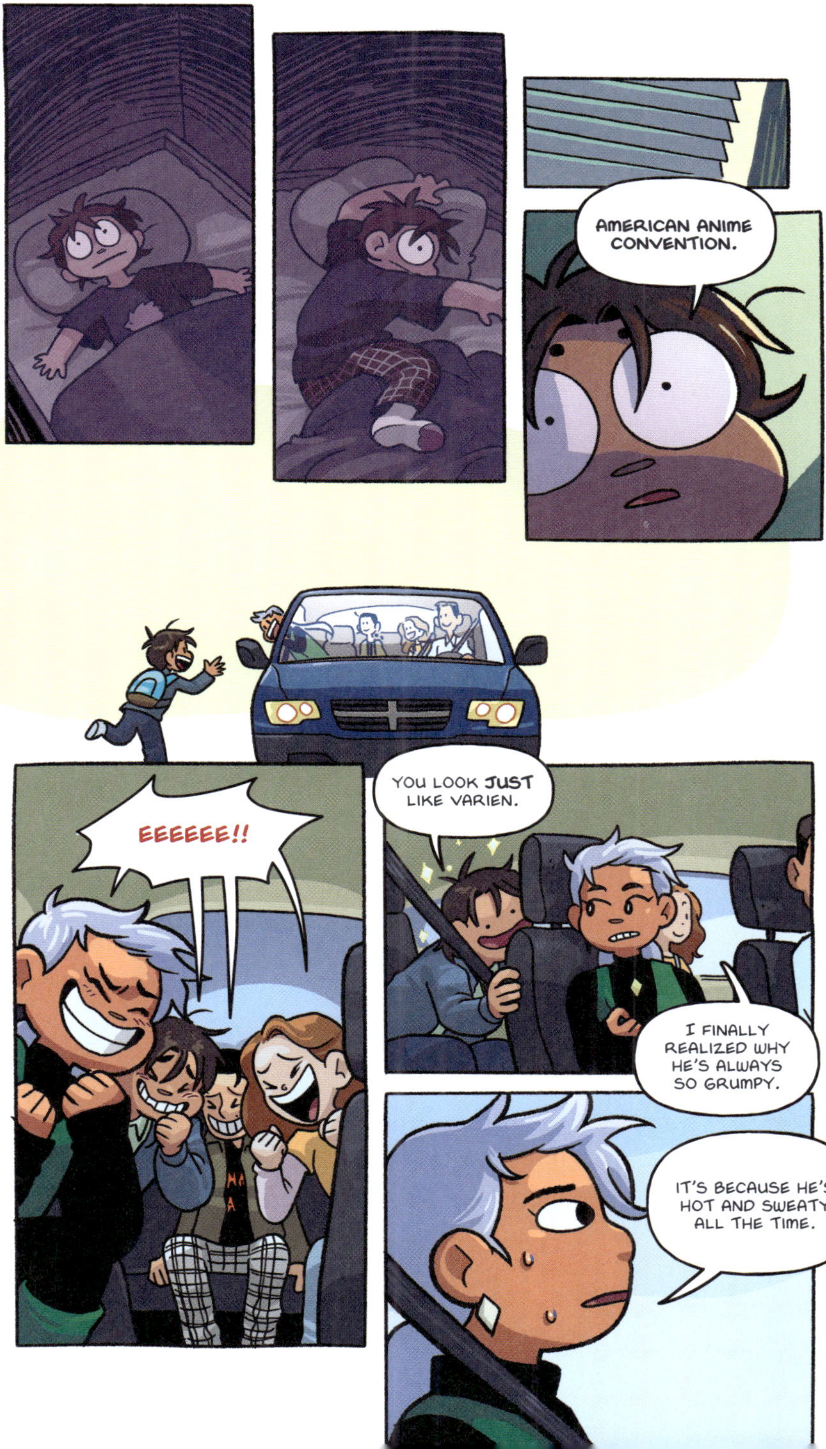
AMERICAN ANIME CONVENTION.
EEEEEE!!
YOU LOOK JUST LIKE VARIEN.
I FINALLY REALIZED WHY HE'S ALWAYS SO GRUMPY.
IT'S BECAUSE HE'S HOT AND SWEATY ALL THE TIME.

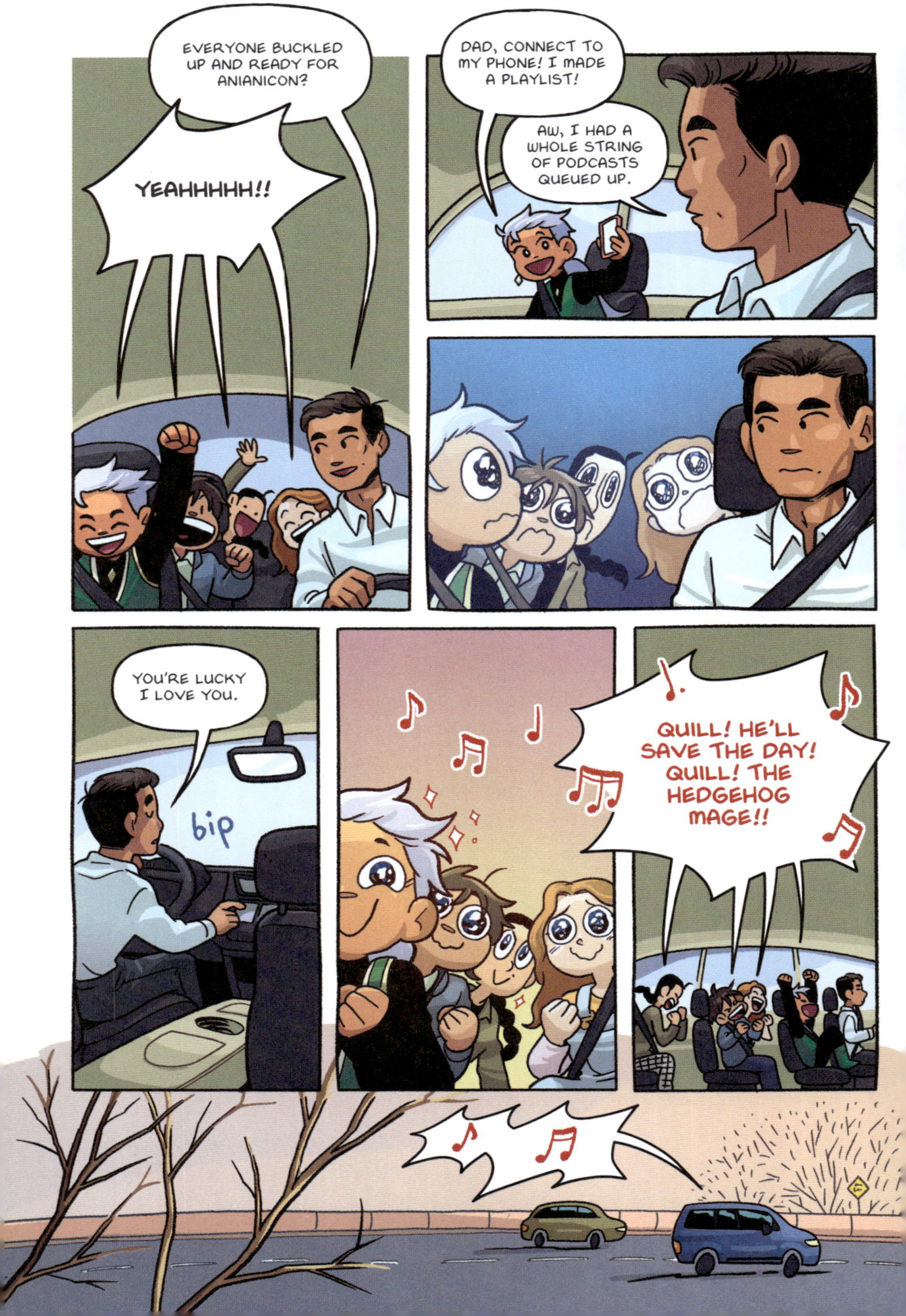
EVERYONE BUCKLED UP AND READY FOR ANIANICON?
YEAHHHHH!!
DAD, CONNECT TO MY PHONE! I MADE A PLAYLIST!
AW, I HAD A WHOLE STRING OF PODCASTS QUEUED UP.
YOU'RE LUCKY I LOVE YOU.
bip
QUILL! HE'LL SAVE THE DAY! QUILL! THE HEDGEHOG MAGE!!

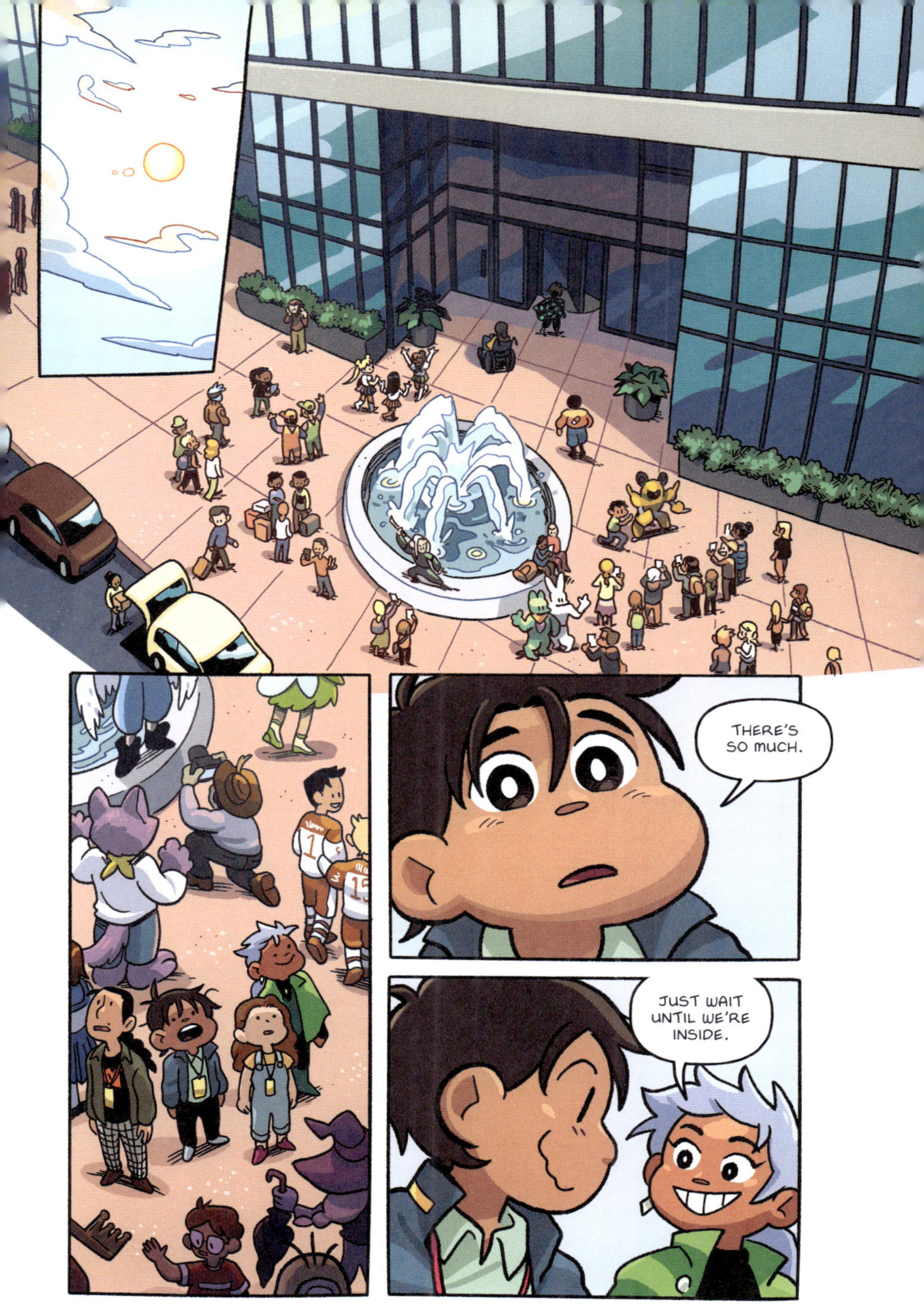
THERE'S SO MUCH.
JUST WAIT UNTIL WE'RE INSIDE.

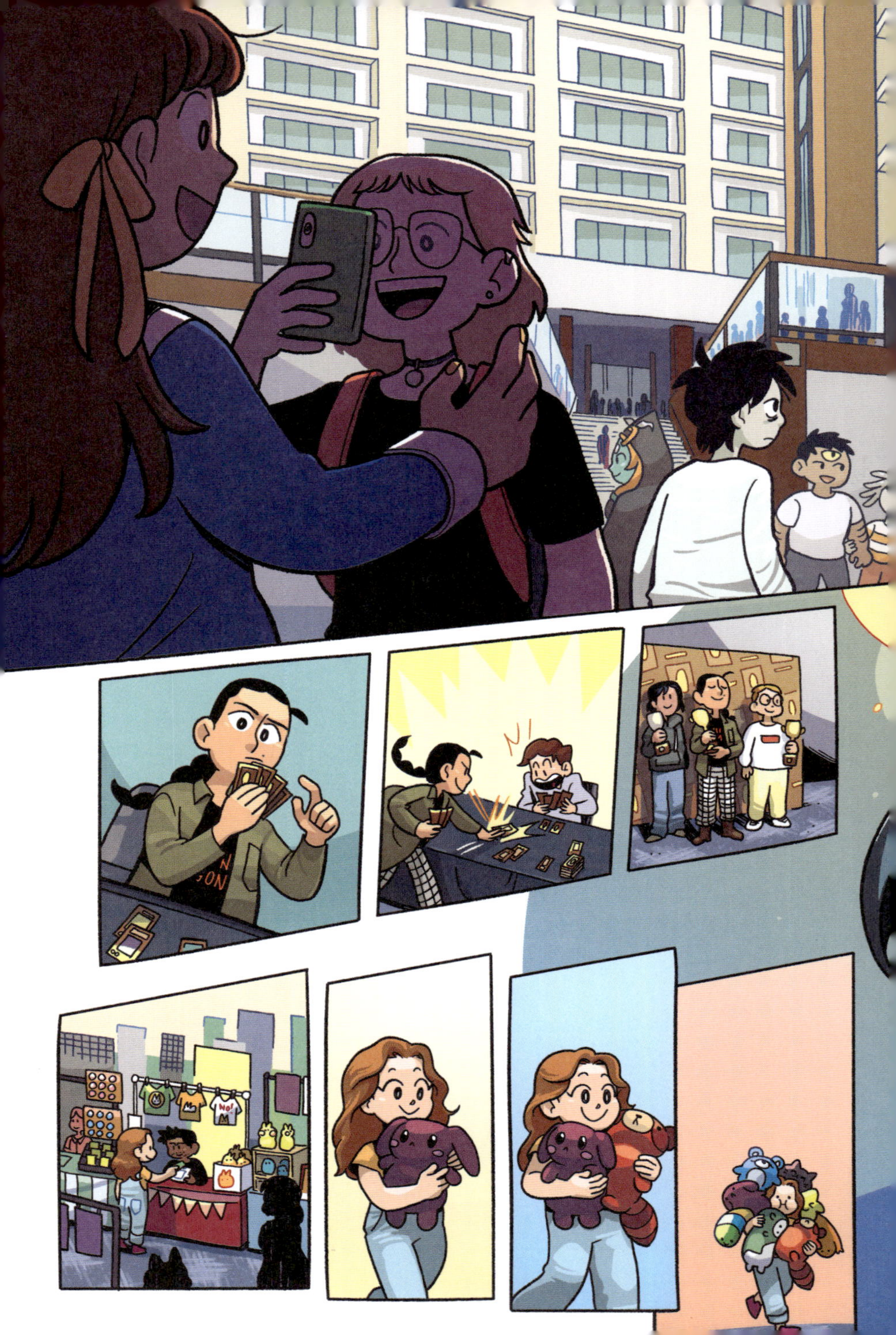

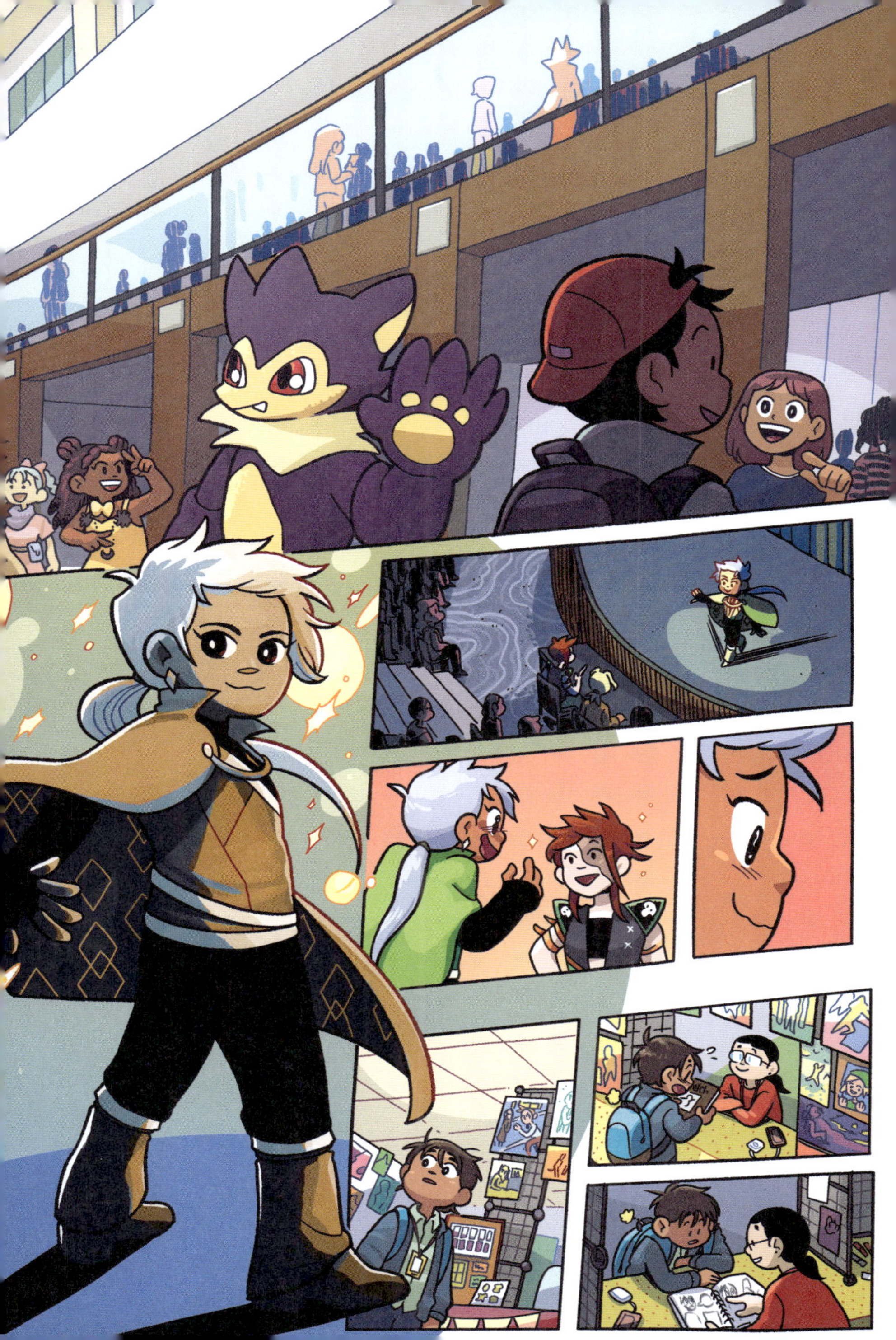

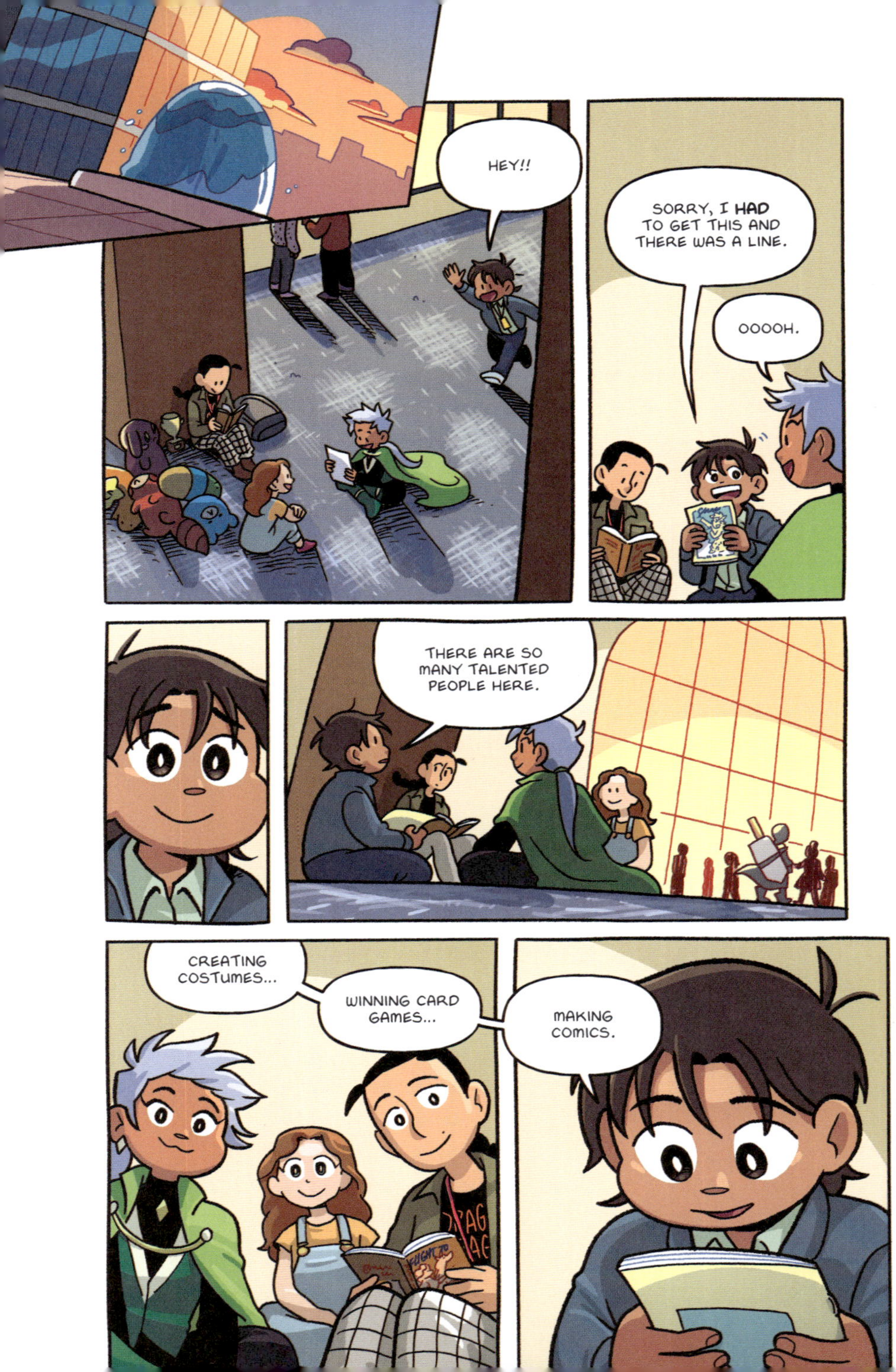
HEY!!
SORRY, I **HAD** TO GET THIS AND THERE WAS A LINE.
OOOOH.
THERE ARE SO MANY TALENTED PEOPLE HERE.
CREATING COSTUMES...
WINNING CARD GAMES...
MAKING COMICS.

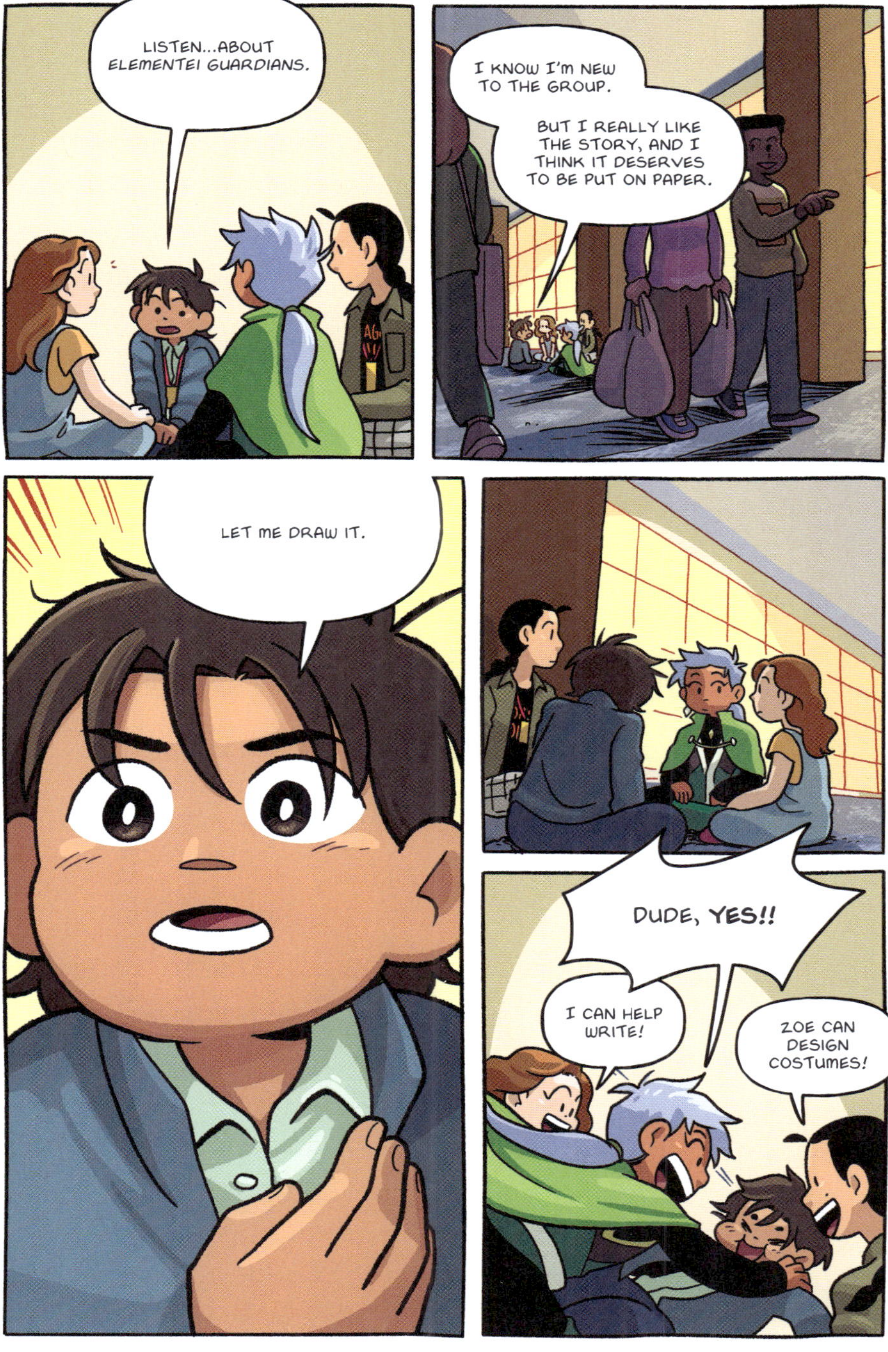
LISTEN...ABOUT ELEMENTEI GUARDIANS.
I KNOW I'M NEW TO THE GROUP.
BUT I REALLY LIKE THE STORY, AND I THINK IT DESERVES TO BE PUT ON PAPER.
LET ME DRAW IT.
DUDE, **YES!!**
I CAN HELP WRITE!
ZOE CAN DESIGN COSTUMES!

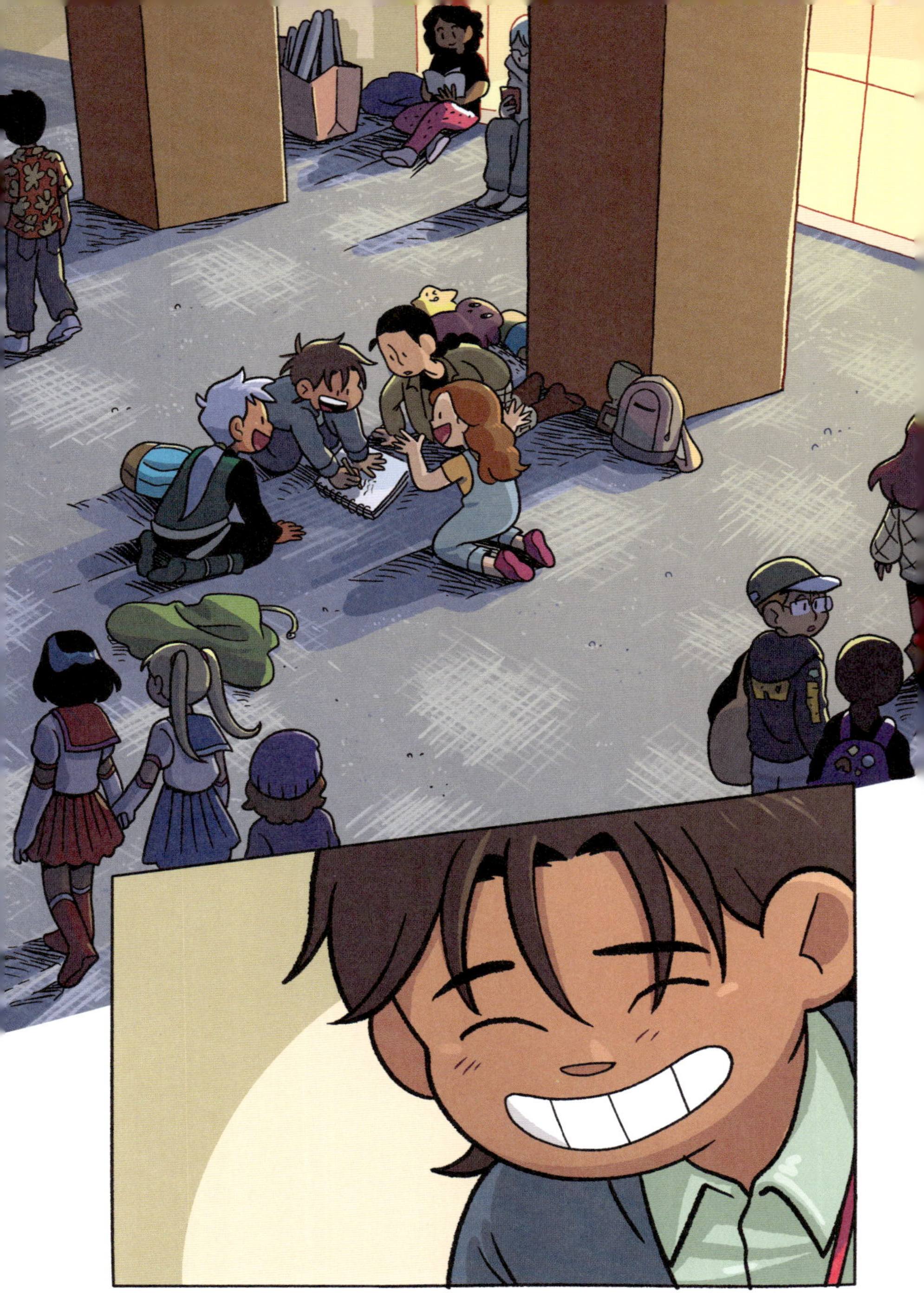

CHAPTER TEN

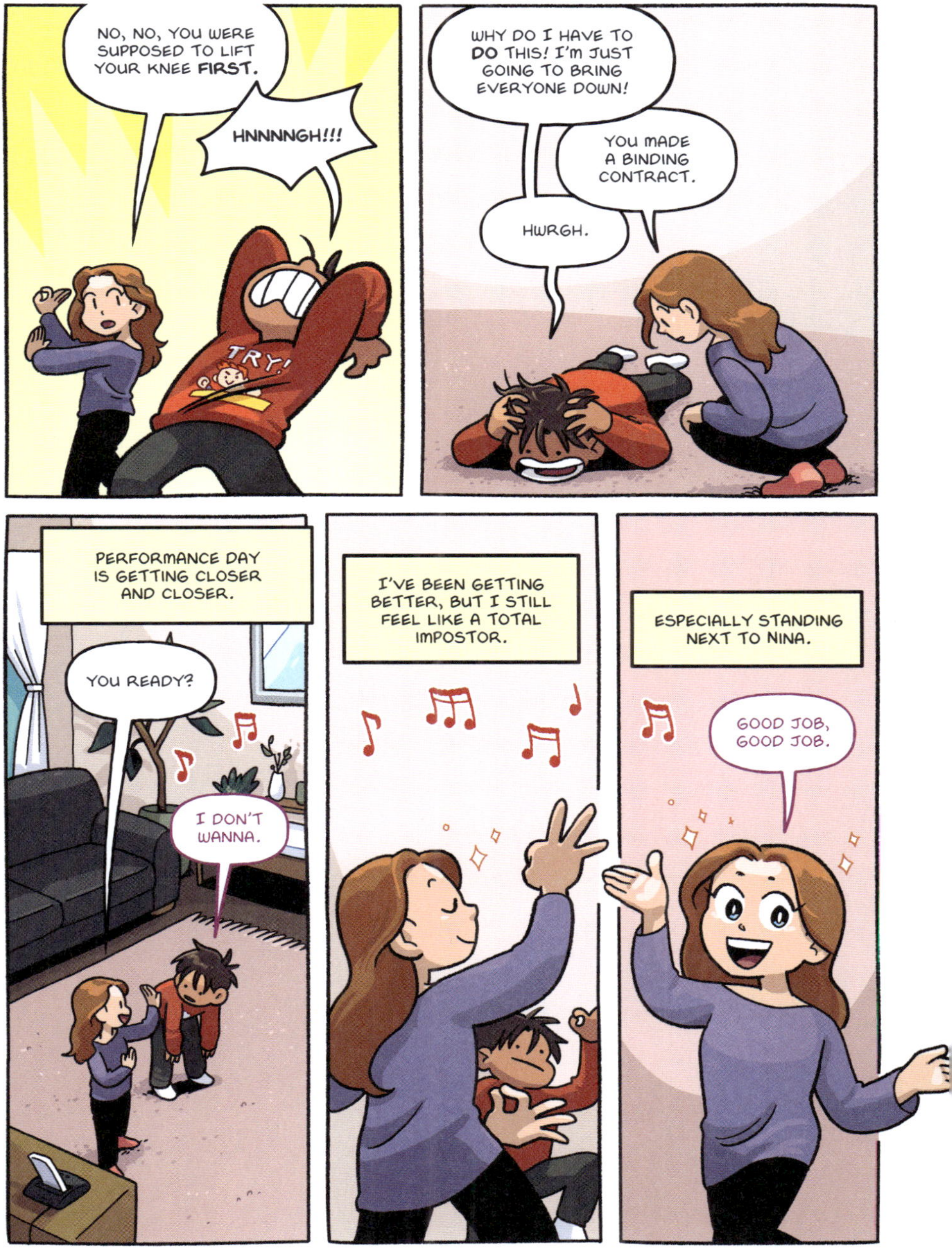

NO, NO, YOU WERE SUPPOSED TO LIFT YOUR KNEE FIRST.
HNNNNGH!!!
WHY DO I HAVE TO DO THIS! I'M JUST GOING TO BRING EVERYONE DOWN!
HWRGH.
YOU MADE A BINDING CONTRACT.
TRY!
PERFORMANCE DAY IS GETTING CLOSER AND CLOSER.
YOU READY?
I DON'T WANNA.
I'VE BEEN GETTING BETTER, BUT I STILL FEEL LIKE A TOTAL IMPOSTOR.
ESPECIALLY STANDING NEXT TO NINA.
GOOD JOB, GOOD JOB.

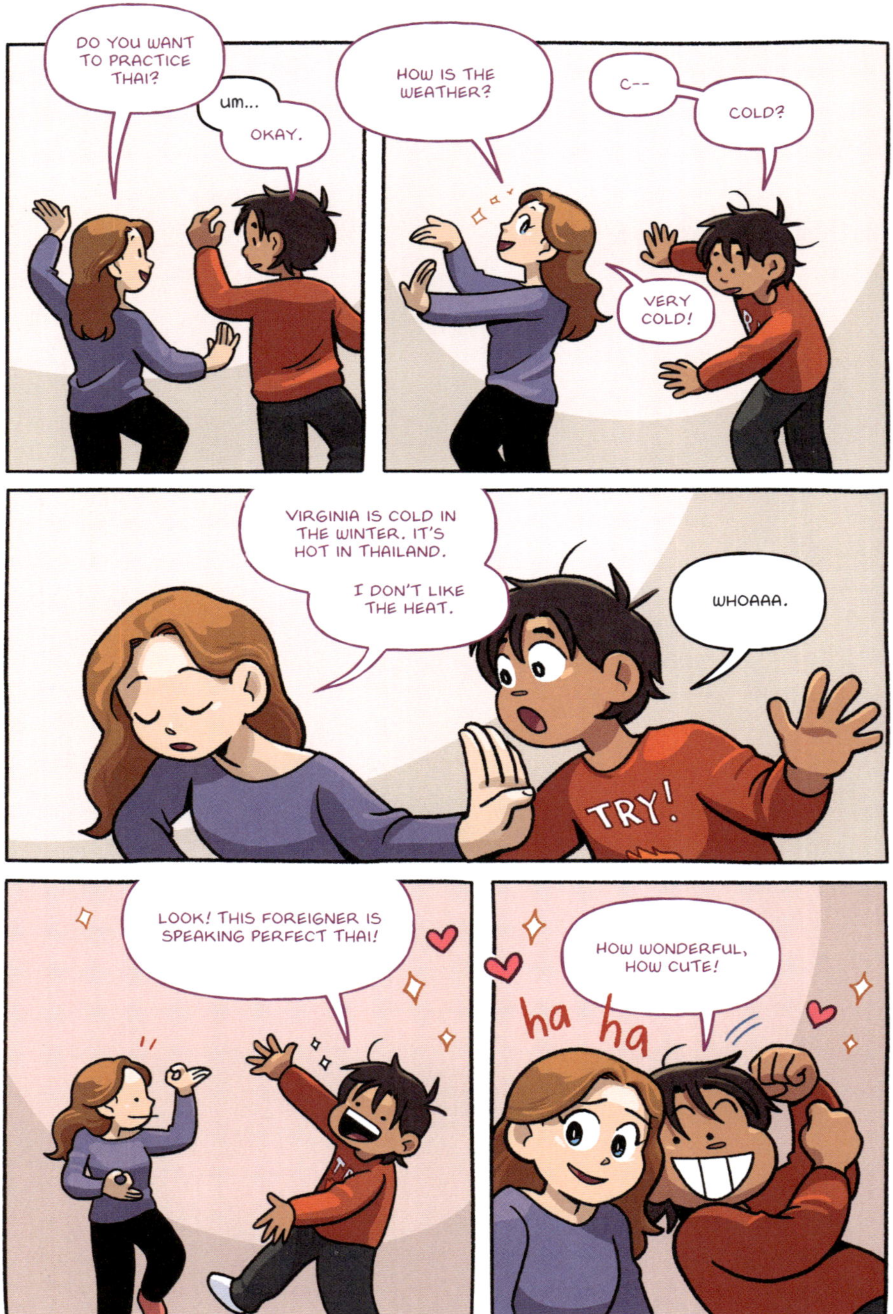
DO YOU WANT TO PRACTICE THAI?
UM... OKAY.
HOW IS THE WEATHER?
C--
COLD?
VERY COLD!
VIRGINIA IS COLD IN THE WINTER. IT'S HOT IN THAILAND.
I DON'T LIKE THE HEAT.
WHOAAA.
TRY!
LOOK! THIS FOREIGNER IS SPEAKING PERFECT THAI!
HOW WONDERFUL, HOW CUTE!
ha ha

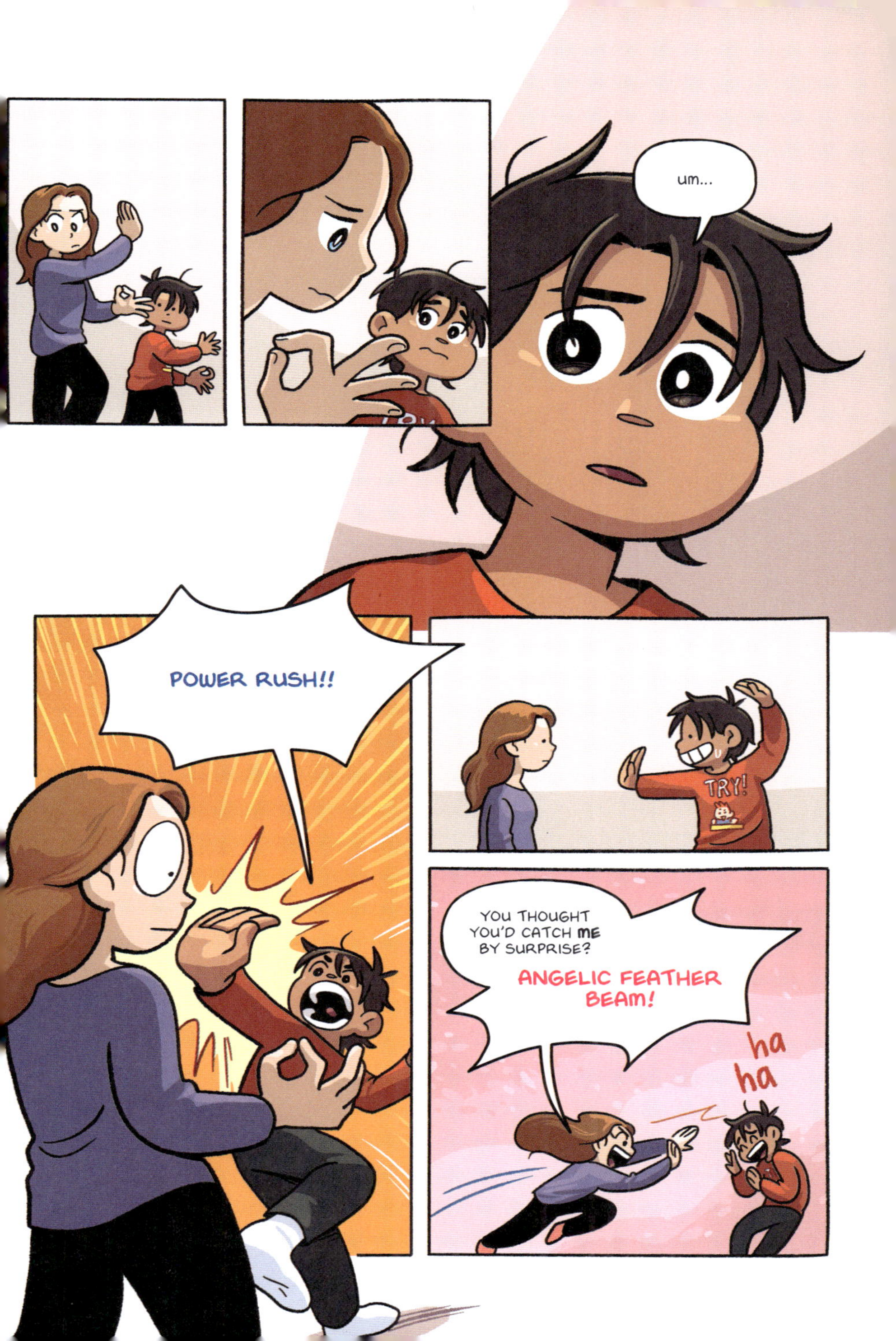
um...
POWER RUSH!!
TRY!
YOU THOUGHT YOU'D CATCH ME BY SURPRISE?
ANGELIC FEATHER BEAM!
ha ha

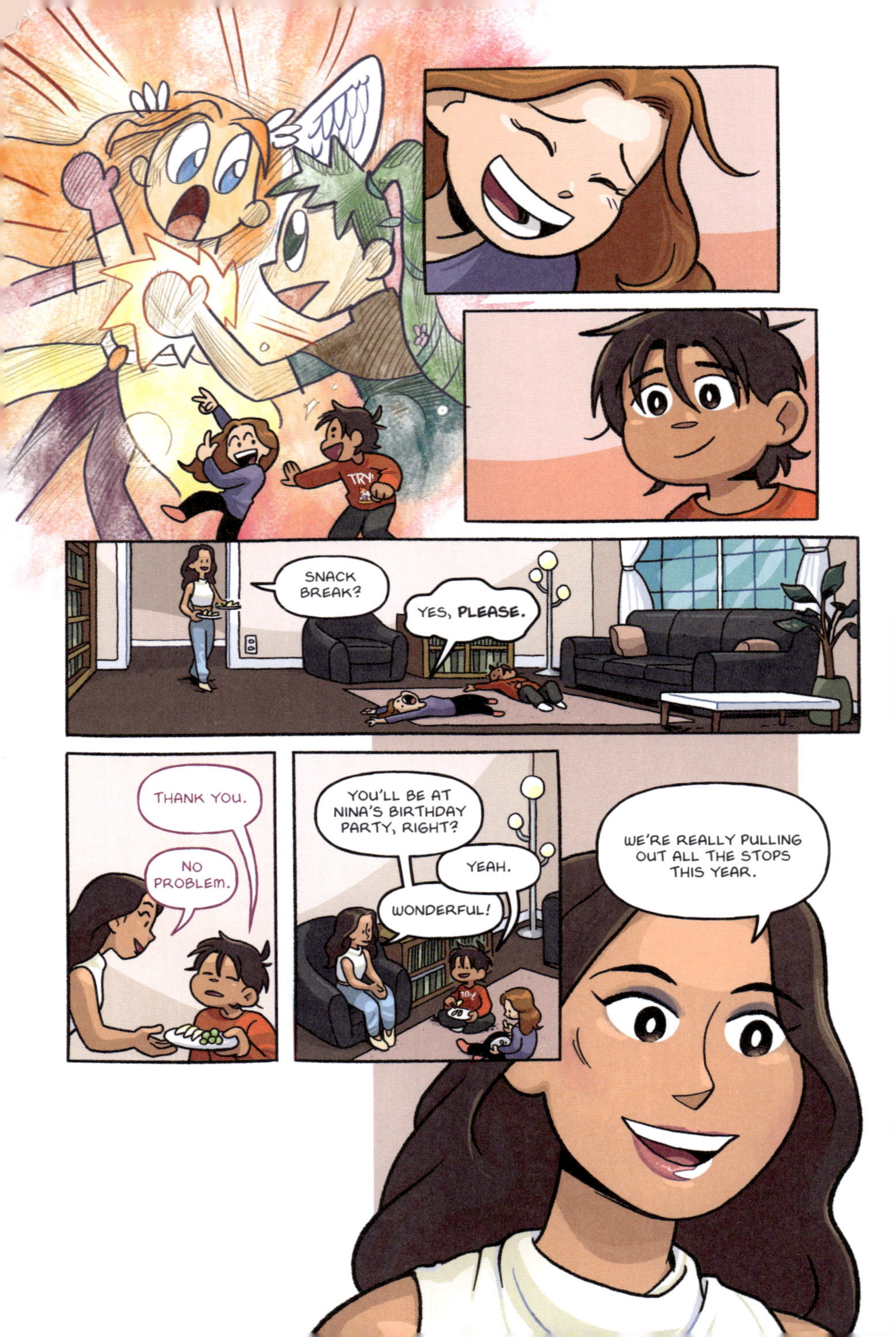
TRY!
SNACK BREAK?
YES, PLEASE.
THANK YOU.
NO PROBLEM.
YOU'LL BE AT NINA'S BIRTHDAY PARTY, RIGHT?
YEAH.
WONDERFUL!
WE'RE REALLY PULLING OUT ALL THE STOPS THIS YEAR.

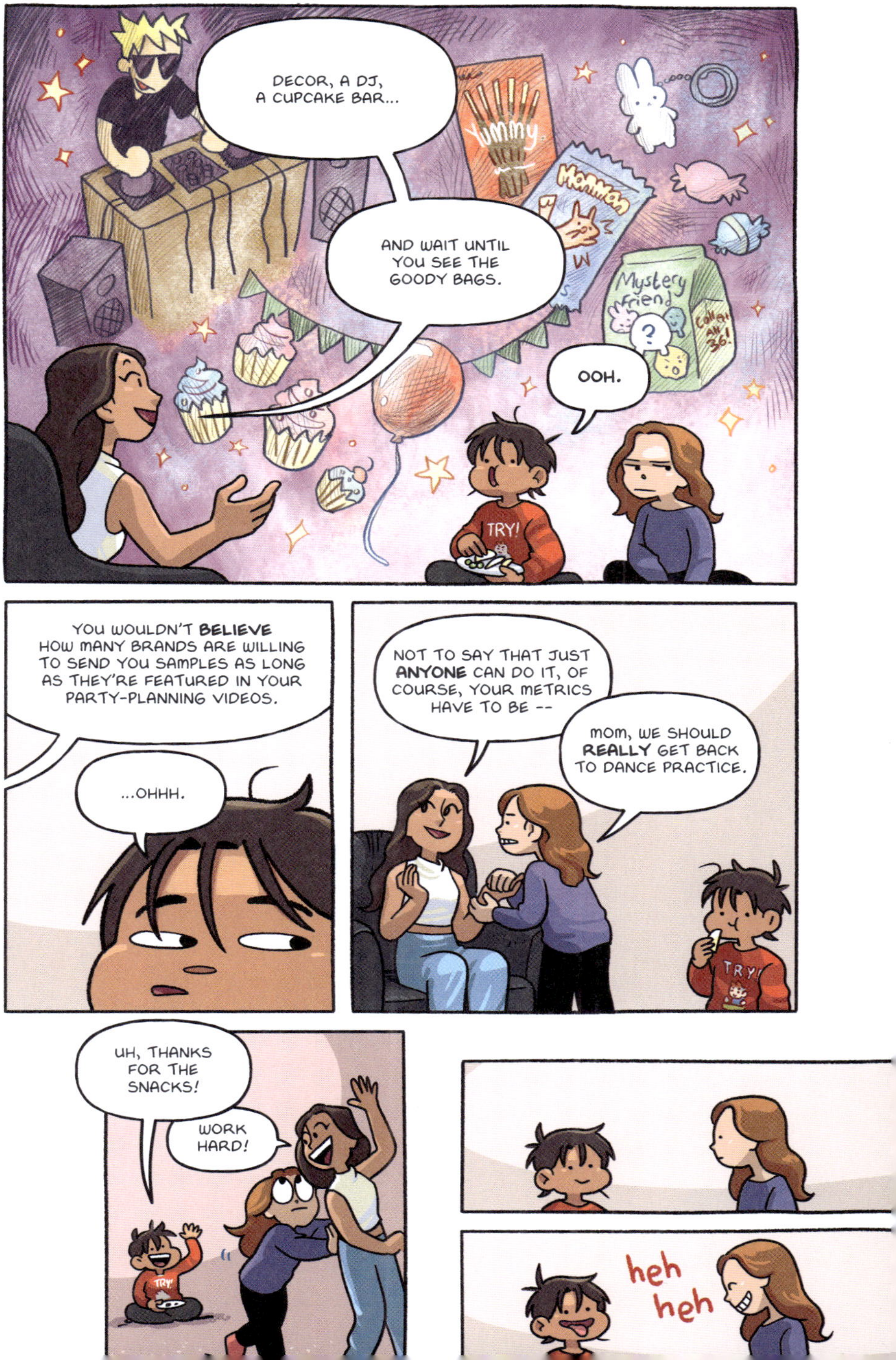

DECOR, A DJ, A CUPCAKE BAR...
AND WAIT UNTIL YOU SEE THE GOODY BAGS.
Yummy
Mystery friend
Collect all 36!
OOH.
TRY!
YOU WOULDN'T BELIEVE HOW MANY BRANDS ARE WILLING TO SEND YOU SAMPLES AS LONG AS THEY'RE FEATURED IN YOUR PARTY-PLANNING VIDEOS.
...OHHH.
NOT TO SAY THAT JUST ANYONE CAN DO IT, OF COURSE, YOUR METRICS HAVE TO BE --
MOM, WE SHOULD REALLY GET BACK TO DANCE PRACTICE.
UH, THANKS FOR THE SNACKS!
WORK HARD!
heh heh

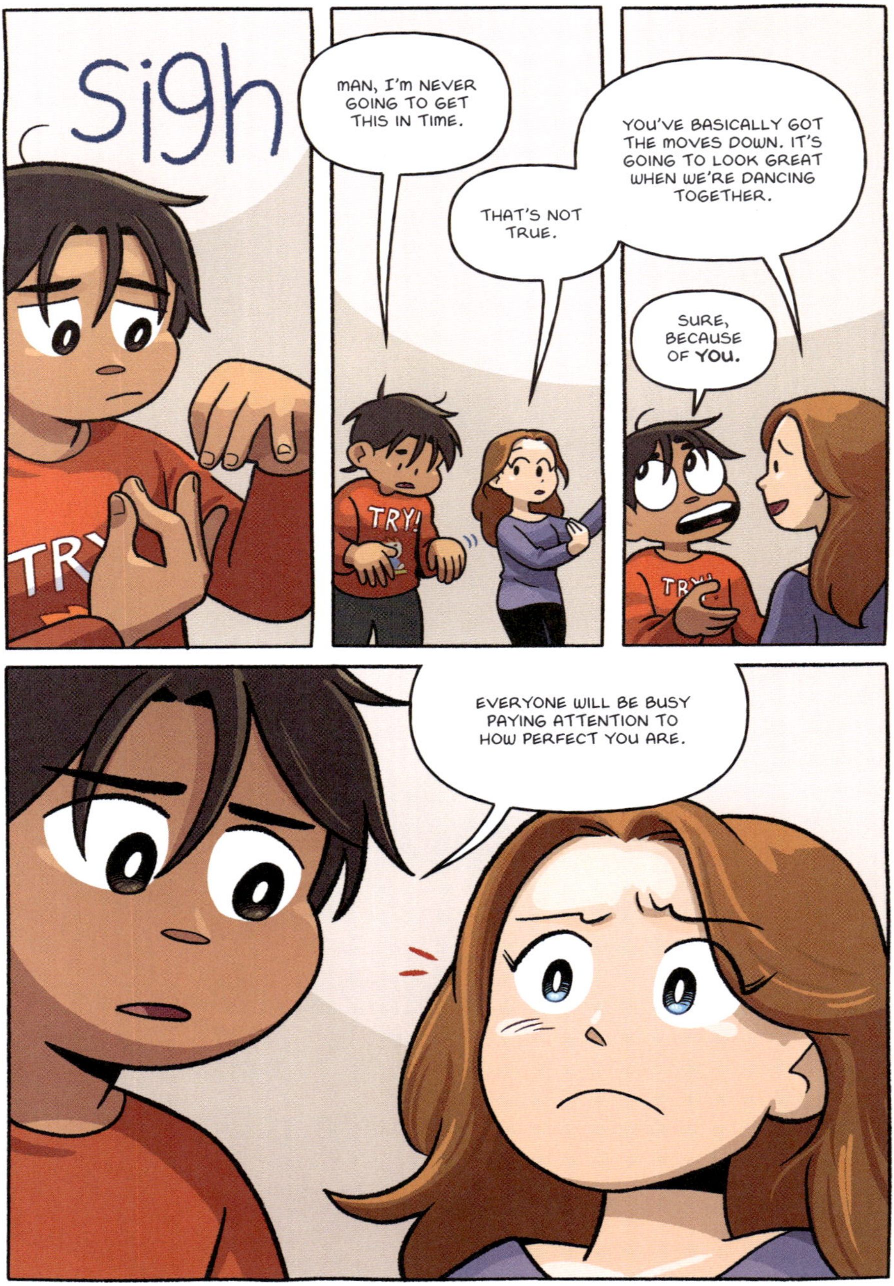
sigh
MAN, I'M NEVER GOING TO GET THIS IN TIME.
THAT'S NOT TRUE.
YOU'VE BASICALLY GOT THE MOVES DOWN. IT'S GOING TO LOOK GREAT WHEN WE'RE DANCING TOGETHER.
SURE, BECAUSE OF **YOU.**
EVERYONE WILL BE BUSY PAYING ATTENTION TO HOW PERFECT YOU ARE.

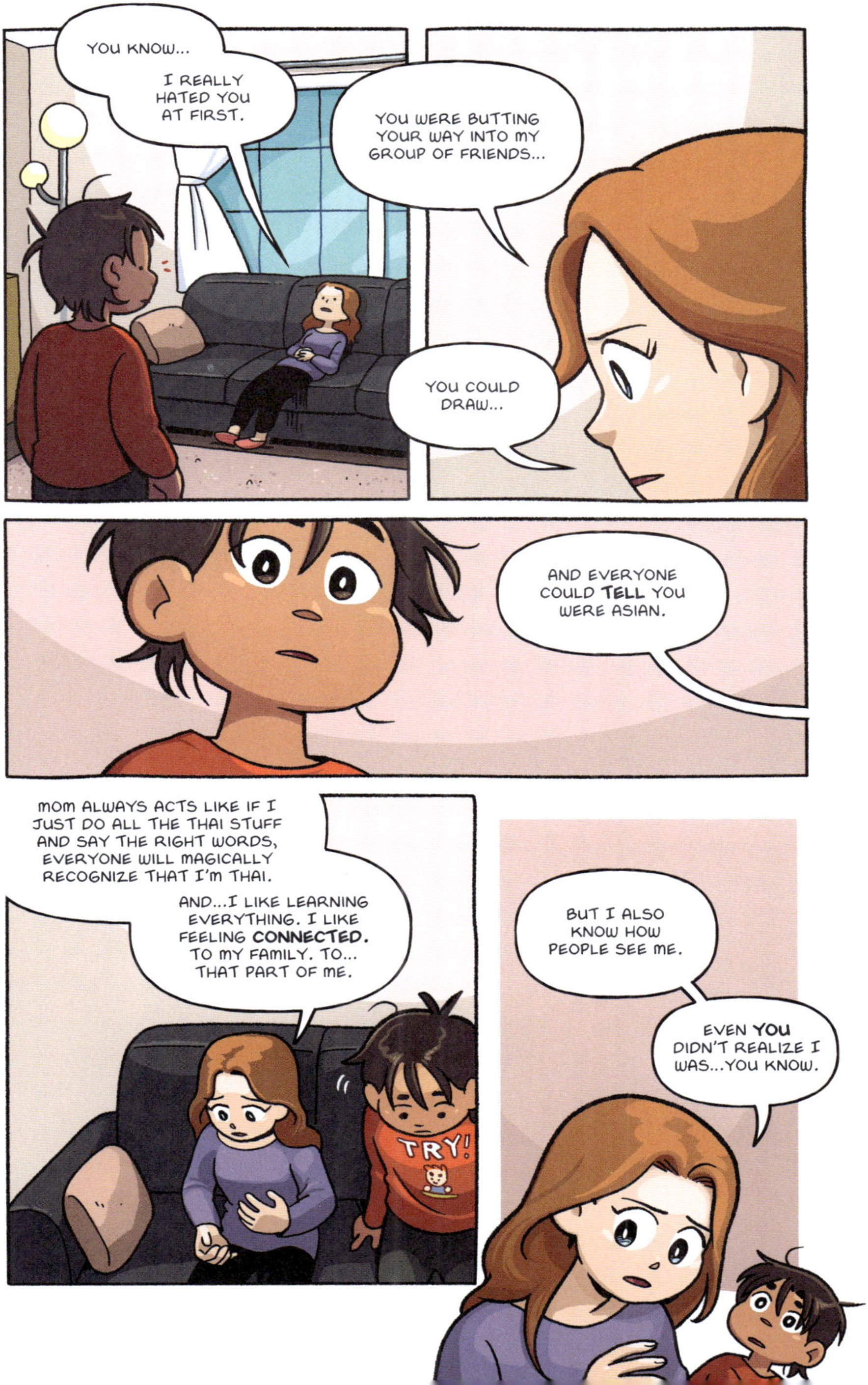
YOU KNOW...
I REALLY HATED YOU AT FIRST.
YOU WERE BUTTING YOUR WAY INTO MY GROUP OF FRIENDS...
YOU COULD DRAW...
AND EVERYONE COULD **TELL** YOU WERE ASIAN.
MOM ALWAYS ACTS LIKE IF I JUST DO ALL THE THAI STUFF AND SAY THE RIGHT WORDS, EVERYONE WILL MAGICALLY RECOGNIZE THAT I'M THAI.
AND...I LIKE LEARNING EVERYTHING. I LIKE FEELING **CONNECTED.** TO MY FAMILY. TO... THAT PART OF ME.
TRY!
BUT I ALSO KNOW HOW PEOPLE SEE ME.
EVEN **YOU** DIDN'T REALIZE I WAS...YOU KNOW.

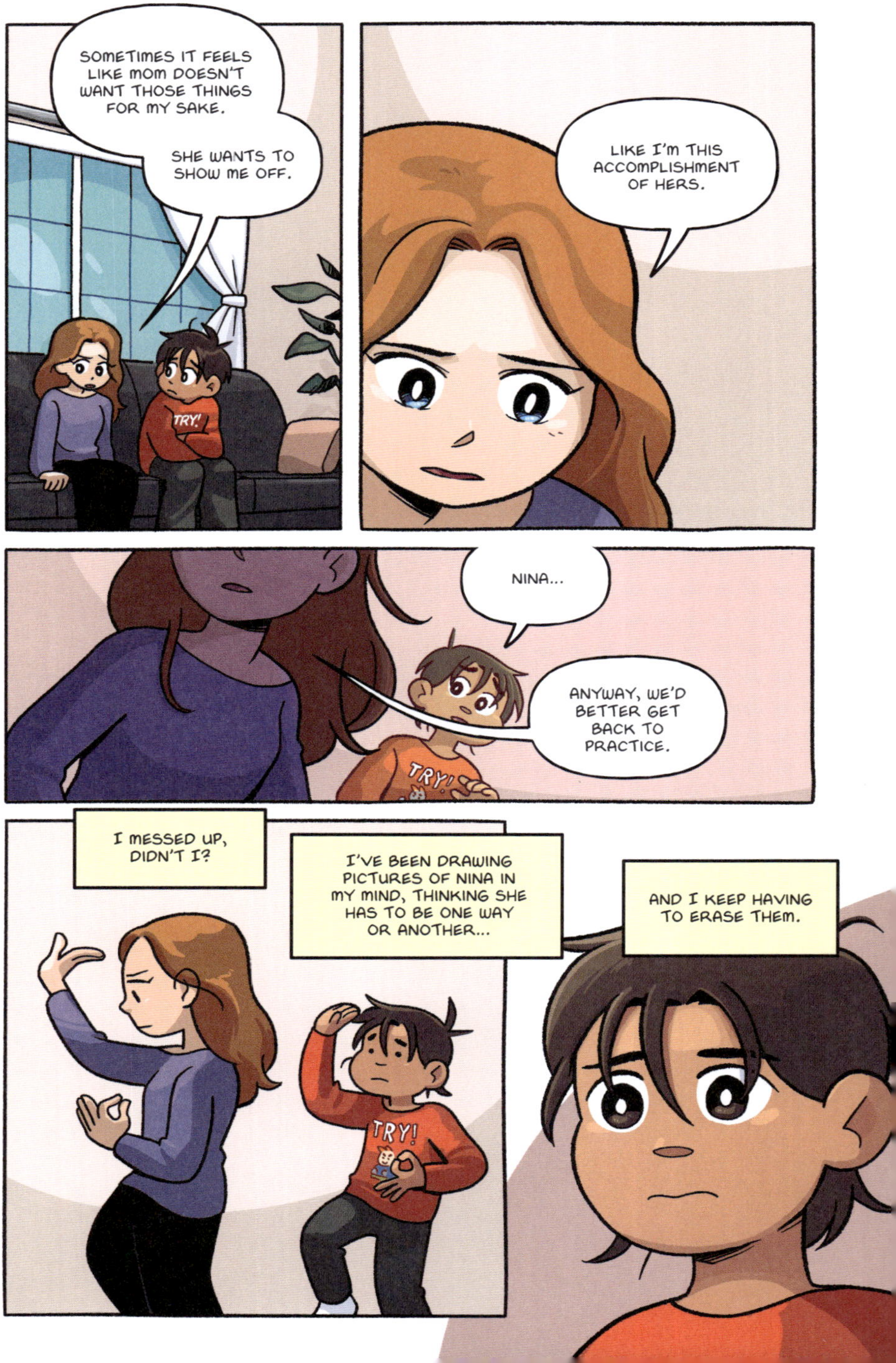
SOMETIMES IT FEELS LIKE MOM DOESN'T WANT THOSE THINGS FOR MY SAKE.
SHE WANTS TO SHOW ME OFF.
TRY!
LIKE I'M THIS ACCOMPLISHMENT OF HERS.
NINA...
ANYWAY, WE'D BETTER GET BACK TO PRACTICE.
TRY!
I MESSED UP, DIDN'T I?
I'VE BEEN DRAWING PICTURES OF NINA IN MY MIND, THINKING SHE HAS TO BE ONE WAY OR ANOTHER...
AND I KEEP HAVING TO ERASE THEM.
TRY!

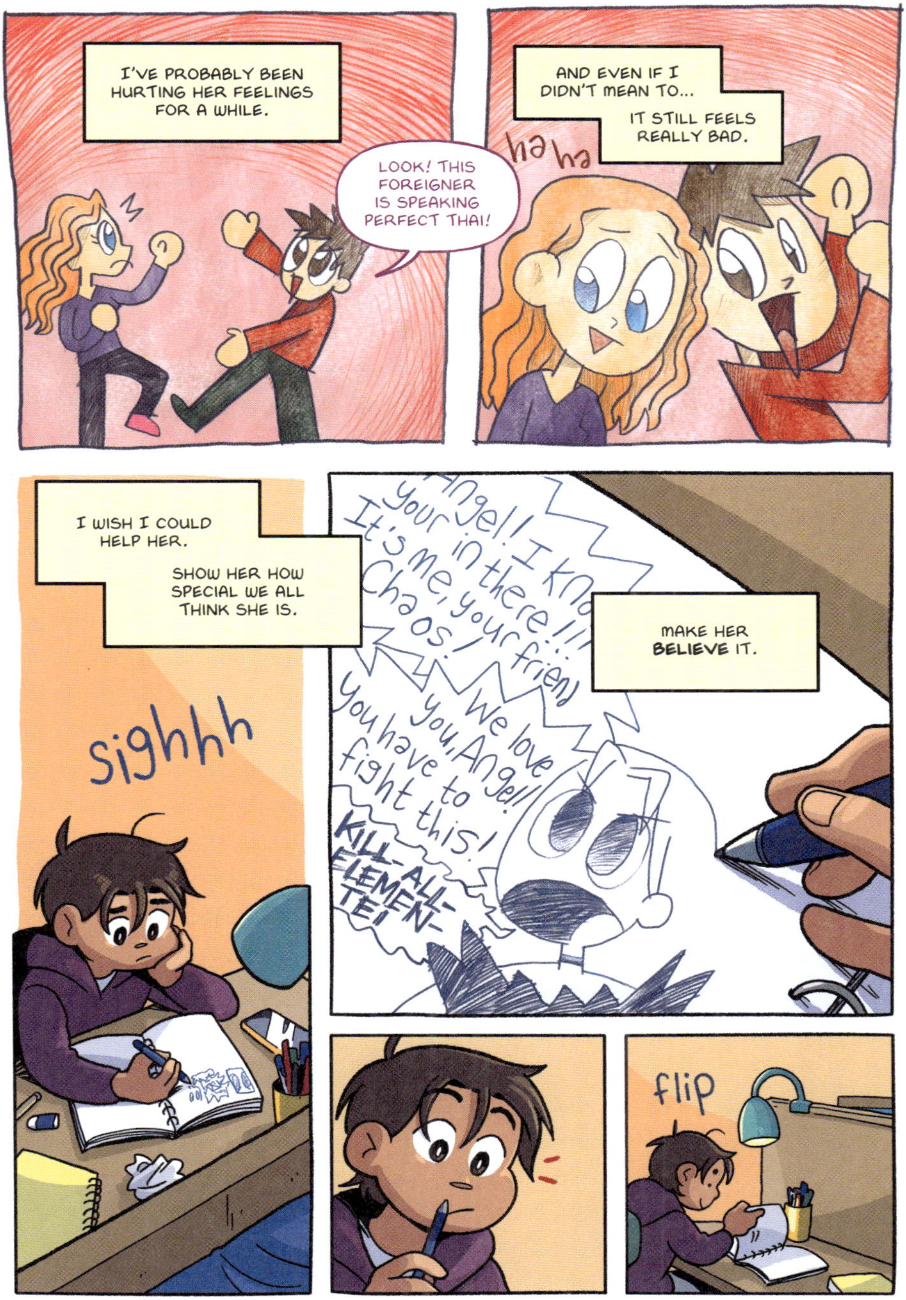
I'VE PROBABLY BEEN HURTING HER FEELINGS FOR A WHILE.
LOOK! THIS FOREIGNER IS SPEAKING PERFECT THAI!
AND EVEN IF I DIDN'T MEAN TO...
IT STILL FEELS REALLY BAD.
ha ha
I WISH I COULD HELP HER.
SHOW HER HOW SPECIAL WE ALL THINK SHE IS.
sighhh
ngel! I kno your in there!!!
It's me, your friend Chaos!
We love you, Angel! You have to fight this!
KILL-ALL-ELEMEN-TEI-
MAKE HER BELIEVE IT.
flip

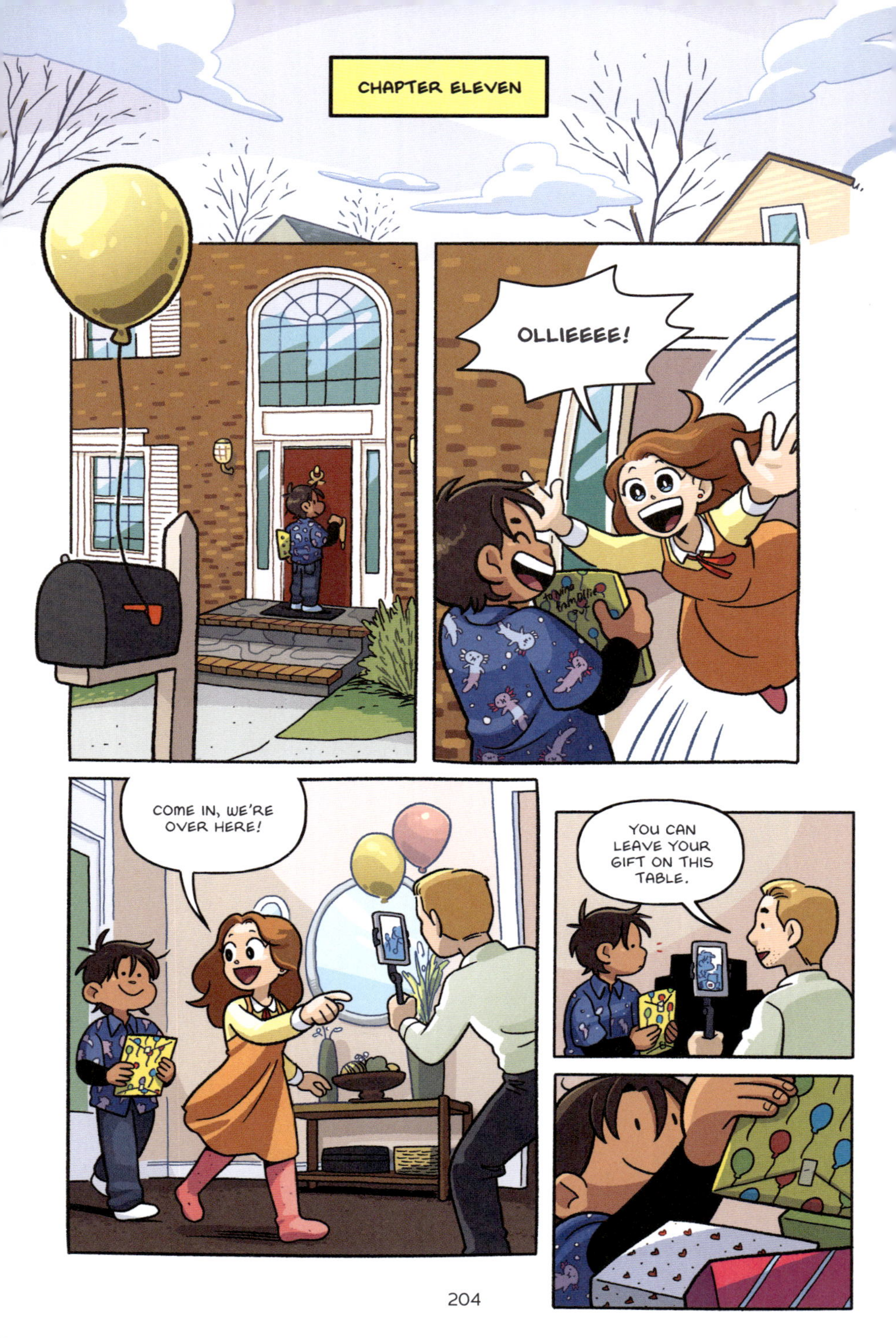
CHAPTER ELEVEN
OLLIEEEE!
COME IN, WE'RE OVER HERE!
YOU CAN LEAVE YOUR GIFT ON THIS TABLE.

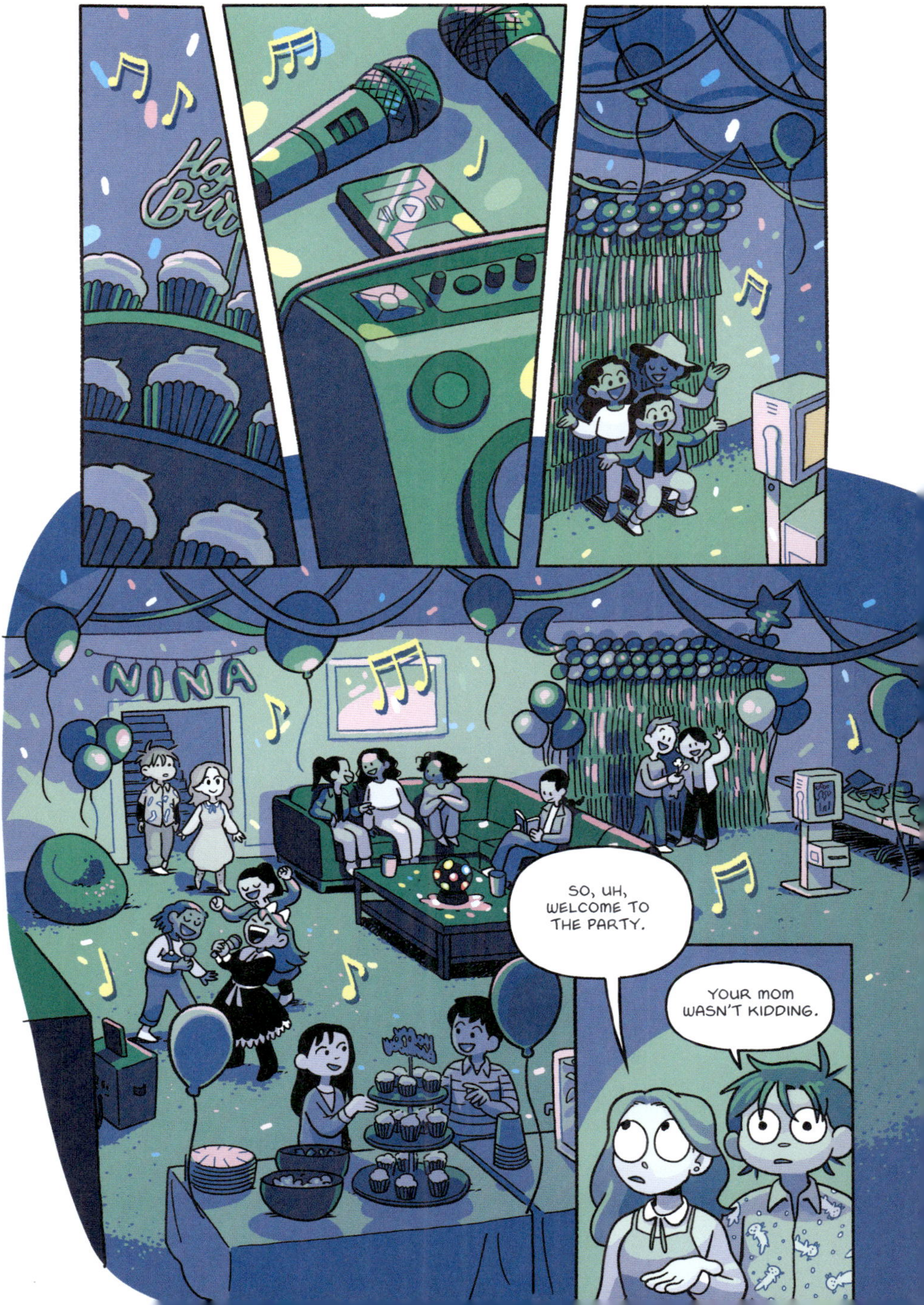
NINA
SO, UH, WELCOME TO THE PARTY.
YOUR MOM WASN'T KIDDING.

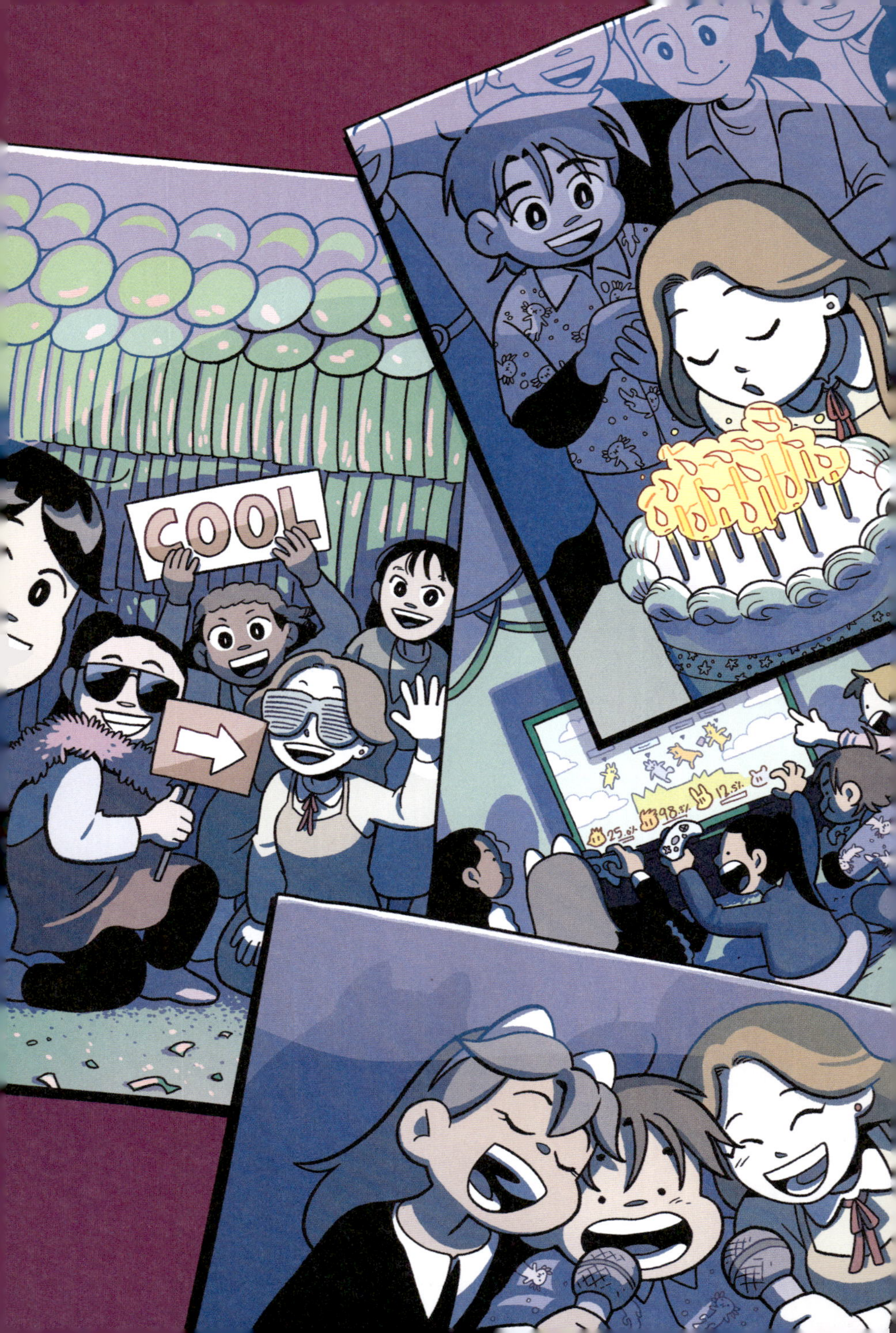
COOL

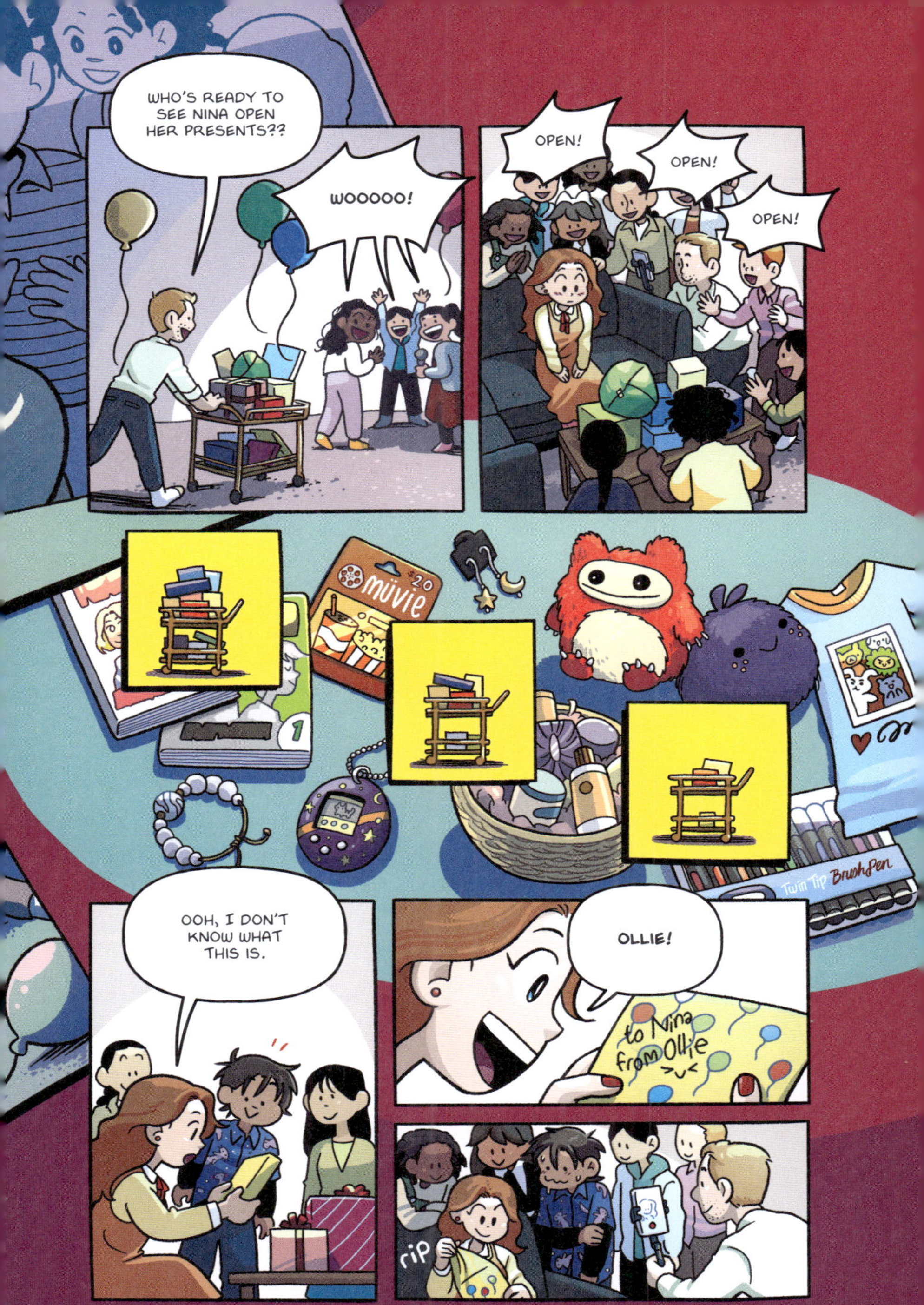

WHO'S READY TO SEE NINA OPEN HER PRESENTS??
WOOOOO!
OPEN!
OPEN!
OPEN!
müvie
$20
Twin Tip BrushPen
OOH, I DON'T KNOW WHAT THIS IS.
OLLIE!
to Nina from Ollie
rip

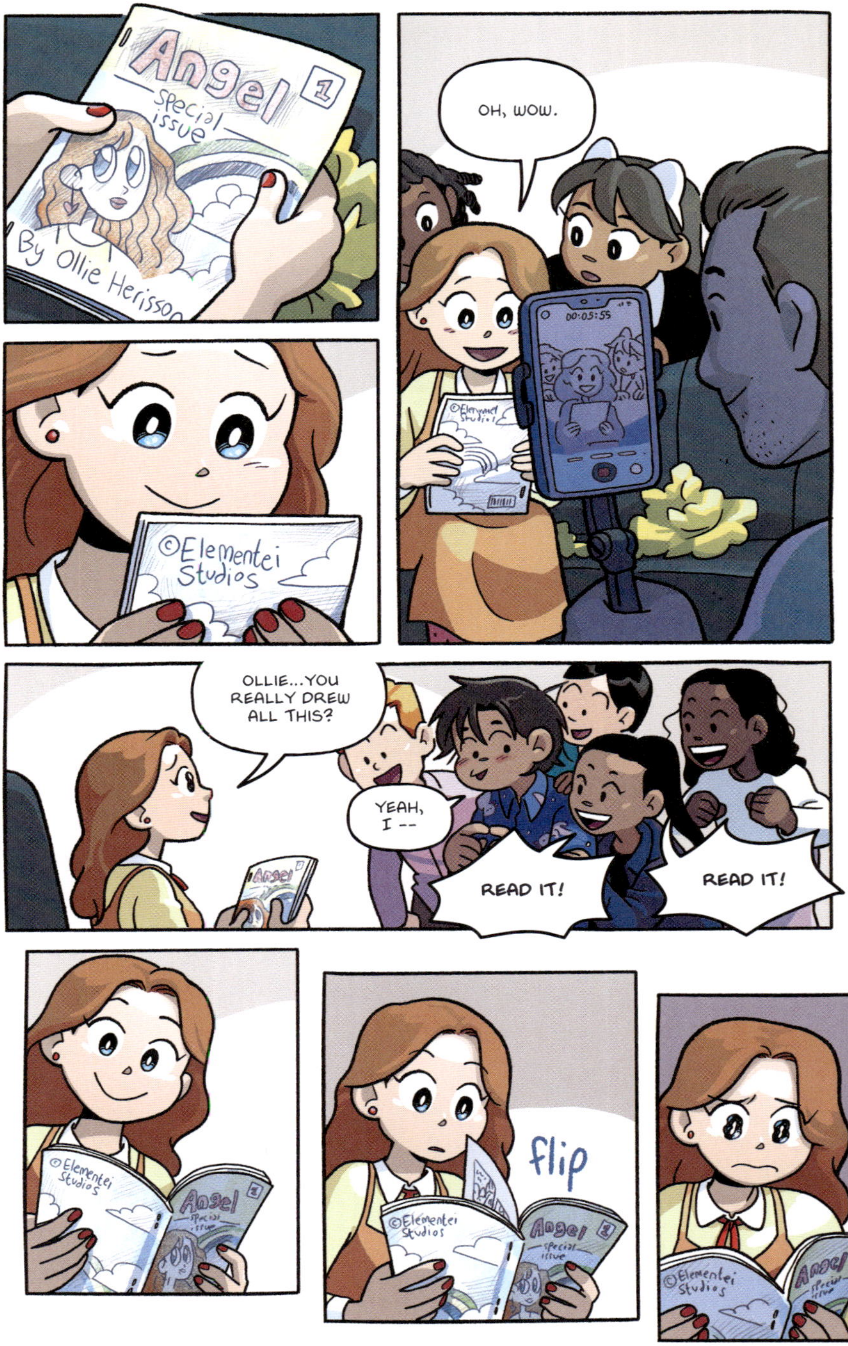
Angel
1
special issue
By Ollie Herisson
OH, WOW.
00:05:55
©Elementei Studios
OLLIE...YOU REALLY DREW ALL THIS?
YEAH, I --
READ IT!
READ IT!
©Elementei Studios
Angel
special issue
flip
©Elementei Studios
Angel
special issue
©Elementei Studios
Angel
special issue

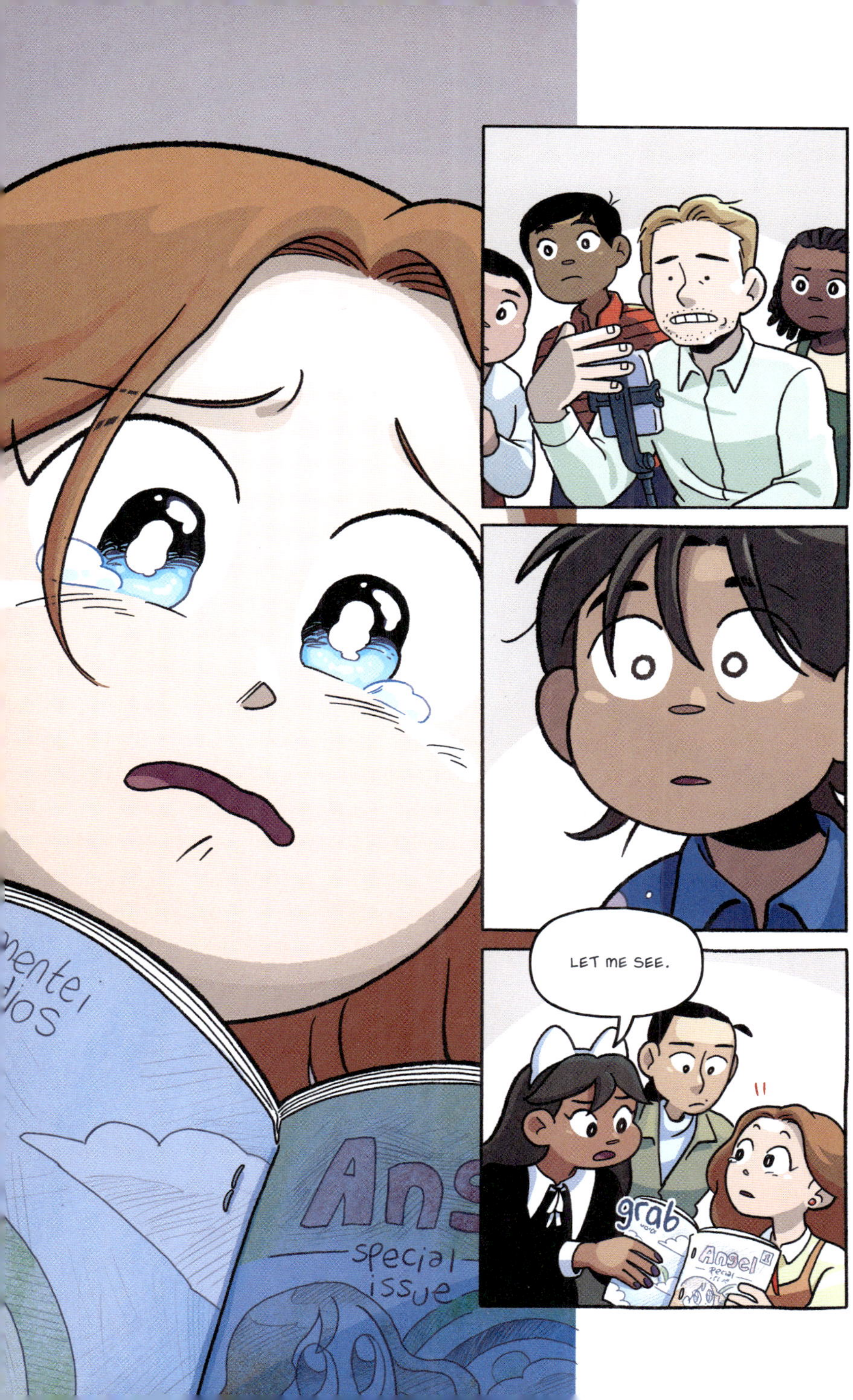
special issue
LET ME SEE.
grab

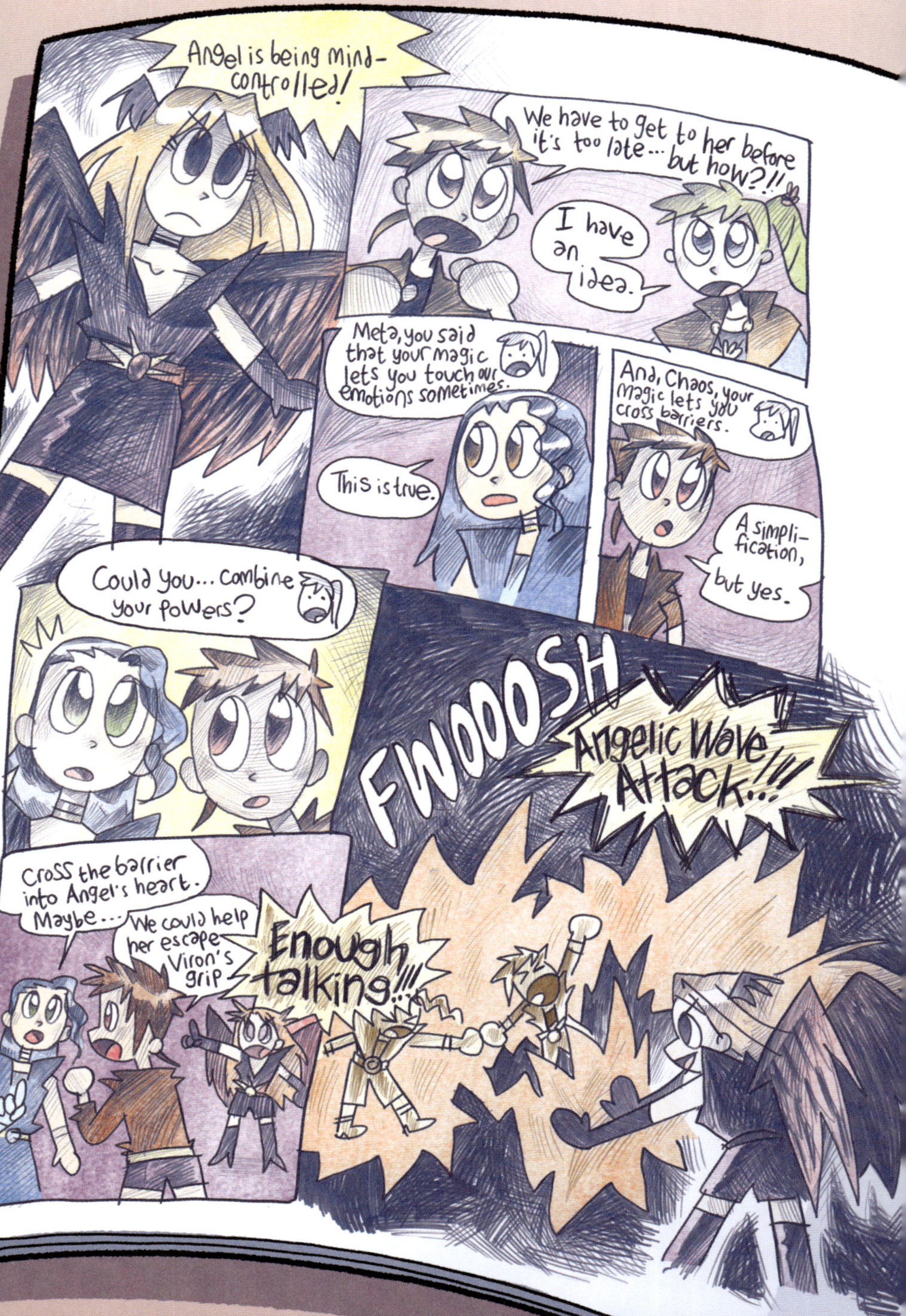
Angel is being mind-controlled!
We have to get to her before it's too late... but how?!!
I have an idea.
Meta, you said that your magic lets you touch our emotions sometimes.
This is true.
And, Chaos, your magic lets you cross barriers.
A simplification, but yes.
Could you... combine your powers?
Cross the barrier into Angel's heart. Maybe...
We could help her escape Viron's grip
Enough talking!!!
FWOOOSH
Angelic Wave Attack!!!!

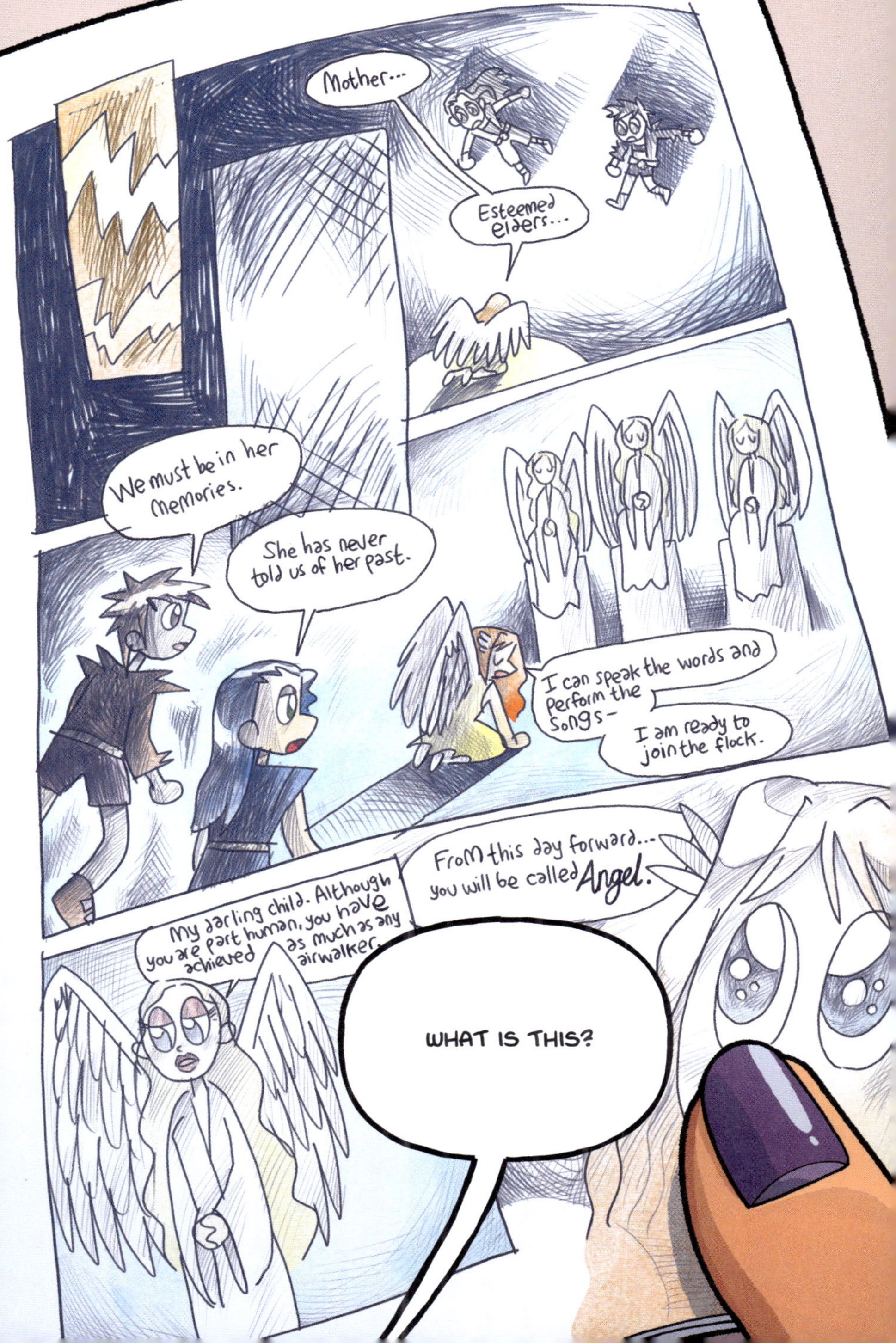
Mother...
Esteemed elders...
We must be in her memories.
She has never told us of her past.
I can speak the words and perform the songs—
I am ready to join the flock.
From this day forward... you will be called Angel.
My darling child. Although you are part human, you have achieved as much as any airwalker.
WHAT IS THIS?

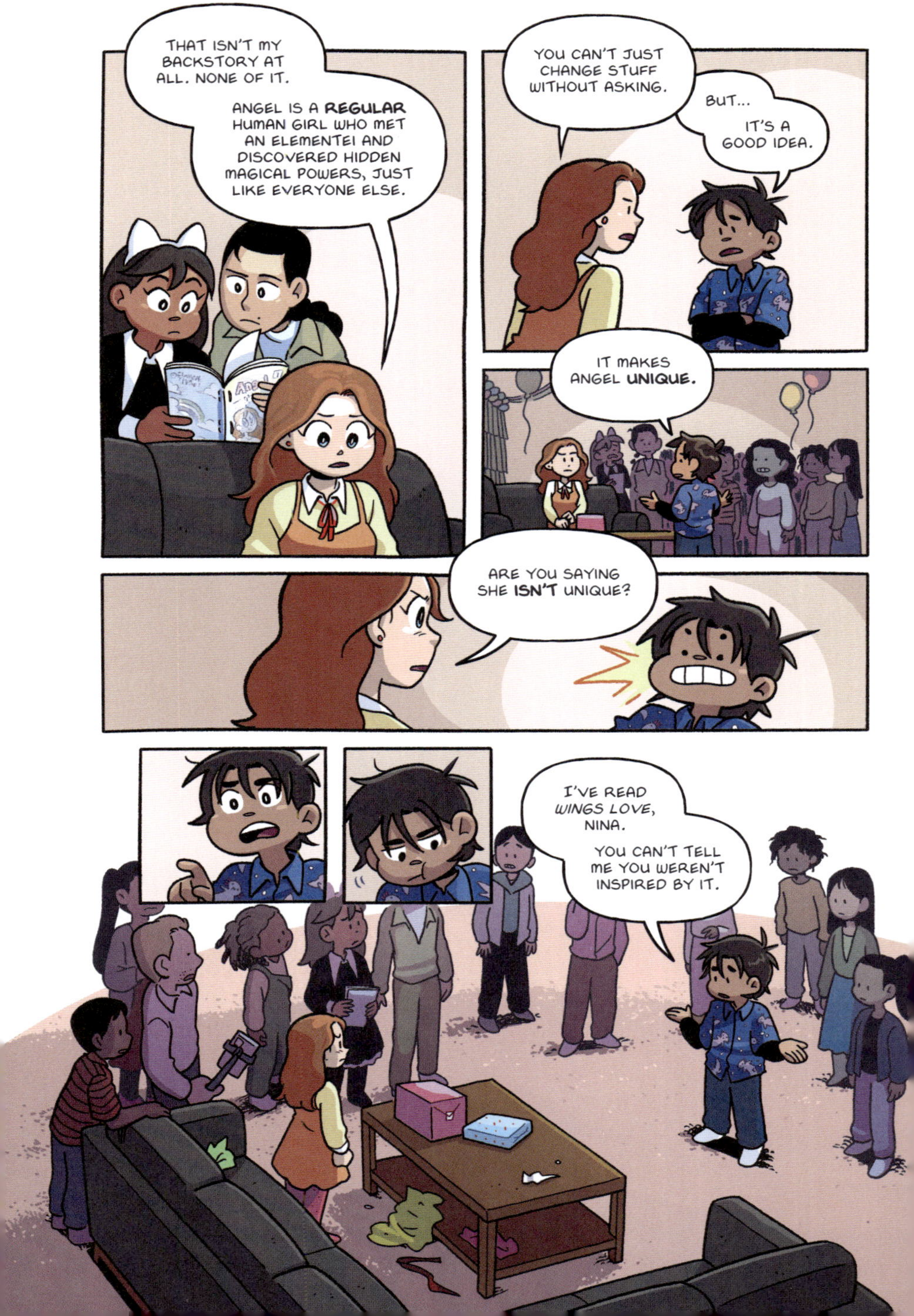
THAT ISN'T MY BACKSTORY AT ALL. NONE OF IT.
ANGEL IS A **REGULAR** HUMAN GIRL WHO MET AN ELEMENTEI AND DISCOVERED HIDDEN MAGICAL POWERS, JUST LIKE EVERYONE ELSE.
YOU CAN'T JUST CHANGE STUFF WITHOUT ASKING.
BUT...
IT'S A GOOD IDEA.
IT MAKES ANGEL **UNIQUE.**
ARE YOU SAYING SHE **ISN'T** UNIQUE?
I'VE READ *WINGS LOVE*, NINA.
YOU CAN'T TELL ME YOU WEREN'T INSPIRED BY IT.

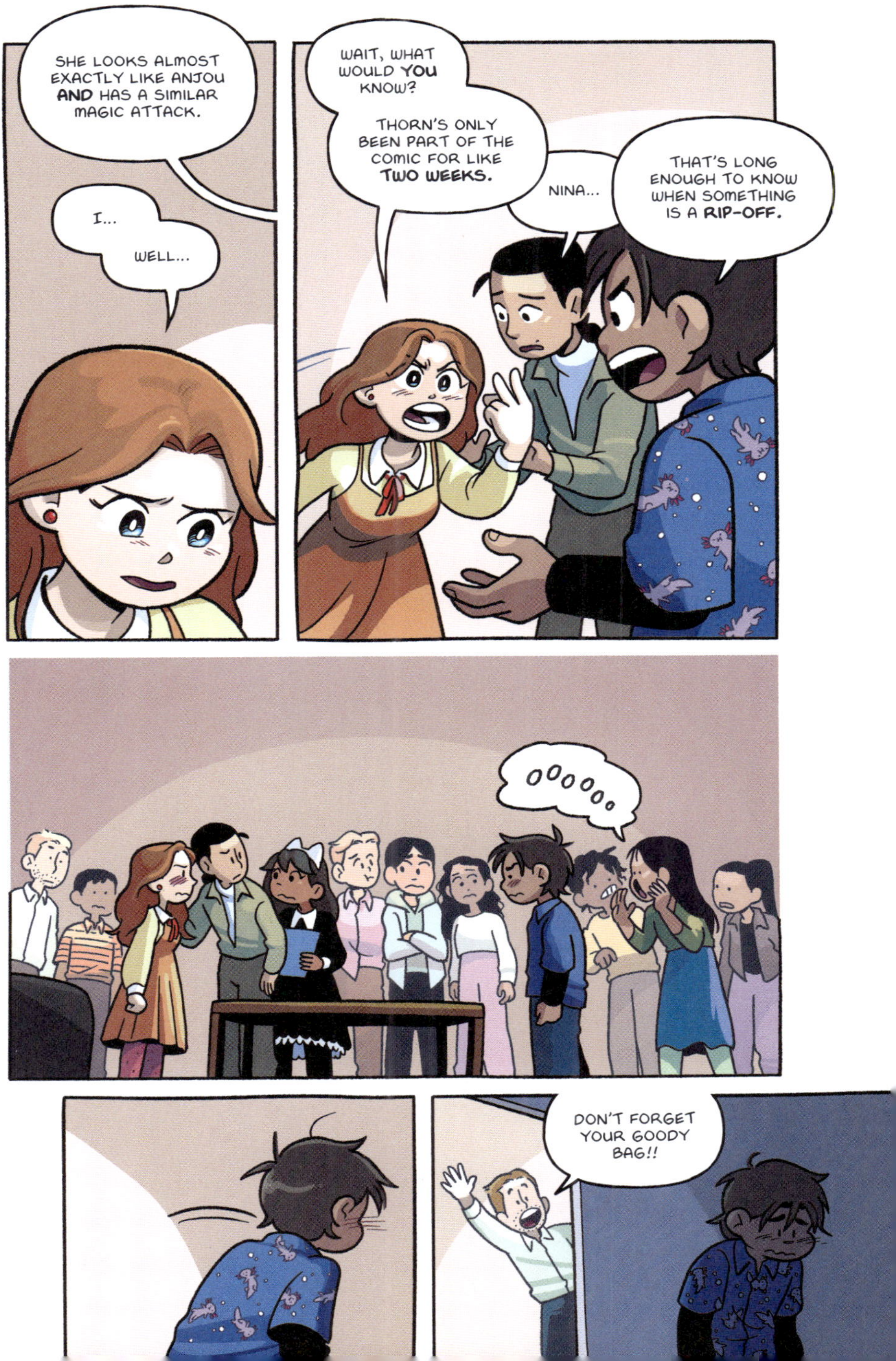
SHE LOOKS ALMOST EXACTLY LIKE ANJOU **AND** HAS A SIMILAR MAGIC ATTACK.
I...
WELL...
WAIT, WHAT WOULD **YOU** KNOW?
THORN'S ONLY BEEN PART OF THE COMIC FOR LIKE **TWO WEEKS.**
NINA...
THAT'S LONG ENOUGH TO KNOW WHEN SOMETHING IS A **RIP-OFF.**
OOOOOO
DON'T FORGET YOUR GOODY BAG!!

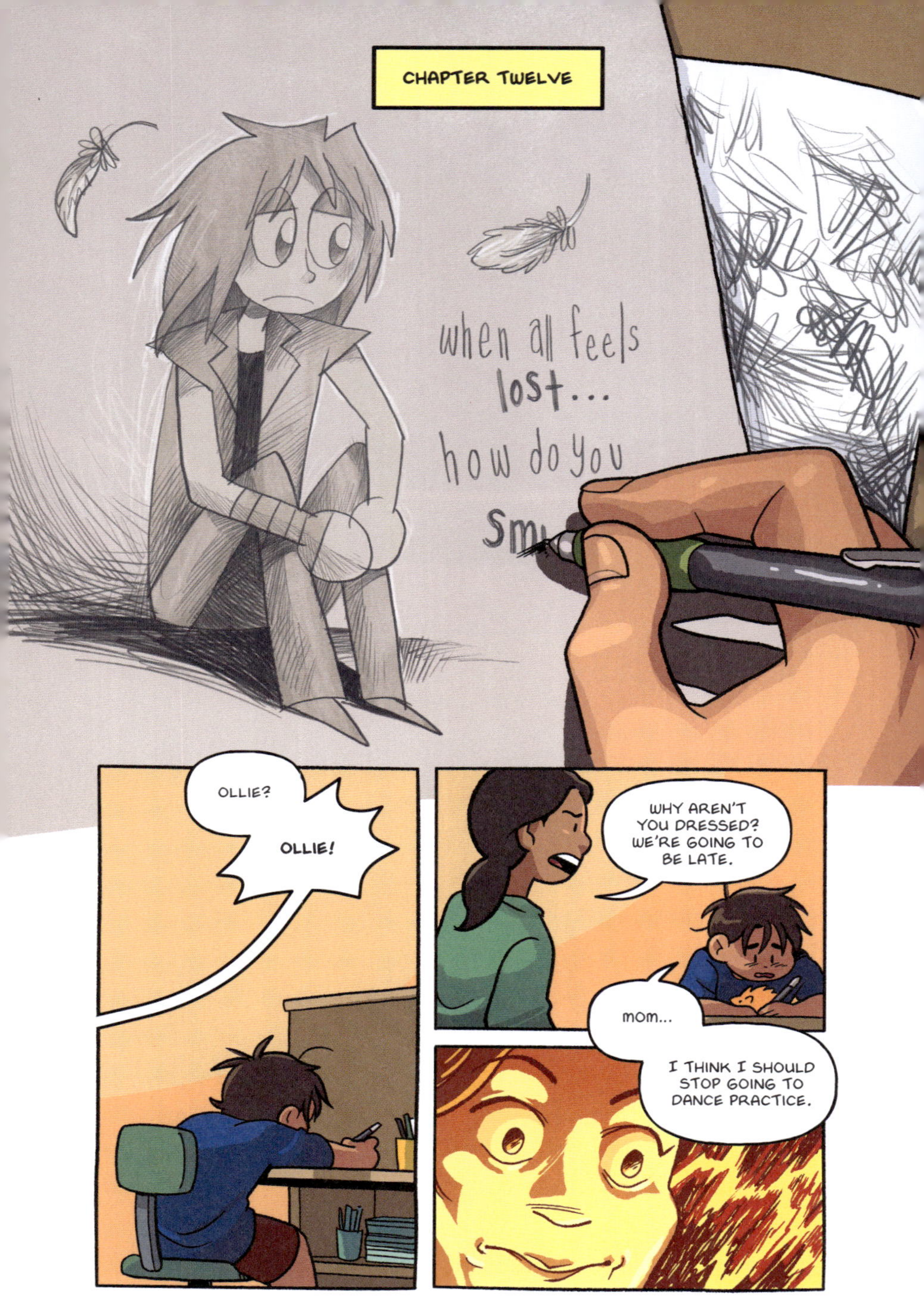
CHAPTER TWELVE
when all feels
lost...
how do you
sm
OLLIE?
OLLIE!
WHY AREN'T YOU DRESSED? WE'RE GOING TO BE LATE.
mom...
I THINK I SHOULD STOP GOING TO DANCE PRACTICE.

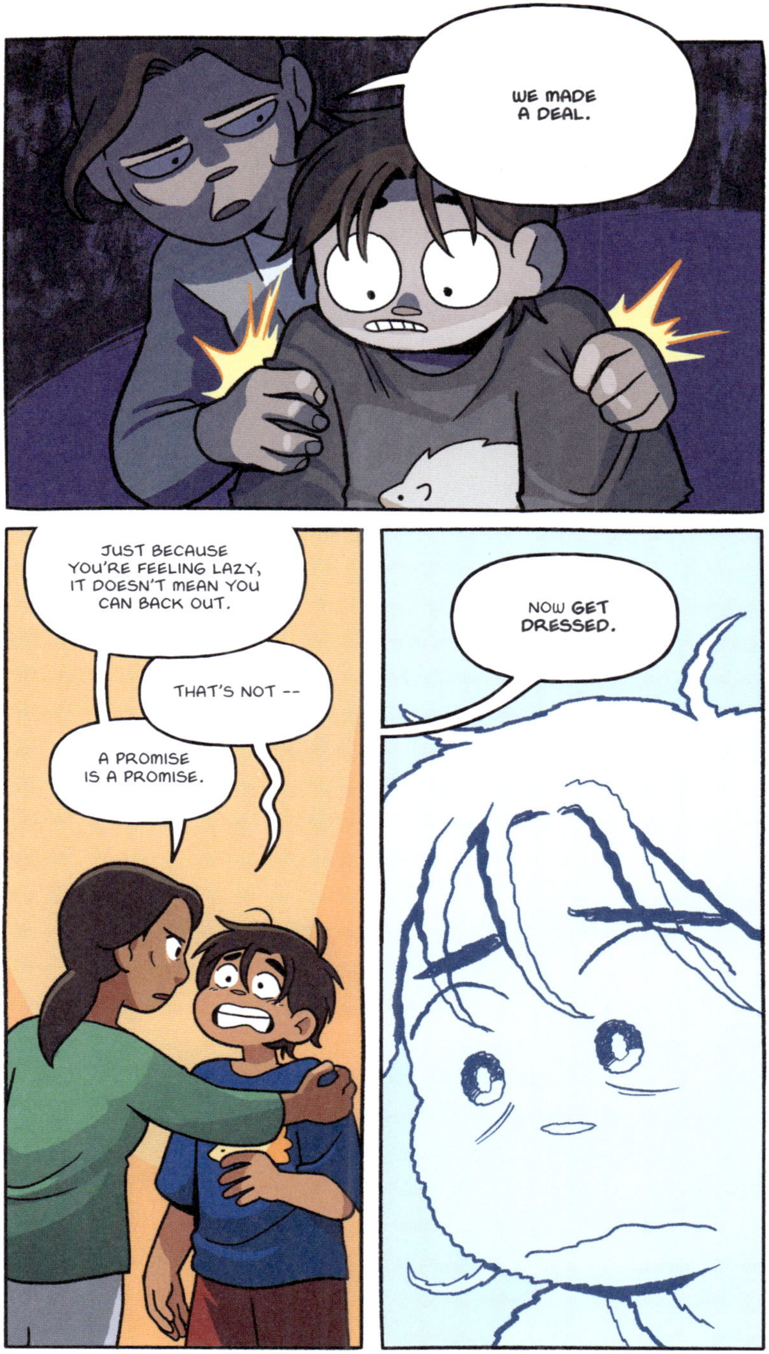
WE MADE A DEAL.
JUST BECAUSE YOU'RE FEELING LAZY, IT DOESN'T MEAN YOU CAN BACK OUT.
THAT'S NOT --
A PROMISE IS A PROMISE.
NOW **GET DRESSED.**

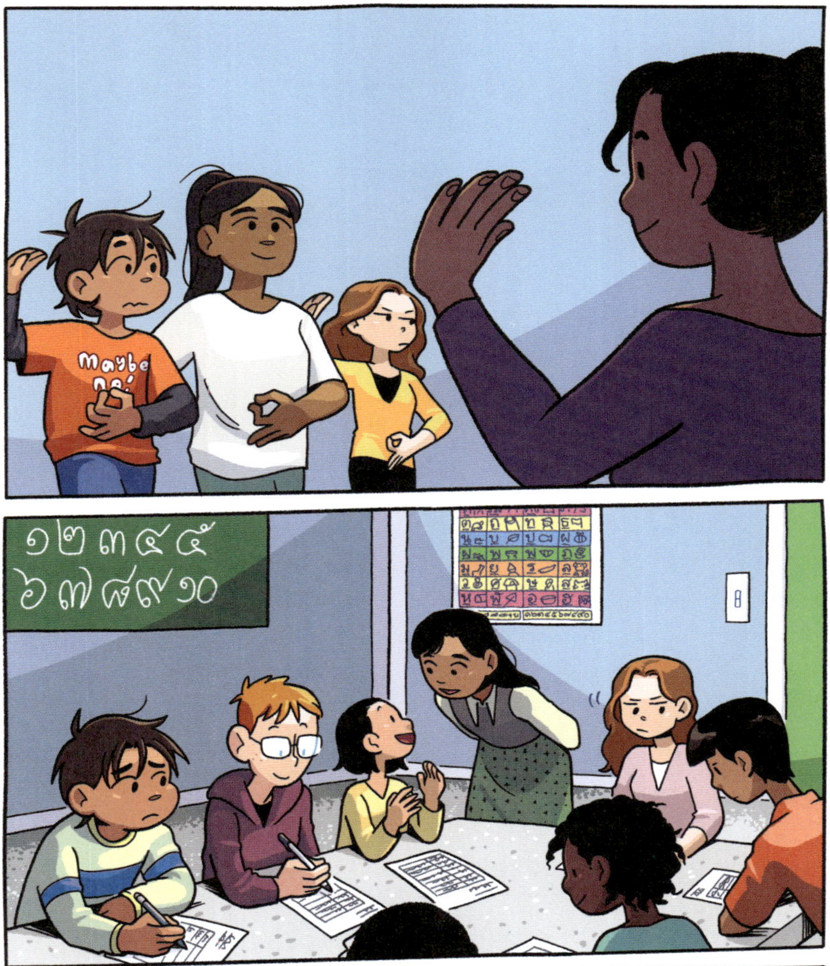
maybe
๑๒๓๔๕
๖๗๘๙๑๐
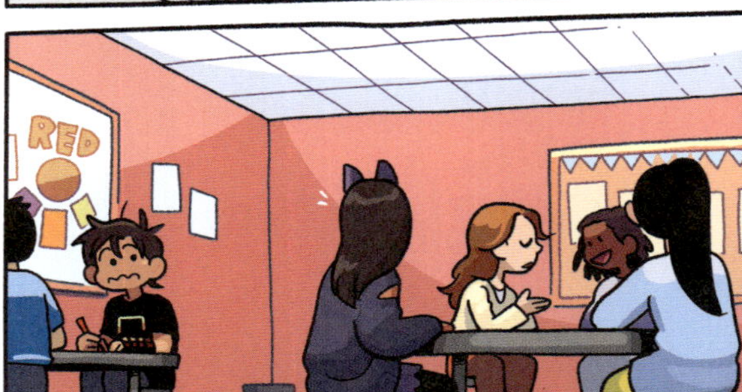
RED
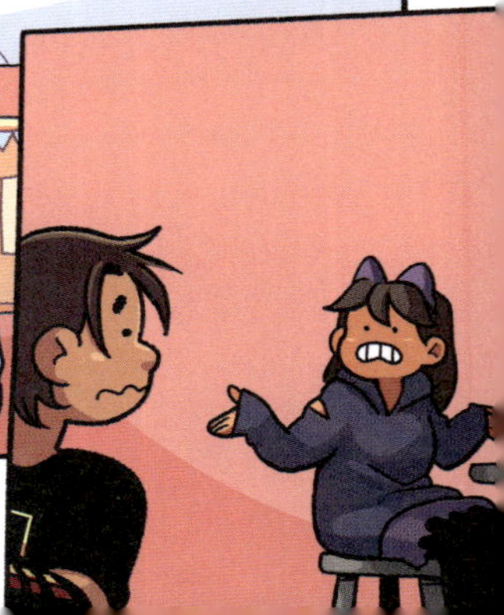

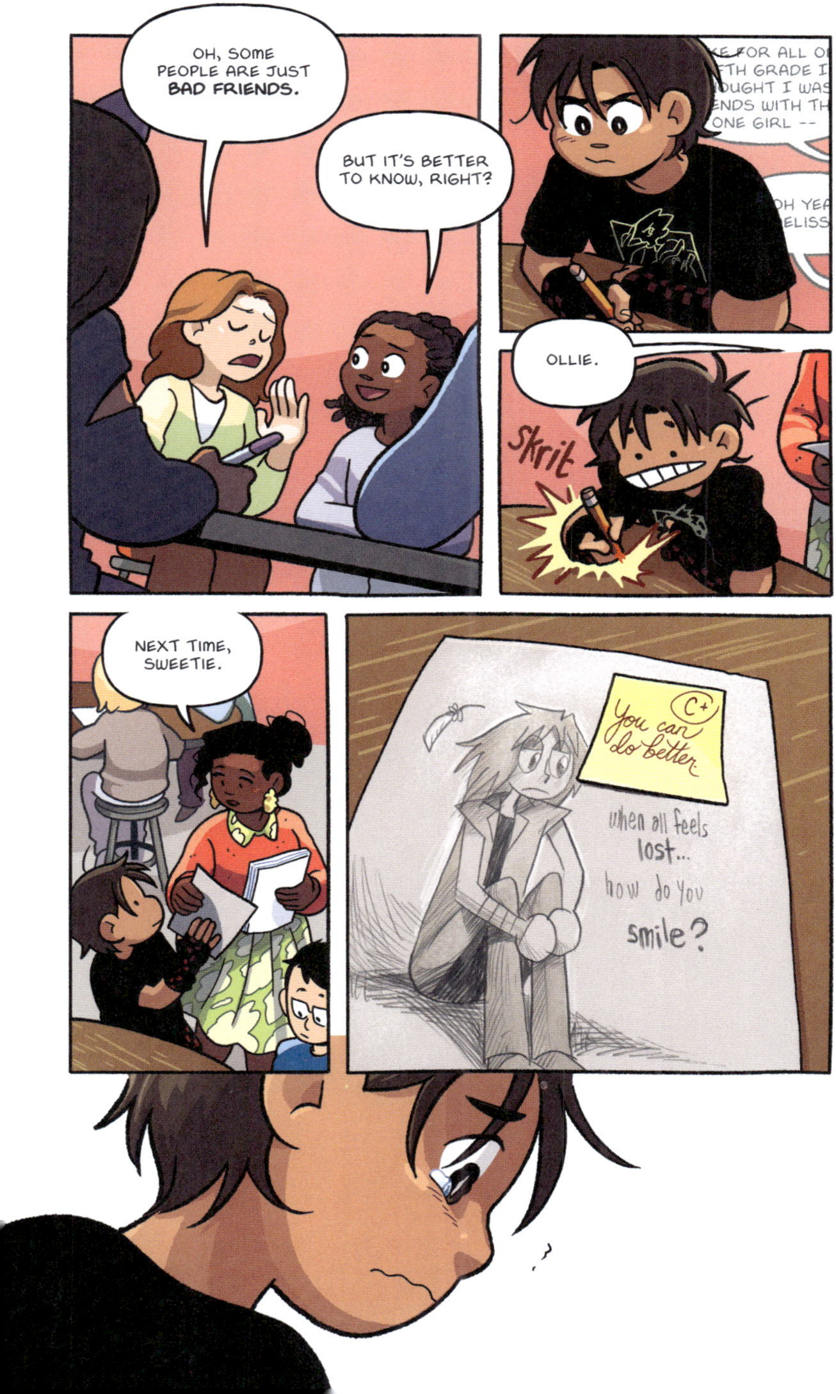
OH, SOME PEOPLE ARE JUST **BAD FRIENDS.**
BUT IT'S BETTER TO KNOW, RIGHT?
KE FOR ALL O FTH GRADE I OUGHT I WAS ENDS WITH TH ONE GIRL --
OH YEA ELISS
OLLIE.
Skrit
NEXT TIME, SWEETIE.
C+
You can do better
when all feels lost... how do you smile?

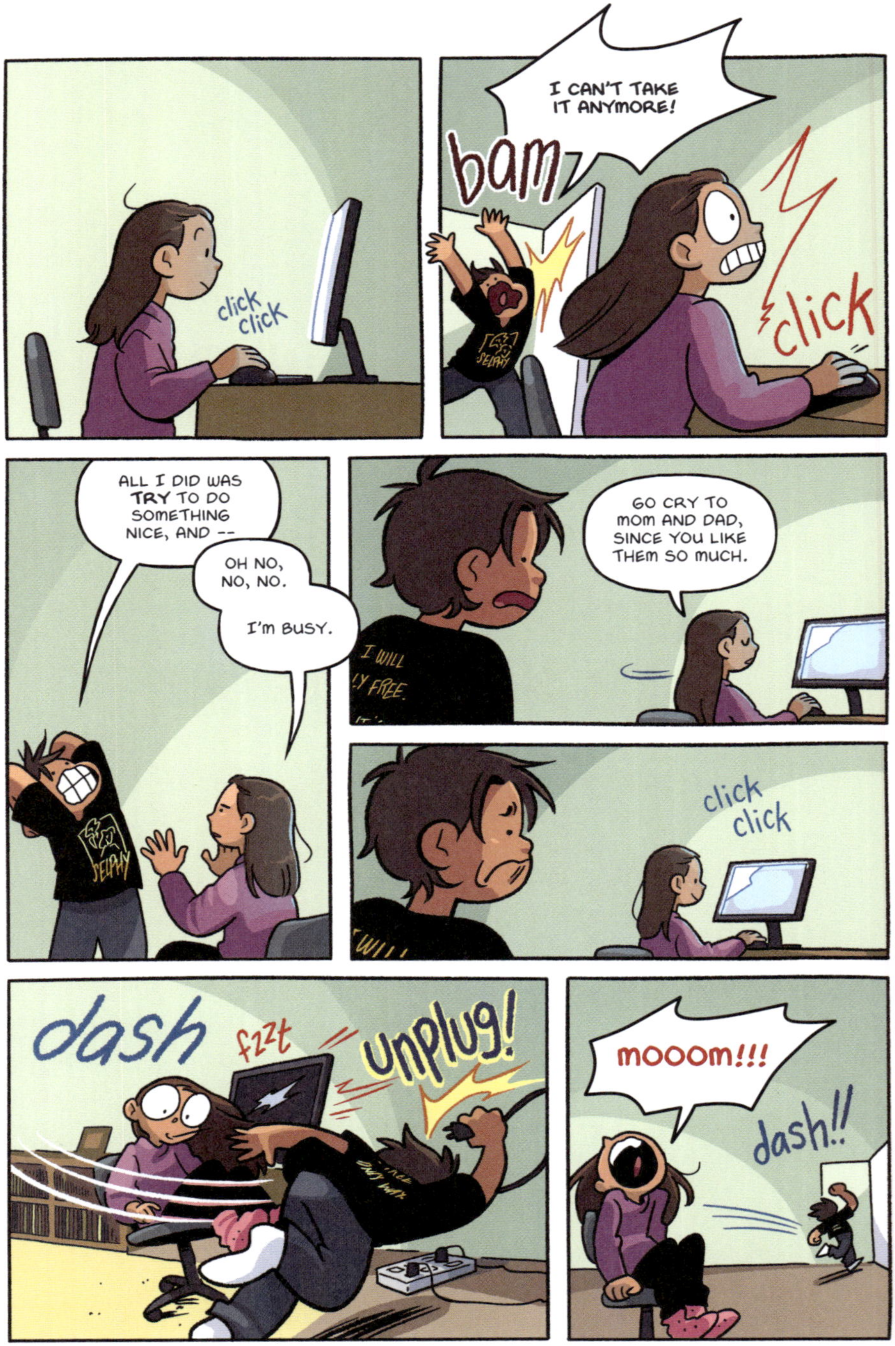
click
click
I CAN'T TAKE IT ANYMORE!
bam
click
ALL I DID WAS **TRY** TO DO SOMETHING NICE, AND --
OH NO, NO, NO.
I'M BUSY.
GO CRY TO MOM AND DAD, SINCE YOU LIKE THEM SO MUCH.
click
click
dash
fzzt
unplug!
mooom!!!
dash!!

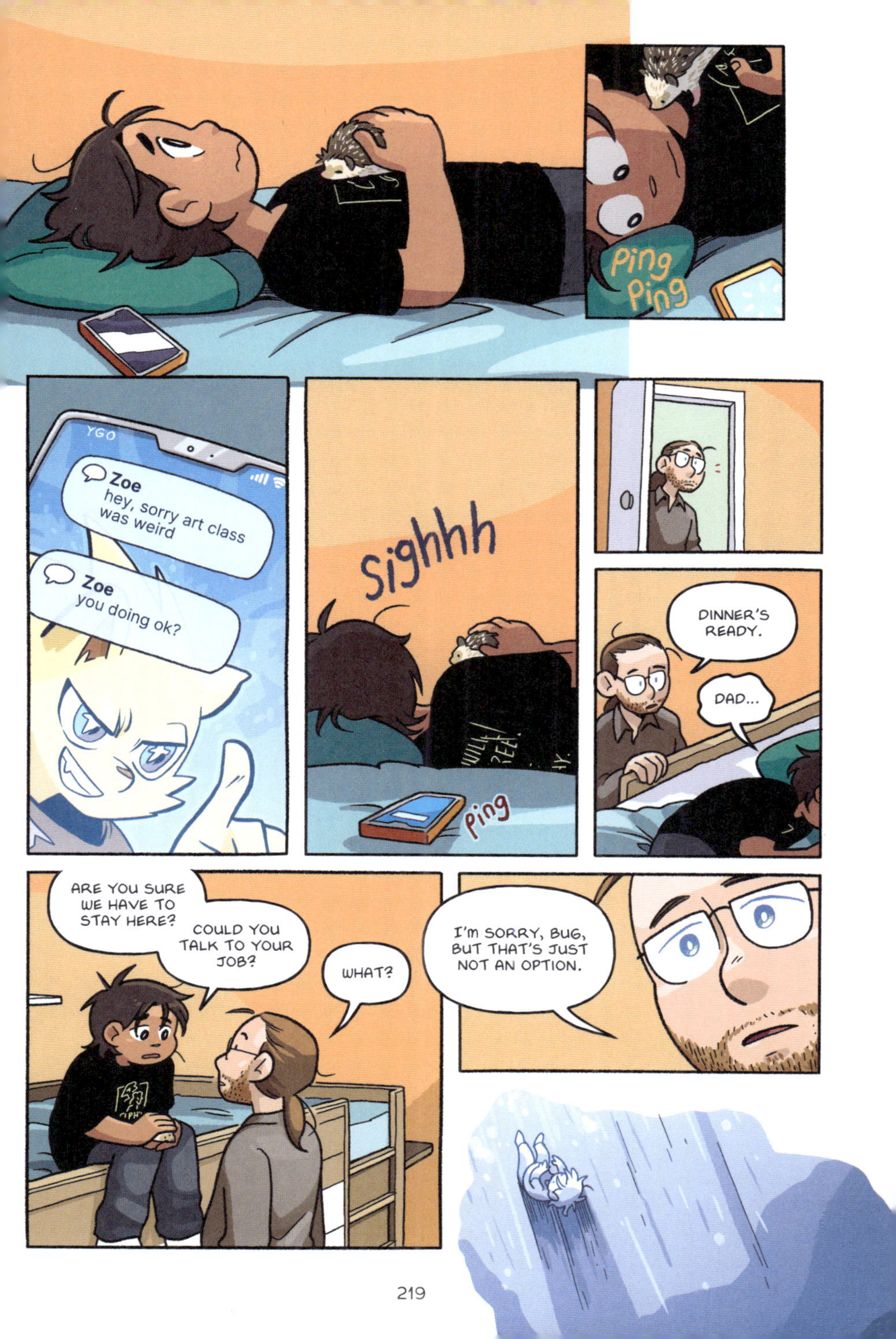
Ping
Ping
YGO
Zoe
hey, sorry art class was weird
Zoe
you doing ok?
sighhh
ping
DINNER'S READY.
DAD...
ARE YOU SURE WE HAVE TO STAY HERE?
COULD YOU TALK TO YOUR JOB?
WHAT?
I'M SORRY, BUG, BUT THAT'S JUST NOT AN OPTION.

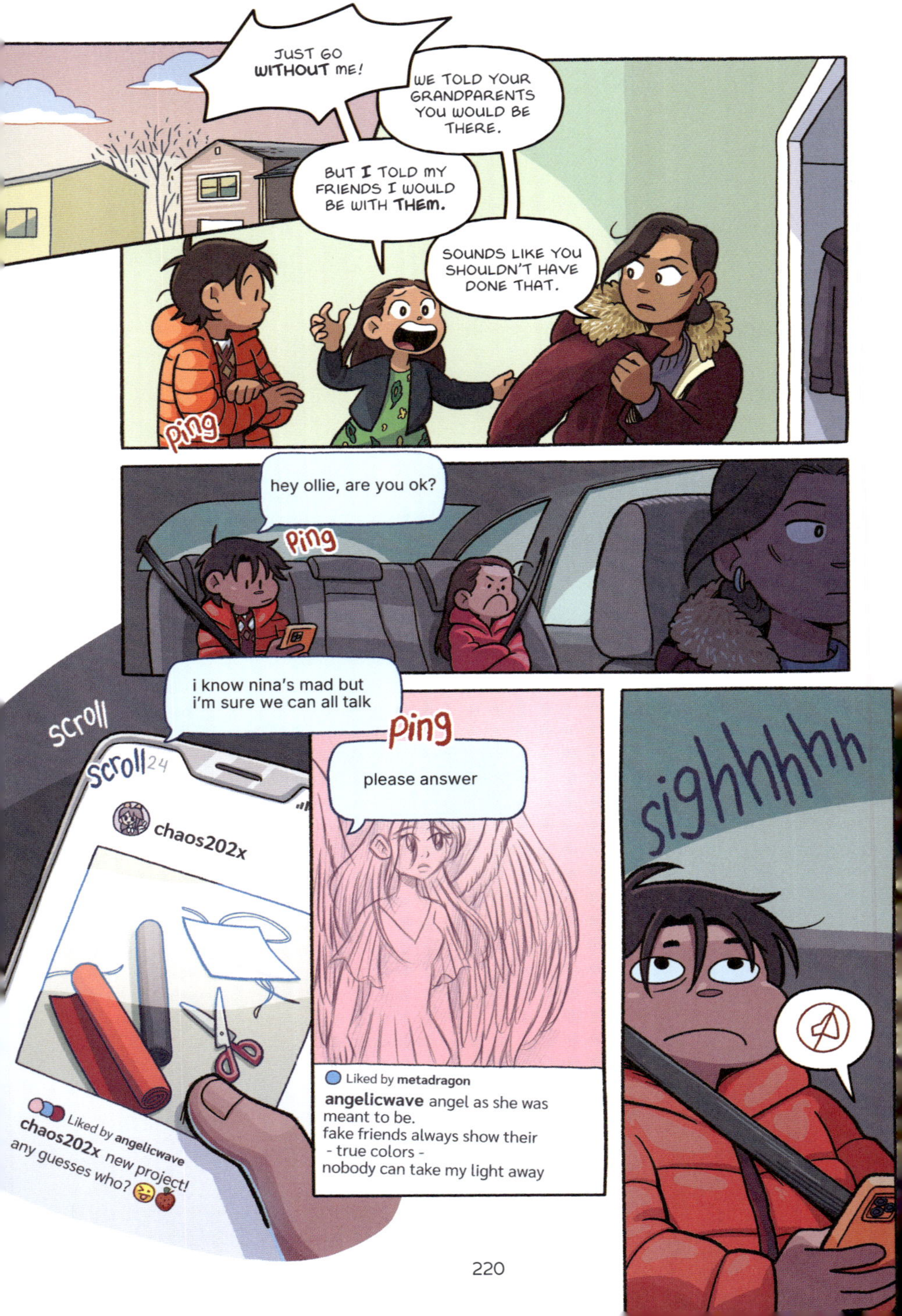
JUST GO **WITHOUT** ME!
WE TOLD YOUR GRANDPARENTS YOU WOULD BE THERE.
BUT **I** TOLD MY FRIENDS I WOULD BE WITH **THEM.**
SOUNDS LIKE YOU SHOULDN'T HAVE DONE THAT.
ping
hey ollie, are you ok?
ping
i know nina's mad but i'm sure we can all talk
scroll
scroll
chaos202x
Liked by angelicwave
chaos202x new project!
any guesses who?
ping
please answer
Liked by metadragon
angelicwave angel as she was meant to be.
fake friends always show their
- true colors -
nobody can take my light away
sighhhhh

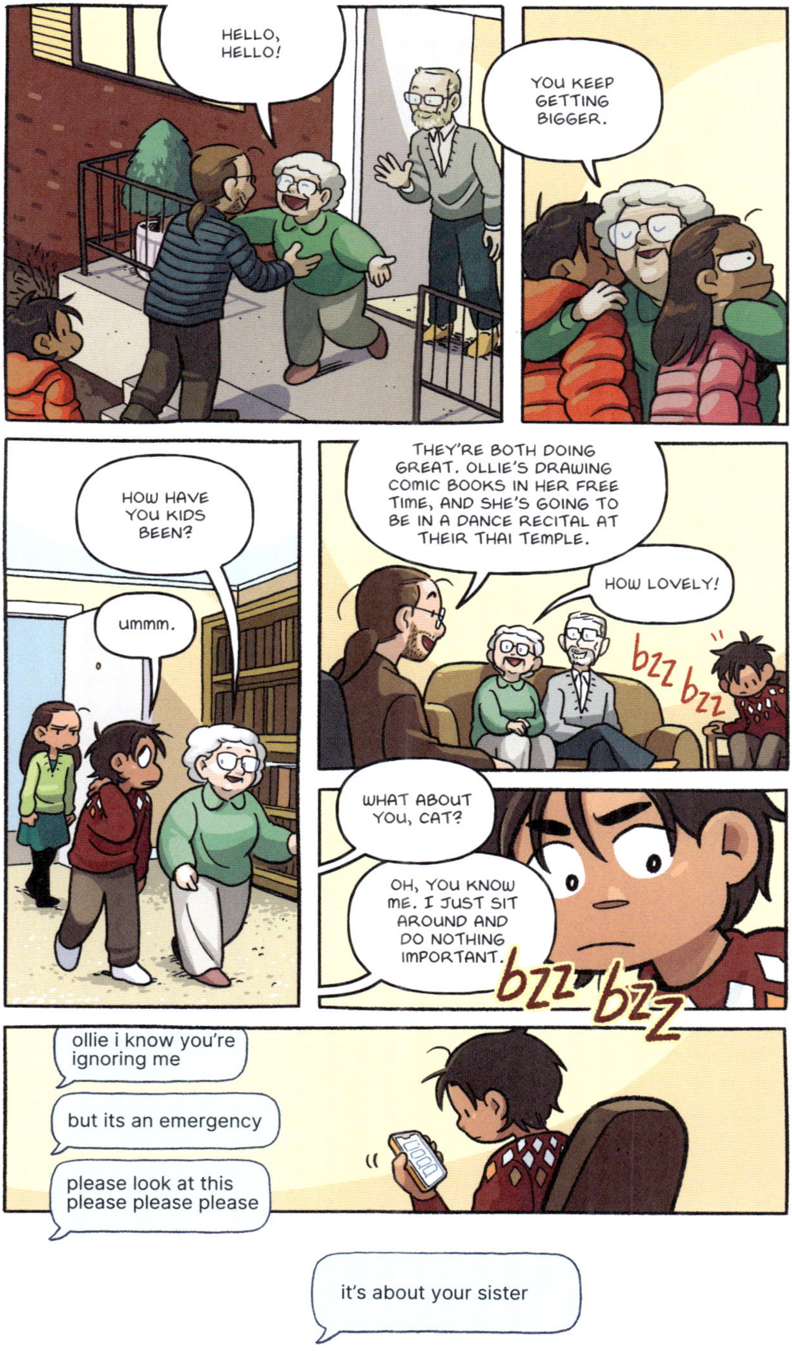
HELLO, HELLO!
YOU KEEP GETTING BIGGER.
HOW HAVE YOU KIDS BEEN?
ummm.
THEY'RE BOTH DOING GREAT. OLLIE'S DRAWING COMIC BOOKS IN HER FREE TIME, AND SHE'S GOING TO BE IN A DANCE RECITAL AT THEIR THAI TEMPLE.
HOW LOVELY!
bzz bzz
WHAT ABOUT YOU, CAT?
OH, YOU KNOW ME. I JUST SIT AROUND AND DO NOTHING IMPORTANT.
bzz bzz
ollie i know you're ignoring me
but its an emergency
please look at this please please please
it's about your sister

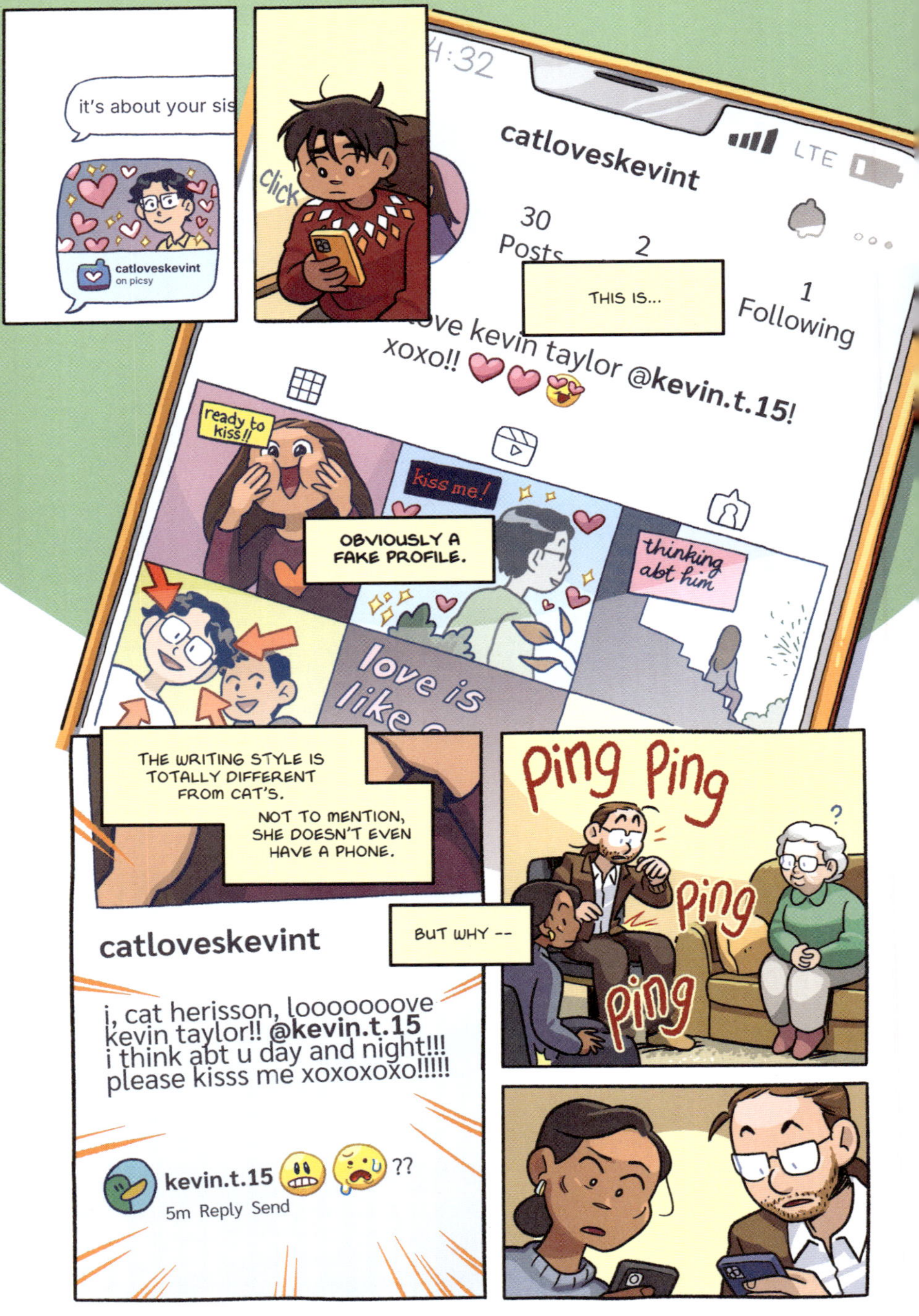
it's about your sis
catloveskevint
on picsy
click
4:32
catloveskevint
LTE
30
Posts
2
1
Following
THIS IS...
ove kevin taylor @kevin.t.15!
xoxo!!
ready to kiss!!
kiss me!
thinking abt him
OBVIOUSLY A FAKE PROFILE.
love is like
THE WRITING STYLE IS TOTALLY DIFFERENT FROM CAT'S.
NOT TO MENTION, SHE DOESN'T EVEN HAVE A PHONE.
catloveskevint
i, cat herisson, looooooove kevin taylor!! @kevin.t.15 i think abt u day and night!!! please kisss me xoxoxoxo!!!!!
kevin.t.15 ??
5m Reply Send
BUT WHY --
ping ping
ping
ping
?

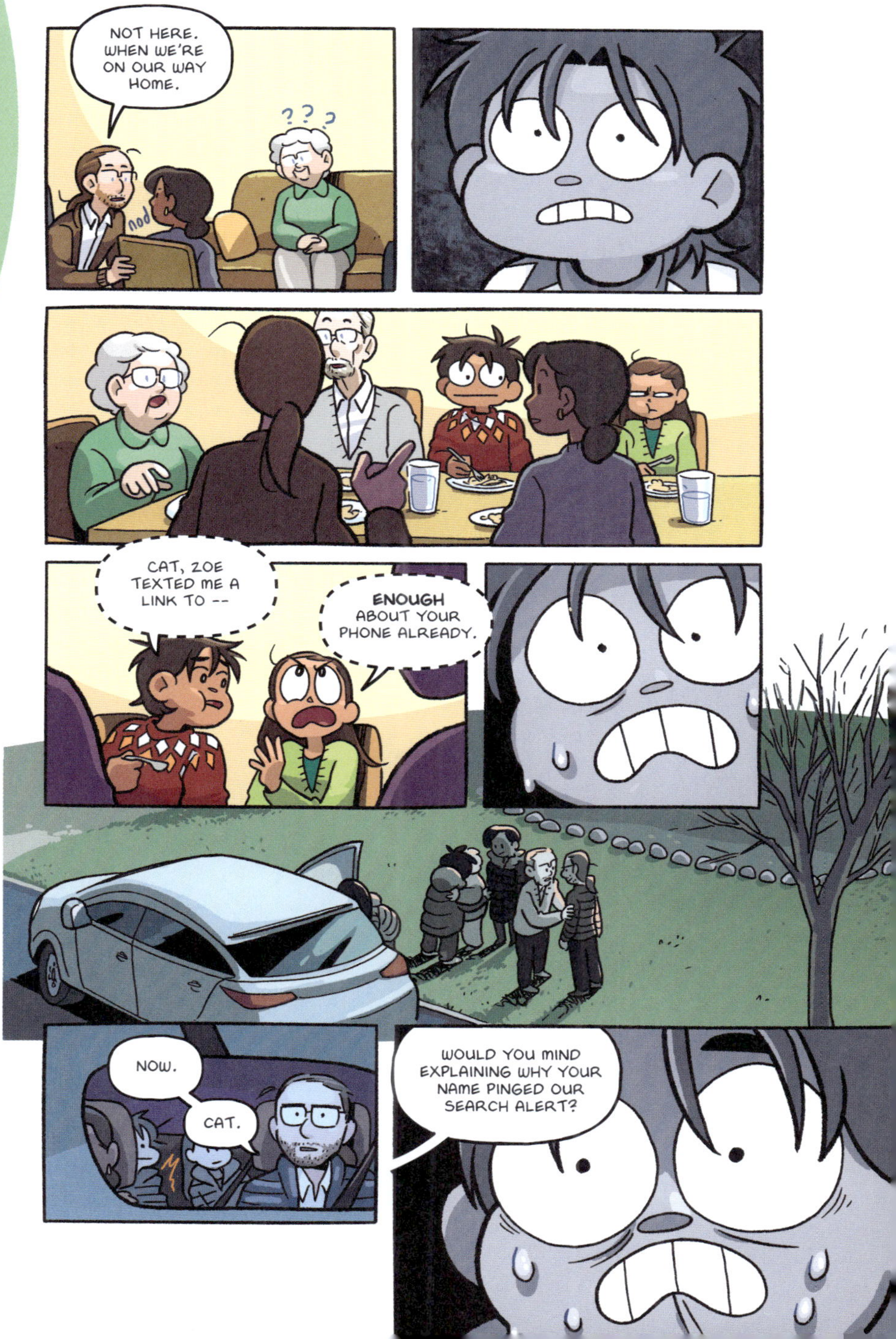
NOT HERE. WHEN WE'RE ON OUR WAY HOME.
nod
? ? ?
CAT, ZOE TEXTED ME A LINK TO --
ENOUGH ABOUT YOUR PHONE ALREADY.
NOW.
CAT.
WOULD YOU MIND EXPLAINING WHY YOUR NAME PINGED OUR SEARCH ALERT?

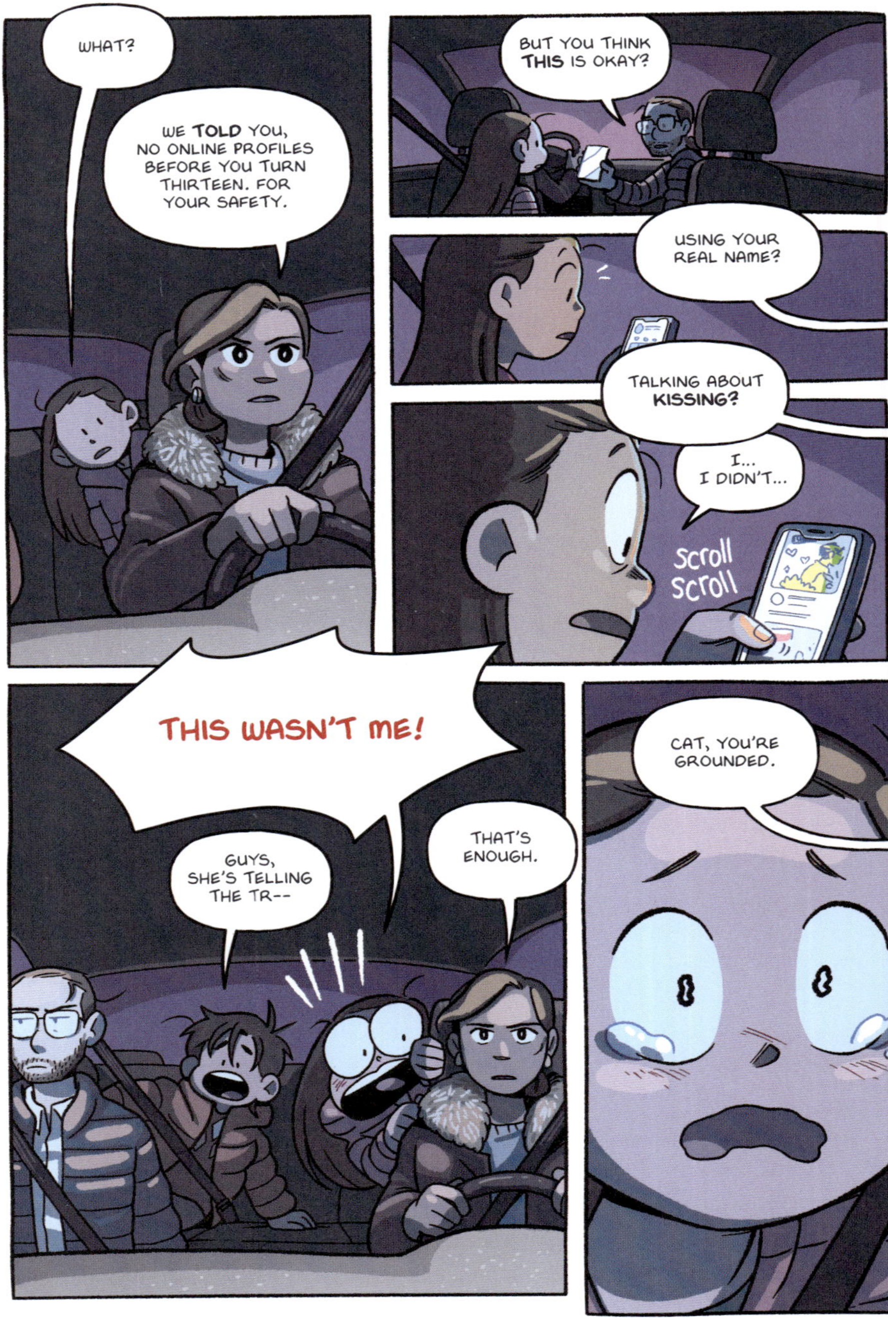
WHAT?
WE TOLD YOU, NO ONLINE PROFILES BEFORE YOU TURN THIRTEEN. FOR YOUR SAFETY.
BUT YOU THINK THIS IS OKAY?
USING YOUR REAL NAME?
TALKING ABOUT KISSING?
I... I DIDN'T...
SCROLL SCROLL
THIS WASN'T ME!
GUYS, SHE'S TELLING THE TR--
THAT'S ENOUGH.
CAT, YOU'RE GROUNDED.

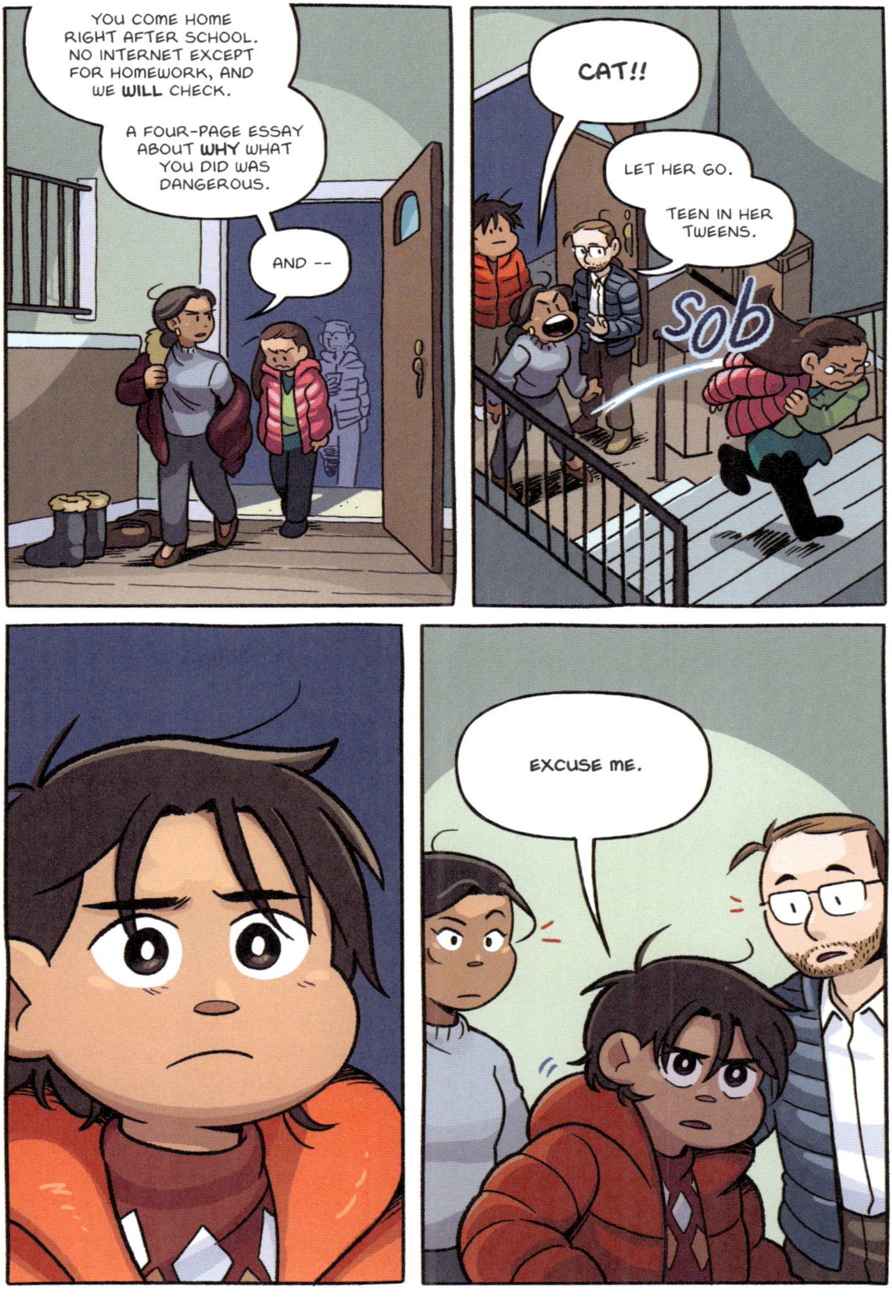
YOU COME HOME RIGHT AFTER SCHOOL. NO INTERNET EXCEPT FOR HOMEWORK, AND WE **WILL** CHECK.
A FOUR-PAGE ESSAY ABOUT **WHY** WHAT YOU DID WAS DANGEROUS.
AND --
CAT!!
LET HER GO.
TEEN IN HER TWEENS.
sob
EXCUSE ME.

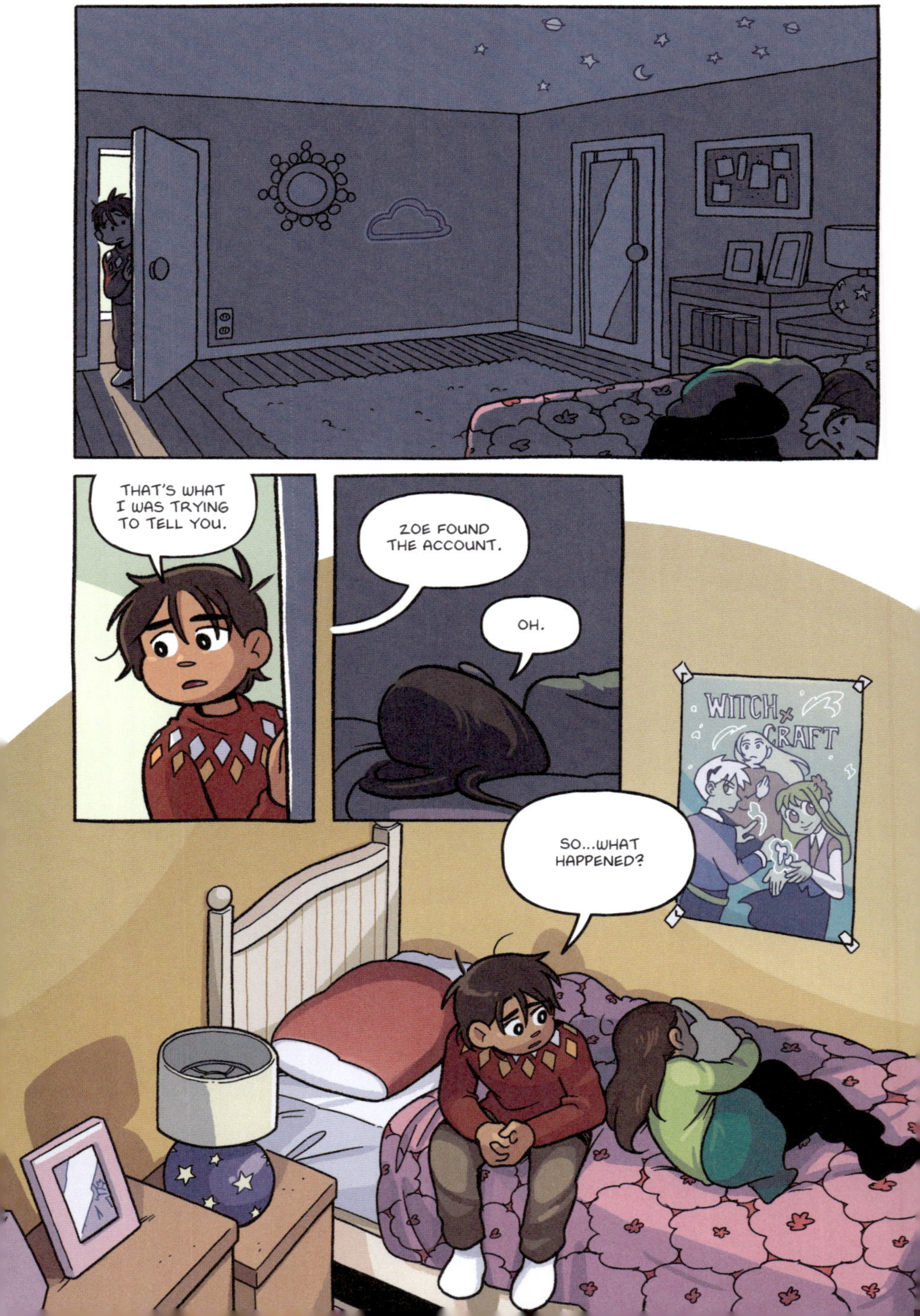
THAT'S WHAT I WAS TRYING TO TELL YOU.
ZOE FOUND THE ACCOUNT.
OH.
WITCH × CRAFT
SO...WHAT HAPPENED?

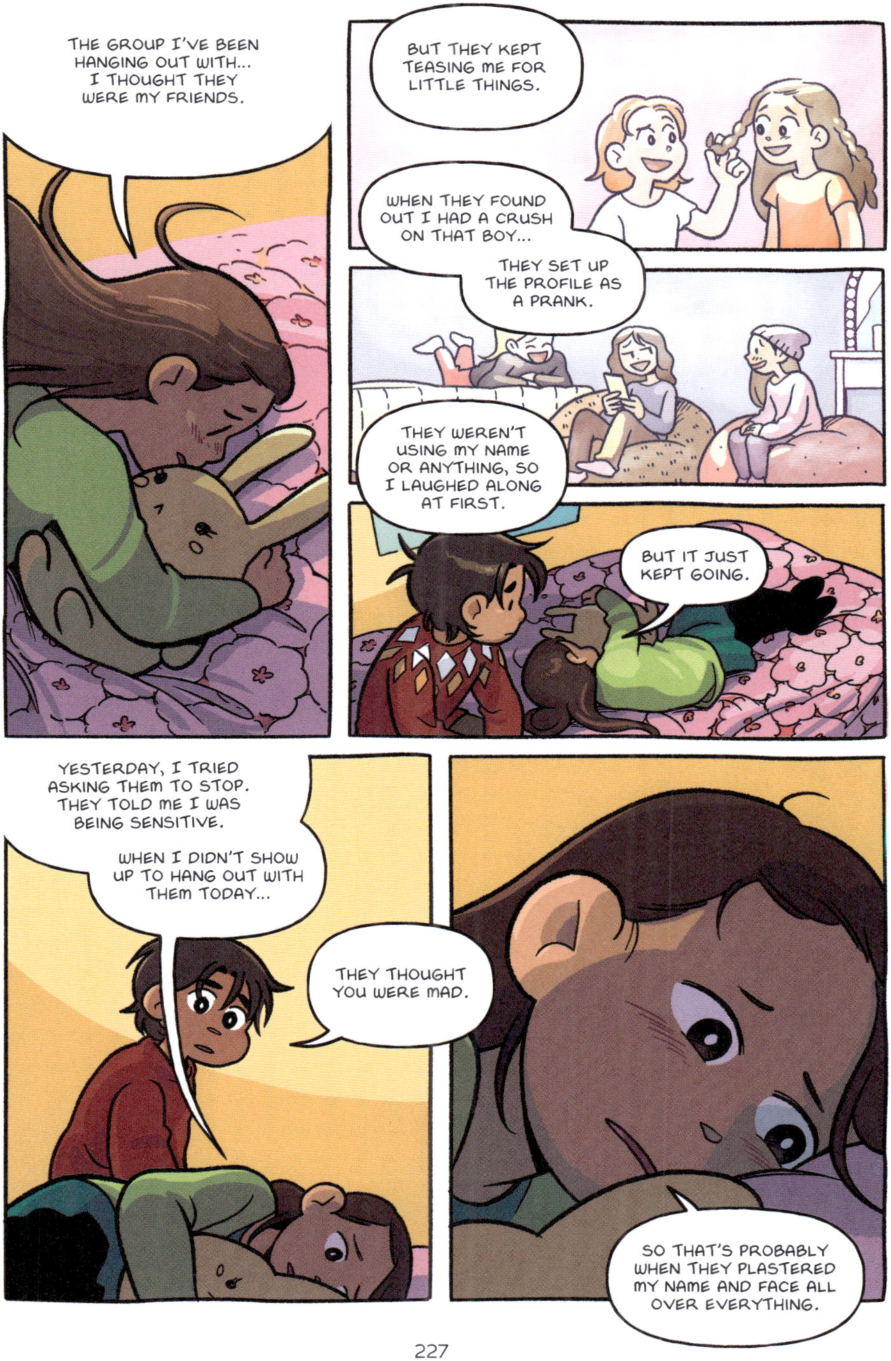
THE GROUP I'VE BEEN HANGING OUT WITH... I THOUGHT THEY WERE MY FRIENDS.
BUT THEY KEPT TEASING ME FOR LITTLE THINGS.
WHEN THEY FOUND OUT I HAD A CRUSH ON THAT BOY...
THEY SET UP THE PROFILE AS A PRANK.
THEY WEREN'T USING MY NAME OR ANYTHING, SO I LAUGHED ALONG AT FIRST.
BUT IT JUST KEPT GOING.
YESTERDAY, I TRIED ASKING THEM TO STOP. THEY TOLD ME I WAS BEING SENSITIVE.
WHEN I DIDN'T SHOW UP TO HANG OUT WITH THEM TODAY...
THEY THOUGHT YOU WERE MAD.
SO THAT'S PROBABLY WHEN THEY PLASTERED MY NAME AND FACE ALL OVER EVERYTHING.

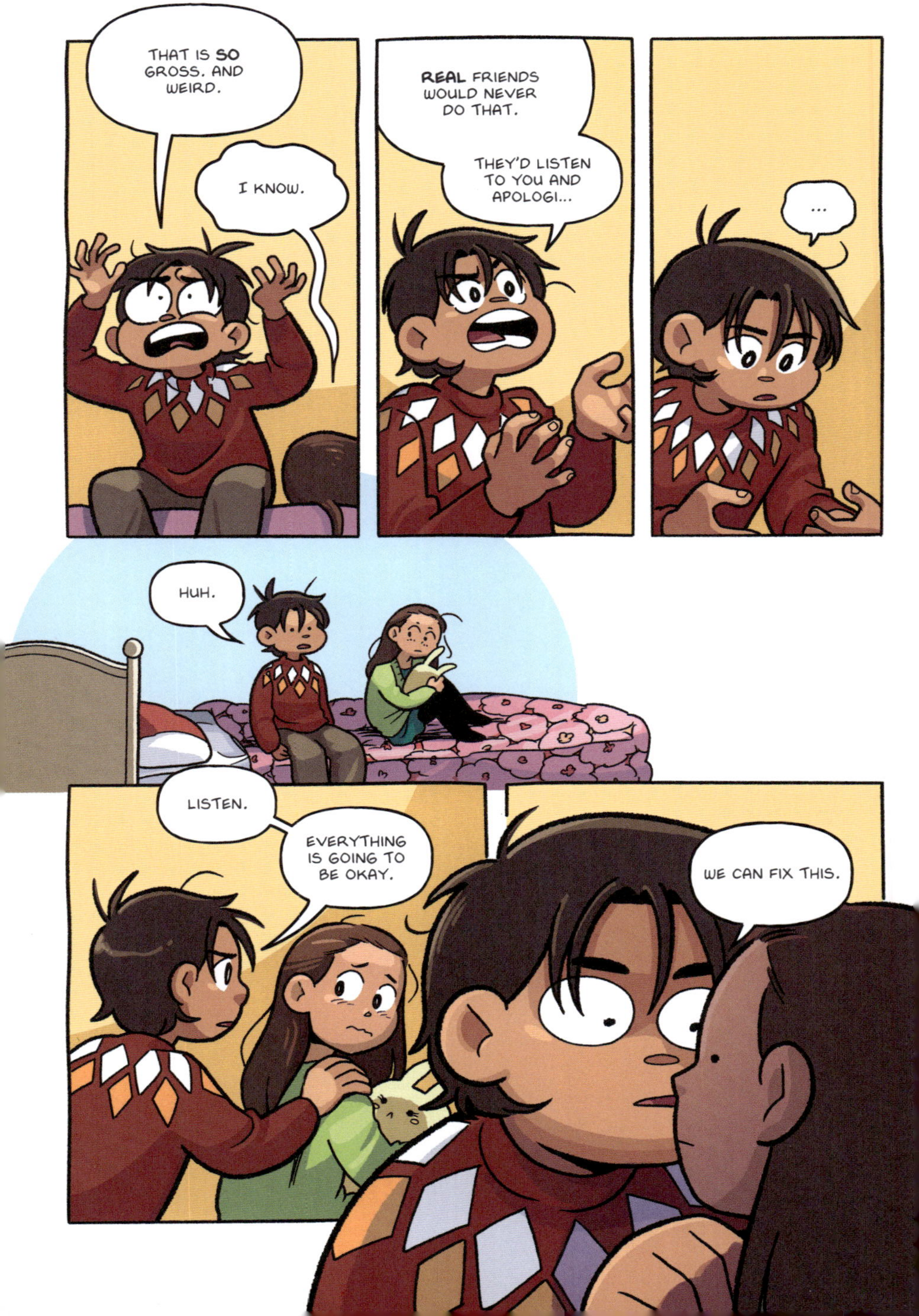
THAT IS **SO** GROSS. AND WEIRD.
I KNOW.
REAL FRIENDS WOULD NEVER DO THAT.
THEY'D LISTEN TO YOU AND APOLOGI...
...
HUH.
LISTEN.
EVERYTHING IS GOING TO BE OKAY.
WE CAN FIX THIS.

CHAPTER THIRTEEN

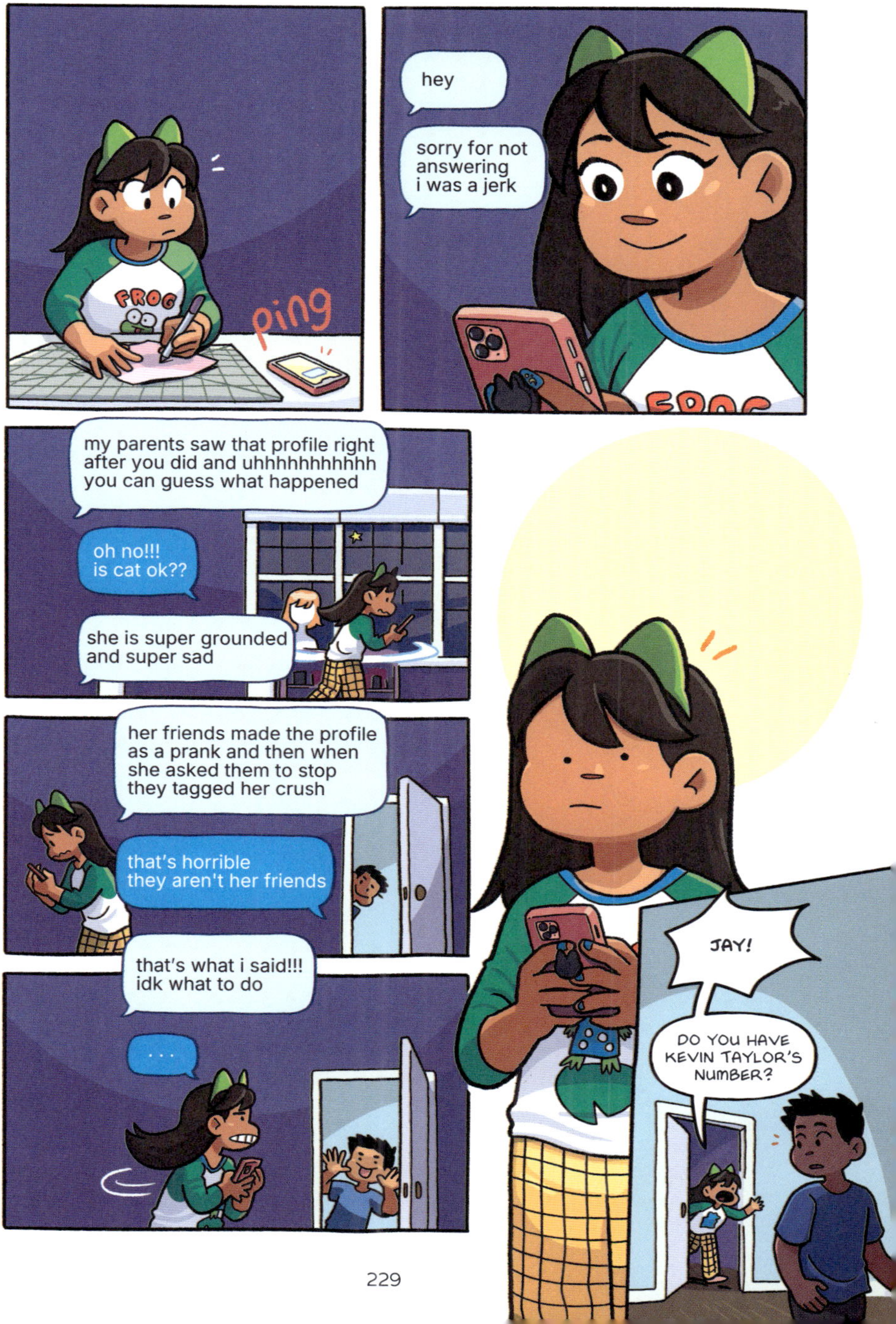
PING
hey
sorry for not answering i was a jerk
my parents saw that profile right after you did and uhhhhhhhhhhh you can guess what happened
oh no!!! is cat ok??
she is super grounded and super sad
her friends made the profile as a prank and then when she asked them to stop they tagged her crush
that's horrible they aren't her friends
that's what i said!!! idk what to do
...
JAY!
DO YOU HAVE KEVIN TAYLOR'S NUMBER?

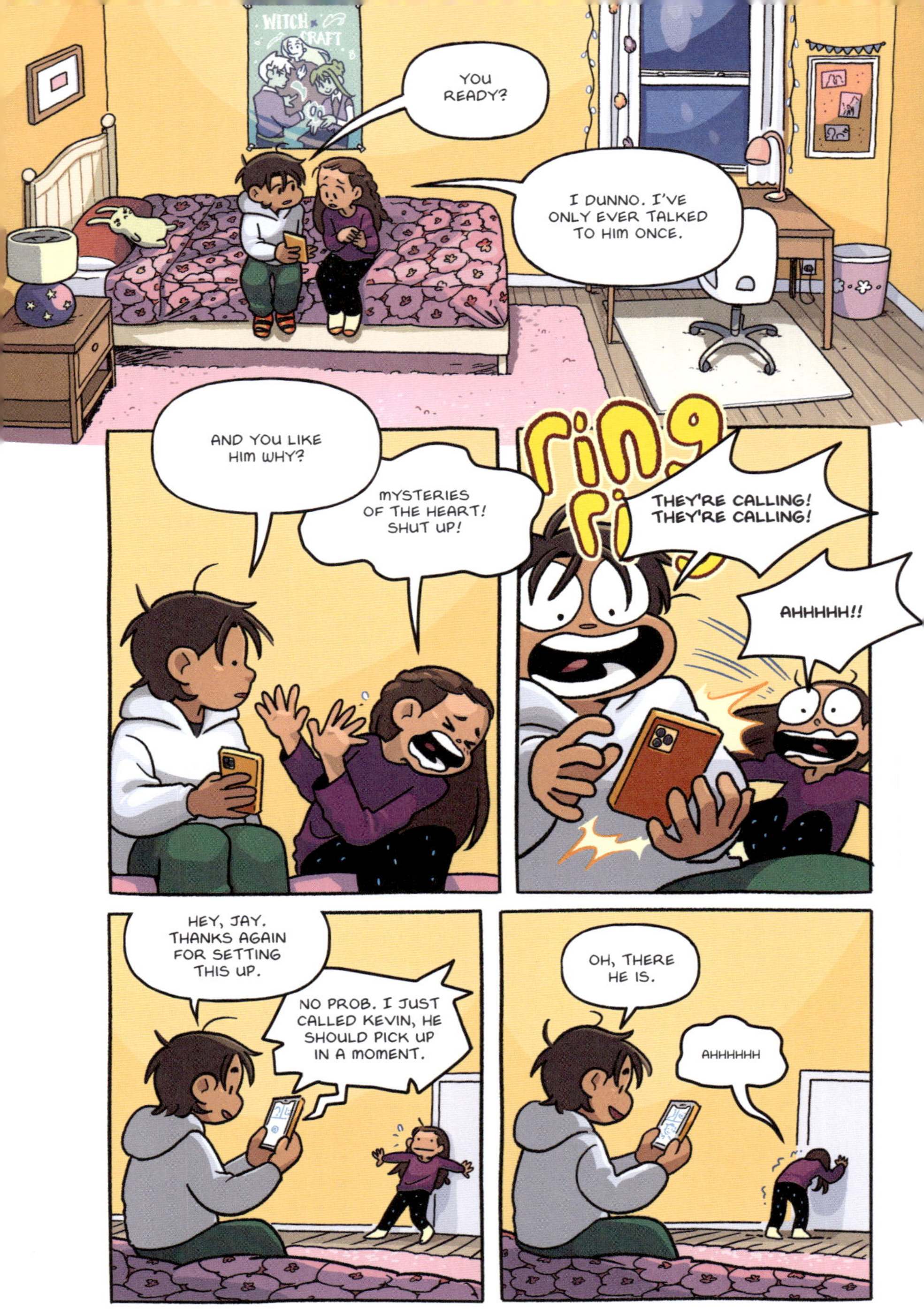

WITCH CRAFT
YOU READY?
I DUNNO. I'VE ONLY EVER TALKED TO HIM ONCE.
AND YOU LIKE HIM WHY?
MYSTERIES OF THE HEART! SHUT UP!
ring ring
THEY'RE CALLING! THEY'RE CALLING!
AHHHHH!!
HEY, JAY. THANKS AGAIN FOR SETTING THIS UP.
NO PROB. I JUST CALLED KEVIN, HE SHOULD PICK UP IN A MOMENT.
OH, THERE HE IS.
AHHHHHH

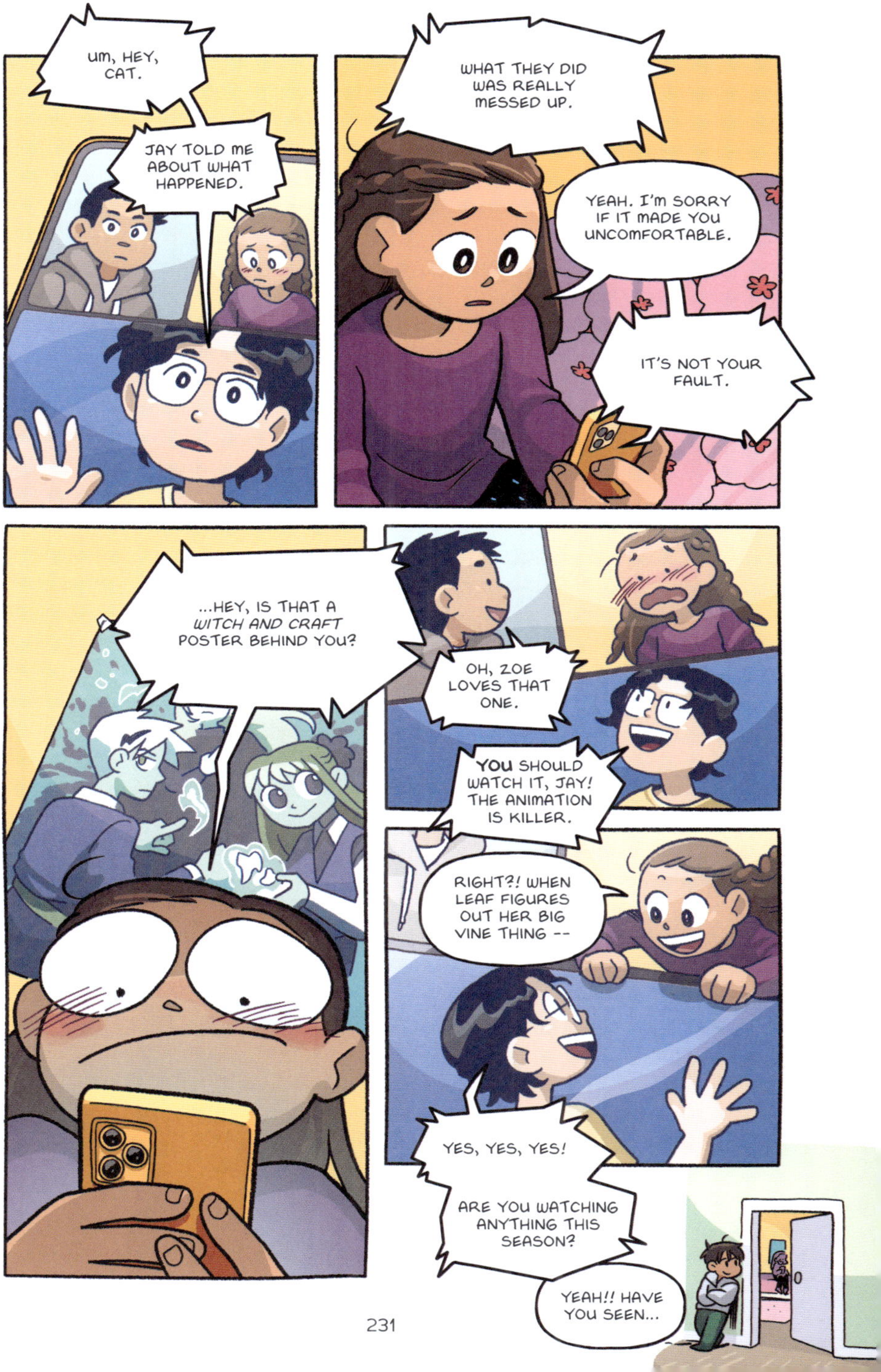
UM, HEY, CAT.
JAY TOLD ME ABOUT WHAT HAPPENED.
WHAT THEY DID WAS REALLY MESSED UP.
YEAH. I'M SORRY IF IT MADE YOU UNCOMFORTABLE.
IT'S NOT YOUR FAULT.
...HEY, IS THAT A *WITCH AND CRAFT* POSTER BEHIND YOU?
OH, ZOE LOVES THAT ONE.
YOU SHOULD WATCH IT, JAY! THE ANIMATION IS KILLER.
RIGHT?! WHEN LEAF FIGURES OUT HER BIG VINE THING --
YES, YES, YES!
ARE YOU WATCHING ANYTHING THIS SEASON?
YEAH!! HAVE YOU SEEN...

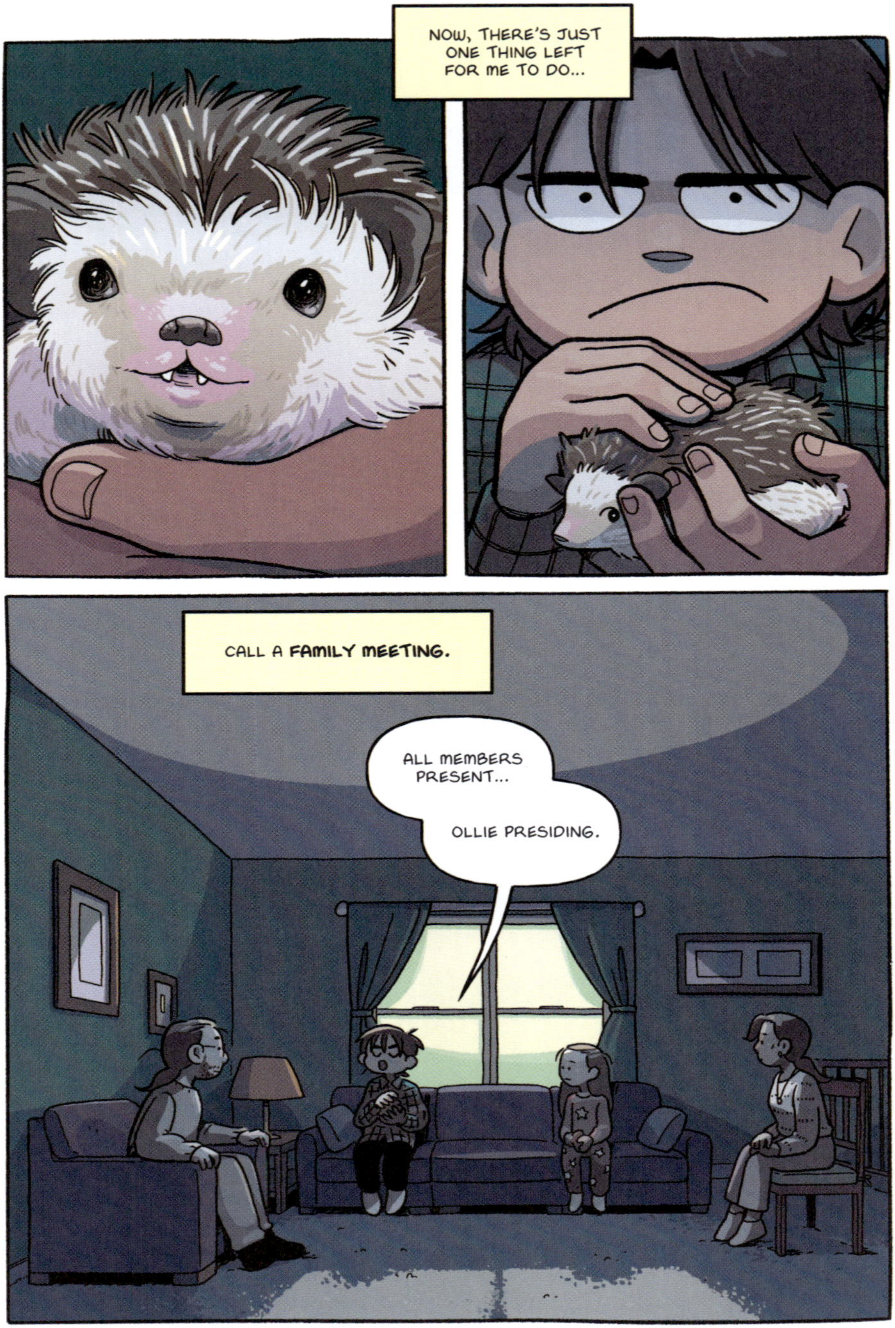
NOW, THERE'S JUST ONE THING LEFT FOR ME TO DO...
CALL A **FAMILY MEETING.**
ALL MEMBERS PRESENT...
OLLIE PRESIDING.

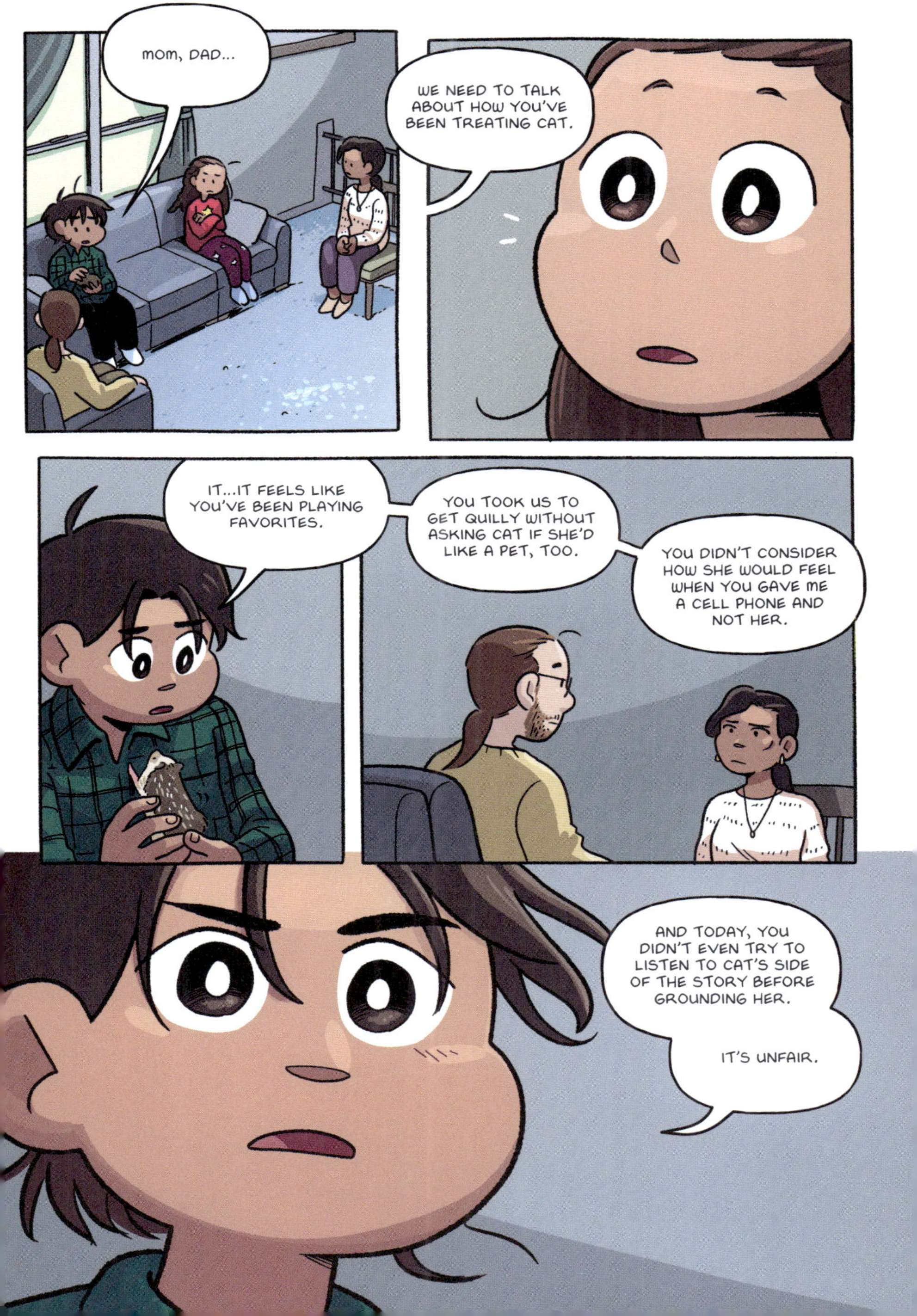
MOM, DAD...
WE NEED TO TALK ABOUT HOW YOU'VE BEEN TREATING CAT.
IT...IT FEELS LIKE YOU'VE BEEN PLAYING FAVORITES.
YOU TOOK US TO GET QUILLY WITHOUT ASKING CAT IF SHE'D LIKE A PET, TOO.
YOU DIDN'T CONSIDER HOW SHE WOULD FEEL WHEN YOU GAVE ME A CELL PHONE AND NOT HER.
AND TODAY, YOU DIDN'T EVEN TRY TO LISTEN TO CAT'S SIDE OF THE STORY BEFORE GROUNDING HER.
IT'S UNFAIR.

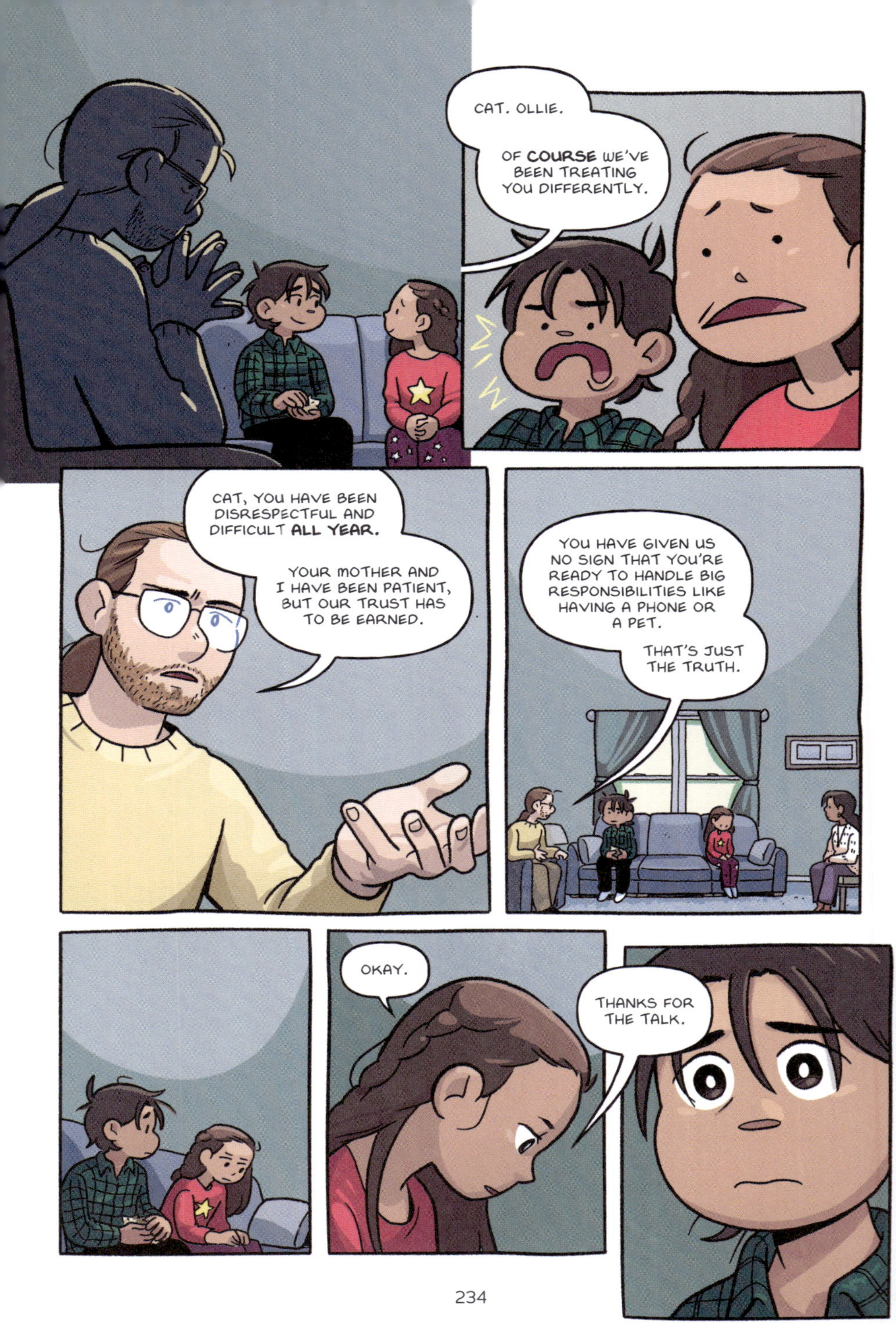
CAT. OLLIE.
OF **COURSE** WE'VE BEEN TREATING YOU DIFFERENTLY.
CAT, YOU HAVE BEEN DISRESPECTFUL AND DIFFICULT **ALL YEAR.**
YOUR MOTHER AND I HAVE BEEN PATIENT, BUT OUR TRUST HAS TO BE EARNED.
YOU HAVE GIVEN US NO SIGN THAT YOU'RE READY TO HANDLE BIG RESPONSIBILITIES LIKE HAVING A PHONE OR A PET.
THAT'S JUST THE TRUTH.
OKAY.
THANKS FOR THE TALK.

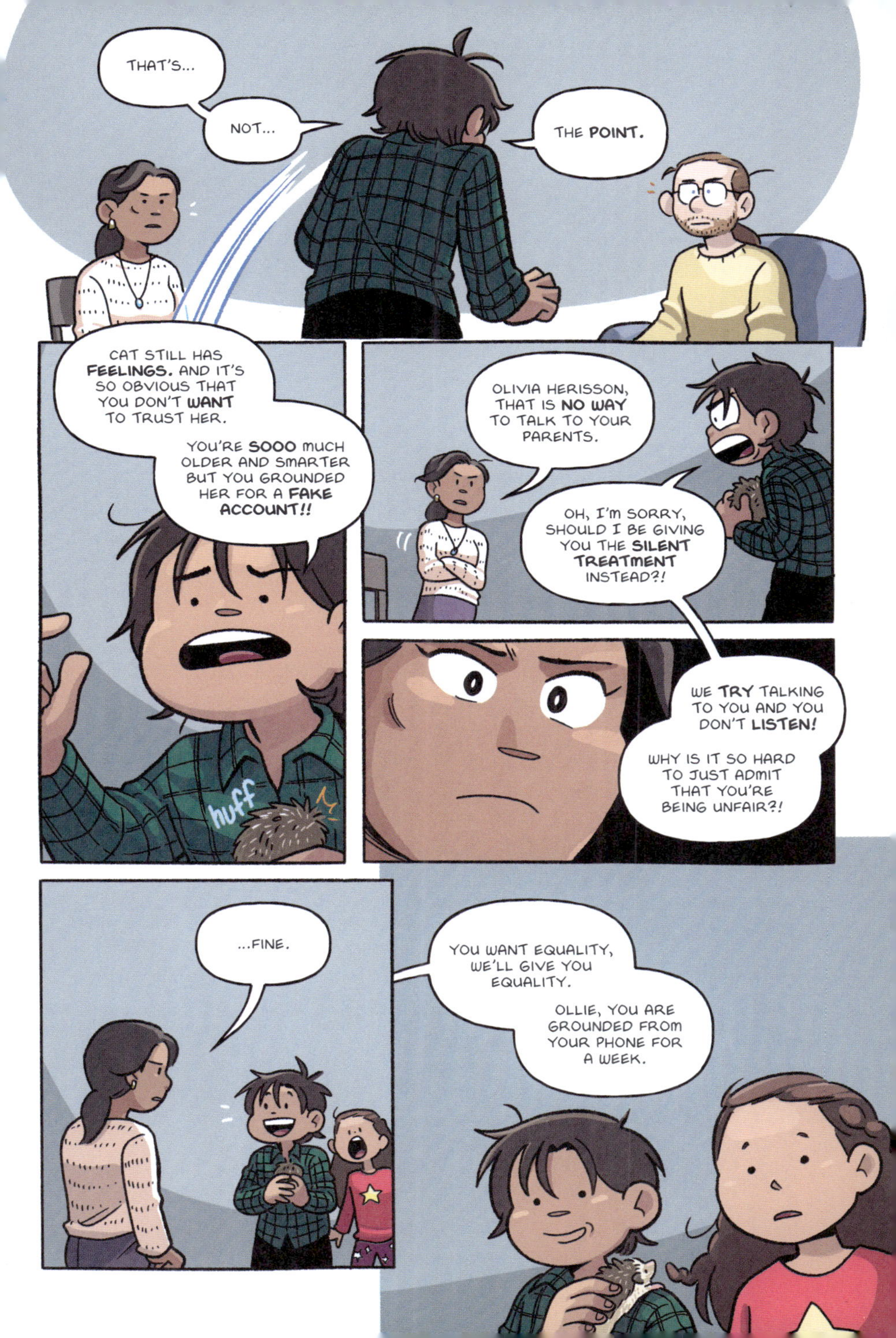

THAT'S...
NOT...
THE **POINT.**
CAT STILL HAS **FEELINGS.** AND IT'S SO OBVIOUS THAT YOU DON'T **WANT** TO TRUST HER.
YOU'RE **SOOO** MUCH OLDER AND SMARTER BUT YOU GROUNDED HER FOR A **FAKE ACCOUNT!!**
huff
OLIVIA HERISSON, THAT IS **NO WAY** TO TALK TO YOUR PARENTS.
OH, I'M SORRY, SHOULD I BE GIVING YOU THE **SILENT TREATMENT** INSTEAD?!
WE **TRY** TALKING TO YOU AND YOU DON'T **LISTEN!**
WHY IS IT SO HARD TO JUST ADMIT THAT YOU'RE BEING UNFAIR?!
...FINE.
YOU WANT EQUALITY, WE'LL GIVE YOU EQUALITY.
OLLIE, YOU ARE GROUNDED FROM YOUR PHONE FOR A WEEK.

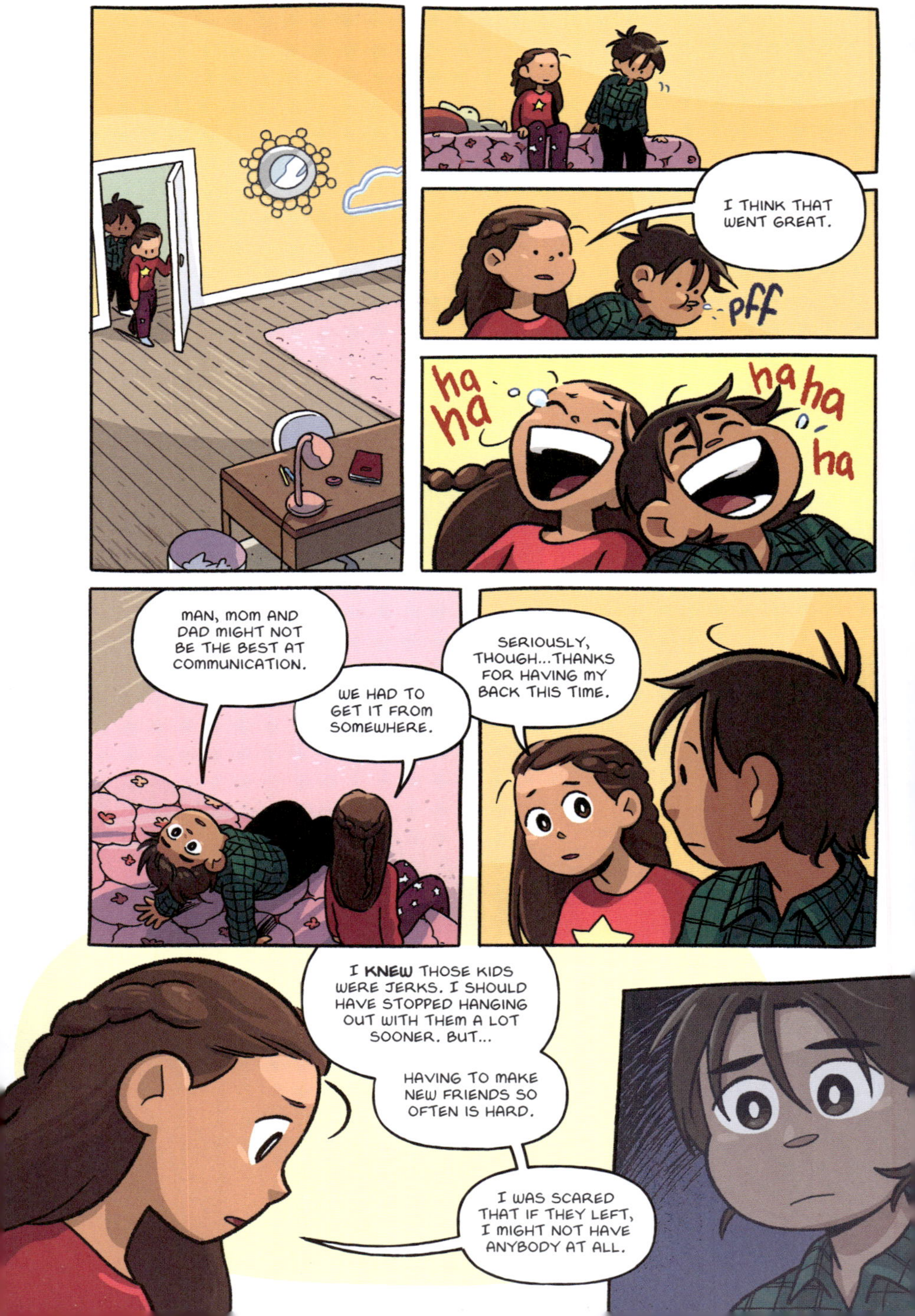
I THINK THAT WENT GREAT.
pff
ha ha
ha ha ha
MAN, MOM AND DAD MIGHT NOT BE THE BEST AT COMMUNICATION.
WE HAD TO GET IT FROM SOMEWHERE.
SERIOUSLY, THOUGH...THANKS FOR HAVING MY BACK THIS TIME.
I **KNEW** THOSE KIDS WERE JERKS. I SHOULD HAVE STOPPED HANGING OUT WITH THEM A LOT SOONER. BUT...
HAVING TO MAKE NEW FRIENDS SO OFTEN IS HARD.
I WAS SCARED THAT IF THEY LEFT, I MIGHT NOT HAVE ANYBODY AT ALL.

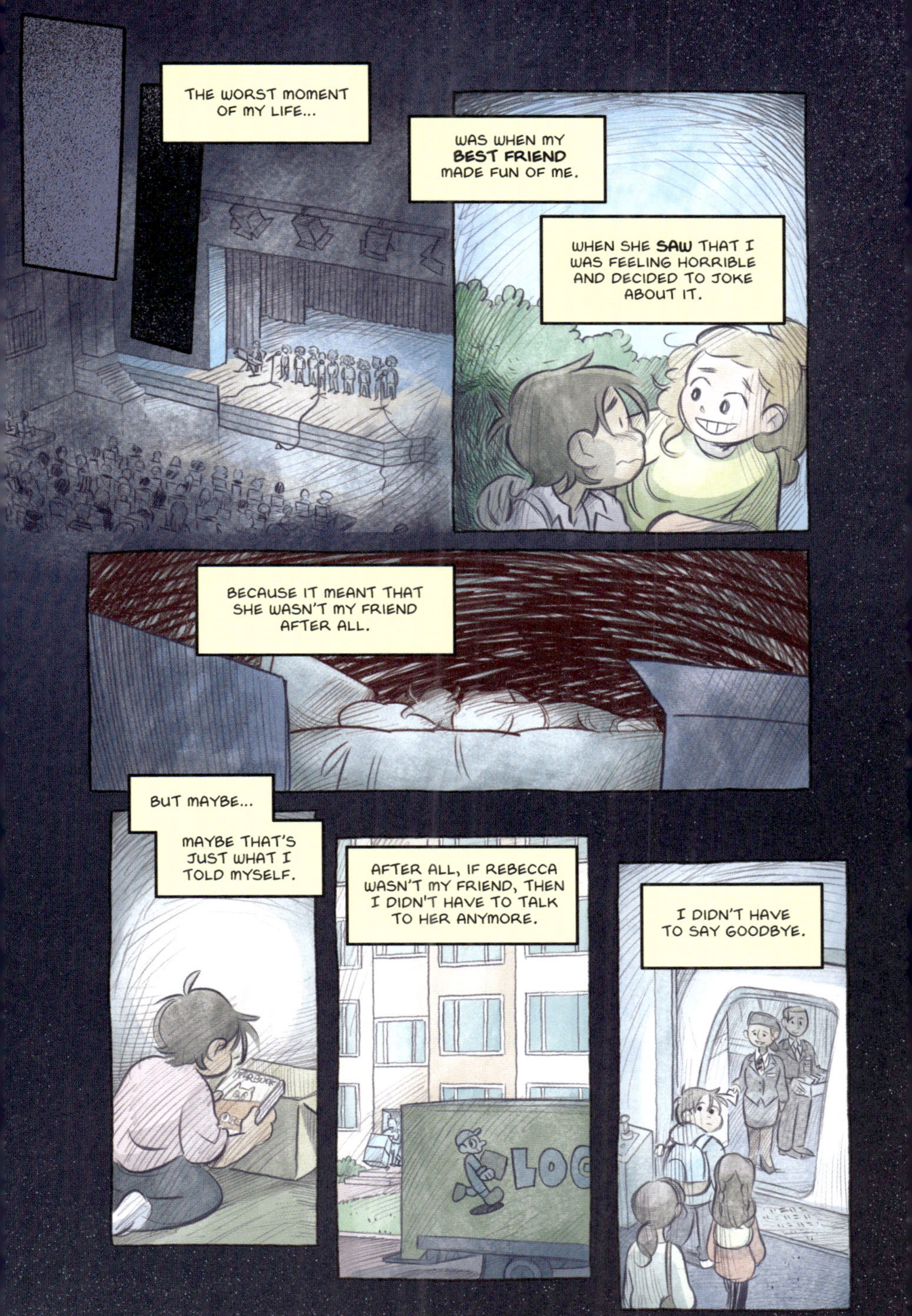
THE WORST MOMENT OF MY LIFE...
WAS WHEN MY BEST FRIEND MADE FUN OF ME.
WHEN SHE SAW THAT I WAS FEELING HORRIBLE AND DECIDED TO JOKE ABOUT IT.
BECAUSE IT MEANT THAT SHE WASN'T MY FRIEND AFTER ALL.
BUT MAYBE...
MAYBE THAT'S JUST WHAT I TOLD MYSELF.
AFTER ALL, IF REBECCA WASN'T MY FRIEND, THEN I DIDN'T HAVE TO TALK TO HER ANYMORE.
I DIDN'T HAVE TO SAY GOODBYE.

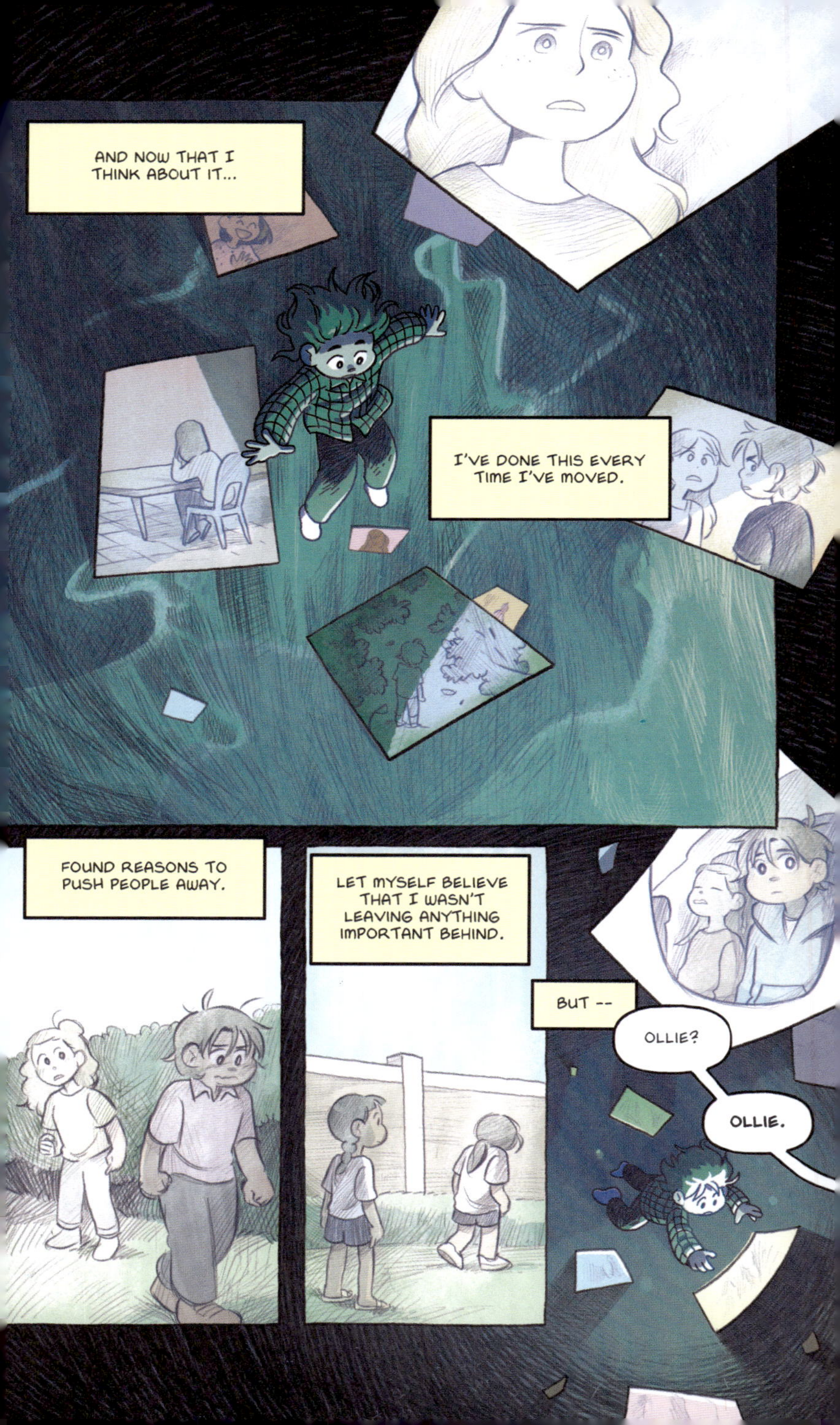
AND NOW THAT I THINK ABOUT IT...
I'VE DONE THIS EVERY TIME I'VE MOVED.
FOUND REASONS TO PUSH PEOPLE AWAY.
LET MYSELF BELIEVE THAT I WASN'T LEAVING ANYTHING IMPORTANT BEHIND.
BUT --
OLLIE?
OLLIE.

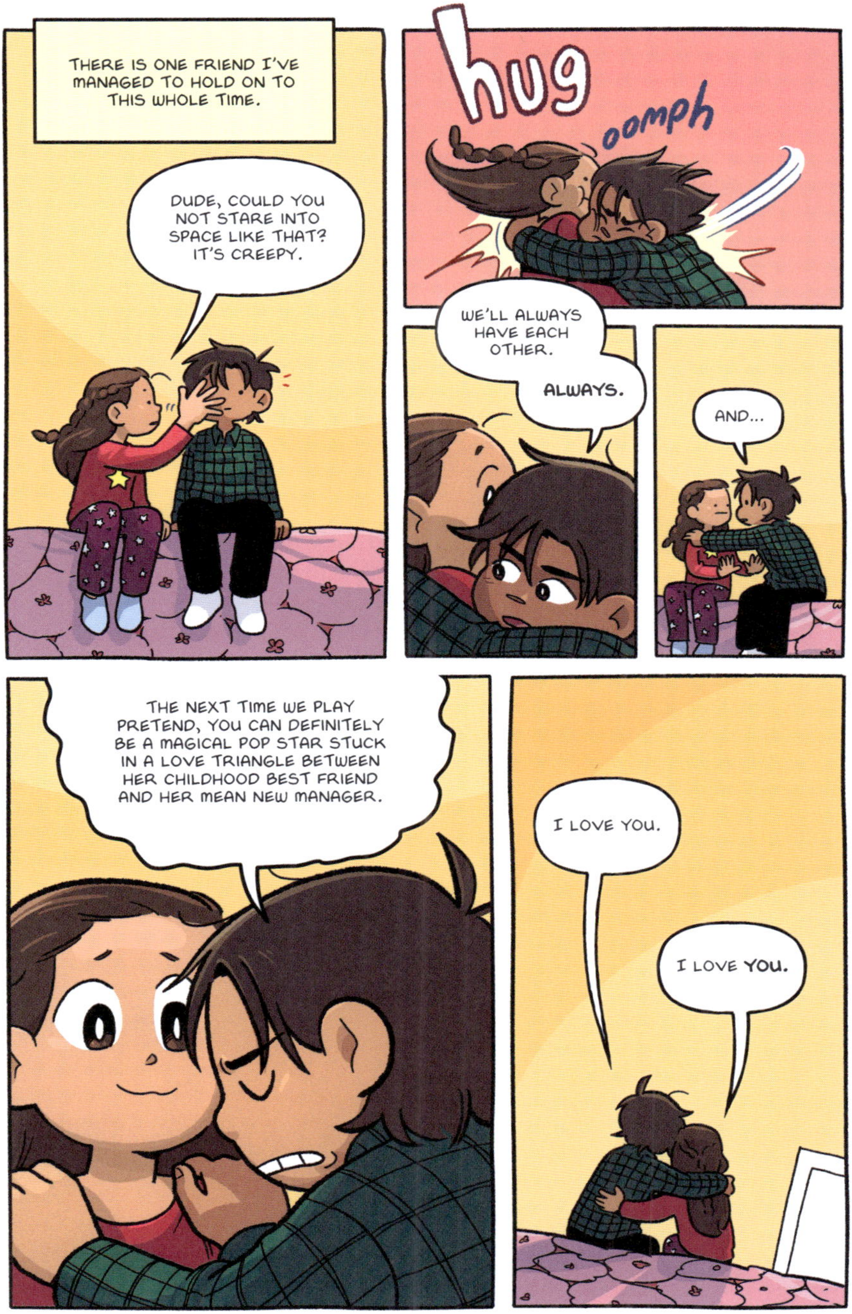
THERE IS ONE FRIEND I'VE MANAGED TO HOLD ON TO THIS WHOLE TIME.
DUDE, COULD YOU NOT STARE INTO SPACE LIKE THAT? IT'S CREEPY.
hug
oomph
WE'LL ALWAYS HAVE EACH OTHER.
ALWAYS.
AND...
THE NEXT TIME WE PLAY PRETEND, YOU CAN DEFINITELY BE A MAGICAL POP STAR STUCK IN A LOVE TRIANGLE BETWEEN HER CHILDHOOD BEST FRIEND AND HER MEAN NEW MANAGER.
I LOVE YOU.
I LOVE YOU.

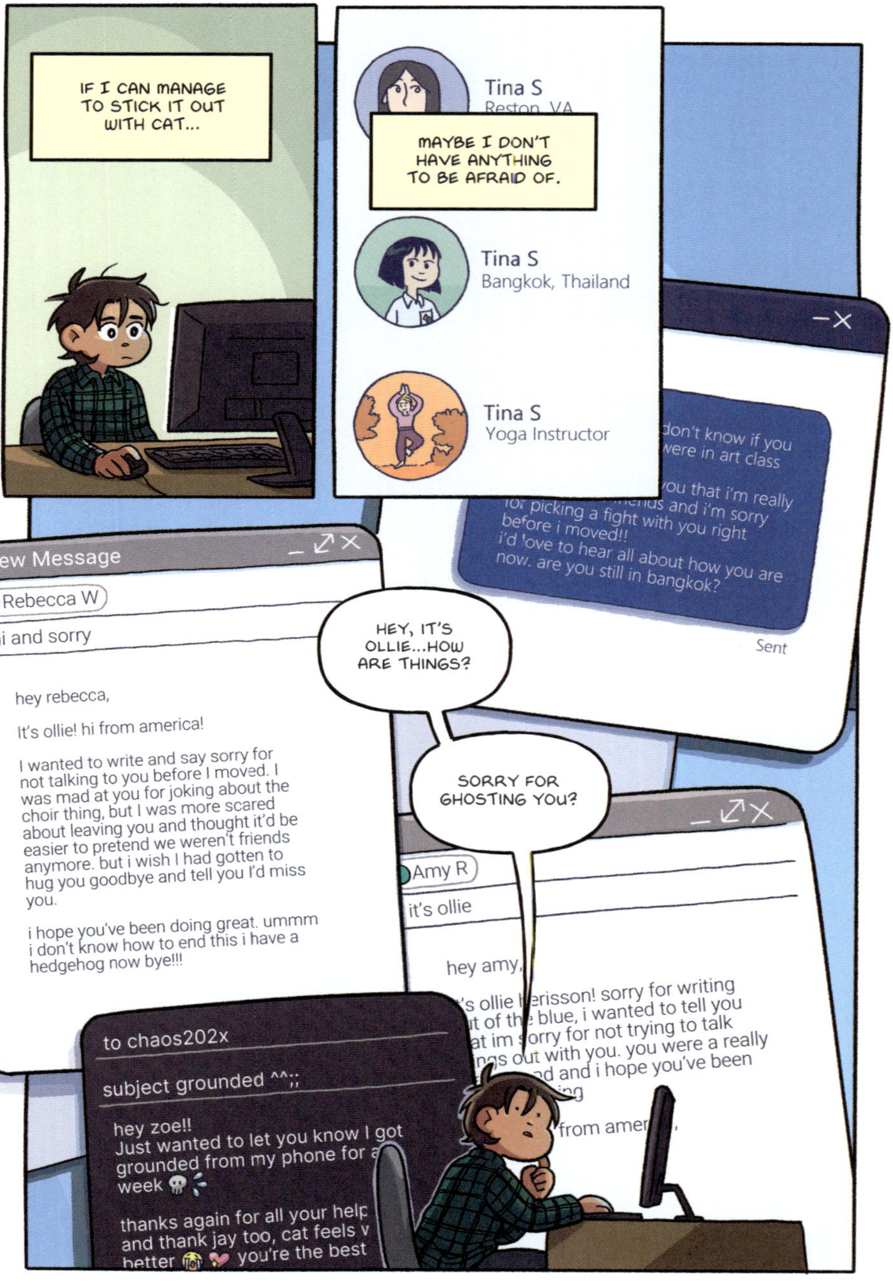
IF I CAN MANAGE TO STICK IT OUT WITH CAT...
Tina S
Reston, VA
MAYBE I DON'T HAVE ANYTHING TO BE AFRAID OF.
Tina S
Bangkok, Thailand
Tina S
Yoga Instructor
don't know if you were in art class
you that i'm really
for picking a fight with you right before i moved!!
i'd love to hear all about how you are now. are you still in bangkok?
Sent
New Message
Rebecca W
hi and sorry
hey rebecca,
It's ollie! hi from america!
I wanted to write and say sorry for not talking to you before I moved. I was mad at you for joking about the choir thing, but I was more scared about leaving you and thought it'd be easier to pretend we weren't friends anymore. but i wish I had gotten to hug you goodbye and tell you I'd miss you.
i hope you've been doing great. ummm i don't know how to end this i have a hedgehog now bye!!!
HEY, IT'S OLLIE...HOW ARE THINGS?
SORRY FOR GHOSTING YOU?
Amy R
it's ollie
hey amy,
sorry for writing
i wanted to tell you
sorry for not trying to talk
out with you. you were a really
and i hope you've been
from amer
to chaos202x
subject grounded ^^;;
hey zoe!!
Just wanted to let you know I got grounded from my phone for a week
thanks again for all your help and thank jay too, cat feels
better you're the best

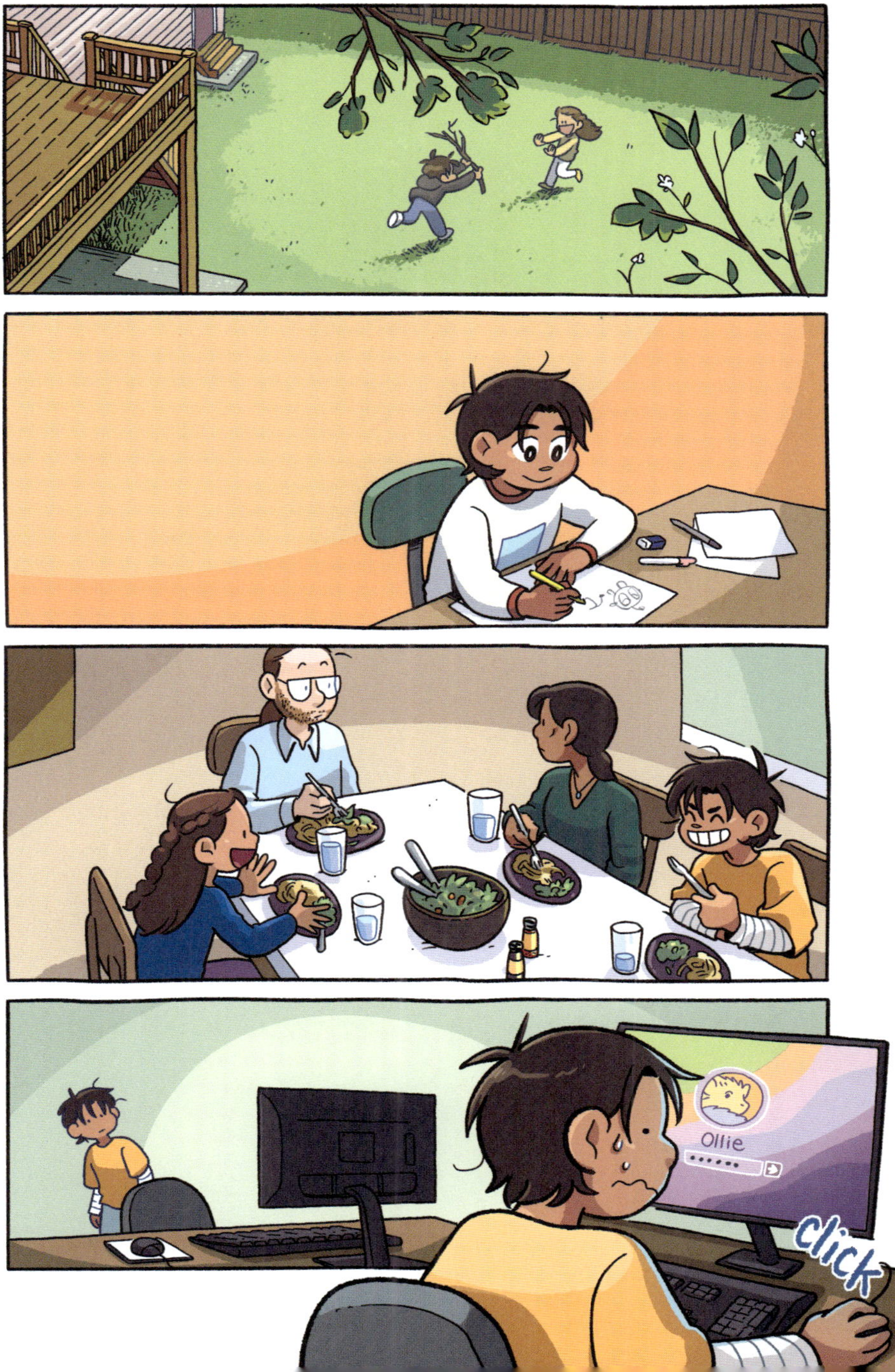
Ollie
click

Inbox
Artsy: Note From chaos202x
nooo you got grounded?!?!?! when
Amy R
Wow hi Ollie! How have you
Tina S
Ollie its been sooo long!
Rebecca W
Hi Ollie,
Rebecca W
Hi Ollie,
Hi Ollie,
It's so good to hear from you!! I've missed you!!!
Thank you for explaining. I was really confused when you stopped talking to me and left. I didn't mean to hurt your feelings and I'm sorry too.
Do you want to video chat sometime? I want to meet your hedgehog!!
Miss you lots.
Xoxo,
Rebecca

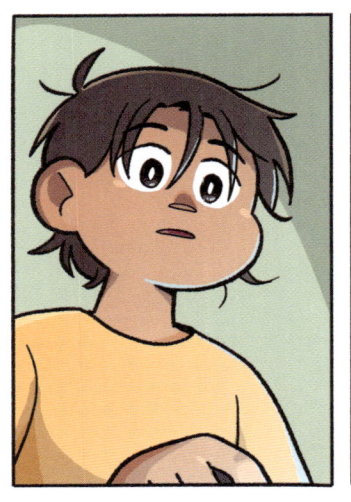

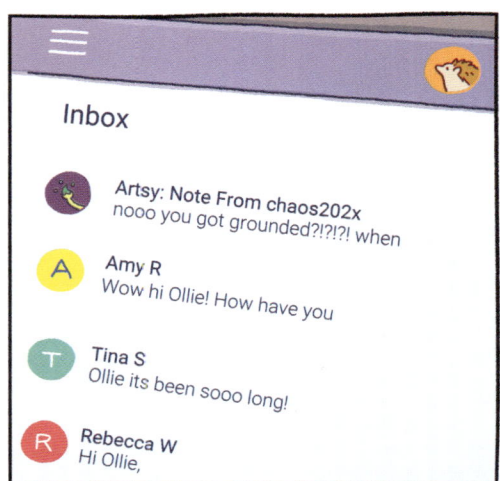

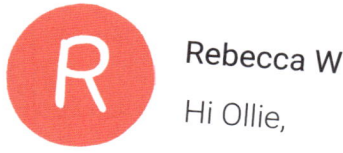

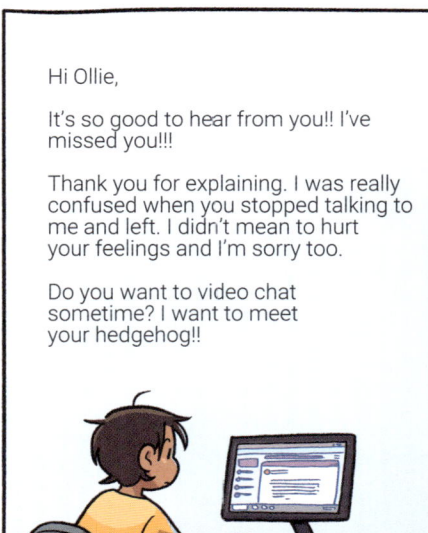

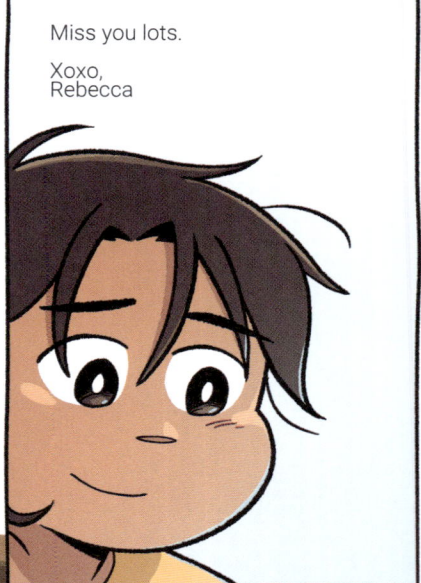

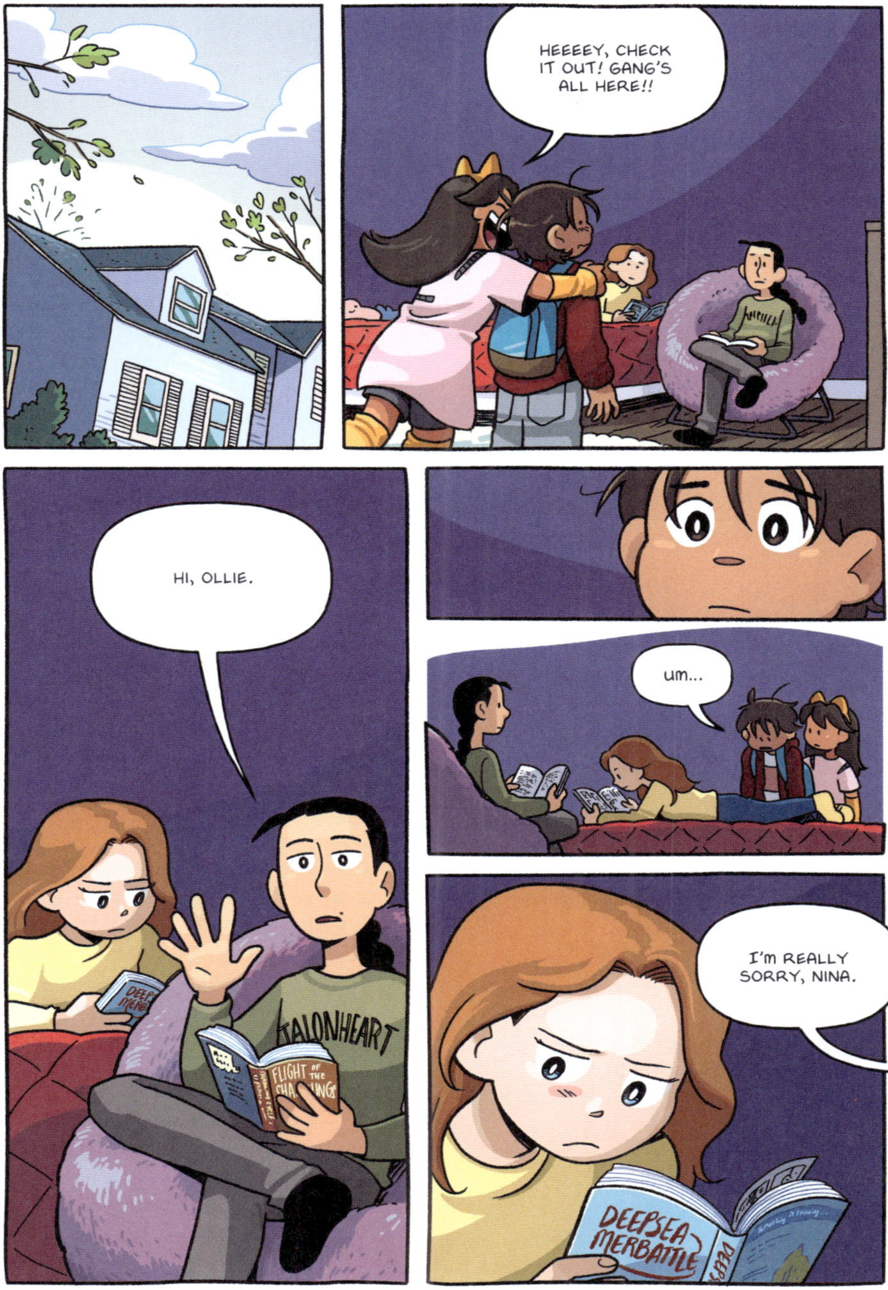
HEEEEY, CHECK IT OUT! GANG'S ALL HERE!!
HI, OLLIE.
TALONHEART
FLIGHT OF THE CHANGELINGS
um...
I'M REALLY SORRY, NINA.
DEEPSEA MERBATTLE

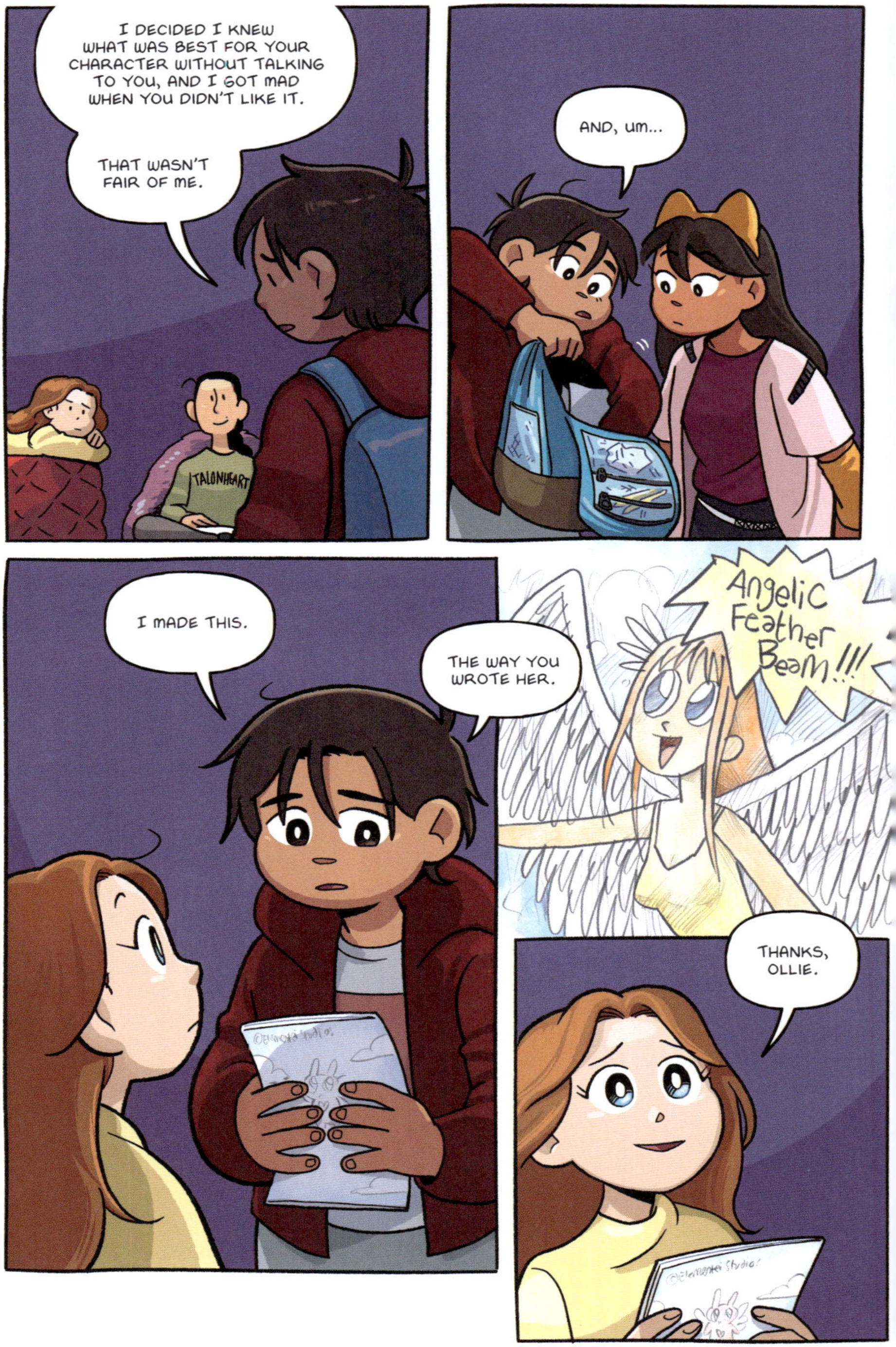
I DECIDED I KNEW WHAT WAS BEST FOR YOUR CHARACTER WITHOUT TALKING TO YOU, AND I GOT MAD WHEN YOU DIDN'T LIKE IT.
THAT WASN'T FAIR OF ME.
TALONHEART
AND, UM...
I MADE THIS.
THE WAY YOU WROTE HER.
Angelic Feather Beam!!!
THANKS, OLLIE.

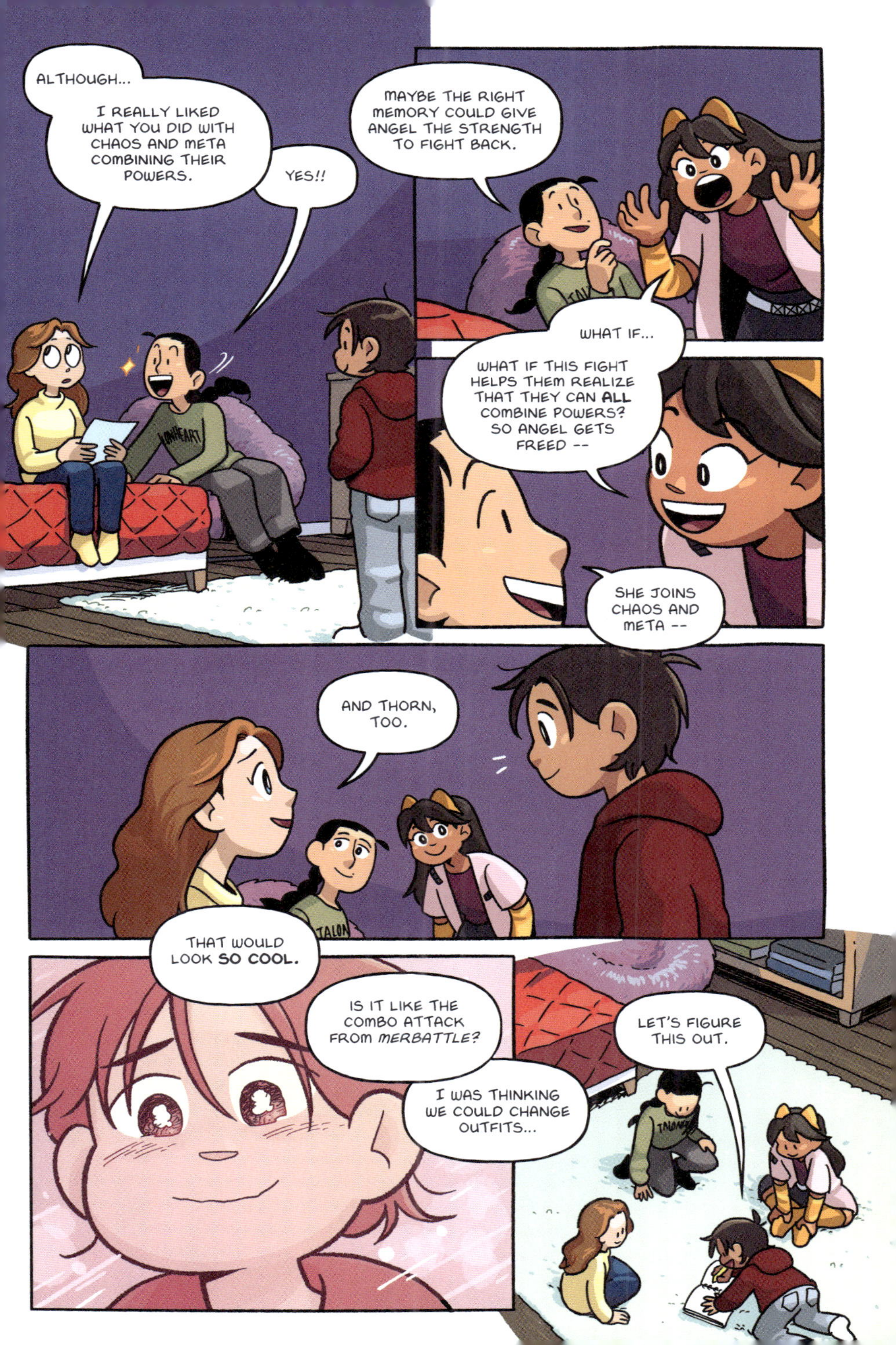
ALTHOUGH...
I REALLY LIKED WHAT YOU DID WITH CHAOS AND META COMBINING THEIR POWERS.
YES!!
TALONHEART
MAYBE THE RIGHT MEMORY COULD GIVE ANGEL THE STRENGTH TO FIGHT BACK.
WHAT IF...
WHAT IF THIS FIGHT HELPS THEM REALIZE THAT THEY CAN **ALL** COMBINE POWERS? SO ANGEL GETS FREED --
SHE JOINS CHAOS AND META --
AND THORN, TOO.
THAT WOULD LOOK **SO COOL.**
IS IT LIKE THE COMBO ATTACK FROM *MERBATTLE*?
I WAS THINKING WE COULD CHANGE OUTFITS...
LET'S FIGURE THIS OUT.

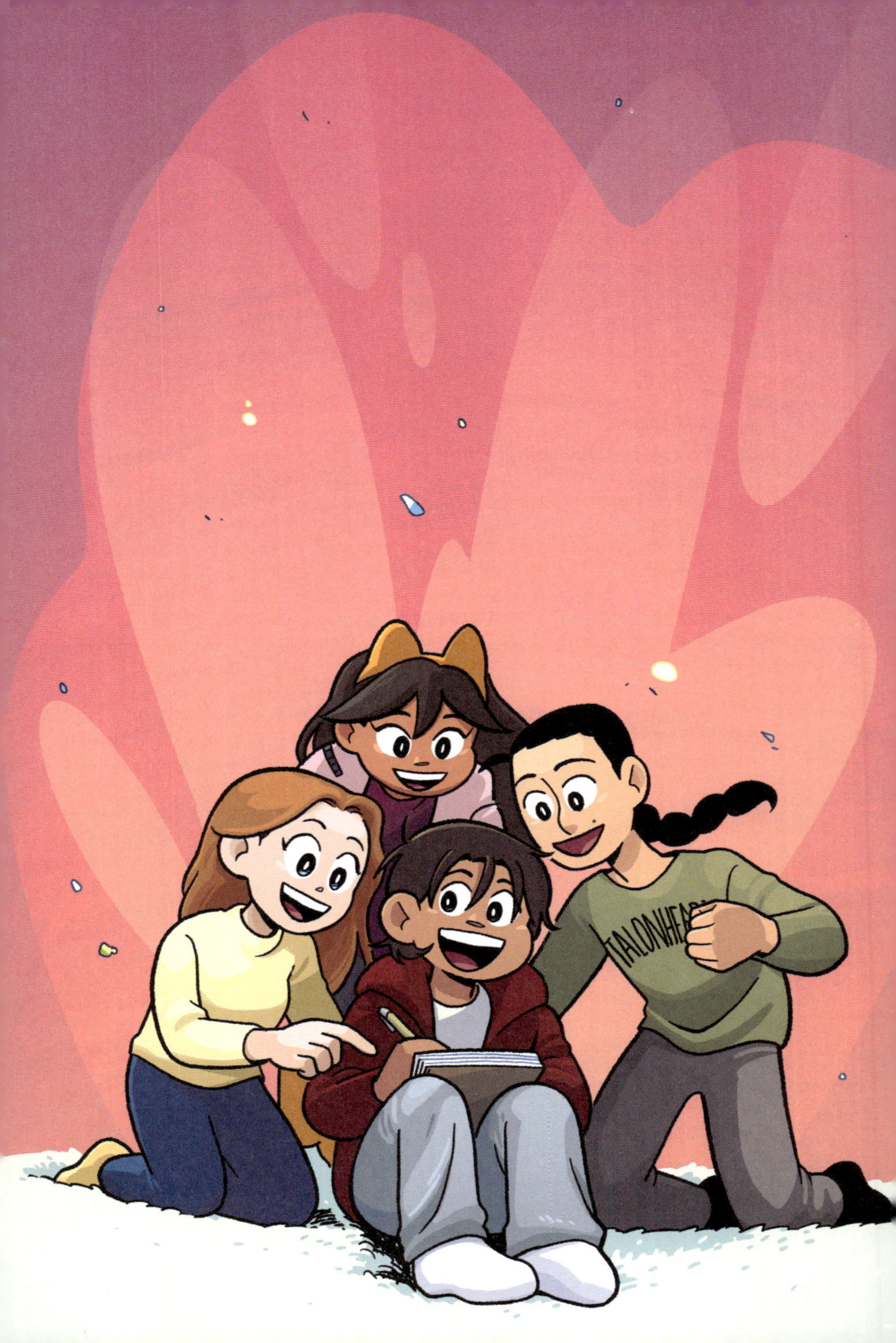

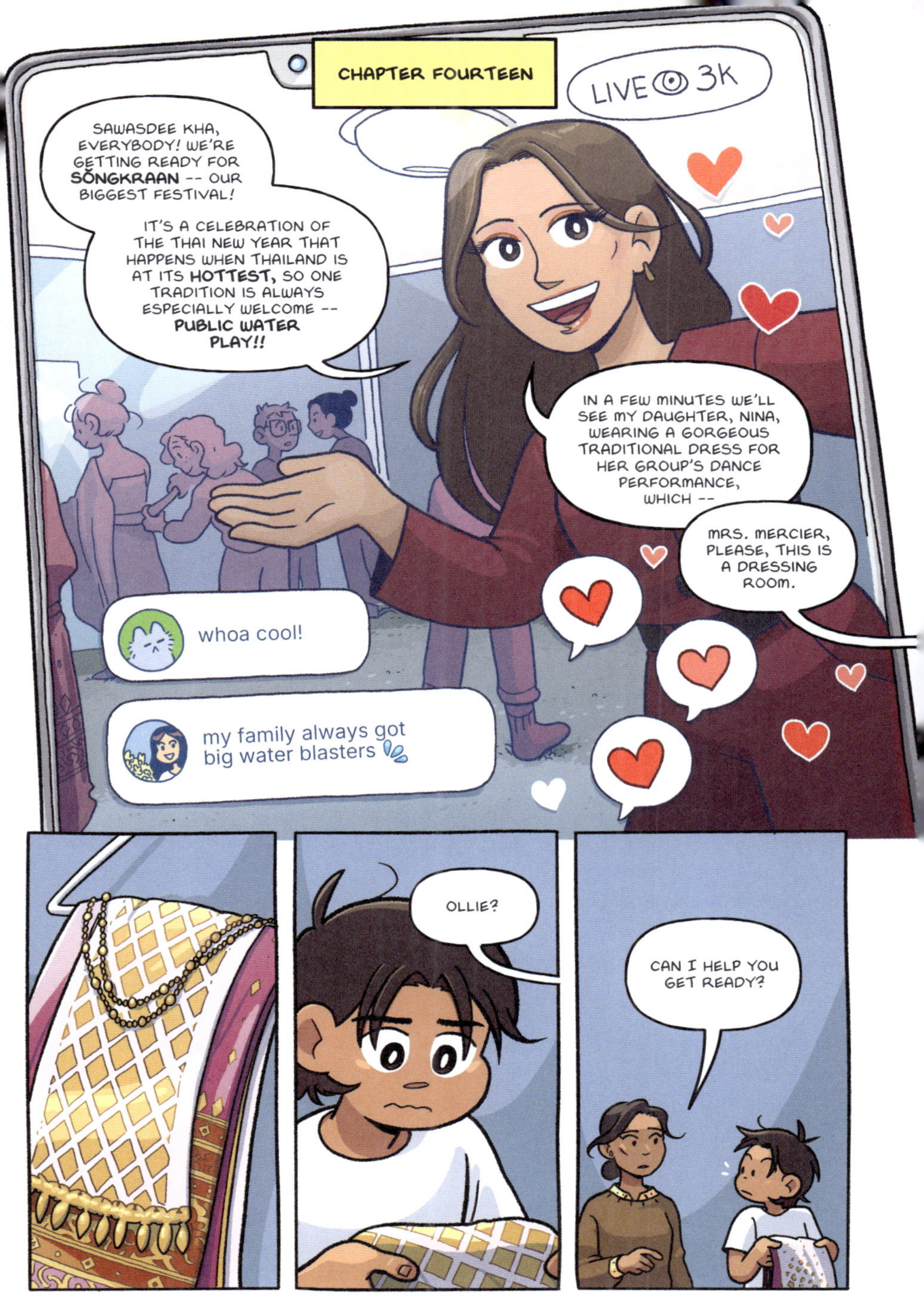
CHAPTER FOURTEEN
LIVE 3K
SAWASDEE KHA, EVERYBODY! WE'RE GETTING READY FOR SŎNGKRAAN -- OUR BIGGEST FESTIVAL!
IT'S A CELEBRATION OF THE THAI NEW YEAR THAT HAPPENS WHEN THAILAND IS AT ITS HOTTEST, SO ONE TRADITION IS ALWAYS ESPECIALLY WELCOME -- PUBLIC WATER PLAY!!
IN A FEW MINUTES WE'LL SEE MY DAUGHTER, NINA, WEARING A GORGEOUS TRADITIONAL DRESS FOR HER GROUP'S DANCE PERFORMANCE, WHICH --
MRS. MERCIER, PLEASE, THIS IS A DRESSING ROOM.
whoa cool!
my family always got big water blasters
OLLIE?
CAN I HELP YOU GET READY?

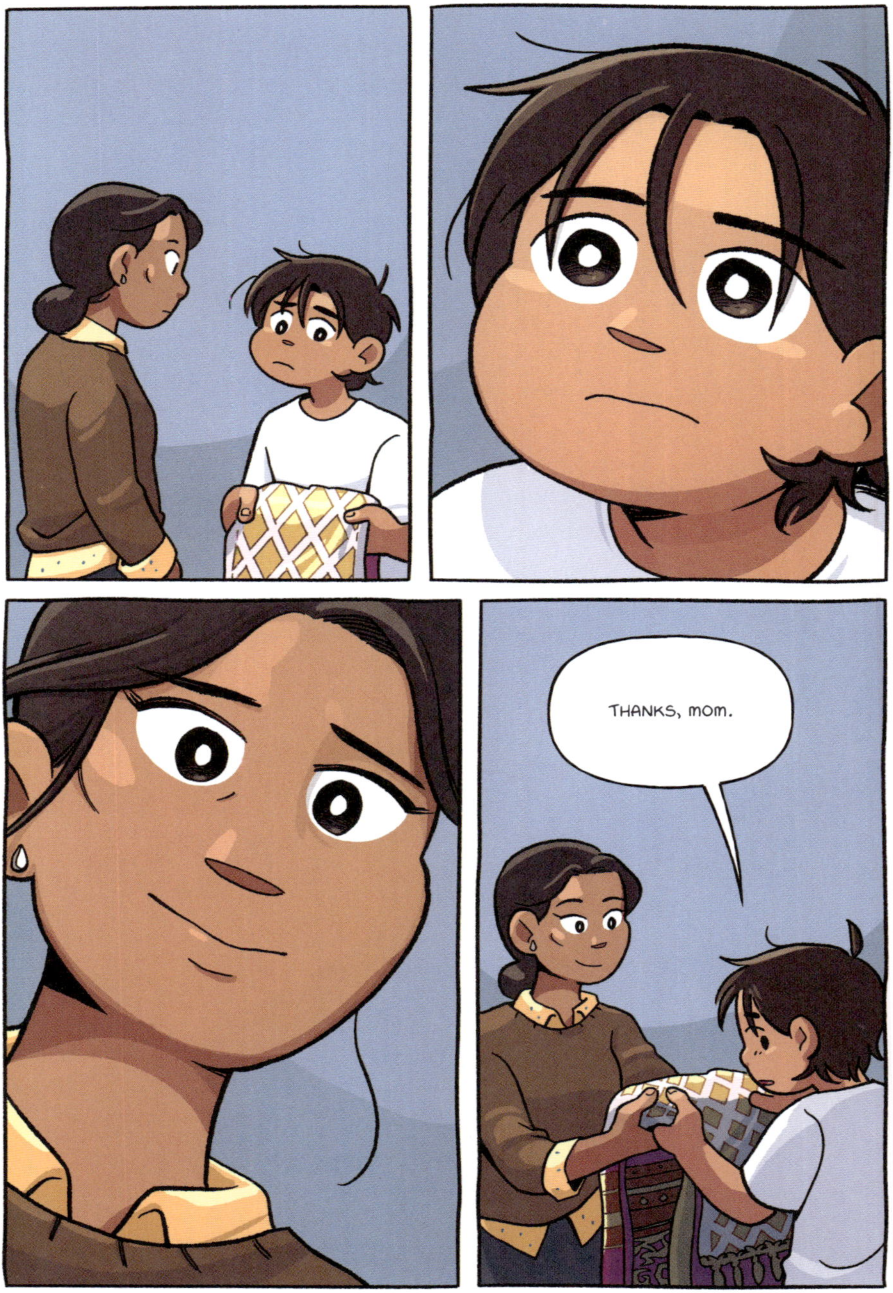
THANKS, MOM.

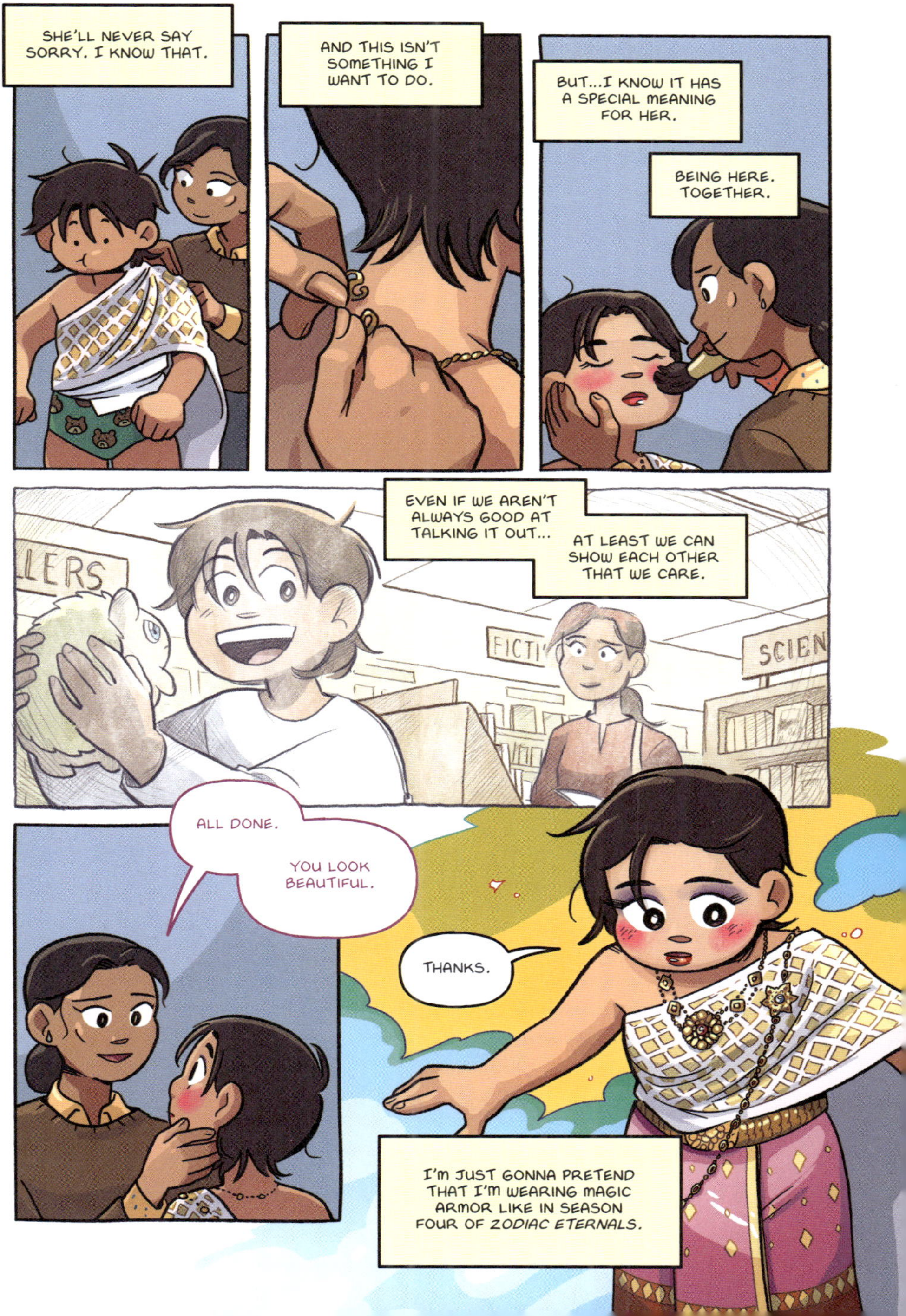

SHE'LL NEVER SAY SORRY. I KNOW THAT.
AND THIS ISN'T SOMETHING I WANT TO DO.
BUT...I KNOW IT HAS A SPECIAL MEANING FOR HER.
BEING HERE. TOGETHER.
EVEN IF WE AREN'T ALWAYS GOOD AT TALKING IT OUT...
AT LEAST WE CAN SHOW EACH OTHER THAT WE CARE.
LERS
FICTI
SCIEN
ALL DONE.
YOU LOOK BEAUTIFUL.
THANKS.
I'M JUST GONNA PRETEND THAT I'M WEARING MAGIC ARMOR LIKE IN SEASON FOUR OF *ZODIAC ETERNALS*.

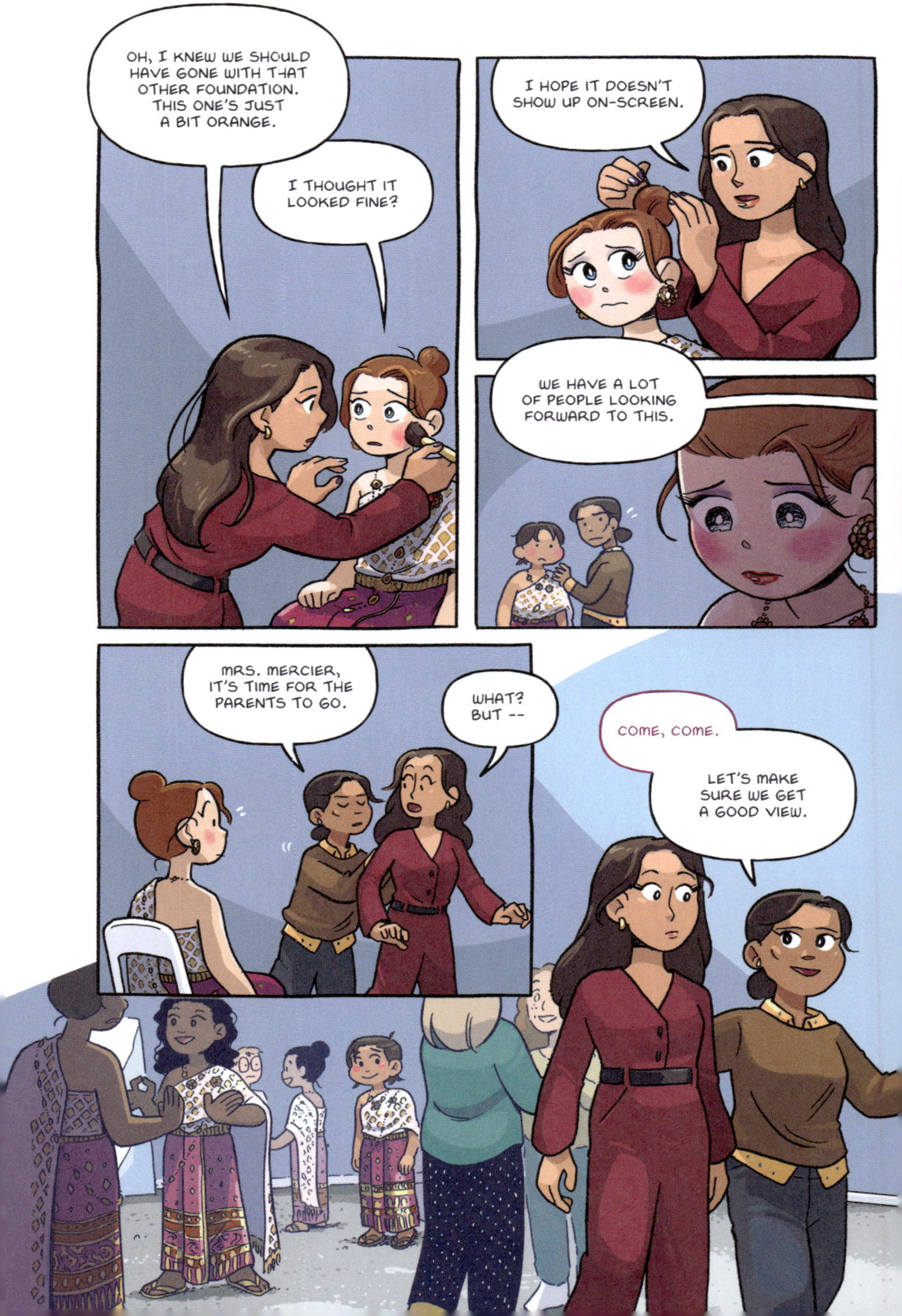
OH, I KNEW WE SHOULD HAVE GONE WITH THAT OTHER FOUNDATION. THIS ONE'S JUST A BIT ORANGE.
I THOUGHT IT LOOKED FINE?
I HOPE IT DOESN'T SHOW UP ON-SCREEN.
WE HAVE A LOT OF PEOPLE LOOKING FORWARD TO THIS.
MRS. MERCIER, IT'S TIME FOR THE PARENTS TO GO.
WHAT? BUT --
COME, COME.
LET'S MAKE SURE WE GET A GOOD VIEW.

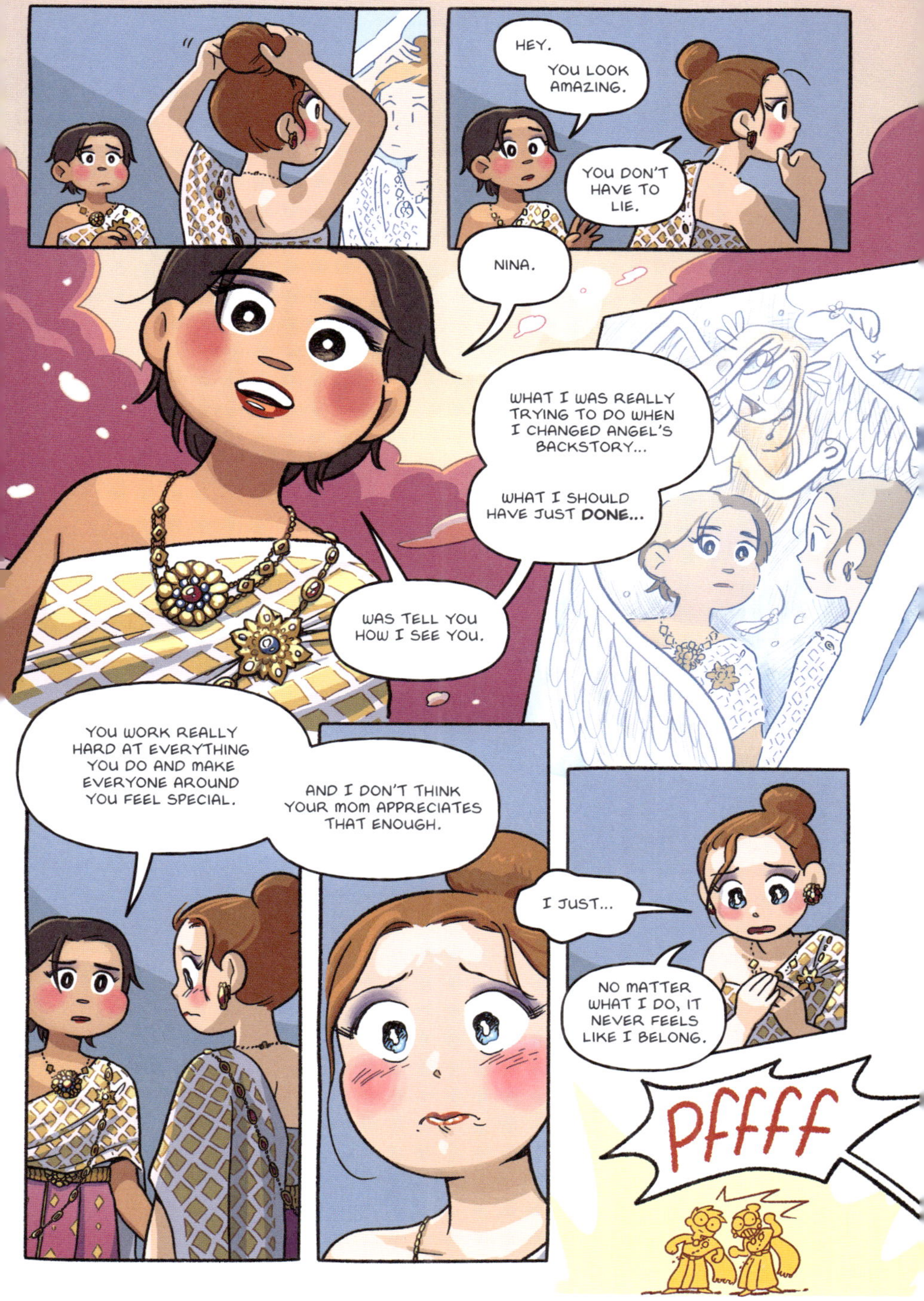
HEY.
YOU LOOK AMAZING.
YOU DON'T HAVE TO LIE.
NINA.
WHAT I WAS REALLY TRYING TO DO WHEN I CHANGED ANGEL'S BACKSTORY...
WHAT I SHOULD HAVE JUST **DONE...**
WAS TELL YOU HOW I SEE YOU.
YOU WORK REALLY HARD AT EVERYTHING YOU DO AND MAKE EVERYONE AROUND YOU FEEL SPECIAL.
AND I DON'T THINK YOUR MOM APPRECIATES THAT ENOUGH.
I JUST...
NO MATTER WHAT I DO, IT NEVER FEELS LIKE I BELONG.
PFFFF

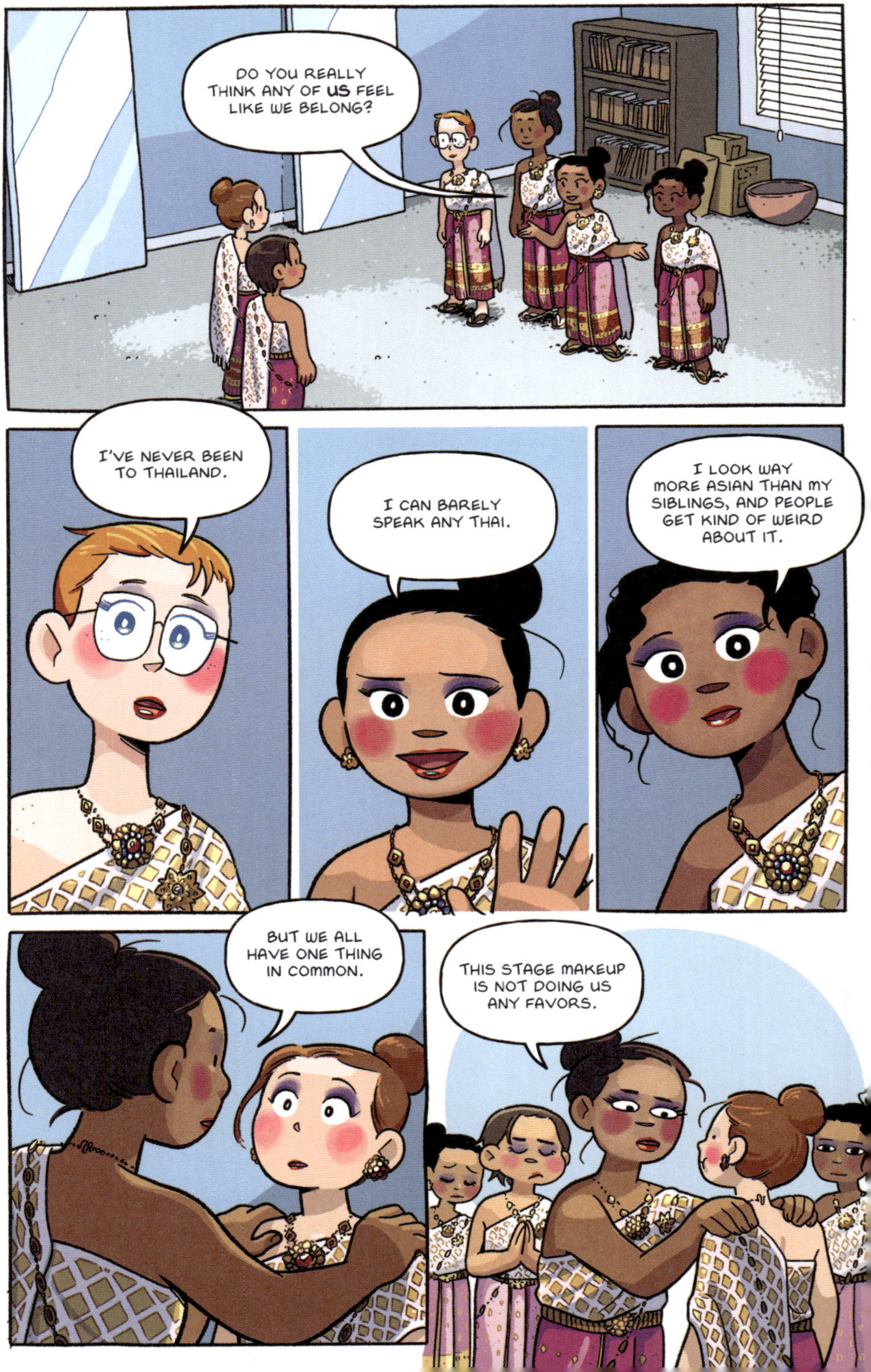
DO YOU REALLY THINK ANY OF **US** FEEL LIKE WE BELONG?
I'VE NEVER BEEN TO THAILAND.
I CAN BARELY SPEAK ANY THAI.
I LOOK WAY MORE ASIAN THAN MY SIBLINGS, AND PEOPLE GET KIND OF WEIRD ABOUT IT.
BUT WE ALL HAVE ONE THING IN COMMON.
THIS STAGE MAKEUP IS NOT DOING US ANY FAVORS.

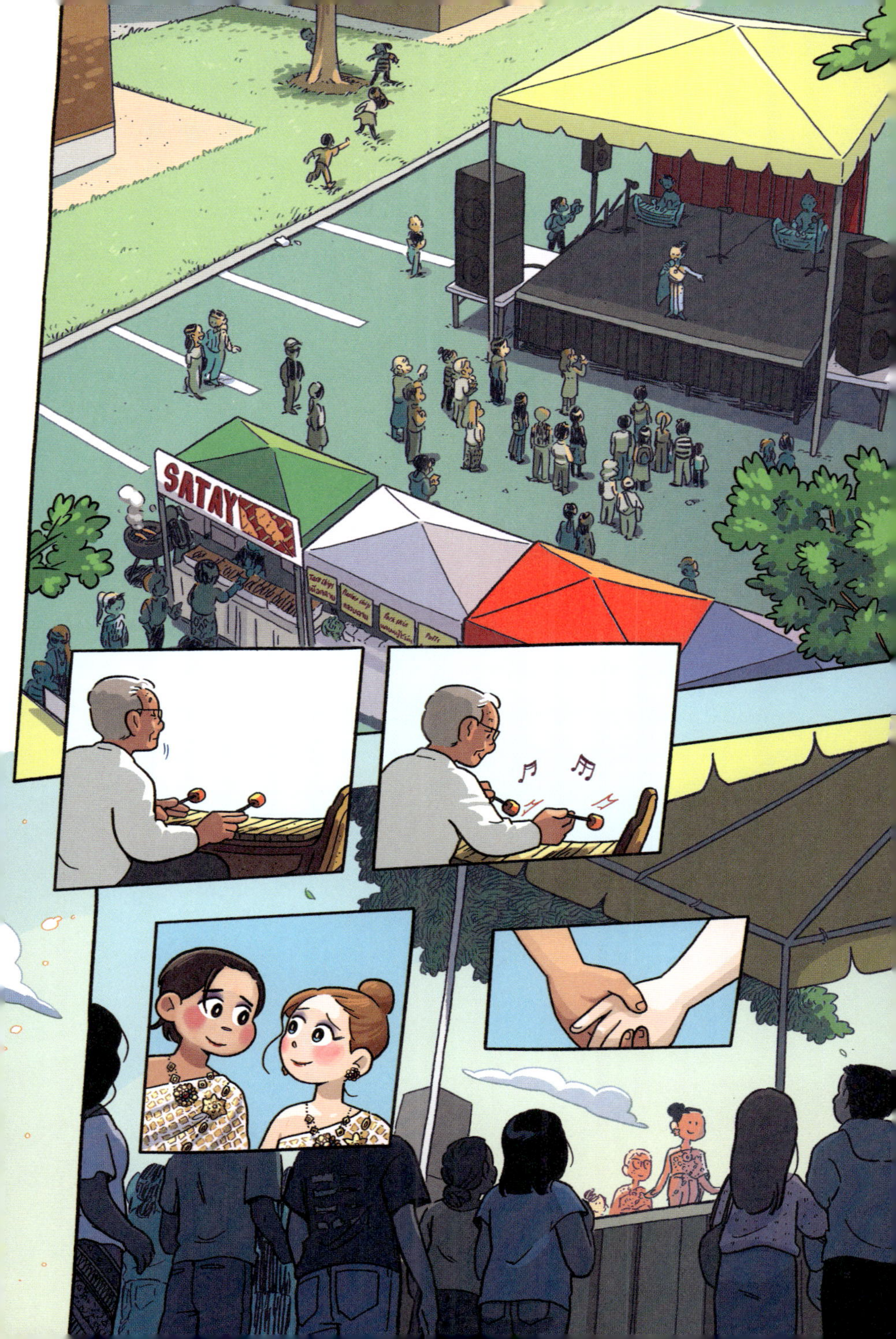
SATAY
Taro chips
Plantain chips
Pork skin
Puffs

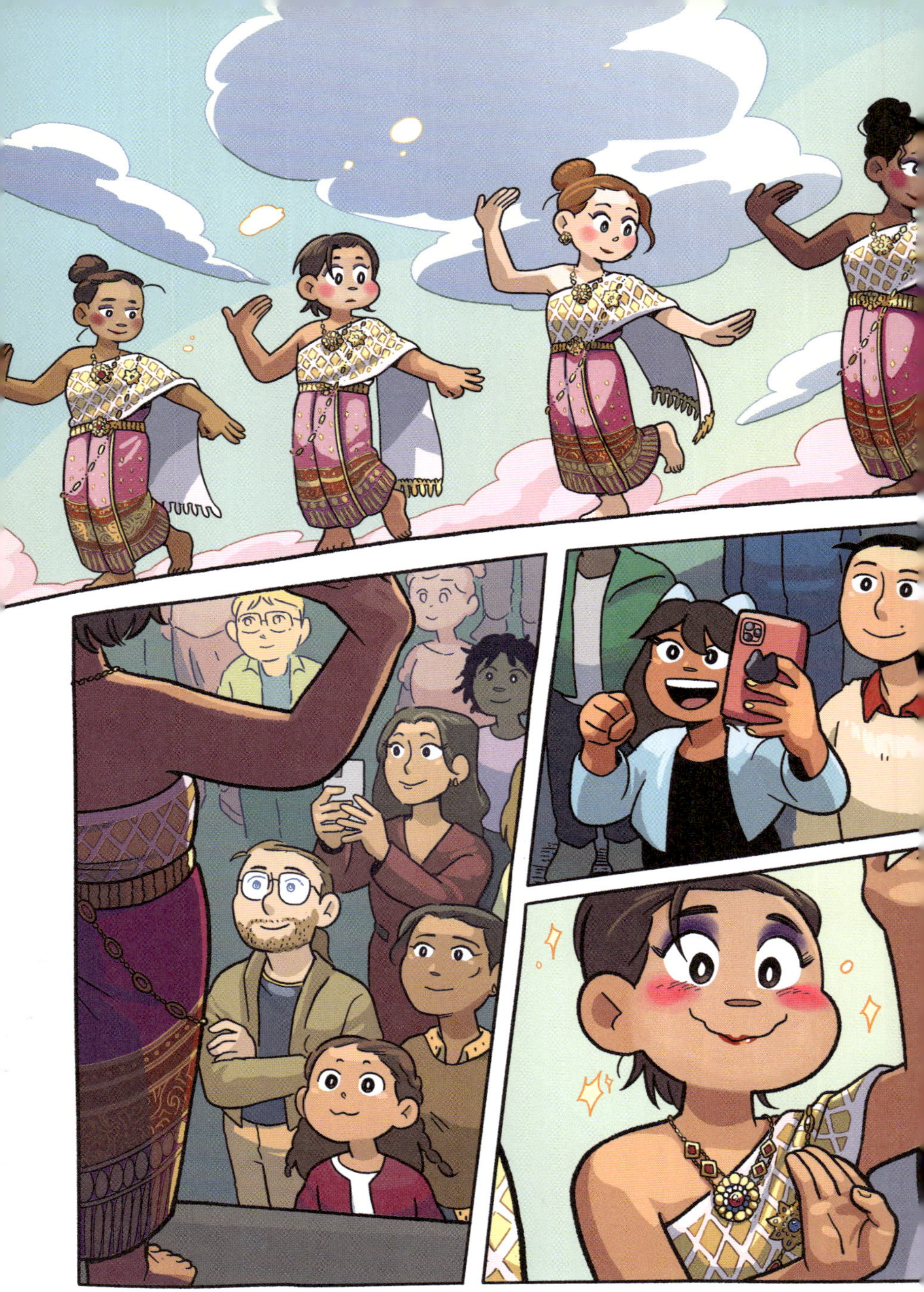

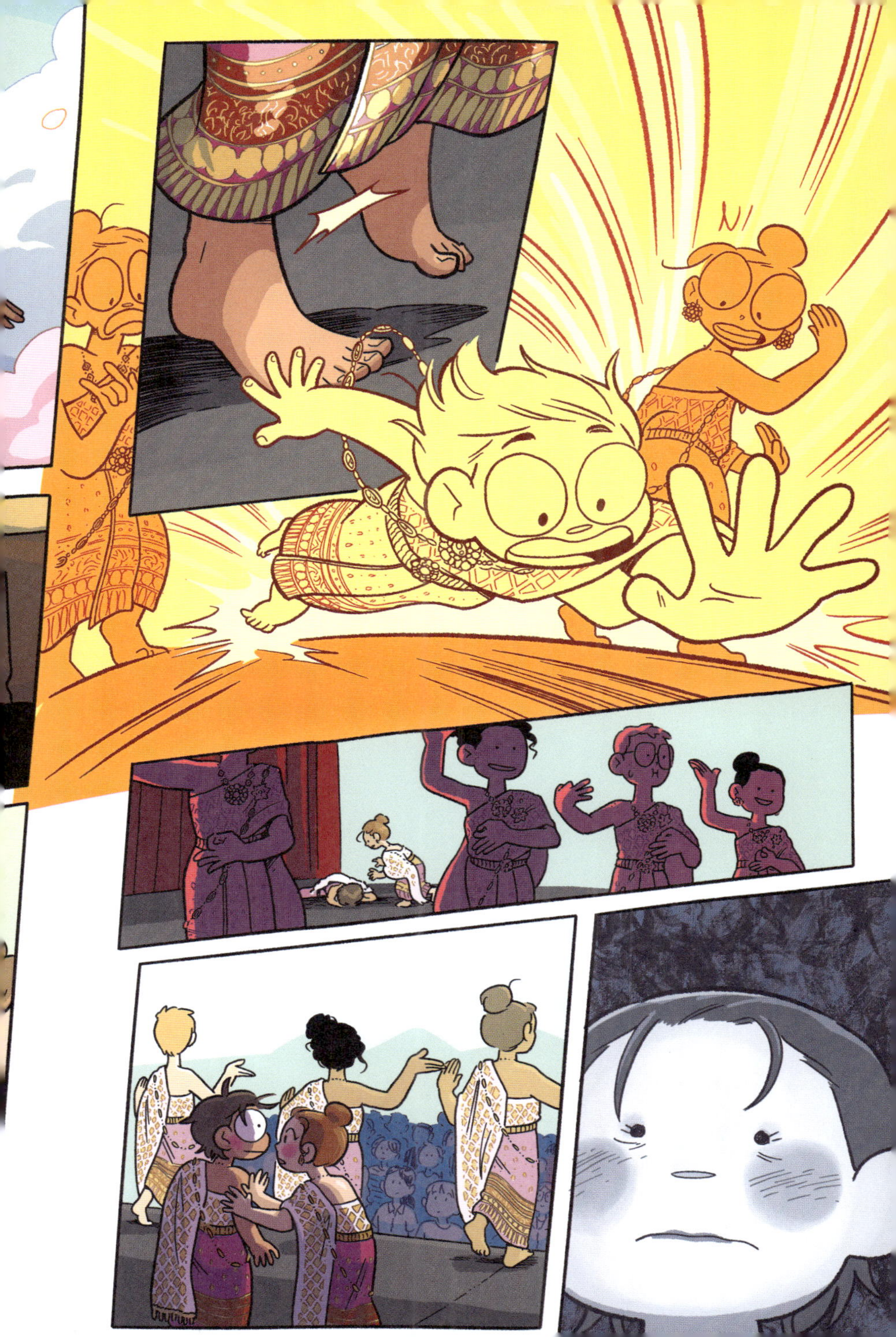

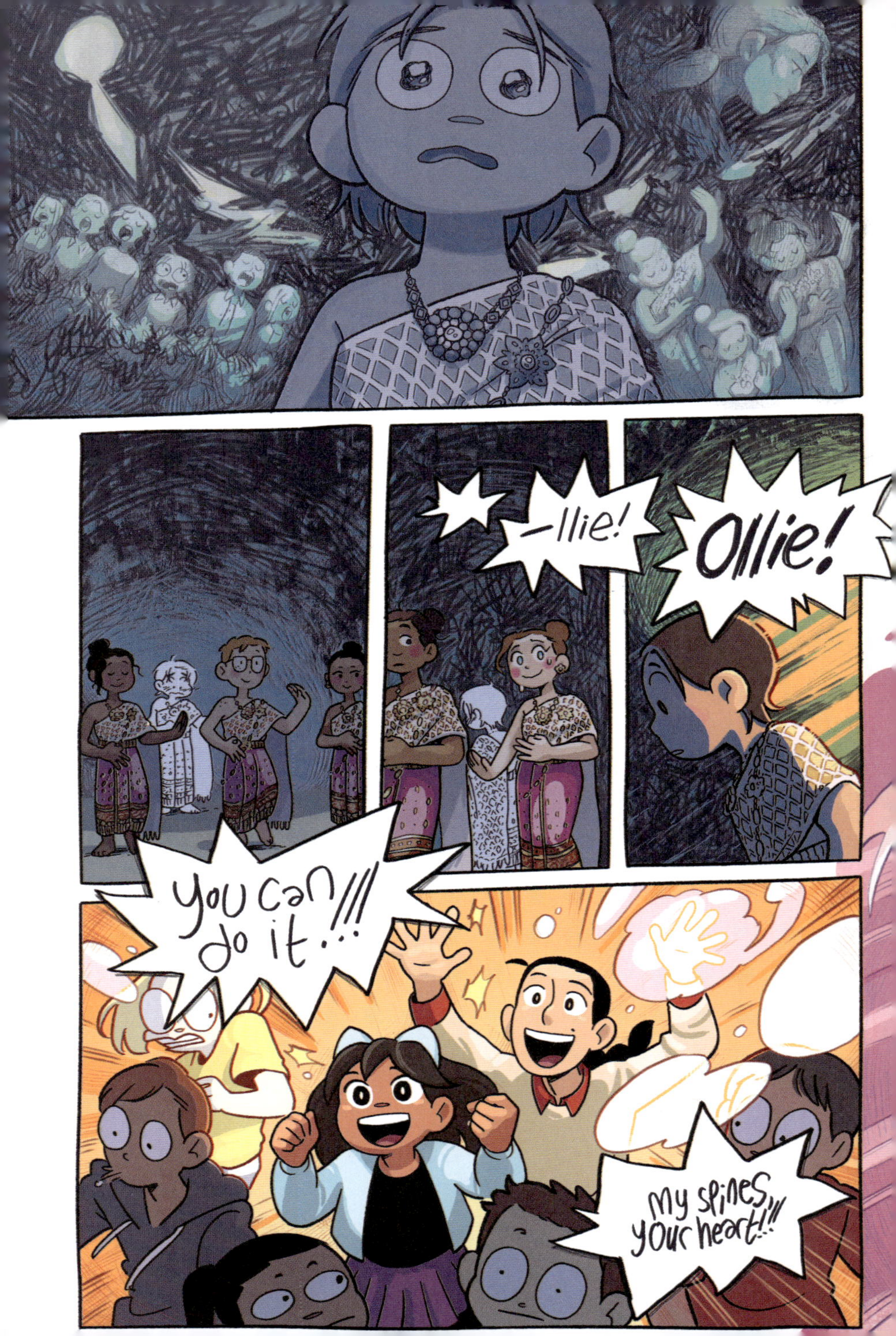
-llie!
Ollie!
You can do it!!!
My spines, your heart!!!

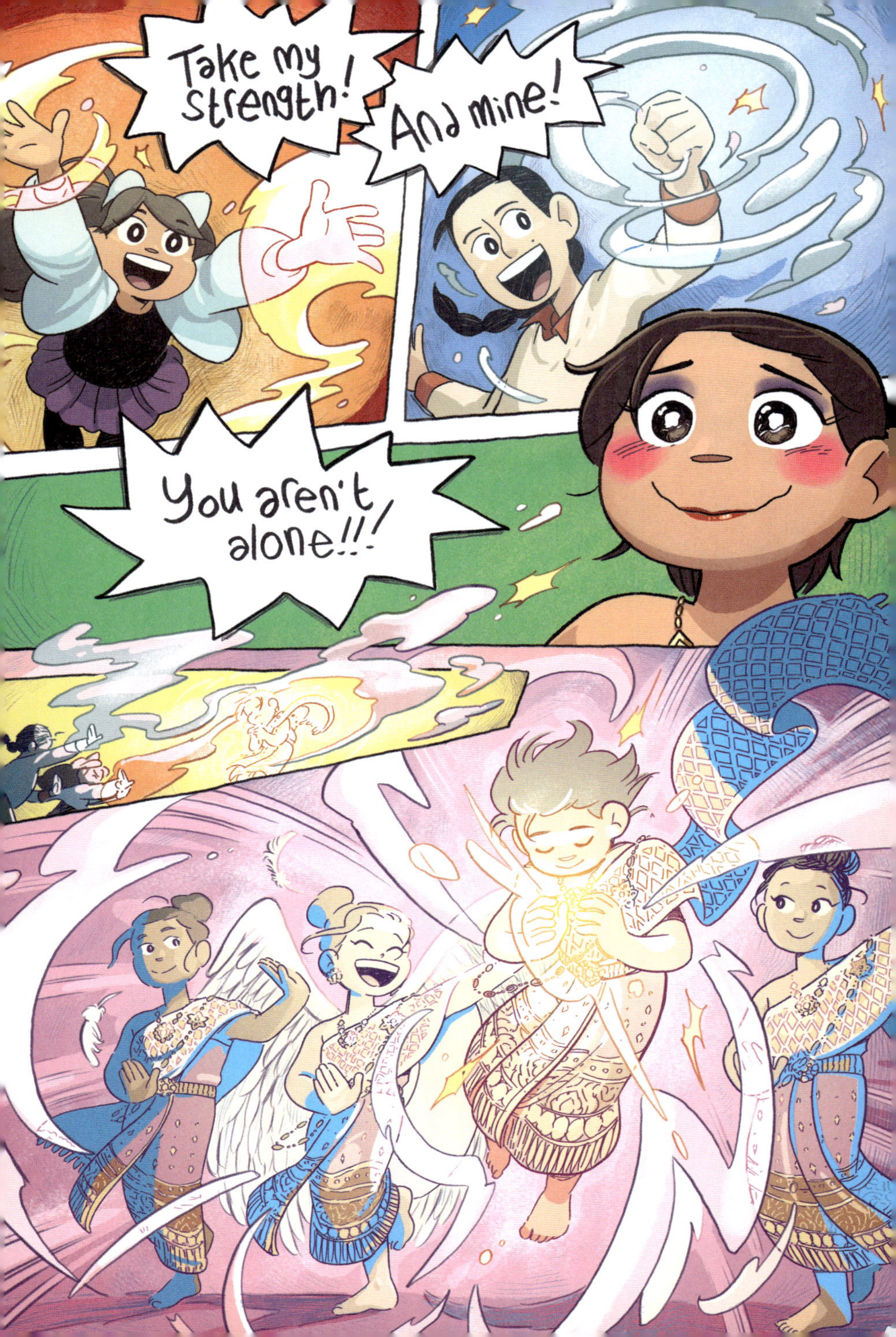
Take my strength!
And mine!
You aren't alone!!!

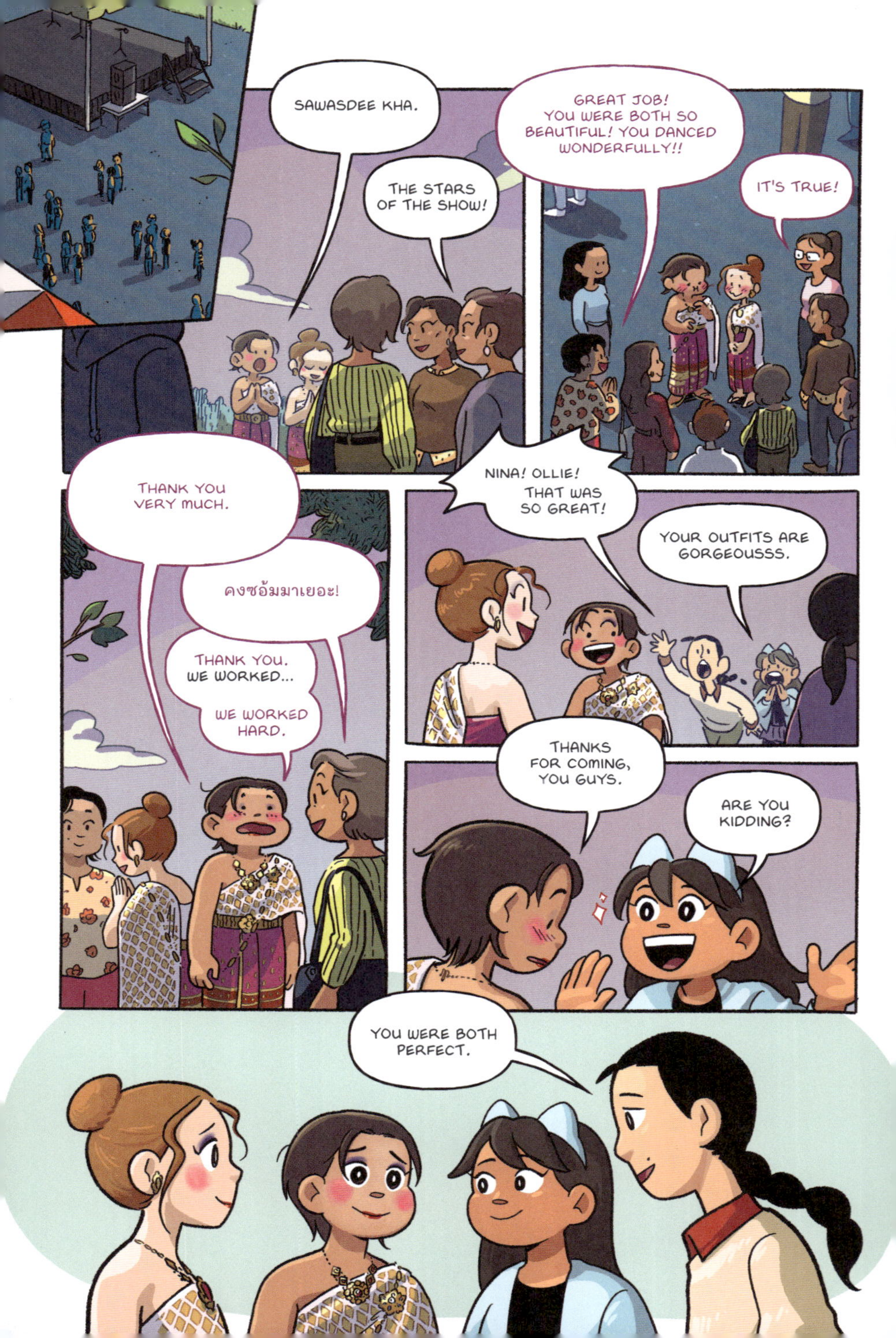
SAWASDEE KHA.
THE STARS OF THE SHOW!
GREAT JOB! YOU WERE BOTH SO BEAUTIFUL! YOU DANCED WONDERFULLY!!
IT'S TRUE!
THANK YOU VERY MUCH.
คงซ้อมมาเยอะ!
THANK YOU. WE WORKED...
WE WORKED HARD.
NINA! OLLIE! THAT WAS SO GREAT!
YOUR OUTFITS ARE GORGEOUSSS.
THANKS FOR COMING, YOU GUYS.
ARE YOU KIDDING?
YOU WERE BOTH PERFECT.

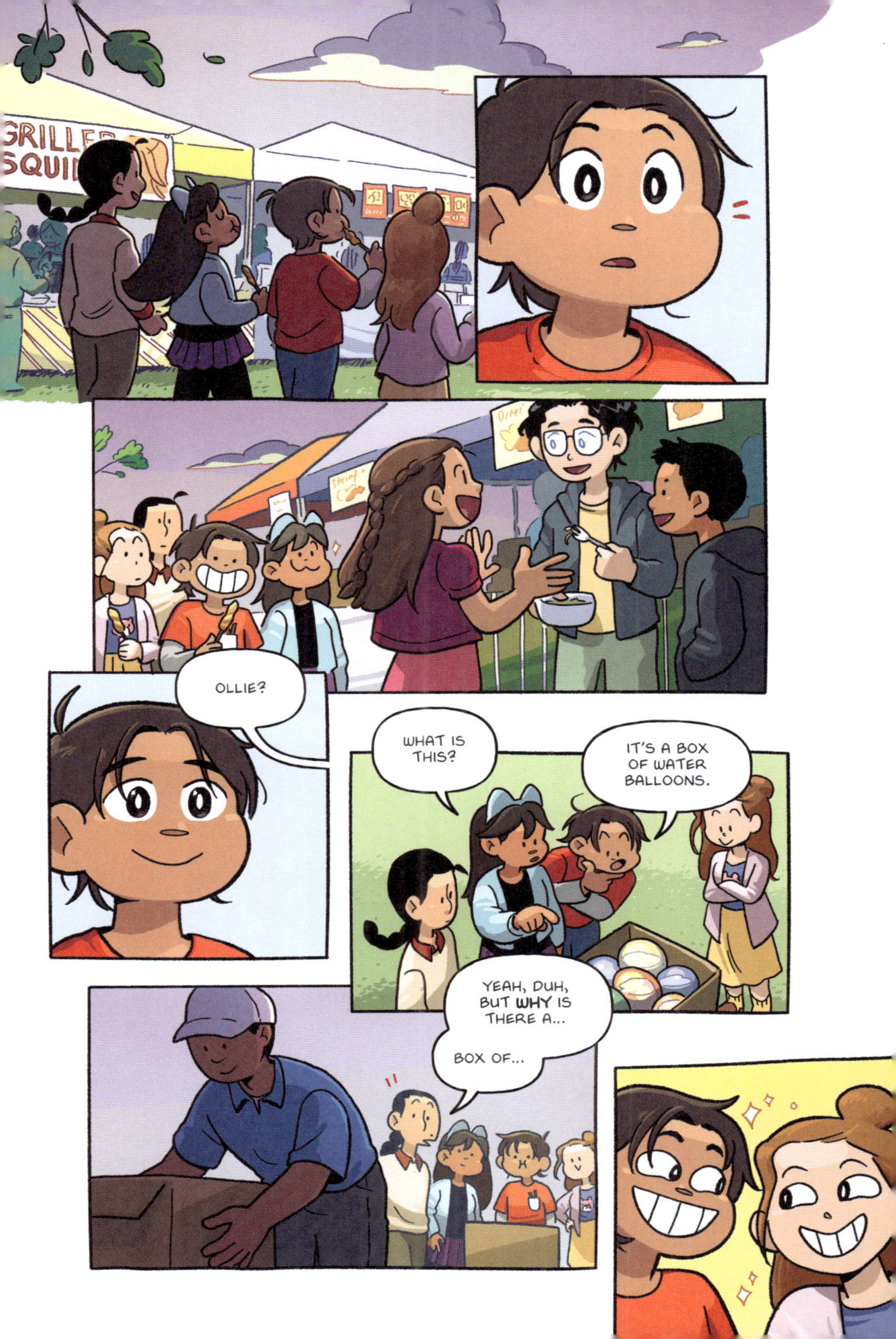
GRILLED SQUID
OLLIE?
WHAT IS THIS?
IT'S A BOX OF WATER BALLOONS.
YEAH, DUH, BUT **WHY** IS THERE A...
BOX OF...

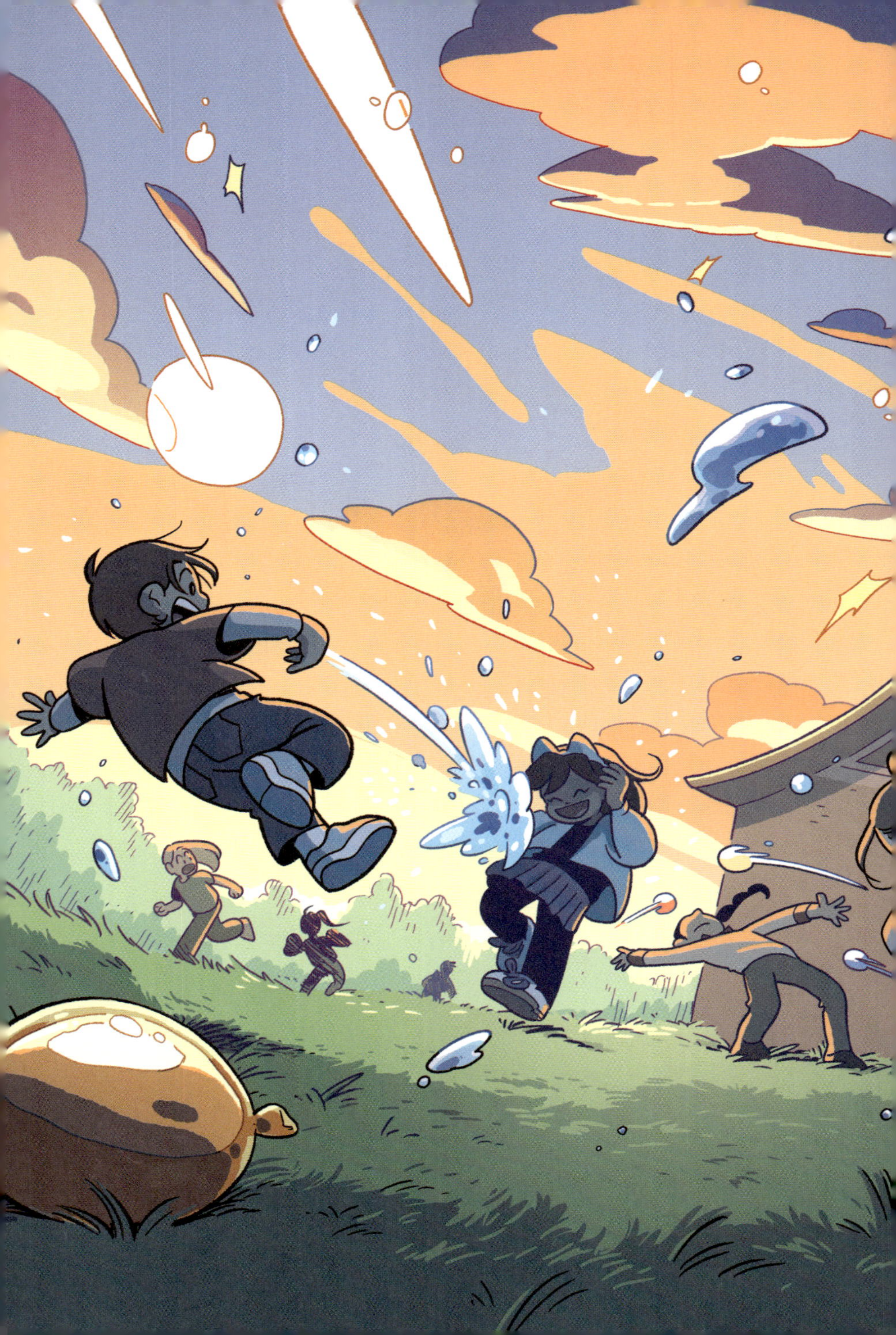

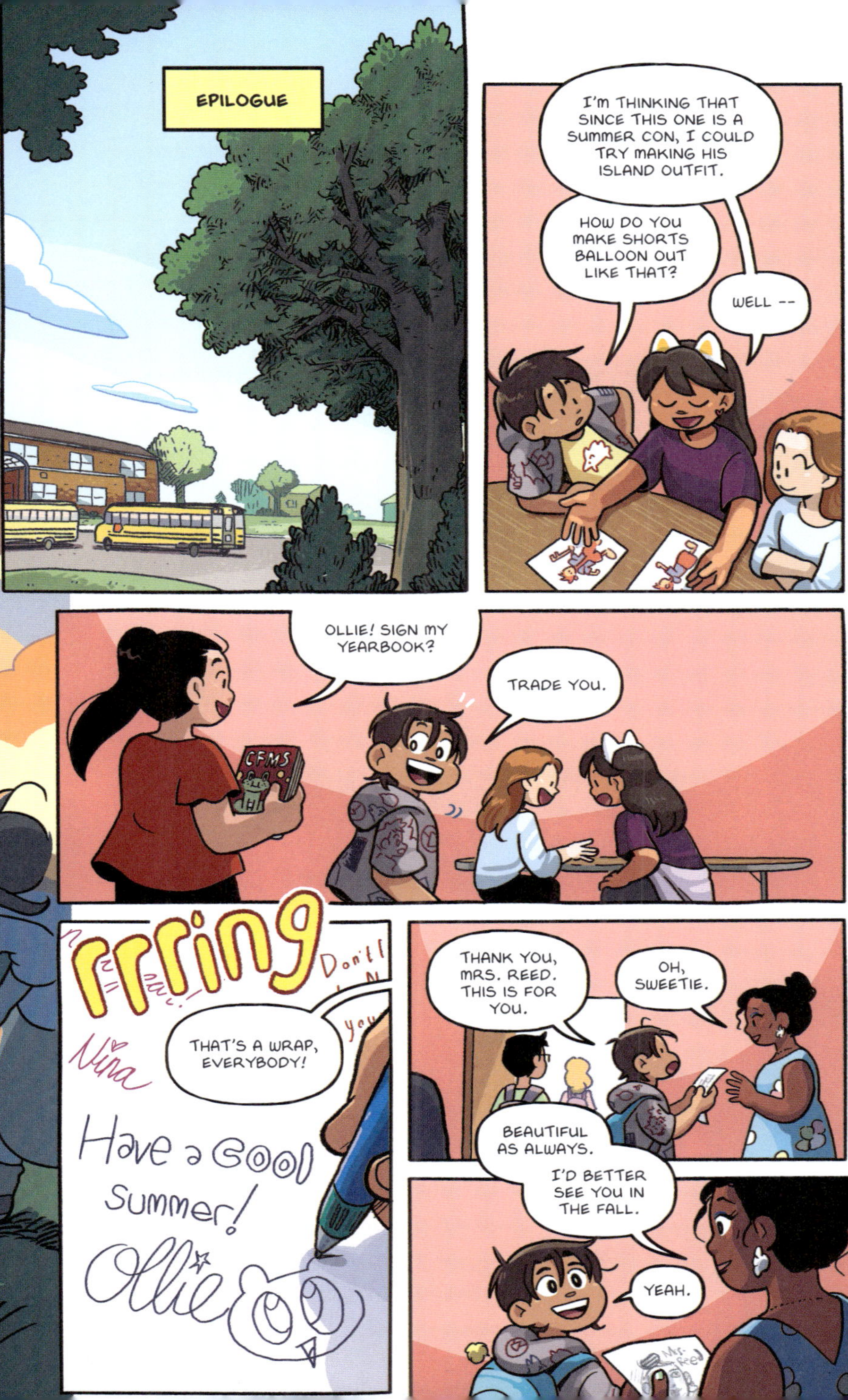
EPILOGUE
I'M THINKING THAT SINCE THIS ONE IS A SUMMER CON, I COULD TRY MAKING HIS ISLAND OUTFIT.
HOW DO YOU MAKE SHORTS BALLOON OUT LIKE THAT?
WELL --
OLLIE! SIGN MY YEARBOOK?
CFMS
TRADE YOU.
rrring
THAT'S A WRAP, EVERYBODY!
Nina
Have a Cool Summer!
Ollie
THANK YOU, MRS. REED. THIS IS FOR YOU.
OH, SWEETIE.
BEAUTIFUL AS ALWAYS.
I'D BETTER SEE YOU IN THE FALL.
YEAH.

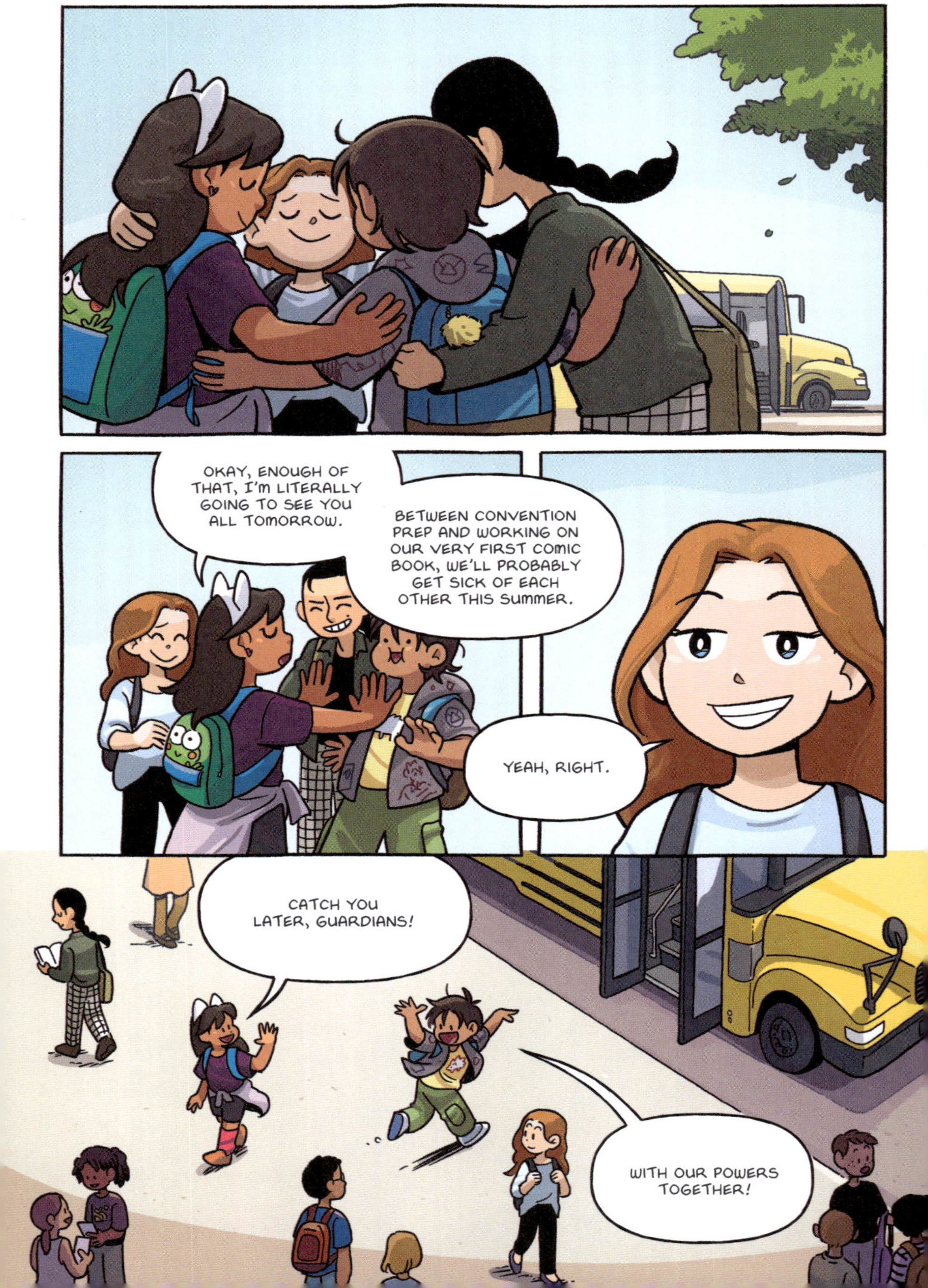
OKAY, ENOUGH OF THAT, I'M LITERALLY GOING TO SEE YOU ALL TOMORROW.
BETWEEN CONVENTION PREP AND WORKING ON OUR VERY FIRST COMIC BOOK, WE'LL PROBABLY GET SICK OF EACH OTHER THIS SUMMER.
YEAH, RIGHT.
CATCH YOU LATER, GUARDIANS!
WITH OUR POWERS TOGETHER!

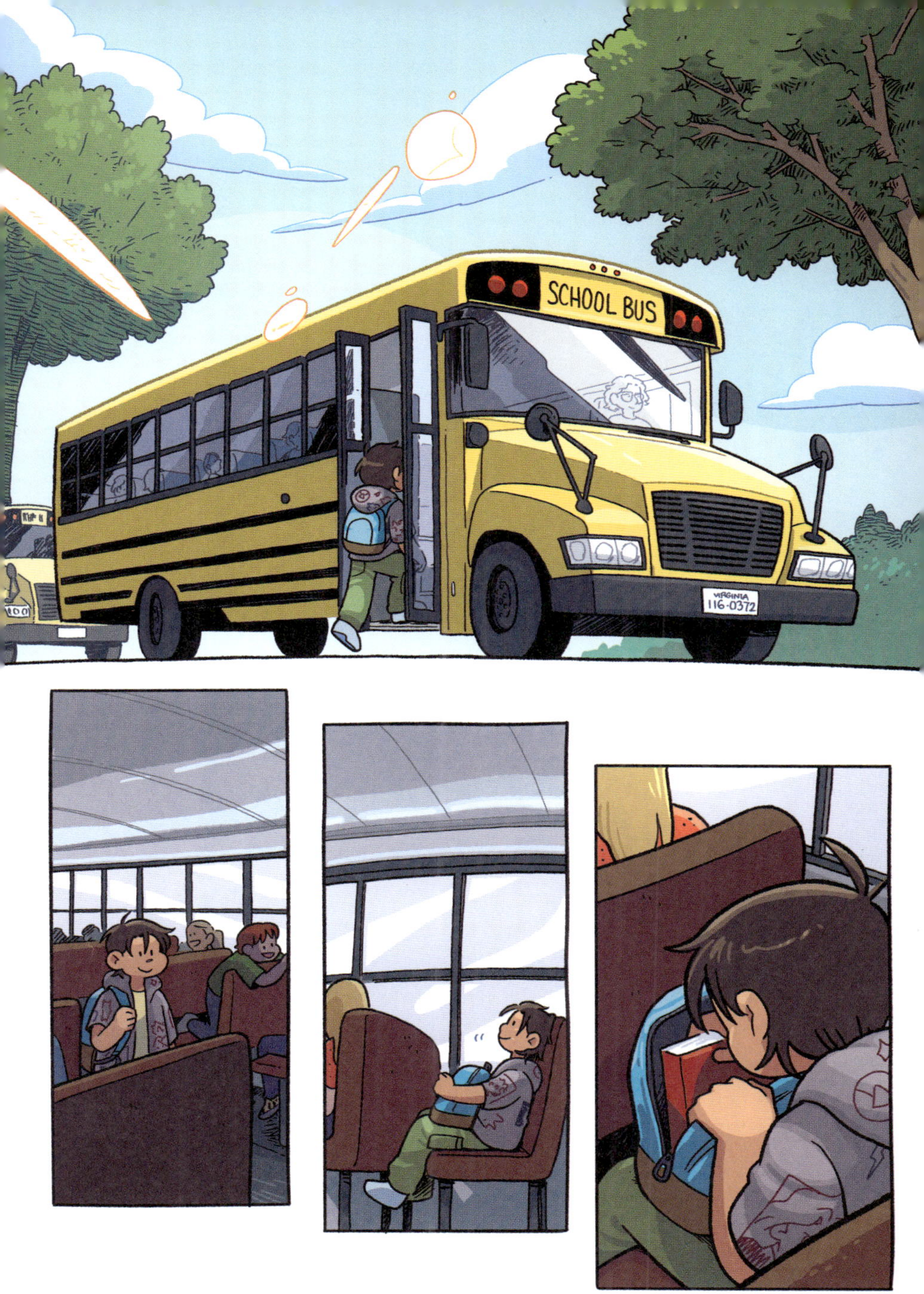
SCHOOL BUS
VIRGINIA
116-0372

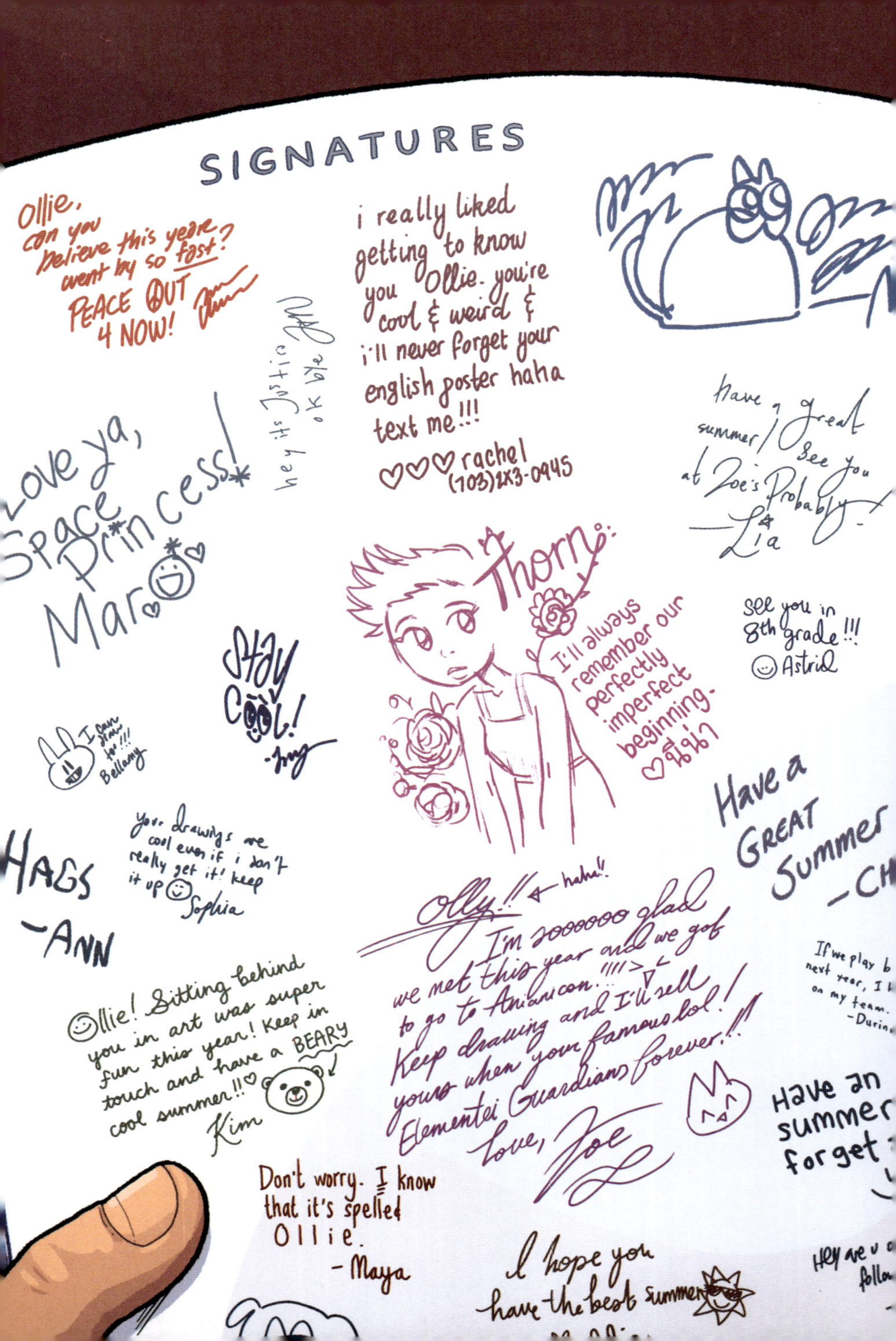
SIGNATURES
Ollie, can you believe this year went by so fast? PEACE OUT 4 NOW!
i really liked getting to know you Ollie. you're cool & weird & i'll never forget your english poster haha text me!!!
♡♡♡ rachel (103)2X3-0945
hey its Justin ok bye
Love ya, Space Princess! Mar
Have a great summer! See you at Zoe's probably -Lia
Thorn: I'll always remember our perfectly imperfect beginning. ♡
See you in 8th grade!!! ☺ Astrid
Stay cool!
I can draw too!!! Bellamy
Your drawings are cool even if i don't really get it! keep it up ☺ Sophia
HAGS -ANN
Have a GREAT Summer -CH
olly!! ← haha!!
I'm soooooo glad we met this year and we got to go to Animicon..!!!! Keep drawing and I'll sell yours when your famous lol! Elementei Guardians forever!!! love, Zoe
If we play b next year, I h on my team. -Durin
Ollie! Sitting behind you in art was super fun this year! Keep in touch and have a BEARY cool summer!! ♡ Kim
Have an summer forget
Don't worry. I know that it's spelled Ollie. - Maya
I hope you have the best summer

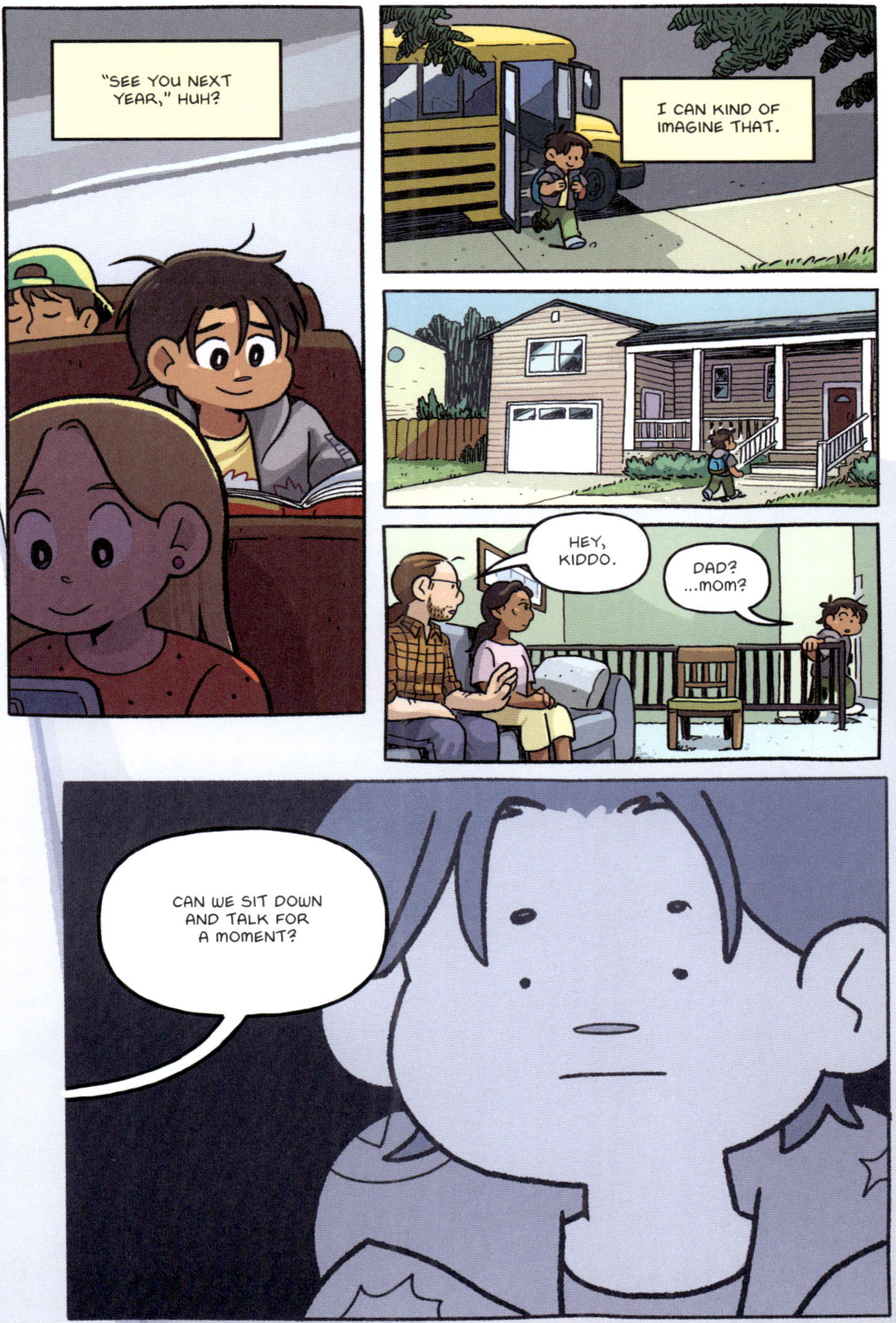
"SEE YOU NEXT YEAR," HUH?
I CAN KIND OF IMAGINE THAT.
HEY, KIDDO.
DAD? ...MOM?
CAN WE SIT DOWN AND TALK FOR A MOMENT?

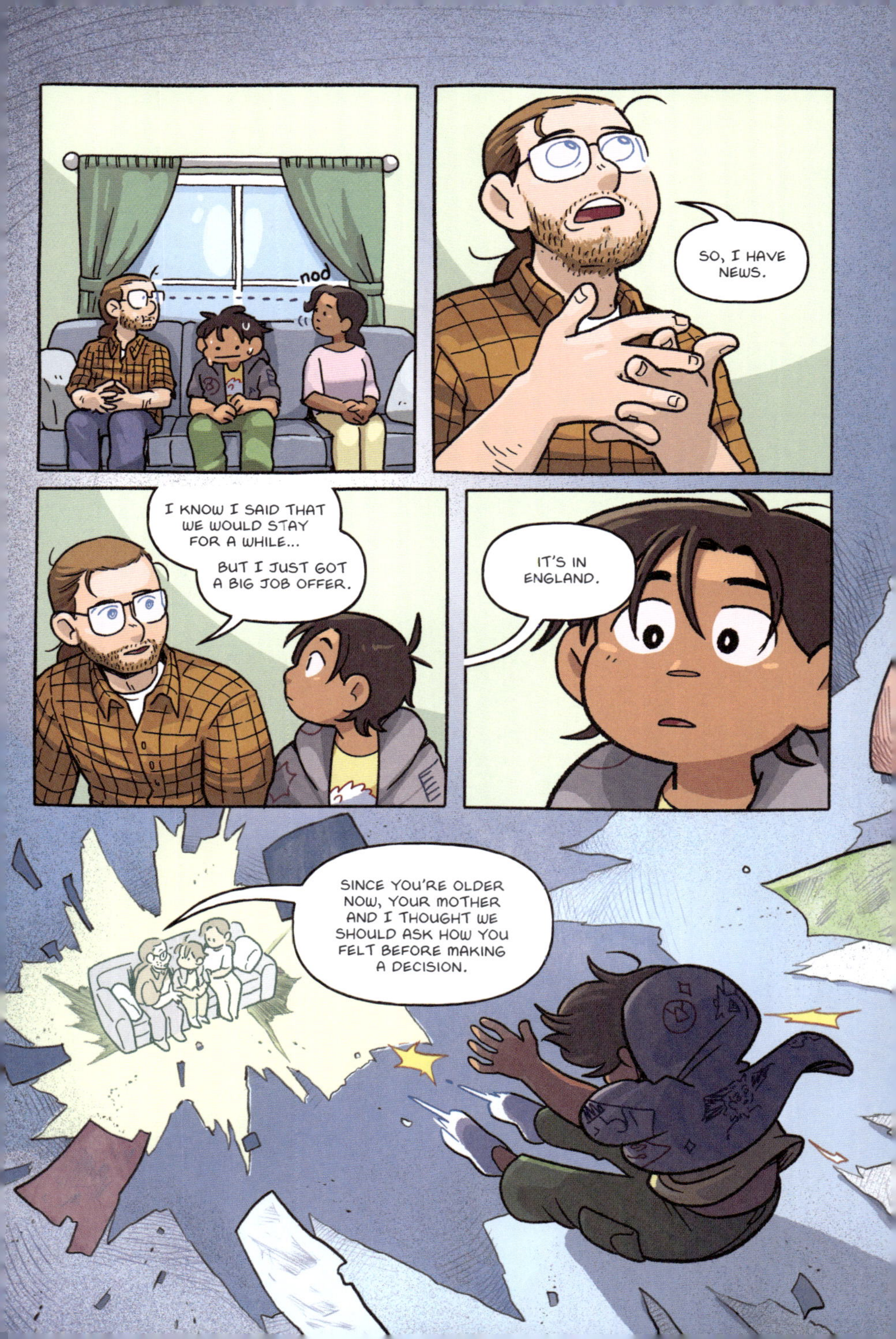
nod
SO, I HAVE NEWS.
I KNOW I SAID THAT WE WOULD STAY FOR A WHILE...
BUT I JUST GOT A BIG JOB OFFER.
IT'S IN ENGLAND.
SINCE YOU'RE OLDER NOW, YOUR MOTHER AND I THOUGHT WE SHOULD ASK HOW YOU FELT BEFORE MAKING A DECISION.

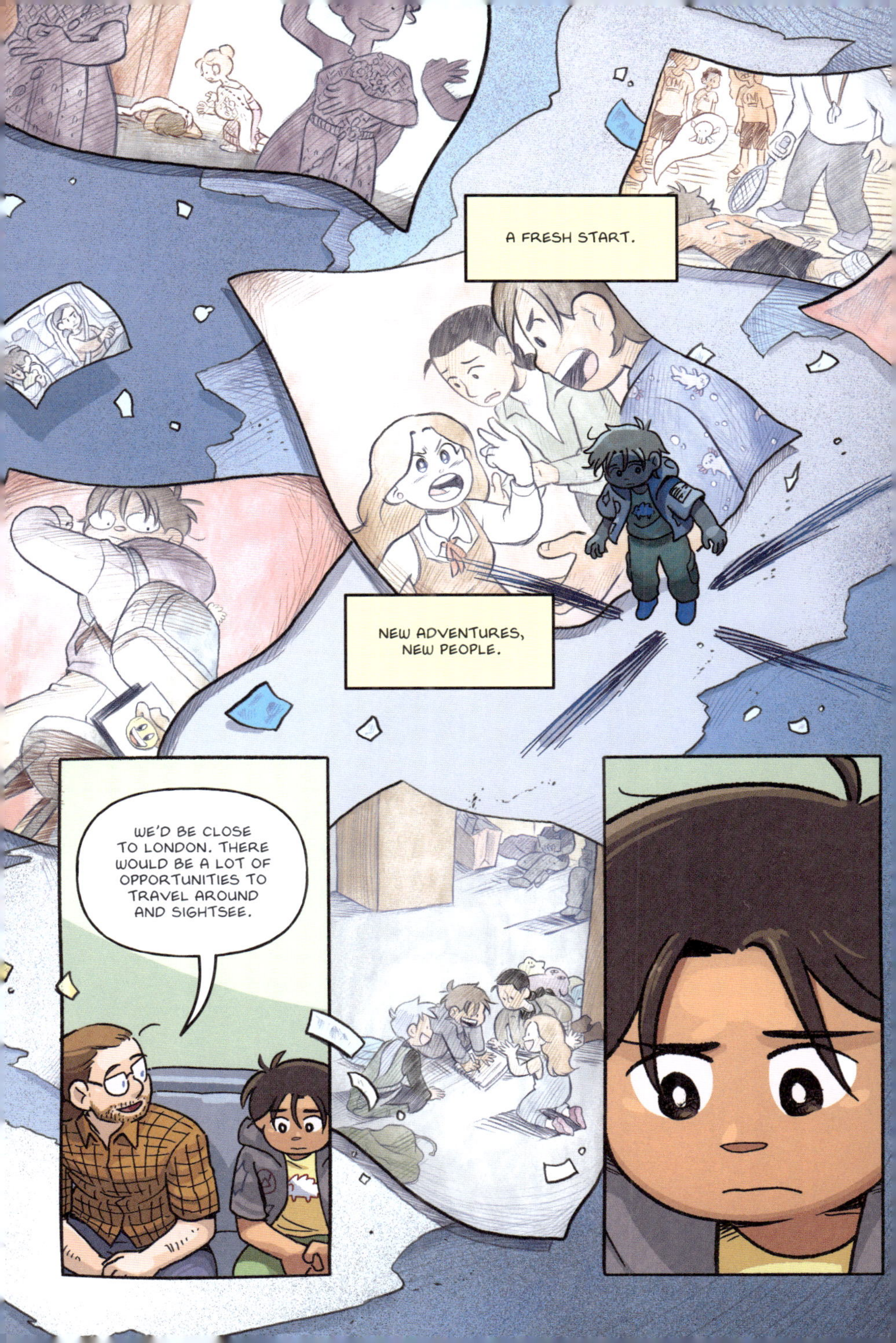
A FRESH START.
NEW ADVENTURES, NEW PEOPLE.
WE'D BE CLOSE TO LONDON. THERE WOULD BE A LOT OF OPPORTUNITIES TO TRAVEL AROUND AND SIGHTSEE.

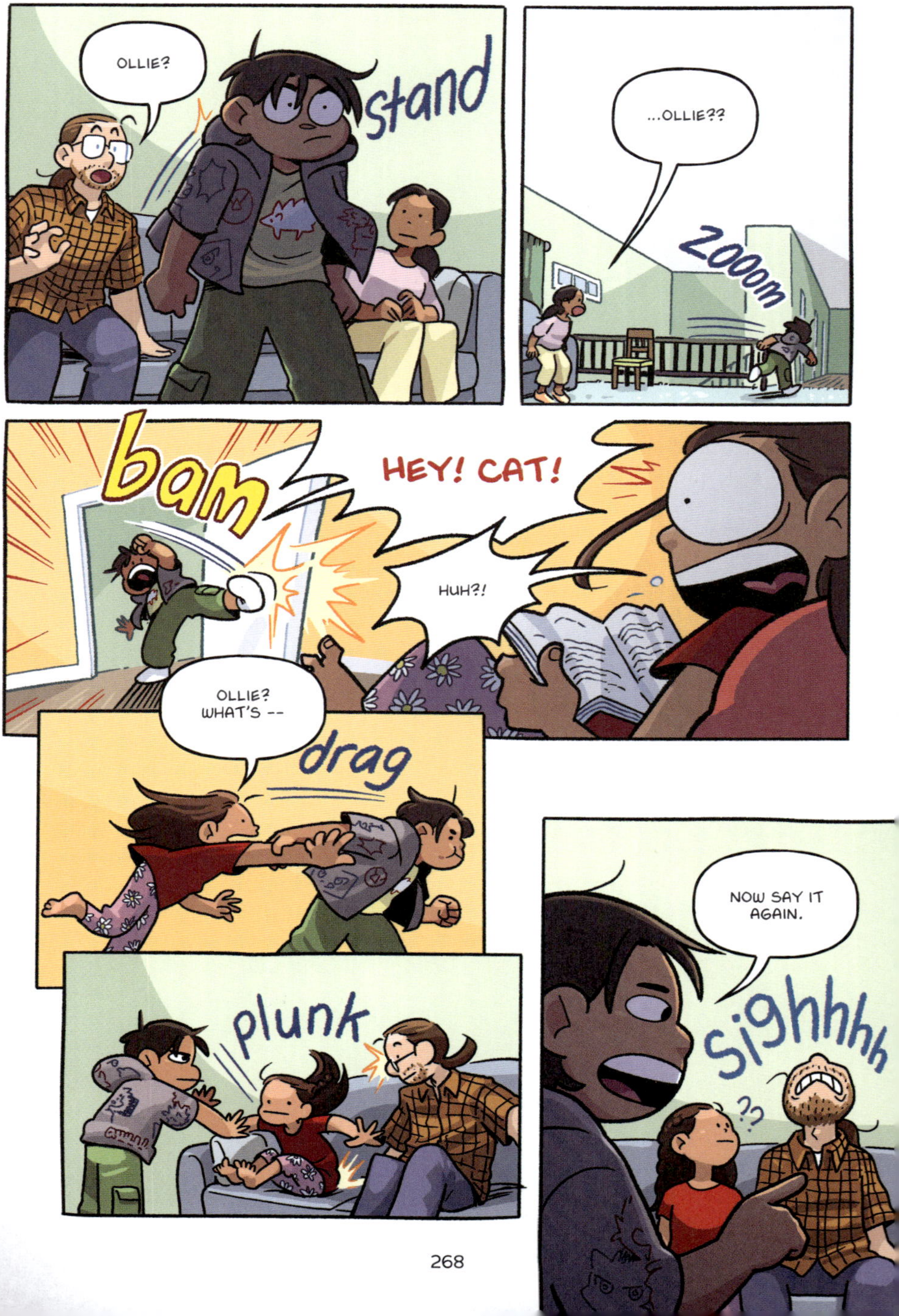
OLLIE?
stand
...OLLIE??
ZOOOM
bam
HEY! CAT!
HUH?!
OLLIE? WHAT'S --
drag
plunk
NOW SAY IT AGAIN.
sighhhh
??

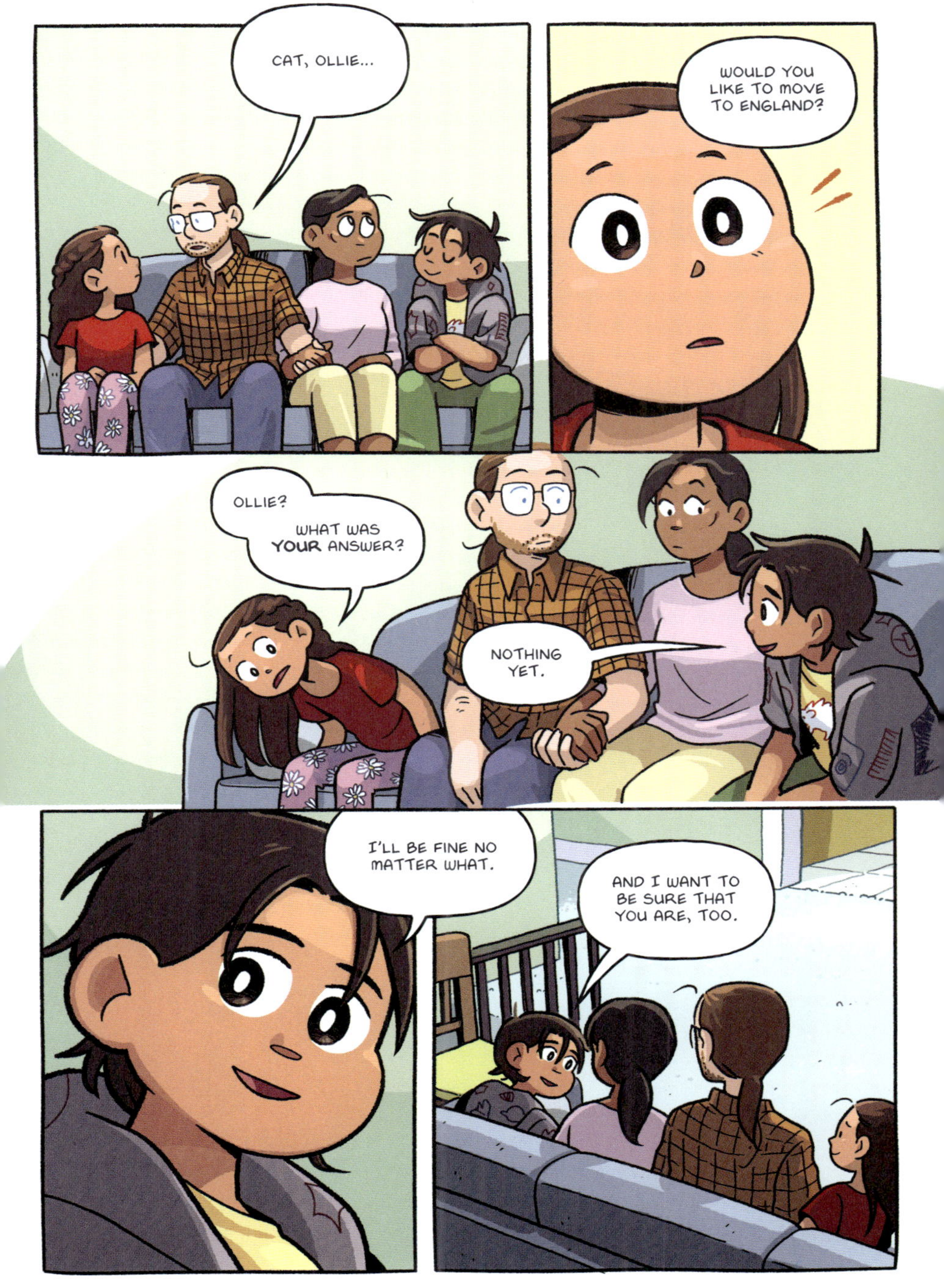
CAT, OLLIE...
WOULD YOU LIKE TO MOVE TO ENGLAND?
OLLIE?
WHAT WAS **YOUR** ANSWER?
NOTHING YET.
I'LL BE FINE NO MATTER WHAT.
AND I WANT TO BE SURE THAT YOU ARE, TOO.

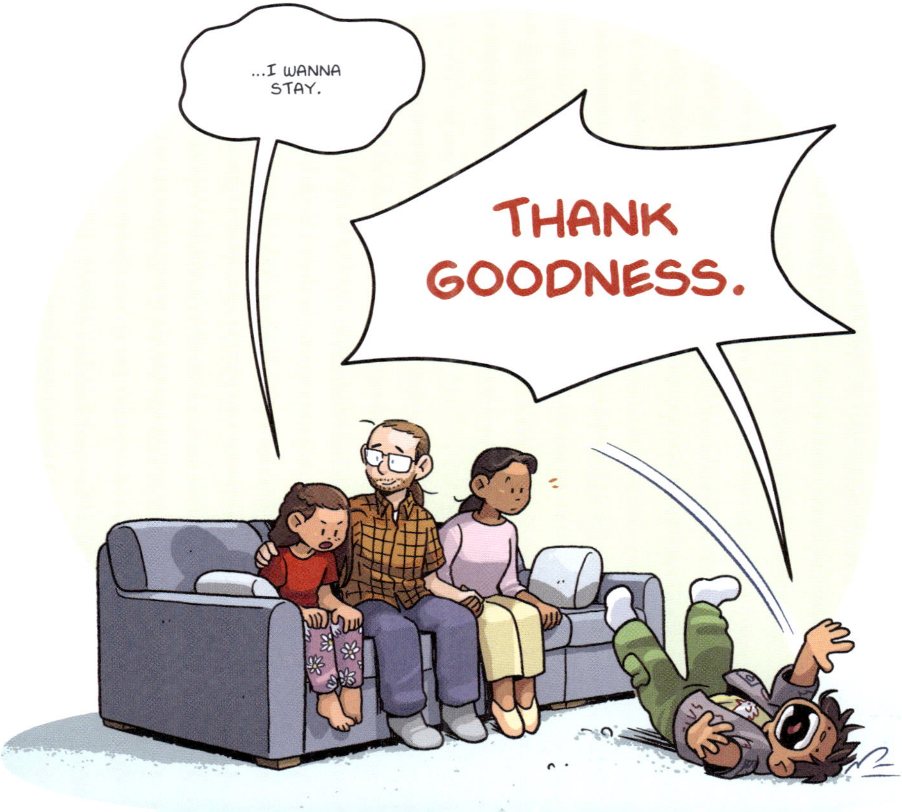
...I WANNA STAY.
THANK GOODNESS.

Author's Note

This book is inspired by my childhood, but it is not completely true to life. Most of the characters in it are mishmashes of a bunch of different people. Some real memories have been shifted around and exaggerated in service of the ideas I want to share. I didn't have a cell phone until sometime in high school, it was the little flippy kind, and texting people cost money so we didn't do it.

However, I need you to know that I *did* actually live through that whole "sang with the wrong choir" thing. When I got back to my seat afterward, my best friend immediately demanded to know what on earth I'd been thinking, and I was mortified to discover the truth. I remember hiding under my extremely 1990s-era windbreaker after school as though nobody would know there was a person in there. I counted the days until we left the country, just like I had every other time we moved.

Because that's another true thing. My dad's job did take us around the world. When I was six, we moved from America to Bangkok, Thailand, where we spent four years; then we lived in Frankfurt, Germany, for two years; then we arrived in Northern Virginia in time for me to start middle school. It was a shock for a lot of reasons. Everyone at school seemed to know each other already. They had all these shared cultural experiences I'd missed out on. And they saw my mixed heritage as something novel, mysterious. *What are you?* I felt caught between worlds.

I think that's one reason I became very enamored with stories about kids with dual identities like *Sailor Moon* and *Yu-Gi-Oh!* These characters had regular school lives, but they were also separate from their peers. Some were bullied or judged for being different. But they found friends who loved them for exactly who they were, and *also*, their differences came with incredible magical powers.

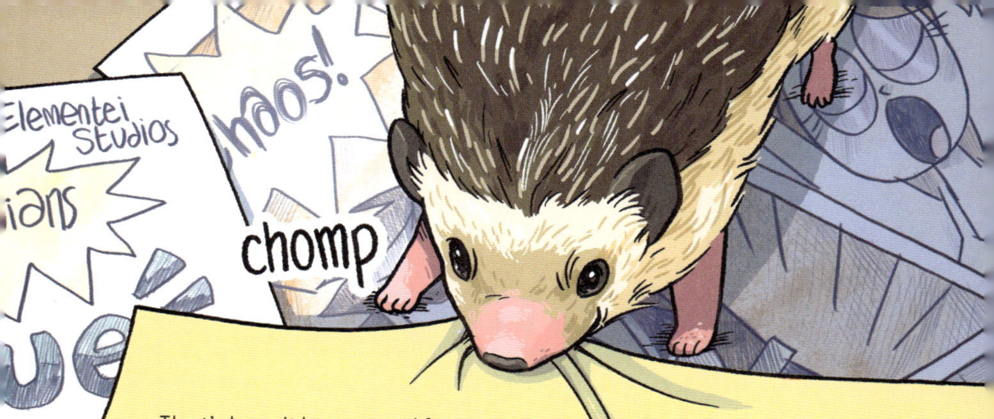
Elementei Studios
chomp

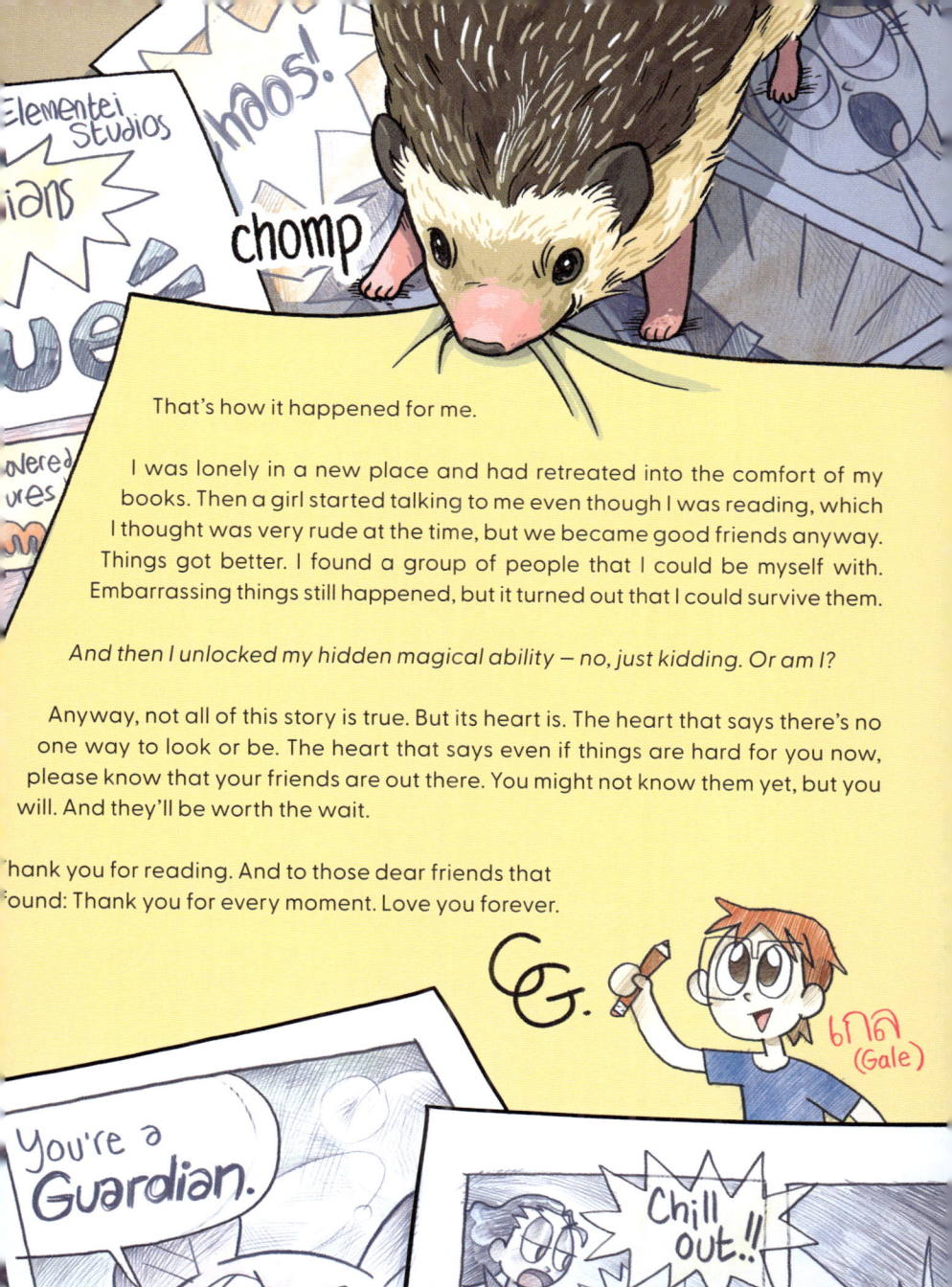

That's how it happened for me.

I was lonely in a new place and had retreated into the comfort of my books. Then a girl started talking to me even though I was reading, which I thought was very rude at the time, but we became good friends anyway. Things got better. I found a group of people that I could be myself with. Embarrassing things still happened, but it turned out that I could survive them.

And then I unlocked my hidden magical ability – no, just kidding. Or am I?

Anyway, not all of this story is true. But its heart is. The heart that says there's no one way to look or be. The heart that says even if things are hard for you now, please know that your friends are out there. You might not know them yet, but you will. And they'll be worth the wait.

hank you for reading. And to those dear friends that
ound: Thank you for every moment. Love you forever.

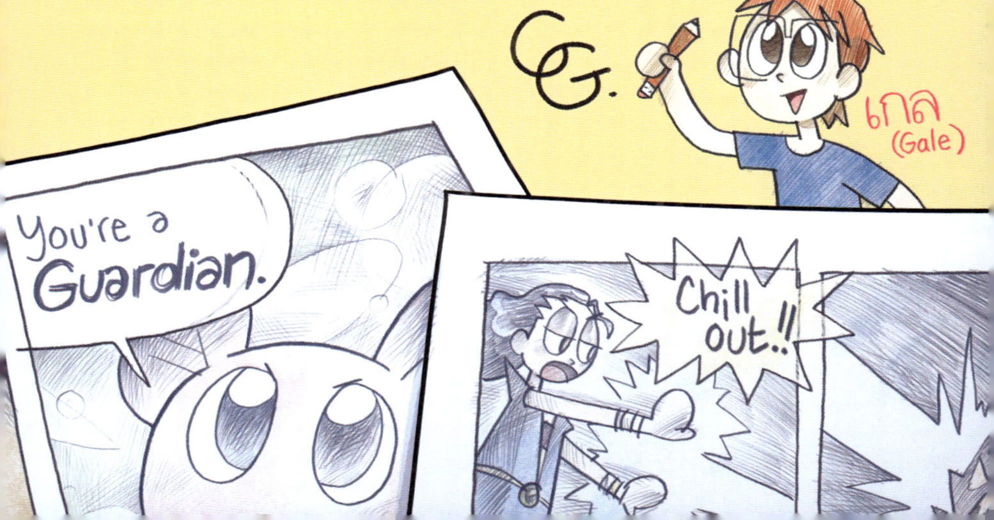
CG.
เกล
(Gale)
You're a Guardian.
Chill out.!!

Bonus Comics!

Behind the scenes

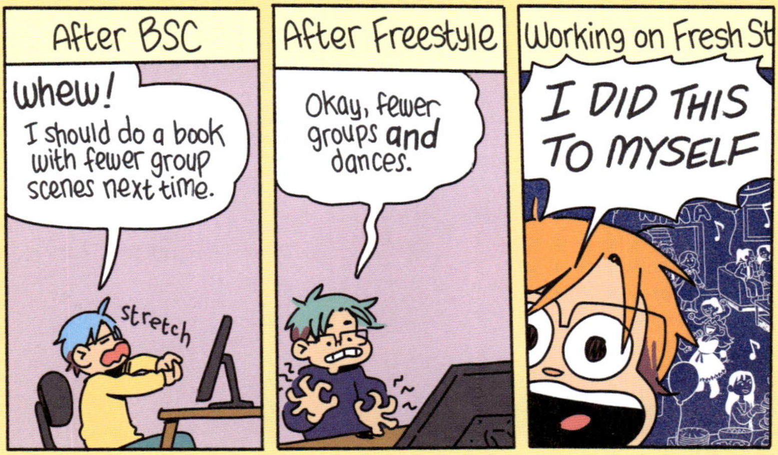
After BSC
whew!
I should do a book with fewer group scenes next time.
stretch
After Freestyle
Okay, fewer groups and dances.
Working on Fresh St
I DID THIS TO MYSELF

Hedgie life

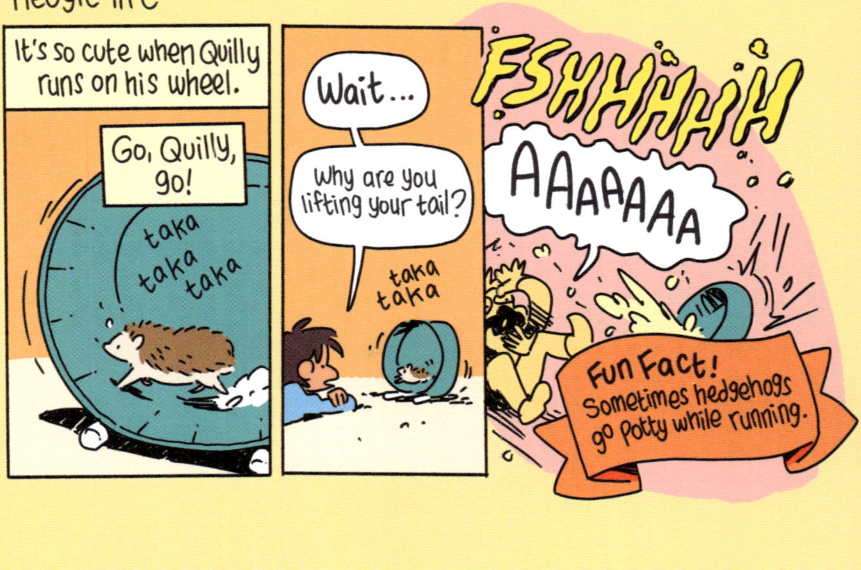
It's so cute when Quilly runs on his wheel.
Go, Quilly, go!
taka taka taka
Wait...
Why are you lifting your tail?
taka taka
FSHHHHH
AAAAAAA
Fun Fact!
Sometimes hedgehogs go potty while running.

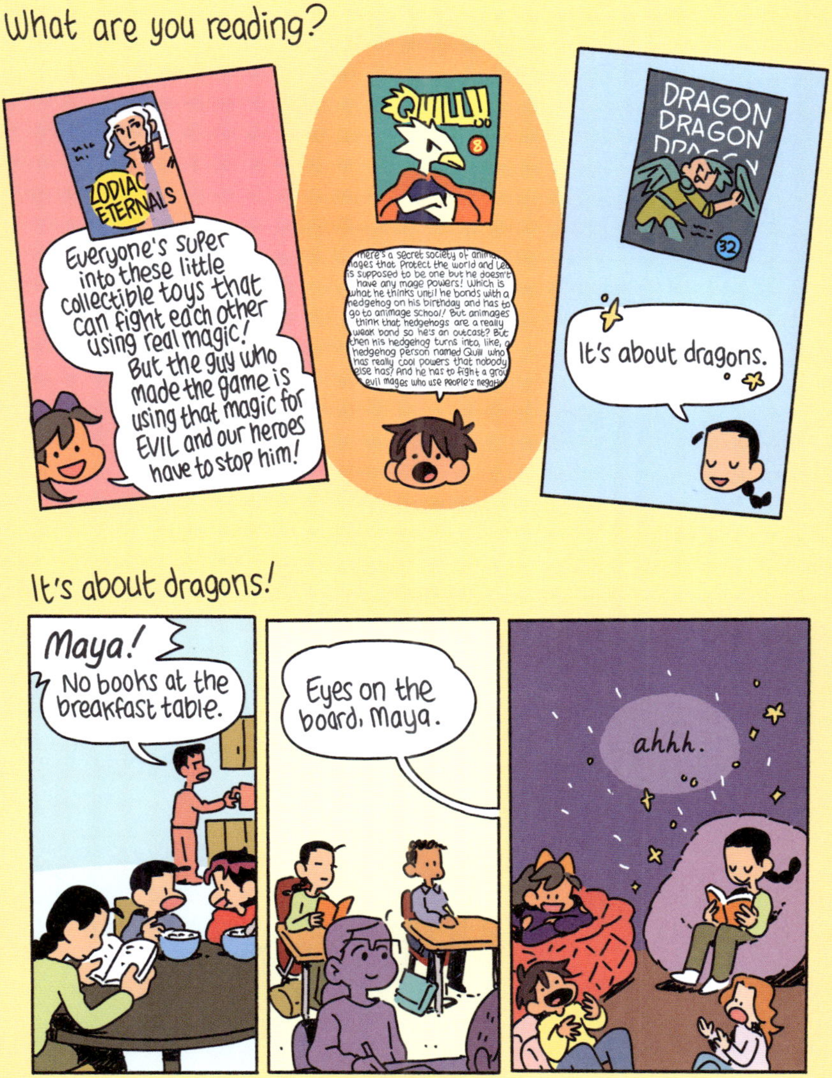
What are you reading?
ZODIAC ETERNALS
Everyone's super into these little collectible toys that can fight each other using real magic! But the guy who made the game is using that magic for EVIL and our heroes have to stop him!
QUILL!! 8
here's a secret society of anim
ages that protect the world and Le
is supposed to be one but he doesn't have any mage powers! Which is what he thinks until he bonds with a hedgehog on his birthday and has to go to animage school! But animages think that hedgehogs are a really weak bond so he's an outcast? But then his hedgehog turns into, like, a hedgehog person named Quill who has really cool powers that nobody else has! And he has to fight a gro
evil mages who use people's negat
DRAGON DRAGON
32
It's about dragons.
It's about dragons!
Maya!
No books at the breakfast table.
Eyes on the board, Maya.
ahhh.

Deleted Valentine's Day scene

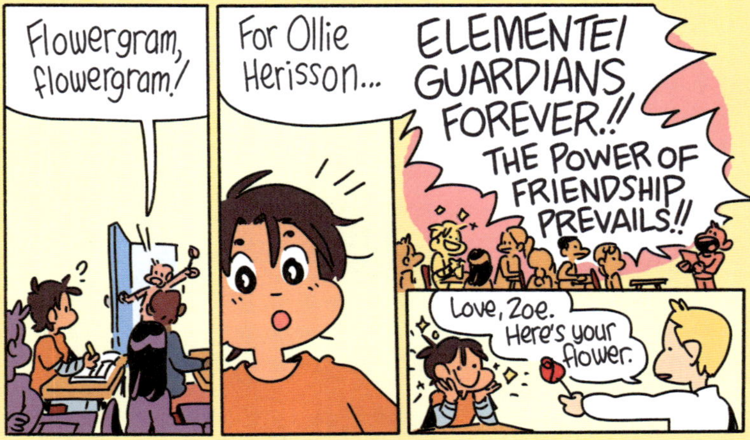
Flowergram, flowergram!
For Ollie Herisson...
ELEMENTEI GUARDIANS FOREVER!!
THE POWER OF FRIENDSHIP PREVAILS!!
Love, Zoe.
Here's your flower.

They still have the costumes!

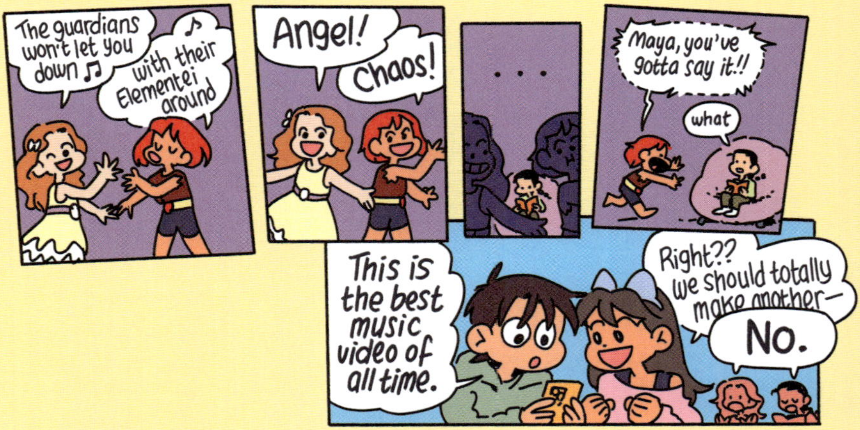
The guardians won't let you down ♫
with their Elementei around
Angel!
Chaos!
. . .
Maya, you've gotta say it!!
what
This is the best music video of all time.
Right?? we should totally make another—
No.

Epilogue #2

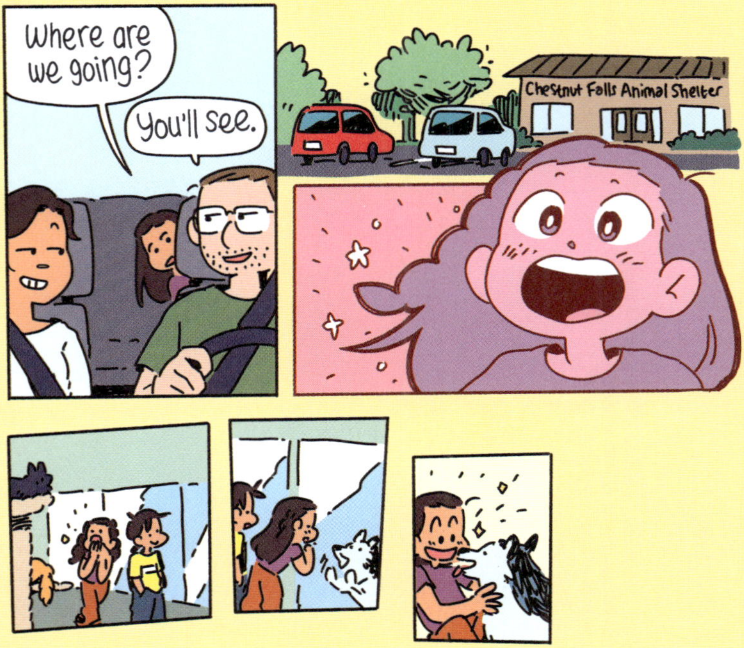
Where are we going?
You'll see.
Chestnut Falls Animal Shelter

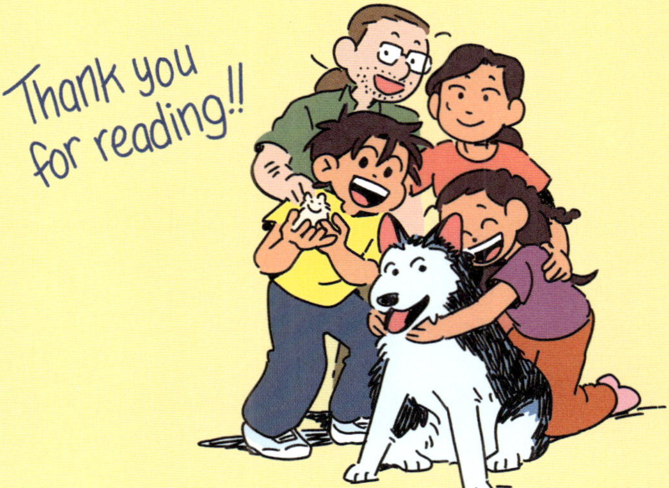
Thank you for reading!!

Photo Album

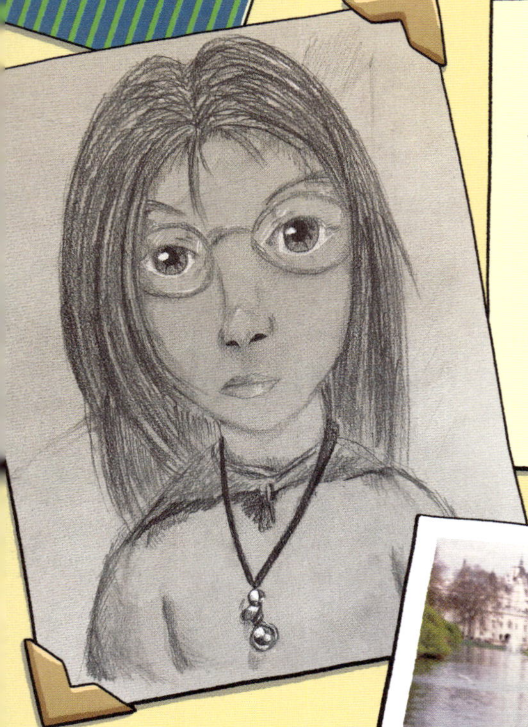

A self-portrait from middle school. I remember the necklace so clearly – it was a pewter dragon whose tail wrapped around a pretty purple marble dangling from a leather cord. I loved stuff like that. Dragons, crystals, tarot. One time, I read that sleeping with a tarot card would help guide my dreams, so I put a card from my *Lord of the Rings* deck into my pillowcase and then forgot about it. Galadriel did not survive the laundering.

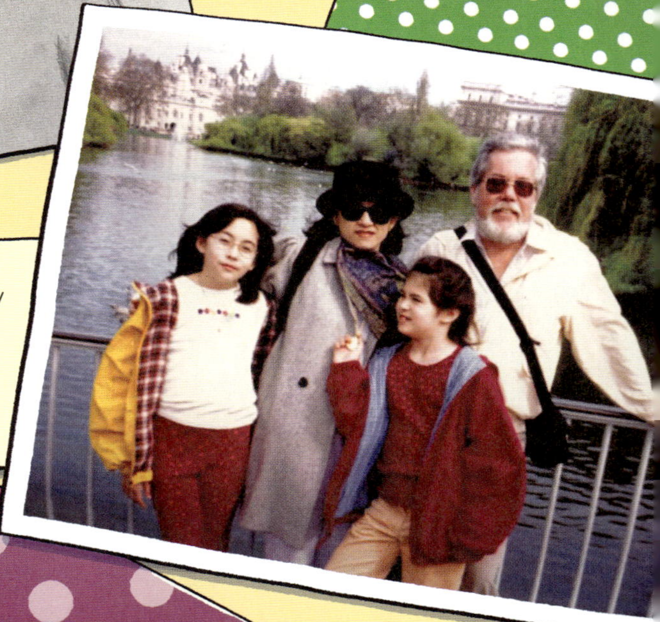

Tween Gale and family in Europe, sometime around the turn of the century, sporting the fashions of the era.

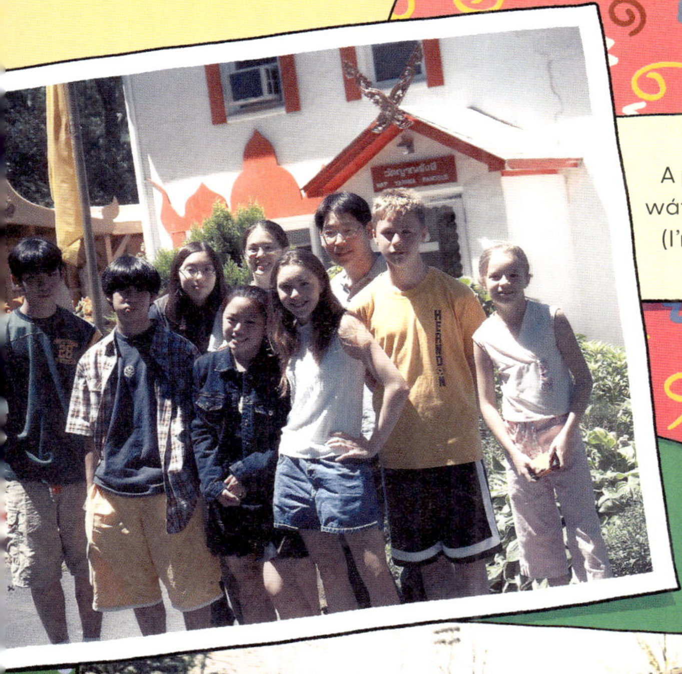

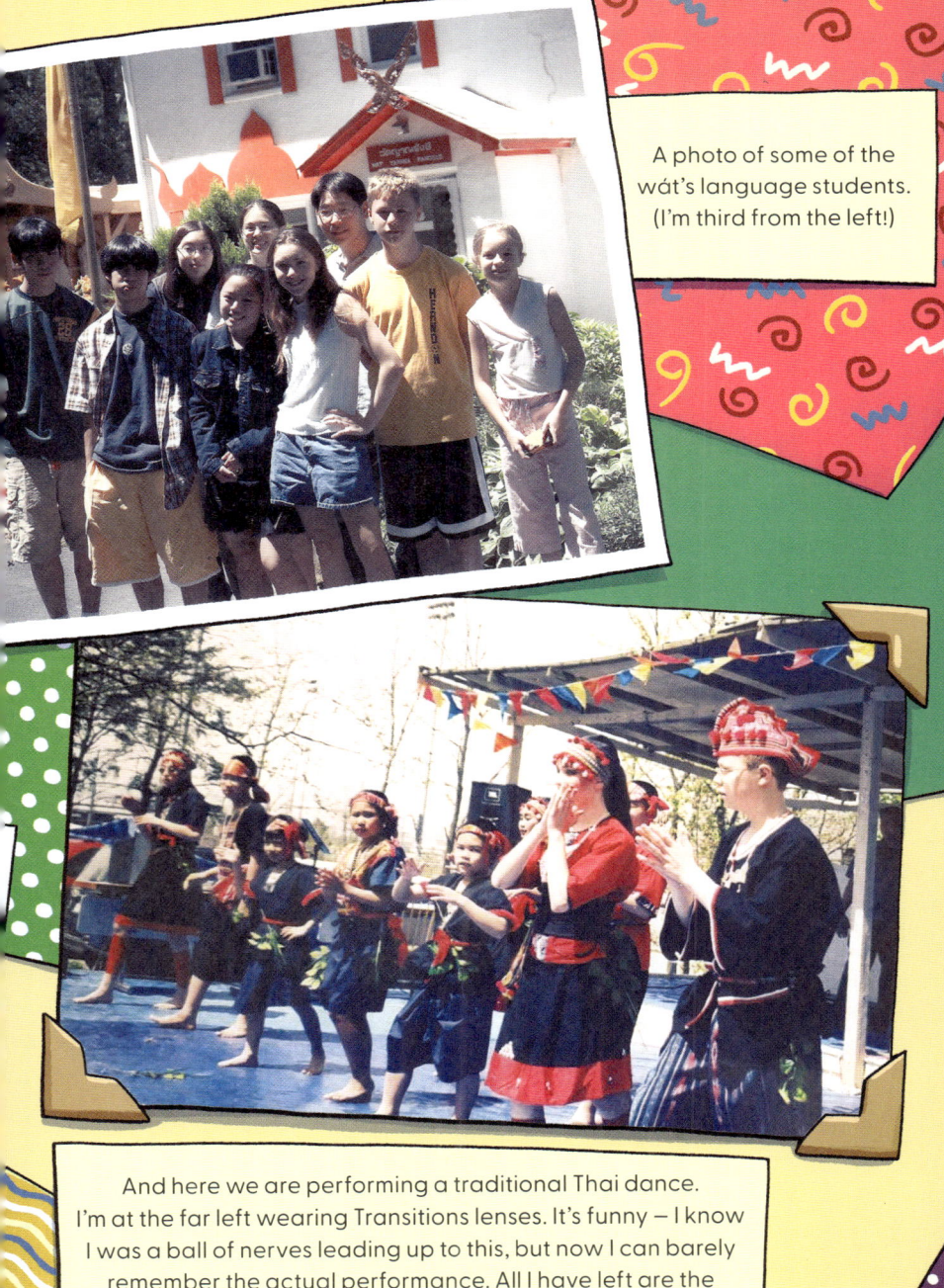

A photo of some of the wát's language students. (I'm third from the left!)

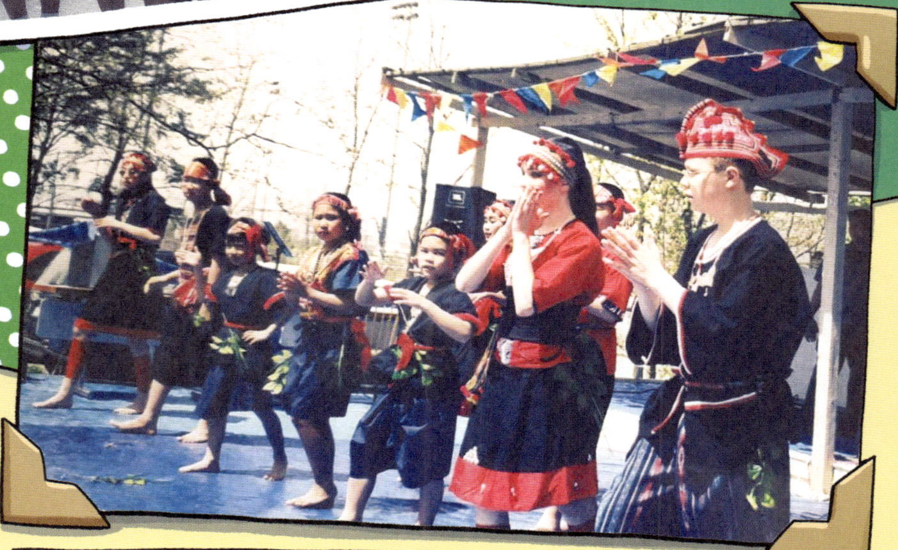

And here we are performing a traditional Thai dance. I'm at the far left wearing Transitions lenses. It's funny – I know I was a ball of nerves leading up to this, but now I can barely remember the actual performance. All I have left are the good memories of practicing with my friend.

More About Thai Language and Traditions

If this is your first time reading a story that includes Thai words or celebrations, or if you've encountered them only briefly in the past, this section is for you. Part of the reason I wanted to make this book was to share a culture that I love with you! But this really only skims the surface, so I encourage you to go out there and enjoy lots of Thai and Thai American media. ♥

In the meantime, here's a little more information about some of the aspects of Thai culture that Ollie encounters in this book. Thank you for reading!!

THAI LANGUAGE

Thai is a *tonal language*. This means that if you change the pitch you use when saying a word, its meaning can change. So if you say "glai" with one tone, it means "near," but if you say it with another tone, it means "far"! If you see a letter with a diacritical mark in this book, like the one over the **o** in **Sǒngkraan**, that means it's spoken with a tone.

Thai also uses a few more specific sounds than English. For example, there are short vowels (ah) and long vowels (ahhhh). To use the **Sǒngkraan** example again: there are two **a**'s at the end because you say the "ah" sound for longer!

Because of these special qualities, people have to make some choices when spelling Thai words with the letters we use for English (this is called romanization). Many Thai Americans don't use an official system and are doing their best based on how they'd personally try to spell words.

For *Fresh Start*, we've chosen to use a modified version of Quincy Surasmith's system. It has handy tone markers and uses letter combinations that are easier for readers to try to sound out themselves. (We've made some exceptions for romanizations that are more familiar to American readers, like **sawasdee**, which would read as **sawàtdii** under Quincy.)

SŎNGKRAAN (OR SONGKRAN)

Sŏngkraan is a festival that starts on April 13 to celebrate the Thai New Year. During this time, Thai people visit family and pay respects to their elders. Those practicing Buddhism will make offerings at temples. Thai people also pour water on Buddha statues and elders as a symbol of washing away the old year. But after the respectful ceremonies, people also get into water play! When I was in Bangkok in the late 1990s, we celebrated by running around the streets with Super Soakers and getting absolutely drenched. What could be better?

(As one more shout-out to Quincy, please look up the video of Conan O'Brien wishing Thai viewers a happy Sŏngkraan. You'll see Quincy translating for Conan!)

LOY KRATHONG
Note: the "th" here is more like the "t" sound you'd encounter in "Thai" or "tone."

Loy Krathong is a festival that usually occurs around November. People celebrate for different reasons. They might be making offerings to the goddess of water, praying to Buddha, or paying respects to their ancestors. But when I lived in Thailand, the main way of celebrating was the same: floating krathongs.

A krathong is a little handmade boat. They're traditionally made with parts of a banana tree, although people also use other biodegradable materials, and you can decorate them however you want. Some people go all out with elaborate arrangements of flowers and fancy carved fruit. Once your krathong is ready, you light candles in the middle and float it down a body of water, creating a beautiful pathway of light — or, in young Ollie's case, a fancy bathtub.

Today, people are much more conscious of the impact that a large number of krathongs might have on their local bodies of water and are developing new solutions to celebrate in a more sustainable and environmentally friendly way.

Acknowledgments

Deepest and most heartfelt thanks to:

Lori, Mom, and Dad, for your love and support.

Patrick and Robin, for every little thing you do.

Judy Hansen, for being a champion.

Cassandra, for continuing this journey with me and helping me to find my strongest stories.

Carina Taylor and Phil Falco, for your incredible design work, and K Czap, for bringing Ollie's world into gorgeous color. This book would not be the same without you.

Manatsu McCluskey at Frankfurt International School, for the virtual tour.

Quincy Surasmith and Anna Naiyapatana, for your expertise and thoughtful feedback.

Rachel, Ngozi, and Dave (quack quack); Carey, Megan, and Aatmaja (snack snack); and The Animal Crackers (TAC TAC). Love you all.

My classmates at the wát for many chaotic Sundays, and Khru Joe, for putting up with us.

The incredible team at Scholastic who have supported this book and shepherded it into the world: David Saylor, Lia Ferrone, Seale Ballenger, Emily Nguyen, Liz Palumbo, Elizabeth Krych, Faith Sagaille, Erin Berger, Meaghan Finnerty, Matt Poulter, Lizette Serrano, Emily Heddleson, Sabrina Montenigro, Ellie Berger, Elizabeth Whiting, and so many more.

And to the librarians, teachers, and guardians putting books in the hands of kids who need them the most. Thank you.

CG.